Praise for The Dark

"King is today's master st
he has latched onto a story worthy of his tale...
—*Los Angeles Daily News*

"Gripping . . . compelling . . .
King mesmerizes the reader."
—*Chicago Sun-Times*

"An impressive work of mythic magnitude.
May turn out to be Stephen King's
greatest literary achievement."
—*The Atlanta Journal-Constitution*

"A compelling whirlpool of a story that draws one
irretrievably to its center."
—*Milwaukee Journal Sentinel*

"King is a master at creating living,
breathing, believable characters."
—*Baltimore Sun*

"Superb . . . through King's vivid imagery
the reader thirsts, cries and nearly dies with Roland."
—*Chicago Herald-Wheaton*

"Enjoyable . . . whets the appetite for more."
—*Bangor Daily News*

"Prime King . . . suspenseful . . .
reams of virtuoso horror writing . . .
an epic in the making."
—*Kirkus Reviews*

Also by Stephen King

THE DARK TOWER IV

STEPHEN KING

WIZARD AND GLASS

SCRIBNER

NEW YORK   LONDON   TORONTO   SYDNEY   NEW DELHI

Scribner
An Imprint of Simon & Schuster, Inc.
1230 Avenue of the Americas
New York, NY 10020

First Scribner trade paperback edition May 2016

SCRIBNER and design are registered trademarks of The Gale Group, Inc.,
used under license by Simon & Schuster, Inc., the publisher of this work.

For information about special discounts for bulk purchases,
please contact Simon & Schuster Special Sales at 1-866-506-1949
or business@simonandschuster.com.

The Simon & Schuster Speakers Bureau can bring authors to your live event.
For more information or to book an event, contact the Simon & Schuster
Speakers Bureau at 1-866-248-3049 or visit our website
at www.simonspeakers.com.

Manufactured in the United States of America

7   9   10   8

Library of Congress Cataloging-in-Publication Data is available.

ISBN 978-1-5011-4355-7
ISBN 978-1-5011-4142-3 (ebook)

Permissions acknowledgments appear on page 895.

This book is dedicated to Julie Eugley
and Marsha DeFilippo. They answer the mail,
and most of the mail for the last couple of years
has been about Roland of Gilead—the gunslinger.
Basically, Julie and Marsha nagged me back
to the word processor. Julie, you nagged
the most effectively, so your name comes first.

CONTENTS

On Being Nineteen
(and a Few Other Things)

I

Hobbits were big when I was nineteen (a number of some import in the stories you are about to read).

There were probably half a dozen Merrys and Pippins slogging through the mud at Max Yasgur's farm during the Great Woodstock Music Festival, twice as many Frodos, and hippie Gandalfs without number. J.R.R. Tolkien's *The Lord of the Rings* was madly popular in those days, and while I never made it to Woodstock (say sorry), I suppose I was at least a halfling-hippie. Enough of one, at any rate, to have read the books and fallen in love with them. The *Dark Tower* books, like most long fantasy tales written by men and women of my generation (*The Chronicles of Thomas Covenant*, by Stephen Donaldson, and *The Sword of Shannara*, by Terry Brooks, are just two of many), were born out of Tolkien's.

But although I read the books in 1966 and 1967, I held off writing. I responded (and with rather touching wholeheartedness) to the sweep of Tolkien's imagination—to the ambition of his story—but I wanted to write my own kind of story, and had I started then, I would have written his. That, as the late Tricky Dick Nixon was fond of saying, would have been wrong. Thanks to Mr. Tolkien, the twentieth century had all the elves and wizards it needed.

In 1967, I didn't have any idea what my kind of story might be, but that didn't matter; I felt positive I'd know it when it passed me on the street. I was nineteen and arrogant. Certainly arrogant enough to feel I could wait a little while on my muse and my masterpiece (as I was sure it would be). At nineteen, it seems to me, one has a right to be arrogant; time has usually not begun its stealthy and rotten subtractions. It takes away your hair and your jump-shot, according to a popular country song, but in truth it takes away a lot more than that. I didn't know it in 1966 and '67, and if I had, I wouldn't have cared. I could imagine—barely—being forty, but fifty? No. *Sixty?* Never! Sixty was out of the question. And at nineteen, that's just the way to be. Nineteen is the age where you say *Look out, world, I'm smokin' TNT and I'm drinkin' dynamite, so if you know what's good for ya, get out of my way—here comes Stevie.*

Nineteen's a selfish age and finds one's cares tightly circumscribed. I had a lot of reach, and I cared about that. I had a lot of ambition, and I cared about that. I had a typewriter that I carried from one shithole apartment to the next, always with a deck of smokes in my pocket and a smile on my face. The compromises of middle age were distant, the insults of old age over the horizon. Like the protagonist in that Bob Seger song they now use to sell the trucks, I felt endlessly powerful and endlessly optimistic; my pockets were empty, but my head was full of things I wanted to say and my heart was full of stories I wanted to tell. Sounds corny now; felt wonderful then. Felt very cool. More than anything else I wanted to get inside my readers' defenses, wanted to rip them and ravish them and change them forever with nothing but story. And I felt I could do those things. I felt I had been *made* to do those things.

How conceited does that sound? A lot or a little? Either way, I don't apologize. I was nineteen. There was not so much as a strand of gray in my beard. I had three pairs of jeans, one pair of boots, the idea that the world was my oyster, and nothing that happened in the next twenty years proved me wrong. Then, around the age of thirty-nine, my troubles set in: drink, drugs, a road accident that changed the way I walked (among other things). I've written about them at length and need not write about them here. Besides, it's the same for you, right? The world eventually sends out a mean-ass Patrol Boy to slow your progress and show you who's boss. You reading this have undoubtedly met yours (or will); I met mine, and I'm sure he'll be back. He's got my address. He's a mean guy, a Bad Lieutenant, the sworn enemy of goofery, fuckery, pride, ambition, loud music, and all things nineteen.

But I still think that's a pretty fine age. Maybe the best age. You can rock and roll all night, but when the music dies out and the beer wears off, you're able to think. And dream big dreams. The mean Patrol Boy cuts you down to size eventually, and if you start out small, why, there's almost nothing left but the cuffs of your pants when he's done with you. "Got another one!" he shouts, and strides on with his citation book in his hand. So a little arrogance (or even a lot) isn't such a bad thing, although your mother undoubtedly told you different. Mine did. *Pride goeth before a fall, Stephen,* she said . . . and then I found out—right around the age that is 19 × 2— that eventually you fall down, anyway. Or get pushed into the ditch. At nineteen they can card you in the bars and tell you to get the fuck out, put your sorry act (and sorrier ass) back on the street, but they can't card you when you sit down to paint a picture, write a poem, or tell a story, by God, and if you reading this happen to be very young, don't let your elders and supposed betters tell you any different. Sure, you've never been to Paris. No, you never ran with the bulls at Pamplona. Yes, you're a pissant who had no hair in your armpits until three years ago—but so what? If you don't start out too big for your britches, how are you gonna fill 'em when you grow up? Let it rip regardless of what anybody tells you, that's my idea; sit down and *smoke* that baby.

II

I think novelists come in two types, and that includes the sort of fledgling novelist I was by 1970. Those who are bound for the more literary or "serious" side of the job examine every possible subject in the light of this question: *What would writing this sort of story mean to me?* Those whose destiny (or ka, if you like) is to include the writing of popular novels are apt to ask a very different one: *What would writing this sort of story mean to others?* The "serious" novelist is looking for answers and keys to the self; the "popular" novelist is looking for an audience. Both kinds of writer are equally selfish. I've known a good many, and will set my watch and warrant upon it.

Anyway, I believe that even at the age of nineteen, I recognized the story of Frodo and his efforts to rid himself of the One Great Ring as one belonging to the second group. They were the adventures of an essentially British band of pilgrims set against a backdrop of vaguely Norse mythology. I liked the idea of the quest—*loved* it, in fact—but I had no interest in either Tolkien's sturdy peasant characters (that's not to say I didn't like them, because I did) or his bosky Scandinavian settings. If I tried going in that direction, I'd get it all wrong.

So I waited. By 1970 I was twenty-two, the first strands of gray had showed up in my beard (I think smoking two and a half packs of Pall Malls a day probably had something to do with that), but even at twenty-two, one can afford to wait. At twenty-two, time is still on one's side, although even then that bad old Patrol Boy's in the neighborhood and asking questions.

Then, in an almost completely empty movie theater (the Bijou, in Bangor, Maine, if it matters), I saw a film directed by Sergio Leone. It was called *The Good, the Bad, and the Ugly,* and before the film was even half over, I realized that what I wanted to write was a novel that contained Tolkien's sense of quest and magic but set against Leone's almost absurdly majestic Western backdrop. If you've only seen this gonzo Western on your television screen, you don't understand what I'm talking about— cry your pardon, but it's true. On a movie screen, projected through the correct Panavision lenses, *TG, TB, & TU* is an epic to rival *Ben-Hur.* Clint Eastwood appears roughly eighteen feet tall, with each wiry jut of stubble on his cheeks looking roughly the size of a young redwood tree. The grooves bracketing Lee Van Cleef's mouth are as deep as canyons, and there could be a thinny (see *Wizard and Glass*) at the bottom of each one. The desert settings appear to stretch at least out as far as the orbit of the planet Neptune. And the barrel of each gun looks to be roughly as large as the Holland Tunnel.

What I wanted even more than the setting was that feeling of epic, apocalyptic *size.* The fact that Leone knew jack shit about American geography (according to one of the characters, Chicago is somewhere in the vicinity of Phoenix, Arizona) added to the film's sense of magnificent dislocation. And in my enthusiasm—the sort only a young person can muster, I think—I wanted to write not just a *long* book, but *the longest popular novel in history.* I did not succeed in doing that, but I feel I had a decent rip; *The Dark Tower,* volumes one through seven, really comprise a single tale, and the first four volumes run to just over two thousand pages in paperback. The final three volumes run another twenty-five hundred in manuscript. I'm not trying to imply here that length has anything whatsoever to do with quality; I'm just saying that I wanted to write an epic, and in some ways, I succeeded. If you were to ask me *why* I wanted to do that, I couldn't tell you. Maybe it's a part of growing up American: build the tallest, dig the deepest, write the longest. And that head-scratching puzzlement when the question of motivation comes up? Seems to me that that is also part of being an American. In the end we are reduced to saying *It seemed like a good idea at the time.*

III

Another thing about being nineteen, do it please ya: it is the age, I think, where a lot of us somehow get stuck (mentally and emotionally, if not physically). The years slide by and one day you find yourself looking into the mirror with real puzzlement. *Why are those lines on my face?* you wonder. *Where did that stupid potbelly come from? Hell, I'm only nineteen!* This is hardly an original concept, but that in no way subtracts from one's amazement.

Time puts gray in your beard, time takes away your jump-shot, and all the while you're thinking—silly you—that it's still on your side. The logical side of you knows better, but your heart refuses to believe it. If you're lucky, the Patrol Boy who cited you for going too fast and having too much fun also gives you a dose of smelling salts. That was more or less what happened to me near the end of the twentieth century. It came in the form of a Plymouth van that knocked me into the ditch beside a road in my hometown.

About three years after that accident I did a book signing for *From a Buick 8* at a Borders store in Dearborn, Michigan. When one guy got to the head of the line, he said he was really, really glad that I was still alive. (I get this a lot, and it beats the *shit* out of "Why the hell didn't you die?")

"I was with this good friend of mine when we heard you got popped," he said. "Man, we just started shaking our heads and saying 'There goes the Tower, it's tilting, it's falling, ahhh, shit, he'll *never* finish it now.' "

A version of the same idea had occurred to me— the troubling idea that, having built the Dark Tower in the collective imagination of a million readers, I might have a responsibility to make it safe for as long as people wanted to read about it. That might be for only five years; for all I know, it might be five hundred. Fantasy stories, the bad as well as the good (even now, someone out there is probably reading *Varney the Vampire* or *The Monk*), seem to have long shelf lives. Roland's way of protecting the tower is to try to remove the threat to the Beams that hold the Tower up. I would have to do it, I realized after my accident, by finishing the gunslinger's story.

During the long pauses between the writing and publication of the first four *Dark Tower* tales, I received hundreds of "pack your bags, we're going on a guilt trip" letters. In 1998 (when I was laboring under the mistaken impression that I was still basically nineteen, in other words), I got one from an "82-yr-old Gramma, don't mean to Bother You w/ My Troubles BUT!! very Sick These Days." The Gramma told me she probably had only a year to live ("14 Mo's at Outside, Cancer all thru Me"), and while she didn't expect me to finish Roland's tale in that time just for her, she wanted to know if I couldn't please (*please*) just tell her how it came out. The line that wrenched my heart (although not quite enough to start writing again) was her promise to "not tell a Single Soul." A year later—probably after the accident that landed me in the hospital—one of my assistants, Marsha DiFilippo, got a letter from a fellow on death row in either Texas or Florida, wanting to know essentially the same thing: how does it come out? (He promised to take the secret to the grave with him, which gave me the creeps.)

I would have given both of these folks what they wanted—a summary of Roland's further adventures—if I could have done, but alas, I couldn't. I had no idea of how things were going to turn out with the gunslinger and his friends. To know, I have to write. I once had an outline, but I lost it along the way. (It probably wasn't worth a tin shit, anyway.) All I had was a few notes (*"Chussit, chissit, chassit,* something-something-*basket"* reads one lying on the desk as I write this). Eventually, starting in July of 2001, I began to write again. I knew by then I was no longer nineteen, nor exempt from any of the ills to which the flesh is heir. I knew I was going to be sixty, maybe even seventy. And I wanted to finish my story before the bad Patrol Boy came for the last time. I had no urge to be filed away with *The Canterbury Tales* and *The Mystery of Edwin Drood.*

The result—for better or worse—lies before you, Constant Reader, whether you reading this are starting with Volume One or are preparing for Volume Five. Like it or hate it, the story of Roland is now done. I hope you enjoy it.

As for me, I had the time of my life.

Stephen King
January 25, 2003

19

REGARD

ARGUMENT

Wizard and Glass is the fourth volume of a longer tale inspired by Robert Browning's narrative poem "Childe Roland to the Dark Tower Came."

The first volume, *The Gunslinger*, tells how Roland of Gilead pursues and at last catches Walter, the man in black, who pretended friendship with Roland's father but who actually served Marten, a great sorcerer. Catching the half-human Walter is not Roland's goal but only a means to an end: Roland wants to reach the Dark Tower, where he hopes the quickening destruction of Mid-World may be halted, perhaps even reversed.

Roland is a kind of knight, the last of his breed, and the Tower is his obsession, his only reason for living when first we meet him. We learn of an early test of manhood forced upon him by Marten, who has seduced Roland's mother. Marten expects Roland to fail this test and to be "sent west," his father's guns forever denied him. Roland, however, lays Marten's plans at nines, passing the test . . . due mostly to his clever choice of weapon.

We discover that the gunslinger's world is related to our own in some fundamental and terrible way. This link is first revealed when Roland meets Jake, a boy from the New York of 1977, at a desert way station. There are doors between Roland's world and our own; one of them is death, and that is how Jake first reaches Mid-World, pushed into Forty-third Street and run over by a car. The pusher was a man named Jack Mort . . . except the thing hiding inside of Mort's head and guiding his murderous hands on this particular occasion was Roland's old enemy, Walter.

Before Jake and Roland reach Walter, Jake dies again . . . this time because the gunslinger, faced with an agonizing choice between this symbolic son and the Dark Tower, chooses the Tower. Jake's last words before plunging into the abyss are "Go, then—there are other worlds than these."

The final confrontation between Roland and Walter occurs near the Western Sea. In a long night of palaver, the man in black tells Roland's future with a strange Tarot deck. Three cards—The Prisoner, The Lady of the Shadows, and Death ("but not for you, gunslinger")—are especially called to Roland's attention.

The second volume, *The Drawing of the Three*, begins on the edge of the Western Sea not long after Roland awakens from his confrontation with his old nemesis and discovers Walter long dead, only more bones in a place of bones. The exhausted gunslinger is attacked by a horde of carnivorous "lobstrosities," and before he can escape them, he has been seriously wounded, losing the first two fingers of his right hand. He is also poisoned by their bites, and as he resumes his trek northward along the Western Sea, Roland is sickening . . . perhaps dying.

On his walk he encounters three doors standing freely on the beach. These open into our city of New York, at three different *whens*. From 1987, Roland draws Eddie Dean, a prisoner of heroin. From 1964, he draws Odetta Susannah Holmes, a woman who has lost her lower legs in a subway mishap . . . one that was no accident. She is indeed a lady of shadows, with a vicious second personality hiding within the socially committed young black woman her friends know. This hidden woman, the violent and crafty Detta Walker, is determined to kill both Roland and Eddie when the gunslinger draws her into Mid-World.

Between these two in time, once again in 1977, Roland enters the hellish mind of Jack Mort, who has hurt Odetta/Detta not once but twice. "Death," the man in black told Roland, "but not for you, gunslinger." Nor is Mort the third of whom Walter foretold; Roland prevents Mort from murdering Jake Chambers, and shortly afterward Mort dies beneath the wheels of the same train which took Odetta's legs in 1959. Roland thus fails to draw the psychotic into Mid-World . . . but, he thinks, who would want such a being in any case?

Yet there's a price to be paid for rebellion against a foretold future; isn't there always? Ka, *maggot,* Roland's old teacher, Cort, might have said; *Such is the great wheel, and always turns. Be not in front of it when it does, or you'll be crushed under it, and so make an end to your stupid brains and useless bags of guts and water.*

Roland thinks that perhaps he has drawn three in just Eddie and Odetta, since Odetta is a double personality, yet when Odetta and Detta merge as one in Susannah (thanks in large part to Eddie Dean's love and courage), the gunslinger knows it's not so. He knows something else as well: he is being tormented by thoughts of Jake, the boy who, dying, spoke of other worlds. Half of the gunslinger's mind, in fact, believes there never *was* a boy. In preventing Jack Mort from pushing Jake in front of the car meant to kill him, Roland has created a temporal paradox which is tearing him apart. And, in our world, it is tearing Jake Chambers apart as well.

The Wastelands, the third volume of the series, begins with this paradox. After killing a gigantic bear named either Mir (by the old people who went in fear of it) or

Shardik (by the Great Old Ones who built it . . . for the bear turns out to be a cyborg), Roland, Eddie, and Susannah backtrack the beast and discover the Path of the Beam. There are six of these beams, running between the twelve portals which mark the edges of Mid-World. At the point where the beams cross—at the center of Roland's world, perhaps the center of all worlds—the gunslinger believes that he and his friends will at last find the Dark Tower.

By now Eddie and Susannah are no longer prisoners in Roland's world. In love and well on the way to becoming gunslingers themselves, they are full participants in the quest and follow him willingly along the Path of the Beam.

In a speaking ring not far from the Portal of the Bear, time is mended, paradox is ended, and the *real* third is at last drawn. Jake reenters Mid-World at the conclusion of a perilous rite where all four—Jake, Eddie, Susannah, and Roland—remember the faces of their fathers and acquit themselves honorably. Not long after, the quartet becomes a quintet, when Jake befriends a billy-bumbler. Bumblers, which look like a combination of badger, raccoon, and dog, have a limited speaking ability. Jake names his new friend Oy.

The way of the pilgrims leads them toward Lud, an urban wasteland where the degenerate survivors of two old factions, the Pubes and the Grays, carry on the vestige of an old conflict. Before reaching the city, they come to a little town called River Crossing, where a few antique residents still remain. They recognize Roland as a remnant of the old days, before the world moved on, and honor him and his companions. After, the old people tell them of a monorail train which may still run from Lud and into the wastelands, along the Path of the Beam and toward the Dark Tower.

Jake is frightened by this news, but not really surprised; before being drawn away from New York, he obtained two books from a bookstore owned by a man with the thought-provoking name of Calvin Tower. One is a book of riddles with the answers torn out. The other, *Charlie the Choo-Choo,* is a children's book about a train. An amusing little tale, most might say . . . but to Jake, there's something about Charlie that isn't amusing at all. Something frightening. Roland knows something else: in the High Speech of his world, the word *char* means death.

Aunt Talitha, the matriarch of the River Crossing folk, gives Roland a silver cross to wear, and the travellers go their course. Before reaching Lud, they discover a downed plane from our world—a German fighter from the 1930s. Jammed into the cockpit is the mummified corpse of a giant, almost certainly the half-mythical outlaw David Quick.

While crossing the dilapidated bridge which spans the River Send, Jake and Oy are nearly lost in an accident. While Roland, Eddie, and Susannah are distracted by this, the party is ambushed by a dying (and very dangerous) outlaw named Gasher. He abducts Jake and takes him underground to the Tick-Tock Man, the last leader of the Grays. Tick-Tock's real name is Andrew Quick; he is the great-grandson of the man who died trying to land an airplane from another world.

While Roland (aided by Oy) goes after Jake, Eddie and Susannah find the Cradle of Lud, where Blaine the Mono awakes. Blaine is the last aboveground tool of the vast computer-system which lies beneath the city of Lud, and it has only one remaining interest: riddles. It promises to take the travellers to the monorail's final stop if they can solve a riddle it poses them. Otherwise, Blaine says, the only trip they'll be taking will be to the place where the path ends in the clearing . . . to their deaths, in other words. In that case they'll have plenty of company, for Blaine is planning to release stocks of nerve-gas which will kill everyone left in Lud: Pubes, Grays, and gunslingers alike.

Roland rescues Jake, leaving the Tick-Tock Man for dead . . . but Andrew Quick is not dead. Half blind, hideously wounded about the face, he is rescued by a man who calls himself Richard Fannin. Fannin, however, also identifies himself as the Ageless Stranger, a demon of whom Roland has been warned by Walter.

Roland and Jake are reunited with Eddie and Susannah in the Cradle of Lud, and Susannah—with a little help from "dat bitch" Detta Walker—is able to solve Blaine's riddle. They gain access to the mono, of necessity ignoring the horrified warnings of Blaine's sane but fatally weak undermind (Eddie calls this voice Little Blaine), only to discover that Blaine means to commit suicide with them aboard. The fact that the actual mind running the mono exists in computers falling farther and farther behind them, running beneath a city which has become a slaughtering-pen, will make no difference when the pink bullet jumps the tracks somewhere along the line at a speed in excess of eight hundred miles an hour.

There is only one chance of survival: Blaine's love of riddles. Roland of Gilead proposes a desperate bargain. It is with this bargain that *The Wastelands* ends; it is with this bargain that *Wizard and Glass* begins.

ROMEO: Lady, by yonder blessed moon I vow,
That tips with silver all these fruit-tree tops—

JULIET: O, swear not by the moon, th' inconstant moon,
That monthly changes in her circled orb,
Lest that thy love prove likewise variable.

ROMEO: What shall I swear by?

JULIET: Do not swear at all.
Or, if thou wilt, swear by thy gracious self,
Which is the god of my idolatry,
And I'll believe thee.

—*Romeo and Juliet*
William Shakespeare

On the fourth day, to [Dorothy's] great joy, Oz sent
for her, and when she entered the Throne Room, he
greeted her pleasantly.

"Sit down, my dear. I think I have found a way to get
you out of this country."

"And back to Kansas?" she asked eagerly.

"Well, I'm not sure about Kansas," said Oz, "for I
haven't the faintest notion which way it lies. . . ."

—*The Wizard of Oz*
L. Frank Baum

I asked one draught of earlier, happier sights,
Ere fitly I could hope to play my part.
Think first, fight afterwards—the soldier's art:
One taste of the old time sets all to rights!

—Childe Roland to the
Dark Tower Came
Robert Browning

BLAİNE

"ASK ME A RIDDLE," Blaine invited.

"Fuck you," Roland said. He did not raise his voice.

"*WHAT* DO YOU SAY?" In its clear disbelief, the voice of Big Blaine had become very close to the voice of its unsuspected twin.

"I said fuck you," Roland said calmly, "but if that puzzles you, Blaine, I can make it clearer. No. The answer is no."

There was no reply from Blaine for a long, long time, and when he did respond, it was not with words. Instead, the walls, floor, and ceiling began to lose their color and solidity again. In a space of ten seconds the Barony Coach once more ceased to exist. They were now flying through the mountain-range they had seen on the horizon: iron-gray peaks rushed toward them at suicidal speed, then fell away to disclose sterile valleys where gigantic beetles crawled about like landlocked turtles. Roland saw something that looked like a huge snake suddenly uncoil from the mouth of a cave. It seized one of the beetles and yanked it back into its lair. Roland had never in his life seen such animals or countryside, and the sight made his skin want to crawl right off his flesh. Blaine might have transported them to some other world.

"PERHAPS I SHOULD DERAIL US HERE," Blaine said. His voice was meditative, but beneath it the gunslinger heard a deep, pulsing rage.

3

"Perhaps you should," the gunslinger said indifferently. Eddie's face was frantic. He mouthed the words *What are you DOING?* Roland ignored him; he had his hands full with Blaine, and he knew perfectly well what he was doing.

"YOU ARE RUDE AND ARROGANT," Blaine said. "THESE MAY SEEM LIKE INTERESTING TRAITS TO YOU, BUT THEY ARE NOT TO ME."

"Oh, I can be much ruder than I have been."

Roland of Gilead unfolded his hands and got slowly to his feet. He stood on what appeared to be nothing, legs apart, his right hand on his hip and his left on the sandalwood grip of his revolver. He stood as he had so many times before, in the dusty streets of a hundred forgotten towns, in a score of rocky canyon killing-zones, in unnumbered dark saloons with their smells of bitter beer and old fried meals. It was just another showdown in another empty street. That was all, and that was enough. It was *khef, ka,* and *ka-tet.* That the showdown always came was the central fact of his life and the axle upon which his own *ka* revolved. That the battle would be fought with words instead of bullets this time made no difference; it would be a battle to the death, just the same. The stench of killing in the air was as clear and definite as the stench of exploded carrion in a swamp. Then the battle-rage descended, as it always did . . . and he was no longer really there to himself at all.

"I can call you a nonsensical, empty-headed, foolish machine. I can call you a stupid, unwise creature whose sense is no more than the sound of a winter wind in a hollow tree."

"STOP IT."

Roland went on in the same serene tone, ignoring Blaine completely. "You're what Eddie calls a 'gadget.' Were you more, I might be ruder yet."

"I AM A GREAT DEAL MORE THAN JUST—"

"I could call you a sucker of cocks, for instance, but you have no mouth. I could say you're viler than the vilest beggar who ever crawled the lowest street in creation, but even such a creature is better than you; you have no knees on which to crawl, and would not fall upon them even if you did, for you have no conception of such a human flaw as mercy. I could even say you fucked your mother, had you one."

Roland paused for breath. His three companions were holding theirs. All around them, suffocating, was Blaine the Mono's thunderstruck silence.

"I *can* call you a faithless creature who let your only companion kill herself, a coward who has delighted in the torture of the foolish and the slaughter of the innocent, a lost and bleating mechanical goblin who—"

"I COMMAND YOU TO STOP IT OR I'LL KILL YOU ALL RIGHT HERE!"

Roland's eyes blazed with such wild blue fire that Eddie shrank away from him. Dimly, he heard Jake and Susannah gasp.

"Kill if you will, but command me nothing!" the gunslinger roared. *"You have forgotten the faces of those who made you! Now either kill us or be silent and listen to me, Roland of Gilead, son of Steven, gunslinger, and lord of ancient lands! I have not come across all the miles and all the years to listen to your childish prating! Do you understand? Now you will listen to ME!"*

There was another moment of shocked silence. No one breathed. Roland stared sternly forward, his head high, his hand on the butt of his gun.

Susannah Dean raised her hand to her mouth and felt the small smile there as a woman might feel some strange new article of clothing—a hat, perhaps—to make sure it is still on straight. She was afraid this was the end of her life, but the feeling which dominated her heart at that moment was not fear but pride. She glanced to her left and saw Eddie regarding Roland with an amazed grin. Jake's expression was even simpler: pure adoration.

"Tell him!" Jake breathed. "Kick his ass! Right!"

"You better pay attention," Eddie agreed. "He really doesn't give much of a fuck, Blaine. They don't call him The Mad Dog of Gilead for nothing."

After a long, long moment, Blaine asked: "DID THEY CALL YOU SO, ROLAND SON OF STEVEN?"

"They may have," Roland replied, standing calmly on thin air above the sterile foothills.

"WHAT GOOD ARE YOU TO ME IF YOU WON'T TELL ME RIDDLES?" Blaine asked. Now he sounded like a grumbling, sulky child who has been allowed to stay up too long past his usual bedtime.

"I didn't say we wouldn't," Roland said.

"NO?" Blaine sounded bewildered. "I DO NOT UNDERSTAND, YET VOICE-PRINT ANALYSIS INDI-CATES RATIONAL DISCOURSE. PLEASE EXPLAIN."

"You said you wanted them right *now*," the gunslinger replied. "*That* was what I was refusing. Your eagerness has made you unseemly."

"I DON'T UNDERSTAND."

"It has made you rude. Do you understand *that*?"

There was a long, thoughtful silence. Centuries had passed since the computer had experienced any human responses other than ignorance, neglect, and superstitious subservience. It had been eons since it had been exposed to simple human courage. Finally: "IF WHAT I SAID STRUCK YOU AS RUDE, I APOLO-GIZE."

"It is accepted, Blaine. But there is a larger problem."

"EXPLAIN."

"Close the carriage again and I will." Roland sat down

as if further argument—and the prospect of immediate death—was now unthinkable.

Blaine did as he was asked. The walls filled with color and the nightmare landscape below was once more blotted out. The blip on the route-map was now blinking close to the dot marked Candleton.

"All right," Roland said. "Rudeness is forgivable, Blaine; so I was taught in my youth. But I was also taught that stupidity is not."

"HOW HAVE I BEEN STUPID, ROLAND OF GILEAD?" Blaine's voice was soft and ominous. Susannah thought of a cat crouched outside a mouse-hole, tail swishing back and forth, green eyes shining with malevolence.

"We have something you want," Roland said, "but the only reward you offer if we give it to you is death. That's *very* stupid."

There was a long, long pause as Blaine thought this over. Then: "WHAT YOU SAY IS TRUE, ROLAND OF GILEAD, BUT THE QUALITY OF YOUR RIDDLES IS NOT PROVEN. I WILL NOT REWARD YOU WITH YOUR LIVES FOR BAD RIDDLES."

Roland nodded. "I understand, Blaine. Listen, now, and take understanding from me. I have told some of this to my friends already. When I was a boy in the Barony of Gilead, there were seven Fair-Days each year— Winter, Wide Earth, Sowing, Mid-Summer, Full Earth, Reaping, and Year's End. Riddling was an important part of every Fair-Day, but it was the most important event of the Fair of Wide Earth and that of Full Earth, for the riddles told were supposed to augur well or ill for the success of the crops."

"THAT IS SUPERSTITION WITH NO BASIS AT ALL IN FACT," Blaine said. "I FIND IT ANNOYING AND UPSETTING."

"Of course it was superstition," Roland agreed, "but

you might be surprised at how well the riddles foresaw the crops. For instance, riddle me this, Blaine: What is the difference between a grandmother and a granary?"

"THAT IS OLD AND NOT VERY INTERESTING," Blaine said, but he sounded happy to have something to solve, just the same. "ONE IS ONE'S BORN KIN; THE OTHER IS ONE'S CORN-BIN. A RIDDLE BASED ON PHONETIC COINCIDENCE. ANOTHER OF THIS TYPE, ONE TOLD ON THE LEVEL WHICH CONTAINS THE BARONY OF NEW YORK, GOES LIKE THIS: WHAT IS THE DIFFERENCE BETWEEN A CAT AND A COMPLEX SENTENCE?"

Jake spoke up. "I know. A cat has claws at the end of its paws, and a complex sentence has a pause at the end of its clause."

"YES," Blaine agreed. "A VERY SILLY OLD RIDDLE, USEFUL ONLY AS A MNEMONIC DEVICE."

"For once I agree with you, Blaine old buddy," Eddie said.

"I AM NOT YOUR BUDDY, EDDIE OF NEW YORK."

"Well, jeez. Kiss my ass and go to heaven."

"THERE IS NO HEAVEN."

Eddie had no comeback for that one.

"I WOULD HEAR MORE OF FAIR-DAY RIDDLING IN GILEAD, ROLAND SON OF STEVEN."

"At noon on Wide Earth and Full Earth, somewhere between sixteen and thirty riddlers would gather in the Hall of the Grandfathers, which was opened for the event. Those were the only times of year when common folk—merchants and farmers and ranchers and such— were allowed into the Hall of the Grandfathers, and on that day they *all* crowded in."

The gunslinger's eyes were far away and dreamy; it was the expression Jake had seen on his face in that misty other life, when Roland had told him of how he and his friends, Cuthbert and Jamie, had once sneaked into the balcony of that same Hall to watch some sort of dance-party. Jake and Roland had been climbing into the mountains when Roland had told him of that time, close on the trail of Walter.

Marten sat next to my mother and father, Roland had said. *I knew them even from so high above—and once she and Marten danced, slowly and revolvingly, and the others cleared the floor for them and clapped when it was over. But the gunslingers did not clap. . . .*

Jake looked curiously at Roland, wondering again where this strange man had come from . . . and why.

"A great barrel was placed in the center of the floor," Roland went on, "and into this each riddler would toss a handful of bark scrolls with riddles writ upon them. Many were old, riddles they had gotten from the elders—even from books, in some cases—but many others were new, made up for the occasion. Three judges, one always a gunslinger, would pass on these when they were told aloud, and they were accepted only if the judges deemed them fair."

"YES, RIDDLES MUST BE FAIR," Blaine agreed.

"So they riddled," the gunslinger said. A faint smile touched his mouth as he thought of those days, days when he had been the age of the bruised boy sitting across from him with the billy-bumbler in his lap. "For hours on end they riddled. A line was formed down the center of the Hall of the Grandfathers. One's position in this line was determined by lot, and since it was much better to be at the end of the line than at the head, everyone hoped for a high draw, although the winner had to answer at least one riddle correctly.

"OF COURSE."

"Each man or woman—for some of Gilead's best riddlers were women—approached the barrel, drew a riddle, and if the riddle was still unanswered after the sands in a three-minute glass had run out, that contestant had to leave the line."

"AND WAS THE SAME RIDDLE ASKED OF THE NEXT PERSON IN THE LINE?"

"Yes."

"SO THE NEXT PERSON HAD EXTRA TIME TO THINK."

"Yes."

"I SEE. IT SOUNDS PRETTY SWELL."

Roland frowned. "Swell?"

"He means it sounds like fun," Susannah said quietly.

Roland shrugged. "It was fun for the onlookers, I suppose, but the contestants took it very seriously. Quite often there were arguments and fistfights after the contest was over and the prize awarded."

"WHAT PRIZE WAS THAT, ROLAND SON OF STEVEN?"

"The largest goose in Barony. And year after year my teacher, Cort, carried that goose home."

"I WISH HE WERE HERE," Blaine said respectfully. "HE MUST HAVE BEEN A GREAT RIDDLER."

"Indeed he was," Roland said. "Are you ready for my proposal, Blaine?"

"OF COURSE. I WILL LISTEN WITH GREAT INTEREST, ROLAND OF GILEAD."

"Let these next few hours be our Fair-Day. You will not riddle us, for you wish to hear new riddles, not tell some of those millions you already know—"

"CORRECT."

"We couldn't solve most of them, anyway," Roland went on. "I'm sure you know riddles that would have stumped even Cort, had they been pulled out of the barrel." He was not sure of it at all, but the time to use the fist had passed and the time to use the feather had come.

"OF COURSE," Blaine agreed.

"Instead of a goose, our lives shall be the prize," Roland said. "We will riddle you as we run, Blaine. If, when we come to Topeka, you have solved every one of our riddles, you may carry out your original plan and kill us. That is your goose. But if *we* pose *you*—if there is a riddle in either Jake's book or one of our heads which you don't know and can't answer—you must take us to Topeka and then free us to pursue our quest. That is *our* goose."

Silence.

"Do you understand?"

"YES."

"Do you agree?"

More silence from Blaine the Mono. Eddie sat stiffly with his arm around Susannah, looking up at the ceiling of the Barony Coach. Susannah's left hand slipped across her belly, stroking the secret which might be hidden there. Jake stroked Oy's fur lightly, avoiding the bloody tangles where the bumbler had been stabbed. They waited while Blaine—the real Blaine, now far behind them, living his quasi-life beneath a city where all the inhabitants lay dead by his hand—considered Roland's proposal.

"YES," Blaine said at last. "I AGREE. IF I SOLVE ALL THE RIDDLES YOU ASK ME, I WILL TAKE YOU WITH ME TO THE PLACE WHERE THE PATH ENDS IN THE CLEARING. IF ONE OF YOU TELLS A RIDDLE I CANNOT SOLVE, I WILL SPARE YOUR LIVES AND LEAVE YOU IN TOPEKA, FROM WHENCE YOU MAY CONTINUE YOUR QUEST FOR THE DARK TOWER, IF YOU SO CHOOSE. HAVE I UNDERSTOOD THE TERMS AND LIMITS OF YOUR PROPOSAL COR-RECTLY, ROLAND SON OF STEVEN?"

"Yes."

"VERY WELL, ROLAND OF GILEAD.

"VERY WELL, EDDIE OF NEW YORK.

"VERY WELL, SUSANNAH OF NEW YORK.

"VERY WELL, JAKE OF NEW YORK.

"VERY WELL, OY OF MID-WORLD."

Oy looked up briefly at the sound of his name.

"YOU ARE *KA-TET;* ONE MADE FROM MANY. SO AM I. WHOSE *KA-TET* IS THE STRONGER IS SOMETHING WE MUST NOW PROVE."

There was a moment of silence, broken only by the hard steady throb of the slo-trans turbines bearing them on across the waste lands, bearing them along the Path of the Beam toward Topeka, where Mid-World ended and End-World began.

"SO," cried the voice of Blaine. "CAST YOUR NETS, WANDERERS! TRY ME WITH YOUR QUESTIONS, AND LET THE CONTEST BEGIN."

PART ONE

RIDDLES

CHAPTER ONE

Beneath the Demon Moon (I)

I

The town of Candleton was a poisoned and irradiated ruin, but not dead; after all the centuries it still twitched with tenebrous life—trundling beetles the size of turtles, birds that looked like small, misshapen dragonlets, a few stumbling robots that passed in and out of the rotten buildings like stainless steel zombies, their joints squalling, their nuclear eyes flickering.

"Show your pass, pard!" cried the one that had been stuck in a corner of the lobby of the Candleton Travellers' Hotel for the last two hundred and thirty-four years. Embossed on the rusty lozenge of its head was a six-pointed star. It had over the years managed to dig a shallow concavity in the steel-sheathed wall blocking its way, but that was all.

"Show your pass, pard! Elevated radiation levels possible south and east of town! Show your pass, pard! Elevated radiation levels possible south and east of town!"

A bloated rat, blind and dragging its guts behind it in a sac like a rotten placenta, struggled over the posse robot's feet. The posse robot took no notice, just went on butting its steel head into the steel wall. "Show your pass, pard! Elevated radiation levels possible, dad rattit and gods cuss it!" Behind it, in the hotel bar, the skulls

15

of men and women who had come in here for one last drink before the cataclysm caught up with them grinned as if they had died laughing. Perhaps some of them had.

When Blaine the Mono blammed overhead, running up the night like a bullet running up the barrel of a gun, windows broke, dust sifted down, and several of the skulls disintegrated like ancient pottery vases. Outside, a brief hurricane of radioactive dust blew up the street, and the hitching-post in front of the Elegant Beef and Pork Restaurant was sucked into the squally updraft like smoke. In the town square, the Candleton Fountain split in two, spilling out not water but only dust, snakes, mutie scorpions, and a few of the blindly trundling turtle-beetles.

Then the shape which had hurtled above the town was gone as if it had never been, Candleton reverted to the mouldering activity which had been its substitute for life over the last two and a half centuries . . . and then the trailing sonic boom caught up, slamming its thunderclap above the town for the first time in seven years, causing enough vibration to tumble the mercantile store on the far side of the fountain. The posse robot tried to voice one final warning: "Elevated rad—" and then quit for good, facing into its corner like a child that has been bad.

Two or three hundred wheels outside Candleton, as one travelled along the Path of the Beam, the radiation levels and concentrations of DEP3 in the soil fell rapidly. Here the mono's track swooped down to less than ten feet off the ground, and here a doe that looked almost normal walked prettily from piney woods to drink from a stream in which the water had three-quarters cleansed itself.

The doe was *not* normal—a stumpish fifth leg dangled down from the center of her lower belly like a teat, waggling bonelessly to and fro when she walked, and a blind third eye peered milkily from the left side of her muzzle.

Yet she was fertile, and her DNA was in reasonably good order for a twelfth-generation mutie. In her six years of life she had given birth to three live young. Two of these fawns had been not just viable but normal—threaded stock, Aunt Talitha of River Crossing would have called them. The third, a skinless, bawling horror, had been killed quickly by its sire.

The world—this part of it, at any rate—had begun to heal itself.

The deer slipped her mouth into the water, began to drink, then looked up, eyes wide, muzzle dripping. Off in the distance she could hear a low humming sound. A moment later it was joined by an eyelash of light. Alarm flared in the doe's nerves, but although her reflexes were fast and the light when first glimpsed was still many wheels away across the desolate countryside, there was never a chance for her to escape. Before she could even begin to fire her muscles, the distant spark had swelled to a searing wolf's eye of light that flooded the stream and the clearing with its glare. With the light came the maddening hum of Blaine's slo-trans engines, running at full capacity. There was a blur of pink above the concrete ridge which bore the rail; a rooster-tail of dust, stones, small dismembered animals, and whirling foliage followed along after. The doe was killed instantly by the concussion of Blaine's passage. Too large to be sucked in the mono's wake, she was still yanked forward almost seventy yards, with water dripping from her muzzle and hoofs. Much of her hide (and the boneless fifth leg) was torn from her body and pulled after Blaine like a discarded garment.

There was brief silence, thin as new skin or early ice on a Year's End pond, and then the sonic boom came rushing after like some noisy creature late for a wedding-feast, tearing the silence apart, knocking a single mutated bird—it might have been a raven—dead out of the air. The bird fell like a stone and splashed into the stream.

In the distance, a dwindling red eye: Blaine's taillight.

Overhead, a full moon came out from behind a scrim of cloud, painting the clearing and the stream in the tawdry hues of pawnshop jewelry. There was a face in the moon, but not one upon which lovers would wish to look. It seemed the scant face of a skull, like those in the Candleton Travellers' Hotel; a face which looked upon those few beings still alive and struggling below with the amusement of a lunatic. In Gilead, before the world had moved on, the full moon of Year's End had been called the Demon Moon, and it was considered ill luck to look directly at it.

Now, however, such did not matter. Now there were demons everywhere.

2

Susannah looked at the route-map and saw that the green dot marking their present position was now almost half-way between Candleton and Rilea, Blaine's next stop. *Except who's stopping?* she thought.

From the route-map she turned to Eddie. His gaze was still directed up at the ceiling of the Barony Coach. She followed it and saw a square which could only be a trap-door (except when you were dealing with futuristic shit like a talking train, she supposed you called it a hatch, or something even cooler). Stencilled on it was a simple red drawing which showed a man stepping through the opening. Susannah tried to imagine following the implied instruction and popping up through that hatch at over eight hundred miles an hour. She got a quick but clear image of a woman's head being ripped from her neck like a flower from its stalk; she saw the head flying backward along the length of the Barony Coach, perhaps bouncing once, and then disappearing into the dark, eyes staring and hair rippling.

She pushed the picture away as fast as she could. The hatch up there was almost certainly locked shut, anyway. Blaine the Mono had no intention of letting them go. They might win their way out, but Susannah didn't think that was a sure thing even if they managed to stump Blaine with a riddle.

Sorry to say this, but you sound like just one more honky motherfucker to me, honey, she thought in a mental voice that was not quite Detta Walker's. *I don't trust your mechanical ass. You apt to be more dangerous beaten than with the blue ribbon pinned to your memory banks.*

Jake was holding his tattered book of riddles out to the gunslinger as if he no longer wanted the responsibility of carrying it. Susannah knew how the kid must feel; their lives might very well be in those grimy, well-thumbed pages. She wasn't sure she would want the responsibility of holding onto it, either.

"Roland!" Jake whispered. "Do you want this?"

"*Ont!*" Oy said, giving the gunslinger a forbidding glance. "*Olan-ont-iss!*" The bumbler fixed his teeth on the book, took it from Jake's hand, and stretched his disproportionately long neck toward Roland, offering him *Riddle-De-Dum! Brain-Twisters and Puzzles for Everyone!*

Roland glanced at it for a moment, his face distant and preoccupied, then shook his head. "Not yet." He looked forward at the route-map. Blaine had no face, so the map had to serve them as a fixing-point. The flashing green dot was closer to Rilea now. Susannah wondered briefly what the countryside through which they were passing looked like, and decided she didn't really want to know. Not after what they'd seen as they left the city of Lud.

"Blaine!" Roland called.

"YES."

"Can you leave the room? We need to confer."

You nuts if you think he's gonna do that, Susannah thought, but Blaine's reply was quick and eager.

"YES, GUNSLINGER. I WILL TURN OFF ALL MY SENSORS IN THE BARONY COACH. WHEN YOUR CONFERENCE IS DONE AND YOU ARE READY TO BEGIN THE RIDDLING, I WILL RETURN."

"Yeah, you and General MacArthur," Eddie muttered.

"WHAT DID YOU SAY, EDDIE OF NEW YORK?"

"Nothing. Talking to myself, that's all."

"TO SUMMON ME, SIMPLY TOUCH THE ROUTE-MAP," said Blaine. "AS LONG AS THE MAP IS RED, MY SENSORS ARE OFF. SEE YOU LATER, ALLIGATOR. AFTER AWHILE, CROCODILE. DON'T FORGET TO WRITE." A pause. Then: "OLIVE OIL BUT NOT CAS-TORIA."

The route-map rectangle at the front of the cabin suddenly turned a red so bright Susannah couldn't look at it without squinting.

"Olive oil but not castoria?" Jake asked. "What the heck does *that* mean?"

"It doesn't matter," Roland said. "We don't have much time. The mono travels just as fast toward its point of ending whether Blaine's with us or not."

"You don't really believe he's gone, do you?" Eddie asked. "A slippery pup like him? Come on, get real. He's peeking, I guarantee you."

"I doubt it very much," Roland said, and Susannah decided she agreed with him. For now, at least. "You could hear how excited he was at the idea of riddling again after all these years. And—"

"And he's confident," Susannah said. "Doesn't expect to have much trouble with the likes of us."

"Will he?" Jake asked the gunslinger. "Will he have trouble with us?"

"I don't know," Roland said. "I don't have a Watch Me hidden up my sleeve, if that's what you're asking. It's a straight game . . . but at least it's a game I've played before. We've *all* played it before, at least to some extent. And there's that." He nodded toward the book which Jake had taken back from Oy. "There are forces at work here, big ones, and not all of them are working to keep us *away* from the Tower."

Susannah heard him, but it was Blaine she was thinking of—Blaine who had gone away and left them alone, like the kid who's been chosen "it" obediently covering his eyes while his playmates hide. And wasn't that what they were? Blaine's playmates? The thought was somehow worse than the image she'd had of trying the escape hatch and having her head torn off.

"So what do we do?" Eddie asked. "You must have an idea, or you never would have sent him away."

"His great intelligence—coupled with his long period of loneliness and forced inactivity—may have combined to make him more human than he knows. That's my hope, anyway. First, we must establish a kind of geography. We must tell, if we can, where he is weak and where he is strong, where he is sure of the game and where not so sure. Riddles are not just about the cleverness of the riddler, never think it. They are also about the blind spots of he who is riddled."

"Does he have blind spots?" Eddie asked.

"If he doesn't," Roland said calmly, "we're going to die on this train."

"I like the way you kind of ease us over the rough spots," Eddie said with a thin smile. "It's one of your many charms."

"We will riddle him four times to begin with," Roland said. "Easy, not so easy, quite hard, very hard. He'll answer all four, of that I am confident, but we will be listening for *how* he answers."

Eddie was nodding, and Susannah felt a small, almost reluctant glimmer of hope. It sounded like the right approach, all right.

"Then we'll send him away again and hold palaver," the gunslinger said. "Mayhap we'll get an idea of what direction to send our horses. These first riddles can come from anywhere, but"—he nodded gravely toward the book—"based on Jake's story of the bookstore, the answer we really need should be in there, not in any memories I have of Fair-Day riddlings. *Must* be in there."

"Question," Susannah said.

Roland looked at her, eyebrows raised over his faded, dangerous eyes.

"It's a *question* we're looking for, not an answer," she said. "This time it's the answers that are apt to get us killed."

The gunslinger nodded. He looked puzzled—frustrated, even—and this was not an expression Susannah liked seeing on his face. But this time when Jake held out the book, Roland took it. He held it for a moment (its faded but still gay red cover looked very strange in his big sunburned hands . . . especially in the right one, with its essential reduction of two fingers), then passed it on to Eddie.

"You're easy," Roland said, turning to Susannah.

"Perhaps," she replied, with a trace of a smile, "but it's still not a very polite thing to say to a lady, Roland."

He turned to Jake. "You'll go second, with one that's a

little harder. I'll go third. You'll go last, Eddie. Pick one from the book that looks hard—"

"The hard ones are toward the back," Jake supplied.

". . . but none of your foolishness, mind. This is life and death. The time for foolishness is past."

Eddie looked at him—old long, tall, and ugly, who'd done God knew how many ugly things in the name of reaching his Tower—and wondered if Roland had any idea at all of how much that hurt. Just that casual admonition not to behave like a child, grinning and cracking jokes, now that their lives were at wager.

He opened his mouth to say something—an Eddie Dean Special, something that would be both funny and stinging at the same time, the kind of remark that always used to drive his brother Henry dogshit—and then closed it again. Maybe long, tall, and ugly was right; maybe it was time to put away the one-liners and dead baby jokes. Maybe it was finally time to grow up.

3

After three more minutes of murmured consultation and some quick flipping through *Riddle-De-Dum!* on Eddie's and Susannah's parts (Jake already knew the one he wanted to try Blaine with first, he'd said), Roland went to the front of the Barony Coach and laid his hand on the fiercely glowing rectangle there. The route-map reappeared at once. Although there was no sensation of movement now that the coach was closed, the green dot was closer to Rilea than ever.

"SO, ROLAND SON OF STEVEN!" Blaine said. To Eddie he sounded more than jovial; he sounded next door to hilarious. "IS YOUR *KA-TET* READY TO BEGIN?"

"Yes. Susannah of New York will begin the first round." He turned to her, lowered his voice a little (not that she reckoned that would do much good if Blaine wanted to listen), and said: "You won't have to step forward like the rest of us, because of your legs, but you must speak fair and address him by name each time you talk to him. If—*when*—he answers your riddle correctly, say 'Than-kee-sai, Blaine, you have answered true.' Then Jake will step into the aisle and have his turn. All right?"

"And if he should get it wrong, or not guess at all?"

Roland smiled grimly. "I think that's one thing we don't have to worry about just yet." He raised his voice again. "Blaine?"

"YES, GUNSLINGER."

Roland took a deep breath. "It starts now."

"EXCELLENT!"

Roland nodded at Susannah. Eddie squeezed one of her hands; Jake patted the other. Oy gazed at her raptly with his gold-ringed eyes.

Susannah smiled at them nervously, then looked up at the route-map. "Hello, Blaine."

"HOWDY, SUSANNAH OF NEW YORK."

Her heart was pounding, her armpits were damp, and here was something she had first discovered way back in the first grade: it was hard to begin. It was hard to stand up in front of the class and be first with your song, your joke, your report on how you spent your summer vacation . . . or your riddle, for that matter. The one she had decided upon was one from Jake Chambers's crazed English essay, which he had recited to them almost ver-batim during their long palaver after leaving the old people of River Crossing. The essay, titled "My Under-standing of Truth," had contained two riddles, one of which Eddie had already used on Blaine.

"SUSANNAH? ARE YOU THERE, L'IL COWGIRL?"

Teasing again, but this time the teasing sounded light, good-natured. *Good-humored.* Blaine could be charming when he got what he wanted. Like certain spoiled children she had known.

"Yes, Blaine, I am, and here is my riddle. What has four wheels and flies?"

There was a peculiar click, as if Blaine were mimicking the sound of a man popping his tongue against the roof of his mouth. It was followed by a brief pause. When Blaine replied, most of the jocularity had gone out of his voice. "THE TOWN GARBAGE WAGON, OF COURSE. A CHILD'S RIDDLE. IF THE REST OF YOUR RIDDLES ARE NO BETTER, I WILL BE EXTREMELY SORRY I SAVED YOUR LIVES FOR EVEN A SHORT WHILE."

The route-map flashed, not red this time but pale pink. "Don't get him mad," the voice of Little Blaine begged. Each time it spoke, Susannah found herself imagining a sweaty little bald man whose every movement was a kind of cringe. The voice of Big Blaine came from everywhere (like the voice of God in a Cecil B. DeMille movie, Susannah thought), but Little Blaine's from only one: the speaker directly over their heads. *"Please* don't make him angry, fellows; he's already got the mono in the red, speedwise, and the track compensators can barely keep up. The trackage has degenerated terribly since the last time we came out this way."

Susannah, who had been on her share of bumpy trolleys and subways in her time, felt nothing—the ride was as smooth now as it had been when they had first pulled out of the Cradle of Lud—but she believed Little Blaine anyway. She guessed that if they *did* feel a bump, it would be the last thing any of them would ever feel.

Roland poked an elbow into her side, bringing her back to her current situation.

"Thankee-sai," she said, and then, as an afterthought,

tapped her throat rapidly three times with the fingers of her right hand. It was what Roland had done when speaking to Aunt Talitha for the first time.

"THANK YOU FOR YOUR COURTESY," Blaine said. He sounded amused again, and Susannah reckoned that was good even if his amusement was at her expense. "I AM NOT FEMALE, HOWEVER. INSOFAR AS I HAVE A SEX, IT IS MALE."

Susannah looked at Roland, bewildered.

"Left hand for men," he said. "On the breastbone." He tapped to demonstrate.

"Oh."

Roland turned to Jake. The boy stood, put Oy on his chair (which did no good; Oy immediately jumped down and followed after Jake when he stepped into the aisle to face the route-map), and turned his attention to Blaine.

"Hello, Blaine, this is Jake. You know, son of Elmer."

"SPEAK YOUR RIDDLE."

"What can run but never walks, has a mouth but never talks, has a bed but never sleeps, has a head but never weeps?"

"NOT BAD! ONE HOPES SUSANNAH WILL LEARN FROM YOUR EXAMPLE, JAKE SON OF ELMER. THE ANSWER MUST BE SELF-EVIDENT TO ANYONE OF ANY INTELLIGENCE AT ALL, BUT A DECENT EFFORT, NEVERTHELESS. A RIVER."

"Thankee-sai, Blaine, you have answered true." He tapped the bunched fingers of his left hand three times against his breastbone and then sat down. Susannah put her arm around him and gave him a brief squeeze. Jake looked at her gratefully.

Now Roland stood up. "Hile, Blaine," he said.

"HILE, GUNSLINGER." Once again Blaine sounded amused . . . possibly by the greeting, which Susannah hadn't heard before. *Heil what?* she wondered. Hitler came to mind, and that made her think of the downed plane they'd found outside Lud. A Focke-Wulf, Jake had claimed. She didn't know about that, but she knew it had contained one *seriously* dead harrier, too old even to stink. "SPEAK YOUR RIDDLE, ROLAND, AND LET IT BE HANDSOME."

"Handsome is as handsome does, Blaine. In any case, here it is: What has four legs in the morning, two legs in the afternoon, and three legs at night?"

"THAT IS INDEED HANDSOME," Blaine allowed. "SIMPLE BUT HANDSOME, JUST THE SAME. THE ANSWER IS A HUMAN BEING, WHO CRAWLS ON HANDS AND KNEES IN BABYHOOD, WALKS ON TWO LEGS DURING ADULTHOOD, AND WHO GOES ABOUT WITH THE HELP OF A CANE IN OLD AGE."

Blaine sounded positively smug, and Susannah suddenly discovered a mildly interesting fact: she loathed the self-satisfied, murderous thing. Machine or not, *it* or *he,* she loathed Blaine. She had an idea she would have felt the same even if he hadn't made them wager their lives in a stupid riddling contest.

Roland, however, did not look the slightest put out of countenance. "Thankee-sai, Blaine, you have answered true." He sat down without tapping his breastbone and looked at Eddie. Eddie stood up and stepped into the aisle.

"What's happening, Blaine my man?" he asked. Roland winced and shook his head, putting his mutilated right hand up briefly to shade his eyes.

Silence from Blaine.

"Blaine? Are you there?"

"YES, BUT IN NO MOOD FOR FRIVOLITY, EDDIE OF NEW YORK. SPEAK YOUR RIDDLE. I SUSPECT IT WILL BE DIFFICULT IN SPITE OF YOUR FOOLISH POSES. I LOOK FORWARD TO IT."

Eddie glanced at Roland, who waved a hand at him—
Go on, for your father's sake, go on!—and then looked back
at the route-map, where the green dot had just passed
the point marked Rilea. Susannah saw that Eddie suspected what she herself all but knew: Blaine understood
they were trying to test his capabilities with a spectrum of
riddles. Blaine knew . . . and welcomed it.

Susannah felt her heart sink as any hopes they might
find a quick and easy way out of this disappeared.

4

"Well," Eddie said, "I don't know how hard it'll seem to
you, but it struck me as a toughie." Nor did he know
the answer, since that section of *Riddle-De-Dum!* had
been torn out, but he didn't think that made any difference; their knowing the answers hadn't been part of the
ground-rules.

"I SHALL HEAR AND ANSWER."

"No sooner spoken than broken. What is it?"

"SILENCE, A THING YOU KNOW LITTLE ABOUT,
EDDIE OF NEW YORK," Blaine said with no pause at all,
and Eddie felt his heart drop a little. There was no need
to consult with the others; the answer was self-evident.
And having it come back at him so quickly was the real
bummer. Eddie never would have said so, but he had
harbored the hope—almost a secret surety—of bringing Blaine down with a single riddle, *ker-smash,* all the
King's horses and all the King's men couldn't put Blaine
together again. The same secret surety, he supposed,
that he had harbored every time he picked up a pair of
dice in some sharpie's back-bedroom crap game, every
time he called for a hit on seventeen while playing black-

jack. That feeling that you couldn't go wrong because you were *you,* the best, the one and only.

"Yeah," he said, sighing. "Silence, a thing I know little about. Thankee-sai, Blaine, you speak truth."

"I HOPE YOU HAVE DISCOVERED SOMETHING WHICH WILL HELP YOU," Blaine said, and Eddie thought: *You fucking mechanical liar.* The complacent tone had returned to Blaine's voice, and Eddie found it of some passing interest that a machine could express such a range of emotion. Had the Great Old Ones built them in, or had Blaine created an emotional rainbow for himself at some point? A little dipolar pretty with which to pass the long decades and centuries? "DO YOU WISH ME TO GO AWAY AGAIN SO YOU MAY CONSULT?"

"Yes," Roland said.

The route-map flashed bright red. Eddie turned toward the gunslinger. Roland composed his face quickly, but before he did, Eddie saw a horrible thing: a brief look of complete hopelessness. Eddie had never seen such a look there before, not when Roland had been dying of the lobstrosities' bites, not when Eddie had been pointing the gunslinger's own revolver at him, not even when the hideous Gasher had taken Jake prisoner and disappeared into Lud with him.

"What do we do next?" Jake asked. "Do another round of the four of us?"

"I think that would serve little purpose," Roland said. "Blaine must know thousands of riddles—perhaps millions—and that is bad. Worse, *far* worse, he understands the *how* of riddling . . . the place the mind has to go to in order to make them and solve them." He turned to Eddie and Susannah, sitting once more with their arms about one another. "Am I right about that?" he asked them. "Do you agree?"

"Yes," Susannah said, and Eddie nodded reluctantly. He didn't *want* to agree . . . but he did.

"So?" Jake asked. "What *do* we do, Roland? I mean, there has to be a way out of this . . . doesn't there?"

Lie to him, you bastard, Eddie sent fiercely in Roland's direction.

Roland, perhaps hearing the thought, did the best he could. He touched Jake's hair with his diminished hand and ruffled through it. "I think there's always an answer, Jake. The real question is whether or not we'll have time to find the right riddle. He said it took him a little under nine hours to run his route—"

"Eight hours, forty-five minutes," Jake put in.

". . . and that's not much time. We've already been running almost an hour—"

"And if that map's right, we're almost halfway to Topeka," Susannah said in a tight voice. "Could be our mechanical pal's been lying to us about the length of the run. Hedging his bets a little."

"Could be," Roland agreed.

"So what do we do?" Jake repeated.

Roland drew in a deep breath, held it, let it out. "Let me riddle him alone, for now. I'll ask him the hardest ones I remember from the Fair-Days of my youth. Then, Jake, if we're approaching the point of . . . if we're approaching Topeka at this same speed with Blaine still unposed, I think you should ask him the last few riddles in your book. The hardest riddles." He rubbed the side of his face distractedly and looked at the ice sculpture. This chilly rendering of his own likeness had now melted to an unrecognizable hulk. "I still think the answer must be in the book. Why else would you have been drawn to it before coming back to this world?"

"And us?" Susannah asked. "What do Eddie and I do?"

"Think," Roland said. *"Think,* for your fathers' sakes."

" 'I do not shoot with my hand,' " Eddie said. He suddenly felt far away, strange to himself. It was the way he'd felt when he had seen first the slingshot and then the key in pieces of wood, just waiting for him to whittle them free . . . and at the same time this feeling was not like that at all.

Roland was looking at him oddly. "Yes, Eddie, you say true. A gunslinger shoots with his mind. What have you thought of?"

"Nothing." He might have said more, but all at once a strange image—a strange *memory*—intervened: Roland hunkering by Jake at one of their stopping-points on the way to Lud. Both of them in front of an unlit campfire. Roland once more at his everlasting lessons. Jake's turn this time. Jake with the flint and steel, trying to quicken the fire. Spark after spark licking out and dying in the dark. And Roland had said that he was being silly. That he was just being . . . well . . . *silly.*

"No," Eddie said. "He didn't say that at all. At least not to the kid, he didn't."

"Eddie?" Susannah. Sounding concerned. Almost frightened.

Well why don't you ask him *what he said, bro?* That was Henry's voice, the voice of the Great Sage and Eminent Junkie. First time in a long time. *Ask him, he's practically sitting right next to you, go on and ask him what he said. Quit dancing around like a baby with a load in his diapers.*

Except that was a bad idea, because that wasn't the way things worked in Roland's world. In Roland's world *everything* was riddles, you didn't shoot with your hand but with your *mind,* your motherfucking *mind,* and what did you say to someone who wasn't getting the spark into the kindling? Move your flint in closer, of course, and that's what Roland had said: *Move your flint in closer, and hold it steady.*

Except none of that was what this was about. It was close, yes, but close only counts in horseshoes, as Henry Dean had been wont to say before he became the Great Sage and Eminent Junkie. Eddie's memory was jinking a little because Roland had embarrassed him . . . shamed him . . . made a joke at his expense . . .

Probably not on purpose, but . . . *something*. Something that had made him feel the way Henry always used to make him feel, of course it was, why else would Henry be here after such a long absence?

All of them looking at him now. Even Oy.

"Go on," he told Roland, sounding a little waspish. "You wanted us to think, we're thinking, already." He himself was thinking so hard

(I shoot with my mind)

that his goddam brains were almost on fire, but he wasn't going to tell old long, tall, and ugly that. "Go on and ask Blaine some riddles. Do your part."

"As you will, Eddie." Roland rose from his seat, went forward, and laid his hand on the scarlet rectangle again. The route-map reappeared at once. The green dot had moved farther beyond Rilea, but it was clear to Eddie that the mono had slowed down significantly, either obeying some built-in program or because Blaine was having too much fun to hurry.

"IS YOUR *KA-TET* READY TO CONTINUE OUR FAIR-DAY RIDDLING, ROLAND SON OF STEVEN?"

"Yes, Blaine," Roland said, and to Eddie his voice sounded heavy. "I will riddle you alone for awhile now. If you have no objection."

"AS *DINH* AND FATHER OF YOUR *KA-TET*, SUCH IS YOUR RIGHT. WILL THESE BE FAIR-DAY RIDDLES?"

"Yes."

"GOOD." Loathsome satisfaction in that voice. "I WOULD HEAR MORE OF THOSE."

"All right." Roland took a deep breath, then began. "Feed me and I live. Give me to drink and I die. What am I?"

"FIRE." No hesitation. Only that insufferable smugness, a tone which said *That was old to me when your grandmother was young, but try again! This is more fun than I've had in centuries, so try again!*

"I pass before the sun, Blaine, yet make no shadow. What am I?"

"WIND." No hesitation.

"You speak true, sai. Next. This is as light as a feather, yet no man can hold it for long."

"ONE'S BREATH." No hesitation.

Yet he did *hesitate,* Eddie thought suddenly. Jake and Susannah were watching Roland with agonized concentration, fists clenched, *willing* him to ask Blaine the right riddle, the stumper, the one with the Get the Fuck Out of Jail Free card hidden inside it; Eddie couldn't look at them—Suze, in particular—and keep his concentration. He lowered his gaze to his own hands, which were also clenched, and forced them to open on his lap. It was surprisingly hard to do. From the aisle he heard Roland continuing to trot out the golden oldies of his youth.

"Riddle me this, Blaine: If you break me, I'll not stop working. If you can touch me, my work is done. If you lose me, you must find me with a ring soon after. What am I?"

Susannah's breath caught for a moment, and although he was looking down, Eddie knew she was thinking what he was thinking: that was a good one, a *damned* good one, maybe—

"THE HUMAN HEART," Blaine said. Still with not a whit of hesitation. "THIS RIDDLE IS BASED IN LARGE PART UPON HUMAN POETIC CONCEITS; SEE FOR INSTANCE JOHN AVERY, SIRONIA HUNTZ,

ONDOLA, WILLIAM BLAKE, JAMES TATE, VERON-
ICA MAYS, AND OTHERS. IT IS REMARKABLE HOW
HUMAN BEINGS PITCH THEIR MINDS ON LOVE.
YET IT IS CONSTANT FROM ONE LEVEL OF THE
TOWER TO THE NEXT, EVEN IN THESE DEGENER-
ATE DAYS. CONTINUE, ROLAND OF GILEAD."

Susannah's breath resumed. Eddie's hands wanted to
clench again, but he wouldn't let them. *Move your flint
in closer,* he thought in Roland's voice. *Move your flint in
closer, for your father's sake!*

And Blaine the Mono ran on, southeast under the
Demon Moon.

CHAPTER TWO

The Falls of the Hounds

I

Jake didn't know how easy or difficult Blaine might find the last ten puzzlers in *Riddle-De-Dum!*, but they looked pretty tough to him. Of course, he reminded himself, he wasn't a thinking-machine with a city-wide bank of computers to draw on. All he could do was go for it; God hates a coward, as Eddie sometimes said. If the last ten failed, he would try Aaron Deepneau's Samson riddle *(Out of the eater came forth meat,* and so on). If that one also failed, he'd probably . . . shit, he didn't know *what* he'd do, or even how he'd feel. *The truth is,* Jake thought, *I'm fried.*

And why not? He had gone through an extraordinary swarm of emotions in the last eight hours or so. First, terror: of being sure he and Oy were going to drop off the suspension bridge and to their deaths in the River Send; of being driven through the crazed maze that was Lud by Gasher; of having to look into the Tick-Tock Man's terrible green eyes and try to answer his unanswerable questions about time, Nazis, and the nature of transitive circuits. Being questioned by Tick-Tock had been like having to take a final exam in hell.

Then the exhilaration of being rescued by Roland (and Oy; without Oy he would almost certainly be toast now), the wonder of all they had seen beneath the city, his awe at the way Susannah had solved Blaine's gate-riddle, and the final mad rush to get aboard the mono before Blaine could release the stocks of nerve-gas stored under Lud.

After surviving all that, a kind of blissed-out surety had settled over him—of *course* Roland would stump Blaine, who would then keep his part of the bargain and set them down safe and sound at his final stop (whatever passed for Topeka in this world). Then they would find the Dark Tower and do whatever they were supposed to do there, right what needed righting, fix what needed fixing. And then? They Lived Happily Ever After, of course. Like folk in a fairy tale.

Except. . .

They shared each other's thoughts, Roland had said; sharing *khef* was part of what *ka-tet* meant. And what had been seeping into Jake's thoughts ever since Roland stepped into the aisle and began to try Blaine with riddles from his young days was a sense of doom. It wasn't coming just from the gunslinger; Susannah was sending out the same grim blue-black vibe. Only Eddie wasn't sending it, and that was because he'd gone off somewhere, was chasing his own thoughts. That might be good, but there were no guarantees, and—

—and Jake began to be scared again. Worse, he felt desperate, like a creature that is pressed deeper and deeper into its final corner by a relentless foe. His fingers worked restlessly in Oy's fur, and when he looked down at them, he realized an amazing thing: the hand which Oy had bitten into to keep from falling off the bridge no longer hurt. He could see the holes the bumbler's teeth had made, and blood was still crusted in his palm and on his wrist, but the hand itself no longer hurt. He flexed it cautiously. There was some pain, but it was low and distant, hardly there at all.

"Blaine, what may go up a chimney down but cannot go down a chimney up?"

"A LADY'S PARASOL," Blaine replied in that tone of jolly complacency which Jake, too, was coming to loathe.

"Thankee-sai, Blaine, once again you have answered true. Next—"

"Roland?"

The gunslinger looked around at Jake, and his look of concentration lightened a bit. It wasn't a smile, but it went a little way in that direction, at least, and Jake was glad.

"What is it, Jake?"

"My hand. It was hurting like crazy, and now it's stopped!"

"SHUCKS," Blaine said in the drawling voice of John Wayne. "I COULDN'T WATCH A HOUND SUFFER WITH A MASHED-UP FOREPAW LIKE THAT, LET ALONE A FINE LITTLE TRAILHAND LIKE YOUR-SELF. SO I FIXED IT UP."

"How?" Jake asked.

"LOOK ON THE ARM OF YOUR SEAT."

Jake did, and saw a faint gridwork of lines. It looked a little like the speaker of the transistor radio he'd had when he was seven or eight.

"ANOTHER BENEFIT OF TRAVELLING BARONY CLASS," Blaine went on in his smug voice. It crossed Jake's mind that Blaine would fit in perfectly at the Piper School. The world's first slo-trans, dipolar nerd. "THE HAND-SCAN SPECTRUM MAGNIFIER IS A DIAGNOS-TIC TOOL ALSO CAPABLE OF ADMINISTERING MINOR FIRST AID, SUCH AS I HAVE PERFORMED ON YOU. IT IS ALSO A NUTRIENT DELIVERY SYSTEM, A BRAIN-PATTERN RECORDING DEVICE, A STRESS-ANALYZER, AND AN EMOTION-ENHANCER WHICH CAN NATURALLY STIMULATE THE PRODUCTION OF ENDORPHINS. HAND-SCAN IS ALSO CAPABLE

OF CREATING VERY BELIEVABLE ILLUSIONS AND HALLUCINATIONS. WOULD YOU CARE TO HAVE YOUR FIRST SEXUAL EXPERIENCE WITH A NOTED SEX-GODDESS FROM YOUR LEVEL OF THE TOWER, JAKE OF NEW YORK? PERHAPS MARILYN MONROE, RAQUEL WELCH, OR EDITH BUNKER?"

Jake laughed. He guessed that laughing at Blaine might be risky, but this time he just couldn't help it. "There *is* no Edith Bunker," he said. "She's just a character on a TV show. The actress's name is, um, Jean Stapleton. Also, she looks like Mrs. Shaw. She's our housekeeper. Nice, but not—you know—a babe."

A long silence from Blaine. When the voice of the computer returned, a certain coldness had replaced the jocose ain't-we-having-fun tone of voice.

"I CRY YOUR PARDON, JAKE OF NEW YORK. I ALSO WITHDRAW MY OFFER OF A SEXUAL EXPERIENCE."

That'll teach me, Jake thought, raising one hand to cover a smile. Aloud (and in what he hoped was a suitably humble tone of voice) he said: "That's okay, Blaine. I think I'm still a little young for that, anyway."

Susannah and Roland were looking at each other. Susannah didn't know who Edith Bunker was—*All in the Family* hadn't been on the tube in her when. But she grasped the essence of the situation just the same; Jake saw her full lips form one soundless word and send it to the gunslinger like a message in a soapbubble:

Mistake.

Yes. Blaine had made a mistake. More, Jake Chambers, a boy of eleven, had picked up on it. And if Blaine had made one, he could make another. Maybe there was hope after all. Jake decided he would treat that possibility as he had treated the *graf* of River Crossing and allow himself just a little.

2

Roland nodded imperceptibly at Susannah, then turned back to the front of the coach, presumably to resume riddling. Before he could open his mouth, Jake felt his body pushed forward. It was funny; you couldn't feel a thing when the mono was running flat-out, but the minute it began to decelerate, you knew.

"HERE IS SOMETHING YOU REALLY OUGHT TO SEE," Blaine said. He sounded cheerful again, but Jake didn't trust that tone; he had sometimes heard his father start telephone conversations that way (usually with some subordinate who had FUB, Fucked Up Big), and by the end Elmer Chambers would be up on his feet, bent over the desk like a man with a stomach cramp and screaming at the top of his lungs, his cheeks red as radishes and the circles of flesh under his eyes as purple as an eggplant. "I HAVE TO STOP HERE, ANYWAY, AS I MUST SWITCH TO BATTERY POWER AT THIS POINT AND THAT MEANS PRE-CHARGING."

The mono stopped with a barely perceptible jerk. The walls around them once more drained of color and then became transparent. Susannah gasped with fear and wonder. Roland moved to his left, felt for the side of the coach so he wouldn't bump his head, then leaned forward with his hands on his knees and his eyes narrowed. Oy began to bark again. Only Eddie seemed unmoved by the breathtaking view which had been provided them by the Barony Coach's visual mode. He glanced around once, face preoccupied and somehow bleary with thought, and then looked down at his hands again. Jake glanced at him with brief curiosity, then stared back out.

They were halfway across a vast chasm and seemed to be hovering on the moon-dusted air. Beyond them Jake could see a wide, boiling river. Not the Send, unless the rivers in Roland's world were somehow able to run in different directions at different points in their courses (and Jake didn't know enough about Mid-World to entirely discount that possibility); also, this river was not placid but raging, a torrent that came tumbling out of the mountains like something that was pissed off and wanted to brawl.

For a moment Jake looked at the trees which dressed the steep slopes along the sides of this river, registering with relief that they looked pretty much all right—the sort of firs you'd expect to see in the mountains of Colorado or Wyoming, say—and then his eyes were dragged back to the lip of the chasm. Here the torrent broke apart and dropped in a waterfall so wide and so deep that Jake thought it made Niagara, where he had gone with his parents (one of three family vacations he could remember; two had been cut short by urgent calls from his father's Network), look like the kind you might see in a third-rate theme-park. The air filling the enclosing semicircle of the falls was further thickened by an uprushing mist that looked like steam; in it half a dozen moonbows gleamed like gaudy, interlocking dream-jewelry. To Jake they looked like the overlapping rings which symbolized the Olympics.

Jutting from the center of the falls, perhaps two hundred feet below the point where the river actually went over the drop, were two enormous stone protrusions. Although Jake had no idea how a sculptor (or a team of them) could have gotten down to where they were, he found it all but impossible to believe they had simply eroded that way. They looked like the heads of enormous, snarling dogs.

The Falls of the Hounds, he thought. There was one

more stop beyond this—Dasherville—and then Topeka. Last stop. Everybody out.

"ONE MOMENT," Blaine said. "I MUST ADJUST THE VOLUME FOR YOU TO ENJOY THE FULL EFFECT."

There was a brief, whispery hooting sound—a kind of mechanical throat-clearing—and then they were assaulted by a vast roar. It was water—a billion gallons a minute, for all Jake knew—pouring over the lip of the chasm and falling perhaps two thousand feet into the deep stone basin at the base of the falls. Streamers of mist floated past the blunt almost-faces of the jutting dogs like steam from the vents of hell. The level of sound kept climbing. Now Jake's whole head vibrated with it, and as he clapped his hands over his ears, he saw Roland, Eddie, and Susannah doing the same. Oy was barking, but Jake couldn't hear him. Susannah's lips were moving again, and again he could read the words—*Stop it, Blaine, stop it!*—but he couldn't hear them any more than he could hear Oy's barks, although he was sure Susannah was screaming at the top of her lungs.

And still Blaine increased the sound of the waterfall, until Jake could feel his eyes shaking in their sockets and he was sure his ears were going to short out like over-stressed stereo speakers.

Then it was over. They still hung above the moon-misty drop, the moonbows still made their slow and dreamlike revolutions before the curtain of endlessly falling water, the wet and brutal stone faces of the dog-guardians continued to jut out of the torrent, but that world-ending thunder was gone.

For a moment Jake thought what he'd feared had happened, that he had gone deaf. Then he realized that he could hear Oy, still barking, and Susannah crying. At first these sounds seemed distant and flat, as if his ears had been packed with cracker-crumbs, but then they began to clarify.

Eddie put his arm around Susannah's shoulders and looked toward the route-map. "Nice guy, Blaine."

"I MERELY THOUGHT YOU WOULD ENJOY HEARING THE SOUND OF THE FALLS AT FULL VOLUME," Blaine said. His booming voice sounded laughing and injured at the same time. "I THOUGHT IT MIGHT HELP YOU TO FORGET MY REGRETTA-BLE MISTAKE IN THE MATTER OF EDITH BUNKER."

My fault, Jake thought. *Blaine may just be a machine, and a suicidal one at that, but he still doesn't like to be laughed at.*

He sat beside Susannah and put his own arm around her. He could still hear the Falls of the Hounds, but the sound was now distant.

"What happens here?" Roland asked. "How do you charge your batteries?"

"YOU WILL SEE SHORTLY, GUNSLINGER. IN THE MEANTIME, TRY ME WITH A RIDDLE."

"All right, Blaine. Here's one of Cort's own making, and has posed many in its time."

"I AWAIT IT WITH GREAT INTEREST."

Roland, pausing perhaps to gather his thoughts, looked up at the place where the roof of the coach had been and where there was now only a starry spill across a black sky (Jake could pick out Aton and Lydia—Old Star and Old Mother—and was oddly comforted by the sight of them, still glaring at each other from their accustomed places). Then the gunslinger looked back at the lighted rectangle which served them as Blaine's face.

" 'We are very little creatures; all of us have different features. One of us in glass is set; one of us you'll find in jet. Another you may see in tin, and a fourth is boxed within. If the fifth you should pursue, it can never fly from you. What are we?' "

"A AND E AND I AND O AND U," Blaine replied.
"THE VOWELS OF THE HIGH SPEECH." Still no hesitation, not so much as a whit. Only that voice, mocking
and just about two steps from laughter; the voice of a
cruel little boy watching bugs run around on top of a hot
stove. "ALTHOUGH THAT PARTICULAR RIDDLE IS
NOT FROM YOUR TEACHER, ROLAND OF GILEAD; I
KNOW IT FROM JONATHAN SWIFT OF LONDON—A
CITY IN THE WORLD YOUR FRIENDS COME FROM."

"Thankee-sai," Roland said, and his sai sounded like a
sigh. "Your answer is true, Blaine, and undoubtedly what
you believe of the riddle's origins is true as well. That
Cort knew of other worlds is something I long suspected.
I think he may have held palaver with the *manni* who
lived outside the city."

"I CARE NOT ABOUT THE *MANNI*, ROLAND OF
GILEAD. THEY WERE ALWAYS A FOOLISH SECT.
TRY ME WITH ANOTHER RIDDLE."

"All right. What has—"

"HOLD, HOLD. THE FORCE OF THE BEAM GATH-
ERS. LOOK NOT DIRECTLY AT THE HOUNDS, MY
INTERESTING NEW FRIENDS! AND SHIELD YOUR
EYES!"

Jake looked away from the colossal rock sculptures jutting from the falls, but didn't get his hand up quite in
time. With his peripheral vision he saw those featureless
heads suddenly develop eyes of a fiercely glowing blue.
Jagged tines of lightning leaped out of them and toward
the mono. Then Jake was lying on the carpeted floor
of the Barony Coach with the heels of his hands pasted
against his closed eyes and the sound of Oy whining in
one faintly ringing ear. Beyond Oy, he heard the crackle
of electricity as it stormed around the mono.

When Jake opened his eyes again, the Falls of the
Hounds were gone; Blaine had opaqued the cabin. He

could still hear the sound, though—a waterfall of electricity, a force somehow drawn from the Beam and shot out through the eyes of the stone heads. Blaine was feeding himself with it, somehow. *When we go on,* Jake thought, *he'll be running on batteries. Then Lud really will be behind us. For good.*

"Blaine," Roland said. "How is the power of the Beam stored in that place? What makes it come from the eyes of yon stone temple-dogs? How do you use it?"

Silence from Blaine.

"And who carved them?" Eddie asked. "Was it the Great Old Ones? It wasn't, was it? There were people even before them. Or . . . *were* they people?"

More silence from Blaine. And maybe that was good. Jake wasn't sure how much he wanted to know about the Falls of the Hounds, or what went on beneath them. He had been in the dark of Roland's world before, and had seen enough to believe that most of what was growing there was neither good nor safe.

"Better not to ask him," the voice of Little Blaine drifted down from over their heads. "Safer."

"Don't ask him silly questions, he won't play silly games," Eddie said. That distant, dreaming look had come onto his face again, and when Susannah spoke his name, he didn't seem to hear.

3

Roland sat down across from Jake and scrubbed his right hand slowly up the stubble on his right cheek, an unconscious gesture he seemed to make only when he was feeling tired or doubtful. "I'm running out of riddles," he said.

Jake looked back at him, startled. The gunslinger had

posed fifty or more to the computer, and Jake supposed that was a lot to just yank out of your head with no preparation, but when you considered that riddling had been such a big deal in the place where Roland had grown up . . .

He seemed to read some of this on Jake's face, for a small smile, lemon-bitter, touched the corners of his mouth, and he nodded as if the boy had spoken out loud. "I don't understand, either. If you'd asked me yesterday or the day before, I would have told you that I had at least a thousand riddles stored up in the junkbin I keep at the back of my mind. Perhaps two thousand. But . . ."

He lifted one shoulder in a shrug, shook his head, rubbed his hand up his cheek again.

"It's not like forgetting. It's as if they were never there in the first place. What's happening to the rest of the world is happening to me, I reckon."

"You're moving on," Susannah said, and looked at Roland with an expression of pity which Roland could look back at for only a second or two; it was as if he felt burned by her regard. "Like everything else here."

"Yes, I fear so." He looked at Jake, lips tight, eyes sharp. "Will you be ready with the riddles from your book when I call on you?"

"Yes."

"Good. And take heart. We're not finished yet."

Outside, the dim crackle of electricity ceased.

"I HAVE FED MY BATTERIES AND ALL IS WELL," Blaine announced.

"Marvelous," Susannah said dryly.

"Luss!" Oy agreed, catching Susannah's sarcastic tone exactly.

"I HAVE A NUMBER OF SWITCHING FUNCTIONS TO PERFORM. THESE WILL TAKE ABOUT

FORTY MINUTES AND ARE LARGELY AUTOMATIC. WHILE THIS SWITCHOVER TAKES PLACE AND THE ACCOMPANYING CHECKLIST IS RUNNING, WE SHALL CONTINUE OUR CONTEST. I AM ENJOYING IT VERY MUCH."

"It's like when you have to switch over from electric to diesel on the train to Boston," Eddie said. He still sounded as if he wasn't quite with them. "At Hartford or New Haven or one of those other places where no one in their right fucking mind would want to live."

"Eddie?" Susannah asked. "What are you—"

Roland touched her shoulder and shook his head.

"NEVER MIND EDDIE OF NEW YORK," Blaine said in his expansive, gosh-but-this-is-fun voice.

"That's right," Eddie said. "Never mind Eddie of New York."

"HE KNOWS NO GOOD RIDDLES. BUT YOU KNOW MANY, ROLAND OF GILEAD. TRY ME WITH ANOTHER."

And, as Roland did just that, Jake thought of his Final Essay. *Blaine is a pain*, he had written there. *Blaine is a pain and that is the truth.* It was the truth, all right.

The *stone* truth.

A little less than an hour later, Blaine the Mono began to move again.

4

Susannah watched with dreadful fascination as the flashing dot approached Dasherville, passed it, and made its final dogleg for home. The dot's movement said that Blaine was moving a bit more slowly now that it had switched over to batteries, and she fancied the lights in the Barony Coach were a little dimmer, but she didn't believe it would make much difference, in the end. Blaine might reach his terminus in Topeka doing six hundred miles an hour instead of eight hundred, but his last load of passengers would be toothpaste either way.

Roland was also slowing down, going deeper and deeper into that mental junkbin of his to find riddles. Yet he *did* find them, and he refused to give up. As always. Ever since he had begun teaching her to shoot, Susannah had felt a reluctant love for Roland of Gilead, a feeling that seemed a mixture of admiration, fear, and pity. She thought she would never really like him (and that the Detta Walker part of her might always hate him for the way he had seized hold of her and dragged her, raving, into the sun), but her love was nonetheless strong. He had, after all, saved Eddie Dean's life and soul; had rescued her beloved. She must love him for that if for nothing else. But she loved him even more, she suspected, for the way he would never, *never* give up. The word *retreat* didn't seem to be in his vocabulary, even when he was discouraged . . . as he so clearly was now.

"Blaine, where may you find roads without carts, forests without trees, cities without houses?"

"ON A MAP."

"You say true, sai. Next. I have a hundred legs but cannot stand, a long neck but no head; I eat the maid's life. What am I?"

"A BROOM, GUNSLINGER. ANOTHER VARIATION ENDS, 'I *EASE* THE MAID'S LIFE.' I LIKE YOURS BETTER."

Roland ignored this. "Cannot be seen, cannot be felt, cannot be heard, cannot be smelt. It lies behind the stars and beneath the hills. Ends life and kills laughter. What is it, Blaine?"

"THE DARK."

"Thankee-sai, you speak true."

The diminished right hand slid up the right cheek—the old fretful gesture—and the minute scratching sound produced by the callused pads of his fingers made Susannah shiver. Jake sat cross-legged on the floor, looking at the gunslinger with a kind of fierce intensity.

"This thing runs but cannot walk, sometimes sings but never talks. Lacks arms, has hands; lacks a head but has a face. What is it, Blaine?"

"A CLOCK."

"Shit," Jake whispered, lips compressing.

Susannah looked over at Eddie and felt a passing ripple of irritation. He seemed to have lost interest in the whole thing—had "zoned out," in his weird 1980s slang. She thought to throw an elbow into his side, wake him up a little, then remembered Roland shaking his head at her and didn't. You wouldn't know he was thinking, not from that slack expression on his face, but maybe he was.

If so, you better hurry it up a little, precious, she thought. The dot on the route-map was still closer to Dasherville than Topeka, but it would reach the halfway point within the next fifteen minutes or so.

And still the match went on, Roland serving questions, Blaine sending the answers whistling right back at him, low over the net and out of reach.

What builds up castles, tears down mountains, makes some blind, helps others to see? SAND.

Thankee-sai.

What lives in winter, dies in summer, and grows with its roots upward? AN ICICLE.

Blaine, you say true.

Man walks over; man walks under; in time of war he burns asunder? A BRIDGE.

Thankee-sai.

A seemingly endless parade of riddles marched past her, one after the other, until she lost all sense of their fun and playfulness. Had it been so in the days of Roland's youth, she wondered, during the riddle contests of Wide Earth and Full Earth, when he and his friends (although she had an idea they hadn't *all* been his friends, no, not by a long chalk) had vied for the Fair-Day goose? She guessed that the answer was probably yes. The winner had probably been the one who could stay fresh longest, keep his poor bludgeoned brains aerated somehow.

The killer was the way Blaine came back with the answer so damned *promptly* each time. No matter how hard the riddle might seem to her, Blaine served it right back to their side of the court, *ka-slam*.

"Blaine, what has eyes yet cannot see?"

"THERE ARE FOUR ANSWERS," Blaine replied. "NEEDLES, STORMS, POTATOES, AND A TRUE LOVER."

"Thankee-sai, Blaine, you speak—"

"LISTEN, ROLAND OF GILEAD. LISTEN, *KA-TET.*"

Roland fell silent at once, his eyes narrowing, his head slightly cocked.

"YOU WILL SHORTLY HEAR MY ENGINES BEGIN TO CYCLE UP," Blaine said. "WE ARE NOW EXACTLY SIXTY MINUTES OUT OF TOPEKA. AT THIS POINT—"

"If we've been riding for seven hours or more, I grew up with the Brady Bunch," Jake said.

Susannah looked around apprehensively, expecting some new terror or small act of cruelty in response to Jake's sarcasm, but Blaine only chuckled. When he spoke again, the voice of Humphrey Bogart had resurfaced.

"TIME'S DIFFERENT HERE, SHWEETHEART. YOU MUST KNOW THAT BY NOW. BUT DON'T WORRY; THE FUNDAMENTAL THINGS APPLY AS TIME GOES BY. WOULD I LIE TO YOU?"

"Yes," Jake muttered.

That apparently struck Blaine's funnybone, because he began to laugh again—the mad, mechanical laughter that made Susannah think of funhouses in sleazy amusement parks and roadside carnivals. When the lights began to pulse in sync with the laughter, she shut her eyes and put her hands over her ears.

"Stop it, Blaine! Stop it!"

"BEG PARDON, MA'AM," drawled the aw-shucks voice of Jimmy Stewart. "AH'M RIGHT SORRY IF I RUINT YOUR EARS WITH MY RISABILITY."

"Ruin this," Jake said, and hoisted his middle finger at the route-map.

Susannah expected Eddie to laugh—you could count on him to be amused by vulgarity at any time of the day or night, she would have said—but Eddie only continued looking down at his lap, his forehead creased, his eyes vacant, his mouth hung slightly agape. He looked a little too much like the village idiot for comfort, Susannah thought, and again had to restrain herself from throwing an elbow into his side to get that doltish look off his face. She wouldn't restrain herself for much longer; if they were going to die at the end of Blaine's run, she wanted Eddie's arms around her when it happened, Eddie's eyes on her, Eddie's mind with hers.

But for now, better let him be.

"AT THIS POINT," Blaine resumed in his normal voice, "I INTEND TO BEGIN WHAT I LIKE TO THINK OF AS MY KAMIKAZE RUN. THIS WILL QUICKLY DRAIN MY BATTERIES, BUT I THINK THE TIME FOR CONSERVATION HAS PASSED, DON'T YOU? WHEN I STRIKE THE TRANSTEEL PIERS AT THE END OF THE TRACK, I SHOULD BE TRAVELLING AT BETTER THAN NINE HUNDRED MILES AN HOUR—FIVE HUNDRED AND THIRTY IN WHEELS, THAT IS. SEE YOU LATER, ALLIGATOR, AFTER AWHILE, CROCODILE, DON'T FORGET TO WRITE. I TELL YOU THIS IN THE SPIRIT OF FAIR PLAY, MY INTER-

ESTING NEW FRIENDS. IF YOU HAVE BEEN SAVING
YOUR BEST RIDDLES FOR LAST, YOU MIGHT DO
WELL TO POSE THEM TO ME NOW."

The unmistakable greed in Blaine's voice—its naked
desire to hear and solve their best riddles before it killed
them—made Susannah feel tired and old.

"I might not have time even so to pose you all my *very*
best ones," Roland said in a casual, considering tone of
voice. "That would be a shame, wouldn't it?"

A pause ensued—brief, but more of a hesitation than
the computer had accorded any of Roland's riddles—
and then Blaine chuckled. Susannah hated the sound
of its mad laughter, but there was a cynical weariness in
this chuckle that chilled her even more deeply. Perhaps
because it was almost sane.

"GOOD, GUNSLINGER. A VALIANT EFFORT. BUT
YOU ARE NOT SCHEHERAZADE, NOR DO WE HAVE
A THOUSAND AND ONE NIGHTS IN WHICH TO
HOLD PALAVER."

"I don't understand you. I know not this Scheherazade."

"NO MATTER. SUSANNAH CAN FILL YOU IN, IF
YOU REALLY WANT TO KNOW. PERHAPS EVEN
EDDIE. THE POINT, ROLAND, IS THAT I'LL NOT BE
DRAWN ON BY THE PROMISE OF MORE RIDDLES.
WE VIE FOR THE GOOSE. COME TOPEKA, IT SHALL
BE AWARDED, ONE WAY OR ANOTHER. DO YOU
UNDERSTAND THAT?"

Once more the diminished hand went up Roland's
cheek; once more Susannah heard the minute rasp of
his fingers against the wiry stubble of his beard.

"We play for keeps. No one cries off."

"CORRECT. NO ONE CRIES OFF."

"All right, Blaine, we play for keeps and no one cries
off. Here's the next."

"AS ALWAYS, I AWAIT IT WITH PLEASURE."

Roland looked down at Jake. "Be ready with yours, Jake; I'm almost at the end of mine."

Jake nodded.

Beneath them, the mono's slo-trans engines continued to cycle up—that beat-beat-beat which Susannah did not so much hear as feel in the hinges of her jaw, the hollows of her temples, the pulse-points of her wrists.

It's not going to happen unless there's a stumper in Jake's book, she thought. *Roland can't pose Blaine, and I think he knows it. I think he knew it an hour ago.*

"Blaine, I occur once in a minute, twice in every moment, but not once in a hundred thousand years. What am I?"

And so the contest would continue, Susannah realized, Roland asking and Blaine answering with his increasingly terrible lack of hesitation, like an all-seeing, all-knowing god. Susannah sat with her cold hands clasped in her lap and watched the glowing dot draw nigh Topeka, the place where all rail service ended, the place where the path of their *ka-tet* would end in the clearing. She thought about the Hounds of the Falls, how they had jutted from the thundering white billows below the dark and starshot sky; she thought of their eyes.

Their electric-blue eyes.

CHAPTER THREE

The Fair-Day Goose

I

Eddie Dean—who did not know Roland sometimes thought of him as *ka-mai, ka*'s fool—heard all of it and heard none of it; saw all of it and saw none of it. The only thing to really make an impression on him once the riddling began in earnest was the fire flashing from the stone eyes of the Hounds; as he raised his hand to shield his eyes from that chain-lightning glare, he thought of the Portal of the Beam in the Clearing of the Bear, how he had pressed his ear against it and heard the distant, dreamy rumble of machinery.

Watching the eyes of the Hounds light up, listening as Blaine drew that current into his batteries, powering up for his final plunge across Mid-World, Eddie had thought: *Not* all *is silent in the halls of the dead and the rooms of ruin. Even now some of the stuff the Old Ones left behind still works. And that's really the horror of it, wouldn't you say? Yes. The exact horror of it.*

Eddie had been with his friends for a short time after that, mentally as well as physically, but then he had fallen back into his thoughts again. *Eddie's zonin,* Henry would have said. *Let 'im be.*

It was the image of Jake striking flint and steel that kept recurring; he would allow his mind to dwell on it

53

for a second or two, like a bee alighting on some sweet flower, and then he would take off again. Because that memory wasn't what he wanted; it was just the way *in* to what he wanted, another door like the ones on the beach of the Western Sea, or the one he had scraped in the dirt of the speaking ring before they had drawn Jake . . . only this door was in his mind. What he wanted was behind it; what he was doing was kind of . . . well . . . diddling the lock.

Zonin, in Henry-speak.

His brother had spent most of his time putting Eddie down—because Henry had been afraid of him and jealous of him, Eddie had finally come to realize—but he remembered one day when Henry had stunned him by saying something that was nice. *Better* than nice, actually; mind-boggling.

A bunch of them had been sitting in the alley behind Dahlie's, some of them eating Popsicles and Hoodsie Rockets, some of them smoking Kents from a pack Jimmie Polino—Jimmie Polio, they had all called him, because he had that fucked-up thing wrong with him, that clubfoot—had hawked out of his mother's dresser drawer. Henry, predictably enough, had been one of the ones smoking.

There were certain ways of referring to things in the gang Henry was a part of (and which Eddie, as his little brother, was also a part of); the argot of their miserable little *ka-tet.* In Henry's gang, you never beat anyone else up; you *sent em home with a fuckin rupture.* You never made out with a girl; you *fucked that skag til she cried.* You never got stoned; you *went on a fuckin bombin-run.* And you never brawled with another gang; you *got in a fuckin pisser.*

The discussion that day had been about who you'd want with you if you got in a fuckin pisser. Jimmie Polio (he got to talk first because he had supplied the cigarettes, which Henry's homeboys called *the fuckin cancersticks*) opted for Skipper Brannigan, because, he said, Skipper wasn't afraid of anyone. One time, Jimmie said, Skipper got pissed off at this teacher—at the Friday night PAL dance, this was—and beat the living shit out of him. Sent *THE FUCKIN CHAPERONE* home with a fuckin rupture, if you could dig it. That was his homie Skipper Brannigan.

Everyone listened to this solemnly, nodding their heads as they ate their Rockets, sucked their Popsicles, or smoked their Kents. Everyone knew that Skipper Brannigan was a fuckin pussy and Jimmie was full of shit, but no one said so. Christ, no. If they didn't pretend to believe Jimmie Polio's outrageous lies, no one would pretend to believe theirs.

Tommy Fredericks opted for John Parelli. Georgie Pratt went for Csaba Drabnik, also known around the nabe as The Mad Fuckin Hungarian. Frank Duganelli nominated Larry McCain, even though Larry was in Juvenile Detention; Larry fuckin *ruled,* Frank said.

By then it was around to Henry Dean. He gave the question the weighty consideration it deserved, then put his arm around his surprised brother's shoulders. *Eddie,* he said. *My little bro. He's the man.*

They all stared at him, stunned—and none more stunned than Eddie. His jaw had been almost down to his belt-buckle. And then Jimmie Polio said, *Come on, Henry, stop fuckin around. This a serious question. Who'd you want watching your back if the shit was gonna come down?*

I am *being serious,* Henry had replied.

Why Eddie? Georgie Pratt had asked, echoing the question which had been in Eddie's own mind. *He couldn't fight his way out of a paper bag. A wet one. So why the fuck?*

Henry thought some more—not, Eddie was convinced, because he didn't know why, but because he had to think about how to articulate it. Then he said: *Because when Eddie's in that fuckin zone, he could talk the devil into setting himself on fire.*

The image of Jake returned, one memory stepping on another. Jake scraping steel on flint, flashing sparks at the kindling of their campfire, sparks that fell short and died before they lit.

He could talk the devil into setting himself on fire.

Move your flint in closer, Roland said, and now there was a third memory, one of Roland at the door they'd come to at the end of the beach, Roland burning with fever, close to death, shaking like a maraca, coughing, his blue bombardier's eyes fixed on Eddie, Roland saying, *Come a little closer, Eddie—come a little closer for your father's sake!*

Because he wanted to grab me, Eddie thought. Faintly, almost as if it were coming through one of those magic doors from some other world, he heard Blaine telling them that the endgame had commenced; if they had been saving their best riddles, now was the time to trot them out. They had an hour.

An hour! Only an hour!

His mind tried to fix on that and Eddie nudged it away. Something was happening inside him (at least he prayed it was), some desperate game of association, and he couldn't let his mind get fucked up with deadlines and consequences and all that crap; if he did, he'd lose whatever chance he had. It was, in a way, like seeing something in a piece of wood, something you could carve out—a bow, a slingshot, perhaps a key to open some unimaginable door. You couldn't look too long, though, at least to start with. You'd lose it if you did. It was almost as if you had to carve while your own back was turned.

He could feel Blaine's engines powering up beneath

him. In his mind's eye he saw the flint flash against the steel, and in his mind's ear he heard Roland telling Jake to move the flint in closer. *And don't hit it with the steel, Jake;* scrape *it.*

Why am I here? If this isn't what I want, why does my mind keep coming back to this place?

Because it's as close as I can get and still stay out of the hurt-zone. Only a medium-sized hurt, actually, but it made me think of Henry. Being put down by Henry.

Henry said you could talk the devil into setting himself on fire.

Yes. I always loved him for that. That was great.

And now Eddie saw Roland move Jake's hands, one holding flint and the other steel, closer to the kindling. Jake was nervous. Eddie could see it; Roland had seen it, too. And in order to ease his nerves, take his mind off the responsibility of lighting the fire, Roland had—

He asked the kid a riddle.

Eddie Dean blew breath into the keyhole of his memory. And this time the tumblers turned.

2

The green dot was closing in on Topeka, and for the first time Jake felt vibration . . . as if the track beneath them had decayed to a point where Blaine's compensators could no longer completely handle the problem. With the sense of vibration there at last came a feeling of speed. The walls and ceiling of the Barony Coach were still opaqued, but Jake found he didn't need to see the countryside blurring past to imagine it. Blaine was rolling full out now, leading his last sonic boom across the waste lands to the place where Mid-World ended, and Jake also found it easy to imagine the transteel piers at the end of the monorail. They would be painted in diagonal stripes of yellow and black. He didn't know how he knew that, but he did.

"TWENTY-FIVE MINUTES," Blaine said complacently. "WOULD YOU TRY ME AGAIN, GUNSLINGER?"

"I think not, Blaine." Roland sounded exhausted. "I've done with you; you've beaten me. Jake?"

Jake got to his feet and faced the route-map. In his chest his heartbeat seemed very slow but very hard, each pulse like a fist slamming on a drumhead. Oy crouched between his feet, looking anxiously up into his face.

"Hello, Blaine," Jake said, and wet his lips.

"HELLO, JAKE OF NEW YORK." The voice was kindly—the voice, perhaps, of a nice old fellow with a habit of molesting the children he from time to time leads into the bushes. "WOULD YOU TRY ME WITH RIDDLES FROM YOUR BOOK? OUR TIME TOGETHER GROWS SHORT."

"Yes," Jake said. "I would try you with these riddles. Give me your understanding of the truth concerning each, Blaine."

"IT IS FAIRLY SPOKEN, JAKE OF NEW YORK. I WILL DO AS YOU ASK."

Jake opened the book to the place he had been keeping with his finger. Ten riddles. Eleven, counting Samson's riddle, which he was saving for last. If Blaine answered them all (as Jake now believed he probably would), Jake would sit down next to Roland, take Oy onto his lap, and wait for the end. There were, after all, other worlds than these.

"Listen, Blaine: In a tunnel of darkness lies a beast of iron. It can only attack when pulled back. What is it?"

"A BULLET." No hesitation.

"Walk on the living, they don't even mumble. Walk on the dead, they mutter and grumble. What are they?"

"FALLEN LEAVES." No hesitation, and if Jake really knew in his heart that the game was lost, why did he feel such despair, such bitterness, such anger?

Because he's a pain, that's why. Blaine is a really BIG pain, and I'd like to push his face in it, just once. I think even making him stop is second to that on my wish-list.

Jake turned the page. He was very close to *Riddle-De-Dum's* torn-out answer section now; he could feel it under his finger, a kind of jagged lump. Very close to the end of the book. He thought of Aaron Deepneau in the Manhattan Restaurant of the Mind, Aaron Deepneau telling him to come back anytime, play a little chess, and oh just by the way, old fatso made a pretty good cup of coffee. A wave of homesickness so strong it was like dying swept over him. He felt he would have sold his soul for a look at New York; hell, he would have sold it for one deep lung-filling breath of Forty-second Street at rush hour.

He fought it off and went to the next riddle.

"I am emeralds and diamonds, lost by the moon. I am found by the sun and picked up soon. What am I?"

"DEW."

Still relentless. Still unhesitating.

The green dot grew closer to Topeka, closing the last of the distance on the route-map. One after another, Jake posed his riddles; one after another, Blaine answered them. When Jake turned to the last page, he saw a boxed message from the author or editor or whatever you called someone who put together books like this: *We hope you've enjoyed the unique combination of imagination and logic known as RIDDLING!*

I haven't Jake thought. *I haven't enjoyed it one little bit, and I hope you choke.* Yet when he looked at the question above the message, he felt a thin thread of hope. It seemed to him that, in this case, at least, they really *had* saved the best for last.

On the route-map, the green dot was now no more than a finger's width from Topeka.

"Hurry up, Jake," Susannah murmured.

"Blaine?"

"YES, JAKE OF NEW YORK."

"With no wings, I fly. With no eyes, I see. With no arms, I climb. More frightening than any beast, stronger than any foe. I am cunning, ruthless, and tall; in the end, I rule all. What am I?"

The gunslinger had looked up, blue eyes gleaming. Susannah began to turn her expectant face from Jake to the route-map. Yet Blaine's answer was as prompt as ever: "THE IMAGINATION OF MAN AND WOMAN."

Jake briefly considered arguing, then thought, *Why waste our time?* As always, the answer, when it was right, seemed almost self-evident. "Thankee-sai, Blaine, you speak true."

"AND THE FAIR-DAY GOOSE IS ALMOST MINE, I WOT. NINETEEN MINUTES AND FIFTY SECONDS TO TERMINATION. WOULD YOU SAY MORE, JAKE OF NEW YORK? VISUAL SENSORS INDICATE YOU HAVE COME TO THE END OF YOUR BOOK, WHICH WAS NOT, I MUST SAY, AS GOOD AS I HAD HOPED."

"Everybody's a goddam critic," Susannah said sotto voce. She wiped a tear from the corner of one eye; without looking directly at her, the gunslinger took her free hand. She clasped it tightly.

"Yes, Blaine, I have one more," Jake said.

"EXCELLENT."

"Out of the eater came forth meat, and out of the strong came sweetness."

"THIS RIDDLE COMES FROM THE HOLY BOOK KNOWN AS 'OLD TESTAMENT BIBLE OF KING JAMES.'" Blaine sounded amused, and Jake felt the last of his hope slip away. He thought he might cry—

not so much out of fear as frustration. "IT WAS MADE
BY SAMSON THE STRONG. THE EATER IS A LION;
THE SWEETNESS IS HONEY, MADE BY BEES WHICH
HIVED IN THE LION'S SKULL. NEXT? YOU STILL
HAVE OVER EIGHTEEN MINUTES, JAKE."

Jake shook his head. He let go of *Riddle-De-Dum!* and
smiled when Oy caught it neatly in his jaws and then
stretched his long neck up to Jake, holding it out again.
"I've told them all. I'm done."

"SHUCKS, L'IL TRAILHAND, THAT'S A PURE-D
SHAME," Blaine said. Jake found this drawly John Wayne
imitation all but unbearable in their current circum-
stances. "LOOKS LIKE I WIN THAT THAR GOOSE,
UNLESS SOMEBODY ELSE CARES TO SPEAK UP.
WHAT ABOUT YOU, OY OF MID-WORLD? GOT ANY
RIDDLES, MY LITTLE BUMBLER BUDDY?"

"Oy!" the billy-bumbler responded, his voice muffled
by the book. Still smiling, Jake took it and sat down next
to Roland, who put an arm around him.

"SUSANNAH OF NEW YORK?"

She shook her head, not looking up. She had turned
Roland's hand over in her own, and was gently tracing
the healed stumps where his first two fingers had been.

"ROLAND SON OF STEVEN? HAVE YOU REMEM-
BERED ANY OTHERS FROM THE FAIR-DAY RID-
DLINGS OF GILEAD?"

Roland also shook his head . . . and then Jake saw that
Eddie Dean was raising his. There was a peculiar smile
on Eddie's face, a peculiar shine in Eddie's eyes, and
Jake found that hope hadn't deserted him, after all. It
suddenly flowered anew in his mind, red and hot and
vivid. Like . . . well, like a rose. A rose in the full fever of
its summer.

"Blaine?" Eddie asked in a low tone. To Jake his voice
sounded queerly choked.

"YES, EDDIE OF NEW YORK." Unmistakable disdain.

"*I* have a couple of riddles," Eddie said. "Just to pass the time between here and Topeka, you understand." No, Jake realized, Eddie didn't sound as if he were choking; he sounded as if he were trying to hold back laughter.

"SPEAK, EDDIE OF NEW YORK."

3

Sitting and listening to Jake run through the last of his riddles, Eddie had mused on Roland's tale of the Fair-Day goose. From there his mind had returned to Henry, travelling from Point A to Point B through the magic of associative thinking. Or, if you wanted to get Zen about it, via Trans-Bird Airlines: goose to turkey. He and Henry had once had a discussion about getting off heroin. Henry had claimed that going cold turkey wasn't the only way; there was also, he said, such a thing as going *cool* turkey. Eddie asked Henry what you called a hype who had just administered a hot shot to himself, and, without missing a beat, Henry had said, *You call that* baked *turkey.* How they had laughed . . . but now, all this long, strange time later, it looked very much as if the joke was going to be on the younger Dean brother, not to mention the younger Dean brother's new friends. Looked like they were all going to be baked turkey before much longer.

Unless you can yank it out of the zone.

Yes.

Then do it, Eddie. It was Henry's voice again, that old resident of his head, but now Henry sounded sober and clear-minded. Henry sounded like his friend instead of his enemy, as if all the old conflicts were finally settled, all the old hatchets buried. *Do it—make the devil set himself*

*on fire. It'll hurt a little, maybe, but you've hurt worse. Hell, I
hurt you worse myself, and you survived. Survived just fine.
And you know where to look.*

Of course. In their palaver around the campfire Jake
had finally managed to light. Roland had asked the kid
a riddle to loosen him up, Jake had struck a spark into
the kindling, and then they had all sat around the fire,
talking. Talking and riddling.

Eddie knew something else, too. Blaine had answered
hundreds of riddles as they ran southeast along the
Path of the Beam, and the others believed that he had
answered every single one of them without hesitation.
Eddie had thought much the same . . . but now, as he
cast his mind back over the contest, he realized an interesting thing: Blaine *had* hesitated.

Once.

He was pissed, too. Like Roland was.

The gunslinger, although often exasperated by Eddie,
had shown real anger toward him just a single time after
the business of carving the key, when Eddie had almost
choked. Roland had tried to cover the depth of that
anger—make it seem like nothing but more exaspera-
tion—but Eddie had sensed what was underneath. He
had lived with Henry Dean for a long time, and was still
exquisitely attuned to all the negative emotions. It had
hurt him, too—not Roland's anger itself, exactly, but the
contempt with which it had been laced. Contempt had
always been one of Henry's favorite weapons.

Why did the dead baby cross the road? Eddie had asked.
Because it was stapled to the chicken, nyuck-nyuck-nyuck!

Later, when Eddie had tried to defend his riddle,
arguing that it was tasteless but not pointless, Roland's
response had been strangely like Blaine's: *I don't care
about taste. It's senseless and unsolvable, and that's what
makes it silly. A good riddle is neither.*

But as Jake finished riddling Blaine, Eddie realized a wonderful, liberating thing: that word *good* was up for grabs. Always had been, always would be. Even if the man using it was maybe a thousand years old and could shoot like Buffalo Bill, that word was still up for grabs. Roland himself had admitted he had never been very good at the riddling game. His tutor claimed that Roland thought too deeply; his father thought it was lack of imagination. Whatever the reason, Roland of Gilead had never won a Fair-Day riddling. He had survived all his contemporaries, and that was certainly a prize of sorts, but he had never carried home a prize goose. *I could always haul a gun faster than any of my mates, but I've never been much good at thinking around corners.*

Eddie remembered trying to tell Roland that jokes were riddles designed to help you build up that often overlooked talent, but Roland had ignored him. The way, Eddie supposed, a color-blind person would ignore someone's description of a rainbow.

Eddie thought Blaine also might have trouble thinking around corners.

He realized he could hear Blaine asking the others if they had any more riddles—even asking Oy. He could hear the mockery in Blaine's voice, could hear it very well. Sure he could. Because he was coming back. Back from that fabled zone. Back to see if he could talk the devil into setting himself on fire. No gun would help this time, but maybe that was all right. Maybe that was all right because—

Because I shoot with my mind. My mind. God help me to shoot this overblown calculator with my mind. Help me shoot it from around the corner.

"Blaine?" he said, and then, when the computer had acknowledged him: "*I* have a couple of riddles." As he spoke, he discovered a wonderful thing: he was struggling to hold back laughter.

4

"SPEAK, EDDIE OF NEW YORK."

No time to tell the others to be on their guard, that anything might happen, and from the look of them, no need, either. Eddie forgot about them and turned his full attention to Blaine.

"What has four wheels and flies?"

"THE TOWN GARBAGE WAGON, AS I HAVE ALREADY SAID." Disapproval—and dislike? Yeah, probably—all but oozing out of that voice. "ARE YOU SO STUPID OR INATTENTIVE THAT YOU DO NOT REMEMBER? IT WAS THE FIRST RIDDLE YOU ASKED ME."

Yes, Eddie thought. *And what we all missed—because we were fixated on stumping you with some brain-buster out of Roland's past or Jake's book—is that the contest almost ended right there.*

"You didn't like that one, did you, Blaine?"

"I FOUND IT EXCEEDINGLY STUPID," Blaine agreed. "PERHAPS THAT'S WHY YOU ASKED IT AGAIN. LIKE CALLS TO LIKE, EDDIE OF NEW YORK, IS IT NOT SO?"

A smile lit Eddie's face; he shook his finger at the route-map. "Sticks and stones may break my bones, but words will never hurt me. Or, as we used to say back in the neighborhood, 'You can rank me to the dogs and back, but I'll never lose the hard-on I use to fuck your mother.' "

"Hurry up!" Jake whispered at him. "If you can do something, *do* it!"

"It doesn't like silly questions," Eddie said. "It doesn't like silly games. And we *knew* that. We knew it from *Charlie the Choo-Choo.* How stupid can you get? Hell, *that* was the book with the answers, not *Riddle-De-Dum,* but we never saw it."

Eddie searched for the other riddle that had been in Jake's Final Essay, found it, posed it.

"Blaine: when is a door not a door?"

Once again, for the first time since Susannah had asked Blaine what had four legs and flies, there came a peculiar clicking sound, like a man popping his tongue on the roof of his mouth. The pause was briefer than the one which had followed Susannah's opening riddle, but it was still there—Eddie heard it. "WHEN IT'S A JAR, OF COURSE," Blaine said. He sounded dour, unhappy. "THIRTEEN MINUTES AND FIVE SECONDS REMAIN BEFORE TERMINATION, EDDIE OF NEW YORK— WOULD YOU DIE WITH SUCH STUPID RIDDLES IN YOUR MOUTH?"

Eddie sat bolt upright, staring at the route-map, and although he could feel warm trickles of sweat running down his back, that smile on his face widened.

"Quit your whining, pal. If you want the privilege of smearing us all over the landscape, you'll just have to put up with a few riddles that aren't quite up to your standards of logic."

"YOU MUST NOT SPEAK TO ME IN SUCH A MAN-NER."

"Or what? You'll kill me? Don't make me laugh. Just play. You agreed to the game; now play it."

Thin pink light flashed briefly out of the route-map. "You're making him angry," Little Blaine mourned. "Oh, you're making him *so* angry."

"Get lost, squirt," Eddie said, not unkindly, and when the pink glow receded, once again revealing a flash-ing green dot that was almost on top of Topeka, Eddie said: "Answer this one, Blaine: the big moron and the little moron were standing on the bridge over the River

Send. The big moron fell off. How come the little moron didn't fall off, too?"

"THAT IS UNWORTHY OF OUR CONTEST. I WILL NOT ANSWER." On the last word Blaine's voice actually dropped into a lower register, making him sound like a fourteen-year-old coping with a change of voice.

Roland's eyes were not just gleaming now but blazing. "What do you say, Blaine? I would understand you well. Are you saying that you cry off?"

"NO! OF COURSE NOT! BUT—"

"Then answer, if you can. Answer the riddle."

"IT'S *NOT* A RIDDLE!" Blaine almost bleated. "IT'S A JOKE, SOMETHING FOR STUPID CHILDREN TO CACKLE OVER IN THE PLAYYARD!"

"Answer now or I declare the contest over and our *ka-tet* the winner," Roland said. He spoke in the dryly confident tone of authority Eddie had first heard in the town of River Crossing. "You must answer, for it is stupidity you complain of, not transgression of the rules, which we agreed upon mutually."

Another of those clicking sounds, but this time it was much louder—so loud, in fact, that Eddie winced. Oy flattened his ears against his skull. It was followed by the longest pause yet; three seconds, at least. Then: "THE LITTLE MORON DID NOT FALL OFF BECAUSE HE WAS A LITTLE MORE ON." Blaine sounded sulky. "MORE PHONETIC COINCIDENCE. TO EVEN ANSWER SUCH AN UNWORTHY RIDDLE MAKES ME FEEL SOILED."

Eddie held up his right hand. He rubbed the thumb and forefinger together.

"WHAT DOES THAT SIGNIFY, FOOLISH CREATURE?"

"It's the world's smallest violin, playing 'My Heart Pumps Purple Piss for You,' " Eddie said. Jake fell into an uncontrollable fit of laughter. "But never mind the cheap New York humor; back to the contest. Why do police lieutenants wear belts?"

The lights in the Barony Coach began to flicker. An odd thing was happening to the walls, as well; they began to fade in and out of true, lunging toward transparency, perhaps, and then opaquing again. Seeing this phenomenon even out of the corner of his eye made Eddie feel a bit whoopsy.

"Blaine? Answer."

"Answer," Roland agreed. "Answer, or I declare the contest at an end and hold you to your promise."

Something touched Eddie's elbow. He looked down and saw Susannah's small and shapely hand. He took it, squeezed it, smiled at her. He hoped the smile was more confident than the man making it felt. They were going to win the contest—he was almost sure of that—but he had no idea what Blaine would do if and when they did.

"TO . . . TO HOLD UP THEIR PANTS?" Blaine's voice firmed, and repeated the question as a statement. "TO HOLD UP THEIR PANTS. A RIDDLE BASED UPON THE EXAGGERATED SIMPLICITY OF—"

"Right. Good one, Blaine, but never mind trying to kill time—it won't work. Next—"

"I INSIST YOU STOP ASKING THESE SILLY—"

"Then stop the mono," Eddie said. "If you're that upset, stop right here, and I will."

"NO."

"Okay, then, on we go. What's Irish and stays out in back of the house, even in the rain?"

There was another of those clicks, this time so loud it felt like having a blunt spike driven against his eardrum. A pause of five seconds. Now the flashing green dot on the route-map was so close to Topeka that it lit the word

like neon each time it flashed. Then: "PADDY O'FUR-
NITURE."

The correct answer to a joke-riddle Eddie had first
heard in the alley behind Dahlie's, or at some similar
gathering-point, but Blaine had apparently paid a price
for forcing his mind into a channel that could conceive
it: the Barony Coach lights were flashing more wildly
than ever, and Eddie could hear a low humming from
inside the walls—the kind of sound your stereo amp
made just before its shit blew up.

Pink light stuttered from the route-map. "Stop!" Little
Blaine cried, his voice so wavery it sounded like the voice
of a character from an old Warner Bros. cartoon. "Stop
it, you're killing him!"

What do you think he's trying to do to us, squirt? Eddie
thought.

He considered shooting Blaine one Jake had told
while they'd been sitting around the campfire that
night—What's green, weighs a hundred tons, and lives at
the bottom of the ocean? Moby Snot!—and then didn't.
He wanted to stick further inside the bounds of logic
than that one allowed . . . and he could do it. He didn't
think he would have to get much more surreal than the
level of, say, a third-grader with a fair-to-good collection
of Garbage Pail Kids cards in order to fuck Blaine up
royally . . . and permanently. Because no matter how
many emotions his fancy dipolar circuits had allowed
him to mimic, *he* was still an *it*—a computer. Even following Eddie this far into riddledom's Twilight Zone had
caused Blaine's sanity to totter.

"Why do people go to bed, Blaine?"

"BECAUSE . . . BECAUSE . . . GODS DAMN YOU,
BECAUSE . . ."

A low squalling started up from beneath them, and
suddenly the Barony Coach swayed violently from right

to left. Susannah screamed. Jake was thrown into her lap. The gunslinger grabbed them both.

"BECAUSE THE BED WON'T COME TO THEM, GODS DAMN YOU! NINE MINUTES AND FIFTY SECONDS!"

"Give up, Blaine," Eddie said. "Stop before I have to blow your mind completely. If you don't quit, it's going to happen. We both know it."

"NO!"

"I got a million of these puppies. Been hearing them my whole life. They stick to my mind the way flies stick to flypaper. Hey, with some people it's recipes. So what do you say? Want to give?"

"NO! NINE MINUTES AND THIRTY SECONDS!"

"Okay, Blaine. You asked for it. Here comes the cruncher. Why did the dead baby cross the road?"

The mono took another of those gigantic lurches; Eddie didn't understand how it could still stay on its track after that, but somehow it did. The screaming from beneath them grew louder; the walls, floor, and ceiling of the car began to cycle madly between opacity and transparency. At one moment they were enclosed, at the next they were rushing over a gray daylight landscape that stretched flat and featureless to a horizon which ran across the world in a straight line.

The voice which came from the speakers was now that of a panicky child: "I KNOW IT, JUST A MOMENT, I KNOW IT, RETRIEVAL IN PROGRESS, ALL LOGIC CIRCUITS IN USE—"

"Answer," Roland said.

"I NEED MORE TIME! YOU MUST GIVE IT TO ME!" Now there was a kind of cracked triumph in that splintered voice. "NO TEMPORAL LIMITS FOR ANSWERING WERE SET, ROLAND OF GILEAD, HATEFUL

GUNSLINGER OUT OF A PAST THAT SHOULD HAVE STAYED DEAD!"

"No," Roland agreed, "no time limits were set, you are quite right. But you may not kill us with a riddle still unanswered, Blaine, and Topeka draws nigh. Answer!"

The Barony Coach cycled into invisibility again, and Eddie saw what appeared to be a tall and rusty grain elevator go flashing past; it was in his view barely long enough for him to identify it. Now he fully appreciated the maniacal speed at which they were travelling; perhaps three hundred miles faster than a commercial jet at cruising speed.

"Let him alone!" moaned the voice of Little Blaine. "You're killing him, I say! *Killing him!*"

"Isn't that 'bout what he wanted?" Susannah asked in the voice of Detta Walker. "To die? That's what he said. We don't mind, either. You not so bad, Little Blaine, but even a world as fucked up as this one has to be better with your big brother gone. It's just him takin us with him we been objectin to all this time."

"Last chance," Roland said. "Answer or give up the goose, Blaine."

"I . . . I . . . YOU . . . SIXTEEN LOG THIRTY-THREE . . . ALL COSINE SUBSCRIPTS . . . ANTI . . . ANTI . . . IN ALL THESE YEARS . . . BEAM . . . FLOOD . . . PYTHAG-OREAN . . . CARTESIAN LOGIC . . . CAN I . . . DARE I . . . A PEACH . . . EAT A PEACH . . . ALLMAN BROTH-ERS . . . PATRICIA . . . CROCODILE AND WHIPLASH SMILE . . . CLOCK OF DIALS . . . TICK-TOCK, ELEVEN O'CLOCK, THE MAN'S IN THE MOON AND HE'S READY TO ROCK . . . *INCESSAMENT* . . . *INCESSA-MENT, MON CHER* . . . OH MY HEAD . . . BLAINE . . . BLAINE DARES . . . BLAINE WILL ANSWER . . . I . . ."

Blaine, now screaming in the voice of an infant, lapsed

into some other language and began to sing. Eddie
thought it was French. He knew none of the words, but
when the drums kicked in, he knew the song perfectly
well: "Velero Fly" by Z.Z. Top.

The glass over the route-map blew out. A moment
later, the route-map itself exploded from its socket,
revealing twinkling lights and a maze of circuit-boards
behind it. The lights pulsed in time to the drums. Suddenly blue fire flashed out, sizzling the surface around
the hole in the wall where the map had been, scorching
it black. From deeper within that wall, toward Blaine's
blunt, bullet-shaped snout, came a thick grinding noise.

"It crossed the road because it was stapled to the
chicken, you dopey fuck!" Eddie yelled. He got to his
feet and started to walk toward the smoking hole where
the route-map had been. Susannah grabbed at the back
of his shirt, but Eddie barely felt it. Barely knew where
he was, in fact. The battle-fire had dropped over him,
burning him everywhere with its righteous heat, sizzling
his sight, frying his synapses and roasting his heart in its
holy glow. He had Blaine in his sights, and although the
thing behind the voice was already mortally wounded,
he was unable to stop squeezing the trigger: *I shoot with
my mind.*

"What's the difference between a truckload of bowling balls and a truckload of dead woodchucks?" Eddie
raved. "You can't unload a truckload of bowling balls
with a pitchfork!"

A terrible shriek of mingled anger and agony issued
from the hole where the route-map had been. It was followed by a gust of blue fire, as if somewhere forward of
the Barony Coach an electric dragon had exhaled violently. Jake called a warning, but Eddie didn't need it;
his reflexes had been replaced with razor-blades. He
ducked, and the burst of electricity went over his right

shoulder, making the hair on that side of his neck stand up. He drew the gun he wore—a heavy .45 with a worn sandalwood grip, one of two revolvers which Roland had brought out of Mid-World's ruin. He kept walking as he bore down on the front of the coach . . . and of course he kept talking. As Roland had said, Eddie would *die* talking. As his old friend Cuthbert had done. Eddie could think of many worse ways to go, and only one better.

"Say, Blaine, you ugly, sadistic fuck! Since we're talking riddles, what is the greatest riddle of the Orient? Many men smoke but Fu Manchu! Get it? No? So solly, Cholly! How about this one? Why'd the woman name her son Seven and a Half? Because she drew his name out of a hat!"

He had reached the pulsing square. Now he lifted Roland's gun and the Barony Coach suddenly filled with its thunder. He put all six rounds into the hole, fanning the hammer with the flat of his hand in the way Roland had shown them, knowing only that this was right, this was proper . . . this was *ka*, goddammit, fucking *ka*, it was the way you ended things if you were a gunslinger. He was one of Roland's tribe, all right, his soul was probably damned to the deepest pit of hell, and he wouldn't have changed it for all the heroin in Asia.

"I HATE YOU!" Blaine cried in his childish voice. The splinters were gone from it now; it was growing soft, mushy. "I HATE YOU FOREVER!"

"It's not dying that bothers you, is it?" Eddie asked. The lights in the hole where the route-map had been were fading. More blue fire flashed, but he hardly had to pull his head back to avoid it; the flame was small and weak. Soon Blaine would be as dead as all the Pubes and Grays in Lud. "It's *losing* that bothers you."

"HATE . . . FORRRRrrrrr . . ."

The word degenerated into a hum. The hum became a kind of stuttery thudding sound. Then it was gone.

Eddie looked around. Roland was there, holding Susannah with one arm curved around her butt, as one might hold a child. Her thighs clasped his waist. Jake stood on the gunslinger's other side, with Oy at his heel.

Drifting out of the hole where the route-map had been was a peculiar charred smell, somehow not unpleasant. To Eddie it smelled like burning leaves in October. Otherwise, the hole was as dead and dark as a corpse's eye. All the lights in there had gone out.

Your goose is cooked, Blaine, Eddie thought, *and your turkey's baked. Happy fuckin Thanksgiving.*

5

The shrieking from beneath the mono stopped. There was one final, grinding thud from up front, and then those sounds ceased, too. Roland felt his legs and hips sway gently forward and put out his free hand to steady himself. His body knew what had happened before his head did: Blaine's engines had quit. They were now simply gliding forward along the track. But—

"Back," he said. "All the way. We're coasting. If we're close enough to Blaine's termination point, we may still crash."

He led them past the puddled remains of Blaine's welcoming ice sculpture and to the back of the coach. "And stay away from that thing," he said, pointing at the instrument which looked like a cross between a piano and a harpsichord. It stood on a small platform. "It may shift. Gods, I wish we could see where we are! Lie down. Wrap your arms over your heads."

They did as he told them. Roland did the same. He lay there with his chin pressing into the nap of the royal blue carpet, eyes shut, thinking about what had just happened.

"I cry your pardon, Eddie," he said. "How the wheel of *ka* turns! Once I had to ask the same of my friend Cuthbert . . . and for the same reason. There's a kind of blindness in me. An *arrogant* blindness."

"I hardly think there's any need of pardon-crying," Eddie said. He sounded uncomfortable.

"There is. I held your jokes in contempt. Now they have saved our lives. I cry your pardon. I have forgotten the face of my father."

"You don't need any pardon and you didn't forget anybody's face," Eddie said. "You can't help your nature, Roland."

The gunslinger considered this carefully, and discovered something which was wonderful and awful at the same time: that idea had never occurred to him. Not once in his whole life. That he was a captive of *ka*—this he had known since earliest childhood. But his *nature . . .* his very *nature . . .*

"Thank you, Eddie. I think—"

Before Roland could say what he thought, Blaine the Mono crashed to a final bitter halt. All four of them were thrown violently up the Barony Coach's central aisle, Oy in Jake's arms and barking. The cabin's front wall buckled and Roland struck it shoulder-first. Even with the padding (the wall was carpeted and, from the feel, undercoated with some resilient stuff), the blow was hard enough to numb him. The chandelier swung forward and tore loose from the ceiling, pelting them with glass pendants. Jake rolled aside, vacating its landing-zone just in time. The harpsichord-piano flew off its podium, struck one of the sofas, and overturned, coming to rest with a discordant *brrrannnggg* sound. The mono tilted to the right and the gunslinger braced himself, meaning to cover both Jake and Susannah with his own body if it overturned completely. Then it settled back, the floor still a little canted, but at rest.

The trip was over.

The gunslinger raised himself up. His shoulder was still numb, but the arm below it supported him, and that was a good sign. On his left, Jake was sitting up and picking glass beads out of his lap with a dazed expression. On his right, Susannah was dabbing a cut under Eddie's left eye. "All right," Roland said. "Who's hur—"

There was an explosion from above them, a hollow *Pow!* that reminded Roland of the big-bangers Cuthbert and Alain had sometimes lit and tossed down drains, or into the privies behind the scullery for a prank. And once Cuthbert had shot some big-bangers with his sling. That had been no prank, no childish folly. That had been—

Susannah uttered a short cry—more of surprise than fear, the gunslinger thought—and then hazy daylight was shining down on his face. It felt good. The taste of the air coming in through the blown emergency exit was even better—sweet with the smell of rain and damp earth.

There was a bony rattle, and a ladder—it appeared to be equipped with rungs made of twisted steel wire—dropped out of a slot up there.

"First they throw the chandelier at you, then they show you the door," Eddie said. He struggled to his feet, then got Susannah up. "Okay, I know when I'm not wanted. Let's make like bees and buzz off."

"Sounds good to me." She reached toward the cut on Eddie's face again. Eddie took her fingers, kissed them, and told her to stop poking the moichandise.

"Jake?" the gunslinger asked. "Okay?"

"Yes," Jake said. "What about you, Oy?"

"Oy!"

"Guess he is," Jake said. He raised his wounded hand and looked at it ruefully.

"Hurting again, is it?" the gunslinger asked.

"Yeah. Whatever Blaine did to it is wearing off. I don't care, though—I'm just glad to still be alive."

"Yes. Life is good. So is *astin*. There's some of it left."

"Aspirin, you mean."

Roland nodded. A pill of magical properties, but one of the words from Jake's world he would never be able to say correctly.

"Nine out of ten doctors recommend Anacin, honey," Susannah said, and when Jake only looked at her quizzically: "Guess they don't use that one anymore in your when, huh? Doesn't matter. We're here, sugarpie, right here and just fine, and that's what matters." She pulled Jake into her arms and gave him a kiss between the eyes, on the nose, and then flush on the mouth. Jake laughed and blushed bright red. "That's what matters, and right now that's the only thing in the world that does."

6

"First aid can wait," Eddie said. He put his arm around Jake's shoulders and led the boy to the ladder. "Can you use that hand to climb with?"

"Yes. But I can't bring Oy. Roland, will you?"

"Yes." Roland picked Oy up and tucked him into his shirt as he had while descending a shaft under the city in pursuit of Jake and Gasher. Oy peeked out at Jake with his bright, gold-ringed eyes. "Up you go."

Jake climbed. Roland followed close enough so that Oy could sniff the kid's heels by stretching out his long neck.

"Suze?" Eddie asked. "Need a boost?"

"And get your nasty hands all over my well-turned fanny? Not likely, white boy!" Then she dropped him a wink and began to climb, pulling herself up easily with her muscular arms and balancing with the stumps of her legs. She went fast, but not too fast for Eddie; he reached up and gave her a soft pinch where the pinching was good. "Oh, my purity!" Susannah cried, laughing and rolling her eyes. Then she was gone. Only Eddie was left, standing by the foot of the ladder and looking around at the luxury coach which he had believed might well be their *ka-tet's* coffin.

You did it, kiddo, Henry said. *Made him set himself on fire. I knew you could, fuckin-A. Remember when I said that to those scag-bags behind Dahlie's? Jimmie Polio and those guys? And how they laughed? But you did it. Sent him home with a fuckin rupture.*

Well, it worked, anyway, Eddie thought, and touched the butt of Roland's gun without even being aware of it. *Well enough for us to walk away one more time.*

He climbed two rungs, then looked back down. The Barony Coach already felt dead. *Long* dead, in fact, just another artifact of a world that had moved on.

"*Adios,* Blaine," Eddie said. "So long, partner."

And he followed his friends out through the emergency exit in the roof.

CHAPTER FOUR

Topeka

I

Jake stood on the slightly tilted roof of Blaine the Mono, looking southeast along the Path of the Beam. The wind riffled his hair (now quite long and decidedly un-Piperish) back from his temples and forehead in waves. His eyes were wide with surprise.

He didn't know what he had expected to see—a smaller and more provincial version of Lud, perhaps—but what he had *not* expected was what loomed above the trees of a nearby park. It was a green roadsign (against the dull gray autumn sky, it almost screamed with color) with a blue shield mounted on it:

Roland joined him, lifted Oy gently out of his shirt, and put him down. The bumbler sniffed the pink surface of Blaine's roof, then looked toward the front of the mono. Here the train's smooth bullet shape was broken by crumpled metal which had peeled back in jagged wings. Two dark slashes—they began at the mono's tip and extended to a point about ten yards from where Jake and Roland stood—gored the roof in parallel lines.

At the end of each was a wide, flat metal pole painted in stripes of yellow and black. These seemed to jut from the top of the mono at a point just forward of the Barony Coach. To Jake they looked a little like football goalposts.

"Those are the piers he talked about hitting," Susannah murmured.

Roland nodded.

"We got off lucky, big boy, you know it? If this thing had been going much faster . . ."

"*Ka,*" Eddie said from behind them. He sounded as if he might be smiling.

Roland nodded. "Just so. *Ka.*"

Jake dismissed the transteel goalposts and turned back toward the sign. He was half-convinced it would be gone, or that it would say something else (MID-WORLD TOLL ROAD, perhaps, or BEWARE OF DEMONS), but it was still there and still said the same thing.

"Eddie? Susannah? Do you see that?"

They looked along his pointing finger. For a moment—one long enough for Jake to fear he was having a hallucination—neither of them said anything. Then, softly, Eddie said: "Holy shit. Are we back home? If we are, where are all the people? And if something like Blaine has been stopping off in Topeka—*our* Topeka, Topeka, Kansas—how come I haven't seen anything about it on *Sixty Minutes?*"

"What's *Sixty Minutes?*" Susannah asked. She was shading her eyes, looking southeast toward the sign.

"TV show," Eddie said. "You missed it by five or ten years. Old white guys in ties. Doesn't matter. That sign—"

"It's Kansas, all right," Susannah said. "*Our* Kansas. I guess." She had spotted another sign, just visible over the trees. Now she pointed until Jake, Eddie, and Roland had all seen it:

"There a Kansas in your world, Roland?"

"No," Roland replied, looking at the signs, "we're far beyond the boundaries of the world I knew. I was far beyond most of the world I knew long before I met you three. This place . . ."

He stopped and cocked his head to one side, as if he was listening to some sound almost too distant to hear. And the expression on his face . . . Jake didn't like it much.

"Say, kiddies!" Eddie said brightly. "Today we're studying Wacky Geography in Mid-World. You see, boys and girls, in Mid-World you start in New York, travel southeast to Kansas, and then continue along the Path of the Beam until you come to the Dark Tower . . . which happens to be smack in the middle of everything. First, fight the giant lobsters! Next, ride the psychotic train! And then, after a visit to our snackbar for a popkin or two—"

"Do you hear anything?" Roland broke in. "Any of you?"

Jake listened. He heard the wind combing through the trees of the nearby park—their leaves had just begun to turn—and he heard the click of Oy's toenails as he strolled back toward them along the roof of the Barony Coach. Then Oy stopped, so even that sound—

A hand seized him by the arm, making him jump. It was Susannah. Her head was tilted, her eyes wide. Eddie was also listening. Oy, too; his ears were up and he was whining far down in his throat.

Jake felt his arms ripple with gooseflesh. At the same time he felt his mouth tighten in a grimace. The sound, though very faint, was the auditory version of biting a lemon. And he'd heard something like it before. Back when he was only five or six, there had been a crazy guy in Central Park who thought he was a musician . . . well, there were *lots* of crazy guys in Central Park who thought they were musicians, but this was the only one Jake had ever seen who played a workshop tool. The guy had had a sign beside his upturned hat which read WORLD'S GREATEST SAW-PLAYER! SOUNDS HAWAIIAN DOESN'T IT! PLEASE CONTRIBUTE TO MY WELFARE!

Greta Shaw had been with Jake the first time he encountered the saw-player, and Jake remembered how she had hurried past the guy. Just sitting there like a cellist in a symphony orchestra he'd been, only with a rust-speckled handsaw spread across his open legs; Jake remembered the expression of comic horror on Mrs. Shaw's face, and the quiver of her pressed-together lips, as if—yes, as if she'd just bitten into a lemon.

This sound wasn't *exactly* like the one

(SOUNDS HAWAIIAN DOESN'T IT)

the guy in the park had made by vibrating the blade of his saw, but it was close: a wavery, trembly, metallic sound that made you feel like your sinuses were filling up and your eyes would shortly begin to gush water. Was it coming from ahead of them? Jake couldn't tell. It seemed to be coming from everywhere and nowhere; at the same time, it was so low he might have been tempted to believe the whole thing was just his imagination, if the others hadn't—

"Watch out!" Eddie cried. "Help me, you guys! I think he's going to faint!"

Jake wheeled toward the gunslinger and saw that his face had gone as white as cottage cheese above the dusty no-color of his shirt. His eyes were wide and blank. One corner of his mouth twitched spastically, as if an invisible fishhook were buried there.

"Jonas and Reynolds and Depape," he said. "The Big

Coffin Hunters. And *her.* The Cöos. They were the ones. They were the ones who—"

Standing on the roof of the mono in his dusty, broken boots, Roland tottered. On his face was the greatest look of misery Jake had ever seen.

"Oh Susan," he said. "Oh, my dear."

2

They caught him, they formed a protective ring around him, and the gunslinger felt hot with guilt and self-loathing. What had he done to deserve such enthusiastic protectors? What, besides tear them out of their known and ordinary lives as ruthlessly as a man might tear weeds out of his garden?

He tried to tell them he was all right, they could stand back, he was fine, but no words would come out; that terrible wavery sound had transported him back to the box canyon west of Hambry all those years ago. Depape and Reynolds and old limping Jonas. Yet most of all it was the woman from the hill he hated, and from black depths of feeling only a very young man can reach. Ah, but how could he have done aught else but hate them? His heart had been broken. And now, all these years later, it seemed to him that the most horrible fact of human existence was that broken hearts mended.

My first thought was, he lied in every word/That hoary cripple, with malicious eye . . .

What words? Whose poem?

He didn't know, but he knew that women could lie, too; women who hopped and grinned and saw too much from the corners of their rheumy old eyes. It didn't matter who had written the lines of poesy; the words were true words, and that was all that mattered. Neither

Eldred Jonas nor the crone on the hill had been of Marten's stature—nor even of Walter's—when it came to evil, but they had been evil enough.

Then, after . . . in the box canyon west of town . . . that sound . . . that, and the screams of wounded men and horses . . . for once in his life, even the normally voluble Cuthbert had been struck silent.

But all that had been long ago, in another *when;* in the here and now, the warbling sound was either gone or had temporarily fallen below the threshold of audibility. They would hear it again, though. He knew that as well as he knew the fact that he walked a road leading to damnation.

He looked up at the others and managed a smile. The trembling at the corner of his mouth had quit, and that was something.

"I'm all right," he said. "But hear me well: this is very close to where Mid-World ends, very close to where End-World begins. The first great course of our quest is finished. We have done well; we have remembered the faces of our fathers; we have stood together and been true to one another. But now we have come to a thinny. We must be very careful."

"A thinny?" Jake asked, looking around nervously.

"Places where the fabric of existence is almost entirely worn away. There are more since the force of the Dark Tower began to fail. Do you remember what we saw below us when we left Lud?"

They nodded solemnly, remembering ground which had fused to black glass, ancient pipes which gleamed with turquoise witchlight, misshapen bird-freaks with wings like great leathern sails. Roland suddenly could not bear to have them grouped around him as they were, looking down on him as folk might look down on a rowdy who had fallen in a barroom brawl.

He lifted his hands to his friends—his new friends. Eddie took them and helped him to his feet. The gunslinger fixed his enormous will on not swaying and stood steady.

"Who was Susan?" Susannah asked. The crease down the center of her forehead suggested she was troubled, and probably by more than a coincidental similarity of names.

Roland looked at her, then at Eddie, then at Jake, who had dropped to one knee so he could scratch behind Oy's ears.

"I'll tell you," he said, "but this isn't the place or time."

"You keep sayin that," Susannah said. "You wouldn't just be putting us off again, would you?"

Roland shook his head. "You shall hear my tale—this part of it, at least—but not on top of this metal carcass."

"Yeah," Jake said. "Being up here is like playing on a dead dinosaur or something. I keep thinking Blaine's going to come back to life and start, I don't know, screwing around with our heads again."

"That sound is gone," Eddie said. "The thing that sounded like a wah-wah pedal."

"It reminded me of this old guy I used to see in Central Park," Jake said.

"The man with the saw?" Susannah asked. Jake looked up at her, his eyes round with surprise, and she nodded. "Only he wasn't old when I used to see him. It's not just the geography that's wacky here. Time's kind of funny, too."

Eddie put an arm around her shoulders and gave her a brief squeeze. "Amen to that."

Susannah turned to Roland. Her look was not accusing, but there was a level and open measurement in her eyes that the gunslinger could not help but admire. "I'm holding you to your promise, Roland. I want to know about this girl that got my name."

"You shall hear," Roland repeated. "For now, though, let's get off this monster's back."

3

That was easier said than done. Blaine had come to rest slightly askew in an outdoor version of the Cradle of Lud (a littered trail of torn pink metal lay along one side of this, marking the end of Blaine's last journey), and it was easily twenty-five feet from the roof of the Barony Coach to the cement. If there was a descent-ladder, like the one which had popped conveniently through the emergency hatch, it had jammed when they crunched to a halt.

Roland unslung his purse, rummaged, and removed the deerskin harness they used for carrying Susannah when the going got too rough for her wheelchair. The chair, at least, would not worry them anymore, the gunslinger reflected; they had left it behind in their mad scramble to board Blaine.

"What you want that for?" Susannah asked truculently. She always sounded truculent when the harness came into view. *I hate them honky mahfahs down in Miss'ippi worse'n I hate that harness,* she had once told Eddie in the voice of Detta Walker, *but sometimes it be a close thing, sugar.*

"Soft, Susannah Dean, soft," the gunslinger said, smiling a little. He unbraided the network of straps which made up the harness, set the seat-piece aside, then pigtailed the straps back together. He wedded this to his last good hank of rope with an old-fashioned sheetbend knot. As he worked, he listened for the warbling of the thinny . . . as the four of them had listened for the god-drums; as he and Eddie had listened for the lobstrosities to begin asking their lawyerly questions ("Dad-a-cham?

Did-a-chee? Dum-a-chum?") as they came tumbling out
of the waves each night.

Ka is a wheel, he thought. Or, as Eddie liked to say,
whatever went around came around.

When the rope was finished, he fashioned a loop at
the bottom of the braided section. Jake stepped a foot
into it with perfect confidence, gripped the rope with
one hand, and settled Oy into the crook of his other
arm. Oy looked around nervously, whined, stretched his
neck, licked Jake's face.

"You're not afraid, are you?" Jake asked the bumbler.

"'Fraid," Oy agreed, but he was quiet enough as
Roland and Eddie lowered Jake down the side of the
Barony Coach. The rope wasn't quite long enough to
take him all the way down, but Jake had no trouble twisting his foot free and dropping the last four feet. He set
Oy down. The bumbler trotted off, sniffing, and lifted
his leg against the side of the terminal building. This was
nowhere near as grand as the Cradle of Lud, but it had
an old-fashioned look that Roland liked—white boards,
overhanging eaves, high, narrow windows, what looked
like slate shingles. It was a *Western* look. Written in gold
gilt on a sign which stretched above the terminal's line
of doors was this message:

ATCHISON, TOPEKA, AND SANTA FE

Towns, Roland supposed, and that last one sounded
familiar to him; had there not been a Santa Fe in the
Barony of Mejis? But that led back toward Susan, lovely
Susan at the window with her hair unbraided and all
down her back, the smell of her like jasmine and rose
and honeysuckle and old sweet hay, smells of which the
oracle in the mountains had been able to make only the
palest mimicry. Susan lying back and looking solemnly
up at him, then smiling and putting her hands behind

her head so that her breasts rose, as if aching for his hands.

If you love me, Roland, then love me . . . bird and bear and hare and fish . . .

". . . next?"

He looked around at Eddie, having to use all of his will to pull himself back from Susan Delgado's when. There were thinnies here in Topeka, all right, and of many sorts. "My mind was wandering, Eddie. Cry your pardon."

"Susannah next? That's what I asked."

Roland shook his head. "You next, then Susannah. I'll go last."

"Will you be okay? With your hand and all?"

"I'll be fine."

Eddie nodded and stuck his foot into the loop. When Eddie had first come into Mid-World, Roland could have lowered him easily by himself, two fingers short the full complement or no, but Eddie had been without his drug for months now, and had put on ten or fifteen pounds of muscle. Roland accepted Susannah's help gladly enough, and together they lowered him down.

"Now you, lady," Roland said, and smiled at her. It felt more natural to smile these days.

"Yes." But for the nonce she only stood there, biting her lower lip.

"What is it?"

Her hand went to her stomach and rubbed there, as if it ached or griped her. He thought she would speak, but she shook her head and said, "Nothing."

"I don't believe that. Why do you rub your belly? Are you hurt? Were you hurt when we stopped?"

She took her hand off her tunic as if the flesh just south of her navel had grown hot. "No. I'm fine."

"Are you?"

Susannah seemed to think this over very carefully. "We'll talk," she said at last. "We'll *palaver*, if you like that better. But you were right before, Roland—this isn't the place or time."

"All four of us, or just you and me and Eddie?"

"Just you and me, Roland," she said, and poked the stump of her leg through the loop. "Just one hen and one rooster, at least to start with. Now lower away, if you please."

He did, frowning down at her, hoping with all his heart that his first idea—the one that had come to mind as soon as he saw that restlessly rubbing hand—was wrong. Because she had been in the speaking ring, and the demon that denned there had had its way with her while Jake was trying to cross between the worlds. Sometimes—*often*—demonic contact changed things.

Never for the better, in Roland's experience.

He pulled his rope back up after Eddie had caught Susannah around the waist and helped her to the platform. The gunslinger walked forward to one of the piers which had torn through the train's bullet snout, fashioning the rope's end into a shake-loop as he went. He tossed this over the pier, snubbed it (being careful not to twitch the rope to the left), and then lowered himself to the platform himself, bent at the waist and leaving boot-tracks on Blaine's pink side.

"Too bad to lose the rope and harness," Eddie remarked when Roland was beside them.

"*I* ain't sorry about that harness," Susannah said. "I'd rather crawl along the pavement until I got chewin-gum all the way up my arms to the elbows."

"We haven't lost anything," Roland said. He snugged his hand into the rawhide foot-loop and snapped it hard to the left. The rope slithered down from the pier, Roland gathering it in almost as fast as it came down.

"Neat trick!" Jake said.

"Eat! Rick!" Oy agreed.

"Cort?" Eddie asked.

"Cort," Roland agreed, smiling.

"The drill instructor from hell," Eddie said. "Better you than me, Roland. Better you than me."

4

As they walked toward the doors leading into the station, that low, liquid warbling sound began again. Roland was amused to see all three of his cohorts wrinkle their noses and pull down the corners of their mouths at the same time; it made them look like blood family as well as *ka-tet*. Susannah pointed toward the park. The signs looming over the trees were wavering slightly, the way things did in a heat-haze.

"Is that from the thinny?" Jake asked.

Roland nodded.

"Will we be able to get around it?"

"Yes. Thinnies are dangerous in much the way that swamps full of quicksand and saligs are dangerous. Do you know those things?"

"We know quicksand," Jake said. "And if saligs are long green things with big teeth, we know them, too."

"That's what they are."

Susannah turned to look back at Blaine one last time. "No silly questions and no silly games. The book was right about that." From Blaine she turned her eyes to Roland. "What about Beryl Evans, the woman who wrote *Charlie the Choo-Choo*? Do you think she's part of this? That we might even meet her? I'd like to thank her. Eddie figured it out, but—"

"It's possible, I suppose," Roland said, "but on measure, I think not. My world is like a huge ship that sank near enough shore for most of the wreckage to wash up on the beach. Much of what we find is fascinating, some of it may be useful, if *ka* allows, but all of it is still wreckage. Senseless wreckage." He looked around. "Like this place, I think."

"I wouldn't exactly call it wrecked," Eddie said. "Look at the paint on the station—it's a little rusty from the gutters up under the eaves, but it hasn't peeled anywhere that I can see." He stood in front of the doors and ran his fingers down one of the glass panels. They left four clear tracks behind. "Dust and plenty of it, but no cracks. I'd say that this building has been left unmaintained at most since . . . the start of the summer, maybe?"

He looked at Roland, who shrugged and nodded. He was listening with only half an ear and paying attention with only half a mind. The rest of him was fixed upon two things: the warble of the thinny, and keeping away the memories that wanted to swamp him.

"But Lud had been going to wrack and ruin for *centuries,*" Susannah said. "This place . . . it may or may not be Topeka, but what it really looks like to me is one of those creepy little towns on *The Twilight Zone.* You boys probably don't remember that one, but—"

"Yes, I do," Eddie and Jake said in perfect unison, then looked at each other and laughed. Eddie stuck out his hand and Jake slapped it.

"They still show the reruns," Jake said.

"Yeah, all the time," Eddie added. "Usually sponsored by bankruptcy lawyers who look like shorthair terriers. And you're right. This place *isn't* like Lud. Why would it be? It's not in the same *world* as Lud. I don't know where we crossed over, but—" He pointed again at the blue Interstate 70 shield, as if that proved his case beyond a shadow of a doubt.

"If it's Topeka, where are the people?" Susannah asked.

Eddie shrugged and raised his hands—who knows?

Jake put his forehead against the glass of the center door, cupped his hands to the sides of his face, and peered in. He looked for several seconds, then saw something that made him pull back fast. "Oh-oh," he said. "No wonder the town's so quiet."

Roland stepped up behind Jake and peered in over the boy's head, cupping his own hands to reduce his reflection. The gunslinger drew two conclusions before even looking at what Jake had seen. The first was that although this was most assuredly a *train* station, it wasn't really a *Blaine* station . . . not a cradle. The other was that the station did indeed belong to Eddie's, Jake's, and Susannah's world . . . but perhaps not to their *where*.

It's the thinny. We'll have to be careful.

Two corpses were leaning together on one of the long benches that filled most of the room; but for their hanging, wrinkled faces and black hands, they might have been revellers who had fallen asleep in the station after an arduous party and missed the last train home. On the wall behind them was a board marked DEPARTURES, with the names of cities and towns and baronies marching down it in a line. DENVER, read one. WICHITA, read another. OMAHA, read a third. Roland had once known a one-eyed gambler named Omaha; he had died with a knife in his throat at a Watch Me table. He had stepped into the clearing at the end of the path with his head thrown back, and his last breath had sprayed blood all the way up to the ceiling. Hanging down from the ceiling of this room (which Roland's stupid and laggard mind insisted on thinking of as a stage rest, as if this were a stop along some half-forgotten road like the one that had brought him to Tull) was a beautiful four-sided clock. Its hands had stopped at 4:14, and Roland supposed they would never move again. It was a sad thought . . . but this was a sad world. He could not see any other dead people, but experience suggested that where there were two dead, there were likely four more dead somewhere out of sight. Or four dozen.

"Should we go in?" Eddie asked.

"Why?" the gunslinger countered. "We have no business here; it doesn't lie along the Path of the Beam."

"You'd make a great tour-guide," Eddie said sourly. " 'Keep up, everyone, and please don't go wandering off into the—' "

Jake interrupted with a request Roland didn't understand. "Do either of you guys have a quarter?" The boy was looking at Eddie and Susannah. Beside him was a square metal box. Written on it in blue was:

The *Topeka Capital-Journal* covers Kansas like no other!
Your hometown paper! *Read it every day!*

Eddie shook his head, amused. "Lost all my change at some point. Probably climbing a tree, just before you joined us, in an all-out effort to avoid becoming snackfood for a robot bear. Sorry."

"Wait a minute . . . wait a minute . . ." Susannah had her purse open and was rummaging through it in a way that made Roland grin broadly in spite of all his preoccupations. It was so damned *womanly,* somehow. She turned over crumpled Kleenex, shook them to make sure there was nothing caught inside, fished out a compact, looked at it, dropped it back, came up with a comb, dropped *that* back—

She was too absorbed to look up as Roland strode past her, drawing his gun from the docker's clutch he had built her as he went. He fired a single time. Susannah let out a little scream, dropping her purse and slapping at the empty holster high up under her left breast.

"Honky, you scared the livin *Jesus* out of me!"

"Take better care of your gun, Susannah, or the next time someone takes it from you, the hole may be between your eyes instead of in a . . . what is it, Jake? A news-telling device of some kind? Or does it hold paper?"

"Both." Jake looked startled. Oy had withdrawn halfway down the platform and was looking at Roland mistrustfully. Jake poked his finger at the bullet-hole in the center of the newspaper box's locking device. A little curl of smoke was drifting from it.

"Go on," Roland said. "Open it."

Jake pulled the handle. It resisted for a moment, then a piece of metal clunked down somewhere inside, and the door opened. The box itself was empty; the sign on the back wall read WHEN ALL PAPERS ARE GONE, PLEASE TAKE DISPLAY COPY. Jake worked it out of its wire holder, and they all gathered round.

"What in God's name . . . ?" Susannah's whisper was both horrified and accusing. "What does it mean? What in God's name *happened*?"

Below the newspaper's name, taking up most of the front page's top half, were screaming black letters:

"CAPTAIN TRIPS" SUPERFLU RAGES UNCHECKED
Govt. Leaders May Have Fled Country Topeka Hospitals Jammed with Sick, Dying Millions Pray for Cure

"Read it aloud," Roland said. "The letters are in your speech, I cannot make them all out, and I would know this story very well."

Jake looked at Eddie, who nodded impatiently.

Jake unfolded the newspaper, revealing a dot-picture (Roland had seen pictures of this type; they were called "fottergrafs") which shocked them all: it showed a lakeside city with its skyline in flames. CLEVELAND FIRES BURN UNCHECKED, the caption beneath read.

"Read, kid!" Eddie told him. Susannah said nothing; she was already reading the story—the only one on the front page—over his shoulder. Jake cleared his throat as if it were suddenly dry, and began.

5

"The byline says John Corcoran, plus staff and AP reports. That means a lot of different people worked on it, Roland. Okay. Here goes. 'America's greatest crisis— and the world's, perhaps—deepened overnight as the so-called superflu, known as Tube-Neck in the Midwest and Captain Trips in California, continues to spread.

" 'Although the death-toll can only be estimated, medical experts say the total at this point is horrible beyond comprehension: twenty to thirty million dead in the continental U.S. alone is the estimate given by Dr. Morris Hackford of Topeka's St. Francis Hospital and Medical Center. Bodies are being burned from Los Angeles, California, to Boston, Massachusetts, in crematoria, factory furnaces, and at landfill sites.

" 'Here in Topeka, the bereaved who are still well enough and strong enough to do so are urged to take their dead to one of three sites: the disposal plant north of Oakland Billard Park; the pit area at Heartland Park Race Track; the landfill on Southeast Sixty-first Street, east of Forbes Field. Landfill users should approach by Berryton Road; California has been blocked by car wrecks and at least one downed Air Force transport plane, sources tell us.' "

Jake glanced up at his friends with frightened eyes,

looked behind him at the silent railway station, then looked back down at the newspaper.

"'Dr. April Montoya of the Stormont-Vail Regional Medical Center points out that the death-toll, horrifying as it is, constitutes only part of this terrible story. "For every person who has died so far as a result of this new flu-strain," Montoya said, "there are another six who are lying ill in their homes, perhaps as many as a dozen. And, so far as we have been able to determine, the recovery rate is zero." Coughing, she then told this reporter: "Speaking personally, I'm not making any plans for the weekend."

"'In other local developments:

"'All commercial flights out of Forbes and Phillip Billard have been cancelled.

"'All Amtrak rail travel has been suspended, not just in Topeka but across all of Kansas. The Gage Boulevard Amtrak station has been closed until further notice.

"'All Topeka schools have also been closed until further notice. This includes Districts 437, 345, 450 (Shawnee Heights), 372, and 501 (metro Topeka). Topeka Lutheran and Topeka Technical College are also closed, as is KU at Lawrence.

"'Topekans must expect brownouts and perhaps blackouts in the days and weeks ahead. Kansas Power and Light has announced a "slow shutdown" of the Kaw River Nuclear Plant in Wamego. Although no one in KawNuke's Office of Public Relations answered this newspaper's calls, a recorded announcement cautions that there is no plant emergency, that this is a safety measure only. KawNuke will return to on-line status, the announcement concludes, "when the current crisis is past." Any comfort afforded by this statement is in large part negated by the recorded statement's final words, which are not "Goodbye" or "Thank you for calling" but "God will help us through our time of trial."'"

Jake paused, following the story to the next page, where there were more pictures: a burned-out panel truck overturned on the steps of the Kansas Museum of Natural History; traffic on San Francisco's Golden Gate Bridge stalled bumper to bumper; piles of corpses in Times Square. One body, Susannah saw, had been hung from a lamppost, and that brought back nightmarish memories of the run for the Cradle of Lud she and Eddie had made after parting from the gunslinger; memories of Luster and Winston and Jeeves and Maud. *When the god-drums started up this time, it was Spanker's stone what came out of the hat,* Maud had said. *We set him to dance.* Except, of course, what she'd meant was that they had set him to *hang.* As they had hung some folks, it seemed, back home in little old New York. When things got weird enough, someone always found a lynchrope, it seemed.

Echoes. Everything echoed now. They bounced back and forth from one world to the other, not fading as ordinary echoes did but growing and becoming more terrible. *Like the god-drums,* Susannah thought, and shuddered.

" 'In national developments,' " Jake read, " 'conviction continues to grow that, after denying the superflu's existence during its early days, when quarantine measures might still have had some effect, national leaders have fled to underground retreats which were created as brain-trust shelters in case of nuclear war. Vice-President Bush and key members of the Reagan cabinet have not been seen during the last forty-eight hours. Reagan himself has not been seen since Sunday morning, when he attended prayer services at Green Valley Methodist Church in San Simeon.

" ' "They have gone to the bunkers like Hitler and the rest of the Nazi sewer-rats at the end of World War II," said Rep. Steve Sloan. When asked if he had any objection to being quoted by name, Kansas's first-term representative, a Republican, laughed and said: "Why should I? I've got a real fine case myself. I'll be so much dust in the wind come this time next week."

" 'Fires, most likely set, continue to ravage Cleveland, Indianapolis, and Terre Haute.

" 'A gigantic explosion centered near Cincinnati's Riverfront Stadium was apparently not nuclear in nature, as was first feared, but occurred as the result of a natural gas buildup caused by unsupervised . . .' "

Jake let the paper drop from his hands. A gust of wind caught it and blew it the length of the platform, the few folded sheets separating as they went. Oy stretched his neck and snagged one of these as it went by. He trotted toward Jake with it in his mouth, as obedient as a dog with a stick.

"No, Oy, I don't want it," Jake said. He sounded ill and very young.

"At least we know where all the folks are," Susannah said, bending and taking the paper from Oy. It was the last two pages. They were crammed with obituaries printed in the tiniest type she had ever seen. No pictures, no causes of death, no announcement of burial services. Just this one died, beloved of so-and-so, that one died, beloved of Jill-n-Joe, t'other one died, beloved of them-and-those. All in that tiny, not-quite-even type. It was the jaggedness of the type which convinced her it was all real.

But how hard they tried to honor their dead, even at the end, she thought, and a lump rose in her throat. *How hard they tried.*

She folded the quarto together and looked on the back—the last page of the *Capital-Journal.* It showed a picture of Jesus Christ, eyes sad, hands outstretched, forehead marked from his crown of thorns. Below it, three stark words in huge type:

PRAY FOR US

She looked up at Eddie, eyes accusing. Then she handed him the newspaper, one brown finger tapping the date at the top. It was June 24, 1986. Eddie had been drawn into the gunslinger's world a year later.

He held it for a long time, fingers slipping back and forth across the date, as if the passage of his finger would somehow cause it to change. Then he looked up at them and shook his head. "No. I can't explain this town, this paper, or the dead people in that station, but I can set you straight about one thing—everything was fine in New York when I left. Wasn't it, Roland?"

The gunslinger looked a trifle sour. "Nothing in your city seemed very fine to me, but the people who lived there did not seem to be survivors of such a plague as this, no."

"There was something called Legionnaires' disease," Eddie said. "And AIDS, of course—"

"That's the sex one, right?" Susannah asked. "Transmitted by fruits and drug addicts?"

"Yes, but calling gays fruits isn't the done thing in my when," Eddie said. He tried a smile, but it felt stiff and unnatural on his face and he put it away again.

"So this . . . this never happened," Jake said, tentatively touching the face of Christ on the back page of the paper.

"But it did," Roland said. "It happened in June-sowing of the year one thousand nine hundred and eighty-six. And here we are, in the aftermath of that plague. If Eddie's right about the length of time that has gone by, the plague of this 'super-flu' was this *past* June-sowing. We're in Topeka, Kansas, in the Reap of eighty-six. That's the *when* of it. As to the *where,* all we know is that it's not Eddie's. It might be yours, Susannah, or yours, Jake, because you left your world before this arrived." He tapped the date on the paper, then looked at Jake. "You said something to me once. I doubt if you remember, but I do; it's one of the most important things anyone has ever said to me: 'Go, then, there are other worlds than these.' "

"More riddles," Eddie said, scowling.

"Is it not a fact that Jake Chambers died once and now stands before us, alive and well? Or do you doubt my story of his death under the mountains? That you have doubted my honesty from time to time is something I know. And I suppose you have your reasons."

Eddie thought it over, then shook his head. "You lie when it suits your purpose, but I think that when you told us about Jake, you were too fucked up to manage anything but the truth."

Roland was startled to find himself hurt by what Eddie had said—*You lie when it suits your purpose*—but he went on. After all, it was essentially true.

"We went back to time's pool," the gunslinger said, "and pulled him out before he could drown."

"You pulled him out," Eddie corrected.

"You helped, though," Roland said, "if only by keeping me alive, you helped, but let that go for now. It's beside the point. What's more to it is that there are many possible worlds, and an infinity of doors leading into them. This is one of those worlds; the thinny we can hear is one of those doors . . . only one much bigger than the ones we found on the beach."

"How big?" Eddie asked. "As big as a warehouse loading door, or as big as the warehouse?"

Roland shook his head and raised his hands palms to the sky—*who knows?*

"This thinny," Susannah said. "We're not just *near* it, are we? We came *through* it. That's how we got here, to this version of Topeka."

"We may have," Roland admitted. "Did any of you feel

something strange? A sensation of vertigo, or transient nausea?"

They shook their heads. Oy, who had been watching Jake closely, also shook his head this time.

"No," Roland said, as if he had expected this. "But we were concentrating on the riddling—"

"Concentrating on not getting killed," Eddie grunted.

"Yes. So perhaps we passed through without being aware. In any case, thinnies aren't natural—they are sores on the skin of existence, able to exist because things are going wrong. Things in *all* worlds."

"Because things are wrong at the Dark Tower," Eddie said.

Roland nodded. "And even if this place—this *when*, this *where*—is not the *ka* of your world now, it might become that *ka*. This plague—or others even worse— could spread. Just as the thinnies will continue to spread, growing in size and number. I've seen perhaps half a dozen in my years of searching for the Tower, and heard maybe two dozen more. The first . . . the first one I ever saw was when I was still very young. Near a town called Hambry." He rubbed his hand up his cheek again, and was not surprised to find sweat amid the bristles. *Love me, Roland. If you love me, then love me.*

"Whatever happened to us, it bumped us out of your world, Roland," Jake said. "We've fallen off the Beam. Look." He pointed at the sky. The clouds were moving slowly above them, but no longer in the direction Blaine's smashed snout was pointing. Southeast was still southeast, but the signs of the Beam which they had grown so used to following were gone.

"Does it matter?" Eddie asked. "I mean . . . the *Beam* may be gone, but the *Tower* exists in all worlds, doesn't it?"

"Yes," Roland said, "but it may not be *accessible* from all worlds."

The year before beginning his wonderful and fulfilling career as a heroin addict, Eddie had done a brief and not-very-successful turn as a bicycle messenger. Now he remembered certain office-building elevators he'd been in while making deliveries, buildings with banks or investment firms in them, mostly. There were some floors where you couldn't stop the car and get off unless you had a special card to swipe through the slot below the numbers. When the elevator came to those locked-off floors, the number in the window was replaced by an X.

"I think," Roland said, "we need to find the Beam again."

"I'm convinced," Eddie said. "Come on, let's get going." He took a couple of steps, then turned back to Roland with one eyebrow raised. "Where?"

"The way we were going," Roland said, as if that should have been obvious, and walked past Eddie in his dusty, broken boots, headed for the park across the way.

CHAPTER FIVE

Turnpikin'

I

Roland walked to the end of the platform, kicking bits of pink metal out of his way as he went. At the stairs, he paused and looked back at them somberly. "More dead. Be ready."

"They're not . . . um . . . runny, are they?" Jake asked.

Roland frowned, then his face cleared as he understood what Jake meant. "No. Not runny. Dry."

"That's all right, then," Jake said, but he held his hand out to Susannah, who was being carried by Eddie for the time being. She gave him a smile and folded her fingers around his.

At the foot of the stairs leading down to the commuter parking lot at the side of the station, half a dozen corpses lay together like a collapsed cornshock. Two were women, three were men. The sixth was a child in a stroller. A summer spent dead in the sun and rain and heat (not to mention at the mercy of any stray cats, coons, or woodchucks that might be passing) had given the toddler a look of ancient wisdom and mystery, like a child mummy discovered in an Incan pyramid. Jake supposed from the faded blue outfit it was wearing that it had been a boy, but it was impossible to tell for sure. Eyeless, lipless, its skin faded to dusky gray, it made a joke of gender—why did the dead baby cross the road? Because it was stapled to the superflu.

Even so, the toddler seemed to have voyaged through Topeka's empty post-plague months better than the adults around it. They were little more than skeletons with hair. In a scrawny bunch of skin-wrapped bones that had once been fingers, one of the men clutched the handle of a suitcase that looked like the Samsonites Jake's parents owned. As with the baby (as with *all* of them), his eyes were gone; huge dark sockets stared at Jake. Below them, a ring of discolored teeth jutted in a pugnacious grin. *What took you so long, kid?* the dead man who was still clutching his suitcase seemed to be asking. *Been waiting for you, and it's been a long hot summer!*

Where were you guys hoping to go? Jake wondered. *Just where in the crispy crap did you think might be safe enough? Des Moines? Sioux City? Fargo? The moon?*

They went down the stairs, Roland first, the others behind him, Jake still holding Susannah's hand with Oy at his heels. The long-bodied bumbler seemed to descend each step in two stages, like a double trailer taking speed-bumps.

"Slow down, Roland," Eddie said. "I want to check the crip spaces before we go on. We might get lucky."

"Crip spaces?" Susannah said. "What're those?"

Jake shrugged. He didn't know. Neither did Roland.

Susannah switched her attention to Eddie. "I only ask, sugarpie, because it sounds a little *on*-pleasant. You know, like calling Negroes 'blacks' or gay folks 'fruits.' I know I'm just a poor ignorant pickaninny from the dark ages of 1964, but—"

"There." Eddie pointed at a rank of signs marking the parking-row closest to the station. There were actually two signs to a post, the top of each pair blue and white, the bottom red and white. When they drew a little closer, Jake saw the one on top was a wheelchair symbol. The one on the bottom was a warning: $200 FINE FOR IMPROPER USE OF HANDICAPPED PARKING SPACE. STRICTLY ENFORCED BY TOPEKA P.D.

"See there!" Susannah said triumphantly. "They shoulda done that a long time ago! Why, back in my when, you're lucky if you can get your damn wheelchair through the doors of anything smaller than the Shop 'n Save. Hell, lucky if you can get it up over the curbs! And special parking? Forget it, sugar!"

The lot was jammed almost to capacity, but even with the end of the world at hand, only two cars that didn't have little wheelchair symbols on their license plates were parked in the row Eddie had called "the crip spaces."

Jake guessed that respecting the "crip spaces" was just one of those things that got a mysterious lifelong hold on people, like putting zip-codes on letters, parting your hair, or brushing your teeth before breakfast.

"And there it is!" Eddie cried. "Hold your cards, folks, but I think we have a Bingo!"

Still carrying Susannah on his hip—a thing he would have been incapable of doing for any extended period of time even a month ago—Eddie hurried over to a boat of a Lincoln. Strapped on the roof was a complicated-looking racing bicycle; poking out of the half-open trunk was a wheelchair. Nor was this the only one; scanning the row of "crip spaces," Jake saw at least four more wheelchairs, most strapped to roof-racks, some stuffed into the backs of vans or station wagons, one (it looked ancient and fearsomely bulky) thrown into the bed of a pickup truck.

Eddie set Susannah down and bent to examine the rig holding the chair in the trunk. There were a lot of criss-crossing elastic cords, plus some sort of locking bar. Eddie drew the Ruger Jake had taken from his father's desk drawer. "Fire in the hole," he said cheerfully, and before any of them could even think of covering their ears, he pulled the trigger and blew the lock off the security-bar. The sound went rolling into the silence, then echoed back. The warbling sound of the thinny returned with it, as if the gunshot had snapped it awake. *Sounds Hawaiian, doesn't it?* Jake thought, and grimaced with distaste. Half an hour ago, he wouldn't have believed that a sound could be as physically upsetting, as . . . well, the smell of rotting meat, say, but he believed it now. He looked up at the turnpike signs. From this angle he could see only their tops, but that was enough to confirm that they were shimmering again. *It throws some kind of field,* Jake thought. *The way mixers and vacuum cleaners make static on the radio or TV, or the way that cyclotron gadget made the hair on my arms stand up when Mr. Kingery brought it to class and then asked for volunteers to come up and stand next to it.*

Eddie wrenched the locking bar aside, and used Roland's knife to cut the elastic cords. Then he drew the wheelchair out of the trunk, examined it, unfolded it, and engaged the support which ran across the back at seat-level. "*Voila!*" he said.

Susannah had propped herself on one hand— Jake thought she looked a little like the woman in this Andrew Wyeth painting he liked, *Christina's World*—and was examining the chair with some wonder.

"God almighty, it looks so little 'n light!"

"Modern technology at its finest, darlin," Eddie said. "It's what we fought Vietnam for. Hop in." He bent to help her. She didn't resist him, but her face was set and frowning as he lowered her into the seat. Like she expected the chair to collapse under her, Jake thought. As she ran her hands over the arms of her new ride, her face gradually relaxed.

Jake wandered off a little, walking down another row

of cars, running his fingers over their hoods, leaving trails of dust. Oy padded after him, pausing once to lift his leg and squirt a tire, as if he had been doing it all his life.

"Make you homesick, honey?" Susannah asked from behind Jake. "Probably thought you'd never see an honest-to-God American automobile again, am I right?"

Jake considered this and decided she was *not* right. It had never crossed his mind that he would remain in Roland's world forever; that he might never see another car. He didn't think that would bother him, actually, but he also didn't think it was in the cards. Not yet, anyway. There was a certain vacant lot in the New York when he had come from. It was on the corner of Second Avenue and Forty-sixth Street. Once there had been a deli there—Tom and Gerry's, Party Platters Our Specialty—but now it was just rubble, and weeds, and broken glass, and . . .

. . . and a rose. Just a single wild rose growing in a vacant lot where a bunch of condos were scheduled to go up at some point, but Jake had an idea that there was nothing quite like it growing anywhere else on Earth. Maybe not on any of those other worlds Roland had mentioned, either. There were roses as one approached the Dark Tower; roses by the billion, according to Eddie, great bloody acres of them. He had seen them in a dream. Still, Jake suspected that his rose was different even from those . . . and that until its fate was decided, one way or the other, he was not done with the world of cars and TVs and policemen who wanted to know if you had any identification and what your parents' names were.

And speaking of parents, I may not be done with them, either, Jake thought. The idea hurried his heartbeat with a mixture of hope and alarm.

They stopped halfway down the row of cars, Jake staring blankly across a wide street (Gage Boulevard, he assumed) as he considered these things. Now Roland and Eddie caught up to them.

"This baby's gonna be great after a couple of months pushing the Iron Maiden," Eddie said with a grin. "Bet you could damn near *puff* it along." He blew a deep breath at the back of the wheelchair to demonstrate. Jake thought of telling Eddie that there were probably others back there in the "crip spaces" with motors in them, then realized what Eddie must have known right away: their batteries would be dead.

Susannah ignored him for the time being; it was Jake she was interested in. "You didn't answer me, sug. All these cars get you homesick?"

"Nah. But I was curious about whether or not they were all cars I knew. I thought maybe . . . if this version of 1986 grew out of some other world than my 1977, there'd be a way to tell. But I *can't* tell. Because things change so darn fast. Even in nine years . . ." He shrugged, then looked at Eddie. "*You* might be able to, though. I mean, you actually *lived* in 1986."

Eddie grunted. "I lived through it, but I didn't exactly *observe* it. I was fucked to the sky most of the time. Still . . . I suppose . . ."

Eddie started pushing Susannah along the smooth macadam of the parking lot again, pointing to cars as they passed them. "Ford Explorer . . . Chevrolet Caprice . . . and that one there's an old Pontiac, you can tell because of the split grille—"

"Pontiac Bonneville," Jake said. He was amused and a little touched by the wonder in Susannah's eyes—most of these cars must look as futuristic to her as Buck Rogers scout-ships. That made him wonder how Roland felt about them, and Jake looked around.

The gunslinger showed no interest in the cars at all. He was gazing across the street, into the park, toward the turnpike . . . except Jake didn't think he was actually looking at any of those things. Jake had an idea that Roland was simply looking into his own thoughts. If so, the expression on his face suggested that he wasn't finding anything good there.

"That's one of those little Chrysler K's," Eddie said, pointing, "and that's a Subaru. Mercedes SEL 450, excellent, the car of champions . . . Mustang . . . Chrysler Imperial, good shape but must be older'n God—"

"Watch it, boy," Susannah said, with a touch of what Jake thought was real asperity in her voice. "I recognize that one. Looks new to me."

"Sorry, Suze. Really. This one's a Cougar . . . another Chevy . . . and one more . . . Topeka loves General Motors, big fuckin surprise there . . . Honda Civic . . . VW Rabbit . . . a Dodge . . . a Ford . . . a—"

Eddie stopped, looking at a little car near the end of the row, white with red trim. "A Takuro," he said, mostly to himself. He went around to look at the trunk. "A Takuro *Spirit*, to be exact. Ever hear of that make and model, Jake of New York?"

Jake shook his head.

"Me, neither," he said. "Me fucking neither."

Eddie began pushing Susannah toward Gage Boulevard (Roland with them but still mostly off in his own private world, walking when they walked, stopping where they stopped). Just shy of the lot's automated entrance (STOP TAKE TICKET), Eddie halted.

"At this rate, we'll be old before we get to yonder park and dead before we raise the turnpike," Susannah said.

This time Eddie didn't apologize, didn't seem even to hear her. He was looking at the bumper sticker on the front of a rusty old AMC Pacer. The sticker was blue and white, like the little wheelchair signs marking the "crip spaces." Jake squatted for a better look, and when

Oy dropped his head on Jake's knee, the boy stroked him absently. With his other hand he reached out and touched the sticker, as if to verify its reality. KANSAS CITY MONARCHS, it said. The O in Monarchs was a baseball with speedlines drawn out behind it, as if it were leaving the park.

Eddie said: "Check me if I'm wrong on this, sport, because I know almost zilch about baseball west of Yankee Stadium, but shouldn't that say Kansas City *Royals?* You know, George Brett and all that?"

Jake nodded. He knew the Royals, and he knew Brett, although he had been a young player in Jake's when and must have been a fairly old one in Eddie's.

"Kansas City *Athletics,* you mean," Susannah said, sounding bewildered. Roland ignored it all; he was still cruising in his own personal ozone layer.

"Not by '86, darlin," Eddie said kindly. "By '86 the Athletics were in Oakland." He glanced from the bumper sticker to Jake. "Minor-league team, maybe?" he asked. "Triple A?"

"The Triple A Royals are still the Royals," Jake said. "They play in Omaha. Come on, let's go."

And although he didn't know about the others, Jake himself went on with a lighter heart. Maybe it was stupid, but he was relieved. He didn't believe that this terrible plague was waiting up ahead for his world, because there were no Kansas City Monarchs in his world. Maybe that wasn't enough information upon which to base a conclusion, but it felt true. And it was an enormous relief to be able to believe that his mother and father weren't slated to die of a germ people called Captain Trips and be burned in a . . . a landfill, or something.

Except that wasn't quite a sure thing, even if this wasn't the 1986 version of his 1977 world. Because even if this awful plague had happened in a world where there were cars called Takuro Spirits and George Brett played for the K.C. Monarchs, Roland said the trouble was spreading . . . that things like the superflu were eating through the fabric of existence like battery acid eating its way into a piece of cloth.

The gunslinger had spoken of time's pool, a phrase which had at first struck Jake as romantic and charming. But suppose the pool was growing stagnant and swampy? And suppose these Bermuda Triangle–type things Roland called thinnies, once great rarities, were becoming the rule rather than the exception? Suppose—oh, and here was a hideous thought, one guaranteed to keep you lying awake until way past three—all of reality was sagging as the structural weaknesses of the Dark Tower grew? Suppose there came a crash, one level falling down into the next . . . and the next . . . and the next . . . until—

When Eddie grasped his shoulder and squeezed, Jake had to bite his tongue to keep from screaming.

"You're giving yourself the hoodoos," Eddie said.

"What do you know about it?" Jake asked. That sounded rude, but he was mad. From being scared or being seen into? He didn't know. Didn't much care, either.

"When it comes to the hoodoos, I'm an old hand," Eddie said. "I don't know exactly what's on your mind, but whatever it is, this would be an *excellent* time to stop thinking about it."

That, Jake decided, was probably good advice. They walked across the street together. Toward Gage Park and one of the greatest shocks of Jake's life.

2

Passing under the wrought-iron arch with GAGE PARK written on it in old-fashioned, curlicued letters, they found themselves on a brick path leading through a garden that was half English Formal and half Ecuadoran Jungle. With no one to tend it through the hot Midwestern summer, it had run to riot; with no one to tend it this fall, it had run to seed. A sign just inside the arch proclaimed this to be the Reinisch Rose Garden, and there were roses, all right; roses everywhere. Most had gone over, but some of the wild ones still throve, making Jake think of the rose in the vacant lot at Forty-sixth and Second with a longing so deep it was an ache.

Off to one side as they entered the park was a beautiful old-time carousel, its prancing steeds and racing stallions now still on their posts. The carousel's very silence, its flashing lights and steamy calliope music stilled forever, gave Jake a chill. Hung over the neck of one horse, dangling from a rawhide strip, was some kid's baseball glove. Jake was barely able to look at it.

Beyond the carousel, the foliage grew even thicker, strangling the path until the travellers edged along single-file, like lost children in a fairy-tale wood. Thorns from overgrown and unpruned rosebushes tore at Jake's clothes. He had somehow gotten into the lead (probably because Roland was still deep inside his own thoughts), and that was why he saw Charlie the Choo-Choo first.

His only thought while approaching the narrow-gauge train-tracks which crossed the path—they were little more than toy tracks, really—was of the gunslinger saying that *ka* was like a wheel, always rolling around to the same place again. *We're haunted by roses and trains,* he thought. *Why? I don't know. I guess it's just another rid—*

Then he looked to his left, and "OhgoodnesstoChrist" fell out of his mouth, all in one word. The strength ran out of his legs and he sat down. His voice sounded watery and distant to his own ears. He didn't quite faint, but the color drained out of the world until the running-to-riot foliage on the west side of the park looked almost as gray as the autumn sky overhead.

"Jake! Jake, what's wrong!" It was Eddie, and Jake could hear the genuine concern in his voice, but it seemed to be coming over a bad long-distance connection. From Beirut, say, or maybe Uranus. And he could feel Roland's steadying hand on his shoulder, but it was as distant as Eddie's voice.

"Jake!" Susannah. "What's wrong, honey? What—"

Then she saw, and stopped talking at him. Eddie saw, and also stopped talking at him. Roland's hand fell away. They all stood looking . . . except for Jake, who *sat* looking. He supposed that strength and feeling would come back into his legs eventually and he would get up, but right now they felt like limp macaroni.

The train was parked fifty feet up, by a toy station that mimicked the one across the street. Hanging from its eaves was a sign which read TOPEKA. The train was Charlie the Choo-Choo, cowcatcher and all; a 402 Big Boy Steam Locomotive. And, Jake knew, if he found enough strength to get up on his feet and go over there, he would find a family of mice nested in the seat where the engineer (whose name had undoubtedly been Bob Something-or-other) had once sat. There would be another family, this one of swallows, nested in the smokestack.

And the dark, oily tears, Jake thought, looking at the tiny train waiting in front of its tiny station with his skin crawling all over his body and his balls hard and his stomach in a knot. *At night it cries those dark, oily tears, and they're rusting the hell out of his fine Stratham headlight. But in your time, Charlie-boy, you pulled your share of kids, right? Around and around Gage Park you went, and the kids laughed, except some of them weren't really laughing; some of them, the ones who were wise to you, were screaming. The way I'd scream now, if I had the strength.*

But his strength was coming back, and when Eddie put a hand under one of his arms and Roland put one under the other, Jake was able to get up. He staggered once, then stood steady.

"Just for the record, I don't blame you," Eddie said. His voice was grim; so was his face. "I feel a little like falling over myself. That's the one in your book; that's it to the life."

"So now we know where Miss Beryl Evans got the idea for *Charlie the Choo-Choo,*" Susannah said. "Either she lived here, or sometime before 1942, when the damned thing was published, she visited Topeka—"

"—and saw the kids' train that goes through Reinisch Rose Garden and around Gage Park," Jake said. He was getting over his scare now, and he—not just an only child but for most of his life a lonely child—felt a burst of love and gratitude for his friends. They had seen what he had seen, they had understood the source of his fright. Of course—they were *ka-tet.*

"It won't answer silly questions, it won't play silly games," Roland said musingly. "Can you go on, Jake?"

"Yes."

"You sure?" Eddie asked, and when Jake nodded, Eddie pushed Susannah across the tracks. Roland went next. Jake paused a moment, remembering a dream he'd had—he and Oy had been at a train-crossing, and the bumbler had suddenly leaped onto the tracks, barking wildly at the oncoming headlight.

Now Jake bent and scooped Oy up. He looked at the rusting train standing silently in its station, its dark headlamp like a dead eye. "I'm not afraid," he said in a low voice. "Not afraid of you."

The headlamp came to life and flashed at him once,

brief but glare-bright, emphatic: *I know different; I know different, my dear little squint.*

Then it went out.

None of the others had seen. Jake glanced once more at the train, expecting the light to flash again—maybe expecting the cursed thing to actually start up and make a run at him—but nothing happened.

Heart thumping hard in his chest, Jake hurried after his companions.

3

The Topeka Zoo (the *World Famous* Topeka Zoo, according to the signs) was full of empty cages and dead animals. Some of the animals that had been freed were gone, but others had died near to hand. The big apes were still in the area marked Gorilla Habitat, and they appeared to have died hand-in-hand. That made Eddie feel like crying, somehow. Since the last of the heroin had washed out of his system, his emotions always seemed on the verge of blowing up into a cyclone. His old pals would have laughed.

Beyond Gorilla Habitat, a gray wolf lay dead on the path. Oy approached it carefully, sniffed, then stretched out his long neck and began to howl.

"Make him quit that, Jake, you hear me?" Eddie said gruffly. He suddenly realized he could smell decaying animals. The aroma was faint, mostly boiled off over the hot days of the summer just passed, but what was left made him feel like upchucking. Not that he could precisely remember the last time he'd eaten.

"Oy! To me!"

Oy howled one final time, then returned to Jake. He stood on the kid's feet, looking up at him with those spooky wedding-ring eyes of his. Jake picked him up, took him in a circle around the wolf, and then set him down again on the brick path.

The path led them to a steep set of steps (weeds had begun to push through the stonework already), and at the top Roland looked back over the zoo and the gardens. From here they could easily see the circuit the toy train-tracks made, allowing Charlie's riders to tour the entire perimeter of Gage Park. Beyond it, fallen leaves clattered down Gage Boulevard before a rush of cold wind.

"So fell Lord Perth," murmured Roland.

"And the countryside did shake with that thunder," Jake finished.

Roland looked down at him with surprise, like a man awakening from a deep sleep, then smiled and put an arm around Jake's shoulders. "I have played Lord Perth in my time," he said.

"Have you?"

"Yes. Very soon now you shall hear."

4

Beyond the steps was an aviary full of dead exotic birds; beyond the aviary was a snackbar advertising (perhaps heartlessly, given the location) TOPEKA'S BEST BUFFALO-BURGER; beyond the snackbar was another wrought iron arch with a sign reading COME BACK TO GAGE PARK REAL SOON! Beyond this was the curving upslope of a limited-access-highway entrance ramp. Above it, the green signs they had first spotted from across the way stood clear.

"Turnpikin' again," Eddie said in a voice almost too low to hear. "Goddam." Then he sighed.

"What's turnpikin', Eddie?"

Jake didn't think Eddie was going to answer; when Susannah craned around to look at him as he stood with his fingers wrapped around the handles of the new wheelchair, Eddie looked away. Then he looked back, first at Susannah, then at Jake. "It's not pretty. Not much about my life before Gary Cooper here yanked me across the Great Divide was."

"You don't have to—"

"It's also no big deal. A bunch of us would get together—me, my brother Henry, Bum O'Hara, usually, 'cause he had a car, Sandra Corbitt, and maybe this friend of Henry's we called Jimmie Polio—and we'd stick all our names in a hat. The one we drew out was the . . . the trip-guide, Henry used to call him. He—she, if it was Sandi—had to stay straight. Relatively, anyway. Everyone else got seriously goobered. Then we'd all pile into Bum's Chrysler and go up I-95 into Connecticut or maybe take the Taconic Parkway into upstate New York . . . only we called it the Catatonic Parkway. Listen to Creedence or Marvin Gaye or maybe even *Elvis's Greatest Hits* on the tape-player.

"It was better at night, best when the moon was full. We'd cruise for hours sometimes with our heads stuck out the windows like dogs do when they're riding, looking up at the moon and watching for shooting stars. We called it turnpikin'." Eddie smiled. It looked like an effort. "A charming life, folks."

"It sounds sort of fun," Jake said. "Not the drug part, I mean, but riding around with your pals at night, looking at the moon and listening to the music . . . that sounds excellent."

"It was, actually," Eddie said. "Even stuffed so full of reds we were as apt to pee on our own shoes as in the bushes, it was excellent." He paused. "That's the horrible part, don't you get it?"

"Turnpikin'," the gunslinger said. "Let's do some."
They left Gage Park and crossed the road to the entrance ramp.

5

Someone had spray-painted over both signs marking the ramp's ascending curve. On the one reading ST. LOUIS 215, someone had slashed

WATCH FOR THE WALKIN DUDE

in black. On the one marked   NEXT REST AREA 10 MI,

ALL HAIL THE CRIMSON KING !

had been written in fat red letters. That scarlet was still bright enough to scream even after an entire summer. Each had been decorated with a symbol—

"Do you know what any of that truck means, Roland?" Susannah asked.
Roland shook his head, but he looked troubled, and that introspective look never left his own eyes.
They went on.

6

At the place where the ramp merged with the turnpike, the two men, the boy, and the bumbler clustered around Susannah in her new wheelchair. All of them looked east.

Eddie didn't know what the traffic situation would be like once they cleared Topeka, but here all the lanes, those headed west as well as the eastbound ones on their side, were crammed with cars and trucks. Most of the vehicles were piled high with possessions gone rusty with a season's worth of rain.

But the traffic was the least of their concerns as they stood there, looking silently eastward. For half a mile or so on either side of them, the city continued—they could see church steeples, a strip of fast food places (Arby's, Wendy's, McD's, Pizza Hut, and one Eddie had never heard of called Boing Boing Burgers), car dealerships, the roof of a bowling alley called Heartland Lanes. They could see another turnpike exit ahead, the sign by the ramp reading TOPEKA STATE HOSPITAL AND S.W. 6TH. Beyond the off-ramp there hulked a massive old red brick edifice with tiny windows peering like desperate eyes out of the climbing ivy. Eddie figured a place that looked so much like Attica *had* to be a hospital, probably the kind of welfare purgatory where poor folks sat in shitty plastic chairs for hours on end, all so some doctor could look at them like they were dogshit.

Beyond the hospital, the city abruptly ended and the thinny began.

To Eddie, it looked like flat water standing in a vast marshland. It crowded up to the raised barrel of I-70 on both sides, silvery and shimmering, making the signs and guardrails and stalled cars waver like mirages; it gave off that liquidy humming sound like a stench.

Susannah put her hands to her ears, her mouth drawn down. "I don't know as I can stand it. Really. I don't mean to be spleeny, but already I feel like vomiting, and I haven't had anything to eat all day."

Eddie felt the same way. Yet, sick as he felt he could hardly take his eyes away from the thinny. It was as if unreality had been given . . . what? A face? No. The vast and humming silver shimmer ahead of them had no face, was the very antithesis of a face, in fact, but it had a body . . . an aspect . . . a *presence.*

Yes; that last was best. It had a presence, as the demon which had come to the circle of stones while they were trying to draw Jake had had a presence.

Roland, meanwhile, was rummaging in the depths of his purse. He appeared to dig all the way to the bottom before finding what he wanted: a fistful of bullets. He plucked Susannah's right hand off the arm of her chair, and put two of the bullets in her palm. Then he took two more and poked them, slug ends first, into his ears. Susannah looked first amazed, then amused, then doubtful. In the end, she followed his example. Almost at once an expression of blissful relief filled her face.

Eddie unshouldered the pack he wore and pulled out the half-full box of .44s that went with Jake's Ruger. The gunslinger shook his head and held out his hand. There were still four bullets in it, two for Eddie and two for Jake.

"What's wrong with these?" Eddie shook a couple of shells from the box that had come from behind the hanging files in Elmer Chambers's desk drawer.

"They're from your world and they won't block out the sound. Don't ask me how I know that; I just do. Try them if you want, but they won't work."

Eddie pointed at the bullets Roland was offering. "Those are from our world, too. The gun-shop on Seventh and Forty-ninth. Clements', wasn't that the name?"

"These didn't come from there. These are mine, Eddie, reloaded often but originally brought from the green land. From Gilead."

"You mean the *wets*?" Eddie asked incredulously. "The last of the wet shells from the beach? The ones that really got soaked?"

Roland nodded.

"You said those would never fire again! No matter how dry they got! That the powder had been . . . what did you say? 'Flattened.' "

Roland nodded again.

"So why'd you save them? Why bring a bunch of useless bullets all this way?"

"What did I teach you to say after a kill, Eddie? In order to focus your mind?"

" 'Father, guide my hands and heart so that no part of the animal will be wasted.' "

Roland nodded a third time. Jake took two shells and put them in his ears. Eddie took the last two, but first he tried the ones he'd shaken from the box. They muffled the sound of the thinny, but it was still there, vibrating in the center of his forehead, making his eyes water the way they did when he had a cold, making the bridge of his nose feel like it was going to explode. He picked them out, and put the bigger slugs—the ones from Roland's ancient revolvers—in their place. *Putting bullets in my ears,* he thought. *Ma would shit.* But that didn't matter. The sound of the thinny was gone—or at least down to a distant drone—and that was what did. When he turned and spoke to Roland, he expected his own voice to sound muffled, the way it did when you were wearing earplugs, but he found he could hear himself pretty well.

"Is there anything you *don't* know?" he asked Roland.

"Yes," Roland said. "Quite a lot."

"What about Oy?" Jake asked.

"Oy will be fine, I think," Roland said. "Come on, let's make some miles before dark."

7

Oy didn't seem bothered by the warble of the thinny, but he stuck close to Jake Chambers all that afternoon, looking mistrustfully at the stalled cars which clogged the eastbound lanes of I-70. And yet, Susannah saw, those cars did not clog the highway completely. The congestion eased as the travellers left downtown behind them, but even where the traffic had been heavy, some of the dead vehicles had been pulled to one side or the other; a number had been pushed right off the highway and onto the median strip, which was a concrete divider in the metro area and grass outside of town.

Somebody's been at work with a wrecker, that's my guess, Susannah thought. The idea made her happy. No one would have bothered clearing a path down the center of the highway while the plague was still raging, and if someone had done it after—if someone had been *around* to do it after—that meant the plague hadn't gotten everyone; those crammed-together obituaries weren't the whole story.

There were corpses in some of the cars, but they, like the ones at the foot of the station steps, were dry, not runny—mummies wearing seatbelts, for the most part. The majority of the cars were empty. A lot of the drivers and passengers caught in the traffic jams had probably tried to walk out of the plague-zone, she supposed, but she guessed that wasn't the only reason they had taken to their feet.

Susannah knew that she herself would have to be chained to the steering wheel to keep her inside a car once she felt the symptoms of some fatal disease setting in; if she was going to die, she would want to do it in God's open air. A hill would be best, someplace with a little elevation, but even a wheatfield would do, came it to that. Anything but coughing your last while smelling the air-freshener dangling from the rearview mirror.

At one time Susannah guessed they would have been able to see many of the corpses of the fleeing dead, but not now. Because of the thinny. They approached it steadily, and she knew exactly when they entered it. A kind of tingling shudder ran through her body, making her draw her shortened legs up, and the wheelchair stopped for a moment. When she turned around she saw Roland, Eddie, and Jake holding their stomachs and grimacing. They looked as if they had all been stricken with the bellyache at the same time. Then Eddie and Roland straightened up. Jake bent to stroke Oy, who had been staring at him anxiously.

"You boys all right?" Susannah asked. The question came out in the half-querulous, half-humorous voice of Detta Walker. Using that voice was nothing she planned; sometimes it just came out.

"Yeah," Jake said. "Feels like I got a bubble in my throat, though." He was staring uneasily at the thinny. Its silvery blankness was all around them now, as if the whole world had turned into a flat Norfolk fen at dawn. Nearby, trees poked out of its silver surface, casting distorted reflections that never stayed quite still or quite in focus. A little farther away, Susannah could see a grain-storage tower, seeming to float. The words GADDISH FEEDS were written on the side in pink letters which might have been red under normal conditions.

"Feels to me like I got a bubble in my *mind*," Eddie said. "Man, look at that shit shimmer."

"Can you still hear it?" Susannah asked.

"Yeah. But faint. I can live with it. Can you?"

"Uh-huh. Let's go."

It was like riding in an open-cockpit plane through broken clouds, Susannah decided. They'd go for what felt like miles through that humming brightness that was not quite fog and not quite water, sometimes seeing shapes (a barn, a tractor, a Stuckey's billboard) loom out of it, then losing everything but the road, which ran consistently above the thinny's bright but somehow indistinct surface.

Then, all at once, they would run into the clear. The humming would fall away to a faint drone; you could even unplug your ears and not be too bothered, at least until you got near the other side of the break. Once again there were vistas . . .

Well, no, that was too grand, Kansas didn't exactly *have* vistas, but there were open fields and the occasional copse of autumn-bright trees marking a spring or cowpond. No Grand Canyon or surf crashing on Portland Headlight, but at least you could see a by-God *horizon* off in the distance, and lose some of that unpleasant feeling of entombment. Then, back into the goop you went. Jake came closest to describing it, she thought, when he said that being in the thinny was like finally reaching the shining water-mirage you could often see far up the highway on hot days.

Whatever it was and however you described it, being inside it was claustrophobic, purgatorial, all the world gone except for the twin barrels of the turnpike and the hulks of the cars, like derelict ships abandoned on a frozen ocean.

Please help us get out of this, Susannah prayed to a God in whom she no longer precisely believed—she still believed in *something,* but since awakening to Roland's world on the beach of the Western Sea, her concept of the invisible world had changed considerably. *Please help us find the Beam again. Please help us escape this world of silence and death.*

They ran into the biggest clear space they had yet come to near a roadsign which read BIG SPRINGS 2 MI. Behind them, in the west, the setting sun shone through a brief rift in the clouds, skipping scarlet splinters across the top of the thinny and lighting the windows and taillights of the stalled cars in tones of fire. On either side of them empty fields stretched away. *Full Earth come and gone,* Susannah thought. *Reaping come and gone, too. This is what Roland calls closing the year.* The thought made her shiver.

"We'll camp here for the night," Roland said soon after they had passed the Big Springs exit ramp. Up ahead they could see the thinny encroaching on the highway again, but that was miles farther on—you could see a damn long way in eastern Kansas, Susannah was discovering. "We can get firewood without going too near the thinny, and the sound won't be too bad. We may even be able to sleep without bullets stuffed into our ears."

Eddie and Jake climbed over the guardrails, descended the bank, and foraged for wood along a dry creekbed, staying together as Roland admonished them to do. When they came back, the clouds had gulped the sun again, and an ashy, uninteresting twilight had begun to creep over the world.

The gunslinger stripped twigs for kindling, then laid his fuel around them in his usual fashion, building a kind of wooden chimney in the breakdown lane. As he did it, Eddie strolled across to the median strip and stood there, hands in pockets, looking east. After a few moments, Jake and Oy joined him.

Roland produced his flint and steel, scraped fire into the shaft of his chimney, and soon the little campfire was burning.

"Roland!" Eddie called. "Suze! Come over here! Look at this!"

Susannah started rolling her chair toward Eddie, then Roland—after a final check of his campfire—took hold of the handles and pushed her.

"Look at what?" Susannah asked.

Eddie pointed. At first Susannah saw nothing, although the turnpike was perfectly visible even beyond the point where the thinny closed in again, perhaps three miles ahead. Then . . . yes, she might see something. Maybe. A kind of shape, at the farthest edge of vision. If not for the fading daylight . . .

"Is it a building?" Jake asked. "Cripes, it looks like it's built right across the highway!"

"What about it, Roland?" Eddie asked. "You've got the best eyes in the universe."

For a time the gunslinger said nothing, only looked up the median strip with his thumbs hooked in his gunbelt. At last he said, "We'll see it better when we get closer."

"Oh, come on!" Eddie said. "I mean, holy shit! Do you know what it is or not?"

"We'll see it better when we get closer," the gunslinger repeated . . . which was, of course, no answer at all. He moseyed back across the eastbound lanes to check on his campfire, bootheels clicking on the pavement. Susannah looked at Jake and Eddie. She shrugged. They shrugged back . . . and then Jake burst into bright peals of laughter. Usually, Susannah thought, the kid acted more like an eighteen-year-old than a boy of eleven, but that laughter made him sound about nine-going-on-ten, and she didn't mind a bit.

She looked down at Oy, who was looking at them earnestly and rolling his shoulders in an effort to shrug.

8

They ate the leaf-wrapped delicacies Eddie called gun-slinger burritos, drawing closer to the fire and feeding it more wood as the dark drew down. Somewhere south a bird cried out—it was just about the loneliest sound he had ever heard in his life, Eddie reckoned. None of them talked much, and it occurred to him that, at this time of their day, hardly anyone ever did. As if the time when the earth swapped day for dark was special, a time that somehow closed them off from the powerful fellow-ship Roland called *ka-tet.*

Jake fed Oy small scraps of dried deermeat from his last burrito; Susannah sat on her bedroll, legs crossed beneath her hide smock, looking dreamily into the fire; Roland lay back on his elbows, looking up at the sky, where the clouds had begun to melt away from the stars. Looking up himself, Eddie saw that Old Star and Old Mother were gone, their places taken by Polaris and the Big Dipper. This might not be his world—Takuro auto-mobiles, the Kansas City Monarchs, and a food franchise called Boing Boing Burgers all suggested it wasn't—but Eddie thought it was too close for comfort. *Maybe,* he thought, *the world next door.*

When the bird cried in the distance again, he roused himself and looked at Roland. "You had something you were going to tell us," he said. "A thrilling tale of your youth, I believe. Susan—that was her name, wasn't it?"

For a moment longer the gunslinger continued to look up at the sky—now it was Roland who must find himself adrift in the constellations, Eddie realized—and then he shifted his gaze to his friends. He looked strangely apologetic, strangely uneasy. "Would you think I was cozening," he said, "if I asked for one more day to think of these things? Or perhaps it's a night to dream of them that I really want. They are old things, dead things, perhaps, but I . . ." He raised his hands in a kind of distracted gesture. "Some things don't rest easy even when they're dead. Their bones cry out from the ground."

"There are ghosts," Jake said, and in his eyes Eddie saw a shadow of the horror he must have felt inside the house in Dutch Hill. The horror he must have felt when the Doorkeeper came out of the wall and reached for him. "Sometimes there are ghosts, and sometimes they come back."

"Yes," Roland said. "Sometimes there are, and sometimes they do."

"Maybe it's better not to brood," Susannah said. "Sometimes—especially when you know a thing's going to be hard—it's better just to get on your horse and ride."

Roland thought this over carefully, then raised his eyes to look at her. "At tomorrow night's fire I will tell you of Susan," he said. "This I promise on my father's name."

"Do we need to hear?" Eddie asked abruptly. He was almost astounded to hear this question coming out of his mouth; no one had been more curious about the gunslinger's past than Eddie himself. "I mean, if it really hurts, Roland . . . hurts big-time . . . maybe . . ."

"I'm not sure you need to hear, but I think I need to tell. Our future is the Tower, and to go toward it with a whole heart, I must put my past to rest as best I may. There's no way I could tell you all of it—in my world even the past is in motion, rearranging itself in many vital ways—but this one story may stand for all the rest."

"Is it a Western?" Jake asked suddenly.

Roland looked at him, puzzled. "I don't take your meaning, Jake. Gilead is a Barony of the Western World, yes, and Mejis as well, but—"

"It'll be a Western," Eddie said. "All Roland's stories

are Westerns, when you get right down to it." He lay back
and pulled his blanket over him. Faintly, from both east
and west, he could hear the warble of the thinny. He
checked in his pocket for the bullets Roland had given
him, and nodded with satisfaction when he felt them.
He reckoned he could sleep without them tonight, but
he would want them again tomorrow. They weren't done
turnpikin' just yet.

Susannah leaned over him, kissed the tip of his nose.
"Done for the day, sugar?"

"Yep," Eddie said, and laced his hands together behind
his head. "It's not every day that I hook a ride on the
world's fastest train, destroy the world's smartest computer, and then discover that everyone's been scragged
by the flu. All before dinner, too. Shit like that makes a
man tired." Eddie smiled and closed his eyes. He was still
smiling when sleep took him.

9

In his dream, they were all standing on the corner of
Second Avenue and Forty-sixth Street, looking over the
short board fence and into the weedy vacant lot behind
it. They were wearing their Mid-World clothes—a mot-
ley combination of deerskin and old shirts, mostly held
together with spit and shoelaces—but none of the pedes-
trians hurrying by on Second seemed to notice. No one
noticed the billy-bumbler in Jake's arms or the artillery
they were packing, either.

Because we're ghosts, Eddie thought. *We're ghosts and we
don't rest easy.*

On the fence there were handbills—one for the Sex
Pistols (a reunion tour, according to the poster, and
Eddie thought that was pretty funny—the Pistols was

one group that was *never* going to get back together), one for a comic, Adam Sandler, that Eddie had never heard of, one for a movie called *The Craft*, about teen-age witches. Beyond that one, written in letters the dusky pink of summer roses, was this:

See the BEAR of fearsome size!
All the WORLD's within his eyes.
TIME grows thin, the past's a riddle;
The TOWER awaits you in the middle.

"There," Jake said, pointing. *"The rose. See how it awaits us, there in the middle of the lot."*

"Yes, it's very beautiful," Susannah said. Then she pointed to the sign standing near the rose and facing Second Avenue. Her voice and her eyes were troubled. *"But what about that?"*

According to the sign, two outfits—Mills Construction and Sombra Real Estate—were going to combine on something called Turtle Bay Condominiums, said con-dos to be erected on this very spot. When? COMING SOON was all the sign had to say in that regard.

"I wouldn't worry about that," Jake said. *"That sign was here before. It's probably old as the hi—"*

At that moment the revving sound of an engine tore into the air. From beyond the fence, on the Forty-sixth Street side of the lot, chugs of dirty brown exhaust ascended like bad-news smoke signals. Suddenly the boards on that side burst open, and a huge red bull-dozer lunged through. Even the blade was red, although the words slashed across its scoop—ALL HAIL THE CRIM-SON KING—were written in a yellow as bright as panic. Sitting in the peak-seat, his rotting face leering at them from above the controls, was the man who had kid-napped Jake from the bridge over the River Send—their old pal Gasher. On the front of his cocked-back hardhat, the words LAMERK FOUNDRY stood out in black. Above them, a single staring eye had been painted.

Gasher lowered the 'dozer's blade. It tore across the lot on a diagonal, smashing brick, pulverizing beer and soda bottles to glittering powder, striking sparks from the rocks. Directly in its path, the rose nodded its delicate head.

"Let's see you ask some of yer silly questions now!" this unwelcome apparition cried. *"Ask all yer wants, my dear little culls, why not? Wery fond of riddles is yer old pal Gasher! Just so you understand that, no matter what yer ask, I'm gointer run that nasty thing over, mash it flat, aye, so I will! Then back over it I'll go! Root and branch, my dear little culls! Aye, root and branch!"*

Susannah shrieked as the scarlet bulldozer blade bore down on the rose, and Eddie grabbed for the fence. He would vault over it, throw himself on the rose, try to protect it . . .

. . . except it was too late. And he knew it.

He looked back up at the cackling thing in the bulldozer's peak-seat and saw that Gasher was gone. Now the man at the controls was Engineer Bob, from *Charlie the Choo-Choo.*

"Stop!" Eddie screamed. *"For Christ's sake, stop!"*

"I can't, Eddie. The world has moved on, and I can't stop. I must move on with it."

And as the shadow of the 'dozer fell over the rose, as the blade tore through one of the posts holding up the sign (Eddie saw COMING SOON had changed to COMING NOW), he realized that the man at the controls wasn't Engineer Bob, either.

It was Roland.

10

Eddie sat up in the breakdown lane of the turnpike, gasping breath he could see in the air and with sweat already chilling on his hot skin. He was sure he had screamed, *must* have screamed, but Susannah still slept beside him with only the top of her head poking out of the bedroll they shared, and Jake was snoring softly off to the left, one arm out of his own blankets and curled around Oy. The bumbler was also sleeping.

Roland wasn't. Roland sat calmly on the far side of the dead campfire, cleaning his guns by starlight and looking at Eddie.

"Bad dreams." Not a question.

"Yeah."

"A visit from your brother?"

Eddie shook his head.

"The Tower, then? The field of roses and the Tower?" Roland's face remained impassive, but Eddie could hear the subtle eagerness which always came into his voice when the subject was the Dark Tower. Eddie had once called the gunslinger a Tower junkie, and Roland hadn't denied it.

"Not this time."

"What, then?"

Eddie shivered. "Cold."

"Yes. Thank your gods there's no rain, at least. Autumn rain's an evil to be avoided whenever one may. What was your dream?"

Still Eddie hesitated. "You'd never betray us, would you, Roland?"

"No man can say that for sure, Eddie, and I have already played the betrayer more than once. To my shame. But . . . I think those days are over. We are one, *ka-tet.* If I betray any one of you—even Jake's furry friend, perhaps—I betray myself. Why do you ask?"

"And you'd never betray your quest."

"Renounce the Tower? No, Eddie. Not that, not ever. Tell me your dream."

Eddie did, omitting nothing. When he had finished, Roland looked down at his guns, frowning. They seemed to have reassembled themselves while Eddie was talking.

"So what does it mean, that I saw you driving that 'dozer at the end? That I still don't trust you? That sub-consciously—"

"Is this ology-of-the-psyche? The cabala I have heard you and Susannah speak of?"

"Yes, I guess it is."

"It's shit," Roland said dismissively. "Mudpies of the mind. Dreams either mean nothing or everything—and when they mean everything, they almost always come as messages from . . . well, from other levels of the Tower." He gazed at Eddie shrewdly. "And not all messages are sent by friends."

"Something or someone is fucking with my head? Is that what you mean?"

"I think it possible. But you must watch me all the same. I bear watching, as you well know."

"I trust you," Eddie said, and the very awkwardness with which he spoke lent his words sincerity. Roland looked touched, almost shaken, and Eddie wondered how he ever could have thought this man an emotion-less robot. Roland might be a little short on imagination, but he had feelings, all right.

"One thing about your dream concerns me very much, Eddie."

"The bulldozer?"

"The machine, yes. The threat to the rose."

"Jake saw the rose, Roland. It was fine."

Roland nodded. "In his when, the when of that particular day, the rose was thriving. But that doesn't mean it will continue to do so. If the construction the sign spoke of comes . . . if the *bulldozer* comes . . ."

"There are other worlds than these," Eddie said. "Remember?"

"Some things may exist only in one. In one *where*, in one *when*." Roland lay down and looked up at the stars. "We must protect that rose," he said. "We must protect it at all costs."

"You think it's another door, don't you? One that opens on the Dark Tower."

The gunslinger looked at him from eyes that ran with starshine. "I think it may *be* the Tower," he said. "And if it's destroyed—"

His eyes closed. He said no more.

Eddie lay awake late.

II

The new day dawned clear and bright and cold. In the strong morning sunlight, the thing Eddie had spotted the evening before was more clearly visible . . . but he still couldn't tell what it was. Another riddle, and he was getting damned sick of them.

He stood squinting at it, shading his eyes from the sun, with Susannah on one side of him and Jake on the other. Roland was back by the campfire, packing what he called their *gunna,* a word which seemed to mean all their worldly goods. He appeared not to be concerned with the thing up ahead, or to know what it was.

How far away? Thirty miles? Fifty? The answer seemed to depend on how far could you see in all this flat land, and Eddie didn't know the answer. One thing he felt quite sure of was that Jake had been right on at least two counts—it was some kind of building, and it sprawled across all four lanes of the highway. It must; how else could they see it? It would have been lost in the thinny . . . wouldn't it?

Maybe it's standing in one of those open patches—what Suze calls "the holes in the clouds." Or maybe the thinny ends before we get that far. Or maybe it's a goddam hallucination. In any case, you might as well put it out of your mind for the time being. Got a little more turnpikin' to do.

Still, the building held him. It looked like an airy Arabian Nights confection of blue and gold . . . except Eddie had an idea that the blue was stolen from the sky and the gold from the newly risen sun.

"Roland, come here a second!"

At first he didn't think the gunslinger would, but then Roland cinched a rawhide lace on Susannah's pack, rose, put his hands in the small of his back, stretched, and walked over to them.

"Gods, one would think no one in this band has the wit to housekeep but me," Roland said.

"We'll pitch in," Eddie said, "we always do, don't we? But look at that thing first."

Roland did, but only with a quick glance, as if he did not even want to acknowledge it.

"It's glass, isn't it?" Eddie asked.

Roland took another brief look. "I wot," he said, a phrase which seemed to mean *Reckon so, partner.*

"We've got lots of glass buildings where I come from, but most of them are office buildings. That thing up ahead looks more like something from Disney World. Do you know what it is?"

"No."

"Then why don't you want to look at it?" Susannah asked.

Roland *did* take another look at the distant blaze of light on glass, but once again it was quick—little more than a peek.

"Because it's trouble," Roland said, "and it's in our road. We'll get there in time. No need to live in trouble until trouble comes."

"Will we get there today?" Jake asked.

Roland shrugged, his face still closed. "There'll be water if God wills it," he said.

"Christ, you could have made a fortune writing fortune cookies," Eddie said. He hoped for a smile, at least, but got none. Roland simply walked back across the road, dropped to one knee, shouldered his purse and his pack, and waited for the others. When they were ready, the pilgrims resumed their walk east along Interstate 70. The gunslinger led, walking with his head down and his eyes on the toes of his boots.

12

Roland was quiet all day, and as the building ahead of them neared (*trouble, and in our road,* he had said), Susannah came to realize it wasn't grumpiness they were seeing, or worry about anything which lay any farther ahead of them than tonight. It was the story he'd promised to tell them that Roland was thinking about, and he was a lot more than worried.

By the time they stopped for their noon meal, they could clearly see the building ahead—a many-turreted palace which appeared to be made entirely of reflective glass. The thinny lay close around it, but the palace rose serenely above all, its turrets trying for the sky. Madly strange here in the flat countryside of eastern Kansas, of course it was, but Susannah thought it the most beautiful building she had ever seen in her life; even more beautiful than the Chrysler Building, and that was going some.

As they drew closer, she found it more and more difficult to look elsewhere. Watching the reflections of the puffy clouds sailing across the glass castle's blue-sky wains and walls was like watching some splendid illusion . . . yet there was a solidity to it, as well. An inarguability. Some of that was probably just the shadow it threw—mirages did not, so far as she knew, create shadows—but not all. It just *was*. She had no idea what such a fabulosity was doing out here in the land of Stuckey's and Hardee's (not to mention Boing Boing Burgers), but there it was. She reckoned that time would tell the rest.

13

They made camp in silence, watched Roland build the wooden chimney that would be their fire in silence, then sat before it in silence, watching the sunset turn the huge glass edifice ahead of them into a castle of fire. Its towers and battlements glowed first a fierce red, then orange, then a gold which cooled rapidly to ocher as Old Star appeared in the firmament above them—

No, she thought in Detta's voice. *Ain't dat one, girl. Not 'tall. That's the North Star. Same one you seen back home, sittin on yo' daddy's lap.*

But it was Old Star she wanted, she discovered; Old Star and Old Mother. She was astounded to find herself homesick for Roland's world, and then wondered why she should be so surprised. It was a world, after all, where no one had called her a nigger bitch (at least not yet), a world where she had found someone to love . . . and made good friends as well. That last made her feel a little bit like crying, and she hugged Jake to her. He let himself be hugged, smiling, his eyes half-closed. At some distance, unpleasant but bearable even without bullet earplugs, the thinny warbled its moaning song.

When the last traces of yellow began to fade from the castle up the road, Roland left them to sit in the turnpike travel lane and returned to his fire. He cooked more leaf-wrapped deermeat, and handed the food around. They ate in silence (Roland actually ate almost nothing, Susannah observed). By the time they were finished, they could see the Milky Way scattered across the walls of the castle ahead of them, fierce points of reflection that burned like fire in still water.

Eddie was the one who finally broke the silence. "You don't have to," he said. "You're excused. Or absolved. Or whatever the hell it is you need to take that look off your face."

Roland ignored him. He drank, tilting the waterskin up on his elbow like some hick drinking moonshine from a jug, head back, eyes on the stars. The last mouthful he spat to the roadside.

"Life for your crop," Eddie said. He did not smile.

Roland said nothing, but his cheek went pale, as if he had seen a ghost. Or heard one.

14

The gunslinger turned to Jake, who looked back at him seriously. "I went through the trial of manhood at the age of fourteen, the youngest of my *ka-tel*—of my class, you would say—and perhaps the youngest ever. I told you some of that, Jake. Do you remember?"

You told all *of us some of that,* Susannah thought, but kept her mouth shut, and warned Eddie with her eyes to do the same. Roland hadn't been himself during that telling; with Jake both dead and alive within his head, the man had been fighting madness.

"You mean when we were chasing Walter," Jake said. "After the way station but before I . . . I took my fall."

"That's right."

"I remember a little, but that's all. The way you remember the stuff you dream about."

Roland nodded. "Listen, then. I would tell you more this time, Jake, because you are older. I suppose we all are."

Susannah was no less fascinated with the story the second time: how the boy Roland had chanced to discover Marten, his father's advisor (his father's *wizard*) in his mother's apartment. Only none of it had been by chance, of course; the boy would have passed her door with no more than a glance had Marten not opened it and invited him in. Marten had told Roland that his mother wanted to see him, but one look at her rueful smile and downcast eyes as she sat in her low-back chair told the boy he was the last person in the world Gabrielle Deschain wanted to see just then.

The flush on her cheek and the love-bite on the side of her neck told him everything else.

Thus had he been goaded by Marten into an early trial of manhood, and by employing a weapon his teacher had not expected—his hawk, David—Roland had defeated Cort, taken his stick . . . and made the enemy of his life in Marten Broadcloak.

Beaten badly, face swelling into something that looked like a child's goblin mask, slipping toward a coma, Cort had fought back unconsciousness long enough to offer his newest apprentice gunslinger counsel: stay away from Marten yet awhile, Cort had said.

"He told me to let the story of our battle grow into a

legend," the gunslinger told Eddie, Susannah, and Jake. "To wait until my shadow had grown hair on its face and haunted Marten in his dreams."

"Did you take his advice?" Susannah asked.

"I never got a chance," Roland said. His face cracked in a rueful, painful smile. "I meant to think about it, and seriously, but before I even got started on my thinking, things . . . changed."

"They have a way of doing that, don't they?" Eddie said. "My goodness, yes."

"I buried my hawk, the first weapon I ever wielded, and perhaps the finest. Then—and this part I'm sure I didn't tell you before, Jake—I went into the lower town. That summer's heat broke in storms full of thunder and hail, and in a room above one of the brothels where Cort had been wont to roister, I lay with a woman for the first time."

He poked a stick thoughtfully into the fire, seemed to become aware of the unconscious symbolism in what he was doing, and threw it away with a lopsided grin. It landed, smoldering, near the tire of an abandoned Dodge Aspen and went out.

"It was good. The sex was good. Not the great thing I and my friends had thought about and whispered about and wondered about, of course—"

"I think store-bought pussy tends to be overrated by the young, sugar," Susannah said.

"I fell asleep listening to the sots downstairs singing along with the piano and to the sound of hail on the window. I awoke the next morning in . . . well . . . let's just say I awoke in a way I never would have expected to awake in such a place."

Jake fed fresh fuel to the fire. It flared up, painting highlights on Roland's cheeks, brushing crescents of shadow beneath his brows and below his lower lip. And

as he talked, Susannah found she could almost see what
had happened on that long-ago morning that must have
smelled of wet cobblestones and rain-sweetened summer air; what had happened in a whore's crib above a
drinking-dive in the lower town of Gilead, Barony seat of
New Canaan, one small mote of land located in the western regions of Mid-World.

One boy, still aching from his battle of the day before
and newly educated in the mysteries of sex. One boy,
now looking twelve instead of fourteen, his lashes dust-
ing down thick upon his cheeks, the lids shuttering those
extraordinary blue eyes; one boy with his hand loosely cupping a whore's breast, his hawk-scarred wrist lying tanned
upon the counterpane. One boy in the final instants of
his life's last good sleep, one boy who will shortly be in
motion, who will be falling as a dislodged pebble falls on
a steep and broken slope of scree; a falling pebble that
strikes another, and another, and another, those pebbles
striking yet more, until the whole slope is in motion and
the earth shakes with the sound of the landslide.

One boy, one pebble on a slope loose and ready to
slide.

A knot exploded in the fire. Somewhere in this dream
of Kansas, an animal yipped. Susannah watched sparks
swirl up past Roland's incredibly ancient face and saw in
that face the sleeping boy of a summer's morn, lying in a
bawd's bed. And then she saw the door crash open, ending Gilead's last troubled dream.

15

The man who strode in, crossing the room to the bed
before Roland could open his eyes (and before the
woman beside him had even begun to register the

sound), was tall, slim, dressed in faded jeans and a dusty shirt of blue chambray. On his head was a dark gray hat with a snakeskin band. Lying low on his hips were two old leather holsters. Jutting from them were the sandalwood grips of the pistols the boy would someday bear to lands of which this scowling man with the furious blue eyes would never dream.

Roland was in motion even before he was able to unseal his eyes, rolling to the left, groping beneath the bed for what was there. He was fast, so fast it was scary, but—and Susannah saw this, too, saw it clearly—the man in the faded jeans was faster yet. He grabbed the boy's shoulder and yanked, turning him naked out of bed and onto the floor. The boy sprawled there, reaching again for what was beneath the bed, lightning-quick. The man in the jeans stamped down on his fingers before they could grasp.

"Bastard!" the boy gasped. "Oh, you bas—"

But now his eyes were open, he looked up, and saw that the invading bastard was his father.

The whore was sitting up now, her eyes puffy, her face slack and petulant. "Here!" she cried. "Here, here! You can't just be a-comin in like that, so you can't! Why, if I was to raise my voice—"

Ignoring her, the man reached beneath the bed and dragged out two gunbelts. Near the end of each was a holstered revolver. They were large, and amazing in this largely gunless world, but they were not so large as those worn by Roland's father, and the grips were eroded metal plates rather than inlaid wood. When the whore saw the guns on the invader's hips and the ones in his hands—the ones her young customer of the night before had been wearing until she had taken him upstairs and divested him of all weapons save for the one with which she was most familiar—the expression of sleepy petulance left her face. What replaced it was the foxlike look of a born survivor. She was up, out of bed, across the floor, and out the door before her bare bum had more than a brief moment to twinkle in the morning sun.

Neither the father standing by the bed nor the son lying naked upon the floor at his feet so much as looked at her. The man in the jeans held out the gunbelts which Roland had taken from the fuzer beneath the apprentices' barracks on the previous afternoon, using Cort's key to open the arsenal door. The man shook the belts under Roland's very nose, as one might hold a torn garment beneath the nose of a feckless puppy that has chewed. He shook them so hard that one of the guns tumbled free. Despite his stupefaction, Roland caught it in midair.

"I thought you were in the west," Roland said. "In Cressia. After Farson and his—"

Roland's father slapped him hard enough to send the boy tumbling across the room and into a corner with blood pouring from one corner of his mouth. Roland's first, appalling instinct was to raise the gun he still held.

Steven Deschain looked at him, hands on hips, reading this thought even before it was fully formed. His lips pulled back in a singularly mirthless grin, one that showed all of his teeth and most of his gums.

"Shoot me if you will. Why not? Make this abortion complete. Ah, gods, I'd welcome it!"

Roland laid the gun on the floor and pushed it away, using the back of his hand to do it. All at once he wanted his fingers nowhere near the trigger of a gun. They were no longer fully under his control, those fingers. He had discovered that yesterday, right around the time he had broken Cort's nose.

"Father, I was tested yesterday. I took Cort's stick. I won. I'm a man."

"You're a fool," his father said. His grin was gone now; he looked haggard and old. He sat down heavily on the whore's bed, looked at the gunbelts he still held, and dropped them between his feet. "You're a fourteen-year-old fool, and that's the worst, most desperate kind." He looked up, angry all over again, but Roland didn't mind; anger was better than that look of weariness. That look of age. "I've known since you toddled that you were no genius, but I never believed until yestereve that you were an idiot. To let him drive you like a cow in a chute! Gods! You have forgotten the face of your father! Say it!"

And that sparked the boy's own anger. Everything he had done the day before he had done with his father's face firmly fixed in his mind.

"That's not true!" he shouted from where he now sat with his bare butt on the splintery boards of the whore's crib and his back against the wall, the sun shining through the window and touching the fuzz on his fair, unscarred cheek.

"It *is* true, you whelp! Foolish whelp! Say your atonement or I'll strip the hide from your very—"

"They were together!" he burst out. "Your wife and your minister—your magician! I saw the mark of his mouth on her neck! *On my mother's neck!*" He reached for the gun and picked it up, but even in his shame and fury was still careful not to let his fingers stray near the trigger; he held the apprentice's revolver only by the plain, undecorated metal of its barrel. "Today I end his treacherous, seducer's life with this, and if you aren't man enough to help me, at least you can stand aside and let m—"

One of the revolvers on Steven's hip was out of its holster and in his hand before Roland's eyes saw any move. There was a single shot, deafening as thunder in the little room; it was a full minute before Roland was able to hear the babble of questions and commotion from below. The 'prentice-gun, meanwhile, was long gone, blown out of his hand and leaving nothing behind but a kind of buzzing tingle. It flew out the window, down and gone, its grip a smashed ruin of metal and its short turn in the gunslinger's long tale at an end.

Roland looked at his father, shocked and amazed. Steven looked back, saying nothing for a long time. But now he wore the face Roland remembered from earliest childhood: calm and sure. The weariness and the look of half-distracted fury had passed away like last night's thunderstorms.

At last his father spoke. "I was wrong in what I said, and I apologize. You did not forget my face, Roland. But still you were foolish—you allowed yourself to be driven by one far slyer than you will ever be in your life. It's only by the grace of the gods and the working of *ka* that you have not been sent west, one more true gunslinger out of Marten's road . . . out of John Farson's road . . . and out of the road which leads to the creature that rules them." He stood and held out his arms. "If I had lost you, Roland, I should have died."

Roland got to his feet and went naked to his father, who embraced him fiercely. When Steven Deschain kissed him first on one cheek and then the other, Roland began to weep. Then, in Roland's ear, Steven Deschain whispered six words.

16

"What?" Susannah asked. "What six words?"

" 'I have known for two years,' " Roland said. "That was what he whispered."

"Holy Christ," Eddie said.

"He told me I couldn't go back to the palace. If I did, I'd be dead by nightfall. He said, 'You have been born to your destiny in spite of all Marten could do; yet he has sworn to kill you before you can grow to be a problem to him. It seems that, winner in the test or no, you must leave Gilead anyway. For only awhile, though, and you'll go east instead of west. I'd not send you alone, either, or without a purpose.' Then, almost as an afterthought, he added: 'Or with a pair of sorry 'prentice revolvers.' "

"What purpose?" Jake asked. He had clearly been captivated by the story; his eyes shone nearly as bright as Oy's. "And which friends?"

"These things you must now hear," Roland said, "and how you judge me will come in time."

He fetched a sigh—the deep sigh of a man who contemplates some arduous piece of work—and then tossed fresh wood on the fire. As the flames flared up, driving the shadows back a little way, he began to talk. All that queerly long night he talked, not finishing the story of Susan Delgado until the sun was rising in the east and painting the glass castle yonder with all the bright hues of a fresh day, and a strange green cast of light which was its own true color.

PART TWO

SUSAN

CHAPTER ONE

Beneath the Kissing Moon

I

A perfect disc of silver—the Kissing Moon, as it was called in Full Earth—hung above the ragged hill five miles east of Hambry and ten miles south of Eyebolt Canyon. Below the hill the late summer heat still held, suffocating even two hours after sundown, but atop the Cöos, it was as if Reap had already come, with its strong breezes and frost-pinched air. For the woman who lived here with no company but a snake and one old mutie cat, it was to be a long night.

Never mind, though; never mind, my dear. Busy hands are happy hands. So they are.

She waited until the hoofbeats of her visitors' horses had faded, sitting quietly by the window in the hut's large room (there was only one other, a bedroom little bigger than a closet). Musty, the six-legged cat, was on her shoulder. Her lap was full of moonlight.

Three horses, bearing away three men. The Big Coffin Hunters, they called themselves.

She snorted. Men were funny, aye, so they were, and the most amusing thing about them was how little they knew it. Men, with their swaggering, belt-hitching names for themselves. Men, so proud of their muscles, their drinking capacities, their eating capacities; so everlastingly proud of their pricks. Yes, even in these times, when a good many of them could shoot nothing but strange, bent seed that produced children fit only to be drowned in the nearest well. Ah, but it was never their fault, was it, dear? No, always it was the woman—her womb, her fault. Men were such cowards. Such grinning cowards. These three had been no different from the general run. The old one with the limp might bear watching—aye, so he might, a clear and overly curious pair of eyes had looked out at her from his head—but she saw nothing in them she could not deal with, came it to that.

Men! She could not understand why so many women feared them. Hadn't the gods made them with the most vulnerable part of their guts hanging right out of their bodies, like a misplaced bit of bowel? Kick them there and they curled up like snails. Caress them there and their brains melted. Anyone who doubted that second bit of wisdom need only look at her night's second bit of business, the one which still lay ahead. Thorin! Mayor of Hambry! Chief Guard o' Barony! No fool like an old fool!

Yet none of these thoughts had any real power over her or any real malice to them, at least not now; the three men who called themselves the Big Coffin Hunters had brought her a marvel, and she would look at it; aye, fill up her eyes with it, so she would.

The gimp, Jonas, had insisted she put it away—he had been told she had a place for such things, not that he wanted to see it himself, not *any* of her secret places, gods forbid (at this sally Depape and Reynolds had laughed like trolls)—and so she had, but the hoofbeats of their horses had been swallowed by the wind now, and she would do as she liked. The girl whose tits had stolen what little there was of Hart Thorin's mind would not be here for another hour, at least (the old woman had insisted that the girl walk from town, citing the purification value of such a moonlit heel-and-toe, actually just wanting to put a safe bumper of time between her two appointments), and during that hour she would do as she liked.

"Oh, it's beautiful, I'm sure 'tis," she whispered, and did she feel a certain heat in that place where her ancient bowlegs came together? A certain moisture in the dry creek which hid there? Gods!

"Aye, even through the box where they hid it I felt its glam. So beautiful, Musty, like you." She took the cat from her shoulder and held it in front of her eyes. The old tom purred and stretched out its pug of a face toward hers. She kissed its nose. The cat closed its milky gray-green eyes in ecstasy. "So beautiful, like you—so y'are, so y'are! Hee!"

She put the cat down. It walked slowly toward the hearth, where a late fire lazed, desultorily eating at a single log. Musty's tail, split at the tip so it looked like the forked tail of a devil in an old drawing, switched back and forth in the room's dim orange air. Its extra legs, dangling from its sides, twitched dreamily. The shadow which trailed across the floor and grew up the wall was a horror: a thing that looked like a cat crossed with a spider.

The old woman rose and went into her sleeping closet, where she had taken the thing Jonas had given her.

"Lose that and you'll lose your head," he'd said.

"Never fear me, my good friend," she'd replied, directing a cringing, servile smile back over her shoulder, all the while thinking: Men! Foolish strutting creatures they were!

Now she went to the foot of her bed, knelt, and passed one hand over the earth floor there. Lines appeared in the sour dirt as she did. They formed a square. She pushed her fingers into one of these lines; it gave before her touch. She lifted the hidden panel (hidden in such

a way that no one without the touch would ever be able
to uncover it), revealing a compartment perhaps a foot
square and two feet deep. Within it was an ironwood box.
Curled atop the box was a slim green snake. When she
touched its back, its head came up. Its mouth yawned in
a silent hiss, displaying four pairs of fangs—two on top,
two on the bottom.

She took the snake up, crooning to it. As she brought
its flat face close to her own, its mouth yawned wider and
its hissing became audible. She opened her own mouth;
from between her wrinkled gray lips she poked the yellowish, bad-smelling mat of her tongue. Two drops of poison—enough to kill an entire dinner-party, if mixed in
the punch—fell on it. She swallowed, feeling her mouth
and throat and chest burn, as if with strong liquor. For
a moment the room swam out of focus, and she could
hear voices murmuring in the stenchy air of the hut—
the voices of those she called "the unseen friends." Her
eyes ran sticky water down the trenches time had drawn
in her cheeks. Then she blew out a breath and the room
steadied. The voices faded.

She kissed Ermot between his lidless eyes (*time o' the
Kissing Moon, all right,* she thought) and then set him
aside. The snake slipped beneath her bed, curled itself
in a circle, and watched as she passed her palms over the
top of the ironwood box. She could feel the muscles in
her upper arms quivering, and that heat in her loins was
more pronounced. Years it had been since she had felt
the call of her sex, but she felt it now, so she did, and it
was not the doing of the Kissing Moon, or not much.

The box was locked and Jonas had given her no key,
but that was nothing to her, who had lived long and studied much and trafficked with creatures that most men,
for all their bold talk and strutting ways, would run from
as if on fire had they caught even the smallest glimpse

of them. She stretched one hand toward the lock, on which was inlaid the shape of an eye and a motto in the High Speech (I SEE WHO OPENS ME), and then withdrew it. All at once she could smell what her nose no longer noticed under ordinary circumstances: must and dust and a dirty mattress and the crumbs of food that had been consumed in bed; the mingled stench of ashes and ancient incense; the odor of an old woman with wet eyes and (ordinarily, at least) a dry pussy. She would not open this box and look at the wonder it contained in here; she would go outside, where the air was clean and the only smells were sage and mesquite.

She would look by the light of the Kissing Moon.

Rhea of Cöos Hill pulled the box from its hole with a grunt, rose to her feet with another grunt (this one from her nether regions), tucked the box under her arm, and left the room.

2

The hut was far enough below the brow of the hill to block off the bitterest gusts of the winter wind which blew almost constantly in these highlands from Reaping until the end of Wide Earth. A path led to the hill's highest vantage; beneath the full moon it was a ditch of silver. The old woman toiled up it, puffing, her white hair standing out around her head in dirty clumps, her old dugs swaying from side to side under her black dress. The cat followed in her shadow, still giving off its rusty purr like a stink.

At the top of the hill, the wind lifted her hair away from her ravaged face and brought her the moaning whisper of the thinny which had eaten its way into the far end of Eyebolt Canyon. It was a sound few cared for, she knew, but she herself loved it; to Rhea of the Cöos, it sounded like a lullabye. Overhead rode the moon, the shadows on its bright skin sketching the faces of lovers kissing . . . if you believed the ordinary fools below, that was. The ordinary fools below saw a different face or set of faces in each full moon, but the hag knew there was only one—the face of the Demon. The face of death.

She herself, however, had never felt more alive.

"Oh, my beauty," she whispered, and touched the lock with her gnarled fingers. A faint glimmer of red light showed between her bunched knuckles, and there was a click. Breathing hard, like a woman who has run a race, she put the box down and opened it.

Rose-colored light, dimmer than that thrown by the Kissing Moon but infinitely more beautiful, spilled out. It touched the ruined face hanging above the box, and for a moment made it the face of a young girl again.

Musty sniffed, head stretched forward, ears laid back, old eyes rimmed with that rose light. Rhea was instantly jealous.

"Get away, foolish, 'tis not for the likes of you!"

She swatted the cat. Musty shied back, hissing like a kettle, and stalked in dudgeon to the hummock which marked the very tip of Cöos Hill. There he sat, affecting disdain and licking one paw as the wind combed ceaselessly through his fur.

Within the box, peeping out of a velvet drawstring bag, was a glass globe. It was filled with that rosy light; it flowed in gentle pulses, like the beat of a satisfied heart.

"Oh, my lovely one," she murmured, lifting it out. She held it up before her; let its pulsing radiance run down her wrinkled face like rain. "Oh, ye live, so ye do!"

Suddenly the color within the globe darkened toward scarlet. She felt it thrum in her hands like an immensely powerful motor, and again she felt that amazing wetness between her legs, that tidal tug she believed had been left behind long ago.

Then the thrumming died, and the light in the globe seemed to furl up like petals. Where it had been there was now a pinkish gloom . . . and three riders coming out of it. At first she thought it was the men who had brought her the globe—Jonas and the others. But no, these were younger, even younger than Depape, who was about twenty-five. The one on the left of the trio appeared to have a bird's skull mounted on the pommel of his saddle—strange but true.

Then that one and the one on the right were gone, darkened away somehow by the power of the glass, leaving only the one in the middle. She took in the jeans and boots he wore, the flat-brimmed hat that hid the upper half of his face, the easy way he sat his horse, and her first alarmed thought was *Gunslinger! Come east from the Inner Baronies, aye, perhaps from Gilead itself!* But she did not have to see the upper half of the rider's face to know he was little more than a child, and there were no guns on his hips. Yet she didn't think the youth came unarmed. If only she could see a little better . . .

She brought the glass almost to the tip of her nose and whispered, "Closer, lovie! Closer still!"

She didn't know what to expect—nothing at all seemed most likely—but within the dark circle of the glass, the figure did come closer. *Swam* closer, almost, like a horse and rider underwater, and she saw there was a quiver of arrows on his back. Before him, on the pommel of his saddle, was not a skull but a shortbow. And to the right side of the saddle, where a gunslinger might have carried a rifle in a scabbard, there was the feather-fluffed shaft of a lance. He was not one of the Old People, his face had none of that look . . . yet she did not think he was of the Outer Arc, either.

"But who *are* ye, cully?" she breathed. "And how shall I know ye? Ye've got yer hat pulled down so far I can't see your God-pounding *eyes,* so ye do! By yer horse, may-hap . . . or p'raps by yer . . . get away, Musty! Why do yer trouble me so? Arrrr!"

The cat had come back from its lookout point and was twining back and forth between her swollen old ankles, *waowing* up at her in a voice even more rusty than its purr. When the old woman kicked out at him, Musty dodged agilely away . . . then immediately came back and started in again, looking up at her with moonstruck eyes and making those soft yowls.

Rhea kicked out at it again, this one just as ineffectual as the first one, then looked into the glass once more. The horse and its interesting young rider were gone. The rose light was gone, as well. It was now just a dead glass ball she held, its only light a reflection borrowed from the moon.

The wind gusted, pressing her dress against the ruination that was her body. Musty, undaunted by the feeble kicks of his mistress, darted forward and began to twine about her ankles again, crying up at her the whole time.

"There, do ye see what you've done, ye nasty bag of fleas and disease? The light's gone out of it, gone out just when I—"

Then she heard a sound from the cart track which led up to her hut, and understood why Musty had been acting out. It was singing she heard. It was the *girl* she heard. The girl was early.

Grimacing horribly—she loathed being caught by surprise, and the little miss down there would pay for doing it—she bent and put the glass back in its box. The inside was lined with padded silk, and the ball fit as neatly as the breakfast egg in His Lordship's cup. And still from down the hill (the cursed wind was wrong or she would have heard it sooner), the sound of the girl singing, now closer than ever:

> *"Love, o love, o careless love,*
> *Can't you see what careless love has done?"*

"I'll give'ee careless love, ye virgin bitch," the old woman said. She could smell the sour reek of sweat from under her arms, but that other moisture had dried up again. "I'll give ye payday for walking in early on old Rhea, so I will!"

She passed her fingers over the lock on the front of the box, but it wouldn't fasten. She supposed she had been overeager to have it open, and had broken something inside it when she used the touch. The eye and the motto seemed to mock her: I SEE WHO OPENS ME. It could be put right, and in a jiffy, but right now even a jiffy was more than she had.

"Pestering cunt!" she whined, lifting her head briefly toward the approaching voice (almost here now, by the gods, and forty-five minutes before her time!). Then she closed the lid of the box. It gave her a pang to do it, because the glass was coming to life again, filling with that rosy glow, but there was no time for looking or dreaming now. Later, perhaps, after the object of Thorin's unseemly late-life prickishness had gone.

And you must restrain yourself from doing anything too awful to the girl, she cautioned herself. *Remember she's here because of him, and at least ain't one of those green girls with a bun in the oven and a boyfriend acting reluctant about the cries o'marriage. It's Thorin's doing, this one's what he thinks about after his ugly old crow of a wife is asleep and he takes himself in his hand and commences the evening milking; it's Thorin's doing, he has the old law on his side, and he has power. Furthermore, what's in that box is his man's business, and if Jonas found out ye looked at it . . . that ye used it . . .*

Aye, but no fear of that. And in the meantime, possession were nine-tenths of the law, were it not?

She hoisted the box under one arm, hoisted her skirts with her free hand, and ran back along the path to the hut. She could still run when she had to, aye, though few there were who'd believe it.

Musty ran at her heels, bounding along with his cloven tail held high and his extra legs flopping up and down in the moonlight.

CHAPTER TWO

Proving Honesty

1

Rhea darted into her hut, crossed in front of the guttering fire, then stood in the doorway to her tiny bedroom, swiping a hand through her hair in a distracted gesture. The bitch hadn't seen her outside the hut—she surely would have stopped caterwauling, or at least faltered in it if she had—and that was good, but the cursed hidey-hole had sealed itself up again, and that was bad. There was no time to open it again, either. Rhea hurried to the bed, knelt, and pushed the box far back into the shadows beneath.

Ay, that would do; until Susy Greengown was gone, it would do very well. Smiling on the right side of her mouth (the left was mostly frozen), Rhea got up, brushed her dress, and went to meet her second appointment of the night.

2

Behind her, the unlocked lid of the box clicked open. It came up less than an inch, but that was enough to allow a sliver of pulsing rose-colored light to shine out.

3

Susan Delgado stopped about forty yards from the witch's hut, the sweat chilling on her arms and the nape of her neck. Had she just spied an old woman (surely the one she had come to see) dart down that last bit of path leading from the top of the hill? She thought she had.

Don't stop singing—when an old lady hurries like that, she doesn't want to be seen. If you stop singing, she'll likely know she was.

For a moment Susan thought she'd stop anyway—that her memory would close up like a startled hand and deny her another verse of the old song which she had been singing since youngest childhood. But the next verse came to her, and she continued on (with feet as well as voice):

> *"Once my cares were far away,*
> *Yes, once my cares were far away,*
> *Now my love has gone from me*
> *And misery is in my heart to stay."*

A bad song for a night such as this, mayhap, but her heart went its own way without much interest in what her head thought or wanted; always had. She was frightened to be out by moonlight, when werewolves were said to walk, she was frightened of her errand, and she was frightened by what that errand portended. Yet when she had gained the Great Road out of Hambry and her heart had demanded she run, she had run—under the light of the Kissing Moon and with her skirt held above her knees she had galloped like a pony, with her shadow galloping right beside her. For a mile or more she had run, until every muscle in her body tingled and the air she pulled down her throat tasted like some sweet heated liquid. And when she reached the upland track leading to this high sinister, she had sung. Because her heart demanded it. And, she supposed, it really hadn't been such a bad idea; if nothing else, it had kept the worst of her megrims away. Singing was good for that much, anyway.

Now she walked to the end of the path, singing the chorus of "Careless Love." As she stepped into the scant light which fell through the open door and onto the stoop, a harsh raincrow voice spoke from the shadows: "Stop yer howling, missy—it catches in my brains like a fishhook!"

Susan, who had been told all her life that she had a fair singing voice, a gift from her gramma, no doubt, fell silent at once, abashed. She stood on the stoop with her hands clasped in front of her apron. Beneath the apron she wore her second-best dress (she only had two). Beneath it, her heart was thumping very hard.

A cat—a hideous thing with two extra legs sticking out of its sides like toasting forks—came into the doorway first. It looked up at her, seemed to measure her, then screwed its face up in a look that was eerily human: contempt. It hissed at her, then flashed away into the night.

Well, good evening to you, too, Susan thought.

The old woman she had been sent to see stepped into the doorway. She looked Susan up and down with that same expression of flat-eyed contempt, then stood back. "Come in. And mind ye clap the door tight. The wind has a way of blowin it open, as ye see!"

Susan stepped inside. She didn't want to close herself into this bad-smelling room with the old woman, but when there was no choice, hesitation was ever a fault. So her father had said, whether the matter under discussion was sums and subtractions or how to deal with boys at barn-dances when their hands became overly adventurous. She pulled the door firmly to, and heard it latch.

"And here y'are," the old woman said, and offered a grotesque smile of welcome. It was a smile guaranteed to make even a brave girl think of stories told in the nursery—Winter's tales of old women with snaggle teeth and bubbling cauldrons full of toad-green liquid. There was no cauldron over the fire in this room (nor was the fire itself much of a shake, in Susan's opinion), but the girl guessed there had been, betimes, and things in it of which it might be better not to think. That this woman was a real witch and not just an old lady posing as one was something Susan had felt sure of from the moment she had seen Rhea darting back inside her hut with the malformed cat at her heels. It was something you could almost smell, like the reeky aroma rising off the hag's skin.

"Yes," she said, smiling. She tried to make it a good one, bright and unafraid. "Here I am."

"And it's early y'are, my little sweeting. Early y'are! Hee!"

"I ran partway. The moon got into my blood, I suppose. That's what my da would have said."

The old woman's horrible smile widened into something that made Susan think of the way eels sometimes seemed to grin, after death and just before the pot. "Aye, but dead he is, dead these five years, Pat Delgado of the red hair and beard, the life mashed out of 'im by 'is own horse, aye, and went into the clearing at the end of the path with the music of his own snapping bones in his ears, so he did!"

The nervous smile slipped from Susan's face as if slapped away. She felt tears, always close at the mere mention of her da's name, burn at the back of her eyes. But she would not let them fall. Not in this heartless old crow's sight, she wouldn't.

"Let our business be quick and be done," she said in a dry voice that was far from her usual one; that voice was usually cheery and merry and ready for fun. But she was Pat Delgado's child, daughter of the best drover ever to work the Western Drop, and she remembered his face very well; she could rise to a stronger nature if required, as it now clearly was. The old woman had meant to reach out and scratch as deep as she could, and the more she saw that her efforts were succeeding, the more she would redouble them.

The hag, meanwhile, was watching Susan shrewdly, her bunch-knuckled hands planted on her hips while her cat twined around her ankles. Her eyes were rheumy, but Susan saw enough of them to realize they were the same gray-green shade as the cat's eyes, and to wonder what sort of fell magic that might be. She felt an urge—a strong one—to drop her eyes, and would not. It was all right to feel fear, but sometimes a very bad idea to show it.

"You look at me pert, missy," Rhea said at last. Her smile was dissolving slowly into a petulant frown.

"Nay, old mother," Susan replied evenly. "Only as one who wishes to do the business she came for and be gone. I have come here at the wish of My Lord Mayor of Mejis, and at that of my Aunt Cordelia, sister of my father. My *dear* father, of whom I would hear no ill spoken."

"I speak as I do," the old woman said. The words were dismissive, yet there was a trace of fawning servility in the hag's voice. Susan set no importance on that; it was a tone such a thing as this had probably adopted her whole life, and came as automatically as breath. "I've lived alone a long time, with no mistress but myself, and once it begins, my tongue goes where it will."

"Then sometimes it might be best not to let it begin at all."

The old woman's eyes flashed uglily. "Curb your own,

stripling girl, lest you find it dead in your mouth, where it will rot and make the Mayor think twice about kissing you when he smells its stink, aye, even under such a moon as this!"

Susan's heart filled with misery and bewilderment. She'd come up here intent on only one thing: getting the business done as quickly as possible, a barely explained rite that was apt to be painful and sure to be shameful. Now this old woman was looking at her with flat and naked hatred. How could things have gone wrong with such suddenness? Or was it always this way with witches?

"We have begun badly, mistress—can we start over?" Susan asked suddenly, and held out her hand.

The hag looked startled, although she did reach out and make brief contact, the wrinkled tips of her fingers touching the short-nailed fingers of the sixteen-year-old girl who stood before her with her clear-skinned face shining and her long hair braided down her back. Susan had to make a real effort not to grimace at the touch, brief as it was. The old woman's fingers were as chilly as those of a corpse, but Susan had touched chilly fingers before ("Cold hands, warm heart," Aunt Cord sometimes said). The real unpleasantness was in the *texture,* the feel of cold flesh spongy and loose on the bones, as if the woman to whom they were attached had drowned and lain long in some pool.

"Nay, nay, there's no starting over," the old woman said, "yet mayhap we'll go on better than we've begun. Ye've a powerful friend in the Mayor, and I'd not have him for my enemy."

She's honest, at least, Susan thought, then had to laugh at herself. This woman would be honest only when she absolutely had to be; left to her own devices and desires, she'd lie about everything—the weather, the crops, the flights of birds come Reaping.

"Ye came before I expected ye, and it's put me out of temper, so it has. Have ye brought me something, missy? Ye have, I'll warrant!" Her eyes were glittering once more, this time not with anger.

Susan reached beneath her apron (so stupid, wearing an apron for an errand on the backside of nowhere, but it was what custom demanded) and into her pocket. There, tied to a string so it could not be easily lost (by young girls suddenly moved to run in the moonlight, perchance), was a cloth bag. Susan broke the binding string and brought the bag out. She put it in the outstretched hand before her, the palm so worn that the lines marking it were now little more than ghosts. She was careful not to touch Rhea again . . . although the old woman would be touching *her* again, and soon.

"Is it the sound o' the wind makes ye shiver?" Rhea asked, although Susan could tell her mind was mostly fixed on the little bag; her fingers were busy tugging out the knot in the drawstring.

"Yes, the wind."

"And so it should. 'Tis the voices of the dead you hear in the wind, and when they scream so, 'tis because they regret—ah!"

The knot gave. She loosened the drawstring and tumbled two gold coins into her hand. They were unevenly milled and crude—no one had made such for generations—but they were heavy, and the eagles engraved upon them had a certain power. Rhea lifted one to her mouth, pulled back her lips to reveal a few gruesome teeth, and bit down. The hag looked at the faint indentations her teeth had left in the gold. For several seconds she gazed, rapt, then closed her fingers over them tightly.

While Rhea's attention was distracted by the coins, Susan happened to look through the open door to her left and into what she assumed was the witch's bedcham-

ber. And here she saw an odd and disquieting thing: a
light under the bed. A pink, pulsing light. It seemed to
be coming from some kind of box, although she could
not quite . . .

The witch looked up, and Susan hastily moved her eyes
to a corner of the room, where a net containing three or
four strange white fruits hung from a hook. Then, as the
old woman moved and her huge shadow danced pon-
derously away from that part of the wall, Susan saw they
were not fruits at all, but skulls. She felt a sickish drop in
her stomach.

"The fire needs building up, missy. Go round to the
side of the house and bring back an armload of wood.
Good-sized sticks are what's wanted, and never mind
whining ye can't lug 'em. Ye're of a strappin good size,
so ye are!"

Susan, who had quit whining about chores around
the time she had quit pissing into her clouts, said nothing . . . although it *did* cross her mind to ask Rhea if
everyone who brought her gold was invited to lug her
wood. In truth, she didn't mind; the air outside would
taste like wine after the stench of the hut.

She had almost reached the door when her foot struck
something hot and yielding. The cat yowled. Susan stumbled and almost fell. From behind her, the old woman
issued a series of gasping, choking sounds which Susan
eventually recognized as laughter.

"Watch Musty, my little sweet one! Tricksy, he is! And
tripsy as well, betimes, so he is! Hee!" And off she went,
in another gale.

The cat looked up at Susan, its ears laid back, its gray-
green eyes wide. It hissed at her. And Susan, unaware
she was going to do it until it was done, hissed back. Like
its expression of contempt, Musty's look of surprise was
eerily—and, in this case, comically—human. It turned

and fled for Rhea's bedroom, its split tail lashing. Susan opened the door and went outside to get the wood. Already she felt as if she had been here a thousand years, and that it might be a thousand more before she could go home.

4

The air was as sweet as she had hoped, perhaps even sweeter, and for a moment she only stood on the stoop, breathing it in, trying to cleanse her lungs . . . and her mind.

After five good breaths, she got herself in motion. Around the side of the house she went . . . but it was the wrong side, it seemed, for there was no woodpile here. There was a narrow excuse for a window, however, half-buried in some tough and unlovely creeper. It was toward the back of the hut, and must look in on the old woman's sleeping closet.

Don't look in there, whatever she's got under her bed isn't your business, and if she were to catch you . . .

She went to the window despite these admonitions, and peeked in.

It was unlikely that Rhea would have seen Susan's face through the dense overgrowth of pig ivy even if the old besom had been looking in that direction, and she wasn't. She was on her knees, the drawstring bag caught in her teeth, reaching under the bed.

She brought out a box and opened its lid, which was already ajar. Her face was flooded with soft pink radiance, and Susan gasped. For one moment it was the face of a young girl—but one filled with cruelty as well as youth, the face of a self-willed child determined to learn all the wrong things for all the wrong reasons. The face of the girl this hag once had been, mayhap. The light appeared to be coming from some sort of glass ball.

The old woman looked at it for several moments, her eyes wide and fascinated. Her lips moved as if she were speaking to it or perhaps even singing to it; the little bag Susan had brought from town, its string still clamped in the hag's mouth, bobbed up and down as she spoke. Then, with what appeared to be great effort of will, she closed the box, cutting off the rosy light. Susan found herself relieved—there was something about it she didn't like.

The old woman cupped one hand over the silver lock in the middle of the lid, and a brief scarlet light spiked out from between her fingers. All this with the draw-string bag still hanging from her mouth. Then she put the box on the bed, knelt, and began running her hands over the dirt just beneath the bed's edge. Although she touched only with her palms, lines appeared as if she had used a drawing tool. These lines darkened, becoming what looked like grooves.

The wood, Susan! Get the wood before she wakes up to how long you've been gone! For your father's sake!

Susan pulled the skirt of her dress all the way up to her waist—she did not want the old woman to see dirt or leaves on her clothing when she came back inside, did not want to answer the questions the sight of such smuts might provoke—and crawled beneath the window with her white cotton drawers flashing in the moonlight. Once she was past, she got to her feet again and hurried quietly around to the far side of the hut. Here she found the woodpile under an old, moldy-smelling hide. She took half a dozen good-sized chunks and walked back toward the front of the house with them in her arms.

When she entered, turning sideways to get her load through the doorway without dropping any, the old woman was back in the main room, staring moodily into the fireplace, where there was now little more than embers. Of the drawstring bag there was no sign.

"Took you long enough, missy," Rhea said. She continued to look into the fireplace, as if Susan were of no account . . . but one foot tapped below the dirty hem of her dress, and her eyebrows were drawn together.

Susan crossed the room, peering over the load of wood in her arms as well as she could while she walked. It wouldn't surprise her a bit to spy the cat lurking near, hoping to trip her up. "I saw a spider," she said. "I flapped my apron at it to make it run away. I hate the look of them, so I do."

"Ye'll see something ye like the look of even less, soon enough," Rhea said, grinning her peculiar one-sided grin. "Out of old Thorin's nightshirt it'll come, stiff as a stick and as red as rhubarb! Hee! Hold a minute, girl; ye gods, ye've brought enough for a Fair-Day bonfire."

Rhea took two fat logs from Susan's pile and tossed them indifferently onto the coals. Embers spiraled up the dark and faintly roaring shaft of the chimney. *There, ye've scattered what's left of yer fire, ye silly old thing, and will likely have to rekindle the whole mess,* Susan thought. Then Rhea reached into the fireplace with one splayed hand, spoke a guttural word, and the logs blazed up as if soaked in oil.

"Put the rest over there," she said, pointing at the woodbox. "And mind ye not be a scatterbark, missy."

What, and dirty all this neat? Susan thought. She bit the insides of her cheeks to kill the smile that wanted to rise on her mouth.

Rhea might have sensed it, however; when Susan straightened again, the old woman was looking at her with a dour, knowing expression.

"All right, mistress, let's do our business and have it done. Do ye know why you're here?"

"I am here at Mayor Thorin's wish," Susan repeated, knowing that was no real answer. She was frightened now—more frightened than when she had looked through the window and seen the old woman crooning to the glass ball. "His wife has come barren to the end of her courses. He wishes to have a son before he is also unable to—"

"Pish-tush, spare me the codswallop and pretty words. He wants tits and arse that don't squish in his hands and a box that'll grip what he pushes. If he's still man enough to push it, that is. If a son come of it, aye, fine, he'll give it over to ye to keep and raise until it's old enough to school, and after that ye'll see it no more. If it's a daughter, he'll likely take it from ye and give it to his new man, the one with the girl's hair and the limp, to drown in the nearest cattle-wallow."

Susan stared at her, shocked out of all measure.

The old woman saw the look and laughed. "Don't like the sound of the truth, do yer? Few do, missy. But that's neither here nor there; yer auntie was ever a trig one, and she'll have done all right out of Thorin and Thorin's treasury. What gold *you* see of it's none o' mine . . . and won't be none o' yours, either, if you don't watch sharp! Hee! Take off that dress!"

I won't was what rose to her lips, but what then? To be turned out of this hut (and to be turned out pretty much as she had come, and not as a lizard or a hopping toad would probably be the best luck she could hope for) and sent west as she was now, without even the two gold coins she'd brought up here? And that was only the small half of it. The large was that she had given her word. At first she had resisted, but when Aunt Cord had invoked her father's name, she had given in. As she always did. Really, she had no choice. And when there was no choice, hesitation was ever a fault.

She brushed the front of her apron, to which small bits of bark now clung, then untied it and took it off. She folded it, laid it on a small, grimy hassock near the hearth, and unbuttoned her dress to the waist. She shivered it from her shoulders, and stepped out. She folded it and laid it atop the apron, trying not to mind the greedy way Rhea of Cöos was staring at her in the firelight. The cat came sashaying across the floor, grotesque extra legs bobbing, and sat at Rhea's feet. Outside, the wind gusted. It was warm on the hearth but Susan was cold just the same, as if that wind had gotten inside her, somehow.

"Hurry, girl, for yer father's sake!"

Susan pulled her shift over her head, folded it atop the dress, then stood in only her drawers, with her arms folded over her bosom. The fire painted warm orange highlights along her thighs; black circles of shadow in the tender folds behind her knees.

"And still she's not nekkid!" the old crow laughed. "Ain't we lahdi-dah! Aye, we are, very fine! Take off those drawers, mistress, and stand as ye slid from yer mother! Although ye had not so many goodies as to interest the likes of Hart Thorin then, did ye? Hee!"

Feeling caught in a nightmare, Susan did as she was bid. With her mound and bush uncovered, her crossed arms seemed foolish. She lowered them to her sides.

"Ah, no wonder he wants ye!" the old woman said. "'Tis beautiful ye are, and true! Is she not, Musty?"

The cat *waowed*.

"There's dirt on yer knees," Rhea said suddenly. "How came it there?"

Susan felt a moment of awful panic. She had lifted her skirts to crawl beneath the hag's window . . . and hung herself by doing it.

Then an answer rose to her lips, and she spoke it

calmly enough. "When I came in sight of your hut, I grew fearful. I knelt to pray, and raised my skirt so as not to soil it."

"I'm touched—to want a clean dress for the likes o' me! How good y'are! Don't you agree, Musty?"

The cat *waowed*, then began to lick one of its forepaws.

"Get on with it," Susan said. "You've been paid and I'll obey, but stop teasing and have done."

"You know what it is I have to do, mistress."

"I *don't*," Susan said. The tears were close again, burning the backs of her eyes, but she would not let them fall. *Would not.* "I have an idea, but when I asked Aunt Cord if I was right, she said that you'd 'take care of my education in that regard.' "

"Wouldn't dirty her mouth with the words, would she? Well, that's all right. Yer Aunt Rhea's not too nice to say what yer Aunt Cordelia won't. I'm to make sure that ye're physically and spiritually intact, missy. Proving honesty is what the old ones called it, and it's a good enough name. So it is. Step to me."

Susan took two reluctant steps forward, so that her bare toes were almost touching the old woman's slippers and her bare breasts were almost touching the old woman's dress.

"If a devil or demon has polluted yer spirit, such a thing as might taint the child you'll likely bear, it leaves a mark behind. Most often it's a suck-mark or a lover's bite, but there's others . . . open yer mouth!"

Susan did, and when the old woman bent closer, the reek of her was so strong that the girl's stomach clenched. She held her breath, praying this would be over soon.

"Run out yer tongue."

Susan ran out her tongue.

"Now send yer breezes into my face."

Susan exhaled her held breath. Rhea breathed it in

and then, mercifully, pulled her head away a little. She had been close enough for Susan to see the lice hopping in her hair.

"Sweet enough," the old woman said. "Aye, good's a meal. Now turn around."

Susan did, and felt the old witch's fingers trail down her back and to her buttocks. Their tips were cold as mud.

"Bend over and spread yer cheeks, missy, be not shy, Rhea's seen more than one pultry in her time!"

Face flushing—she could feel the beat of her heart in the center of her forehead and in the hollows of her temples—Susan did as told. And then she felt one of those corpselike fingers prod its way into her anus. Susan bit her lips to keep from screaming.

The invasion was mercifully short . . . but there would be another, Susan feared.

"Turn around."

She turned. The old woman passed her hands over Susan's breasts, flicked lightly at the nipples with her thumbs, then examined the undersides carefully. Rhea slipped a finger into the cup of the girl's navel, then hitched up her own skirt and dropped to her knees with a grunt of effort. She passed her hands down Susan's legs, first front, then back. She seemed to take special pains with the area just below the calves, where the tendons ran.

"Lift yer right foot, girl."

Susan did, and uttered a nervous, screamy laugh as Rhea ran a thumbnail down her instep to her heel. The old woman parted her toes, looking between each pair.

After this process had been repeated with the other foot, the old woman—still on her knees—said: "You know what comes next."

"Aye." The word came out of her in a little trembling rush.

"Hold ye still, missy—all else is well, clean as a willow-strip, ye are, but now we've come to the cozy nook that's all Thorin cares for; we've come to where honesty must really be proved. So hold ye still!"

Susan closed her eyes and thought of horses running along the Drop—nominally they were the Barony's horse, overlooked by Rimer, Thorin's Chancellor and the Barony's Minister of Inventory, but the horses didn't know that; they thought they were free, and if you were free in your mind, what else mattered?

Let me be free in my mind, as free as the horses along the Drop, and don't let her hurt me. Please, don't let her hurt me. And if she does, please help me to bear it in decent silence.

Cold fingers parted the downy hair below her navel; there was a pause, and then two cold fingers slipped inside her. There *was* pain, but only a moment of it, and not bad; she'd hurt herself worse stubbing her toe or barking her shin on the way to the privy in the middle of the night. The humiliation was the bad part, and the revulsion of Rhea's ancient touch.

"Caulked tight, ye are!" Rhea cried. "Good as ever was! But Thorin'll see to that, so he will! As for you, my girl, I'll tell yer a secret yer prissy aunt with her long nose 'n tight purse 'n little goosebump tits never knew: even a girl who's intact don't need to lack for a shiver now 'n then, if she knows how!"

The hag's withdrawing fingers closed gently around the little nubbin of flesh at the head of Susan's cleft. For one terrible second Susan thought they would pinch that sensitive place, which sometimes made her draw in a breath if it rubbed just so against the pommel of her saddle when she was riding, but instead the fingers caressed . . . then pressed . . . and the girl was horrified to feel a heat which was far from unpleasant kindle in her belly.

"Like a little bud o' silk," the old woman crooned, and

her meddling fingers moved faster. Susan felt her hips sway forward, as if with a mind and life of their own, and then she thought of the old woman's greedy, self-willed face, pink as the face of a whore by gaslight as it hung over the open box; she thought of the way the drawstring bag with the gold pieces in it had hung from the wrinkled mouth like some disgorged piece of flesh, and the heat she felt was gone. She drew back, trembling, her arms and belly and breasts breaking out in gooseflesh.

"You've finished what you were paid to do," Susan said. Her voice was dry and harsh.

Rhea's face knotted. "Ye'll not tell me aye, no, yes, or maybe, impudent stripling of a girl! *I* know when I'm done, *I*, Rhea, the Weirding of Cöos, and—"

"Be still, and be on your feet before I kick you into the fire, unnatural thing."

The old woman's lips wriggled back from her few remaining teeth in a doglike sneer, and now, Susan realized, she and the witch-woman were back where they had been at the start: ready to claw each other's eyes out.

"Raise hand or foot to me, you impudent cunt, and what leaves my house will leave handless, footless, and blind of eye."

"I do not much doubt you could do it, but Thorin should be vexed," Susan said. It was the first time in her life she had ever invoked a man's name for protection. Realizing this made her feel ashamed . . . small, somehow. She didn't know why that should be, especially since she had agreed to sleep in his bed and bear his child, but it was.

The old woman stared, her seamed face working until it folded into a parody of a smile that was worse than her snarl. Puffing and pulling at the arm of her chair, Rhea got to her feet. As she did, Susan quickly began to dress.

"Aye, vexed he would be. Perhaps you know best after

all, missy; I've had a strange night, and it's wakened parts of me better left asleep. Anything else that might have happened, take it as a compliment to yer youth 'n purity . . . and to yer beauty as well. Aye. You're a beautiful thing, and there's no doubtin it. Yer hair, now . . . when yer let it down, as ye will for Thorin, I wot, when ye lay with him . . . it glows like the sun, doesn't it?"

Susan did not want to force the old hag out of her posturing, but she didn't want to encourage these fawning compliments, either. Not when she could still see the hate in Rhea's rheumy eyes, not when she could feel the old woman's touch still crawling like beetles on her skin. She said nothing, only stepped into her dress, set it on her shoulders, and began to button up the front.

Rhea perhaps understood the run of her thoughts, for the smile dropped off her mouth and her manner grew businesslike. Susan found this a great relief.

"Well, never mind it. Ye've proved honest; ye may dress yerself and go. But not a word of what passed between us to Thorin, mind ye! Words between women need trouble no man's ear, especially one as great as he." Yet at this Rhea could not forbear a certain spasming sneer. Susan didn't know if the old woman was aware of it or not. "Are we agreed?"

Anything, anything, just as long as I can be out of here and away.

"You declare me proved?"

"Aye, Susan, daughter of Patrick. So I do. But it's not what I *say* that matters. Now . . . wait . . . somewhere here . . ."

She scrabbled along the mantel, pushing stubs of candles stuck on cracked saucers this way and that, lifting first a kerosene lantern and then a battery flashlight, looking fixedly for a moment at a drawing of a young boy and then putting it aside.

"Where . . . where . . . *arrrr* . . . here!"

She snatched up a pad of paper with a sooty cover (CITGO stamped on it in ancient gold letters) and a stub of pencil. She paged almost to the end of the pad before finding a blank sheet. On it she scrawled something, then tore the sheet off the spiral of wire at the top of the pad. She held the sheet out to Susan, who took it and looked at it. Scrawled there was a word she did not understand at first:

Below it was a symbol:

"What's this?" she asked, tapping the little drawing.

"Rhea, her mark. Known for six Baronies around, it is, and can't be copied. Show that paper to yer aunt. Then to Thorin. If yer aunt wants to take it and show it to Thorin herself—I know her, y'see, and her bossy ways—tell her no, Rhea says no, she's not to have the keeping of it."

"And if Thorin wants it?"

Rhea shrugged dismissively. "Let him keep it or burn it or wipe his bum with it, for all of me. It's nothing to you, either, for you knew you were honest all along, so you did. True?"

Susan nodded. Once, walking home after a dance, she had let a boy slip his hand inside her shirt for a moment or two, but what of that? She was honest. And in more ways than this nasty creature meant.

"But don't lose that paper. Unless you'd see me again, that is, and go through the same business a second time."

Gods perish even the thought, Susan thought, and managed not to shudder. She put the paper in her pocket, where the drawstring bag had been.

"Now, come to the door, missy." She looked as if she wanted to grasp Susan's arm, then thought better of it. The two of them walked side by side to the door, not touching in such a careful way that it made them look awkward. Once there, Rhea did grip Susan's arm. Then, with her other hand, she pointed to the bright silver disc hanging over the top of the Cöos.

"The Kissing Moon," Rhea said. " 'Tis midsummer."

"Yes."

"Tell Thorin he's not to have you in his bed—or in a haystack, or on the scullery floor, or anywhere else—until Demon Moon rises full in the sky."

"Not until Reaping?" That was three months—a lifetime, it seemed to her. Susan tried not to show her delight at this reprieve. She'd thought Thorin would put an end to her virginity by moonrise the next night. She wasn't blind to the way he looked at her.

Rhea, meanwhile, was looking at the moon, seeming to calculate. Her hand went to the long tail of Susan's hair and stroked it. Susan bore this as well as she could, and just when she felt she could bear it no longer, Rhea dropped her hand back to her side and nodded. "Aye, not just Reaping, but true *fin de año*—Fair-Night, tell him. Say that he may have you after the bonfire. You understand?"

"True *fin de año,* yes." She could barely contain her joy.

"When the fire in Green Heart burns low and the last of the red-handed men are ashes," Rhea said. "Then and not *until* then. You must tell him so."

"I will."

The hand came out and began to stroke her hair again. Susan bore it. After such good news, she thought, it would have been mean-spirited to do otherwise. "The

time between now and Reaping you will use to meditate,
and to gather your forces to produce the male child the
Mayor wants . . . or mayhap just to ride along the Drop
and gather the last flowers of your maidenhood. Do you
understand?"

"Yes." She dropped a curtsey. "Thankee-sai."

Rhea waved this off as if it were a flattery. "Speak not
of what passed between us, mind. 'Tis no one's affair but
our own."

"I won't. And our business is done?"

"Well . . . mayhap there's one more *small* thing . . ." Rhea
smiled to show it was indeed small, then raised her left
hand in front of Susan's eyes with three fingers together
and one apart. Glimmering in the fork between was a silver medallion, seemingly produced from nowhere. The
girl's eyes fastened on it at once. Until Rhea spoke a single guttural word, that was.

Then they closed.

5

Rhea looked at the girl who stood asleep on her stoop
in the moonlight. As she replaced the medallion within
her sleeve (her fingers were old and bunchy, but they
moved dextrously enough when it was required, oh,
aye), the businesslike expression fell from her face, and
was replaced by a look of squint-eyed fury. *Kick me into the
fire, would you, you trull? Tattle to Thorin?* But her threats
and impudence weren't the worst. The worst had been
the expression of revulsion on her face when she had
pulled back from Rhea's touch.

Too good for Rhea, she was! And thought herself
too good for Thorin as well, no doubt, she with sixteen
years' worth of fine blonde hair hanging down from her

head, hair Thorin no doubt dreamed of plunging his hands into even as he plunged and reared and plowed down below.

She couldn't hurt the girl, much as she wanted to and much as the girl deserved it; if nothing else, Thorin might take the glass ball away from her, and Rhea couldn't bear that. Not yet, anyway. So she could not hurt the girl, but she *could* do something that would spoil his pleasure in her, at least for awhile.

Rhea leaned close to the girl, grasped the long braid which lay down her back, and began to slip it through her fist, enjoying its silky smoothness.

"Susan," she whispered. "Do'ee hear me, Susan, daughter of Patrick?"

"Yes." The eyes did not open.

"Then listen." The light of the Kissing Moon fell on Rhea's face and turned it into a silver skull. "Listen to me well, and remember. Remember in the deep cave where yer waking mind never goes."

She pulled the braid through her hand again and again. Silky and smooth. Like the little bud between her legs.

"Remember," the girl in the doorway said.

"Aye. There's something ye'll do after he takes yer virginity. Ye'll do it right away, without even thinking about it. Now listen to me, Susan, daughter of Patrick, and hear me very well."

Still stroking the girl's hair, Rhea put her wrinkled lips to the smooth cup of Susan's ear and whispered in the moonlight.

CHAPTER THREE

A Meeting on the Road

I

She had never in her life had such a strange night, and it was probably not surprising that she didn't hear the rider approaching from behind until he was almost upon her.

The thing that troubled her most as she made her way back toward town was her new understanding of the compact she had made. It was good to have a reprieve—months yet before she would have to live up to her end of the bargain—but a reprieve didn't change the basic fact: when the Demon Moon was full, she would lose her virginity to Mayor Thorin, a skinny, twitchy man with fluffy white hair rising like a cloud around the bald spot on top of his head. A man whose wife regarded him with a certain weary sadness that was painful to look at. Hart Thorin was a man who laughed uproariously when a company of players put on an entertainment involving head-knocking or pretend punching or rotten fruit-throwing, but who only looked puzzled at a story which was pathetic or tragical. A knuckle-cracker, a back-slapper, a dinner-table belcher, a man who had a way of looking anxiously toward his Chancellor at almost every other word, as if to make sure he hadn't offended Rimer in some way.

Susan had observed all these things often; her father had for years been in charge of the Barony's horse and had gone to Seafront often on business. Many times he had taken his much loved daughter with him. Oh, she had seen a lot of Hart Thorin over the years, and he had seen a lot of her, as well. Too much, mayhap! For what now seemed the most important fact about him was that he was almost fifty years older than the girl who would perhaps bear his son.

She had made the bargain lightly enough—

No, not lightly, that was being unfair to herself . . . but she had lost little sleep over it, that much was true. She had thought, after listening to all Aunt Cord's arguments: *Well, it's little enough, really, to have the indenture off the lands; to finally own our little piece of the Drop in fact as well as in tradition . . . to actually have papers, one in our house and one in Rimer's files, saying it's ours. Aye, and to have horses again. Only three, 'tis true, but that's three more than we have now. And against that? To lie with him a time or two, and to bear a child, which millions of women have done before me with no harm. 'Tis not, after all, a mutant or a leper I'm being asked to partner with but just an old man with noisy knuckles. 'Tis not forever, and, as Aunt Cord says, I may still marry, if time and* ka *decree; I should not be the first woman to come to her husband's bed as a mother. And does it make me a whore to do such? The law says not, but never mind that; my heart's law is what matters, and my heart says that if I may gain the land that was my da's and three horses to run on it by being such, then it's a whore I'll be.*

There was something else: Aunt Cord had capitalized—rather ruthlessly, Susan now saw—on a child's innocence. It was the *baby* Aunt Cord had harped on, *the cunning little baby* she would have. Aunt Cord had known that Susan, the dolls of her childhood put aside not all that long ago, would love the idea of her own baby, a little living doll to dress and feed and sleep with in the heat of the afternoon.

What Cordelia had ignored (*perhaps she's too innocent*

even to have considered it, Susan thought, but didn't quite believe) was what the hag-woman had made brutally clear to her this evening: Thorin wanted more than a child.

He wants tits and arse that don't squish in his hands and a box that'll grip what he pushes.

Just thinking of those words made her face throb as she walked through the post-moonset dark toward town (no high-spirited running this time; no singing, either). She had agreed with vague thoughts of how managed livestock mated—they were allowed to go at it "until the seed took," then separated again. But now she knew that Thorin might want her again and again, probably *would* want her again and again, and common law going back like iron for two hundred generations said that he could continue to lie with her until she who had proved the consort honest should prove her honestly with child as well, and that child honest in and of itself . . . not, that was, a mutant aberration. Susan had made discreet enquiries and knew that this second proving usually came around the fourth month of pregnancy . . . around the time she would begin to show, even with her clothes on. It would be up to Rhea to make the judgment . . . and Rhea didn't like her.

Now that it was too late—now that she had accepted the compact formally tendered by the Chancellor, now that she had been proved honest by yon strange bitch— she rued the bargain. Mostly what she thought of was how Thorin would look with his pants off, his legs white and skinny, like the legs of a stork, and how, as they lay together, she would hear his long bones crackling: knees and back and elbows and neck.

And knuckles. Don't forget his knuckles.

Yes. Big old man's knuckles with hair growing out of them. Susan chuckled at the thought, it was that comical, but at the same time a warm tear ran unnoticed

from the corner of one eye and tracked down her cheek.
She wiped it away without knowing it, any more than she
heard the clip-clip of approaching hoofs in the soft road-
dust. Her mind was still far away, returning to the odd
thing she had seen through the old woman's bedroom
window—the soft but somehow unpleasant light coming
from the pink globe, the hypnotized way the hag had
been looking down at it . . .

When Susan at last heard the approaching horse, her
first alarmed thought was that she must get into the copse
of trees she was currently passing and hide. The chances
of anyone aboveboard being on the road this late seemed
small to her, especially now that such bad times had come
to Mid-World—but it was too late for that.

The ditch, then, and sprawled flat. With the moon
down, there was at least a chance that whoever it was
would pass without—

But before she could even begin in that direction, the
rider who had sneaked up behind her while she was thinking her long and rueful thoughts had hailed her. "Goodeven, lady, and may your days be long upon the earth."

She turned, thinking: *What if it's one of the new men
always lounging about Mayor's House or in the Travellers' Rest?
Not the oldest one, the voice isn't wavery like his, but maybe one
of the others . . . it could be the one they call Depape . . .*

"Goodeven," she heard herself saying to the man-
shape on the tall horse. "May yours be long also."

Her voice didn't tremble, not that she could hear. She
didn't think it was Depape, or the one named Reynolds,
either. The only thing she could tell about the fellow for
sure was that he wore a flat-brimmed hat, the sort she
associated with men of the Inner Baronies, back when
travel between east and west had been more common
than it was now. Back before John Farson came—the
Good Man—and the bloodletting began.

As the stranger came up beside her, she forgave herself a little for not hearing him approach—there was no buckle or bell on his gear that she could see, and everything was tied down so as not to snap or flap. It was almost the rig of an outlaw or a harrier (she had the idea that Jonas, he of the wavery voice, and his two friends might have been both, in other times and other climes) or even a gunslinger. But this man bore no guns, unless they were hidden. A bow on the pommel of his saddle and what looked like a lance in a scabbard, that was all. And there had never, she reckoned, been a gunslinger as young as this.

He clucked sidemouth at the horse just as her da had always done (and she herself, of course), and it stopped at once. As he swung one leg over his saddle, lifting it high and with unconscious grace, Susan said: "Nay, nay, don't trouble yerself, stranger, but go as ye would!"

If he heard the alarm in her voice, he paid no heed to it. He slipped off the horse, not bothering with the tied-down stirrup, and landed neatly in front of her, the dust of the road puffing about his square-toed boots. By starlight she saw that he was young indeed, close to her own age on one side or the other. His clothes were those of a working cowboy, although new.

"Will Dearborn, at your service," he said, then doffed his hat, extended a foot on one bootheel, and bowed as they did in the Inner Baronies.

Such absurd courtliness out here in the middle of nowhere, with the acrid smell of the oilpatch on the edge of town already in her nostrils, startled her out of her fear and into a laugh. She thought it would likely offend him, but he smiled instead. A good smile, honest and artless, its inner part lined with even teeth.

She dropped him a little curtsey, holding out one side of her dress. "Susan Delgado, at yours."

He tapped his throat thrice with his right hand. "Thankee-sai, Susan Delgado. We're well met, I hope. I didn't mean to startle you—"

"Ye did, a little."

"Yes, I thought I had. I'm sorry."

Yes. Not *aye* but *yes.* A young man, from the Inner Baronies, by the sound. She looked at him with new interest.

"Nay, ye need not apologize, for I was deep in my own thoughts," she said. "I'd been to see a . . . friend . . . and hadn't realized how much time had passed until I saw the moon was down. If ye stopped out of concern, I thankee, stranger, but ye may be on yer way as I would be on mine. It's only to the edge of the village I go— Hambry. It's close, now."

"Pretty speech and lovely sentiments," he answered with a grin, "but it's late, you're alone, and I think we may as well pass on together. Do you ride, sai?"

"Yes, but really—"

"Step over and meet my friend Rusher, then. He shall carry you the last two miles. He's gelded, sai, and gentle."

She looked at Will Dearborn with a mixture of amusement and irritation. The thought which crossed her mind was *If he calls me sai again, as though I were a schoolteacher or his doddery old great aunt, I'm going to take off this stupid apron and swat him with it.* "I never minded a bit of temper in a horse docile enough to wear a saddle. Until his death, my father managed the Mayor's horses . . . and the Mayor in these parts is also Guard o' Barony. I've ridden my whole life."

She thought he might apologize, perhaps even stutter, but he only nodded with a calm thoughtfulness that she rather liked. "Then step to the stirrup, my lady. I'll walk beside and trouble you with no conversation, if you'd rather not have it. It's late, and talk palls after moonset, some say."

She shook her head, softening her refusal with a smile. "Nay. I thank ye for yer kindness, but it would not be well, mayhap, for me to be seen riding a strange young man's horse at eleven o' the clock. Lemon-juice won't take the stain out of a lady's reputation the way it will out of a shirtwaist, you know."

"There's no one out here to see you," the young man said in a maddeningly reasonable voice. "And that you're tired, I can tell. Come, sai—"

"Please don't call me that. It makes me feel as ancient as a . . ." She hesitated for a brief moment, rethinking the word

(witch)

that first came to her mind. ". . . as an old woman."

"Miss Delgado, then. Are you sure you won't ride?"

"Sure as can be. I'd not ride cross-saddle in a dress in any case, Mr. Dearborn—not even if you were my own brother. 'Twouldn't be proper."

He stood in the stirrup himself, reached over to the far side of his saddle (Rusher stood docilely enough at this, only flicking his ears, which Susan would have been happy to flick herself had she been Rusher—they were that beautiful), and stepped back down with a rolled garment in his hands. It was tied with a rawhide hank. She thought it was a poncho.

"You may spread this over your lap and legs like a duster," he said. "There's quite enough of it for decorum's sake—it was my father's, and he's taller than me." He looked off toward the western hills for a moment, and she saw he was handsome, in a hard sort of way that jagged against his youth. She felt a little shiver inside her, and wished for the thousandth time that the foul old woman had kept her hands strictly on her business, as unpleasant as that business had been. Susan didn't want to look at this handsome stranger and remember Rhea's touch.

"Nay," she said gently. "Thankee again, I recognize yer kindness, but I must refuse."

"Then I'll walk along beside, and Rusher'll be our chaperone," he said cheerfully. "As far as the edge of town, at least, there'll be no eyes to see and think ill of a perfectly proper young woman and a more-or-less proper young man. And once there, I'll tip my hat and wish you a very good night."

"I wish ye wouldn't. Really." She brushed a hand across her forehead. "Easy for you to say there are no eyes to see, but sometimes there are eyes even where there shouldn't be. And my position is . . . a little delicate just now."

"I'll walk with you, however," he repeated, and now his face was somber. "These are not good times, Miss Delgado. Here in Mejis you are far from the worst of the troubles, but sometimes trouble reaches out."

She opened her mouth—to protest again, she supposed, perhaps to tell him that Pat Delgado's daughter could take care of herself—and then she thought of the Mayor's new men, and the cold way they had run their eyes over her when Thorin's attention had been elsewhere. She had seen those three this very night as she left on her way to the witch's hut. Them she *had* heard approaching, and in plenty of time for her to leave the road and rest behind a handy *piñón* tree (she refused to think of it as hiding, exactly). Back toward town they had gone, and she supposed they were drinking at the Travellers' Rest right now—and would continue to until Stanley Ruiz closed the bar—but she had no way of knowing that for sure. They could come back.

"If I can't dissuade ye, very well," she said, sighing with a vexed resignation she didn't really feel. "But only to the first mailbox—Mrs. Beech's. That marks the edge of town."

He tapped his throat again, and made another of those absurd, enchanting bows—foot stuck out as if he would trip someone, heel planted in the dirt. "Thankee, Miss Delgado!"

At least he didn't call me sai, she thought. *That's a start.*

2

She thought he'd chatter away like a magpie in spite of his promise to be silent, because that was what boys did around her—she was not vain of her looks, but she thought she *was* good-looking, if only because the boys could not shut up or stop shuffling their feet when they were around her. And this one would be full of questions the town boys didn't need to ask—how old was she, had she always lived in Hambry, were her parents alive, half a hundred others just as boring—but they would all circle in on the same one: did she have a steady fellow?

But Will Dearborn of the Inner Baronies didn't ask her about her schooling or family or friends (the most common way of approaching any romantic rivals, she had found). Will Dearborn simply walked along beside her, one hand wrapped around Rusher's bridle, looking off east toward the Clean Sea. They were close enough to it now so that the teary smell of salt mingled with the tarry stench of oil, even though the wind was from the south.

They were passing Citgo now, and she was glad for Will Dearborn's presence, even if his silence was a little irritating. She had always found the oilpatch, with its skeletal forest of gantries, a little spooky. Most of those steel towers had stopped pumping long since, and there was neither the parts, the need, nor the understanding to repair them. And those which did still labor along—nineteen out of about two hundred—could not be stopped. They just pumped and pumped, the supplies of oil beneath them seemingly inexhaustible. A little was still used, but a very little—most simply ran back down into the wells beneath the dead pumping stations. The world had moved on, and this place reminded her of a strange mechanical graveyard where some of the corpses hadn't quite—

Something cold and smooth nuzzled the small of her back, and she wasn't quite able to stifle a little shriek. Will Dearborn wheeled toward her, his hands dropping toward his belt. Then he relaxed and smiled.

"Rusher's way of saying he feels ignored. I'm sorry, Miss Delgado."

She looked at the horse. Rusher looked back mildly, then dipped his head as if to say he was also sorry for having startled her.

Foolishness, girl, she thought, hearing the hearty, no-nonsense voice of her father. *He wants to know why you're being so standoffy, that's all And so do I. 'Tisn't like you, so it's not.*

"Mr. Dearborn, I've changed my mind," she said. "I'd like to ride."

3

He turned his back and stood looking out at Citgo with his hands in his pockets while Susan first laid the poncho over the cantle of the saddle (the plain black saddle of a working cowboy, without a Barony brand or even a ranch brand to mark it), and then mounted into the stirrup. She lifted her skirt and glanced around sharply, sure he would be stealing a peek, but his back was still to her. He seemed fascinated with the rusty oil derricks.

What's so interesting about them, cully? she thought, a trifle crossly—it was the lateness of the hour and the residue of her stirred-up emotions, she supposed. *Filthy old things have been there six centuries and more, and I've been smelling their stink my whole life.*

"Stand easy now, my boy," she said once she had her foot fixed in the stirrup. One hand held the top of the saddle's pommel, the other the reins. Rusher, meanwhile, flicked his ears as if to say he would stand easy all night, were that what she required.

She swung up, one long bare thigh flashing in the starlight, and felt the exhilaration of being horsed that she always felt . . . only tonight it seemed a little stronger, a little sweeter, a little sharper. Perhaps because the horse was such a beauty, perhaps because the horse was a stranger . . .

Perhaps because the horse's owner is a stranger, she thought, *and fair.*

That was nonsense, of course . . . and potentially dangerous nonsense. Yet it was also true. He *was* fair.

As she opened the poncho and spread it over her legs, Dearborn began to whistle. And she realized, with a mixture of surprise and superstitious fear, what the tune was: "Careless Love." The very lay she had been singing on her way up to Rhea's hut.

Mayhap it's ka, *girl,* her father's voice whispered.

No such thing, she thought right back at him. *I'll not see* ka *in every passing wind and shadow, like the old ladies who gather in Green Heart of a summer's evening. It's an old tune; everyone knows it.*

Mayhap better if you're right, Pat Delgado's voice returned. *For if it's* ka, *it'll come like a wind, and your plans will stand before it no more than my da's barn stood before the cyclone when it came.*

Not *ka*; she would not be seduced by the dark and the shadows and the grim shapes of the oil derricks into believing it was. Not *ka* but only a chance meeting with a nice young man on the lonely road back to town.

"I've made myself decent," she said in a dry voice that didn't sound much like her own. "Ye may turn back if you like, Mr. Dearborn."

He did turn and gazed at her. For a moment he said nothing, but she could see the look in his eyes well enough to know that he found her fair as well. And although this disquieted her—perhaps because of what he'd been whistling—she was also glad. Then he said, "You look well up there. You sit well."

"And I shall have horses of my own to sit before long," she said. *Now the questions will come,* she thought.

But he only nodded, as though he had known this about her already, and began to walk toward town again. Feeling a little disappointed and not knowing exactly why, she clucked sidemouth at Rusher and twitched her knees at him. He got moving, catching up with his master, who gave Rusher's muzzle a companionable little caress.

"What do they call that place yonder?" he asked, pointing at the derricks.

"The oilpatch? Citgo."

"Some of the derricks still pump?"

"Aye, and no way to stop them. Not that anyone still knows."

"Oh," he said, and that was all—just *oh*. But he left his place by Rusher's head for a moment when they came to the weedy track leading into Citgo, walking across to look at the old disused guard-hut. In her childhood there had been a sign on it reading AUTHORIZED PERSONNEL ONLY, but it had blown away in some windstorm or other. Will Dearborn had his look and then came ambling back to the horse, boots puffing up summer dust, easy in his new clothes.

They went toward town, a young walking man in a

flat-crowned hat, a young riding woman with a poncho spread over her lap and legs. The starlight rained down on them as it has on young men and women since time's first hour, and once she looked up and saw a meteor flash overhead—a brief and brilliant orange streak across the vault of heaven. Susan thought to wish on it, and then, with something like panic, realized she had no idea what to wish for. None at all.

4

She kept her own silence until they were a mile or so from town, and then asked the question which had been on her mind. She had planned to ask hers after he had begun asking his, and it irked her to be the one to break the silence, but in the end her curiosity was too much.

"Where do ye come from, Mr. Dearborn, and what brings ye to our little bit o' Mid-World . . . if ye don't mind me asking?"

"Not at all," he said, looking up at her with a smile. "I'm glad to talk and was only trying to think how to begin. Talk's not a specialty of mine." *Then what is, Will Dearborn?* she wondered. Yes, she wondered very much, for in adjusting her position on the saddle, she had put her hand on the rolled blanket behind . . . and had touched something hidden inside that blanket. Something that felt like a gun. It didn't *have* to be, of course, but she remembered the way his hands had dropped instinctively toward his belt when she had cried out in surprise.

"I come from the In-World. I've an idea you probably guessed that much on your own. We have our own way of talking."

"Aye. Which Barony is yer home, might I ask?"

"New Canaan."

She felt a flash of real excitement at that. New Canaan! Center of the Affiliation! That did not mean all it once had, of course, but still—

"Not Gilead?" she asked, detesting the hint of a girlish gush she heard in her voice. And more than just a hint, mayhap.

"No," he said with a laugh. "Nothing so grand as Gilead. Only Hemphill, a village forty or so wheels west of there. Smaller than Hambry, I wot."

Wheels, she thought, marvelling at the archaism. *He said wheels.*

"And what brings ye to Hambry, then? May ye tell?"

"Why not? I've come with two of my friends, Mr. Richard Stockworth of Pennilton, New Canaan, and Mr. Arthur Heath, a hilarious young man who actually does come from Gilead. We're here at the order of the Affiliation, and have come as counters."

"Counters of what?"

"Counters of anything and everything which may aid the Affiliation in the coming years," he said, and she heard no lightness in his voice now. "The business with the Good Man has grown serious."

"Has it? We hear little real news this far to the south and east of the hub."

He nodded. "The Barony's distance from the hub is the chief reason we're here. Mejis has been ever loyal to the Affiliation, and if supplies need to be drawn from this part of the Outers, they'll be sent. The question that needs answering is how much the Affiliation can count on."

"How much of what?"

"Yes," he agreed, as if she'd made a statement instead of asking a question. "And how much of what."

"Ye speak as though the Good Man were a real threat.

He's just a bandit, surely, frosting his thefts and murders with talk of 'democracy' and 'equality'?"

Dearborn shrugged, and she thought for a moment that would be his only comment on the matter, but then he said, reluctantly: " 'Twas once so, perhaps. Times have changed. At some point the bandit became a general, and now the general would become a ruler in the name of the people." He paused, then added gravely, "The Northern and West'rd Baronies are in flames, lady."

"But those are thousands of miles away, surely!" This talk was upsetting, and yet strangely exciting, too. Mostly it seemed *exotic,* after the pokey all-days-the-same world of Hambry, where someone's dry well was good for three days of animated conversation.

"Yes," he said. Not *aye* but *yes*—the sound was both strange and pleasing to her ear. "But the wind is blowing in this direction." He turned to her and smiled. Once more it softened his hard good looks, and made him seem no more than a child, up too late after his bedtime. "But I don't think we'll see John Farson tonight, do you?"

She smiled back. "If we did, Mr. Dearborn, would ye protect me from him?"

"No doubt," he said, still smiling, "but I should do so with greater enthusiasm, I wot, if you were to let me call you by the name your father gave you."

"Then, in the interests of my own safety, ye may do so. And I suppose I must call ye Will, in those same interests."

" 'Tis both wise and prettily put," he said, the smile becoming a grin, wide and engaging. "I—" Then, walking as he was with his face turned back and up to her, Susan's new friend tripped over a rock jutting out of the road and almost fell. Rusher whinnied through his nose and reared a little. Susan laughed merrily. The poncho shifted, revealing one bare leg, and she took a moment before putting matters right again. She liked him, aye, so she did. And what harm could there be in it? He was only a boy, after all. When he smiled, she could see he was only a year or two removed from jumping in haystacks. (The thought that she had recently graduated from haystack-jumping herself had somehow fled her mind.)

"I'm usually not clumsy," he said. "I hope I didn't startle you."

Not at all, Will; boys have been stubbing their toes around me ever since I grew my breasts.

"Not at all," she said, and returned to the previous topic. It interested her greatly. "So ye and yer friends come at the behest of the Affiliation to count our goods, do you?"

"Yes. The reason I took particular note of yon oilpatch is because one of us will have to come back and count the working derricks—"

"I can spare ye that, Will. There are nineteen."

He nodded. "I'm in your debt. But we'll also need to make out—if we can—how much oil those nineteen pumps are bringing up."

"Are there so many oil-fired machines still working in New Canaan that such news matters? And do ye have the alchemy to change the oil into the stuff yer machines can use?"

"It's called refinery rather than alchemy in this case—at least I think so—and I believe there is one that still works. But no, we haven't that many machines, although there are still a few working filament-lights in the Great Hall at Gilead."

"Fancy it!" she said, delighted. She had seen pictures of filament-lights and electric flambeaux, but never the lights themselves. The last ones in Hambry (they had been called "spark-lights" in this part of the world, but she felt sure they were the same) had burned out two generations ago.

"You said your father managed the Mayor's horses until his death," Will Dearborn said. "Was his name Patrick Delgado? It was, wasn't it?"

She looked down at him, badly startled and brought back to reality in an instant. "How do ye know that?"

"His name was in our lessons of calling. We're to count cattle, sheep, pigs, oxen . . . and horses. Of all your livestock, horses are the most important. Patrick Delgado was the man we were to see in that regard. I'm sorry to hear he's come to the clearing at the end of the path, Susan. Will you accept my condolence?"

"Aye, and with thanks."

"Was it an accident?"

"Aye." Hoping her voice said what she wanted it to say, which was *leave this subject, ask no more.*

"Let me be honest with you," he said, and for the first time she thought she heard a false note there. Perhaps it was only her imagination. Certainly she had little experience of the world (Aunt Cord reminded her of this almost daily), but she had an idea that people who set on by saying *Let me be honest with you* were apt to *go* on by telling you straight-faced that rain fell up, money grew on trees, and babies were brought by the Grand Featherex.

"Aye, Will Dearborn," she said, her tone just the tiniest bit dry. "They say honesty's the best policy, so they do."

He looked at her a bit doubtfully, and then his smile shone out again. That smile was dangerous, she thought—a quicksand smile if ever there was one. Easy to wander in; perhaps more difficult to wander back out.

"There's not much Affiliation in the Affiliation these days. That's part of the reason Farson's gone on as long as he has; that's what has allowed his ambitions to grow. He's come a far way from the harrier who began as a stage-robber in Garlan and Desoy, and he'll come farther yet if the Affiliation isn't revitalized. Maybe all the way to Mejis."

She couldn't imagine what the Good Man could possibly want with her own sleepy little town in the Barony which lay closest to the Clean Sea, but she kept silent.

"In any case, it wasn't really the Affiliation that sent us," he said. "Not all this way to count cows and oil derricks and hectares of land under cultivation."

He paused a moment, looking down at the road (as if for more rocks in the way of his boots) and stroking Rusher's nose with absentminded gentleness. She thought he was embarrassed, perhaps even 'shamed. "We were sent by our fathers."

"Yer—" Then she understood. Bad boys, they were, sent out on a make-work quest that wasn't quite exile. She guessed their real job in Hambry might be to rehabilitate their reputations. *Well,* she thought, *it certainly explains the quicksand smile, doesn't it? 'Ware this one, Susan; he's the sort to burn bridges and upset mail-carts, then go on his merry way without a single look back. Not in meanness but in plain old boy-carelessness.*

That made her think of the old song again, the one she'd been singing, the one he'd been whistling.

"Our fathers, yes."

Susan Delgado had cut a caper or two (or perhaps it was two dozen) of her own in her time, and she felt sympathy for Will Dearborn as well as caution. And interest. Bad boys could be amusing . . . up to a point. The question was, how bad had Will and his cronies been?

"Helling?" she asked.

"Helling," he agreed, still sounding glum but perhaps brightening just a bit about the eyes and mouth. "We were warned; yes, warned very well. There was . . . a certain amount of drinking."

And a few girls to squeeze with the hand not busy squeezing the ale-pot? It was a question no nice girl could outright ask, but one that couldn't help occurring to her mind.

Now the smile which had played briefly around the corners of his mouth dropped away. "We pushed it too far and the fun stopped. Fools have a way of doing that. One night there was a race. One *moonless* night. After midnight. All of us drunk. One of the horses caught his hoof in a gopher-hole and snapped a foreleg. He had to be put down."

Susan winced. It wasn't the worst thing she could think of, but bad enough. And when he opened his mouth again, it got worse.

"The horse was a thoroughbred, one of just three owned by my friend Richard's father, who is not well-to-do. There were scenes in our households which I haven't any desire to remember, let alone talk about. I'll make a long story short and say that, after much talk and many proposals for punishment, we were sent here, on this errand. It was Arthur's father's idea. I think Arthur's da has always been a bit appalled by Arthur. Certainly Arthur's ructions didn't come from George Heath's side."

Susan smiled to herself, thinking of Aunt Cordelia saying, "She certainly doesn't get it from *our* side of the family." Then the calculated pause, followed by: "She had a great-aunt on her mother's side who ran crazy . . . you didn't know? Yes! Set herself on fire and threw herself over the Drop. In the year of the comet, it was."

"Anyway," Will resumed, "Mr. Heath set us on with a saying from his own father—'One should meditate in purgatory.' And here we are."

"Hambry's far from purgatory."

He sketched his funny little bow again. "If it were, all should want to be bad enough to come here and meet the pretty denizens."

"Work on that one a bit," she said in her driest voice. "It's still rough, I fear. Perhaps—"

She fell silent as a dismaying realization occurred to her: she was going to have to hope this boy would enter into a limited conspiracy with her. Otherwise, she was apt to be embarrassed.

"Susan?"

"I was just thinking. Are you here yet, Will? Officially, I mean?"

"No," he said, taking her meaning at once. And likely already seeing where this was going. He seemed sharp enough, in his way. "We only arrived in Barony this afternoon, and you're the first person any of us has spoken to . . . unless, that is, Richard and Arthur have met folks. I couldn't sleep, and so came out to ride and to think things over a little. We're camped over there." He pointed to the right. "On that long slope that runs toward the sea."

"Aye, the Drop, it's called." She realized that Will and his mates might even be camped on what would be her own land by law before much more time had passed. The thought was amusing and exciting and a little startling.

"Tomorrow we ride into town and present our compliments to My Lord Mayor, Hart Thorin. He's a bit of a fool, according to what we were told before leaving New Canaan."

"Were ye indeed told so?" she asked, raising one eyebrow.

"Yes—apt to blabber, fond of strong drink, even more fond of young girls," Will said. "Is it true, would you say?"

"I think ye must judge for yerself," said she, stifling a smile with some effort.

"In any case, we'll also be presenting to the Honorable Kimba Rimer, Thorin's Chancellor, and I understand he knows his beans. And *counts* his beans, as well."

"Thorin will have ye to dinner at Mayor's House," Susan said. "Perhaps not tomorrow night, but surely the night after."

"A dinner of state in Hambry," Will said, smiling and still stroking Rusher's nose. "Gods, how shall I bear the agony of my anticipation?"

"Never mind yer nettlesome mouth," she said, "but only listen, if ye'd be my friend. This is important."

His smile dropped away, and she saw again—as she had for a moment or two before—the man he'd be before too many more years had passed. The hard face, the concentrated eyes, the merciless mouth. It was a frightening face, in a way—a frightening *prospect*—and yet, still, the place the old hag had touched felt warm and she found it difficult to take her eyes off him. What, she wondered, was his hair like under that stupid hat he wore?

"Tell me, Susan."

"If you and yer friends come to table at Thorin's, ye may see me. If ye see me, Will, see me for the first time. See Miss Delgado, as I shall see Mr. Dearborn. Do'ee take my meaning?"

"To the letter." He was looking at her thoughtfully. "Do you serve? Surely, if your father was the Barony's chief drover, you do not—"

"Never mind what I do or don't do. Just promise that if we meet at Seafront, we meet for the first time."

"I promise. But—"

"No more questions. We've nearly come to the place where we must part ways, and I want to give ye a warning—fair payment for the ride on this nice mount of yours, mayhap. If ye dine with Thorin and Rimer, ye'll not be the only new folk at his table. There'll likely be three others, men Thorin has hired to serve as private guards o' the house."

"Not as Sheriff's deputies?"

"Nay, they answer to none but Thorin . . . or, mayhap, to Rimer. Their names are Jonas, Depape, and Reynolds. They look like hard boys to me . . . although Jonas's boyhood is so long behind him that I imagine he's forgot he ever had one."

"Jonas is the leader?"

"Aye. He limps, has hair that falls to his shoulders pretty as any girl's, and the quavery voice of an old gaffer who spends his days polishing the chimney-corner . . . but I think he's the most dangerous of the three all the same. I'd guess these three have forgot more about helling than you and yer friends will ever learn."

Now why had she told him all that? She didn't know, exactly. Gratitude, perhaps. He had promised to keep the secret of this late-night meeting, and he had the look of a promise-keeper, in hack with his father or not.

"I'll watch them. And I thank you for the advice." They were now climbing a long, gentle slope. Overhead, Old Mother blazed relentlessly. "Bodyguards," he mused. "Bodyguards in sleepy little Hambry. It's strange times, Susan. Strange indeed."

"Aye." She had wondered about Jonas, Depape, and Reynolds herself, and could think of no good reason for them to be in town. Had they been Rimer's doing, Rimer's decision? It seemed likely—Thorin wasn't the sort of man to even *think* about bodyguards, she would have said; the High Sheriff had always done well enough for him—but still . . . why?

They breasted the hill. Below them lay a nestle of buildings—the village of Hambry. Only a few lights still shone. The brightest cluster marked the Travellers' Rest. From here, on the warm breeze, she could hear the piano beating out "Hey Jude" and a score of drunken voices gleefully murdering the chorus. Not the three men of whom she had warned Will Dearborn, though; they would be standing at the bar, watching the room with their flat eyes. Not the singing type were those three. Each had a small blue coffin-shape tattooed on his right hand, burned into the webbing between thumb and forefinger. She thought to tell Will this, then realized he'd see for himself soon enough. Instead, she pointed a little way down the slope, at a dark shape which overhung the road on a chain. "Do ye see that?"

"Yes." He heaved a large and rather comical sigh. "Is it the object I fear beyond all others? Is it the dread shape of Mrs. Beech's mailbox?"

"Aye. And it's there we must part."

"If you say we must, we must. Yet I wish—" Just then the wind shifted, as it sometimes did in the summer, and blew a strong gust out of the west. The smell of sea-salt was gone in an instant, and so was the sound of the drunken, singing voices. What replaced them was a sound infinitely more sinister, one that never failed to produce a scutter of gooseflesh up her back: a low, atonal noise, like the warble of a siren being turned by a man without much longer to live.

Will took a step backward, eyes widening, and again she noticed his hands take a dip toward his belt, as if reaching for something not there.

"What in gods' name is that?"

"It's a thinny," she said quietly. "In Eyebolt Canyon. Have ye never heard of such?"

"Heard of, yes, but never *heard* until now. Gods, how do you stand it? It sounds *alive!*"

She had never thought of it quite like that, but now, in a way listening with his ears instead of her own, she thought he was right. It was as if some sick part of the night had gained a voice and was actually trying to sing.

She shivered. Rusher felt the momentary increased pressure of her knees and whickered softly, craning his head around to look at her.

"We don't often hear it so clearly at this time of year," she said. "In the fall, the men burn it to quiet."

"I don't understand."

Who did? Who understood anything anymore? Gods, they couldn't even turn off the few oil-pumps in Citgo that still worked, although half of them squealed like pigs in a slaughtering chute. These days you were usually just grateful to find things that still worked at all.

"In the summer, when there's time, drovers and cowboys drag loads of brush to the mouth of Eyebolt," she said. "Dead brush is all right, but live is better, for it's smoke that's wanted, and the heavier the better. Eyebolt's a box canyon, very short and steep-walled. Almost like a chimney lying on its side, you see?"

"Yes."

"The traditional time for burning is Reap Morn—the day after the fair and the feast and the fire."

"The first day of winter."

"Aye, although in these parts it doesn't feel like winter so soon. In any case it's no tradition; the brush is sometimes lit sooner, if the winds have been prankish or if the sound's particularly strong. It upsets the livestock, you know—cows give poorly when the noise of the thinny's strong—and it makes sleep difficult."

"I should think it would." Will was still looking north, and a stronger gust of wind blew his hat off. It fell to his back, the rawhide tugstring pulling against the line of his throat. The hair so revealed was a little long, and as black as a crow's wing. She felt a sudden, greedy desire to run her hands through it, to let her fingers tell its texture—rough or smooth or silky? And how would it smell? At this she felt another shiver of heat down low in her belly. He turned to her as though he had read her mind, and she flushed, grateful that he wouldn't be able to see the darkening of her cheek.

"How long has it been there?"

"Since before I was born," she said, "but not before my da was born. He said that the ground shook in an earthquake just before it came. Some say the earthquake brought it, some say that's superstitious nonsense. All I know is that it's always been there. The smoke quiets it awhile, the way it will quiet a hive of bees or wasps, but the sound always comes back. The brush piled at the mouth helps to keep any wandering livestock out, too—sometimes they're drawn to it, gods know why. But if a cow or sheep *does* happen to get in—after the burning and before the next year's pile has started to grow, mayhap— it doesn't come back out. Whatever it is, it's hungry."

She put his poncho aside, lifted her right leg over the saddle without so much as touching the horn, and slipped off Rusher—all this in a single liquid movement. It was a stunt made for pants rather than a dress, and she knew from the further widening of his eyes that he'd seen a good lot of her . . . but nothing she had to wash with the bathroom door closed, so what of that? And that quick dismount had ever been a favorite trick of hers when she was in a showoffy mood.

"Pretty!" he exclaimed.

"I learned it from my da," she said, responding to the more innocent interpretation of his compliment. Her smile as she handed him the reins, however, suggested that she was willing to accept the compliment any way it was meant.

"Susan? Have you ever seen the thinny?"

"Aye, once or twice. From above."

"What does it look like?"

"Ugly," she responded at once. Until tonight, when

she had observed Rhea's smile up close and endured her twiddling, meddling fingers, she would have said it was the ugliest thing she had ever seen. "It looks a little like a slow-burning peat fire, and a little like a swamp full of scummy green water. There's a mist that rises off it. Sometimes it looks like long, skinny arms. With hands at the end of em."

"Is it growing?"

"Aye, they say it is, that every thinny grows, but it grows slowly. 'Twon't escape Eyebolt Canyon in your time or mine."

She looked up at the sky, and saw that the constellations had continued to tilt along their tracks as they spoke. She felt she could talk to him all night—about the thinny, or Citgo, or her irritating aunt, or just about anything—and the idea dismayed her. Why should this happen to her now, for the gods' sake? After three years of dismissing the Hambry boys, why should she now meet a boy who interested her so strangely? Why was life so unfair?

Her earlier thought, the one she'd heard in her father's voice, recurred to her: *If it's* ka, *it'll come like a wind, and your plans will stand before it no more than a barn before a cyclone.*

But no. And no. And no. So set she, with all her considerable determination, her mind against the idea. This was no barn; this was her *life.*

Susan reached out and touched the rusty tin of Mrs. Beech's mailbox, as if to steady herself in the world. Her little hopes and daydreams didn't mean so much, perhaps, but her father had taught her to measure herself by her ability to do the things she'd said she would do, and she would not overthrow his teachings simply because she happened to encounter a good-looking boy at a time when her body and her emotions were in a stew.

"I'll leave ye here to either rejoin yer friends or resume

yer ride," she said. The gravity she heard in her voice
made her feel a bit sad, for it was an adult gravity. "But
remember yer promise, Will—if ye see me at Seafront—
Mayor's House—and if ye'd be my friend, see me there
for the first time. As I'd see you."

He nodded, and she saw her seriousness now mirrored
in his own face. And the sadness, mayhap. "I've never
asked a girl to ride out with me, or if she'd accept a visit
of me. I'd ask of you, Susan, daughter of Patrick—I'd
even bring you flowers to sweeten my chances—but it
would do no good, I think."

She shook her head. "Nay. 'Twouldn't."

"Are you promised in marriage? It's forward of me to
ask, I know, but I mean no harm."

"I'm sure ye don't, but I'd as soon not answer. My position is a delicate one just now, as I told ye. Besides, it's
late. Here's where we part, Will. But stay . . . one more
moment . . ."

She rummaged in the pocket of her apron and brought
out half a cake wrapped in a piece of green leaf. The
other half she had eaten on her way up to the Cöos . . .
in what now felt like the other half of her life. She held
what was left of her little evening meal out to Rusher,
who sniffed it, then ate it and nuzzled her hand. She
smiled, liking the velvet tickle in the cup of her palm.
"Aye, thee's a good horse, so ye are."

She looked at Will Dearborn, who stood in the road,
shuffling his dusty boots and gazing at her unhappily. The
hard look was gone from his face, now; he looked her
age again, or younger. "We were well met, weren't we?"
he asked.

She stepped forward, and before she could let herself
think about what she was doing, she put her hands on
his shoulders, stood on her toes, and kissed him on the
mouth. The kiss was brief but not sisterly.

"Aye, very well met, Will." But when he moved toward her (as thoughtlessly as a flower turning its face to follow the sun), wishing to repeat the experience, she pushed him back a step, gently but firmly.

"Nay, that was only a thank-you, and one thank-you should be enough for a gentleman. Go yer course in peace, Will."

He took up the reins like a man in a dream, looked at them for a moment as if he didn't know what in the world they were, and then looked back at her. She could see him working to clear his mind and emotions of the impact her kiss had made. She liked him for it. And she was very glad she had done it.

"And you yours," he said, swinging into the saddle. "I look forward to meeting you for the first time."

He smiled at her, and she saw both longing and wishes in that smile. Then he gigged the horse, turned him, and started back the way they'd come—to have another look at the oilpatch, mayhap. She stood where she was, by Mrs. Beech's mailbox, willing him to turn around and wave so she could see his face once more. She felt sure he would . . . but he didn't. Then, just as she was about to turn away and start down the hill to town, he *did* turn, and his hand lifted, fluttering for a moment in the dark like a moth.

Susan lifted her own in return and then went her way, feeling happy and unhappy at the same time. Yet— and this was perhaps the most important thing—she no longer felt soiled. When she had touched the boy's lips, Rhea's touch seemed to have left her skin. A small magic, perhaps, but she welcomed it.

She walked on, smiling a little and looking up at the stars more frequently than was her habit when out after dark.

CHAPTER FOUR

Long After Moonset

I

He rode restlessly for nearly two hours back and forth along what she called the Drop, never pushing Rusher above a trot, although what he wanted to do was gallop the big gelding under the stars until his own blood began to cool a little.

It'll cool plenty if you draw attention to yourself, he thought, *and likely you won't even have to cool it yourself. Fools are the only folk on the earth who can absolutely count on getting what they deserve.* That old saying made him think of the scarred and bowlegged man who had been his life's greatest teacher, and he smiled.

At last he turned his horse down the slope to the trickle of brook which ran there, and followed it a mile and a half upstream (past several gathers of horse; they looked at Rusher with a kind of sleepy, wall-eyed surprise) to a grove of willows. From the hollow within, a horse whickered softly. Rusher whickered in return, stamping one hoof and nodding his head up and down.

His rider ducked his own head as he passed through the willow fronds, and suddenly there was a narrow and inhuman white face hanging before him, its upper half all but swallowed by black, pupilless eyes.

He dipped for his guns—the third time tonight he'd

done that, and for the third time there was nothing there. Not that it mattered; already he recognized what was hanging before him on a string: that idiotic rook's skull.

The young man who was currently calling himself Arthur Heath had taken it off his saddle (it amused him to call the skull so perched their lookout, "ugly as an old gammer, but perfect cheap to feed") and hung it here as a prank greeting. Him and his jokes! Rusher's master batted it aside hard enough to break the string and send the skull flying into the dark.

"Fie, Roland," said a voice from the shadows. It was reproachful, but there was laughter bubbling just beneath . . . as there always was. Cuthbert was his oldest friend—the marks of their first teeth had been embedded on many of the same toys—but Roland had in some ways never understood him. Nor was it just his laughter; on the long-ago day when Hax, the palace cook, was to be hung for a traitor on Gallows Hill, Cuthbert had been in an agony of terror and remorse. He'd told Roland he couldn't stay, couldn't watch . . . but in the end he had done both. Because neither the stupid jokes nor the easy surface emotions were the truth of Cuthbert Allgood.

As Roland entered the hollow at the center of the grove, a dark shape stepped out from behind the tree where it had been keeping. Halfway across the clearing, it resolved itself into a tall, narrow-hipped boy who was barefooted below his jeans and barechested above them. In one hand he held an enormous antique revolver—a kind which was sometimes called a beer-barrel because of the cylinder's size.

"Fie," Cuthbert repeated, as if he liked the sound of this word, not archaic only in forgotten backwaters like Mejis. "That's a fine way to treat the guard o' the watch, smacking the poor thin-faced fellow halfway to the nearest mountain-range!"

"If I'd been wearing a gun, I likely would have blown it to smithereens and woken half the countryside."

"I knew you wouldn't be going about strapped," Cuthbert answered mildly. "You're remarkably ill-looking, Roland son of Steven, but nobody's fool even as you approach the ancient age of fifteen."

"I thought we agreed we'd use the names we're travelling under. Even among ourselves."

Cuthbert stuck out his leg, bare heel planted in the turf, and bowed with his arms outstretched and his hands strenuously bent at the wrist—an inspired imitation of the sort of man for whom court has become career. He also looked remarkably like a heron standing in a marsh, and Roland snorted laughter in spite of himself. Then he touched the inside of his left wrist to his forehead, to see if he had a fever. He felt feverish enough inside his head, gods knew, but the skin above his eyes felt cool.

"I cry your pardon, gunslinger," Cuthbert said, his eyes and hands still turned humbly down.

The smile on Roland's face died. "And don't call me that again, Cuthbert. Please. Not here, not anywhere. Not if you value me."

Cuthbert dropped his pose at once and came quickly to where Roland sat his horse. He looked honestly humbled.

"Roland—Will—I'm sorry."

Roland clapped him on the shoulder. "No harm done. Just remember from here on out. Mejis may be at the end of the world . . . but it still *is* the world. Where's Alain?"

"Dick, do you mean? Where do you think?" Cuthbert pointed across the clearing, to where a dark hulk was either snoring or slowly choking to death.

"That one," Cuthbert said, "would sleep through an earthquake."

"But you heard me coming and woke."

"Yes," Cuthbert said. His eyes were on Roland's face, searching it with an intensity that made Roland feel a little uneasy. "Did something happen to you? You look different."

"Do I?"

"Yes. Excited. Aired out, somehow."

If he was going to tell Cuthbert about Susan, now was the time. He decided without really thinking about it (most of his decisions, certainly the best of them, were made in this same way) not to tell. If he met her at Mayor's House, it would be the first time as far as Cuthbert and Alain knew, as well. What harm in that?

"I've been properly aired, all right," he said, dismounting and bending to uncinch the girths of his saddle. "I've seen some interesting things, too."

"Ah? Speak, companion of my bosom's dearest tenant."

"I'll wait until tomorrow, I think, when yon hibernating bear is finally awake. Then I only have to tell once. Besides, I'm tired. I'll share you one thing, though: there are too many horses in these parts, even for a Barony renowned for its horseflesh. Too many by far."

Before Cuthbert could ask any questions, Roland pulled the saddle from Rusher's back and set it down beside three small wicker cages which had been bound together with rawhide, making them into a carrier which could be secured to a horse's back. Inside, three pigeons with white rings around their necks cooed sleepily. One took his head out from beneath his wing, had a peek at Roland, and then tucked himself away again.

"These fellows all right?" Roland asked.

"Fine. Pecking and shitting happily in their straw. As far as they're concerned, they're on vacation. What did you mean about—"

"Tomorrow," Roland said, and Cuthbert, seeing that

there would be no more, only nodded and went to find his lean and bony lookout.

Twenty minutes later, Rusher unloaded and rubbed down and set to forage with Buckskin and Glue Boy (Cuthbert could not even name his horse as a normal person would), Roland lay on his back in his bedroll, looking up at the late stars overhead. Cuthbert had gone back to sleep as easily as he had awakened at the sound of Rusher's hoofs, but Roland had never felt less sleepy in his life.

His mind turned back a month, to the whore's room, to his father sitting on the whore's bed and watching him dress. The words his father had spoken—*I have known for two years*—had reverberated like a struck gong in Roland's head. He suspected they might continue to do so for the rest of his life.

But his father had had much more to say. About Marten. About Roland's mother, who was, perhaps, more sinned against than sinning. About harriers who called themselves patriots. And about John Farson, who had indeed been in Cressia, and who was gone from that place now—vanished, as he had a way of doing, like smoke in a high wind. Before leaving, he and his men had burned Indrie, the Barony seat, pretty much to the ground. The slaughter had been in the hundreds, and perhaps it was no surprise that Cressia had since repudiated the Affiliation and spoken for the Good Man. The Barony Governor, the Mayor of Indrie, and the High Sheriff had all ended the early summer day which concluded Farson's visit with their heads on the wall guarding the town's entrance. That was, Steven Deschain had said, "pretty persuasive politics."

It was a game of Castles where both armies had come out from behind their Hillocks and the final moves had commenced, Roland's father had said, and as was so often the case with popular revolutions, that game was apt to be over before many in the Baronies of Mid-World had begun to realize that John Farson was a serious threat . . . or, if you were one of those who believed passionately in his vision of democracy and an end to what he called "class slavery and ancient fairy-tales," a serious agent of change.

His father and his father's small *ka-tet* of gunslingers, Roland was amazed to learn, cared little about Farson in either light; they looked upon him as small cheese. Looked upon the Affiliation itself as small cheese, come to that.

I'm going to send you away, Steven had said, sitting there on the bed and looking somberly at his only son, the one who had lived. *There is no true safe place left in Mid-World, but the Barony of Mejis on the Clean Sea is as close to true safety as any place may be these days . . . so it's there you'll go, along with at least two of your mates. Alain, I suppose, for one. Just not that laughing boy for the other, I beg of you. You'd be better off with a barking dog.*

Roland, who on any other day in his life would have been overjoyed at the prospect of seeing some of the wider world, had protested hotly. If the final battles against the Good Man were at hand, he wanted to fight them at his father's side. He was a gunslinger now, after all, if only a 'prentice, and—

His father had shaken his head, slowly and emphatically. *No, Roland. You don't understand. You shall, however; as well as possible, you shall.*

Later, the two of them had walked the high battlements above Mid-World's last living city—green and gorgeous Gilead in the morning sun, with its pennons flapping and the vendors in the streets of the Old Quarter and horses trotting on the bridle paths which radiated out from the palace standing at the heart of everything. His father had told him more (not everything), and he had understood more (far from everything—nor did his father understand everything). The Dark Tower had not been mentioned by either of them, but already it hung in Roland's mind, a possibility like a storm-cloud far away on the horizon.

Was the Tower what all of this was really about? Not a jumped-up harrier with dreams of ruling Mid-World, not the wizard who had enchanted his mother, not the glass ball which Steven and his posse had hoped to find in Cressia . . . but the Dark Tower?

He hadn't asked.

He hadn't *dared* ask.

Now he shifted in his bedroll and closed his eyes. He saw the girl's face at once; he felt her lips pressed firmly against his own again, and smelled the scent of her skin. He was instantly hot from the top of his head to the base of his spine, cold from the base of his spine to the tips of his toes. Then he thought of the way her legs had flashed as she slid from Rusher's back (also the glimmer of the undergarments beneath her briefly raised dress), and his hot half and cold half changed places.

The whore had taken his virginity but wouldn't kiss him; had turned her face aside when he tried to kiss her. She'd allowed him to do whatever else he wanted, but not that. At the time he'd been bitterly disappointed. Now he was glad.

The eye of his adolescent mind, both restless and clear, considered the braid which fell down her back to her waist, the soft dimples which had formed at the corners of her mouth when she smiled, the lilt of her voice, her old-fashioned way of saying aye and nay, ye and yer and da. He thought of how her hands had felt on his shoulders as she stretched up to kiss him, and thought he would give everything he owned to feel her hands there again, so light and so firm. And her mouth on his. It was a mouth that knew only a little about kissing, he guessed, but that was a little more than he knew himself.

Be careful, Roland—don't let your feeling for this girl tip anything over. She's not free, anyway—she said as much. Not married, but spoken for in some other way.

Roland was far from the relentless creature he would eventually become, but the seeds of that relentlessness were there—small, stony things that would, in their time, grow into trees with deep roots . . . and bitter fruit. Now one of these seeds cracked open and sent up its first sharp blade.

What's been spoken for may be unspoken, and what's done may be undone. Nothing's sure, but . . . I want her.

Yes. That was the one thing he did know, and he knew it as well as he knew the face of his father: he wanted her. Not as he had wanted the whore when she lay naked on her bed with her legs spread and her half-lidded eyes looking up at him, but in the way he wanted food when he was hungry or water when he was thirsty. In the way, he supposed, that he wanted to drag Marten's dusty body behind his horse down Gilead's High Road in payment for what the wizard had done to his mother.

He wanted her; he wanted the girl Susan.

Roland turned over on his other side, closed his eyes, and fell asleep. His rest was thin and lit by the crudely poetic dreams only adolescent boys have, dreams where sexual attraction and romantic love come together and resonate more powerfully than they ever will again. In these thirsty visions Susan Delgado put her hands on Roland's shoulders over and over, kissed his mouth over and over, told him over and over to come to her for the first time, to be with her for the first time, to see her for the first time, to see her very well.

2

Five miles or so from where Roland slept and dreamed his dreams, Susan Delgado lay in her bed and looked out her window and watched Old Star begin to grow pale with the approaching dawn. Sleep was no closer now than it had been when she lay down, and there was a throb between her legs where the old woman had touched her. It was distracting but no longer unpleasant, because she now associated it with the boy she'd met on the road and impulsively kissed by starlight. Every time she shifted her legs, that throb flared into a brief sweet ache.

When she'd got home, Aunt Cord (who would have been in her own bed an hour before on any ordinary night) had been sitting in her rocking chair by the fireplace—dead and cold and swept clean of ashes at this time of year—with a lapful of lace that looked like wave-froth against her dowdy black dress. She was edging it with a speed that seemed almost supernatural to Susan, and she hadn't looked up when the door opened and her niece came in on a swirl of breeze.

"I expected ye an hour ago," Aunt Cord said. And then, although she didn't sound it: "I was worried."

"Aye?" Susan said, and said no more. She thought that on any other night she would have offered one of her fumbling excuses which always sounded like a lie to her own ears—it was the effect Aunt Cord had had on her all her life—but this hadn't been an ordinary night. Never in her life had there been a night like this. She found she could not get Will Dearborn out of her mind.

Aunt Cord had looked up then, her close-set, rather beady eyes sharp and inquisitive above her narrow blade of a nose. Some things hadn't changed since Susan had set out for the Cöos; she had still been able to feel her aunt's eyes brushing across her face and down her body, like little whisk-brooms with sharp bristles.

"What took ye so long?" Aunt Cord had asked. "Was there trouble?"

"No trouble," Susan had replied, but for a moment she thought of how the witch had stood beside her in the doorway, pulling her braid through the gnarled tube of one loosely clenched fist. She remembered wanting to go, and she remembered asking Rhea if their business was done.

Mayhap there's one more little thing, the old woman had said . . . or so Susan thought. But what had that one more little thing been? She couldn't remember. And, really, what did it matter? She was shut of Rhea until her belly began to rise with Thorin's child . . . and if there could be no baby-making until Reap-Night, she'd not be returning to the Cöos until late winter at the soonest. An age! And it would be longer than that, were she slow to kindle . . .

"I walked slowly coming home, Aunt. That's all."

"Then why look ye so?" Aunt Cord had asked, scant brows knitting toward the vertical line which creased her brow.

"How so?" Susan had asked, taking off her apron and knotting the strings and hanging it on the hook just inside the kitchen door.

"Flushy. Frothy. Like milk fresh out of the cow."

She'd almost laughed. Aunt Cord, who knew as little about men as Susan did about the stars and planets, had struck it directly. Flushy and frothy was exactly how she felt. "Only the night air, I suppose," she had said. "I saw a meteor, Aunt. And heard the thinny. The sound's strong tonight."

"Aye?" her aunt asked without interest, then returned to the subject which did interest her. "Did it hurt?"

"A little."

"Did ye cry?"

Susan shook her head.

"Good. Better not. Always better. She likes it when they cry, I've heard. Now, Sue—did she give you something? Did the old pussy give you something?"

"Aye." She reached into her pocket and brought out the paper with

on͵ɹest

written upon it. She held it out and her aunt snatched it away with a greedy look. Cordelia had been quite the sugarplum over the last month or so, but now that she had what she wanted (and now that Susan had come too far and promised too much to have a change of heart), she'd reverted to the sour, supercilious, often suspicious woman Susan had grown up with; the one who'd been driven into almost weekly bouts of rage by her phlegmatic, life-goes-as-'twill brother. In a way, it was a relief. It had been nervewracking to have Aunt Cord playing Cybilla Good-Sprite day after day.

"Aye, aye, there's her mark, all right," her aunt had said, tracing her fingers over the bottom of the sheet. "A devil's hoof's what it means, some say, but what do we care, eh, Sue? Nasty, horrid creature that she is, she's still made it possible for two women to get on in the world a little longer. And ye'll only have to see her once more, probably around Year's End, when ye've caught proper."

"It will be later than that," Susan had told her. "I'm not to lie with him until the full of the Demon Moon. After the Reaping Fair and the bonfire."

Aunt Cord had stared, eyes wide, mouth open. "Said she so?"

Are you calling me a liar, Auntie? she had thought with a sharpness that wasn't much like her; usually her nature was more like her father's.

"Aye."

"But why? Why so *long?*" Aunt Cord was obviously upset, obviously disappointed. There had so far been eight pieces of silver and four of gold out of this; they were tucked up wherever it was that Aunt Cord squirreled her money away (and Susan suspected there was a fair amount of it, although Cordelia liked to plead poverty at every opportunity), and twice that much was still owed . . . or would be, once the bloodstained sheet went to the Mayor's House laundress. That same amount would be paid yet again when Rhea had confirmed the baby, and the baby's honesty. A lot of money, all told. A *great* lot, for a little place like this and little folk like them. And now, to have the paying of it put back so far . . .

Then came a sin Susan had prayed over (although without much enthusiasm) before getting into her bed: she had rather enjoyed the cheated, frustrated look on Aunt Cord's face—the look of the thwarted miser.

"Why so *long?*" she repeated.

"I suppose you could go up the Cöos and ask her."

Cordelia Delgado's lips, thin to begin with, had pressed together so tightly they almost disappeared. "Are you pert, missy? Are you pert with me?"

"No. I'm much too tired to be pert with anyone. I want to wash—I can still feel her hands on me, so I can—and go to bed."

"Then do so. Perhaps in the morning we can discuss this in more ladylike fashion. And we must go and see Hart, of course." She folded the paper Rhea had given Susan, looking pleased at the prospect of visiting Hart Thorin, and moved her hand toward her dress pocket.

"No," Susan said, and her voice had been unusually

sharp—enough so to freeze her aunt's hand in mid-air. Cordelia had looked at her, frankly startled. Susan had felt a little embarrassed by that look, but she hadn't dropped her eyes, and when she held out her own hand, it had been steady enough.

"I'm to have the keeping of that, Aunt."

"Who tells ye to speak so?" Aunt Cord had asked, her voice almost whining with outrage—it was close to blasphemy, Susan supposed, but for a moment Aunt Cord's voice had reminded her of the sound the thinny made. "Who tells ye to speak so to the woman who raised a motherless girl? To the sister of that girl's poor dead father?"

"You know who," Susan said. She still held her hand out. "I'm to keep it, and I'm to give it to Mayor Thorin. She said she didn't care what happened to it then, he could wipe his bum with it for all of her," (the flush which suffused her aunt's face at that had been very enjoyable) "but *until* then, it was to be in my keeping."

"I never heard of such a thing," Aunt Cordelia had huffed . . . but she had handed the grimy scrap of paper back. "Giving the keep of such an important document to a mere scrap of a girl."

Yet not too mere a scrap to be his gilly, am I? To lie under him and listen to his bones creak and take his seed and mayhap bear his child.

She'd dropped her eyes to her pocket as she put the paper away again, not wanting Aunt Cord to see the resentment in them.

"Go up," Aunt Cord had said, brushing the froth of lace off her lap and into her workbasket, where it lay in an unaccustomed tangle. "And when you wash, do your mouth with especial care. Cleanse it of its impudence and disrespect toward those who have given up much for love of its owner."

Susan had gone silently, biting back a thousand retorts, mounting the stairs as she had so often, throbbing with a mixture of shame and resentment.

And now here she was, in her bed and still awake as the stars paled away and the first brighter shades began to color the sky. The events of the night just past slipped through her mind in a kind of fantastical blur, like shuffled playing cards—and the one which turned up with the most persistence was the face of Will Dearborn. She thought of how that face could be hard at one moment and soften so unexpectedly at the next. And was it a handsome face? Aye, she thought so. For herself, she knew so.

I've never asked a girl to ride out with me, or if she would accept a visit of me. I would ask you, Susan, daughter of Patrick.

Why now? Why should I meet him now, when no good can come of it?

If it's ka, it'll come like a wind. Like a cyclone.

She tossed from one side of the bed to the other, then at last rolled onto her back again. There would be no sleep for her in what remained of this night, she thought. She might as well walk out on the Drop and watch the sun come up.

Yet she continued to lie in bed, feeling somehow sick and well at the same time, looking into the shadows and listening to the first cries of the morning birds, thinking of how his mouth had felt against hers, the tender grain of it and the feeling of his teeth below his lips; the smell of his skin, the rough texture of his shirt under her palms.

She now put those palms against the top of her shift and cupped her breasts with her fingers. The nipples were hard, like little pebbles. And when she touched them, the heat between her legs flared suddenly and urgently.

She *could* sleep, she thought. She could, if she took care of that heat. If she knew how.

And she did. The old woman had shown her. *Even a girl who's intact don't need to lack for a shiver now 'n then . . . Like a little bud o' silk, so it is.*

Susan shifted in bed and slipped a hand deep beneath the sheet. She forced the old woman's bright eyes and hollow cheeks out of her mind—it wasn't hard to do at all once you set your mind to it, she discovered—and replaced it with the face of the boy with the big gelding and the silly flat-crowned hat. For a moment the vision of her mind became so clear and so sweet that it was real, and all the rest of her life only a drab dream. In this vision he kissed her over and over, their mouths widening, their tongues touching; what he breathed out, she breathed in.

She burned. She burned in her bed like a torch. And when the sun finally came over the horizon some short time later, she lay deeply asleep, with a faint smile on her lips and her unbraided hair lying across the side of her face and her pillow like loose gold.

3

In the last hour before dawn, the public room of the Travellers' Rest was as quiet as it ever became. The gas-lights which turned the chandelier into a brilliant jewel until two of the clock or so on most nights were now turned down to guttering blue points, and the long, high room was shadowy and spectral.

In one corner lay a jumble of kindling—the remains of a couple of chairs smashed in a fight over a Watch Me game (the combatants were currently residing in the High Sheriff's drunk-cell). In another corner was a fairly large puddle of congealing puke. On the raised platform at the east end of the room stood a battered piano; propped against its bench was the ironwood club which belonged to Barkie, the saloon's bouncer and all-around tough man. Barkie himself, the naked mound of his scarred stomach rising above the waistband of his corduroy pants like a clot of bread dough, lay under the bench, snoring. In one hand he held a playing card: the deuce of diamonds.

At the west end of the room were the card tables. Two drunks lay with their heads on one of these, snoring and drooling on the green felt, their outstretched hands touching. Above them, on the wall, was a picture of Arthur, the Great King of Eld astride his white stallion, and a sign which read (in a curious mixture of High and Low Speech): ARGYOU NOT ABOUT THE HAND YOU ARE DELT IN CARDS OR LIFE.

Mounted behind the bar, which ran the length of the room, was a monstrous trophy: a two-headed elk with a rack of antlers like a forest grove and four glaring eyes. This beast was known to local habitues of the Travellers' as The Romp. None could have said why. Some wit had carefully drawn a pair of sow-titty condoms over the prongs of two of its antlers. Lying on the bar itself and directly beneath The Romp's disapproving gaze was Pettie the Trotter, one of the Travellers' dancers and gilly-girls . . . although Pettie's actual girlhood was well behind her now, and soon she would be reduced to doing her business on her knees behind the Travellers' rather than upstairs in one of the tiny cribs. Her plump legs were spread, one dangling over the bar on the inside, one on the outside, the filthy tangle of her skirt frothed up between. She breathed in long snores, occasionally twitching at the feet and fat fingers. The only other sounds were the hot summer wind outside and the soft, regular snap of cards being turned one by one.

A small table stood by itself near the batwing doors which gave upon the Hambry High Street; it was here that Coral Thorin, owner of the Travellers' Rest (and the Mayor's sister), sat on the nights when she descended from her suite "to be a part of the company." When she came down, she came down early—when there were still more steaks than whiskey being served across the old scratched bar—and went back up around the time that Sheb, the piano player, sat down and began to pound his hideous instrument. The Mayor himself never came in at all, although it was well-known that he owned at least a half-interest in the Travellers'. Clan Thorin enjoyed the money the place brought in; they just didn't enjoy the look of it after midnight, when the sawdust spread on the floor began to soak up the spilled beer and the spilled blood. Yet there was a hard streak in Coral, who had twenty years before been what was called "a wild child." She was younger than her political brother, not so thin, and good-looking in a large-eyed, weasel-headed way. No one sat at her table during the saloon's operating hours—Barkie would have put a stop to anyone who tried, and double-quick—but operating hours were over now, the drunks mostly gone or passed out upstairs, Sheb curled up and fast asleep in the corner behind his piano. The softheaded boy who cleaned the place had been gone since two o' the clock or so (chased out by jeers and insults and a few flying beer-glasses, as he always was; Roy Depape in particular had no love in his heart for that particular lad). He would be back around nine or so, to begin readying the old party-palace for another night of hilarity, but until then the man sitting at Mistress Thorin's table had the place to himself.

A game of Patience was laid out before him: black on

red, red on black, the partially formed Square o' Court above all, just as it was in the affairs of men. In his left hand the player held the remains of the deck. As he flipped the cards up, one by one, the tattoo on his right hand moved. It was disconcerting somehow, as if the coffin were breathing. The card-player was an oldish fellow, not as thin as the Mayor or his sister, but thin. His long white hair straggled down his back. He was deeply tanned, except for his neck, where he always burned; the flesh there hung in scant wattles. He wore a mustache so long the ragged white ends hung nearly to his jaw—a sham gunslinger's mustache, many thought it, but no one used the word "sham" to Eldred Jonas's face. He wore a white silk shirt, and a black-handled revolver hung low on his hip. His large, red-rimmed eyes looked sad on first glance. A second, closer look showed them only to be watery. Of emotion they were as dead as the eyes of The Romp.

He turned up the Ace of Wands. No place for it. "Pah, you bugger," he said in an odd, reedy voice. It quavered, as well, like the voice of a man on the verge of tears. It fit perfectly with his damp and red-rimmed eyes. He swept the cards together.

Before he could reshuffle, a door opened and closed softly upstairs. Jonas put the cards aside and dropped his hand to the butt of his gun. Then, as he recognized the sound of Reynolds's boots coming along the gallery, he let go of the gun and drew his tobacco-pouch from his belt instead. The hem of the cloak Reynolds always wore came into view, and then he was coming down the stairs, his face freshly washed and his curly red hair hanging about his ears. Vain of his looks was dear old Mr. Reynolds, and why not? He'd sent his cock on its exploring way up more damp and cozy cracks than Jonas had ever seen in his life, and Jonas was twice his age.

At the bottom of the stairs Reynolds walked along the

bar, pausing to squeeze one of Pettie's plump thighs, and then crossed to where Jonas sat with his makings and his deck of cards.

"Evening, Eldred."

"Morning, Clay." Jonas opened the sack, took out a paper, and sprinkled tobacco into it. His voice shook, but his hands were steady. "Like a smoke?"

"I could do with one."

Reynolds pulled out a chair, turned it around, and sat with his forearms crossed on its back. When Jonas handed him the cigarette, Reynolds danced it along the backs of his fingers, an old gunslinger trick. The Big Coffin Hunters were full of old gunslinger tricks.

"Where's Roy? With Her Nibs?" They had been in Hambry a little over a month now, and in that time Depape had conceived a passion for a fifteen-year-old whore named Deborah. Her bowlegged clumping walk and her way of squinting off into the distance led Jonas to suspect she was just another cowgirl from a long line of them, but she had high-hat ways. It was Clay who had started calling the girl Her Nibs, or Her Majesty, or sometimes (when drunk) "Roy's Coronation Cunt."

Reynolds now nodded. "It's like he's drunk on her."

"He'll be all right. He ain't throwing us over for some little snuggle-bunny with pimples on her tits. Why, she's so ignorant she can't spell cat. Not so much as cat, no. I asked her."

Jonas made a second cigarette, drew a sulfur match from the sack, and popped it alight with his thumbnail. He lit Reynolds's first, then his own.

A small yellow cur came in under the batwing doors. The men watched it in silence, smoking. It crossed the room, first sniffed at the curdled vomit in the corner, then began to eat it. Its stub of a tail wagged back and forth as it dined.

Reynolds nodded toward the admonition not to argue about the cards you were dealt. "That mutt'd understand that, I'd say."

"Not at all, not at all," Jonas demurred. "Just a dog is all he is, a spew-eating dog. I heard a horse twenty minutes ago. First on the come, then on the go. Would it have been one of our hired watchmen?"

"You don't miss a trick, do you?"

"Don't pay to, no, don't pay a bit. Was it?"

"Yep. Fellow who works for one of the small freeholders out along the east end of the Drop. He seen 'em come in. Three. Young. Babies." Reynolds pronounced this last as they did in the North'rd Baronies: *babbies.* "Nothing to worry of."

"Now, now, we don't know that," Jonas said, his quavering voice making him sound like a temporizing old man. "Young eyes see far, they say."

"Young eyes see what they're pointed at," Reynolds replied. The dog trotted past him, licking its chops. Reynolds helped it on its way with a kick the cur was not quite quick enough to avoid. It scuttled back out under the batwings, uttering little *yike-yike* sounds that made Barkie snort thickly from his place of rest beneath the piano bench. His hand opened and the playing card dropped out of it.

"Maybe so, maybe not," Jonas said. "In any case, they're Affiliation brats, sons of big estates off in the Green Somewhere, if Rimer and that fool he works for have it straight. That means we'll be very, very careful. Walk easy, like on eggshells. Why, we've got three more months here, at least! And those young'uns may be here that whole time, counting this 'n counting that and putting it all down on paper. Folks counting things ain't good for us right now. Not for men in the resupply business."

"Come on! It's make-work, that's all—a slap on the wrist for getting in trouble. Their daddies—"

"Their daddies know Farson's in charge of the whole Southwest Edge now, and sitting on high ground. The brats may know the same—that playtime's purt' near over for the Affiliation and all its pukesome royalty. Can't know, Clay. With folks like these, you can't know which way they'll jump. At the very least, they may try to do a half-decent job just to try and get on the good side o' their parents again. We'll know better when we see em, but I tell you one thing: we can't just put guns to the backs of their heads and drop them like broke-leg hosses if they see the wrong thing. Their daddies might be mad at em alive, but I think they'd be very tender of em dead—that's just the way daddies are. We'll want to be trig, Clay; as trig as we can be."

"Better leave Depape out of it, then."

"Roy will be fine," Jonas said in his quavery voice. He dropped the stub of his cigarette to the floor and crushed it under his bootheel. He looked up at The Romp's glassy eyes and squinted, as if calculating. "Tonight, your friend said? They arrived tonight, these brats?"

"Yep."

"They'll be in to see Avery tomorrow, then, I reckon." This was Herk Avery, High Sheriff of Mejis and Chief Constable of Hambry, a large man who was as loose as a trundle of laundry.

"Reckon so," Clay Reynolds said. "To present their papers 'n all."

"Yes, sir, yes indeedy. How-d'you-do, and how-d'you-do, and how-d'you-do again."

Reynolds said nothing. He often didn't understand Jonas, but he had been riding with him since the age of fifteen, and knew it was usually better not to ask for enlightenment. If you did, you were apt to end up listening to a cult-manni lecture about the other worlds the old buzzard had visited through what he called "the special doors." As far as Reynolds was concerned, there were enough ordinary doors in the world to keep him busy.

"I'll speak to Rimer and Rimer'll talk to the Sheriff about where they should stay," Jonas said. "I think the bunkhouse at the old Bar K ranch. You know where I mean?"

Reynolds did. In a Barony like Mejis, you got to know the few landmarks in a hurry. The Bar K was a deserted spread of land northwest of town, not too far from that weird squalling canyon. They burned at the mouth of the canyon every fall, and once, six or seven years ago, the wind had shifted and gone back wrong and burned most of the Bar K to the ground—barns, stables, the home place. It had spared the bunkhouse, however, and that would be a good spot for three tenderfeet from the Inners. It was away from the Drop; it was also away from the oilpatch.

"Ye like it, don't ye?" Jonas asked, putting on a hick Hambry accent. "Aye, ye like it very much, I can see ye do, my cully. Ye know what they say in Cressia? 'If ye'd steal the silver from the dining room, first put the dog in the pantry.' "

Reynolds nodded. It was good advice. "And those trucks? Those what-do-you-callums, tankers?"

"Fine where they are," Jonas said. "Not that we could move em now without attracting the wrong kind of attention, eh? You and Roy want to go out there and cover them with brush. Lay it on nice and thick. Day after tomorrow you'll do it."

"And where will you be while we're flexing our muscles out at Citgo?"

"By daylight? Preparing for dinner at Mayor's House, you clod—the dinner Thorin will be giving to introduce his guests from the Great World to the shitpicky society of the smaller one." Jonas began making another cigarette. He gazed up at The Romp rather than at what he was doing, and still spilled barely a scrap of tobacco. "A bath, a shave, a trim of these tangled old man's locks . . . I might even wax my mustache, Clay, what do you say to that?"

"Don't strain yourself, Eldred."

Jonas laughed, the sound shrill enough to make Barkie mutter and Pettie stir uneasily on her makeshift bar-top bed.

"So Roy and I aren't invited to this fancy do."

"You'll be invited, oh yes, you'll be invited very warmly," Jonas said, and handed Reynolds the fresh cigarette. He began making another for himself. "I'll offer your excuses. I'll do you boys proud, count on me. Strong men may weep."

"All so we can spend the day out there in the dust and stink, covering those hulks. You're too kind, Jonas."

"I'll be asking questions, as well," Jonas said dreamily. "Drifting here and there . . . looking spruce, smelling of bayberries . . . and asking my little questions. I've known folks in our line of trade who'll go to a fat, jolly fellow to find out the gossip—a saloon-keeper or bartender, perhaps a livery stable owner or one of the chubby fellows who always hangs about the jail or the courthouse with his thumbs tucked into his vest pockets. As for myself, Clay, I find that a woman's best, and the narrower the better—one with more nose than tits sticking off her. I look for one who don't paint her lips and keeps her hair scooped back against her head."

"You have someone in mind?"

"Yar. Cordelia Delgado's her name."

"Delgado?"

"You know the name, it's on the lips of everyone in this town, I reckon. Susan Delgado, our esteemed Mayor's

soon-to-be gilly. Cordelia's her auntie. Now here's a fact
of human nature I've found: folk are more apt to talk to
someone like her, who plays them close, than they are
to the local jolly types who'll buy you a drink. And that
lady plays them close. I'm going to slip in next to her at
that dinner, and I'm going to compliment her on the perfume I doubt like hell she'll be wearing, and I'm going to
keep her wineglass full. Now, how sounds that for a plan?"

"A plan for what? That's what I want to know."

"For the game of Castles we may have to play," Jonas
said, and all the lightness dropped out of his voice.
"We're to believe that these boys have been sent here
more as punishment than to do any real job of work. It
sounds plausible, too. I've known rakes in my time, and
it sounds plausible, indeed. I believe it each day until
about three in the morning, and then a little doubt sets
in. And do you know what, Clay?"

Reynolds shook his head.

"I'm *right* to doubt. Just as I was right to go with Rimer
to old man Thorin and convince him that Farson's glass
would be better with the witch-woman, for the nonce.
She'll keep it in a place where a *gunslinger* couldn't find
it, let alone a nosy lad who's yet to have his first piece
of arse. These are strange times. A storm's coming. And
when you know the wind is going to blow, it's best to
keep your gear battened down."

He looked at the cigarette he had made. He had been
dancing it along the backs of his knuckles, as Reynolds
had done earlier. Jonas pushed back the fall of his hair
and tucked the cigarette behind his ear.

"I don't want to smoke," he said, standing up and
stretching. His back made small crackling sounds. "I'm
crazy to smoke at this hour of the morning. Too many
cigarettes are apt to keep an old man like me awake."

He walked toward the stairs, squeezing Pettie's bare

leg as he went by, also as Reynolds had done. At the foot of the stairs he looked back.

"I don't want to kill them. Things are delicate enough without that. I'll smell quite a little wrong on them and not lift a finger, no, not a single finger of my hand. But . . . I'd like to make them clear on their place in the great scheme o' things."

"Give them a sore paw."

Jonas brightened. "Yessir, partner, maybe a sore paw's just what I'd like to give them. Make them think twice about tangling with the Big Coffin Hunters later on, when it matters. Make them swing wide around us when they see us in their road. Yessir, that's something to think about. It really is."

He started up the stairs, chuckling a little, his limp quite pronounced—it got worse late at night. It was a limp Roland's old teacher, Cort, might have recognized, for Cort had seen the blow which caused it. Cort's own father had dealt it with an ironwood club, breaking Eldred Jonas's leg in the yard behind the Great Hall of Gilead before taking the boy's weapon and sending him west, gunless, into exile.

Eventually, the man the boy had become had found a gun, of course; the exiles always did, if they looked hard enough. That such guns could never be quite the same as the big ones with the sandalwood grips might haunt them for the rest of their lives, but those who needed guns could still find them, even in this world.

Reynolds watched until he was gone, then took his seat at Coral Thorin's desk, shuffled the cards, and continued the game which Jonas had left half-finished.

Outside, the sun was coming up.

CHAPTER FIVE

Welcome To Town

I

Two nights after arriving in the Barony of Mejis, Roland, Cuthbert, and Alain rode their mounts beneath an adobe arch with the words COME IN PEACE inscribed above it. Beyond was a cobblestone courtyard lit with torches. The resin which coated these had been doctored somehow so that the torches glowed different colors: green, orangey-red, a kind of sputtery pink that made Roland think of fireworks. He could hear the sound of guitars, the murmur of voices, the laughter of women. The air was redolent of those smells which would always remind him of Mejis: sea-salt, oil, and pine.

"I don't know if I can do this," Alain muttered. He was a big boy with a mop of unruly blond hair spilling out from under his stockman's hat. He had cleaned up well—they all had—but Alain, no social butterfly under the best of circumstances, looked scared to death. Cuthbert was doing better, but Roland guessed his old friend's patina of insouciance didn't go very deep. If there was to be leading done here, he would have to do it.

"You'll be fine," he told Alain. "Just—"

"Oh, he *looks* fine," Cuthbert said with a nervous laugh as they crossed the courtyard. Beyond it was Mayor's House, a sprawling, many-winged adobe hacienda that seemed to spill light and laughter from every window. "White as a sheet, ugly as a—"

"Shut up," Roland said curtly, and the teasing smile tumbled off Cuthbert's face at once. Roland noted this, then turned to Alain again. "Just don't drink anything with alcohol in it. You know what to say on that account. Remember the rest of our story, too. Smile. Be pleasant. Use what social graces you have. Remember how the Sheriff fell all over himself to make us feel welcome."

Alain nodded at that, looking a little more confident.

"In the matter of social graces," Cuthbert said, "they won't have many themselves, so we should all be a step ahead."

Roland nodded, then saw that the bird's skull was back on the horn of Cuthbert's saddle. "And get rid of that!"

Looking guilty, Cuthbert stuffed "the lookout" hurriedly into his saddlebag. Two men wearing white jackets, white pants, and sandals were coming forward, bowing and smiling.

"Keep your heads," Roland said, lowering his voice. "Both of you. Remember why you're here. And remember the faces of your fathers." He clapped Alain, who still looked doubtful, on the shoulder. Then he turned to the hostlers. "Goodeven, gents," he said. "May your days be long upon the earth."

They both grinned, their teeth flashing in the extravagant torchlight. The older one bowed. "And your own as well, young masters. Welcome to Mayor's House."

2

The High Sheriff had welcomed them the day before every bit as happily as the hostlers.

So far *everyone* had greeted them happily, even the carters they had passed on their way into town, and that alone made Roland feel suspicious and on his guard. He told himself he was likely being foolish—of *course* the locals were friendly and helpful, that was why they had been sent here, because Mejis was both out-of-the-way and loyal to the Affiliation—and it probably *was* foolish, but he thought it best to be on close watch, just the same. To be a trifle nervous. The three of them were little more than children, after all, and if they fell into trouble here, it was apt to be as a result of taking things at face value.

The combined Sheriff's office and jail o' Barony was on Hill Street, overlooking the bay. Roland didn't know for sure, but guessed that few if any hungover drunks and wife-beaters anywhere else in Mid-World woke up to such picturesque views: a line of many-colored boathouses to the south, the docks directly below, with boys and old men line-fishing while the women mended nets and sails; beyond them, Hambry's small fleet moving back and forth on the sparkling blue water of the bay, setting their nets in the morning, pulling them in the afternoon.

Most buildings on the High Street were adobe, but up here, overlooking Hambry's business section, they were as squat and bricky as any narrow lane in Gilead's Old Quarter. Well kept, too, with wrought-iron gates in front of most and tree-shaded paths. The roofs were orange tile, the shutters closed against the summer sun. It was hard to believe, riding down this street with their horses' hoofs clocking on the swept cobbles, that the northwestern side of the Affiliation—the ancient land of Eld, Arthur's kingdom—could be on fire and in danger of falling.

The jailhouse was just a larger version of the post office and land office; a smaller version of the Town Gathering

Hall. Except, of course, for the bars on the windows facing down toward the small harbor.

Sheriff Herk Avery was a big-bellied man in a lawman's khaki pants and shirt. He must have been watching them approach through the spyhole in the center of the jail's iron-banded front door, because the door was thrown open before Roland could even reach for the turn-bell in the center. Sheriff Avery appeared on the stoop, his belly preceding him as a baliff may precede My Lord Judge into court. His arms were thrown wide in the most amiable of greetings.

He bowed deeply to them (Cuthbert said later he was afraid the man might overbalance and go rolling down the steps; perhaps go rolling all the way down to the harbor) and wished them repeated goodmorns, tapping away at the base of his throat like a madman the whole while. His smile was so wide it looked as if it might cut his head clean in two. Three deputies with a distinctly farmerish look about them, dressed in khaki like the Sheriff, crowded into the door behind Avery and gawked. That was what it was, all right, a gawk; there was just no other word for that sort of openly curious and totally unself-conscious stare.

Avery shook each boy by the hand, continuing to bow as he did so, and nothing Roland said could get him to stop until he was done. When he finally was, he showed them inside. The office was delightfully cool in spite of the beating midsummer sun. That was the advantage of brick, of course. It was big as well, and cleaner than any High Sheriff's office Roland had ever been in before . . . and he had been in at least half a dozen over the last three years, accompanying his father on several short trips and one longer patrol-swing.

There was a rolltop desk in the center, a notice-board to the right of the door (the same sheets of foolscap had been scribbled on over and over; paper was a rare commodity in Mid-World), and, in the far corner, two rifles in a padlocked case. These were such ancient blunderbusses that Roland wondered if there was ammunition for them. He wondered if they would fire, come to that. To the left of the gun-case, an open door gave on the jail itself—three cells on each side of a short corridor, and a smell of strong lye soap drifting out.

They've cleaned for our coming, Roland thought. He was amused, touched, and uneasy. *Cleaned it as though we were a troop of Inner Barony horse—career soldiers who might want to stage a hard inspection instead of three lads serving punishment detail.*

But was such nervous care on the part of their hosts really so strange? They were from New Canaan, after all, and folk in this tucked-away corner of the world might well see them as a species of visiting royalty.

Sheriff Avery introduced his deputies. Roland shook hands with all of them, not trying to memorize their names. It was Cuthbert who took care of names, and it was a rare occasion when he dropped one. The third, a bald fellow with a monocle hanging around his neck on a ribbon, actually dropped to one knee before them.

"Don't do that, ye great idiot!" Avery cried, yanking him back up by the scruff of his neck. "What kind of a bumpkin will they think ye? Besides, you've embarrassed them, so ye have!"

"That's all right," Roland said (he was, in fact, very embarrassed, although trying not to show it). "We're really nothing at all special, you know—"

"Nothing special!" Avery said, laughing. His belly, Roland noticed, did not shake as one might have expected it to do; it was harder than it looked. The same might be true of its owner. "Nothing special, he says! Five hundred mile or more from the In-World they've come, our first official visitors from the Affiliation since a gunslinger passed through on the Great Road four year ago, and yet he says they're nothing special! Would ye sit, my boys? I've got *graf*, which ye won't want so early in the day— p'raps not at all, given your ages (and if you'll forgive me for statin so bald the obvious fact of yer youth, for youth's not a thing to be ashamed of, so it's not, we were all young once), and I also have white iced tea, which I recommend most hearty, as Dave's wife makes it and she's a dab hand with most any potable."

Roland looked at Cuthbert and Alain, who nodded and smiled (and tried not to look all at sea), then back at Sheriff Avery. White tea would go down a treat in a dusty throat, he said.

One of the deputies went to fetch it, chairs were produced and set in a row at one side of Sheriff Avery's roll-top, and the business of the day commenced.

"You know who ye are and where ye hail from, and I know the same," Sheriff Avery said, sitting down in his own chair (it uttered a feeble groan beneath his bulk but held steady). "I can hear In-World in yer voices, but more important, I can see it in yer faces.

"Yet we hold to the old ways here in Hambry, sleepy and rural as we may be; aye, we hold to our course and remember the faces of our fathers as well's we can. So, although I'd not keep yer long from yer duties, and if ye'll forgive me for the impertinence, I'd like a look at any papers and documents of passage ye might just happen to've brought into town with ye."

They just "happened" to have brought *all* of their papers into town with them, as Roland was sure Sheriff Avery well knew they would. He went through them quite slowly for a man who'd promised not to hold them from their duties, tracing the well-folded sheets (the linen content so high that the documents were perhaps closer to cloth than paper) with one pudgy finger, his lips moving. Every now and then the finger would reverse as he reread a line. The two other deputies stood behind him, looking sagely down over his large shoulders. Roland wondered if either could actually read.

William Dearborn. Drover's son.

Richard Stockworth. Rancher's son.

Arthur Heath. Stockline breeder's son.

The identification document belonging to each was signed by an attestor—James Reed (of Hemphill) in the case of Dearborn, Piet Ravenhead (of Pennilton) in the case of Stockworth, Lucas Rivers (of Gilead) in the case of Heath. All in order, descriptions nicely matched. The papers were handed back with profuse thanks. Roland next handed Avery a letter which he took from his wallet with some care. Avery handled it in the same fashion, his eyes growing wide as he saw the frank at the bottom. "'Pon my soul, boys! 'Twas a gunslinger wrote this!"

"Aye, so it was," Cuthbert agreed in a voice of wonder. Roland kicked his ankle—hard—without taking his respectful eyes from Avery's face.

The letter above the frank was from one Steven Deschain of Gilead, a gunslinger (which was to say a knight, squire, peacemaker, and Baron . . . the last title having almost no meaning in the modern day, despite all John Farson's ranting) of the twenty-ninth generation descended from Arthur of Eld, on the side line of descent (the long-descended get of one of Arthur's many gillies, in other words). To Mayor Hartwell Thorin, Chancellor Kimba Rimer, and High Sheriff Herkimer Avery, it sent greetings and recommended to their notice the three young men who delivered this document, Masters Dearborn, Stockworth, and Heath. These had been sent on special mission from the Affiliation to serve as counters of all materials which might serve the Affiliation in time of need (the word *war* was omitted from the document, but glowed between every line). Steven Deschain, on behalf of the Affiliation of Baronies, exhorted Misters Thorin, Rimer, and Avery to afford the Affiliation's nominated counters every help in their service, and to be particularly careful in the enumerations of all livestock, all supplies of food, and all forms of transport. Dearborn, Stockworth, and Heath would be in Mejis for at least three months, Deschain wrote, possibly as long as a year. The document finished by inviting any or all of the addressed public officials to "write us word of these young men and their deportment, in all detail as you shall imagine of interest to us." And, it begged, "Do not stint in this matter, if you love us."

Tell us if they behaved themselves, in other words. Tell us if they've learned their lesson.

The deputy with the monocle came back while the High Sheriff was perusing this document. He carried a tray loaded with four glasses of white tea and bent down with it like a butler. Roland murmured thanks and handed the glasses around. He took the last for himself, raised it to his lips, and saw Alain looking at him, his blue eyes bright in his stolid face.

Alain shook his glass slightly—just enough to make the ice tinkle—and Roland responded with the barest sliver of a nod. He had expected cool tea from a jug kept in a nearby spring-house, but there were actual chunks of ice in the glasses. Ice in high summer. It was interesting.

And the tea was, as promised, delicious.

Avery finished the letter and handed it back to Roland with the air of one passing on a holy relic. "Ye want to keep that safe about yer person, Will Dearborn—aye, very safe indeed!"

"Yes, sir." He tucked the letter and his identification

back into his purse. His friends "Richard" and "Arthur" were doing the same.

"This is excellent white tea, sir," Alain said. "I've never had better."

"Aye," Avery said, sipping from his own glass. " 'Tis the honey that makes it so fearsome. Eh, Dave?"

The deputy with the monocle smiled from his place by the notice-board. "I believe so, but Judy don't like to say. She had the recipe from her mother."

"Aye, we must remember the faces of our mothers, too, so we must." Sheriff Avery looked sentimental for a moment, but Roland had an idea that the face of his mother was the furthest thing from the big man's mind just then. He turned to Alain, and sentiment was replaced by a surprising shrewdness.

"Ye're wondering about the ice, Master Stockworth."

Alain started. "Well, I . . ."

"Ye expected no such amenity in a backwater like Hambry, I'll warrant," Avery said, and although there was a joshing quality on top of his voice, Roland thought there was something else entirely underneath.

He doesn't like us. He doesn't like what he thinks of as our "city ways." He hasn't known us long enough to know what kind of ways we have, if any at all, but already he doesn't like them. He thinks we're a trio of snotnoses; that we see him and everyone else here as country bumpkins.

"Not just Hambry," Alain said quietly. "Ice is as rare in the Inner Arc these days as anywhere else, Sheriff Avery. When I grew up, I saw it mostly as a special treat at birthday parties and such."

"There was always ice on Glowing Day," Cuthbert put in. He spoke with very un-Cuthbertian quiet. "Except for the fireworks, that's what we liked about it most."

"Is that so, is that so," Sheriff Avery said in an amazed,

wonders-will-never-cease tone. Avery perhaps didn't like them riding in like this, didn't like having to take up what he would probably call "half the damn morning" with them; he didn't like their clothes, their fancy identification papers, their accents, or their youth. Least of all their youth. Roland could understand all that, but wondered if it was the whole story. If there was something else going on here, what was it?

"There's a gas-fired refrigerator and stove in the Town Gathering Hall," Avery said. "Both work. There's plenty of earth-gas out at Citgo—that's the oilpatch east of town. Yer passed it on yer way in, I wot."

They nodded.

"Stove's nobbut a curiosity these days—a history lesson for the schoolchildren—but the refrigerator comes in handy, so it does." Avery held up his glass and looked through the side. "'Specially in summer." He sipped some tea, smacked his lips, and smiled at Alain. "You see? No mystery."

"I'm surprised you haven't found use for the oil," Roland said. "No generators in town, Sheriff?"

"Aye, there be four or five," Avery said. "The biggest is out at Francis Lengyll's Rocking B ranch, and I recall when it useter run. It's HONDA. Do ye kennit that name, boys? HONDA?"

"I've seen it once or twice," Roland said, "on old motor-driven bicycles."

"Aye? In any case, none of the generators will run on the oil from the Citgo patch. 'Tis too thick. Tarry goo, is all. We have no refineries here."

"I see," Alain said. "In any case, ice in summer's a treat. However it comes to the glass." He let one of the chunks slip into his mouth, and crunched it between his teeth.

Avery looked at him a moment longer, as if to make sure the subject was closed, then switched his gaze back to Roland. His fat face was once more radiant with his broad, untrustworthy smile.

"Mayor Thorin has asked me to extend ye his very best greetings, and convey his regrets for not bein here today—very busy is our Lord Mayor, very busy indeed. But he's laid on a dinner-party at Mayor's House tomorrow evening—seven o' the clock for most folk, eight for you young fellows . . . so you can make a bit of an entrance, I imagine, add a touch o' drama, like. And I need not tell such as yourselves, who've probably attended more such parties than I've had hot dinners, that it would be best to arrive pretty much on the dot."

"Is it *fancy*-dress?" Cuthbert asked uneasily. "Because we've come a long way, almost four hundred wheels, and we didn't pack formal wear and sashes, none of us."

Avery was chuckling—more honestly this time, Roland thought, perhaps because he felt "Arthur" had displayed a streak of unsophistication and insecurity. "Nay, young master, Thorin understands ye've come to do a job—next door to workin cowboys, ye be! 'Ware they don't have ye out draggin nets in the bay next!"

From the corner, Dave—the deputy with the monocle—honked unexpected laughter. Perhaps it was the sort of joke you had to be local to understand, Roland thought.

"Wear the best ye have, and ye'll be fine. There'll be no one there in sashes, in any case—that's not how things are done in Hambry." Again Roland was struck by the man's constant smiling denigration of his town and Barony . . . and the resentment of the outsiders which lay just beneath it.

"In any case, ye'll find yerselves working more than playing tomorrow night, I imagine. Hart's invited all the large ranchers, stockliners, and livestock owners from this part of the Barony . . . not that there's so many, you understand, bein as how Mejis is next door to desert once you get west o' the Drop. But everyone whose goods and chattel you've been sent to count will be there, and I think you'll find all of them loyal Affiliation men, ready and eager to help. There's Francis Lengyll of the Rocking B . . . John Croydon of the Piano Ranch . . . Henry Wertner, who's the Barony's stockliner as well as a horse-breeder in his own right . . . Hash Renfrew, who owns the Lazy Susan, the biggest horse-ranch in Mejis (not that it's much by the standards you fellows are used to, I wot) . . . and there'll be others, as well. Rimer'll introduce you, and get you about your business right smart."

Roland nodded and turned to Cuthbert. "You'll want to be on your mettle tomorrow night."

Cuthbert nodded. "Don't fear me, Will, I'll note em all."

Avery sipped more tea, eyeing them over his glass with a roguish expression so false it made Roland want to squirm.

"Most of em's got daughters of marriageable age, and they'll bring em. You boys want to look out."

Roland decided he'd had enough tea and hypocrisy for one morning. He nodded, emptied his glass, smiled (hoping his looked more genuine than Avery's now looked to him), and got to his feet. Cuthbert and Alain took the cue and did likewise.

"Thank you for the tea, and for the welcome," Roland said. "Please send a message to Mayor Thorin, thanking him for his kindness and telling him that he'll see us tomorrow, at eight o' the clock, prompt."

"Aye. So I will."

Roland then turned to Dave. That worthy was so surprised to be noticed again that he recoiled, almost bumping his head on the notice-board. "And please thank your wife for the tea. It was wonderful."

"I will. Thankee-sai."

They went back outside, High Sheriff Avery herding them along like a genial, overweight sheepdog.

"As to where you'll locate—" he began as they descended the steps and started down the walk. As soon as they hit the sunshine, he began to sweat.

"Oh, land, I forgot to ask you about that," Roland said, knocking the heel of his hand against his forehead. "We've camped out on that long slope, lots of horses as you go down the turf, I'm sure you know where I mean—"

"The Drop, aye."

"—but without permission, because we don't yet know who to ask."

"That'd be John Croydon's land, and I'm sure he wouldn't begrudge ye, but we mean to do ye better than that. There's a spread northwest of here, the Bar K. Used to b'long to the Garber family, but they gave it up and moved on after a fire. Now it b'longs to the Horsemen's Association—that's a little local group of farmers and ranchers. I spoke to Francis Lengyll about you fellows— he's the H.A. president just current—and he said 'We'll put em out to the old Garber place, why not?' "

"Why not?" Cuthbert agreed in a gentle, musing voice. Roland shot him a sharp glance, but Cuthbert was looking down at the harbor, where the small fishing boats skittered to and fro like waterbugs.

"Aye, just what I said, 'Why not, indeed?' I said. The home place burned to a cinder, but the bunkhouse still stands; so does the stable and the cook-shack next door to it. On Mayor Thorin's orders, I've taken the liberty of stocking the larder and having the bunkhouse swept out and spruced up a little. Ye may see the occasional bug, but nothing that'll bite or sting . . . and no snakes, unless there's a few under the floor, and if there are, let em stay there's what I say. Hey, boys? Let em stay there!"

"Let em stay there, right under the floor where they're happy," Cuthbert agreed, still gazing down at the harbor with his arms folded over his chest.

Avery gave him a brief, uncertain glance, his smile flickering a bit at the corners. Then he turned back to Roland, and the smile shone out strongly once more. "There's no holes in the roof, lad, and if it rains, ye'll be dry. What think ye of that? Does it sound well to ye?"

"Better than we deserve. I think that you've been very efficient and Mayor Thorin's been far too kind." And he *did* think that. The question was why. "But we appreciate his thoughtfulness. Don't we, boys?"

Cuthbert and Alain made vigorous assent.

"And we accept with thanks."

Avery nodded. "I'll tell him. Go safely, boys."

They had reached the hitching rail. Avery once more shook hands all around, this time saving his keenest looks for their horses.

"Until tomorrow night, then, young gents?"

"Tomorrow night," Roland agreed.

"Will ye be able to find the Bar K on your own, do yer think?"

Again Roland was struck by the man's unspoken contempt and unconscious condescension. Yet perhaps it was to the good. If the High Sheriff thought they were stupid, who knew what might come of it?

"We'll find it," Cuthbert said, mounting up. Avery was looking suspiciously at the rook's skull on the horn of Cuthbert's saddle. Cuthbert saw him looking, but for once managed to keep his mouth shut. Roland was both amazed and pleased by this unexpected reticence. "Fare you well, Sheriff."

"And you, boy."

He stood there by the hitching post, a large man in a khaki shirt with sweat-stains around the armpits and black boots that looked too shiny for a working sheriff's feet. *And where's the horse that could support him through a day of range-riding?* Roland thought. *I'd like to see the cut of that Cayuse.*

Avery waved to them as they went. The other deputies came down the walk, Deputy Dave in the forefront. They waved, too.

3

The moment the Affliation brats mounted on their fathers' expensive horseflesh were around the corner and headed downhill to the High Street, the sheriff and the deputies stopped waving. Avery turned to Dave Hollis, whose expression of slightly stupid awe had been replaced by one marginally more intelligent.

"What think ye, Dave?"

Dave lifted his monocle to his mouth and began to nibble nervously at its brass edging, a habit about which Sheriff Avery had long since ceased to nag him. Even Dave's wife, Judy, had given up on that score, and Judy Hollis—Judy Wertner that was—was a fair engine when it came to getting her own way.

"Soft," Dave said. "Soft as eggs just dropped out of a chicken's ass."

"Mayhap," Avery said, putting his thumbs in his belt and rocking enormously back and forth, "but the one did most of the talking, him in the flathead hat, he doesn't *think* he's soft."

"Don't matter what he *thinks*," Dave said, still nibbling at his eyeglass. "He's in Hambry, now. He may have to change his way of thinking to our'n."

Behind him, the other deputies laughed. Even Avery smiled. They would leave the rich boys alone if the rich boys left them alone—those were orders, straight from Mayor's House—but Avery had to admit that he wouldn't mind a little dust-up with them, so he wouldn't. He would enjoy putting his boot into the balls of the one with that idiotic bird's skull on his saddle-horn—standing there and mocking him, he'd been, thinking all the while that Herk Avery was too country-dumb to know what he was up to— but the thing he'd *really* enjoy would be beating the cool look from the eyes of the boy in the flathead preacher's hat, seeing a hotter expression of fear rise up in them as Mr. Will Dearborn of Hemphill realized that New Canaan was far away and his rich father couldn't help him.

"Aye," he said, clapping Dave on the shoulder. "Mayhap he'll have to change his way of thinking." He smiled—one very different from any of those he had shown the Affiliation counters. "Mayhap they all will."

4

The three boys rode in single file until they were past the Travellers' Rest (a young and obviously retarded man with kinky black hair looked up from scrubbing the brick stoop and waved to them; they waved back). Then they moved up abreast, Roland in the middle.

"What did you think of our new friend, the High Sheriff?" Roland asked.

"I have no opinion," Cuthbert said brightly. "No, none at all. Opinion is politics, and politics is an evil which has caused many a fellow to be hung while he's still young and pretty." He leaned forward and tapped the rook's skull with his knuckles. "The lookout didn't care for him, though. I'm sorry to say that our faithful lookout thought Sheriff Avery a fat bag of guts without a trustworthy bone in his body."

Roland turned to Alain. "And you, young Master Stockworth?"

Alain considered it for some time, as was his way, chewing a piece of grass he'd bent oversaddle to pluck from his side of the road. At last he said: "If he came upon us burning in the street, I don't think he'd piss on us to put us out."

Cuthbert laughed heartily at that. "And you, Will? How do you say, dear captain?"

"He doesn't interest me much . . . but one thing he said does. Given that the horse-meadow they call the Drop has to be at least thirty wheels long and runs five or more to the dusty desert, how do you suppose Sheriff Avery knew we were on the part of it that belongs to Croydon's Piano Ranch?"

They looked at him, first with surprise, then speculation. After a moment Cuthbert leaned forward and rapped once more on the rook's skull. "We're being watched, and you never reported it? No supper for you, sir, and it'll be the stockade the next time it happens!"

But before they had gone much farther, Roland's thoughts of Sheriff Avery gave way to more pleasant ones of Susan Delgado. He would see her the following night, of that he was sure. He wondered if her hair would be down.

He couldn't wait to find out.

5

Now here they were, at Mayor's House. *Let the game begin,* Roland thought, not clear on what that meant even as the phrase went through his mind, surely not thinking of Castles . . . not then.

The hostlers led their mounts away, and for a moment

the three of them stood at the foot of the steps—huddled, almost, as horses do in unfriendly weather—their beardless faces washed by the light of the torches. From inside, the guitars played and voices were raised in a fresh eddy of laughter.

"Do we knock?" Cuthbert asked. "Or just open and march in?"

Roland was spared answering. The main door of the *haci* was thrown open and two women stepped out, both wearing long white-collared dresses that reminded all three boys of the dresses stockmen's wives wore in their own part of the world. Their hair was caught back in snoods that sparkled with some bright diamondy stuff in the light of the torches.

The plumper of the two stepped forward, smiling, and dropped them a deep curtsey. Her earrings, which looked like square-cut firedims, flashed and bobbed. "You are the young men from the Affiliation, so you are, and welcome you are, as well. Goodeven, sirs, and may your days be long upon the earth!"

They bowed in unison, boots forward, and thanked her in an unintended chorus that made her laugh and clap her hands. The tall woman beside her offered them a smile as spare as her frame.

"I am Olive Thorin," the plump woman said, "the Mayor's wife. This is my sister-in-law, Coral."

Coral Thorin, still with that narrow smile (it barely creased her lips and touched her eyes not at all), dipped them a token curtsey. Roland, Cuthbert, and Alain bowed again over their outstretched legs.

"I welcome you to Seafront," Olive Thorin said, her dignity leavened and made pleasant by her artless smile, her obvious dazzlement at the appearance of her young visitors from In-World. "Come to our house with joy. I say so with all my heart, so I do."

"And so we will, madam," Roland said, "for your greeting has made us joyful." He took her hand, and, with no calculation whatever, raised it to his lips and kissed it. Her delighted laughter made him smile. He liked Olive Thorin on sight, and it was perhaps well he met someone of that sort early on, for, with the problematic exception of Susan Delgado, he met no one else he liked, no one else he trusted, all that night.

6

It was warm enough even with the Seabreeze, and the cloak- and coat-collector in the foyer looked as though he'd had little or no custom. Roland wasn't entirely surprised to see that it was Deputy Dave, his remaining bits of hair slicked back with some sort of gleaming grease and his monocle now lying on the snow-white breast of a houseman's jacket. Roland gave him a nod. Dave, his hands clasped behind his back, returned it.

Two men—Sheriff Avery and an elderly gent as gaunt as Old Doctor Death in a cartoon—came toward them. Beyond, through a pair of double doors now open wide, a whole roomful of people stood about with crystal punch-cups in their hands, talking and taking little bits of food from the trays which were circulating.

Roland had time for just one narrow-eyed glance toward Cuthbert: *Everything. Every name, every face . . . every nuance. Especially those.*

Cuthbert raised an eyebrow—his discreet version of a nod—and then Roland was pulled, willy-nilly, into the evening, his first real evening of service as a working gunslinger. And he had rarely worked harder.

Old Doctor Death turned out to be Kimba Rimer, Thorin's Chancellor and Minister of Inventory (Roland suspected the title had been made up special for their visit). He was easily five inches taller than Roland, who was considered tall in Gilead, and his skin was pale as candlewax. Not unhealthy-looking; just pale. Wings of iron-gray hair floated away from either side of his head, gossamer as cobwebs. The top of his skull was completely bald. Balanced on his whelk of a nose was a pince-nez.

"My boys!" he said, when the introductions had been made. He had the smooth, sadly sincere voice of a politician or an undertaker. "Welcome to Mejis! To Hambry! And to Seafront, our humble Mayor's House!"

"If this is humble, I should wonder at the palace your folk might build," Roland said. It was a mild enough remark, more pleasantry than witticism (he ordinarily left the wit to Bert), but Chancellor Rimer laughed hard. So did Sheriff Avery.

"Come, boys!" Rimer said, when he apparently felt he had expressed enough amusement. "The Mayor awaits you with impatience, I'm sure."

"Aye," said a timid voice from behind them. The skinny sister-in-law, Coral, had disappeared, but Olive Thorin was still there, looking up at the newcomers with her hands decorously clasped before that area of her body which might once have been her waist. She was still smiling her hopeful, pleasant smile. "Very eager to meet you, Hart is, very eager, indeed. Shall I conduct them, Kimba, or—"

"Nay, nay, you mustn't trouble yourself with so many other guests to attend," Rimer said.

"I suppose you're right." She curtseyed to Roland and his companions a final time, and although she still smiled and although the smile looked completely genuine to Roland, he thought: *She's unhappy about something, all the same. Desperately so, I think.*

"Gentlemen?" Rimer asked. The teeth in his smile were almost disconcertingly huge. "Will ye come?"

He led them past the grinning Sheriff and into the reception hall.

7

Roland was hardly overwhelmed by it; he had, after all, been in the Great Hall of Gilead—the Hall of the Grandfathers, it was sometimes called—and had even peeped down on the great party which was held there each year, the so-called Dance of Easterling, which marked the end of Wide Earth and the advent of Sowing. There were five chandeliers in the Great Hall instead of just one, and lit with electric bulbs rather than oil lamps. The dress of the partygoers (many of them expensive young men and women who had never done a hand's turn of work in their lives, a fact of which John Farson spoke at every opportunity) had been richer, the music had been fuller, the company of older and nobler lines which grew closer and closer together as they stretched back toward Arthur Eld, he of the white horse and unifying sword.

Yet there was life here, and plenty of it. There was a robustness that had been missing in Gilead, and not just at Easterling, either. The texture he felt as he stepped into the Mayor's House reception room was the sort of thing, Roland reflected, that you didn't entirely miss when it was gone, because it slipped away quietly and painlessly. Like blood from a vein cut in a tub filled with hot water.

The room—almost but not quite grand enough to be a hall—was circular, its panelled walls decorated by paintings (most quite bad) of previous Mayors. On a raised stand to the right of the doors leading into the dining area, four grinning guitarists in *tati* jackets and sombreros were playing something that sounded like a waltz with pepper on it. In the center of the floor was a table supporting two cut-glass punchbowls, one vast and grand, the other smaller and plainer. The white-jacketed fellow in charge of the dipping-out operations was another of Avery's deputies.

Contrary to what the High Sheriff had told them the day before, several of the men were wearing sashes of various colors, but Roland didn't feel too out of place in his white silk shirt, black string tie, and one pair of stove-pipe dress trousers. For every man wearing a sash, he saw three wearing the sort of dowdy, box-tailed coats that he associated with stockmen at church, and he saw several others (younger men, for the most part) who weren't wearing coats at all. Some of the women wore jewelry (though nothing so expensive as sai Thorin's firedim earrings), and few looked as if they'd missed many meals, but they also wore clothes Roland recognized: the long, round-collared dresses, usually with the lace fringe of a colored underskirt showing below the hem, the dark shoes with low heels, the snoods (most sparkling with gem-dust, as those of Olive and Coral Thorin had been).

And then he saw one who was very different.

It was Susan Delgado, of course, shimmering and almost too beautiful to look at in a blue silk dress with a high waist and a square-cut bodice which showed the tops of her breasts. Around her neck was a sapphire pendant that made Olive Thorin's earrings look like paste. She stood next to a man wearing a sash the color of coals in a hot woodfire. That deep orange-red was the Barony's color, and Roland supposed that the man was their host, but for the moment Roland barely saw him. His eye was held by Susan Delgado: the blue dress, the tanned skin, the triangles of color, too pale and perfect to be makeup, which ran lightly up her cheeks; most of all her hair, which was unbound tonight and fell to her waist like a shimmer of palest silk. He wanted her, suddenly and completely, with a desperate depth of feeling that felt like sickness. Everything he was and everything he had come for, it seemed, was secondary to her.

She turned a little, then, and spied him. Her eyes (they were gray, he saw) widened the tiniest bit. He thought that the color in her cheeks deepened a little. Her lips— lips that had touched his as they stood on a dark road, he thought with wonder—parted a little. Then the man standing next to Thorin (also tall, also skinny, with a mustache and long white hair lying on the dark shoulders of his coat) said something, and she turned back to him. A moment later the group around Thorin was laughing, Susan included. The man with the white hair didn't join them, but smiled thinly.

Roland, hoping his face did not give away the fact that his heart was pounding like a hammer, was led directly to this group, which stood close to the punchbowls. Distantly, he could feel Rimer's bony confederation of fingers clamped to his arm above the elbow. More clearly he could smell mingled perfumes, the oil from the lamps on the walls, the aroma of the ocean. And thought, for no reason at all, *Oh, I am dying. I am dying.*

Take hold of yourself, Roland of Gilead. Stop this foolishness, for your father's sake. Take hold!

He tried . . . to some degree succeeded . . . and knew he would be lost the next time she looked at him. It was her eyes. The other night, in the dark, he hadn't been able to see those fog-colored eyes. *I didn't know how lucky I was,* he thought wryly.

"Mayor Thorin?" Rimer asked. "May I present our guests from the Inner Baronies?"

Thorin turned away from the man with the long white hair and the woman standing next to him, his face brightening. He was shorter than his Chancellor but just as thin, and his build was peculiar: a short and narrow-shouldered upper body over impossibly long and skinny legs. He looked, Roland thought, like the sort of bird you should glimpse in a marsh at dawn, bobbing for its breakfast.

"Aye, you may!" he cried in a strong, high voice. "Indeed you may, we've been waiting with impatience, *great* impatience, for this moment! Well met we are, very well met! Welcome, sirs! May your evening in this house of which I am the fleeting proprietor be happy, and may your days be long upon the earth!"

Roland took the bony outstretched hand, heard the knuckles crack beneath his grip, looked for an expression of discomfort on the Mayor's face, and was relieved to see none. He bowed low over his outstretched leg.

"William Dearborn, Mayor Thorin, at your service. Thank you for your welcome, and may your own days be long upon the earth."

"Arthur Heath" made his manners next, then "Richard Stockworth." Thorin's smile widened at each deep bow. Rimer did his best to beam, but looked unused to it. The man with the long white hair took a glass of punch, passed it to his female companion, and continued to smile thinly. Roland was aware that everyone in the room—the guests numbered perhaps fifty in all—was looking at them, but what he felt most upon his skin, beating like a soft wing, was *her* regard. He could see the blue silk of her dress from the side of one eye, but did not dare look at her more directly.

"Was your trip difficult?" Thorin was asking. "Did you have adventures and experience perils? We would hear all the details at dinner, so we would, for we have few guests from the Inner Arc these days." His eager, slightly fatuous smile faded; his tufted brows drew together. "Did ye encounter patrols of Farson?"

"No, Excellency," Roland said. "We—"

"Nay, lad, nay—no Excellency, I won't have it, and the fisherfolk and hoss-drovers I serve wouldn't, even if I would. Just Mayor Thorin, if you please."

"Thank you. We saw many strange things on our journey, Mayor Thorin, but no Good Men."

"Good Men!" Rimer jerked out, and his upper lip lifted in a smile which made him look doglike. "Good Men, indeed!"

"We would hear it all, every word," Thorin said. "But before I forget my manners in my eagerness, young gentlemen, let me introduce you to these close around me. Kimba you've met; this formidable fellow to my left is Eldred Jonas, chief of my newly installed security staff." Thorin's smile looked momentarily embarrassed. "I'm not convinced that I need extra security, Sheriff Avery's always been quite enough to keep the peace in our corner of the world, but Kimba insists. And when Kimba insists, the Mayor must bow."

"Very wise, sir," Rimer said, and bowed himself. They all laughed, save for Jonas, who simply held onto his narrow smile.

Jonas nodded. "Pleased, gents, I'm sure." The voice was a reedy quaver. He then wished them long days upon the earth, all three, coming to Roland last in his round of handshaking. His grip was dry and firm, utterly untouched by the tremor in his voice. And now Roland noticed the queer blue shape tattooed on the back of the man's right hand, in the webbing between thumb and first finger. It looked like a coffin.

"Long days, pleasant nights," Roland said with hardly a thought. It was a greeting from his childhood, and it was only later that he would realize it was one more apt to be associated with Gilead than with any such rural place as Hemphill. Just a small slip, but he was beginning to believe that their margin for such slips might be a good deal less than his father had thought when he had sent Roland here to get him out of Marten's way.

"And to you," Jonas said. His bright eyes measured Roland with a thoroughness that was close to insolence, still holding his hand. Then he released it and stepped back.

"Cordelia Delgado," Mayor Thorin said, next bowing to the woman who had been speaking to Jonas. As Roland also bowed in her direction, he saw the family resemblance . . . except that what looked generous and lovely on Susan's face looked pinched and folded on the face before him now. Not the girl's mother; Roland guessed that Cordelia Delgado was a bit too young for that.

"And our especial friend, Miss Susan Delgado," Thorin finished, sounding flustered (Roland supposed she would have that effect on any man, even an old one like the Mayor). Thorin urged her forward, bobbing his head and grinning, one of his knuckle-choked hands pressed against the small of her back, and Roland felt an instant of poisonous jealousy. Ridiculous, given this man's age and his plump, pleasant wife, but it was there, all right, and it was sharp. Sharp as a bee's ass, Cort would have said.

Then her face tilted up to his, and he was looking into her eyes again. He had heard of drowning in a woman's eyes in some poem or story, and thought it ridiculous. He still thought it ridiculous, but understood it was perfectly possible, nonetheless. And she knew it. He saw concern in her eyes, perhaps even fear.

Promise me that if we meet at Mayor's House, we meet for the first time.

The memory of those words had a sobering, clarifying effect, and seemed to widen his vision a little. Enough for him to be aware that the woman beside Jonas, the one who shared some of Susan's features, was looking at the girl with a mixture of curiosity and alarm.

He bowed low, but did little more than touch her ring-less outstretched hand. Even so, he felt something like a spark jump between their fingers. From the momentary widening of those eyes, he thought that she felt it, too.

"Pleased to meet you, sai," he said. His attempt to be casual sounded tinny and false in his own ears. Still, he was begun, it felt like the whole world was watching him *(them)*, and there was nothing to do but go on with it. He tapped his throat three times. "May your days be long—"

"Aye, and yours, Mr. Dearborn. Thankee-sai."

She turned to Alain with a rapidity that was almost rude, then to Cuthbert, who bowed, tapped, then said gravely: "Might I recline briefly at your feet, miss? Your beauty has loosened my knees. I'm sure a few moments spent looking up at your profile from below, with the back of my head on these cool tiles, would put me right."

They all laughed at that—even Jonas and Miss Cordelia. Susan blushed prettily and slapped the back of Cuthbert's hand. For once Roland blessed his friend's relentless sense of foolery.

Another man joined the party by the punchbowl. This newcomer was blocky and blessedly un-thin in his box-tail coat. His cheeks burned with high color that looked like windburn rather than drink, and his pale eyes lay in nets of wrinkles. A rancher; Roland had ridden often enough with his father to know the look.

"There'll be maids a-plenty to meet you boys tonight," the newcomer said with a friendly enough smile. "Ye'll find y'selves drunk on perfume if ye're not careful. But I'd like my crack at you before you meet em. Fran Lengyll, at your service."

His grip was strong and quick; no bowing or other nonsense went with it.

"I own the Rocking B . . . or it owns me, whichever way ye want to look at it. I'm also boss of the Horsemen's Association, at least until they fire me. The Bar K was my idea. Hope it's all right."

"It's perfect, sir," Alain said. "Clean and dry and room for twenty. Thank you. You've been too kind."

"Nonsense," Lengyll said, looking pleased all the same as he knocked back a glass of punch. "We're all in this together, boy. John Farson's but one bad straw in a field of wrongheadedness these days. The world's moved on, folks say. Huh! So it has, aye, and a good piece down the road to hell is where it's moved on to. Our job is to hold the hay out of the furnace as well as we can, as long as we can. For the sake of our children even more than for that of our fathers."

"Hear, hear," Mayor Thorin said in a voice that strove for the high ground of solemnity and fell with a splash into fatuity instead. Roland noticed the scrawny old fellow was gripping one of Susan's hands (she seemed almost unaware of it; was looking intently at Lengyll instead), and suddenly he understood: the Mayor was either her uncle or perhaps a cousin of some close degree. Lengyll ignored both, looking at the three newcomers instead, scrutinizing each in turn and finishing with Roland.

"Anything us in Mejis can do to help, lad, just ask—me, John Croydon, Hash Renfrew, Jake White, Hank Wertner, any or all. Ye'll meet em tonight, aye, their wives and sons and daughters as well, and ye need only ask. We may be a good piece out from the hub of New Canaan here, but we're strong for the Affiliation, all the same. Aye, very strong."

"Well spoken," Rimer said quietly.

"And now," Lengyll said, "we'll toast your arrival proper. And ye've had to wait too long already for a dip of punch. It's dry as dust ye must be."

He turned to the punchbowls and reached for the ladle in the larger and more ornate of the two, waving off the attendant, clearly wanting to honor them by serving them himself.

"Mr. Lengyll," Roland said quietly. Yet there was a force of command in that voice; Fran Lengyll heard it and turned.

"The smaller bowl is soft punch, is it not?"

Lengyll considered this, at first not understanding. Then his eyebrow went up. For the first time he seemed to consider Roland and the others not as living symbols of the Affiliation and the Inner Baronies, but as actual human beings. Young ones. Only boys, when you got right down to it.

"Aye?"

"Draw ours from that, if you'd be so kind." He felt all eyes upon them now. *Her* eyes particularly. He kept his own firmly fixed on the rancher, but his peripheral vision was good, and he was very aware that Jonas's thin smile had resurfaced. Jonas knew what this was about already. Roland supposed Thorin and Rimer did, as well. These country mice knew a lot. More than they should, and he would need to think about that carefully later. It was the least of his concerns at the current moment, however.

"We have forgotten the faces of our fathers in a matter that has some bearing on our posting to Hambry." Roland was uncomfortably aware that he was now making a speech, like it or not. It wasn't the whole room he was addressing—thank the gods for little blessings—but the circle of listeners had grown well beyond the original group. Yet there was nothing for it but to finish; the boat was launched. "I needn't go into details—nor would you expect them, I know—but I should say that we promised not to indulge in spirits during our time here. As penance, you see."

Her gaze. He could still feel it on his skin, it seemed.

For a moment there was complete quiet in the little group around the punchbowls, and then Lengyll said: "Your father would be proud to hear ye speak so frank, Will Dearborn—aye, so he would. And what boy worth his salt didn't get up to a little noise 'n wind from time to time?" He clapped Roland on the shoulder, and although the grip of his hand was firm and his smile looked genuine, his eyes were hard to read, only gleams of speculation deep in those beds of wrinkles. "In his place, may I be proud for him?"

"Yes," Roland said, smiling in return. "And with my thanks."

"And mine," Cuthbert said.

"Mine as well," Alain said quietly, taking the offered cup of soft punch and bowing to Lengyll.

Lengyll filled more cups and handed them rapidly around. Those already holding cups found them plucked away and replaced with fresh cups of the soft punch. When each of the immediate group had one, Lengyll turned, apparently intending to offer the toast himself. Rimer tapped him on the shoulder, shook his head slightly, and cut his eyes toward the Mayor. That worthy was looking at them with his eyes rather popped and his jaw slightly dropped. To Roland he looked like an enthralled playgoer in a penny seat; all he needed was a lapful of orange-peel. Lengyll followed the Chancellor's glance and then nodded.

Rimer next caught the eye of the guitar player standing at the center of the musicians. He stopped playing; so did the others. The guests looked that way, then back to the center of the room when Thorin began speaking. There was nothing ridiculous about his voice when he put it to use as he now did—it was carrying and pleasant.

"Ladies and gentlemen, my friends," he said. "I would

ask you to help me in welcoming three *new* friends—
young men from the Inner Baronies, fine young men
who have dared great distances and many perils on behalf
of the Affiliation, and in the service of order and peace."

Susan Delgado set her punch-cup aside, retrieved her
hand (with some difficulty) from her uncle's grip, and
began to clap. Others joined in. The applause which
swept the room was brief but warm. Eldred Jonas did
not, Roland noticed, put his cup aside to join in.

Thorin turned to Roland, smiling. He raised his cup.
"May I set you on with a word, Will Dearborn?"

"Aye, so you may, and with thanks," Roland said. There
was laughter and fresh applause at his usage.

Thorin raised his cup even higher. Everyone else in
the room followed suit; crystal gleamed like starpoints in
the light of the chandelier.

"Ladies and gentlemen, I give you William Dearborn
of Hemphill, Richard Stockworth of Pennilton, and
Arthur Heath of Gilead."

Gasps and murmurs at that last, as if their Mayor had
announced Arthur Heath of Heaven.

"Take of them well, give to them well, make their days
in Mejis sweet, and their memories sweeter. Help them
in their work and to advance the causes which are so
dear to all of us. May their days be long upon the earth.
So says your Mayor."

"*SO SAY WE ALL!*" they thundered back.

Thorin drank; the rest followed his example. There
was fresh applause. Roland turned, helpless to stop himself, and found Susan's eyes again at once. For a moment
she looked at him fully, and in her frank gaze he saw that
she was nearly as shaken by his presence as he was by
hers. Then the older woman who looked like her bent
and murmured something into her ear. Susan turned
away, her face a composed mask . . . but he had seen

her regard in her eyes. And thought again that what was done might be undone, and what was spoken might be unspoken.

8

As they passed into the dining hall, which had tonight been set with four long trestle tables (so close there was barely room to move between them), Cordelia tugged her niece's hand, pulling her back from the Mayor and Jonas, who had fallen into conversation with Fran Lengyll.

"Why looked you at him so, miss?" Cordelia whispered furiously. The vertical line had appeared on her forehead. Tonight it looked as deep as a trench. "What ails thy pretty, stupid head?" *Thy.* Just that was enough to tell Susan that her aunt was in a fine rage.

"Looked at who? And how?" Her tone sounded right, she thought, but oh, her heart—

The hand over hers clamped down, hurting. "Play no fiddle with me, Miss Oh So Young and Pretty! Have ye ever seen that fine-turned row of pins before? Tell me the truth!"

"No, how could I? Aunt, you're hurting me."

Aunt Cord smiled balefully and clamped down harder. "Better a small hurt now than a large one later. Curb your impudence. And curb your flirtatious eyes."

"Aunt, I don't know what you—"

"I think you do," Cordelia said grimly, pressing her niece close to the wood panelling to allow the guests to stream past them. When the rancher who owned the boathouse next to theirs said hello, Aunt Cord smiled pleasantly at him and wished him goodeven before turning back to Susan.

"Mind me, miss—mind me well. If I saw yer cow's eyes,

ye may be sure that half the company saw. Well, what's done is done, but it stops now. Your time for such child-maid games is over. Do you understand?"

Susan was silent, her face setting in those stubborn lines Cordelia hated most of all; it was an expression that always made her feel like slapping her headstrong niece until her nose bled and her great gray doe's eyes gushed tears.

"Ye've made a vow and a contract. Papers have been passed, the weird-woman has been consulted, money has changed hands. *And ye've given your promise.* If that means nothing to such as yerself, girl, remember what it'd mean to yer father."

Tears rose in Susan's eyes again, and Cordelia was glad to see them. Her brother had been an improvident irritation, capable of producing only this far too pretty womanchild . . . but he had his uses, even dead.

"Now promise ye'll keep yer eyes to yourself, and that if ye see that boy coming, ye'll swing wide—aye, wide's you can—to stay out of his way."

"I promise, Aunt," Susan whispered. "I do."

Cordelia smiled. She was really quite pretty when she smiled. "It's well, then. Let's go in. We're being looked at. Hold my arm, child!"

Susan clasped her aunt's powdered arm. They entered the room side by side, their dresses rustling, the sapphire pendant on the swell of Susan's breast flashing, and many there were who remarked upon how alike they looked, and how well pleased poor old Pat Delgado would have been with them.

9

Roland was seated near the head of the center table, between Hash Renfrew (a rancher even bigger and blockier than Lengyll) and Thorin's rather morose sister, Coral. Renfrew had been handy with the punch; now, as the soup was brought to table, he set about proving himself equally adept with the ale.

He talked about the fishing trade ("not what it useter be, boy, although it's less muties they pull up in their nets these days, 'n that's a blessin"), the farming trade ("folks round here can grow most anythin, long's it's corn or beans"), and finally about those things clearly closest to his heart: horsin, coursin, and ranchin. Those businesses went on as always, aye, so they did, although times had been hard in the grass-and-seacoast Baronies for forty year or more.

Weren't the bloodlines clarifying? Roland asked. For they had begun to do so where he came from.

Aye, Renfrew agreed, ignoring his potato soup and gobbling barbecued beef-strips instead. These he scooped up with a bare hand and washed down with more ale. Aye, young master, bloodlines was clarifying wonderful well, indeed they were, three colts out of every five were threaded stock—in thoroughbred as well as common lines, kennit—and the fourth could be kept and worked if not bred. Only one in five these days born with extra legs or extra eyes or its guts on the outside, and that was good. But the birth-rates were way down, so they were; the stallions had as much ram as ever in their ramrods, it seemed, but not as much powder and ball.

"Beggin your pardon, ma'am," Renfrew said, leaning briefly across Roland to Coral Thorin. She smiled her thin smile (it reminded Roland of Jonas's), trudged her spoon through her soup, and said nothing. Renfrew emptied his ale-cup, smacked his lips heartily, and held the cup out again. As it was recharged, he turned back to Roland.

Things weren't good, not as they once had been, but

they could be worse. *Would* be worse, if that bugger Farson had his way. (This time he didn't bother excusing himself to sai Thorin.) They all had to pull together, that was the ticket—rich and poor, great and small, while pulling could still do some good. And then he seconded Lengyll, telling Roland that whatever he and his friends wanted, whatever they needed, they had only to name it.

"Information should be enough," Roland said. "Numbers of things."

"Aye, can't be a counter without numbers," Renfrew agreed, and sprayed beery laughter. On Roland's left hand, Coral Thorin nibbled a bit of green (the beef-strips she had not so much as touched), smiled her narrow smile, and went on boating with her spoon. Roland guessed there was nothing wrong with her ears, though, and that her brother might get a complete report of their conversation. Or possibly it would be Rimer to get the report. For, while it was too early to say for sure, Roland had an idea that Rimer might be the real force here. Along, perhaps, with sai Jonas.

"For instance," Roland said, "how many riding horses do you think we may be able to report back to the Affiliation?"

"Tithe or total?"

"Total."

Renfrew put his cup down and appeared to calculate. As he did, Roland looked across the table and saw Lengyll and Henry Wertner, the Barony's stockliner, exchange a quick glance. They had heard. And he saw something else as well, when he returned his attention to his seatmate: Hash Renfrew was drunk, but likely not as drunk as he wanted young Will Dearborn to believe.

"Total, ye say—not just what we owe the Affiliation, or might be able to send along in a pinch."

"Yes."

"Well, let's see, young sai. Fran must run a hundred 'n forty head; John Croydon's got near a hundred. Hank Wertner's got forty on his own hook, and must run sixty more out along the Drop for the Barony. Gov'mint hoss-flesh, Mr. Dearborn."

Roland smiled. "I know it well. Split hoofs, low necks, no speed, bottomless bellies."

Renfrew laughed hard at that, nodding . . . but Roland found himself wondering if the man was really amused. In Hambry, the waters on top and the waters down below seemed to run in different directions.

"As for myself, I've had a bad ten or twelve year—sand-eye, brain fever, cabbards. At one time there was two hundred head of running horses out there on the Drop with the Lazy Susan brand on em; now there can't be more than eighty."

Roland nodded. "So we're speaking of four hundred and twenty head."

"Oh, more'n that," Renfrew said with a laugh. He went to pick up his ale-cup, struck it with the side of one work- and weather-reddened hand, knocked it over, cursed, picked it up, then cursed the aleboy who came slow to refill it.

"More than that?" Roland prompted, when Renfrew was finally cocked and locked and ready to resume action.

"Ye have to remember, Mr. Dearborn, that this is hoss-country more than it's fisher-country. We josh each other, we and the fishers, but there's many a scale-scraper got a nag put away behind his house, or in the Barony stables if they have no roof of their own to keep the rain off a hoss's head. 'Twas her poor da useter keep the Barony stables."

Renfrew nodded toward Susan, who was seated across and three seats up from Roland himself—just a table's turn from the Mayor, who was, of course, seated at the

head. Roland found her placement there passing peculiar, especially given the fact that the Mayor's missus had
been seated almost all the way at the far end of the table,
with Cuthbert on one side of her and some rancher to
whom they had not yet been introduced on her other.

Roland supposed an old fellow like Thorin might like
to have a pretty young relation near at hand to help
draw attention to him, or to cheer up his own eye, but it
still seemed odd. Almost an insult to one's wife. If he was
tired of her conversation, why not put her at the head of
another table?

*They have their own customs, that's all, and the customs of
the country aren't your concern. This man's crazy horse-count
is your concern.*

"How many other running horses, would you say?" he
asked Renfrew. "In all?"

Renfrew gazed at him shrewdly. "An honest answer'll
not come back to haunt me, will it, sonny? I'm an Affiliation man—so I am, Affiliation to the core, they'll carve
Excalibur on my gravehead, like as not—but I'd not see
Hambry and Mejis stripped of all its treasure."

"That won't happen, sai. How could we force you to
give up what you don't want to in any case? Such forces
as we have are all committed in the north and west,
against the Good Man."

Renfrew considered this, then nodded.

"And may I not be Will to you?"

Renfrew brightened, nodded, and offered his hand
a second time. He grinned broadly when Roland this
time shook it in both of his, the over-and-under grip preferred by drovers and cowboys.

"These're bad times we live in, Will, and they've bred
bad manners. I'd guess there are probably another hundred and fifty head of horse in and about Mejis. Good
ones is what I mean."

"Big-hat stock."

Renfrew nodded, clapped Roland on the back, ingested a goodly quaff of ale. "Big-hats, aye."

From the top of their table there came a burst of laughter. Jonas had apparently said something funny. Susan laughed without reservation, her head tilted back and her hands clasped before the sapphire pendant. Cordelia, who sat with the girl on her left and Jonas on her right, was also laughing. Thorin was absolutely convulsed, rocking back and forth in his chair, wiping his eyes with a napkin.

"Yon's a lovely girl," Renfrew said. He spoke almost reverently. Roland could not quite swear that a small sound—a womanly *hmmpf*, perhaps—had come from his other side. He glanced in that direction and saw sai Thorin still sporting with her soup. He looked back toward the head of the table.

"Is the Mayor her uncle, or perhaps her cousin?" Roland asked.

What happened next had a heightened clarity in his memory, as if someone had turned up all the colors and sounds of the world. The velvet swags behind Susan suddenly seemed a brighter red; the caw of laughter which came from Coral Thorin was the sound of a breaking branch. It was surely loud enough to make everyone in the vicinity stop their conversations and look at her, Roland thought . . . except only Renfrew and the two ranchers across the table did.

"Her *uncle!*" It was her first conversation of the evening. "Her *uncle*, that's good. Eh, Rennie?"

Renfrew said nothing, only pushed his ale-cup away and finally began to eat his soup.

"I'm surprised at ye, young man, so I am. Ye may be from the In-World, but oh goodness, whoever tended to your education of the *real* world—the one outside of books 'n maps—stopped a mite short, I'd say. She's his—" And then a word so thick with dialect that Roland had no idea what it was. *Seefin*, it sounded, or perhaps *sheevin*.

"I beg pardon?" He was smiling, but the smile felt cold and false on his mouth. There was a heaviness in his belly, as if the punch and the soup and the single beef-strip he had eaten for politeness' sake had all lumped together in his stomach. *Do you serve?* he'd asked her, meaning did she serve at table. Mayhap she *did* serve, but likely she did it in a room rather more private than this. Suddenly he wanted to hear no more; had not the slightest interest in the meaning of the word the Mayor's sister had used.

Another burst of laughter rocked the top of the table. Susan laughed with her head back, her cheeks glowing, her eyes sparkling. One strap of her dress had slipped down her arm, disclosing the tender hollow of her shoulder. As he watched, his heart full of fear and longing, she brushed it absently back into place with the palm of her hand.

"It means 'quiet little woman,'" Renfrew said, clearly uncomfortable. "It's an old term, not used much these days—"

"Stop it, Rennie," said Coral Thorin. Then, to Roland: "He's just an old cowboy, and can't quit shovelling horse-shit even when he's away from his beloved nags. *Sheevin* means side-wife. In the time of my great-grandmother, it meant whore . . . but one of a certain kind." She looked with a pale eye at Susan, who was now sipping ale, then turned back to Roland. There was a species of baleful amusement in her gaze, an expression that Roland liked little. "The kind of whore you had to pay for in coin, the kind too fine for the trade of simple folk."

"She's his gilly?" Roland asked through lips which felt as if they had been iced.

"Aye," Coral said. "Not consummated, not until the Reap—and none too happy about that is my brother, I'll warrant—but bought and paid for just as in the old days. So she is." Coral paused, then said, "Her father would die of shame if he could see her." She spoke with a kind of melancholy satisfaction.

"I hardly think we should judge the Mayor too harshly," Renfrew said in an embarrassed, pontificating voice.

Coral ignored him. She studied the line of Susan's jaw, the soft swell of her bosom above the silken edge of her bodice, the fall of her hair. The thin humor was gone from Coral Thorin's face. In it now was a somehow chilling species of contempt.

In spite of himself, Roland found himself imagining the Mayor's knuckle-bunchy hands pushing down the straps of Susan's dress, crawling over her naked shoulders, plunging like gray crabs into the cave beneath her hair. He looked away, toward the table's lower end, and what he saw there was no better. It was Olive Thorin that his eye found—Olive, who had been relegated to the foot of the table, Olive, looking up at the laughing folk who sat at its head. Looking up at her husband, who had replaced her with a beautiful young girl, and gifted that girl with a pendant which made her own firedim earrings look dowdy by comparison. There was none of Coral's hatred and angry contempt on her face. Looking at her might have been easier if that were so. She only gazed at her husband with eyes that were humble, hopeful, and unhappy. Now Roland understood why he had thought her sad. She had every reason to be sad.

More laughter from the Mayor's party; Rimer had leaned over from the next table, where he was presiding, to contribute some witticism. It must have been a good one. This time even Jonas was laughing. Susan put a hand to her bosom, then took her napkin and raised it to wipe a tear of laughter from the corner of her eye. Thorin covered her other hand. She looked toward Roland and met his eyes, still laughing. He thought of Olive Thorin, sitting down there at the foot of the table, with the salt and spices, an untouched bowl of soup before her and that unhappy smile on her face. Seated where the girl could see her, as well. And he thought that, had he been wearing his guns, he might well have drawn one and put a bullet in Susan Delgado's cold and whoring little heart.

And thought: *Who do you hope to fool?*

Then one of the serving boys was there, putting a plate of fish in front of him. Roland thought he had never felt less like eating in his life . . . but he *would* eat, just the same, just as he would turn his mind to the questions raised by his conversation with Hash Renfrew of the Lazy Susan Ranch. He would remember the face of his father.

Yes, I'll remember it very well, he thought. *If only I could forget the one above yon sapphire.*

10

The dinner was interminable, and there was no escape afterward. The table at the center of the reception room had been removed, and when the guests came back that way—like a tide which has surged as high as it can and now ebbs—they formed two adjacent circles at the direction of a sprightly little redhaired man whom Cuthbert later dubbed Mayor Thorin's Minister of Fun.

The boy-girl, boy-girl, boy-girl circling was accomplished with much laughter and some difficulty (Roland guessed that about three-quarters of the guests were now fairly well shottered), and then the guitarists struck up a *quesa*. This proved to be a simple sort of reel. The circles revolved in opposite directions, all holding hands, until the music stopped for a moment. Then the couple created at the place where the two circles touched danced at the center of the female partner's circle, while everyone else clapped and cheered.

The lead musician managed this old and clearly well-loved tradition with a keen eye to the ridiculous, stopping his *muchachos* in order to create the most amusing couples: tall woman-short man, fat woman-skinny man, old woman-young man (Cuthbert ended up side-kicking with a woman as old as his great-granddame, to the sai's breathless cackles and the company's general roars of approval).

Then, just when Roland was thinking this stupid dance would never end, the music stopped and he found himself facing Susan Delgado.

For a moment he could do nothing but stare at her, feeling that his eyes must burst from their sockets, feeling that he could move neither of his stupid feet. Then she raised her arms, the music began, the circle (this one included Mayor Thorin and the watchful, narrowly smiling Eldred Jonas) applauded, and he led her into the dance.

At first, as he spun her through a figure (his feet moved with all their usual grace and precision, numb or not), he felt like a man made of glass. Then he became aware of her body touching his, and the rustle of her dress, and he was all too human again.

She moved closer for just a moment, and when she spoke, her breath tickled in his ear. He wondered if a woman could drive you mad—literally mad. He wouldn't have believed so before tonight, but tonight everything had changed.

"Thank you for your discretion and your propriety," she whispered.

He pulled back from her a little and at the same time

twirled her, his hand against the small of her back—palm resting on cool satin, fingers touching warm skin. Her feet followed his with never a pause or stutter; they moved with perfect grace, unafraid of his great and booted clod-stompers even in their flimsy silk slippers.

"I can be discreet, sai," he said. "As for propriety? I'm amazed you even know the word."

She looked up into his cold face, her smile fading. He saw anger come in to fill it, but before anger there was hurt, as if he had slapped her. He felt both glad and sorry at the same time.

"Why do you speak so?" she whispered.

The music stopped before he could answer . . . although how he might have answered, he had no idea. She curtseyed and he bowed, while those surrounding them clapped and whistled. They went back to their places, to their separate circles, and the guitars began again. Roland felt his hands grasped on either side and began to turn with the circle once more.

Laughing. Kicking. Clapping on the beat. Feeling her somewhere behind him, doing the same. Wondering if she wanted as badly as he did to be out of here, to be in the dark, to be alone in the dark, where he could put his false face aside before the real one beneath could grow hot enough to set it afire.

CHAPTER SIX

Sheemie

I

Around ten o' the clock, the trio of young men from the Inner Baronies made their manners to host and hostess, then slipped off into the fragrant summer night. Cordelia Delgado, who happened to be standing near Henry Wertner, the Barony's stockliner, remarked that they must be tired. Wertner laughed at this and replied in an accent so thick it was almost comic: "Nay, ma'am, byes that age're like rats explorin en woodpile after hokkut rain, so they are. It'll be hours yet before the bunks out'ta Bar K sees em."

Olive Thorin left the public rooms shortly after the boys, pleading a headache. She was pale enough to be almost believable.

By eleven, the Mayor, his Chancellor, and the chief of his newly inaugurated security staff were conversing in the Mayor's study with the last few late-staying guests (all ranchers, all members of the Horsemen's Association). The talk was brief but intense. Several of the ranchers present expressed relief that the Affiliation's emissaries were so young. Eldred Jonas said nothing to this, only looked down at his pale, long-fingered hands and smiled his narrow smile.

By midnight, Susan was at home and undressing for

bed. She didn't have the sapphire to worry about, at least; that was a Barony jewel, and had been tucked back into the strongbox at Mayor's House before she left, despite what Mr. Ain't-We-Fine Will Dearborn might think about it and her. Mayor Thorin (she couldn't bring herself to call him Hart, although he had asked her to do so—not even to herself could she do it) had taken it back from her himself. In the hallway just off from the reception room, that had been, by the tapestry showing Arthur Eld carrying his sword out of the pyramid in which it had been entombed. And he (Thorin, not the Eld) had taken the opportunity to kiss her mouth and have a quick fumble at her breasts—a part of her that had felt much too naked during that entire interminable evening. "I burn for Reaping," he had whispered melodramatically in her ear. His breath had been redolent of brandy. "Each day of this summer seems an age."

Now, in her room, brushing her hair with harsh, quick strokes and looking out at the waning moon, she thought she had never been so angry in her life as she was at this moment: angry at Thorin, angry at Aunt Cord, *furious* with that self-righteous prig of a Will Dearborn. Most of all, however, she was angry at herself.

"There's three things ye can do in any situation, girl," her father had told her once. "Ye can decide to do a thing, ye can decide *not* to do a thing . . . or ye can decide not to decide." That last, her da had never quite come out and said (he hadn't needed to) was the choice of weaklings and fools. She had promised herself she would never elect it herself . . . and yet she had allowed herself to drift into this ugly situation. Now all the choices seemed bad and honorless, all the roads either filled with rocks or hub-deep in mud.

In her room at Mayor's House (she had not shared a chamber with Hart for ten years, or a bed, even briefly,

for five), Olive sat in a nightdress of undecorated white
cotton, also looking out at the waning moon. After
closing herself into this safe and private place, she had
wept . . . but not for long. Now she was dry-eyed, and felt
as hollow as a dead tree.

And what was the worst? That Hart didn't understand how humiliated she was, and not just for herself.
He was too busy strutting and preening (also too busy
trying to look down the front of sai Delgado's dress at
every opportunity) to know that people—his own Chancellor among them—were laughing at him behind his
back. That might stop when the girl had returned to her
aunt's with a big belly, but that wouldn't be for months
yet. The witch had seen to that. It would be even longer
if the girl kindled slowly. And what was the silliest, most
humilating thing of all? That she, John Haverty's daughter Olive, still loved her husband. Hart was an overween-
ing, vainglorious, prancing loon of a man, but she still
loved him.

There was something else, something quite apart
from the matter of Hart's turning into George o' Goats
in his late middle age: she thought there was an intrigue
of some sort going on, something dangerous and quite
likely dishonorable. Hart knew a little about it, but she
guessed he knew only what Kimba Rimer and that hideous limping man *wanted* him to know.

There was a time, and not so long ago, when Hart
wouldn't have allowed himself to be fobbed off in such
fashion by the likes of Rimer, a time when he would have
taken one look at Eldred Jonas and his friends and sent
them west ere they had so much as a single hot dinner
in them. But that was before Hart had become besotted
with sai Delgado's gray eyes, high bosom, and flat belly.

Olive turned down the lamp, blew out the flame, and
crept off to bed, where she would lie wakeful until dawn.

By one o' the clock, no one was left in the public rooms of Mayor's House except for a quartet of cleaning women, who performed their chores silently (and nervously) beneath the eye of Eldred Jonas. When one of them looked up and saw him gone from the window-seat where he had been sitting and smoking, she murmured softly to her friends, and they all loosened up a little. But there was no singing, no laughter. *Il spectro,* the man with the blue coffin on his hand, might only have stepped back into the shadows. He might still be watching.

By two o' the clock, even the cleaning women were gone. It was an hour at which a party in Gilead would just have been reaching its apogee of glitter and gossip, but Gilead was far away, not just in another Barony but almost in another world. This was the Outer Arc, and in the Outers, even gentry went to bed early.

There was no gentry on view at the Travellers' Rest, however, and beneath the all-encompassing gaze of The Romp, the night was still fairly young.

2

At one end of the saloon, fishermen still wearing their rolled-down boots drank and played Watch Me for small stakes. To their right was a poker table; to their left, a knot of yelling, exhorting men—cowpokes, mostly— stood along Satan's Alley, watching the dice bounce down the velvet incline. At the room's other end, Sheb McCurdy was pounding out jagged boogie, right hand flying, left hand pumping, the sweat pouring down his neck and pale cheeks. Beside and above him, standing drunk on a stool, Pettie the Trotter shook her enormous bottom and bawled out the words to the song at the top of her voice: *"Come on over, baby, we got chicken in the barn,*

*what barn, whose barn, my barn! Come on over, baby, baby got
the bull by the horns . . . "*

Sheemie stopped beside the piano, the camel bucket
in one hand, grinning up at her and attempting to sing
along. Pettie swatted him on his way, never missing a
word, bump, or grind, and Sheemie went with his peculiar laugh, which was shrill but somehow not unpleasant.

A game of darts was in progress; in a booth near the
back, a whore who styled herself Countess Julian of
Up'ard Killian (exiled royalty from distant Garlan, my
dears, oh how special we are) was managing to give two
handjobs at the same time while smoking a pipe. And
at the bar, a whole line of assorted toughs, drifters, cow-
punchers, drovers, drivers, carters, wheelwrights, stagies,
carpenters, conmen, stockmen, boatmen, and gunmen
drank beneath The Romp's double head.

The only *real* gunmen in the place were at the end of
the bar, a pair drinking by themselves. No one attempted
to join them, and not just because they wore shooting
irons in holsters that were slung low and tied down gunslinger fashion. Guns were uncommon but not unknown
in Mejis at that time, and not necessarily feared, but
these two had the sullen look of men who have spent a
long day doing work they didn't want to do—the look of
men who would pick a fight on no account at all, and be
glad to end their day by sending some new widow's husband home in a hurry-up wagon.

Stanley the bartender served them whiskey after whiskey with no attempt to make conversation, not so much
as a "Hot day, gents, wa'n't it?" They reeked of sweat,
and their hands were pitchy with pine-gum. Not enough
to keep Stanley from being able to see the blue cof-
fin-shapes tattooed on them, though. Their friend, the
old limping buzzard with the girl's hair and the gimp
leg, wasn't here, at least. In Stanley's view, Jonas was eas-

ily the worst of the Big Coffin Hunters, but these two were bad enough, and he had no intention of getting aslant of them if he could help it. With luck, no one would; they looked tired enough to call it a night early.

Reynolds and Depape were tired, all right—they had spent the day out at Citgo, camouflaging a line of empty steel tankers with nonsense words (TEXACO, CITGO, SUNOCO, EXXON) printed on their sides, a billion pine-boughs they'd hauled and stacked, it seemed—but they had no consequent plans to finish their drinking early. Depape might have done so if Her Nibs had been available, but that young beauty (actual name: Gert Moggins) had a ranch-job and wouldn't be back until two nights hence. "And it'll be a week if there's hard cash on offer," Depape said morosely. He pushed his spectacles up on his nose.

"Fuck her," Reynolds said.

"That's just what I'd do if I could, but I can't."

"I'm going to get me a plate of that free lunch," Reynolds said, pointing down to the other end of the bar, where a tin bucket of steamed clams had just come out of the kitchen. "You want some?"

"Them look like hocks of snot and go down the same way. Bring me a strip of beef jerky."

"All right, partner." Reynolds went off down the bar. People gave him wide passage; gave even his silk-lined cloak wide passage.

Depape, more morose than ever now that he had thought of Her Nibs gobbling cowboy spareribs out there at the Piano Ranch, downed his drink, winced at the stench of pine-gum on his hand, then held his glass out in Stanley Ruiz's direction. "Fill this up, you dog!" he shouted. A cowhand leaning with his back, butt, and elbows against the bar jerked forward at the sound of Depape's bellow, and that was all it took to start trouble.

Sheemie was bustling toward the passthrough from which the steamers had just appeared, now holding the camel bucket out before him in both hands. Later, when the Travellers' began to empty out, his job would be to clean up. For now, however, it was simply to circulate with the camel bucket, dumping in every unfinished drink he found. This combined elixir ended up in a jug behind the bar. The jug was labelled fairly enough— CAMEL PISS—and a double shot could be obtained for three pennies. It was a drink only for the reckless or the impecunious, but a fair number of both passed beneath the stern gaze of The Romp each night; Stanley rarely had a problem emptying the jug. And if it wasn't empty at the end of the night, why, there was always a fresh night coming along. Not to mention a fresh supply of thirsty fools.

But on this occasion Sheemie never made it to the Camel Piss jug behind the end of the bar. He tripped over the boot of the cowboy who had jerked forward, and went to his knees with a grunt of surprise. The contents of the bucket sloshed out ahead of him, and, following Satan's First Law of Malignity— to wit, if the worst can happen, it usually will—they drenched Roy Depape from the knees down in an eyewatering mixture of beer, *graf,* and white lightning.

Conversation at the bar stopped, and that stopped the talk of the men gathered around the dice-chute. Sheb turned, saw Sheemie kneeling before one of Jonas's men, and stopped playing. Pettie, her eyes squeezed shut as she poured her entire soul into her singing, continued on a capella for three or four bars before registering the silence which was spreading out like a ripple. She stopped singing and opened her eyes. That sort of silence usually meant that someone was going to be killed. If so, she didn't intend to miss it.

Depape stood perfectly still, inhaling the raw stench of alcohol as it rose. He didn't mind the smell; on the whole, it had the stink of pine-gum beat six ways to the Peddler. He didn't mind the way his pants were sticking to his knees, either. It might have been a bit of an irritation if some of that joy-juice had gotten down inside his boots, but none had.

His hand fell to the butt of his gun. Here, by god and by goddess, was something to take his mind off his sticky hands and absent whore. And good entertainment was ever worth a little wetting.

Silence blanketed the place now. Stanley stood as stiff as a soldier behind the bar, nervously plucking at one of his arm-garters. At the bar's other end, Reynolds looked back toward his partner with bright interest. He took a clam from the steaming bucket and cracked it on the edge of the bar like a boiled egg. At Depape's feet, Sheemie looked up, his eyes big and fearful beneath the wild snarl of his black hair. He was trying his best to smile.

"Wellnow, boy," Depape said. "You have wet me considerable."

"Sorry, big fella, I go trippy-trip." Sheemie jerked a hand back over his shoulder; a little spray of camel piss flew from the tips of his fingers. Somewhere someone cleared his throat nervously—*raa-aach!* The room was full of eyes, and quiet enough so that they all could hear both the wind in the eaves and the waves breaking on the rocks of Hambry Point, two miles away.

"The hell you did," said the cowpoke who had jerked. He was about twenty, and suddenly afraid he might never see his mother again. "Don't you go tryin to put your trouble off on me, you damned feeb."

"I don't care *how* it happened," Depape said. He was aware he was playing for an audience, and knew that what an audience mostly wants is to be entertained. Sai R. B. Depape, always a trouper, intended to oblige.

He pinched the corduroy of his pants above the knees and pulled the legs up, revealing the toes of his boots. They were shiny and wet.

"See there. Look at what you got on my boots."

Sheemie looked up at him, grinning and terrified.

Stanley Ruiz decided he couldn't let this happen without at least trying to stop it. He had known Dolores Sheemer, the boy's mother; there was even a possibility that he himself was the boy's father. In any case, he liked Sheemie. The boy was foolish, but his heart was good, he never took a drink, and he always did his work. Also, he could find a smile for you even on the coldest, foggiest winter's day. That was a talent many people of normal intelligence did not have.

"Sai Depape," he said, taking a step forward and speaking in a low, respectful tone. "I'm very sorry about that. I'll be happy to buy your drinks for the rest of the evening if we can just forget this regrettable—"

Depape's movement was a blur almost too fast to see, but that wasn't what amazed the people who were in the Rest that night; they would have expected a man running with Jonas to be fast. What amazed them was the fact that *he never looked around to set his target.* He located Stanley by his voice alone.

Depape drew his gun and swept it to the right in a rising arc. It struck Stanley Ruiz dead in the mouth, mashing his lips and shattering three of his teeth. Blood splashed the backbar mirror; several high-flying drops decorated the tip of The Romp's lefthand nose. Stanley screamed, clapped his hands to his face, and staggered back against the shelf behind him. In the silence, the chattery clink of the bottles was very loud.

Down the bar, Reynolds cracked another clam and watched, fascinated. Good as a play, it was.

Depape turned his attention back to the kneeling boy. "Clean my boots," he said.

A look of muddled relief came onto Sheemie's face. Clean his boots! Yes! You bet! Right away! He pulled the rag he always kept in his back pocket. It wasn't even dirty yet. Not very, at least.

"No," Depape said patiently. Sheemie looked up at him, gaping and puzzled. "Put that nasty clout back where it come from—I don't even want to look at it."

Sheemie tucked it into his back pocket again.

"Lick em," Depape said in that same patient voice. "That's what I want. You lick my boots until they're dry again, and so clean you can see your stupid rabbit's face in em."

Sheemie hesitated, as if still not sure what was required of him. Or perhaps he was only processing the information.

"I'd do it, boy," Barkie Callahan said from what he hoped was a safe place behind Sheb's piano. "If you want to see the sun come up, I'd surely do it."

Depape had already decided the mush-brain wasn't going to see another sunrise, not in *this* world, but kept quiet. He had never had his boots licked. He wanted to see what it felt like. If it was nice—kind of sexy-like—he could maybe try Her Nibs out on it.

"Does I have to?" Sheemie's eyes were filling with tears. "Can't just I-sorry and polish em real good?"

"*Lick*, you feeble-minded donkey," Depape said.

Sheemie's hair fell across his forehead. His tongue poked tentatively out between his lips, and as he bent his head toward Depape's boots, the first of his tears fell.

"Stop it, stop it, stop it," a voice said. It was shocking in the silence—not because it was sudden, and certainly not because it was angry. It was shocking because it was amused. "I simply can't allow that. Nope. I would if I could, but I can't. Unsanitary, you see. Who knows what disease might be spread in such fashion? The mind quails! Ab-so-lutely *cuh-wails!*"

Standing just inside the batwing doors was the purveyor of this idiotic and potentially fatal screed: a young man of middling height, his flat-crowned hat pushed back to reveal a tumbled comma of brown hair. Except *young man* didn't really cover him, Depape realized; *young man* was drawing it heavy. He was only a kid. Around his neck, gods knew why, he wore a bird's skull like an enormous comical pendant. It was hung on a chain that ran through the eyeholes. And in his hands was not a gun (*where would an unwhiskered dribble like him get a gun in the first place?* Depape wondered) but a goddam slingshot. Depape burst out laughing.

The kid laughed as well, nodding as if he understood how ridiculous the whole thing looked, how ridiculous the whole thing *was*. His laughter was infectious; Pettie, still up on her stool, tittered herself before clapping her hands over her mouth.

"This is no place for a boy such as you," Depape said. His revolver, an old five-shooter, was still out; it lay in his fist on the bar, with Stanley Ruiz's blood dripping off the gunsight. Depape, without raising it from the ironwood, waggled it slightly. "Boys who come to places like this learn bad habits, kid. Dying is apt to be one of them. So I give you this one chance. Get out of here."

"Thank you, sir, I appreciate my one chance," the boy said. He spoke with great and winning sincerity . . . but didn't move. Still he stood just inside the batwing doors, with the wide elastic strap of his sling pulled back. Depape couldn't quite make out what was in the cup, but it glittered in the gaslight. A metal ball of some sort.

"Well, then?" Depape snarled. This was getting old, and fast.

"I know I'm being a pain in the neck, sir—not to mention an ache in the ass and a milky drip from the tip of a sore dick—but if it's all the same to you, my dear friend, I'd like to give my chance to the young fellow on his knees before you. Let him apologize, let him polish your boots with his clout until you are entirely satisfied, and let him go on living his life."

There was an unfocused murmur of approval at this from the area where the card-players were watching. Depape didn't like the sound of it at all, and he made a sudden decision. The boy would die as well, executed for the crime of impertinence. The swabby who had spilled the bucket of dregs on him was clearly retarded. Yon brat had not even that excuse. He just thought he was funny.

From the corner of his eye, Depape saw Reynolds moving to flank the boy, smooth as oiled silk. Depape appreciated the thought, but didn't believe he'd need much help with the slingshot specialist.

"Boy, I think you've made a mistake," he said in a kindly voice. "I really believe—" The cup of the slingshot dipped a little . . . or Depape fancied it did. He made his move.

3

They talked about it in Hambry for years to come; three decades after the fall of Gilead and the end of the Affiliation, they were still talking. By that time there were better than five hundred old gaffers (and a few old gammers) claiming that they were drinking a beer in the Rest that night, and saw it all.

Depape was young, and had the speed of a snake. Nevertheless, he never came close to getting a shot off at Cuthbert Allgood. There was a *thip-TWANG!* as the elastic was released, a steel gleam that drew itself across the saloon's smoky air like a line on a slateboard, and then Depape screamed. His revolver tumbled to the floor, and a foot spun it away from him across the sawdust (no one would claim that foot while the Big Coffin Hunters were still in Hambry; hundreds claimed it after they were gone). Still screaming—he could not bear pain— Depape raised his bleeding hand and looked at it with agonized, unbelieving eyes. Actually, he had been lucky. Cuthbert's ball had smashed the tip of the second finger and torn off the nail. Lower, and Depape would have been able to blow smoke-rings through his own palm.

Cuthbert, meanwhile, had already reloaded the cup of his slingshot and drawn the elastic back again. "Now," he said, "if I have your attention, good sir—"

"I can't speak for his," Reynolds said from behind him, "but you got mine, partner. I don't know if you're good with that thing or just shitass lucky, but either way, you're done with it now. Relax the draw on it and put it down. That table in front of you's the place I want to see it."

"I've been blindsided," Cuthbert said sadly. "Betrayed once more by my own callow youth."

"I don't know nothing about your callow youth, brother, but you've been blindsided, all right," Reynolds agreed. He stood behind and slightly to the left of Cuthbert, and now he moved his gun forward until the boy could feel the muzzle against the back of his head. Reynolds thumbed the hammer. In the pool of silence which the Travellers' Rest had become, the sound was very loud. "Now put that twanger down."

"I think, good sir, that I must offer my regrets and decline."

"What?"

"You see, I've got my trusty sling aimed at your pleasant friend's head—" Cuthbert began, and when Depape shifted uneasily against the bar, Cuthbert's voice rose in a whipcrack that did not sound callow in the least. *"Stand still! Move again and you're a dead man!"*

Depape subsided, holding his bloody hand against his pine-tacky shirt. For the first time he looked frightened, and for the first time that night—for the first time since hooking up with Jonas, in fact—Reynolds felt mastery of a situation on the verge of slipping away . . . except how could it be? How could it be when he'd been able to circle around this smart-talking squint and get the drop on him? This should be *over.*

Lowering his voice to its former conversational—not to say playful—pitch, Cuthbert said: "If you shoot me, the ball flies and your friend dies, too."

"I don't believe that," Reynolds said, but he didn't like what he heard in his own voice. It sounded like doubt. "No man could make a shot like that."

"Why don't we let your friend decide?" Cuthbert raised his voice in a good-humored hail. "Hi-ho, there, Mr. Spectacles! Would you like your pal to shoot me?"

"No!" Depape's cry was shrill, verging on panic. "No, Clay! Don't shoot!"

"So it's a standoff," Reynolds said, bemused. And then bemusement changed to horror as he felt the blade of a very large knife slip against his throat. It pressed the tender skin just over his adam's apple.

"No, it's not," Alain said softly. "Put the gun down, my friend, or I'll cut your throat."

4

Standing outside the batwing doors, having arrived by simple good fortune in time for this Pinch and Jilly show, Jonas watched with amazement, contempt, and something close to horror. First one of the Affiliation brats gets the drop on Depape, and when Reynolds covers that one, the big kid with the round face and the plowboy's shoulders puts a knife to Reynolds's throat. Neither of the brats a day over fifteen, and neither with a gun. Marvelous. He would have thought it better than a travelling circus, if not for the problems that would follow if this were not put right. What sort of work could they do in Hambry if it got around that the boogeymen were afraid of the children, instead of vice-versa?

There's time to stop this before there's killing, mayhap. If you want to. Do you?

Jonas decided he did; that they could walk out winners if they played it just right. He also decided the Affiliation brats would not, unless they were very lucky indeed, be leaving Mejis Barony alive.

Where's the other one? Dearborn?

A good question. An *important* question. Embarrassment would become outright humiliation if he found himself trumped in the same fashion as Roy and Clay.

Dearborn wasn't in the bar, and that was sure. Jonas turned on his heels, scanning the South High Street in both directions. It was almost day-bright under a Kissing Moon only two nights past the full. No one there, not in the street, not on the far side, where Hambry's mercantile store stood. The mercantile had a porch, but there was nothing on it save for a line of carved totems illustrating Guardians of the Beam: Bear, Turtle, Fish, Eagle, Lion, Bat, and Wolf. Seven of twelve, bright as marble in the moonlight, and no doubt great favorites of the kiddies. No men over there, though. Good. Lovely.

Jonas peered hard into the thread of alley between the mercantile and the butcher's, glimpsed a shadow behind a tumble of cast-off boxes, tensed, then relaxed as he saw a cat's shining green eyes. He nodded and turned to the business at hand, pushing back the lefthand batwing and stepping into the Travellers' Rest. Alain heard the squeak of a hinge, but Jonas's gun was at his temple before he could even begin to turn.

"Sonny, unless you're a barber, I think you'd better put that pigsticker down. You don't get a second warning."

"No," Alain said.

Jonas, who had expected nothing but compliance and had been prepared for nothing else, was thunderstruck. *"What?"*

"You heard me," Alain said. "I said no."

5

After making their manners and excusing themselves from Seafront, Roland had left his friends to their own amusements—they would finish up at the Travellers' Rest, he supposed, but wouldn't stay long or get into much trouble when they had no money for cards and could drink nothing more exciting than cold tea. He had ridden into town another way, tethered his mount at a public post in the lower of the two town squares (Rusher had offered a single puzzled nicker at this treatment, but no more), and had since been tramping the empty, sleeping streets with his hat yanked low over his eyes and his hands clasped into an aching knot at the small of his back.

His mind was full of questions—things were wrong here, very wrong. At first he'd thought that was just his imagination, the childish part of him finding make-believe troubles and storybook intrigue because he had been removed from the heart of the real action. But after his talk with "Rennie" Renfrew, he knew better. There were questions, outright mysteries, and the most hellish thing of all was that he couldn't concentrate on them, let alone go any distance toward making sense of them. Every time he tried, Susan Delgado's face intruded . . . her face, or the sweep of her hair, or even the pretty, fear-less way her silk-slippered feet had followed his boots in the dance, never lagging or hesitating. Again and again he heard the last thing he had said to her, speaking in the stilted, priggish voice of a boy preacher. He would have given almost anything to take back both the tone and the words themselves. She'd be on Thorin's pillow come Reaptide, and kindle him a child before the first snow flew, perhaps a male heir, and what of it? Rich men, famous men, and well-blooded men had taken gilly-girls since the beginning of time; Arthur Eld had had better than forty himself, according to the tales. So, really, what was it to him?

I think I've gone and fallen in love with her. That's what it is to me.

A dismaying idea, but not a dismissable one; he knew the landscape of his own heart too well. He loved her, very likely it was so, but part of him also hated her, and held to the shocking thought he'd had at dinner: that he could have shot Susan Delgado through the heart if he'd come armed. Some of this was jealousy, but not all; perhaps not even the greater part. He had made some indefinable but powerful connection between Olive Thorin—her sad but game little smile from the foot of the table—and his own mother. Hadn't some of that same woeful, rueful look been in his mother's eyes on the day when he had come upon her and his father's advisor? Marten in an open-throated shirt, Gabrielle Deschain in a sacque that had slipped off one shoulder, the whole room reeking of what they had been up to that hot morning?

His mind, tough as it already was, shrank from the image, horrified. It returned instead to that of Susan Delgado—her gray eyes and shining hair. He saw her laughing, chin uptilted, hands clasped before the sapphire Thorin had given her.

Roland could forgive her the gilly business, he supposed. What he could not forgive, in spite of his attraction to Susan, was that awful smile on Olive Thorin's face as she watched the girl sitting in what should have been her place. Sitting in her place and laughing.

These were the things that chased through his head as he paced off acres of moonlight. He had no business with such thoughts, Susan Delgado was not the reason he was here, nor was the ridiculous knuckle-cracking Mayor and his pitiable country-Mary of a wife . . . yet he couldn't put them away and get to what *was* his business. He had forgotten the face of his father, and walked in the moonlight, hoping to find it again.

In such fashion he came along the sleeping, silver-gilded High Street, walking north to south, thinking vaguely that he would perhaps stand Cuthbert and Alain to a taste of something wet and toss the dice down Satan's Alley a time or two before going back to get Rusher and call it a night. And so it was that he happened to spy Jonas—the man's gaunt figure and fall of long white hair were impossible to mistake—standing outside the batwings of the Travellers' Rest and peering in. Jonas did this with one hand on the butt of his gun and a tense set of body that put everything else from

Roland's mind at once. Something was going on, and if Bert and Alain were in there, it might involve them. They were the strangers in town, after all, and it was possible—even likely—that not everyone in Hambry loved the Affiliation with the fervor that had been professed at tonight's dinner. Or perhaps it was Jonas's friends who were in trouble. *Something* was brewing, in any case.

With no clear thought as to why he was doing it, Roland went softly up the steps to the mercantile's porch. There was a line of carved animals there (and probably spiked firmly to the boards, so that drunken wags from the saloon across the street couldn't carry them away, chanting the nursery rhymes of their childhood as they went). Roland stepped behind the last one in line—it was the Bear—and bent his knees so that the crown of his hat wouldn't show. Then he went as still as the carving. He could see Jonas turn, look across the street, then look to his left, peering at something—

Very low, a sound: *Waow! Waow!*

It's a cat. In the alley.

Jonas looked a moment longer, then stepped into the Rest. Roland was out from behind the carved bear, down the steps, and into the street at once. He hadn't Alain's gift of the touch, but he had intuitions that were sometimes very strong. This one was telling him he must hurry.

Overhead, the Kissing Moon drifted behind a cloud.

6

Pettie the Trotter still stood on her stool, but she no longer felt drunk and singing was the last thing on her mind. She could hardly believe what she was seeing: Jonas had the drop on a boy who had the drop on Reynolds who had the drop on *another* boy (this last one wearing a bird's skull around his neck on a chain) who had the drop on Roy Depape. Who had, in fact, drawn some of Roy Depape's blood. And when Jonas had told the big boy to put down the knife he was holding to Reynolds's throat, *the big boy had refused.*

You can blow my lights out and send me to the clearing at the end of the path, thought Pettie, *for now I've seen it all, so I have.* She supposed she should get off the stool—there was apt to be shooting any second now, and likely a great lot of it—but sometimes you just had to take your chances.

Because some things were just too good to miss.

7

"We're in this town on Affiliation business," Alain said. He had one hand buried deep in Reynolds's sweaty hair; the other maintained a steady pressure on the knife at Reynolds's throat. Not quite enough to break the skin. "If you harm us, the Affiliation will take note. So will our fathers. You'll be hunted like dogs and hung upside down, like as not, when you're caught."

"Sonny, there's not an Affiliation patrol within two hundred wheels of here, probably three hundred," Jonas said, "and I wouldn't care a fart in a windstorm if there was one just over yon hill. Nor do your fathers mean a squitter to me. Put that knife down or I'll blow your fucking brains out."

"No."

"Future developments in this matter should be quite wonderful," Cuthbert said cheerily . . . although there was now a beat of nerves under his prattle. Not fear, perhaps not even nervous-*ness*, just nerves. The good kind, more likely than not, Jonas thought sourly. He had underestimated these boys at meat; if nothing else was clear, that was. "You shoot Richard, and Richard cuts Mr. Cloak's throat just as Mr. Cloak shoots me; my poor dying fingers release my sling's elastic and put a steel ball in what passes for Mr. Spectacles's brain. *You'll* walk away, at least, and I suppose that will be a great comfort to your dead friends."

"Call it a draw," Alain said to the man with the gun at his temple. "We all stand back and walk away."

"No, sonny," Jonas said. His voice was patient, and he didn't think his anger showed, but it was rising. Gods, to be outfaced like this, even temporarily! "No one does like that to the Big Coffin Hunters. This is your last chance to—"

Something hard and cold and very much to the point pressed against the back of Jonas's shirt, dead center between the shoulderblades. He knew what it was and who held it at once, understood the game was lost, but couldn't understand how such a ludicrous, maddening turn of events could have happened.

"Holster the gun," the voice behind the sharp tip of metal said. It was empty, somehow—not just calm, but emotionless. "Do it now, or this goes in your heart. No more talk. Talking's done. Do it or die."

Jonas heard two things in that voice: youth and truth. He holstered his gun.

"You with the black hair. Take your gun out of my friend's ear and put it back in your holster. Now."

Clay Reynolds didn't have to be invited twice, and he uttered a long, shaky sigh when Alain took the blade off his throat and stood back. Cuthbert did not look around, only stood with the elastic of his slingshot pulled and his elbow cocked.

"You at the bar," Roland said. "Holster up."

Depape did so, grimacing with pain as he bumped his

hurt finger against his gunbelt. Only when this gun was put away did Cuthbert relax his hold on his sling and drop the ball from the cup into the palm of his hand.

The cause of all this had been forgotten as the effects played themselves out. Now Sheemie got to his feet and pelted across the room. His cheeks were wet with tears. He grasped one of Cuthbert's hands, kissed it several times (loud smacking noises that would have been comic under other circumstances), and held the hand to his cheek for a moment. Then he dodged past Reynolds, pushed open the righthand batwing, and flew right into the arms of a sleepy-eyed and still half-drunk Sheriff. Avery had been fetched by Sheb from the jailhouse, where the Sheriff o' Barony had been sleeping off the Mayor's ceremonial dinner in one of his own cells.

8

"This is a nice mess, isn't it?"

Avery speaking. No one answering. He hadn't expected they would, not if they knew what was good for them.

The office area of the jail was too small to hold three men, three strapping not-quite-men, and one extra-large Sheriff comfortably, so Avery had herded them into the nearby Town Gathering Hall, which echoed to the soft flutter of the pigeons in the rafters and the steady beat-beat-beat of the grandfather clock behind the podium.

It was a plain room, but an inspired choice all the same. It was where the townsfolk and Barony landowners had come for hundreds of years to make their decisions, pass their laws, and occasionally send some especially troublesome person west. There was a feeling of seriousness in its moon-glimmered darkness, and Roland thought even the old man, Jonas, felt a little of it. Certainly it invested Sheriff Herk Avery with an authority he might not otherwise have been able to project.

The room was filled with what were in that place and time called "bareback benches"—oaken pews with no cushions for either butt *or* back. There were sixty in all, thirty on each side of a wide center aisle. Jonas, Depape, and Reynolds sat on the front bench to the left of the aisle. Roland, Cuthbert, and Alain sat across from them on the right. Reynolds and Depape looked sullen and embarrassed; Jonas looked remote and composed. Will Dearborn's little crew was quiet. Roland had given Cuthbert a look which he hoped the boy could read: *One smart remark and I'll rip the tongue right out of your head.* He thought the message had been received. Bert had stowed his idiotic "lookout" somewhere, which was a good sign.

"A nice mess," Avery repeated, and blew liquor-scented wind at them in a deep sigh. He was sitting on the edge of the stage with his short legs hanging down, looking at them with a kind of disgusted wonder.

The side door opened and in came Deputy Dave, his white service jacket laid aside, his monocle tucked into the pocket of his more usual khaki shirt. In one hand he carried a mug; in the other a folded scrap of what looked to Roland like birch-bark.

"Did ye boil the first half, David?" Avery asked. He now wore a put-upon expression.

"Aye."

"Boiled it twice?"

"Aye, twice."

"For that was the directions."

"Aye," Dave repeated in a resigned voice. He handed Avery the cup and dumped the remaining contents of the birch-bark scrap in when the Sheriff held the cup out for them.

Avery swirled the liquid, peered in with a doubtful, resigned expression, then drank. He grimaced. "Oh, foul!" he cried. "What's so nasty as this?"

"What is it?" Jonas asked.

"Headache powder. *Hangover* powder, ye might say. From the old witch. The one who lives up the Cöos. Know where I mean?" Avery gave Jonas a knowing look. The old gunny pretended not to see it, but Roland thought he had. And what did it mean? Another mystery.

Depape looked up at the word *Cöos*, then went back to sucking his wounded finger. Beyond Depape, Reynolds sat with his cloak drawn about him, looking grimly down at his lap.

"Does it work?" Roland asked.

"Aye, boy, but ye pay a price for witch's medicine. Remember that: ye always pay. This 'un takes away the headache if ye drink too much of Mayor Thorin's damned punch, but it gripes the bowels somethin fierce, so it does. And the farts—!" He waved a hand in front of his face to demonstrate, took another sip from the cup, then set it aside. He returned to his former gravity, but the mood in the room had lightened just a little; they all felt it. "Now what are we to do about this business?"

Herk Avery swept them slowly with his eyes, from Reynolds on his far right to Alain—"Richard Stockworth"—on his far left. "Eh, boys? We've got the Mayor's men on one side and the Affiliation's . . . men . . . on the other, six fellows at the point of murder, and over what? A halfwit and a spilled bucket of slops." He pointed first at the Big Coffin Hunters, then to the Affiliation's counters. "Two powderkegs and one fat sheriff in the middle. So what's yer thoughts on't? Speak up, don't be shy, you wasn't shy in Coral's whoreden down the road, don't be shy in here!"

No one said anything. Avery sipped some more of his

foul drink, then set it down and looked at them decisively. What he said next didn't surprise Roland much; it was exactly what he would have expected of a man like Avery, right down to the tone which implied that he considered himself a man who could make the hard decisions when he had to, by the gods.

"I'll tell yer what we're going to do: We're going to forget it."

He now assumed the air of one who expects an uproar and is prepared to handle it. When no one spoke or even shuffled a foot, he looked discomfited. Yet he had a job to do, and the night was growing old. He squared his shoulders and pushed on.

"I'll not spend the next three or four months waiting to see who among you's killed who. Nay! Nor will I be put in a position where I might have to take the punishment for your stupid quarrel over that halfwit Sheemie.

"I appeal to your practical natures, boys, when I point out that I may be either your friend or your enemy during your time here . . . but I'd be wrong if I didn't also appeal to your more noble natures, which I am sure are both large and sensitive."

The Sheriff now tried on an exalted expression, which was not, in Roland's estimation, notably successful. Avery turned his attention to Jonas.

"Sai, I can't believe ye'll want to be causin trouble for three young men from the Affiliation—the Affiliation that's been like mother's milk and father's shelterin hand since aye or oh fifty generations back; ye'd not be so disrespectful as all that, would ye?"

Jonas shook his head, smiling his thin smile.

Avery nodded again. Things were going along well, that nod said. "Ye've all yer own cakes to bake and oats to roll, and none of ye wants something like this to get in the way of doin yer jobs, do yer?"

They all shook their heads this time.

"So what I want you to do is to stand up, face each other, shake hands, and cry each other's pardon. If ye don't do that, ye can all ride west out of town by sunrise, far as I'm concerned."

He picked up the mug and took a bigger drink this time. Roland saw that the man's hand was trembling the tiniest bit, and wasn't surprised. It was all bluff and blow, of course. The Sheriff would have understood that Jonas, Reynolds, and Depape were beyond his authority as soon as he saw the small blue coffins on their hands; after tonight, he must feel the same way about Dearborn, Stockworth, and Heath. He could only hope that all would see where their self-interest lay. Roland did. So, apparently, did Jonas, for even as Roland got up, Jonas did the same.

Avery recoiled a little bit, as if expecting Jonas to go for his gun and Dearborn for the knife in his belt, the one he'd been holding against Jonas's back when Avery came puffing up to the saloon.

There was no gun or knife drawn, however. Jonas turned toward Roland and held out his hand.

"He's right, lad," Jonas said in his reedy, quavering voice.

"Yes."

"Will you shake with an old man, and vow to start over?"

"Yes." Roland held out his hand.

Jonas took it. "I cry your pardon."

"I cry your own, Mr. Jonas." Roland tapped left-hand at his throat, as was proper when addressing an elder in such fashion.

As the two of them sat down, Alain and Reynolds rose, as neatly as men in a prerehearsed ceremony. Last of all,

Cuthbert and Depape rose. Roland was all but positive that Cuthbert's foolishness would pop out like Jack from his box—the idiot would simply not be able to help himself, although he must surely realize that Depape was no man to make sport of tonight.

"Cry your pardon," Bert said, with an admirable lack of laughter in his voice.

"Cryerown," Depape mumbled, and held out his blood-streaked hand. Roland had a nightmare vision of Bert squeezing down on it as hard as he could, making the redhead yowl like an owl on a hot stove, but Bert's grip was as restrained as his voice.

Avery sat on the edge of the stage with his pudgy legs hanging down, watching it all with avuncular good cheer. Even Deputy Dave was smiling.

"Now I propose to shake hands with yer all myself, 'n then send yer on yer ways, for the hour's late, so it is, and such as me needs my beauty rest." He chuckled, and again looked uncomfortable when no one joined in. But he slipped off the stage and began to shake hands, doing so with the enthusiasm of a minister who has finally succeeded in marrying a headstrong couple after a long and stormy courtship.

9

When they stepped outside, the moon was down and the first lightening in the sky had begun to show at the far edge of the Clean Sea.

"Mayhap we'll meet again, sai," Jonas said.

"Mayhap we will," Roland said, and swung up into his saddle.

10

The Big Coffin Hunters were staying in the watchman's house about a mile south of Seafront—five miles out of town, this was.

Halfway there, Jonas stopped at a turnout beside the road. From here the land made a steep, rocky descent to the brightening sea.

"Get down, mister," he said. It was Depape he was looking at.

"Jonas . . . Jonas, I . . ."

"Get down."

Biting his lip nervously, Depape got down.

"Take off your spectacles."

"Jonas, what's this about? I don't—"

"Or if you want em broke, leave em on. It's all the same to me."

Biting his lip harder now, Depape took off his gold-rimmed spectacles. They were barely in his hand before Jonas had fetched him a terrific clip on the side of the head. Depape cried out and reeled toward the drop. Jonas drove forward, moving as fast as he had struck, and seized him by the shirt just before he went tumbling over the edge. Jonas twisted his hand into the shirt material and yanked Depape toward him. He breathed deep, inhaling the scent of pine-tar and Depape's sweat.

"I ought to toss you right over the edge," he breathed. "Do you know how much harm you've done?"

"I . . . Jonas, I never meant . . . just a little fun is all I . . . how was we supposed to know they . . ."

Slowly, Jonas's hand relaxed. That last bit of babble had gone home. How was they supposed to know, that was ungrammatical but right. And if not for tonight, they might *not* have known. If you looked at it that way, Depape had actually done them a favor. The devil you knew was always preferable to the devil you didn't. Still, word would get around, and people would laugh. Maybe even that was all right, though. The laughter would stop in due time.

"Jonas, I cry your pardon."

"Shut up," Jonas said. In the east, the sun would shortly heave itself over the horizon, casting its first gleams on a new day in this world of toil and sorrow. "I ain't going to toss you over, because then I'd have to toss Clay over and follow along myself. They got the drop on us the same as you, right?"

Depape wanted to agree, but thought it might be dangerous to do so. He was prudently silent.

"Get down here, Clay."

Clay slid off his mount.

"Now hunker."

The three of them hunkered on their bootsoles, heels up. Jonas plucked a shoot of grass and put it between his lips. "Affiliation brats is what we were told, and we had no reason not to believe it," he said. "The bad boys are sent all the way to Mejis, a sleepy Barony on the Clean Sea, on a make-work detail that's two parts penance and three parts punishment. Ain't that what we were told?"

They nodded.

"Either of you believe it after tonight?"

Depape shook his head. So did Clay.

"They may be rich boys, but that's not all they are," Depape said. "The way they were tonight . . . they were like . . ." He trailed off, not quite willing to finish the thought. It was too absurd.

Jonas was willing. "They acted like gunslingers."

Neither Jonas nor Reynolds replied at first. Then Clay

Reynolds said, "They're too young, Eldred. Too young by *years*."

"Not too young to be 'prentices, mayhap. In any case, we're going to find out." He turned to Depape. "You've got some riding to do, cully."

"Aww, Jonas—!"

"None of us exactly covered ourselves with glory, but you were the fool that started the pot boiling." He looked at Depape, but Depape only looked down at the ground between them. "You're going to ride their backtrail, Roy, and you're going to ask questions until you've got the answers you think will satisfy my curiosity. Clay and I are mostly going to wait. And watch. Play Castles with em, if you like. When I feel like enough time's gone by for us to be able to do a little snooping without being trigged, mayhap we'll do it."

He bit on the piece of grass in his mouth. The larger piece tumbled out and lay between his boots.

"Do you know why I shook his hand? That boy Dearborn's damned hand? Because we can't rock the boat, boys. Not just when it's edging in toward harbor. Latigo and the folks we've been waiting for will be moving toward us very soon, now. Until they get into these parts, it's in our interest to keep the peace. But I tell you this: no one puts a knife to Eldred Jonas's back and lives. Now listen, Roy. Don't make me tell you any of this twice."

Jonas began to speak, leaning forward over his knees toward Depape as he did. After awhile, Depape began to nod. He might like a little trip, actually. After the recent comedy in the Travellers' Rest, a change of air might be just the ticket.

II

The boys were almost back to the Bar K and the sun was coming over the horizon before Cuthbert broke the silence. "Well! That was an amusing and instructive evening, was it not?" Neither Roland nor Alain replied, so Cuthbert leaned over to the rook's skull, which he had returned to its former place on the horn of his saddle. "What say *you*, old friend? Did we enjoy our evening? Dinner, a circle-dance, and almost killed to top things off. Did you enjoy?"

The lookout only stared ahead of Cuthbert's horse with its great dark eyes.

"He says he's too tired for talk," Cuthbert said, then yawned. "So'm I, actually." He looked at Roland. "I got a good look into Mr. Jonas's eyes after he shook hands with you, Will. He means to kill you."

Roland nodded.

"They mean to kill all of us," Alain said.

Roland nodded again. "We'll make it hard for them, but they know more about us now than they did at dinner. We'll not get behind them that way again."

He stopped, just as Jonas had stopped not three miles from where they now were. Only instead of looking directly out over the Clean Sea, Roland and his friends were looking down the long slope of the Drop. A herd of horses was moving from west to east, barely more than shadows in this light.

"What do you see, Roland?" Alain asked, almost timidly.

"Trouble," Roland said, "and in our road." Then he gigged his horse and rode on. Before they got back to the Bar K bunkhouse, he was thinking about Susan again. Five minutes after he dropped his head on his flat burlap pillow, he was dreaming of her.

CHAPTER SEVEN

On the Drop

I

Three weeks had passed since the welcoming dinner at Mayor's House and the incident at the Travellers' Rest. There had been no more trouble between Roland's *ka-tet* and Jonas's. In the night sky, Kissing Moon had waned and Peddler's Moon had made its first thin appearance. The days were bright and warm; even the oldtimers admitted it was one of the most beautiful summers in memory.

On a mid-morning as beautiful as any that summer, Susan Delgado galloped a two-year-old *rosillo* named Pylon north along the Drop. The wind dried the tears on her cheeks and yanked her unbound hair out behind her as she went. She urged Pylon to go faster yet, lightly thumping his sides with her spurless boots. Pylon turned it up a notch at once, ears flattening, tail flagging. Susan, dressed in jeans and the faded, oversized khaki shirt (one of her da's) that had caused all the trouble, leaned over the light practice saddle, holding to the horn with one hand and rubbing the other down the side of the horse's strong, silky neck.

"More!" she whispered. "More and faster! Go on, boy!"

Pylon let it out yet another notch. That he had at least one more in him she knew; that he had even one more beyond that she suspected.

They sped along the Drop's highest ridge, and she barely saw the magnificent slope of land below her, all green and gold, or the way it faded into the blue haze of the Clean Sea. On any other day the view and the cool, salt-smelling breeze would have uplifted her. Today she only wanted to hear the steady low thunder of Pylon's hoofs and feel the flex of his muscles beneath her; today she wanted to outrun her own thoughts.

And all because she had come downstairs this morning dressed for riding in one of her father's old shirts.

2

Aunt Cord had been at the stove, wrapped in her dressing gown and with her hair still netted. She dished herself up a bowl of oatmeal and brought it to the table. Susan had known things weren't good as soon as her aunt turned toward her, bowl in hand; she could see the discontented twitch of Aunt Cord's lips, and the disapproving glance she shot at the orange Susan was peeling. Her aunt was still rankled by the silver and gold she had expected to have in hand by now, coins which would be withheld yet awhile due to the witch's prankish decree that Susan should remain a virgin until autumn.

But that wasn't the main thing, and Susan knew it. Quite simply put, the two of them had had enough of each other. The money was only one of Aunt Cord's disappointed expectations; she had counted on having the house at the edge of the Drop to herself this summer . . . except, perhaps, for the occasional visit from Mr. Eldred Jonas, with whom Cordelia seemed quite taken. Instead, here they still were, one woman growing toward the end of her courses, thin, disapproving lips in a thin, disapproving face, tiny apple-breasts under her high-necked dresses with their choker collars (The Neck, she frequently told Susan, is the First Thing to Go), her hair losing its former chestnut shine and showing wire-threads of gray; the other young, intelligent, agile, and rounding toward the peak of her physical beauty. They grated against each other, each word seeming to produce a spark, and that was not surprising. The man who had loved them both enough to make them love each other was gone.

"Are ye going out on that horse?" Aunt Cord had said, putting her bowl down and sitting in a shaft of early sun. It was a bad location, one she never would have allowed herself to be caught in had Mr. Jonas been in attendance. The strong light made her face look like a carved mask. There was a cold-sore growing at one corner of her mouth; she always got them when she was not sleeping well.

"Aye," Susan said.

"Ye should eat more'n that, then. 'Twon't keep ye til nine o' the clock, girl."

"It'll keep me fine," Susan had replied, eating the sections of orange faster. She could see where this was tending, could see the look of dislike and disapproval in her aunt's eyes, and wanted to get away from the table before trouble could begin.

"Why not let me get ye a dish of this?" Aunt Cord asked, and plopped her spoon into her oatmeal. To Susan it sounded like a horse's hoof stamping down in mud—or shit—and her stomach clenched. "It'll hold ye to lunch, if ye plan to ride so long. I suppose a fine young lady such as yerself can't be bothered with chores—"

"They're done." *And you know they're done,* she did not add. *I did em while you were sitting before your glass, poking at that sore on your mouth.*

Aunt Cord dropped a chunk of creamery butter into

her muck—Susan had no idea how the woman stayed so thin, really she didn't—and watched it begin to melt. For a moment it seemed that breakfast might end on a reasonably civilized note, after all.

Then the shirt business had begun.

"Before ye go out, Susan, I want ye to take off that rag you're wearing and put on one of the new riding blouses Thorin sent ye week before last. It's the least ye can do to show yer—"

Anything her aunt might have said past that point would have been lost in anger even if Susan hadn't interrupted. She passed a hand down the sleeve of her shirt, loving its texture—it was almost velvety from so many washings. "This *rag* belonged to my father!"

"Aye, Pat's." Aunt Cord sniffed. "It's too big for ye, and worn out, and not proper, in any case. When you were young it was mayhap all right to wear a man's button-shirt, but now that ye have a woman's bustline . . ."

The riding blouses were on hangers in the corner; they had come four days ago and Susan hadn't even deigned to take them up to her room. There were three of them, one red, one green, one blue, all silk, all undoubtedly worth a small fortune. She loathed their pretension, and the overblown, blushy-frilly look of them: full sleeves to flutter artistically in the wind, great floppy foolish collars . . . and, of course, the low-scooped fronts which were probably all Thorin would see if she appeared before him dressed in one. As she wouldn't, if she could possibly help it.

"My 'woman's bust-line,' as you call it, is of no interest to me and can't possibly be of any interest to anyone else when I'm out riding," Susan said.

"Perhaps, perhaps not. If one of the Barony's drovers should see you—even Rennie, he's out that way all the time, as ye well know—it wouldn't hurt for him to mention to Hart that he saw ye wearing one of the *camisas* that he so kindly gave to ye. Now would it? Why do ye have to be such a stiffkins, girl? Why always so unwilling, so unfair?"

"What does it matter to ye, one way or t'other?" Susan had asked. "Ye have the money, don't ye? And ye'll have more yet. After he fucks me."

Aunt Cord, her face white and shocked and furious, had leaned across the table and slapped her. "How dare thee use that word in my house, ye *malhablada*? How *dare* ye?"

That was when her tears began to flow—at hearing her call it her house. "It was my *father's* house! His and mine! Ye were all on yer own with no real place to go, except perhaps to the Quarters, and he took ye in! *He took ye in, Aunt!*"

The last two orange sections were still in her hand. She threw them into her aunt's face, then pushed herself back from the table so violently that her chair tottered, tipped, and spilled her to the floor. Her aunt's shadow fell over her. Susan crawled frantically out of it, her hair hanging, her slapped cheek throbbing, her eyes burning with tears, her throat swelled and hot. At last she found her feet.

"Ye ungrateful girl," her aunt said. Her voice was soft and so full of venom it was almost caressing. "After all I have done for thee, and all Hart Thorin has done for thee. Why, the very nag ye mean to ride this morning was Hart's gift of respect to—"

"*PYLON WAS OURS!*" she shrieked, almost maddened with fury at this deliberate blurring of the truth. "*ALL OF THEM WERE! THE HORSES, THE LAND—THEY WERE OURS!*"

"Lower thy voice," Aunt Cord said.

Susan took a deep breath and tried to find some control. She swept her hair back from her face, revealing the red print of Aunt Cord's hand on her cheek. Cordelia flinched a little at the sight of it.

"My father never would have allowed this," Susan said. "He never would have allowed me to go as Hart Thorin's gilly. Whatever he might have felt about Hart as the Mayor . . . or as his *patrono* . . . he never would have allowed this. And ye know it. *Thee* knows it."

Aunt Cord rolled her eyes, then twirled a finger around her ear as if Susan had gone mad. "Thee agreed to it yerself, Miss Oh So Young and Pretty. Aye, so ye did. And if yer girlish megrims now cause ye to want to cry off what's been done—"

"Aye," Susan agreed. "I agreed to the bargain, so I did. After ye'd dunned me about it day and night, after ye'd come to me in tears—"

"I never did!" Cordelia cried, stung.

"Have ye forgotten so quick, Aunt? Aye, I suppose. As by tonight ye'll have forgotten slapping me at breakfast. Well, *I* haven't forgotten. Thee cried, all right, cried and told me ye feared we might be turned off the land, since we had no more legal right to it, that we'd be on the road, thee wept and said—"

"Stop calling me that!" Aunt Cord shouted. Nothing on earth maddened her so much as having her own thees and thous turned back at her. "Thee has no more right to the old tongue than thee has to thy stupid sheep's complaints! Go on! Get out!"

But Susan went on. Her rage was at the flood and would not be turned aside.

"Thee wept and said we'd be turned out, turned west, that we'd never see my da's homestead or Hambry again . . . and then, when I was frightened enough, ye talked of the cunning little baby I'd have. The land that was ours to begin with given back again. The horses that were ours likewise given back. As a sign of the Mayor's honesty, I have a horse *I myself helped to foal.* And what have I done to deserve these things that would have been mine in any case, but for the loss of a single paper? What have I done so that he should give ye money? What have I done save promise to fuck him while his wife of forty year sleeps down the hall?"

"Is it the money ye want, then?" Aunt Cord asked, smiling furiously. "Do ye and do ye and aye? Ye shall have it, then. Take it, keep it, lose it, feed it to the swine, I care not!"

She turned to her purse, which hung on a post by the stove. She began to fumble in it, but her motions quickly lost speed and conviction. There was an oval of mirror mounted to the left of the kitchen doorway, and in it Susan caught sight of her aunt's face. What she saw there—a mixture of hatred, dismay, and greed—made her heart sink.

"Never mind, Aunt. I see thee's loath to give it up, and I wouldn't have it, anyway. It's whore's money."

Aunt Cord turned back to her, face shocked, her purse conveniently forgotten. " 'Tis not whoring, ye stupid get! Why, some of the greatest women in history have been gillys, and some of the greatest men have been born *of* gillys. *'Tis not whoring!*"

Susan ripped the red silk blouse from where it hung and held it up. The shirt moulded itself to her breasts as if it had been longing all the while to touch them. "Then why does he send me these whore's clothes?"

"Susan!" Tears stood in Aunt Cord's eyes.

Susan flung the shirt at her as she had the orange slices. It landed on her shoes. "Pick it up and put it on yerself, if ye fancy. *You* spread yer legs for him, if ye fancy."

She turned and hurled herself out the door. Her aunt's half-hysterical shriek had followed her: "Don't thee go off thinking foolish thoughts, Susan! Foolish thoughts lead to foolish deeds, and it's too late for either! Thee's agreed!"

She knew that. And however fast she rode Pylon along the Drop, she could not outrace her knowing. She had agreed, and no matter how horrified Pat Delgado might have been at the fix she had gotten herself into, he would have seen one thing clear—she had made a promise, and promises must be kept. Hell awaited those who would not do so.

3

She eased the *rosillo* back while he still had plenty of wind. She looked behind her, saw that she had come nearly a mile, and brought him down further—to a canter, a trot, a fast walk. She took a deep breath and let it out. For the first time that morning she registered the day's bright beauty—gulls circling in the hazy air off to the west, high grasses all around her, and flowers in every shaded cranny: cornflowers and lupin and phlox and her favorites, the delicate blue silkflowers. From everywhere came the somnolent buzz of bees. The sound soothed her, and with the high surge of her emotions subsiding a little, she was able to admit something to herself . . . admit it, and then voice it aloud.

"Will Dearborn," she said, and shivered at the sound of his name on her lips, even though there was no one to hear it but Pylon and the bees. So she said it again, and when the words were out she abruptly turned her own wrist inward to her mouth and kissed it where the blood beat close to the surface. The action shocked her because she hadn't known she was going to do it, and shocked her more because the taste of her own skin and sweat aroused her immediately. She felt an urge to cool herself off as she had in her bed after meeting him. The way she felt, it would be short work.

Instead, she growled her father's favorite cuss—"Oh, bite it!"—and spat past her boot. Will Dearborn had been responsible for all too much upset in her life these last three weeks; Will Dearborn with his unsettling blue eyes, his dark tumble of hair, and his stiff-necked, judgmental attitude. *I can be discreet, madam. As for propriety? I'm amazed you even know the word.*

Every time she thought of that, her blood sang with anger and shame. Mostly anger. How dare he presume to make judgments? He who had grown up possessing every luxury, no doubt with servants to tend his every whim and so much gold that he likely didn't even need it—he would be given the things he wanted free, as a way of currying favor. What would a boy like that—for that was all he was, really, just a boy—know about the hard choices she had made? For that matter, how could such as Mr. Will Dearborn of Hemphill understand that she hadn't really made those choices at all? That she had been carried to them the way a mother cat carries a wayward kitten back to the nesting-box, by the scruff of the neck?

Still, he wouldn't leave her mind; she knew, even if Aunt Cord didn't, that there had been an unseen third present at their quarrel this morning.

She knew something else as well, something that would have upset her aunt to no end.

Will Dearborn hadn't forgotten her, either.

4

About a week after the welcoming dinner and Dearborn's disastrous, hurtful remark to her, the retarded slops-fella

from the Travellers' Rest—Sheemie, folks called him—
had appeared at the house Susan and her aunt shared.
In his hands he held a large bouquet, mostly made up
of the wildflowers that grew out on the Drop, but with a
scattering of dusky wild roses, as well. They looked like
pink punctuation marks. On the boy's face there had
been a wide, sunny grin as he swung the gate open, not
waiting for an invitation.

Susan had been sweeping the front walk at the time;
Aunt Cord had been out back, in the garden. That was
fortunate, but not very surprising; these days the two of
them got on best when they kept apart as much as they
could.

Susan had watched Sheemie come up the walk, his
grin beaming out from behind his upheld freight of
flowers, with a mixture of fascination and horror.

"G'day, Susan Delgado, daughter of Pat," Sheemie
said cheerfully. "I come to you on an errand and cry yer
pardon at any troubleation I be, oh aye, for I am a problem for folks, and know it same as them. These be for
you. Here."

He thrust them out, and she saw a small, folded envelope tucked amongst them.

"Susan?" Aunt Cord's voice, from around the side of
the house . . . and getting closer. "Susan, did I hear the
gate?"

"Yes, Aunt!" she called back. Curse the woman's sharp
ears! Susan nimbly plucked the envelope from its place
among the phlox and daisies. Into her dress pocket it
went.

"They from my third-best friend," Sheemie said. "I got
three different friends now. This many." He held up two
fingers, frowned, added two more, and then grinned
splendidly. "Arthur Heath my first-best friend, Dick Stockworth my second-best friend. My third-best friend—"

"Hush!" Susan said in a low, fierce voice that made Shee-mie's smile fade. "Not a word about your three friends."

A funny little flush, almost like a pocket fever, raced across her skin—it seemed to run down her neck from her cheeks, then slip all the way to her feet. There had been a lot of talk in Hambry about Sheemie's new friends during the past week—talk about little else, it seemed. The stories she had heard were outlandish, but if they weren't true, why did the versions told by so many different witnesses sound so much alike?

Susan was still trying to get herself back under control when Aunt Cord swept around the corner. Sheemie fell back a step at the sight of her, puzzlement becoming out-right dismay. Her aunt was allergic to beestings, and was presently swaddled from the top of her straw 'brera to the hem of her faded garden dress in gauzy stuff that made her look peculiar in strong light and downright eerie in shade. Adding a final touch to her costume, she carried a pair of dirt-streaked garden shears in one gloved hand.

She saw the bouquet and bore down on it, shears raised. When she reached her niece, she slid the scissors into a loop on her belt (almost reluctantly, it seemed to the niece herself) and parted the veil on her face. "Who sent ye those?"

"I don't know, Aunt," Susan said, much more calmly than she felt. 'This is the young man from the inn—"

"Inn!" Aunt Cord snorted.

"He doesn't seem to know who sent him," Susan carried on. If only she could get him out of here! "He's, well, I suppose you'd say he's—"

"He's a fool, yes, I know that." Aunt Cord cast Susan a brief, irritated look, then bent her attention on Sheemie. Talking with her gloved hands upon her knees, shouting directly into his face, she asked: *"WHO . . . SENT . . . THESE . . . FLOWERS . . . YOUNG . . . MAN?"*

The wings of her face-veil, which had been pushed aside, now fell back into place. Sheemie took another step backward. He looked frightened.

"*WAS IT . . . PERHAPS . . . SOMEONE FROM . . . SEA-FRONT? . . . FROM . . . MAYOR . . . THORIN? . . . TELL . . . ME . . . AND . . . I'LL . . . GIVE . . . YOU . . . A PENNY.*"

Susan's heart sank, sure he would tell—he'd not have the wit to understand he'd be getting her into trouble. Will, too, likely.

But Sheemie only shook his head. "Don't 'member. I got a empty head, sai, so I do. Stanley says I a bugwit."

His grin shone out again, a splendid thing full of white, even teeth. Aunt Cord answered it with a grimace. "Oh, foo! Be gone, then. Straight back to town, too—don't be hanging around hoping for a goose-feather. For a boy who can't remember deserves not so much as a penny! And don't you come back here again, no matter who wants you to carry flowers for the young sai. Do you hear me?"

Sheemie had nodded energetically. Then: "Sai?"

Aunt Cord glowered at him. The vertical line on her forehead had been very prominent that day.

"Why you all wropped up in cobwebbies, sai?"

"Get out of here, ye impudent cull!" Aunt Cord cried. She had a good loud voice when she wanted to use it, and Sheemie jumped back from her in alarm. When she was sure he was headed back down the High Street toward town and had no intention of returning to their gate and hanging about in hopes of a tip, Aunt Cord had turned to Susan.

"Get those in some water before they wilt, Miss Oh So Young and Pretty, and don't go mooning about, wondering who yer secret admirer might be."

Then Aunt Cord had smiled. A *real* smile. What hurt Susan the most, confused her the most, was that her aunt was no cradle-story ogre, no witch like Rhea of the Cöos. There was no monster here, only a maiden lady with some few social pretensions, a love of gold and silver, and a fear of being turned out, penniless, into the world.

"For folks such as us, Susie-pie," she said, speaking with a terrible heavy kindness, " 'tis best to stick to our housework and leave dreams to them as can afford them."

5

She had been sure the flowers were from Will, and she was right. His note was written in a hand which was clear and passing fair.

> Dear Susan Delgado,
>   I spoke out of turn the other night, and cry your pardon. May I see you and speak to you? It must be private. *This is a matter of importance.* If you will see me, get a message to the boy who brings this. He is safe.
>
>   Will Dearborn

A matter of importance. Underlined. She felt a strong desire to know what was so important to him, and cautioned herself against doing anything foolish. Perhaps he was smitten with her . . . and if so, whose fault was that? Who had talked to him, ridden his horse, showed him her legs in a flashy carnival dismount? Who had put her hands on his shoulders and kissed him?

Her cheeks and forehead burned at the thought of that, and another hot ring seemed to go slipping down her body. She wasn't sure she regretted the kiss, but it had been a mistake, regrets or no regrets. Seeing him again now would be a worse one.

Yet she wanted to see him, and knew in her deepest heart that she was ready to set her anger at him aside. But there was the promise she had made.

The wretched promise.

That night she lay sleepless, tossing about in her bed, first thinking it would be better, more dignified, just to keep her silence, then composing mental notes anyway—some haughty, some cold, some with a lace-edge of flirtation.

When she heard the midnight bell ring, passing the old day out and calling the new one in, she decided enough was enough. She'd thrown herself from her bed, gone to her door, opened it, and thrust her head out into the hall. When she heard Aunt Cord's flutelike snores, she had closed her door again, crossed to her little desk by the window, and lit her lamp. She took one of her sheets of parchment paper from the top drawer, tore it in half (in Hambry, the only crime greater than wasting paper was wasting threaded stockline), and then wrote quickly, sensing that the slightest hesitation might condemn her to more hours of indecision. With no salutation and no signature, her response took only a breath to write:

I may not see you. 'Twould not be proper.

She had folded it small, blew out her lamp, and returned to bed with the note safely tucked under her pillow. She was asleep in two minutes. The following day, when the marketing took her to town, she had gone by the Travellers' Rest, which, at eleven in the morning, had all the charm of something which has died badly at the side of the road.

The saloon's dooryard was a beaten dirt square bisected by a long hitching rail with a watering trough

beneath. Sheemie was trundling a wheelbarrow along
the rail, picking up last night's horse-droppings with a
shovel. He was wearing a comical pink *sombrera* and singing "Golden Slippers." Susan doubted if many of the
Rest's patrons would wake up feeling as well as Sheemie
obviously did this morning . . . so who, when you came
right down to it, was more soft-headed?

She looked around to make sure no one was paying
heed to her, then went over to Sheemie and tapped
him on the shoulder. He looked frightened at first, and
Susan didn't blame him—according to the stories she'd
been hearing, Jonas's friend Depape had almost killed
the poor kid for spilling a drink on his boots.

Then Sheemie recognized her. "Hello, Susan Delgado
from out there by the edge of town," he said companionably. "It's a good day I wish you, sai."

He bowed—an amusing imitation of the Inner Baronies bow favored by his three new friends. Smiling, she
dropped him a bit of curtsey (wearing jeans, she had to
pretend at the skirt-holding part, but women in Mejis
got used to curtseying in pretend skirts).

"See my flowers, sai?" he asked, and pointed toward
the unpainted side of the Rest. What she saw touched
her deeply: a line of mixed blue and white silkflowers
growing along the base of the building. They looked
both brave and pathetic, flurrying there in the faint
morning breeze with the bald, turd-littered yard before
them and the splintery public house behind them.

"Did you grow those, Sheemie?"

"Aye, so I did. And Mr. Arthur Heath of Gilead has
promised me yellow ones."

"I've never seen yellow silkflowers."

"Noey-no, me neither, but Mr. Arthur Heath says they
have them in Gilead." He looked at Susan solemnly, the
shovel held in his hands as a soldier would hold a gun or

spear at port arms. "Mr. Arthur Heath saved my life. I'd do anything for him."

"Would you, Sheemie?" she asked, touched.

"Also, he has a lookout! It's a bird's head! And when he talks to it, tendy-pretend, do I laugh? Aye, fit to split!"

She looked around again to make sure no one was watching (save for the carved totems across the street), then removed her note, folded small, from her jeans pocket.

"Would you give this to Mr. Dearborn for me? He's also your friend, is he not?"

"Will? Aye!" He took the note and put it carefully into his own pocket.

"And tell no one."

"Shhhhh!" he agreed, and put a finger to his lips. His eyes had been amusingly round beneath the ridiculous pink lady's straw he wore. "Like when I brought you the flowers. Hushaboo!"

"That's right, hushaboo. Fare ye well, Sheemie."

"And you, Susan Delgado."

He went back to his cleanup operations. Susan had stood watching him for a moment, feeling uneasy and out of sorts with herself. Now that the note was success-fully passed, she felt an urge to ask Sheemie to give it back, to scratch out what she had written, and promise to meet him. If only to see his steady blue eyes again, looking into her face.

Then Jonas's other friend, the one with the cloak, came sauntering out of the mercantile. She was sure he didn't see her—his head was down and he was rolling a cigarette—but she had no intention of pressing her luck. Reynolds talked to Jonas, and Jonas talked—all too much!—to Aunt Cord. If Aunt Cord heard she had been passing the time of day with the boy who had brought her the flowers, there were apt to be questions. Ones she didn't want to answer.

6

All that's history now, Susan—water under the bridge. Best to get your thoughts out of the past.

She brought Pylon to a stop and looked down the length of the Drop at the horses that moved and grazed there. Quite a surprising number of them this morning.

It wasn't working. Her mind kept turning back to Will Dearborn.

What bad luck meeting him had been! If not for that chance encounter on her way back down from the Cöos, she might well have made peace with her situation by now—she was a practical girl, after all, and a promise was a promise. She certainly never would have expected herself to get all goosy-gushy over losing her maidenhead, and the prospect of carrying and bearing a child actually excited her.

But Will Dearborn had changed things; had gotten into her head and now lodged there, a tenant who defied eviction. His remark to her as they danced stayed with her like a song you can't stop humming, even though you hate it. It had been cruel and stupidly self-righteous, that remark . . . but was there not also a grain of truth in it? Rhea had been right about Hart Thorin, of that much Susan no longer had any doubt. She supposed that witches were right about men's lusts even when they were wrong about everything else. Not a happy thought, but likely a true one.

It was Will Be Damned to You Dearborn who had made it difficult for her to accept what needed accepting, who had goaded her into arguments in which she could hardly recognize her own shrill and desperate voice, who came to her in her dreams—dreams where he put his arms around her waist and kissed her, kissed her, kissed her.

She dismounted and walked downhill a little way with the reins looped in her fist. Pylon followed willingly enough, and when she stopped to look off into the blue haze to the southwest, he lowered his head and began to crop again.

She thought she needed to see Will Dearborn once more, if only to give her innate practicality a chance to reassert itself. She needed to see him at his right size, instead of the one her mind had created for him in her warm thoughts and warmer dreams. Once that was done, she could get on with her life and do what needed doing. Perhaps that was why she had taken this path— the same one she'd ridden yesterday, and the day before yesterday, and the day before that. He rode this part of the Drop; that much she had heard in the lower market.

She turned away from the Drop, suddenly knowing he would be there, as if her thought had called him—or her *ka*.

She saw only blue sky and low ridgeline hills that curved gently like the line of a woman's thigh and hip and waist as she lies on her side in bed. Susan felt a bitter disappointment fill her. She could almost taste it in her mouth, like wet tea leaves.

She started back to Pylon, meaning to return to the house and take care of the apology she reckoned she must make. The sooner she did it, the sooner it would be done. She reached for her left stirrup, which was twisted a little, and as she did, a rider came over the horizon, breaking against the sky at the place which looked to her like a woman's hip. He sat there, only a silhouette on horseback, but she knew who it was at once.

Run! she told herself in a sudden panic. *Mount and gallop! Get out of here! Quickly! Before something terrible happens . . . before it really is* ka, *come like a wind to take you and all your plans over the sky and far away!*

She didn't run. She stood with Pylon's reins in one hand, and murmured to him when the *rosillo* looked up and nickered a greeting to the big bay-colored gelding coming down the hill.

Then Will was there, first above her and looking down, then dismounted in an easy, liquid motion she didn't think she could have matched, for all her years of horsemanship. This time there was no kicked-out leg and planted heel, no hat swept over a comically solemn bow; this time the gaze he gave her was steady and serious and disquietingly adult.

They looked at each other in the Drop's big silence, Roland of Gilead and Susan of Mejis, and in her heart she felt a wind begin to blow. She feared it and welcomed it in equal measure.

7

"Goodmorn, Susan," he said. "I'm glad to see you again."

She said nothing, waiting and watching. Could he hear her heart beating as clearly as she could? Of course not; that was so much romantic twaddle. Yet it still seemed to her that everything within a fifty-yard radius should be able to hear that thumping.

Will took a step forward. She took a step back, looking at him mistrustfully. He lowered his head for a moment, then looked up again, his lips set.

"I cry your pardon," he said.

"Do you?" Her voice was cool.

"What I said that night was unwarranted."

At that she felt a spark of real anger. "I care not that it was unwarranted; I care that it was unfair. That it hurt me."

A tear overbrimmed her left eye and slipped down her cheek. She wasn't all cried out after all, it seemed.

She thought what she said would perhaps shame him, but although faint color came into his cheeks, his eyes remained firmly on hers.

"I fell in love with you," he said. "That's why I said it. It happened even before you kissed me, I think."

She laughed at that . . . but the simplicity with which he had spoken made her laughter sound false in her own ears. Tinny. "Mr. Dearborn—"

"Will. Please."

"Mr. Dearborn," she said, patiently as a teacher working with a dull student, "the idea is ridiculous. On the basis of one single meeting? One single kiss? A *sister's* kiss?" Now she was the one who was blushing, but she hurried on. "Such things happen in stories, but in real life? I think not."

But his eyes never left hers, and in them she saw some of Roland's truth: the deep romance of his nature, buried like a fabulous streak of alien metal in the granite of his practicality. He accepted love as a fact rather than a flower, and it rendered her genial contempt powerless over both of them.

"I cry your pardon," he repeated. There was a kind of brute stubbornness in him. It exasperated her, amused her, and appalled her, all at the same time. "I don't ask you to return my love, that's not why I spoke. You told me your affairs were complicated . . ." Now his eyes did leave hers, and he looked off toward the Drop. He even laughed a little. "I called him a bit of a fool, didn't I? To your face. So who's the fool, after all?"

She smiled; couldn't help it. "Ye also said ye'd heard he was fond of strong drink and berry-girls."

Roland hit his forehead with the heel of his hand. If his friend Arthur Heath had done that, she would have taken it as a deliberate, comic gesture. Not with Will. She had an idea he wasn't much for comedy.

Silence between them again, this time not so uncomfortable. The two horses, Rusher and Pylon, cropping contentedly, side by side. *If we were horses, all this would be much easier,* she thought, and almost giggled.

"Mr. Dearborn, ye understand that I have agreed to an arrangement?"

"Aye." He smiled when she raised her eyebrows in surprise. "It's not mockery but the dialect. It just . . . seeps in."

"Who told ye of my business?"

"The Mayor's sister."

"Coral." She wrinkled her nose and decided she wasn't surprised. And she supposed there were others who could have explained her situation even more crudely. Eldred Jonas, for one. Rhea of the Cöos, for another. Best to leave it. "So if ye understand, and if ye don't ask me to return your . . . whatever it is ye think ye feel . . . why are we talking? Why do ye seek me out? I think it makes ye passing uncomfortable—"

"Yes," he said, and then, as if stating a simple fact: "It makes me uncomfortable, all right. I can barely look at you and keep my head."

"Then mayhap it'd be best not to look, not to speak, not to think!" Her voice was both sharp and a little shaky. How could he have the courage to say such things, to just state them straight out and starey-eyed like that? "Why did ye send me the bouquet and that note? Are ye not aware of the trouble ye could've gotten me into? If y'knew my aunt . . . ! She's already spoken to me about ye, and if she knew about the note . . . or saw us together out here . . ."

She looked around, verifying that they were still unobserved. They were, at least as best she could tell. He reached out, touched her shoulder. She looked at him, and he pulled his fingers back as if he had put them on something hot.

"I said what I did so you'd understand," he said. "That's all. I feel how I feel, and you're not responsible for that."

But I am, she thought. *I kissed you. I think I'm more than a little responsible for how we both feel, Will.*

"What I said while we were dancing I regret with all my heart. Won't you give me your pardon?"

"Aye," she said, and if he had taken her in his arms at that moment, she would have let him, and damn the consequences. But he only took off his hat and made her a charming little bow, and the wind died.

"Thankee-sai."

"Don't call me that. I hate it. My name is Susan."

"Will you call me Will?"

She nodded.

"Good. Susan, I want to ask you something—not as the fellow who insulted you and hurt you because he was jealous. This is something else entirely. May I?"

"Aye, I suppose," she said warily.

"Are you for the Affiliation?"

She looked at him, flabbergasted. It was the last question in the world she had expected . . . but he was looking at her seriously.

"I'd expected ye and yer friends to count cows and guns and spears and boats and who knows what else," she said, "but I didn't think thee would also count Affiliation supporters."

She saw his look of surprise, and a little smile at the corners of his mouth. This time the smile made him look older than he could possibly be. Susan thought back across what she'd just said, realized what must have

struck him, and gave a small, embarrassed laugh. "My
aunt has a way of lapsing into thee and thou. My father
did, too. It's from a sect of the Old People who called
themselves Friends."

"I know. We have the Friendly Folk in my part of the
world still."

"Do you?"

"Yes . . . or aye, if you like the sound of that better; I'm
coming to. And I like the way the Friends talk. It has a
lovely sound."

"Not when my aunt uses it," Susan said, thinking back
to the argument over the shirt. "To answer your question,
aye—I'm for the Affiliation, I suppose. Because my da
was. If ye ask am I *strong* for the Affiliation, I suppose not.
We see and hear little enough of them, these days. Mostly
rumors and stories carried by drifters and far-travelling
drummers. Now that there's no railway . . ." She shrugged.

"Most of the ordinary day-to-day folk I've spoken to
seem to feel the same. And yet your Mayor Thorin—"

"He's not *my* Mayor Thorin," she said, more sharply
than she had intended.

"And yet the *Barony's* Mayor Thorin has given us every
help we've asked for, and some we haven't. I have only
to snap my fingers, and Kimba Rimer stands before me."

"Then don't snap them," she said, looking around in
spite of herself. She tried to smile and show it was a joke,
but didn't make much success of it.

"The townsfolk, the fisherfolk, the farmers, the cowboys . . . they all speak well of the Affiliation, but distantly. Yet the Mayor, his Chancellor, and the members
of the Horsemen's Association, Lengyll and Garber and
that lot—"

"I know them," she said shortly.

"They're absolutely enthusiastic in their support.
Mention the Affiliation to Sheriff Avery and he all but

dances. In every ranch parlor we're offered a drink from an Eld commemorative cup, it seems."

"A drink of what?" she asked, a trifle roguishly. "Beer? Ale? *Graf?*"

"Also wine, whiskey, and pettibone," he said, not responding to her smile. "It's almost as if they wish us to break our vow. Does that strike you as strange?"

"Aye, a little; or just as Hambry hospitality. In these parts, when someone—especially a young man—says he's taken the pledge, folks tend to think him coy, not serious."

"And this joyful support of the Affiliation amongst the movers and the shakers? How does *that* strike you?"

"Queer."

And it did. Pat Delgado's work had brought him in almost daily contact with these landowners and horse-breeders, and so she, who had tagged after her da any time he would let her, had seen plenty of them. She thought them a cold bunch, by and large. She couldn't imagine John Croydon or Jake White waving an Arthur Eld stein in a sentimental toast . . . especially not in the middle of the day, when there was stock to be run and sold.

Will's eyes were full upon her, as if he were reading these thoughts.

"But you probably don't see as much of the big fellas as you once did," he said. "Before your father passed, I mean."

"Perhaps not . . . but do bumblers learn to speak back-ward?"

No cautious smile this time; this time he outright grinned. It lit his whole face. Gods, how handsome he was! "I suppose not. No more than cats change their spots, as we say. And Mayor Thorin doesn't speak of such as us—me and my friends—to you when you two are alone? Or is that question beyond what I have a right to ask? I suppose it is."

"I care not about that," she said, tossing her head pertly enough to make her long braid swing. "I understand little of propriety, as some have been good enough to point out." But she didn't care as much for his downcast look and flush of embarrassment as she had expected. She knew girls who liked to tease as well as flirt—and to tease hard, some of them—but it seemed she had no taste for it. Certainly she had no desire to set her claws in him, and when she went on, she spoke gently. "I'm not alone with him, in any case."

And oh how ye do lie, she thought mournfully, remembering how Thorin had embraced her in the hall on the night of the party, groping at her breasts like a child trying to get his hand into a candy-jar; telling her that he burned for her. *Oh ye great liar.*

"In any case, Will, Hart's opinion of you and yer friends can hardly concern ye, can it? Ye have a job to do, that's all. If he helps ye, why not just accept and be grateful?"

"Because something's wrong here," he said, and the serious, almost somber quality of his voice frightened her a little.

"Wrong? With the Mayor? With the Horsemen's Association? What are ye talking about?"

He looked at her steadily, then seemed to decide something. "I'm going to trust you, Susan."

"I'm not sure I want thy trust any more than I want thy love," she said.

He nodded. "And yet, to do the job I was sent to do, I have to trust *someone.* Can you understand that?"

She looked into his eyes, then nodded.

He stepped next to her, so close she fancied she could feel the warmth of his skin. "Look down there. Tell me what you see."

She looked, then shrugged. "The Drop. Same as always." She smiled a little. "And as beautiful. This has always been my favorite place in all the world."

"Aye, it's beautiful, all right. What else do you see?"

"Horses, of courses." She smiled to show this was a joke (an old one of her da's, in fact), but he didn't smile back. Fair to look at, and courageous, if the stories they were already telling about town were true—quick in both thought and movement, too. Really not much sense of humor, though. Well, there were worse failings. Grabbing a girl's bosom when she wasn't expecting it might be one of them.

"Horses. Yes. But does it look like the right *number* of them? You've been seeing horses on the Drop all your life, and surely no one who's not in the Horsemen's Association is better qualified to say."

"And ye don't trust them?"

"They've given us everything we've asked for, and they're as friendly as dogs under the dinner-table, but no—I don't think I do."

"Yet ye'd trust me."

He looked at her steadily with his beautiful and frightening eyes—a darker blue than they would later be, not yet faded out by the suns of ten thousand drifting days. "I have to trust someone," he repeated.

She looked down, almost as though he had rebuked her. He reached out, put gentle fingers beneath her chin, and tipped her face up again. "Does it seem the right number? Think carefully!"

But now that he'd brought it to her attention, she hardly needed to think about it at all. She had been aware of the change for some time, she supposed, but it had been gradual, easy to overlook.

"No," she said at last. "It's not right."

"Too few or too many? Which?"

She paused for a moment. Drew in breath. Let it out in a long sigh. "Too many. Far too many."

Will Dearborn raised his clenched fists to shoulder-height and gave them a single hard shake. His blue eyes blazed like the spark-lights of which her grand-da had told her. "I knew it," he said. "I *knew* it."

8

"How many horses are down there?" he asked.

"Below us? Or on the whole Drop?"

"Just below us."

She looked carefully, making no attempt to actually count. That didn't work; it only confused you. She saw four good-sized groups of about twenty horses each, moving about on the green almost exactly as birds moved about in the blue above them. There were perhaps nine smaller groups, ranging from octets to quartets . . . several pairs (they reminded her of lovers, but everything did today, it seemed) . . . a few galloping loners—young stallions, mostly . . .

"A hundred and sixty?" he asked in a low, almost hesitant voice.

She looked at him, surprised. "Aye. A hundred sixty's the number I had in mind. To a pin."

"And how much of the Drop are we looking at? A quarter? A third?"

"Much less." She tilted him a small smile. "As I think thee knows. A sixth of the total open graze, perhaps."

"If there are a hundred and sixty horses free-grazing on each sixth, that comes to . . ."

She waited for him to come up with nine hundred and sixty. When he did, she nodded. He looked down a moment longer, and grunted with surprise when Rusher nosed him in the small of the back. Susan put a curled hand to her mouth to stifle a laugh. From the impatient way he pushed the horse's muzzle away, she guessed he still saw little that was funny.

"How many more are stabled or training or working, do you reckon?" he asked.

"One for every three down there. At a guess."

"So we'd be talking twelve hundred head of horses. All threaded stock, no muties."

She looked at him with faint surprise. "Aye. There's almost no mutie stock here in Mejis . . . in *any* of the Outer Baronies, for that matter."

"You true-breed more than three out of every five?"

"We breed em *all*! Of course every now and then we get a freak that has to be put down, but—"

"Not one freak out of every five livebirths? One out of five born with—" How had Renfrew put it? "With extra legs or its guts on the outside?"

Her shocked look was enough answer. "Who's been telling ye such?"

"Renfrew. He also told me that there was about five hundred and seventy head of threaded stock here in Mejis."

"That's just . . ." She gave a bewildered little laugh. "Just crazy! If my da was here—"

"But he's not," Roland said, his tone as dry as a snapping twig. "He's dead."

For a moment she seemed not to register the change in that tone. Then, as if an eclipse had begun to happen somewhere inside her head, her entire aspect darkened. "My da had an accident. Do you understand that, Will Dearborn? An *accident*. It was terribly sad, but the sort of thing that happens, sometimes. A horse rolled on him. Ocean Foam. Fran says Foam saw a snake in the grass."

"Fran Lengyll?"

"Aye." Her skin was pale, except for two wild roses—pink, like those in the bouquet he'd sent her by way of Sheemie—glowing high up on her cheekbones. "Fran rode many miles with my father. They weren't great friends—they were of different classes, for one thing—but they rode together. I've a cap put away somewhere that Fran's first wife made for my christening. They rode the trail together. I can't believe Fran Lengyll would lie about how my da died, let alone that he had . . . anything to do with it."

Yet she looked doubtfully down at the running horses. So many. *Too* many. Her da would have seen. And her da would have wondered what she was wondering now: whose brands were on the extras?

"It so happens Fran Lengyll and my friend Stockworth had a discussion about horses," Will said. His voice sounded almost casual, but there was nothing casual on his face. "Over glasses of spring water, after beer had been offered and refused. They spoke of them much as I did with Renfrew at Mayor Thorin's welcoming dinner. When Richard asked sai Lengyll to estimate riding horses, he said perhaps four hundred."

"Insane."

"It would seem so," Will agreed.

"Do they not kennit the horses are out here where ye can see em?"

"They know we've barely gotten started," he said, "and that we've begun with the fisherfolk. We'll be a month yet, I'm sure they think, before we start to concern ourselves with the horseflesh hereabouts. And in the meantime, they have an attitude about us of . . . how shall I put it? Well, never mind how I'd put it. I'm not very good with words, but my friend Arthur calls it 'genial contempt.' They leave the horses out in front of our eyes, I think, because they don't believe we'll know what we're looking at. Or because they think we won't believe what we're seeing. I'm very glad I found you out here."

Just so I could give you a more accurate horse-count? Is that the only reason?

"But ye *will* get around to counting the horses. Eventually. I mean, that must surely be one of the Affiliation's main needs."

He gave her an odd look, as if she had missed something that should have been obvious. It made her feel self-conscious.

"What? What is it?"

"Perhaps they expect the extra horses to be gone by the time we get around to this side of the Barony's business."

"Gone *where?*"

"I don't know. But I don't like this. Susan, you will keep this just between the two of us, won't you?"

She nodded. *She'd* be insane to tell anyone she had been with Will Dearborn, unchaperoned except by Rusher and Pylon, out on the Drop.

"It may all turn out to be nothing, but if it doesn't, knowing could be dangerous."

Which led back to her da again. Lengyll had told her and Aunt Cord that Pat had been thrown, and that Ocean Foam had then rolled upon him. Neither of them had had any reason to doubt the man's story. But Fran Lengyll had also told Will's friend that there were only four hundred head of riding stock in Mejis, and that was a bald lie.

Will turned to his horse, and she was glad.

Part of her wanted him to stay—to stand close to her while the clouds sent their long shadows flying across the grassland—but they had been together out here too long already. There was no reason to think anyone would come along and see them, but instead of comforting her, that idea for some reason made her more nervous than ever.

He straightened the stirrup hanging beside the scab-barded shaft of his lance (Rusher whickered way back in his throat, as if to say *About time we got going*), then turned to her again. She felt actually faint as his gaze fell upon her, and now the idea of *ka* was almost too strong to deny. She tried to tell herself it was just the dim— that feeling of having lived a thing before—but it wasn't the dim; it was a sense of finding a road one had been searching for all along.

"There's something else I want to say. I don't like returning to where we started, but I must."

"No," she said faintly. "That's closed, surely."

"I told you that I loved you, and that I was jealous," he said, and for the first time his voice had come unan-chored a little, wavering in his throat. She was alarmed to see that there were tears standing in his eyes. "There was more. Something more."

"Will, I don't want to—" She turned blindly for her horse. He took her shoulder and turned her back. It wasn't a harsh touch, but there was an inexorability to it that was dreadful. She looked helplessly up into his face, saw that he was young and far from home, and sud-denly understood she could not stand against him for long. She wanted him so badly that she ached with it. She would have given a year of her life just to be able to put her palms on his cheeks and feel his skin.

"You miss your father, Susan?"

"Aye," she whispered. "With all my heart I do."

"I miss my mother the same way." He held her by both shoulders now. One eye overbrimmed; one tear drew a silver line down his cheek.

"Is she dead?"

"No, but something happened. About her. To her. *Shit!* How can I talk about it when I don't even know how to *think* about it? In a way, she *did* die. For me."

"Will, that's terrible."

He nodded. "The last time I saw her, she looked at me in a way that will haunt me to my grave. Shame and love and hope, all of them bound up together. Shame at what I'd seen and knew about her, hope, maybe, that I'd understand and forgive . . ." He took a deep breath. "The night of the party, toward the end of the meal, Rimer said something funny. You all laughed—"

"If I did, it was only because it would have looked strange if I was the only one who didn't," Susan said. "I don't like him. I think he's a schemer and a conniver."

"You all laughed, and I happened to look down toward the end of the table. Toward Olive Thorin. And for a moment—only a moment—I thought she was my mother. The expression was the same, you see. The same one I saw on the morning when I opened the wrong door at the wrong time and came upon my mother and her—"

"Stop it!" she cried, pulling back from his hands. Inside her, everything was suddenly in motion, all the mooring-lines and buckles and clamps she'd been using to hold herself together seeming to melt at once. "Stop it, just stop it, I can't listen to you talk about her!"

She groped out for Pylon, but now the whole world was wet prisms. She began to sob. She felt his hands on her shoulders, turning her again, and she did not resist them.

"I'm so ashamed," she said. "I'm so ashamed and so frightened and I'm sorry. I've forgotten my father's face and . . . and . . ."

And I'll never be able to find it again, she wanted to say, but she didn't have to say anything. He stopped her mouth with his kisses. At first she just let herself be kissed . . . and then she was kissing him back, kissing him almost furiously. She wiped the wetness from beneath his eyes with soft little sweeps of her thumbs, then slipped her palms up his cheeks as she had longed to do. The feeling was exquisite; even the soft rasp of the stubble close to the skin was exquisite. She slid her arms around his neck, her open mouth on his, holding him and kissing him as hard as she could, kissing him there between the horses, who simply looked at each other and then went back to cropping grass.

9

They were the best kisses of his whole life, and never forgotten: the yielding pliancy of her lips and the strong shape of her teeth under them, urgent and not shy in the least; the fragrance of her breath, the sweet line of her body pressed against his. He slipped a hand up to her left breast, squeezed it gently, and felt her heart speeding under it. His other hand went to her hair and combed along the side of it, silk at her temple. He never forgot its texture.

Then she was standing away from him, her face flaming with blush and passion, one hand going to her lips, which he had kissed until they were swollen. A little trickle of blood ran from the corner of the lower one. Her eyes, wide on his. Her bosom rising and falling as if she had just run a race. And between them a current that was like nothing he had ever felt in his life. It ran like a river and shook like a fever.

"No more," she said in a trembling voice. "No more, please. If you really do love me, don't let me dishonor myself. I've made a promise. Anything might come later, after that promise was fulfilled, I suppose . . . if you still wanted me . . ."

"I would wait forever," he said calmly, "and do anything for you but stand away and watch you go with another man."

"Then if you love me, go away from me. Please, Will!"

"Another kiss."

She stepped forward at once, raising her face trustingly up to his, and he understood he could do whatever he wanted with her. She was, at least for the moment, no longer her own mistress; she might consequently be his. He could do to her what Marten had done to his own mother, if that was his fancy.

The thought broke his passion apart, turned it to coals that fell in a bright shower, winking out one by one in a dark bewilderment. His father's acceptance

(I have known for two years)

was in many ways the worst part of what had happened to him this year; how could he fall in love with this girl—any girl—in a world where such evils of the heart seemed necessary, and might even be repeated?

Yet he did love her.

Instead of the passionate kiss he wanted, he placed his lips lightly on the corner of her mouth where the little rill of blood flowed. He kissed, tasting salt like the taste of his own tears. He closed his eyes and shivered when her hand stroked the hair at the nape of his neck.

"I'd not hurt Olive Thorin for the world," she whispered in his ear. "No more than I'd hurt thee, Will. I didn't understand, and now 'tis too late to be put right. But thank you for not . . . not taking what you could. And I'll remember you always. How it was to be kissed by you. It's the best thing that ever happened to me, I think. Like heaven and earth all wrapped up together, aye."

"I'll remember, too." He watched her swing up into the saddle, and remembered how her bare legs had flashed in the dark on the night he had met her. And suddenly he couldn't let her go. He reached forward, touched her boot.

"Susan—"

"No," she said. "Please."

He stood back. Somehow.

"This is our secret," she said. "Yes?"

"Aye."

She smiled at that . . . but it was a sad smile. "Stay away from me from now on, Will. Please. And I'll stay away from you."

He thought about it. "If we can."

"We must, Will. We must."

She rode away fast. Roland stood beside Rusher's stirrup, watching her go. And when she was out of sight over the horizon, still he watched.

10

Sheriff Avery, Deputy Dave, and Deputy George Riggins were sitting on the porch in front of the Sheriff's office and jail when Mr. Stockworth and Mr. Heath (the latter with that idiotic bird's skull still mounted on the horn of his saddle) went past at a steady walk. The bell o' noon had rung fifteen minutes before, and Sheriff Avery reckoned they were on their way to lunch, perhaps at The Millbank, or perhaps at the Rest, which put on a fair noon meal. Popkins and such. Avery liked something a little more filling; half a chicken or a haunch of beef suited him just fine.

Mr. Heath gave them a wave and a grin. "Good day, gents! Long life! Gentle breezes! Happy siestas!"

They waved and smiled back. When they were out of sight, Dave said: "They spent all mornin down there on the piers, countin nets. *Nets!* Do you believe it?"

"Yessir," Sheriff Avery said, lifting one massive cheek a bit out of his rocker and letting off a noisy pre-luncheon fart. "Yessir, I do. Aye."

George said: "If not for them facing off Jonas's boys the way they done, I'd think they was a pack of fools."

"Nor would they likely mind," Avery said. He looked at Dave, who was twirling his monocle on the end of its ribbon and looking off in the direction the boys had taken. There were folks in town who had begun calling the Affiliation brats Little Coffin Hunters. Avery wasn't sure what to make of that. He'd soothed it down between them and Thorin's hard boys, and had gotten both a commendation and a piece of gold from Rimer for his efforts, but still . . . what to make of them?

"The day they came in," he said to Dave, "ye thought they were soft. How do ye say now?"

"Now?" Dave twirled his monocle a final time, then popped it in his eye and stared at the Sheriff through it. "Now I think they might have been a little harder than I thought, after all."

Yes indeed, Avery thought. *But hard don't mean smart, thank the gods. Aye, thank the gods for that.*

"I'm hungry as a bull, so I am," he said, getting up. He bent, put his hands on his knees, and ripped off another loud fart. Dave and George looked at each other. George fanned a hand in front of his face. Sheriff Herkimer Avery, Barony Sheriff, straightened up, looking both relieved and anticipatory. "More room out than there is in," he said. "Come on, boys. Let's go downstreet and tuck into a little."

II

Not even sunset could do much to improve the view from the porch of the Bar K bunkhouse. The building—

except for the cook-shack and the stable, the only one still standing on what had been the home acre—was L-shaped, and the porch was built on the inside of the short arm. Left for them on it had been just the right number of seats: two splintery rockers and a wooden crate to which an unstable board back had been nailed.

On this evening, Alain sat in one of the rockers and Cuthbert sat on the box-seat, which he seemed to fancy. On the rail, peering across the beaten dirt of the door-yard and toward the burned-out hulk of the Garber home place, was the lookout.

Alain was bone-tired, and although both of them had bathed in the stream near the west end of the home acre, he thought he still smelled fish and seaweed on himself. They had spent the day counting nets. He was not averse to hard work, even when it was monotonous, but he didn't like pointless work. Which this was. Hambry came in two parts: the fishers and the horse-breeders. There was nothing for them among the fishers, and after three weeks all three of them knew it. Their answers were out on the Drop, at which they had so far done no more than look. At Roland's order.

The wind gusted, and for a moment they could hear the low, grumbling, squealing sound of the thinny.

"I hate that sound," Alain said.

Cuthbert, unusually silent and introspective tonight, nodded and said only "Aye." They were all saying that now, not to mention *So you do* and *So I am* and *So it is.* Alain suspected the three of them would have Hambry on their tongues long after they had wiped its dust from their boots.

From behind them, inside the bunkhouse door, came a less unpleasant sound—the cooing of pigeons. And then, from around the side of the bunkhouse, a third, for which he and Cuthbert had unconsciously been listening as they sat watching the sun go down: horse's hoofs. Rusher's.

Roland came around the corner, riding easy, and as he did, something happened that struck Alain as oddly portentous . . . a kind of omen. There was a flurry-flutter of wings, a dark shape in the air, and suddenly a bird was roosting on Roland's shoulder.

He didn't jump; barely looked around. He rode up to the hitching rail and sat there, holding out his hand. "Hile," he said softly, and the pigeon stepped into his palm. Bound to one of its legs was a capsule. Roland removed it, opened it, and took out a tiny strip of paper, which had been rolled tight. In his other hand he held the pigeon out.

"Hile," Alain said, holding out his own hand. The pigeon flew to it. As Roland dismounted, Alain took the pigeon into the bunkhouse, where the cages had been placed beneath an open window. He ungated the center one and held out his hand. The pigeon which had just arrived hopped in; the pigeon in the cage hopped out and into his palm. Alain shut the cage door, latched it, crossed the room, and turned up the pillow of Bert's bunk. Beneath it was a linen envelope containing a number of blank paper strips and a tiny storage-pen. He took one of the strips and the pen, which held its own small reservoir of ink and did not have to be dipped. He went back out on the porch. Roland and Cuthbert were studying the unrolled strip of paper the pigeon had delivered from Gilead. On it was a line of tiny geometric shapes:

$$\square \, \flat \, \flat \, \bigcirc \, \flat \, \mathsf{C} \, \mathsf{J} \, \square \, \mathsf{J} \, \mathsf{C} \, \mathsf{V} \, \triangledown \, \bigcirc \, \square \, \square \, \mathsf{G}$$

"What does it say?" Alain asked. The code was simple enough, but he could not get it by heart or read it on sight, as Roland and Bert had been able to, almost immediately. Alain's talents—his ability to track, his easy access to the touch—lay in other directions.

" 'Farson moves east,' " Cuthbert read. " 'Forces split, one big, one small. Do you see anything unusual.' " He looked at Roland, almost offended. "Anything unusual, what does that mean?"

Roland shook his head. He didn't know. He doubted if the men who had sent the message—of whom his own father was almost surely one—did, either.

Alain handed Cuthbert the strip and the pen. With one finger Bert stroked the head of the softly cooing pigeon. It ruffled its wings as if already anxious to be off to the west.

"What shall I write?" Cuthbert asked. "The same?"

Roland nodded.

"But we *have* seen things that are unusual!" Alain said. "And we know things are wrong here! The horses . . . and at that small ranch way south . . . I can't remember the name . . ."

Cuthbert could. "The Rocking H."

"Aye, the Rocking H. There are *oxen* there. *Oxen!* My gods, I've never seen them, except for pictures in a book!"

Roland looked alarmed. "Does anyone know you saw?"

Alain shrugged impatiently. "I don't think so. There were drovers about—three, maybe four—"

"Four, aye," Cuthbert said quietly.

"—but they paid no attention to us. Even when we see things, they think we don't."

"And that's the way it must stay." Roland's eyes swept them, but there was a kind of absence in his face, as if his thoughts were far away. He turned to look toward the sunset, and Alain saw something on the collar of his shirt. He plucked it, a move made so quickly and nimbly that not even Roland felt it. *Bert couldn't have done that,* Alain thought with some pride.

"Aye, but—"

"Same message," Roland said. He sat down on the top step and looked off toward the evening redness in the west. "Patience, Mr. Richard Stockworth and Mr. Arthur Heath. We know certain things and we believe certain other things. But would John Farson come all this way simply to resupply horses? I don't think so. I'm not sure, horses are valuable, aye, so they are . . . but I'm not sure. So we wait."

"All right, all right, same message." Cuthbert smoothed the scrap of paper flat on the porch rail, then made a small series of symbols on it. Alain could read this message; he had seen the same sequence several times since they had come to Hambry. "Message received. We are fine. Nothing to report at this time."

The message was put in the capsule and attached to the pigeon's leg. Alain went down the steps, stood beside Rusher (still waiting patiently to be unsaddled), and held the bird up toward the fading sunset. "Hile!"

It was up and gone in a flutter of wings. For a moment only they saw it, a dark shape against the deepening sky.

Roland sat looking after. The dreamy expression was still on his face. Alain found himself wondering if Roland had made the right decision this evening. He had never in his life had such a thought. Nor expected to have one.

"Roland?"

"Hmmm?" Like a man half-awakened from some deep sleep.

"I'll unsaddle him, if you want." He nodded at Rusher. "And rub him down."

No answer for a long time. Alain was about to ask again when Roland said, "No. I'll do it. In a minute or two." And went back to looking at the sunset.

Alain climbed the porch steps and sat down in his rocker. Bert had resumed his place on the box-seat. They were behind Roland now, and Cuthbert looked at Alain with his eyebrows raised. He pointed to Roland and then looked at Alain again.

Alain passed over what he had plucked from Roland's collar. Although it was almost too fine to be seen in this light, Cuthbert's eyes were gunslinger's eyes, and he took it easily, with no fumbling.

It was a long strand of hair, the color of spun gold. He could see from Bert's face that Bert knew whose head it had come from. Since arriving in Hambry, they'd met only one girl with long blonde hair. The two boys' eyes met. In Bert's Alain saw dismay and laughter in equal measure.

Cuthbert Allgood raised his forefinger to his temple and mimed pulling the trigger.

Alain nodded.

Sitting on the steps with his back to them, Roland looked toward the dying sunset with dreaming eyes.

CHAPTER EIGHT

Beneath the Peddler's Moon

I

The town of Ritzy, nearly four hundred miles west of Mejis, was anything but. Roy Depape reached it three nights before the Peddler's Moon—called Late-summer's Moon by some—came full, and left it a day later.

Ritzy was, in fact, a miserable little mining village on the eastern slope of the Vi Castis Mountains, about fifty miles from Vi Castis Cut. The town had but one street; it was engraved with iron-hard wheelruts now, and would become a lake of mud roughly three days after the storms of autumn set in. There was the Bear and Turtle Mercantile & Sundrie Items, where miners were forbidden by the Vi Castis Company to shop, and a company store where no one but grubbies *would* shop; there was a combined jailhouse and Town Gathering Hall with a windmill-cum-gallows out front; there were six roaring barrooms, each more sordid, desperate, and dangerous than the last.

Ritzy was like an ugly lowered head between a pair of huge shrugged shoulders—the foothills. Above town to the south were the clapped-out shacks where the Company housed its miners; each puff of breeze brought the stench of their un-limed communal privies. To the north were the mines themselves: dangerous, under-shored scratch drifts that went down fifty feet or so and then spread like fingers clutching for gold and silver and copper and the occasional nest of firedims. From the outside they were just holes punched into the bare and rocky earth, holes like staring eyes, each with its own pile of till and scrapings beside the adit.

Once there had been freehold mines up there, but they were all gone, regulated out by the Vi Castis Company. Depape knew all about it, because the Big Coffin Hunters had been a part of that little spin and raree. Just after he'd hooked up with Jonas and Reynolds, that had been. Why, they had gotten those coffins tattooed on their hands not fifty miles from here, in the town of Wind, a mudpen even less ritzy than Ritzy. How long ago? He couldn't rightly say, although it seemed to him that he should be able to. But when it came to reckoning times past, Depape often felt lost. It was hard even to remember how old he was. Because the world had moved on, and time was different, now. *Softer.*

One thing he had no trouble remembering at all—his recollection was refreshed by the miserable flare of pain he suffered each time he bumped his wounded finger. That one thing was a promise to himself that he would see Dearborn, Stockworth, and Heath laid out dead in a row, hand to outstretched hand like a little girl's paper dolls. He intended to unlimber the part of him which had longed so bootlessly for Her Nibs these last three weeks and use it to hose down their dead faces. The majority of his squirt would be saved for Arthur Heath of Gilead, New Canaan. That laughing chatterbox motherfucker had a *serious* hosing-down coming.

Depape rode out the sunrise end of Ritzy's only street, trotted his horse up the flank of the first hill, and paused at the top for a single look back. Last night, when he'd been talking to the old bastard behind Hattigan's, Ritzy had been roaring. This morning at seven, it looked as ghostly as the Peddler's Moon, which still hung in the sky above the rim of the plundered hills. He could hear the mines tink-tonking away, though. You bet. Those babies tink-tonked away seven days a week. No rest for the wicked . . . and he supposed that included him. He dragged his horse's head around with his usual unthinking and ham-handed force, booted its flanks, and headed east, thinking of the old bastard as he went. He had treated the old bastard passing fair, he reckoned. A reward had been promised, and had been paid for information given.

"Yar," Depape said, his glasses flashing in the new sun (it was a rare morning when he had no hangover, and he felt quite cheerful), "I reckon the old bugger can't complain."

Depape had had no trouble following the young culls' backtrail; they had come east on the Great Road the whole way from New Canaan, it appeared, and at every town where they had stopped, they had been marked. In most they were marked if they did no more than pass through. And why not? Young men on good horses, no scars on their faces, no regulator tattoos on their hands, good clothes on their backs, expensive hats on their heads. They were remembered especially well at the inns and saloons, where they had stopped to refresh themselves but had drunk no hard liquor. No beer or *graf*, either, for that matter. Yes, they were remembered. Boys on the road, boys that seemed almost to shine. As if they had come from an earlier, better time.

Piss in their faces, Depape thought as he rode. *One by one. Mr. Arthur "Ha-Ha" Heath last. I'll save enough so it'd drown you, were you not already at the end of the path and into the clearing.*

They had been noticed, all right, but that wasn't good

enough—if he went back to Hambry with no more than that, Jonas would likely shoot his nose off. And he would deserve it. *They may be rich boys, but that's not all they are.* Depape had said that himself. The question was, what else were they? And finally, in the shit-and-sulfur stench of Ritzy, he had found out. Not everything, perhaps, but enough to allow him to turn his horse around before he found himself all the way back in fucking New Canaan.

He had hit two other saloons, sipping watered beer in each, before rolling into Hattigan's. He ordered yet another watered beer, and prepared to engage the bartender in conversation. Before he even began to shake the tree, however, the apple he wanted fell off and dropped into his hand, neat as you please.

It was an old man's voice (an old *bastard's* voice), speaking with the shrill, head-hurting intensity which is the sole province of old bastards in their cups. He was talking about the old days, as old bastards always did, and about how the world had moved on, and how things had been ever so much better when he was a boy. Then he had said something which caused Depape's ears to prick up: something about how the old days might be coming again, for hadn't he seen three young lords not two months a-gone, mayhap less, and even bought one of them a drink, even if 'twas only sasparilly soda?

"You wouldn't know a young lord from a young turd," said a miss who appeared to have all of four teeth left in her charming young head.

There was general laughter at this. The old bastard looked around, offended. "I know, all right," he said. "I've forgot more than you'll ever learn, so I have. One of them at least came from the Eld line, for I saw his father in his face . . . just as clear as I see your saggy tits, Jolene." And then the old bastard had done something Depape rather admired—yanked out the front of the saloon-whore's blouse and poured the remainder of his beer down it. Even the roars of laughter and heavy applause which greeted this couldn't entirely drown the girl's caw of rage, or the old man's cries when she began to slap and punch him about the head and shoulders. These latter cries were only indignant at first, but when the girl grabbed the old bastard's own beer-stein and shattered it against the side of his head, they became screams of pain. Blood—mixed with a few watery dregs of beer—began to run down the old bastard's face.

"Get out of here!" she yelled, and gave him a shove toward the door. Several healthy kicks from the miners in attendance (who had changed sides as easily as the wind changes directions) helped him along. "And don't come back! I can smell the weed on your breath, you old cocksucker! Get out and take your gods-cussed stories of old days and young lords with you!"

The old bastard was in such manner conveyed across the room, past the tootling trumpet-player who served as entertainment for the patrons of Hattigan's (that young bowler-hatted worthy added his own kick in the seat of the old bastard's dusty trousers without ever missing so much as a single note of "Play, Ladies, Play"), and out through the batwing doors, where he collapsed face-first into the street.

Depape had sauntered after him and helped him up. As he did so, he smelled an acrid odor—not beer—on the old man's breath, and saw the telltale greenish-gray discolorations at the corners of his lips. Weed, all right. The old bastard was probably just getting started on it (and for the usual reason: devil-grass was free in the hills, unlike the beer and whiskey that was sold in town), but once they started, the finish came quick.

"They got no respect," the old bastard said thickly. "Nor understanding, either."

"Aye, so they don't," said Depape, who had not yet gotten the accents of the seacoast and the Drop out of his speech.

The old bastard stood swaying, looking up at him, wiping ineffectually at the blood which ran down his wrinkled cheeks from his lacerated scalp. "Son, do you have the price of a drink? Remember the face of your father and give an old soul the price of a drink!"

"I'm not much for charity, old-timer," Depape said, "but mayhap you could earn yourself the price of a drink. Step on over here, into my office, and let's us see."

He'd led the old bastard out of the street and back to the boardwalk, angling well to the left of the black batwings with their golden shafts of light spilling out above and below. He waited for a trio of miners to go by, singing at the top of their lungs (*"Woman I love . . . is long and tall . . . she moves her body . . . like a cannonball . . ."*), and then, still holding the old bastard by the elbow, had guided him into the alley between Hattigan's and the undertaking establishment next door. For some people, Depape mused, a visit to Ritzy could damn near amount to one-stop shopping: get your drink, get your bullet, get laid out next door.

"Yer office," the old bastard cackled as Depape led him down the alley toward the board fence and the heaps of rubbish at the far end. The wind blew, stinging Depape's nose with odors of sulfur and carbolic from the mines. From their right, the sounds of drunken revelry pounded through the side of Hattigan's. "Your office, that's good."

"Aye, my office."

The old man gazed at him in the light of the moon, which rode the slot of sky above the alley. "Are you from Mejis? Or Tepachi?"

"Maybe one, maybe t'other, maybe neither."

"Do I know you?" The old bastard was looking at him even more closely, standing on tiptoe as if hoping for a kiss. Ugh.

Depape pushed him away. "Not so close, dad." Yet he felt marginally encouraged. He and Jonas and Reynolds *had* been here before, and if the old man remembered his face, likely he wasn't talking through his hat about fellows he'd seen much more recently.

"Tell me about the three young lords, old dad." Depape rapped on the wall of Hattigan's. "Them in there may not be interested, but I am."

The old bastard looked at him with a bleary, calculating eye. "Might there be a bit o' metal in it for me?"

"Yar," Depape said. "If you tell me what I want to hear, I'll give you metal."

"Gold?"

"Tell me, and we'll see."

"No, sir. Dicker first, tell second."

Depape seized him by the arm, whirled him around, and yanked a wrist which felt like a bundle of sticks up to the old bastard's scrawny shoulderblades. "Fuck with me, dad, and we'll start by breaking your arm."

"Let go!" the old bastard screamed breathlessly. "Let go, I'll trust to your generosity, young sir, for you have a generous face! Yes! Yes indeed!"

Depape let him go. The old bastard eyed him warily, rubbing his shoulder. In the moonlight the blood drying on his cheeks looked black.

"Three of them, there were," he said. "Fine-born lads."

"Lads or lords? Which is it, dad?"

The old bastard had taken the question thoughtfully. The whack on the head, the night air, and having his arm twisted seemed to have sobered him up, at least temporarily.

"Both, I do believe," he said at last. "One was a lord for

sure, whether them in there believe it or not. For I saw his father, and his father bore the guns. Not such poor things such as you wear—beggin your pardon, I know they're the best to be had these days—but *real* guns, such as were seen when my own dad was a boy. The big ones with the sandalwood grips."

Depape had stared at the old man, feeling a rise of excitement . . . and a species of reluctant awe, as well. *They acted like gunslingers,* Jonas had said. When Reynolds protested they were too young, Jonas had said they might be apprentices, and now it seemed the boss had likely been right.

"*Sandalwood* grips?" he had asked. "*Sandalwood* grips, old dad?"

"Yep." The old man saw his excitement, and his belief. He expanded visibly.

"A gunslinger, you mean. This one young fellow's father carried the big irons."

"Yep, a gunslinger. One of the last lords. Their line is passing, now, but my dad knew him well enough. Steven Deschain, of Gilead. Steven, son of Henry."

"And this one you saw not long ago—"

"His son, Henry the Tall's grandson. The others looked well-born, as if they might also come from the line of lords, but the one I saw come down all the way from Arthur Eld, by one line or another. Sure as you walk on two legs. Have I earned my metal yet?"

Depape thought to say yes, then realized he didn't know which of the three culls this old bastard was talking about.

"Three young men," he mused. "Three high-borns. And did they have guns?"

"Not out where the drift-diggers of *this* town could see em," the old bastard said, and laughed nastily. "But they had em, all right. Probably hid in their bedrolls. I'd set my watch and warrant on it."

"Aye," Depape said. "I suppose you would. Three young men, one the son of a lord. Of a *gunslinger*, you think. Steven of Gilead." And the name was familiar to him, aye, it was.

"Steven Deschain of Gilead, that's it."

"And what name did he give, this young lord?"

The old bastard had screwed his face up alarmingly in an effort to remember. "Deerfield? Deerstine? I don't quite remember—"

"That's all right, I know it. And you've earned your metal."

"Have I?" The old bastard had edged close again, his breath gagging-sweet with the weed. "Gold or silver? Which is it, my friend?"

"Lead," Depape replied, then hauled leather and shot the old man twice in the chest. Doing him a favor, really.

Now he rode back toward Mejis—it would be a faster trip without having to stop in every dipshit little town and ask questions.

There was a flurry of wings close above his head. A pigeon—dark gray, it was, with a white ring around its neck—fluttered down on a rock just ahead of him, as if to rest. An interesting-looking bird. Not, Depape thought, a wild pigeon. Someone's escaped pet? He couldn't imagine anyone in this desolate quarter of the world keeping anything but a half-wild dog to bite the squash off any would-be robber (although what these folks might have worth robbing was another question he couldn't answer), but he supposed anything was possible. In any case, roast pigeon would go down a treat when he stopped for the night.

Depape drew his gun, but before he could cock the

hammer, the pigeon was off and flying east. Depape took a shot after it, anyway. Sometimes you got lucky, but apparently not this time; the pigeon dipped a little, then straightened out and disappeared in the direction Depape himself was going. He sat astride his horse for a moment, not much put out of countenance; he thought Jonas was going to be very pleased with what he had found out.

After a bit, he booted his horse in the sides and began to canter east along the Barony Sea Road, back toward Mejis, where the boys who had embarrassed him were waiting to be dealt with. Lords they might be, sons of gunslingers they might be, but in these latter days, even such as those could die. As the old bastard himself would undoubtedly have pointed out, the world had moved on.

2

On a late afternoon three days after Roy Depape left Ritzy and headed his horse toward Hambry again, Roland, Cuthbert, and Alain rode north and west of town, first down the long swell of the Drop, then into the freeland Hambry folk called the Bad Grass, then into desert waste lands. Ahead of them and clearly visible once they were back in the open were crumbled and eroded bluffs. In the center of these was a dark, almost vaginal cleft, its edges so splintered it looked as if it had been whacked into reality by an ill-tempered god wielding a hatchet.

The distance between the end of the Drop and the bluffs was perhaps six miles. Three quarters of the way across, they passed the flatlands' only real geographic feature: a jutting upthrust of rock that looked like a finger bent at the first knuckle. Below it was a small, boomerang-shaped greensward, and when Cuthbert gave a ululating yell to hear his voice bounce back at him from the bluffs ahead, a pack of chattering billy-bumblers broke from this greenplace and went racing back southeast, toward the Drop.

"That's Hanging Rock," Roland said. "There's a spring at the base of it—only one in these parts, they say."

It was all the talk that passed between them on the ride out, but a look of unmistakable relief passed between Cuthbert and Alain behind Roland's back. For the last three weeks they had pretty much marched in place as summer rolled around them and past them. It was all well for Roland to say they must wait, they must pay great-est attention to the things that didn't matter and count the things which did from the corners of their eyes, but neither of them quite trusted the dreamy, disconnected air which Roland wore these days like his own special ver-sion of Clay Reynolds's cloak. They didn't talk about this between themselves; they didn't have to. Both knew that if Roland began courting the pretty girl whom Mayor Thorin meant for his gilly (and who else could that long blonde hair have belonged to?), they would be in very bad trouble. But Roland showed no courting plumage, neither of them spied any more blonde hairs on his shirt-collars, and tonight he seemed more himself, as if he had put that cloak of abstraction aside. Temporarily, mayhap. Permanently, if they were lucky. They could only wait and see. In the end, *ka* would tell, as it always did.

A mile or so from the bluffs, the strong sea breeze which had been at their backs for the whole ride sud-denly dropped, and they heard the low, atonal squall-ing from the cleft that was Eyebolt Canyon. Alain pulled up, grimacing like a man who has bitten into a fruit of extravagant sourness. All he could think of was a hand-ful of sharp pebbles, squeezed and ground together in a strong hand. Buzzards circled above the canyon as if drawn to the sound.

"The lookout don't like it, Will," Cuthbert said, knocking his knuckles on the skull. "I don't like it much, either. What are we out here for?"

"To count," Roland said. "We were sent to count everything and see everything, and this is something to count and see."

"Oh, aye," Cuthbert said. He held his horse in with some effort; the low, grinding wail of the thinny had made it skittish. "Sixteen hundred and fourteen fishing nets, seven hundred and ten boats small, two hundred and fourteen boats large, seventy oxen that nobody will admit to, and, on the north of town, one thinny. Whatever the hell *that* is."

"We're going to find out," Roland said.

They rode into the sound, and although none of them liked it, no one suggested they go back. They had come all the way out here, and Roland was right—this was their job. Besides, they were curious.

The mouth of the canyon had been pretty well stopped up with brush, as Susan had told Roland it would be. Come fall, most of it would probably be dead, but now the stacked branches still bore leaves and made it hard to see into the canyon. A path led through the center of the brushpile, but it was narrow for the horses (who might have balked at going through, anyway), and in the failing light Roland could make out hardly anything.

"Are we going in?" Cuthbert asked. "Let the Recording Angel note that I'm against, although I'll offer no mutiny."

Roland had no intention of taking them through the brush and toward the source of that sound. Not when he had only the vaguest idea of what a thinny was. He had asked a few questions about it over the last few weeks, and gotten little useful response. "I'd stay away," was the extent of Sheriff Avery's advice. So far his best information was still what he had gotten from Susan on the night he met her.

"Sit easy, Bert. We're not going in."

"Good," Alain said softly, and Roland smiled.

There was a path up the canyon's west side, steep and narrow, but passable if they were careful. They went single file, stopping once to clear a rockfall, pitching splintered chunks of shale and hornfels into the groaning trench to their right. When this was done and just as the three of them were preparing to mount up again, a large bird of some sort—perhaps a grouse, perhaps a prairie chicken—rose above the lip of the canyon in an explosive whir of feathers. Roland dipped for his guns, and saw both Cuthbert and Alain doing the same. Quite funny, considering that their firearms were wrapped in protective oilcloth and secreted beneath the floorboards of the Bar K bunkhouse.

They looked at each other, said nothing (except with their eyes, which said plenty), and went on. Roland found that the effect of being this close to the thinny was cumulative—it wasn't a sound you could get used to. Quite the contrary, in fact: the longer you were in the immediate vicinity of Eyebolt Canyon, the more that sound scraped away at your brain. It got into your teeth as well as your ears; it vibrated in the knot of nerves below the breastbone and seemed to eat at the damp and delicate tissue behind the eyes. Most of all, though, it got into your head, telling you that everything you had ever been afraid of was just behind the next curve of the trail or yonder pile of tumbled rock, waiting to snake out of its place and get you.

Once they got to the flat and barren ground at the top of the path and the sky opened out above them again it was a little better, but by then the light was almost gone, and when they dismounted and walked to the canyon's crumbling edge, they could see little but shadows.

"No good," Cuthbert said disgustedly. "We should have left earlier, Roland . . . Will, I mean. What dummies we are!"

"I can be Roland to you out here, if you like. And we'll see what we came to see and count what we came to count—one thinny, just as you said. Only wait."

They waited, and not twenty minutes later the Peddler's Moon rose above the horizon—a perfect summer moon, huge and orange. It loomed in the darkening violet swim of the sky like a crashing planet. On its face, as clear as anyone had ever seen it, was the Peddler, he who came out of Nones with his sackful of squealing souls. A hunched figure made of smudged shadows with a pack clearly visible over one cringing shoulder. Behind it, the orange light seemed to flame like hellfire.

"Ugh," Cuthbert said. "That's an ill sight to see with that sound coming up from below."

Yet they held their ground (and their horses, which periodically yanked back on their reins as if to tell them they should already be gone from this place), and the moon rose in the sky, shrinking a little as it went and turning silver. Eventually it rose enough to cast its bony light into Eyebolt Canyon. The three boys stood looking down. None of them spoke. Roland didn't know about his friends, but he didn't think he himself could have spoken even if called on to do so.

A box canyon, very short and steep-sided, Susan had said, and the description was perfectly accurate. She'd also said Eyebolt looked like a chimney lying on its side, and Roland supposed that was also true, if you allowed that a falling chimney might break up a little on impact, and lie with one crooked place in its middle.

Up to that crook, the canyon floor looked ordinary enough; even the litter of bones the moon showed them was not extraordinary. Many animals which wandered into box canyons hadn't the wit to find their way back out again, and with Eyebolt the possibility of escape was further reduced by the choke of brush piled at the canyon's mouth. The sides were much too steep to climb except maybe for one place, just before that crooked little jog. There Roland saw a kind of groove running up the canyon wall, with enough jutting spurs inside it to—maybe!—provide handholds. There was no real reason for him to note this; he just did, as he would go on noting potential escape-routes his entire life.

Beyond the jag in the canyon floor was something none of them had ever seen before . . . and when they got back to the bunkhouse several hours later, they all agreed that they weren't sure exactly what they *had* seen. The latter part of Eyebolt Canyon was obscured by a sullen, silvery liquescence from which snakes of smoke or mist were rising in streamers. The liquid seemed to move sluggishly, lapping at the walls which held it in. Later, they would discover that both liquid and mist were a light green; it was only the moonlight that had made them look silver.

As they watched, a dark flying shape—perhaps it was the same one that had frightened them before—skimmed down toward the surface of the thinny. It snatched something out of the air—a bug? another, smaller, bird?—and then began to rise again. Before it could, a silvery arm of liquid rose from the canyon's floor. For a moment that soupy, grinding grumble rose a notch, and became almost a voice. It snatched the bird out of the air and dragged it down. Greenish light, brief and unfocused, flashed across the surface of the thinny like electricity, and was gone.

The three boys stared at each other with frightened eyes.

Jump in, gunslinger, a voice suddenly called. It was

the voice of the thinny; it was the voice of his father; it was also the voice of Marten the enchanter, Marten the seducer. Most terrible of all, it was his own voice.

Jump in and let all these cares cease. There is no love of girls to worry you here, and no mourning of lost mothers to weigh your child's heart. Only the hum of the growing cavity at the center of the universe; only the punky sweetness of rotting flesh.

Come, gunslinger. Be a part of the thinny.

Dreamy-faced and blank-eyed, Alain began walking along the edge of the drop, his right boot so close to it that the heel puffed little clouds of dust over the chasm and sent clusters of pebbles down into it. Before he could get more than five steps, Roland grabbed him by the belt and yanked him roughly back.

"Where do you think you're going?"

Alain looked at him with sleepwalker's eyes. They began to clear, but slowly. "I don't . . . know, Roland."

Below them, the thinny hummed and growled and sang. There was a sound, as well: an oozing, sludgy mutter.

"*I* know," Cuthbert said. "I know where we're all going. Back to the Bar K. Come on, let's get out of here." He looked pleadingly at Roland. "Please. It's awful."

"All right."

But before he led them back to the path, he stepped to the edge and looked down at the smoky silver ooze below him. "Counting," he said with a kind of clear defiance. "Counting one thinny." Then, lowering his voice: "And be damned to you."

3

Their composure returned as they rode back—the sea-breeze in their faces was wonderfully restorative after the dead and somehow *baked* smell of the canyon and the thinny.

As they rode up the Drop (on a long diagonal, so as to save the horses a little), Alain said: "What do we do next, Roland? Do you know?"

"No. As a matter of fact, I don't."

"Supper would be a start," Cuthbert said brightly, and tapped the lookout's hollow skull for emphasis.

"You know what I mean."

"Yes," Cuthbert agreed. "And I'll tell you something, Roland—"

"Will, please. Now that we're back on the Drop, let me be Will."

"Aye, fine. I'll tell you something, Will: we can't go on counting nets and boats and looms and wheel-irons much longer. We're running out of things that don't matter. I believe that looking stupid will become a good deal harder once we move to the horse-breeding side of life as it's lived in Hambry."

"Aye," Roland said. He stopped Rusher and looked back the way they had come. He was momentarily enchanted by the sight of horses, apparently infected with a kind of moon-madness, frolicking and racing across the silvery grass. "But I tell you both again, *this is not just about horses.* Does Farson need them? Aye, may-hap. So does the Affiliation. Oxen as well. But there are horses everywhere—perhaps not as good as these, I'll admit, but any port does in a storm, so they say. So, if it's not horses, what is it? Until we know, or decide we'll *never* know, we go on as we are."

Part of the answer was waiting for them back at the Bar K. It was perched on the hitching rail and flicking its tail saucily. When the pigeon hopped into Roland's hand, he saw that one of its wings was oddly frayed. Some animal—likely a cat—had crept up on it close enough to pounce, he reckoned.

The note curled against the pigeon's leg was short, but it explained a good deal of what they hadn't understood.

I'll have to see her again, Roland thought after reading it, and felt a surge of gladness. His pulse quickened, and in the cold silver light of the Peddler's Moon, he smiled.

CHAPTER NINE

Citgo

I

The Peddler's Moon began to wane; it would take the hottest, fairest part of the summer with it when it went. On an afternoon four days past the full, the old *mozo* from Mayor's House (Miguel had been there long before Hart Thorin's time and would likely be there long after Thorin had gone back to his ranch) showed up at the house Susan shared with her aunt. He was leading a beautiful chestnut mare by a hack'. It was the second of the three promised horses, and Susan recognized Felicia at once. The mare had been one of her childhood's favorites.

Susan embraced Miguel and covered his bearded cheeks with kisses. The old man's wide grin would have showed every tooth in his head, if he'd had any left to show. *"Gracias, gracias,* a thousand thanks, old father," she told him.

"Da nada," he replied, and handed her the bridle. "It is the Mayor's earnest gift."

She watched him away, the smile slowly fading from her lips. Felicia stood docilely beside her, her dark brown coat shining like a dream in the summer sunlight. But this was no dream. It had seemed like one at first— that sense of unreality had been another inducement to walk into the trap, she now understood—but it was no dream. She had been proved honest; now she found herself the recipient of "earnest gifts" from a rich man. The phrase was a sop to conventionality, of course . . . or a bitter joke, depending on one's mood and outlook. Felicia was no more a gift than Pylon had been—they were step-by-step fulfillments of the contract into which she had entered. Aunt Cord could express shock, but Susan knew the truth: what lay directly ahead was whoring, pure and simple.

Aunt Cord was in the kitchen window as Susan walked her gift (which was really just returned property, in her view) to the stable. She called out something passing cheery about how the horse was a good thing, that caring for it would give Susan less time for her megrims. Susan felt a hot reply rise to her lips and held it back. There had been a wary truce between the two of them since the shouting match about the shirts, and Susan didn't want to be the one to break it. There was too much on her mind and heart. She thought that one more argument with her aunt and she might simply snap like a dry twig under a boot. *Because often silence is best,* her father had told her when, at age ten or so, she had asked him why he was always so quiet. The answer had puzzled her then, but now she understood better.

She stabled Felicia next to Pylon, rubbed her down, fed her. While the mare munched oats, Susan examined her hooves. She didn't care much for the look of the iron the mare was wearing—that was Seafront for you—and so she took her father's shoebag from its nail beside the stable door, slung the strap over her head and shoulder so the bag hung on her hip, and walked the two miles to Hookey's Stable and Fancy Livery. Feeling the leather bag bang against her hip brought back her father in a way so fresh and clear that grief pricked her again and made her feel like crying. She thought he would have been appalled at her current situation, perhaps even disgusted. And he would have liked Will Dearborn, of that she was sure—liked him and approved of him for her. It was the final miserable touch.

2

She had known how to shoe most of her life, and even enjoyed it, when her mood was right; it was dusty, elemental work, with always the possibility of a healthy kick in the slats to relieve the boredom and bring a girl back to reality. But of *making* shoes she knew nothing, nor wished to. Brian Hookey made them at the forge behind his barn and hostelry, however; Susan easily picked out four new ones of the right size, enjoying the smell of horseflesh and fresh hay as she did. Fresh paint, too. Hookey's Stable & Smithy looked very well, indeed. Glancing up, she saw not so much as a single hole in the barn roof. Times had been good for Hookey, it seemed.

He wrote the new shoes up on a beam, still wearing his blacksmith's apron and squinting horribly out of one eye at his own figures. When Susan began to speak haltingly to him about payment, he laughed, told her he knew she'd settle her accounts as soon as she could, gods bless her, yes. 'Sides, they weren't any of them going anywhere, were they? Nawp, nawp. All the time gently propelling her through the fragrant smells of hay and horses toward the door. He would not have treated even so small a matter as four iron shoes in such a carefree manner a year ago, but now she was Mayor Thorin's good friend, and things had changed.

The afternoon sunlight was dazzling after the dimness of Hookey's barn, and she was momentarily blinded, groping forward toward the street with the leather bag bouncing on her hip and the shoes clashing softly inside. She had just a moment to register a shape looming in the brightness, and then it thumped into her hard enough to rattle her teeth and make Felicia's new shoes clang. She would have fallen, but for strong hands that quickly reached out and grasped her shoulders. By then her eyes were adjusting and she saw with dismay and amusement that the young man who had almost knocked her sprawling into the dirt was one of Will's friends—Richard Stockworth.

"Oh, sai, your pardon!" he said, brushing the arms of her dress as if he *had* knocked her over. "Are you well? Are you quite well?"

"Quite well," she said, smiling. "Please don't apologize." She felt a sudden wild impulse to stand on tiptoe and kiss his mouth and say, *Give that to Will and tell him to never mind what I said! Tell him there are a thousand more where that came from! Tell him to come and get every one!*

Instead, she fixed on a comic image: this Richard Stockworth smacking Will full on the mouth and saying it was from Susan Delgado. She began to giggle. She put her hands to her mouth, but it did no good. Sai Stockworth smiled back at her . . . tentatively, cautiously. *He probably thinks I'm mad . . . and I am! I am!*

"Good day, Mr. Stockworth," she said, and passed on before she could embarrass herself further.

"Good day, Susan Delgado," he called in return.

She looked back once, when she was fifty yards or so farther up the street, but he was already gone. Not into Hookey's, though; of that she was quite sure. She wondered what Mr. Stockworth had been doing at that end of town to begin with.

Half an hour later, as she took the new iron from her da's shoebag, she found out. There was a folded scrap of paper tucked between two of the shoes, and even before she unfolded it, she understood that her collision with Mr. Stockworth hadn't been an accident.

She recognized Will's handwriting at once from the note in the bouquet.

Susan,

Can you meet me at Citgo this evening or tomorrow evening? Very important. Has to do with what we discussed before. Please.

W.

P.S. Best you burn this note.

She burned it at once, and as she watched the flames first flash up and then die down, she murmured over and over the one word in it which had struck her the hardest: *Please.*

3

She and Aunt Cord ate a simple, silent evening meal—bread and soup—and when it was done, Susan rode Felicia out to the Drop and watched the sun go down. She would not be meeting him this evening, no. She already owed too much sorrow to impulsive, unthinking behavior. But tomorrow?

Why Citgo?

Has to do with what we discussed before.

Yes, probably. She did not doubt his honor, although she had much come to wonder if he and his friends were who they said they were. He probably did want to see her for some reason which bore on his mission (although how the oilpatch could have anything to do with too many horses on the Drop she did not know), but there was something between them now, something sweet and dangerous. They might start off talking but would likely end up kissing . . . and kissing would just be the start. Knowing didn't change feeling, though; she wanted to see him. *Needed* to see him.

So she sat astride her new horse—another of Hart Thorin's payments-in-advance on her virginity—and watched the sun swell and turn red in the west. She listened to the faint grumble of the thinny, and for the first time in her sixteen years was truly torn by indecision. All she wanted stood against all she believed of honor, and her mind roared with conflict. Around all, like a rising wind around an unstable house, she felt the idea of *ka* growing. Yet to give over one's honor for that reason was so easy, wasn't it? To excuse the fall of virtue by invoking all-powerful *ka*. It was soft thinking.

Susan felt as blind as she'd been when leaving the darkness of Brian Hookey's barn for the brightness of the street. At one point she cried silently in frustration without even being aware of it, and pervading her every effort to think clearly and rationally was her desire to kiss him again, and to feel his hand cupping her breast.

She had never been a religious girl, had little faith in the dim gods of Mid-World, so at the last of it, with the sun gone and the sky above its point of exit going from red to purple, she tried to pray to her father. And an answer came, although whether from him or from her own heart she didn't know.

Let ka *mind itself,* the voice in her mind said. *It will, anyway; it always does. If* ka *should overrule your honor, so it will be; in the meantime, Susan, there's no one to mind it but yourself. Let* ka *go and mind the virtue of your promise, hard as that may be.*

"All right," she said. In her current state she discovered that any decision—even one that would cost her another chance to see Will—was a relief. "I'll honor my promise. *Ka* can take care of itself."

In the gathering shadows, she clucked sidemouth to Felicia and turned for home.

4

The next day was Sanday, the traditional cowboys' day of rest. Roland's little band took this day off as well. "It's fair enough that we should," Cuthbert said, "since we don't know what the hell we're doing in the first place."

On this particular Sanday—their sixth since coming to Hambry—Cuthbert was in the upper market (lower market was cheaper, by and large, but too fishy-smelling for his liking), looking at brightly colored *serapes* and trying not to cry. For his mother had a *serape*, it was a great favorite of hers, and thinking of how she would ride out sometimes with it flowing back from her shoulders had filled him with homesickness so strong it was savage. "Arthur Heath," Roland's *ka-mai*, missing his mama so badly his eyes were wet! It was a joke worthy of . . . well, worthy of Cuthbert Allgood.

As he stood so, looking at the *serapes* and a hanging rack of *dolina* blankets with his hands clasped behind his back like a patron in an art gallery (and blinking back tears all the while), there came a light tap on his shoulder. He turned, and there was the girl with the blonde hair.

Cuthbert wasn't surprised that Roland was smitten with her. She was nothing short of breathtaking, even dressed in jeans and a farmshirt. Her hair was tied back with a series of rough rawhide hanks, and she had eyes of the brightest gray Cuthbert had ever seen. Cuthbert thought it was a wonder that Roland had been able to continue with any other aspect of his life at all, even down to the washing of his teeth. Certainly she came with a cure for Cuthbert; sentimental thoughts of his mother disappeared in an instant.

"Sai," he said. It was all he could manage, at least to start with.

She nodded and held out what the folk of Mejis called a *corvette*—"little packet" was the literal definition; "little purse" was the practical one. These small leather accessories, big enough for a few coins but not much more, were more often carried by ladies than gentlemen, although that was not a hard-and-fast rule of fashion.

"Ye dropped this, cully," she said.

"Nay, thankee-sai." This one well might have been the property of a man—plain black leather, and unadorned by foofraws—but he had never seen it before. Never carried a *corvette,* for that matter.

"It's yours," she said, and her eyes were now so intense that her gaze felt hot on his skin. He should have understood at once, but he had been blinded by her unexpected appearance. Also, he admitted, by her cleverness. You somehow didn't expect cleverness from a girl this beautiful; beautiful girls did not, as a rule, have to be clever. So far as Bert could tell, all beautiful girls had to do was wake up in the morning. "It *is.* "

"Oh, aye," he said, almost snatching the little purse from her. He could feel a foolish grin overspreading his face. "Now that you mention it, sai—"

"Susan." Her eyes were grave and watchful above her smile. "Let me be Susan to you, I pray."

"With pleasure. I cry your pardon, Susan, it's just that my mind and memory, realizing it's Sanday, have joined hands and gone off on holiday together—eloped, you might say—and left me temporarily without a brain in my head."

He might well have rattled on like that for another hour (he had before; to that both Roland and Alain could testify), but she stopped him with the easy briskness of an older sister. "I can easily believe ye have no control over yer mind, Mr. Heath—or the tongue hung below it—but perhaps ye'll take better care of yer purse in the future. Good day." She was gone before he could get another word out.

5

Bert found Roland where he so often was these days: out on the part of the Drop that was called Town Lookout by many of the locals. It gave a fair view of Hambry, dreaming away its Sanday afternoon in a blue haze, but Cuthbert rather doubted the Hambry view was what drew his oldest friend back here time after time. He thought that its view of the Delgado house was the more likely reason.

This day Roland was with Alain, neither of them saying a word. Cuthbert had no trouble *accepting* the idea that some people could go long periods of time without talking to each other, but he did not think he would ever *understand* it.

He came riding up to them at a gallop, reached inside his shirt, and pulled out the *corvette*. "From Susan Delgado. She gave it to me in the upper market. She's beautiful, and she's also as wily as a snake. I say that with utmost admiration."

Roland's face filled with light and life. When Cuthbert tossed him the *corvette*, he caught it one-handed and pulled the lace-tie with his teeth. Inside, where a travelling man would have kept his few scraps of money, there was a single folded piece of paper. Roland read this quickly, the light going out of his eyes, the smile fading off his mouth.

"What does it say?" Alain asked.

Roland handed it to him and then went back to looking out at the Drop. It wasn't until he saw the very real desolation in his friend's eyes that Cuthbert fully realized how far into Roland's life—and hence into all their lives—Susan Delgado had come.

Alain handed him the note. It was only a single line, two sentences:

It's best we don't meet. I'm sorry.

Cuthbert read it twice, as if rereading might change it, then handed it back to Roland. Roland put the note back into the *corvette*, tied the lace, and then tucked the little purse into his own shirt.

Cuthbert hated silence worse than danger (it *was* danger, to his mind), but every conversational opening he tried in his mind seemed callow and unfeeling, given the look on his friend's face. It was as if Roland had been poisoned. Cuthbert was disgusted at the thought of that lovely young girl bumping hips with the long and bony Mayor of Hambry, but the look on Roland's face now called up stronger emotions. For that he could hate her.

At last Alain spoke up, almost timidly. "And now, Roland? Shall we have a hunt out there at the oilpatch without her?"

Cuthbert admired that. Upon first meeting him, many people dismissed Alain Johns as something of a dullard. That was very far from the truth. Now, in a diplomatic way Cuthbert could never have matched, he had pointed out that Roland's unhappy first experience with love did not change their responsibilities.

And Roland responded, raising himself off the saddlehorn and sitting up straight. The strong golden light of that summer's afternoon lit his face in harsh contrasts, and for a moment that face was haunted by the ghost of the man he would become. Cuthbert saw that ghost and shivered—not knowing what he saw, only knowing that it was awful.

"The Big Coffin Hunters," he said. "Did you see them in town?"

"Jonas and Reynolds," Cuthbert answered. "Still no sign of Depape. I think Jonas must have choked him and thrown him over the sea cliffs in a fit of pique after that night in the bar."

Roland shook his head. "Jonas needs the men he trusts too much to waste them—he's as far out on thin ice as we are. No, Depape's just been sent off for awhile."

"Sent where?" Alain asked.

"Where he'll have to shit in the bushes and sleep in the rain if the weather's bad." Roland laughed shortly, without much humor. "Jonas has got Depape running our backtrail, more likely than not."

Alain grunted softly, in surprise that wasn't really surprise. Roland sat easily astride Rusher, looking out over the dreamy depths of land, at the grazing horses. With one hand he unconsciously rubbed the *corvette* he had tucked into his shirt. At last he looked around at them again.

"We'll wait a bit longer," he said. "Perhaps she'll change her mind."

"Roland—" Alain began, and his tone was deadly in its gentleness.

Roland raised his hands before Alain could go on. "Doubt me not, Alain—I speak as my father's son."

"All right." Alain reached out and briefly gripped Roland's shoulder. As for Cuthbert, he reserved judgment. Roland might or might not be acting as his father's son; Cuthbert guessed that at this point Roland hardly knew his own mind at all.

"Do you remember what Cort used to say was the primary weakness of maggots such as us?" Roland asked with a trace of a smile.

" 'You run without consideration and fall in a hole,' " Alain quoted in a gruff imitation that made Cuthbert laugh aloud.

Roland's smile broadened a touch. "Aye. They're words I mean to remember, boys. I'll not upset this cart in order to see what's in it . . . not unless there's no other choice. Susan may come around yet, given time to think. I believe she would have agreed to meet me already, if not for . . . other matters between us."

He paused, and for a little while there was quiet among them.

"I wish our fathers hadn't sent us," Alain said at last . . . although it was *Roland's* father who had sent them, and all three knew it. "We're too young for matters such as these. Too young by years."

"We did all right that night in the Rest," Cuthbert said.

"That was training, not guile—and they didn't take us seriously. That won't happen again."

"They wouldn't have sent us—not my father, not yours—if they'd known what we'd find," Roland said. "But now we've found it, and now we're for it. Yes?"

Alain and Cuthbert nodded. They were for it, all right—there no longer seemed any doubt of that.

"In any case, it's too late to worry about it now. We'll wait and hope for Susan. I'd rather not go near Citgo without someone from Hambry who knows the lay of the place . . . but if Depape comes back, we'll have to take our chance. God knows what he may find out, or what stories he may invent to please Jonas, or what Jonas may do after they palaver. There may be shooting."

"After all this creeping around, I'd almost welcome it," Cuthbert said.

"Will you send her another note, Will Dearborn?" Alain asked.

Roland thought about it. Cuthbert laid an interior bet with himself on which way Roland would go. And lost.

"No," he said at last. "We'll have to give her time, hard as that is. And hope her curiosity will bring her around."

With that he turned Rusher toward the abandoned bunk-house which now served them as home. Cuthbert and Alain followed.

6

Susan worked herself hard the rest of that Sunday, mucking out the stables, carrying water, washing down all the steps. Aunt Cord watched all this in silence, her expression one of mingled doubt and amazement. Susan cared not a bit for how her aunt looked—she wanted only to exhaust herself and avoid another sleepless night. It was over. Will would know it as well now, and that was to the good. Let done be done.

"Are ye daft, girl?" was all Aunt Cord asked her as Susan dumped her last pail of dirty rinse-water behind the kitchen. "It's Sanday!"

"Not daft a bit," she replied shortly, without looking around.

She accomplished the first half of her aim, going to bed just after moonrise with tired arms, aching legs, and a throbbing back—but sleep still did not come. She lay in bed wide-eyed and unhappy. The hours passed, the moon set, and still Susan couldn't sleep. She looked into the dark and wondered if there was any possibility, even the slightest, that her father had been murdered. To stop his mouth, to close his eyes.

Finally she reached the conclusion Roland had already

come to: if there had been no attraction for her in those eyes of his, or the touch of his hands and lips, she would have agreed in a flash to the meeting he wanted. If only to set her troubled mind to rest.

At this realization, relief overspread her and she was able to sleep.

7

Late the next afternoon, while Roland and his friends were at fives in the Travellers' Rest (cold beef sandwiches and gallons of white iced tea—not as good as that made by Deputy Dave's wife, but not bad), Sheemie came in from outside, where he had been watering his flowers. He was wearing his pink *sombrera* and a wide grin. In one hand he held a little packet.

"Hello, there, you Little Coffin Hunters!" he cried cheerfully, and made a bow which was an amusingly good imitation of their own. Cuthbert particularly enjoyed seeing such a bow done in gardening sandals. "How be you? Well, I'm hoping, so I do!"

"Right as rainbarrels," Cuthbert said, "but none of us enjoys being called Little Coffin Hunters, so maybe you could just play soft on that, all right?"

"Aye," Sheemie said, as cheerful as ever. "Aye, Mr. Arthur Heath, good fella who saved my life!" He paused and looked puzzled for a moment, as if unable to remember why he had approached them in the first place. Then his eyes cleared, his grin shone out, and he held the packet out to Roland. "For you, Will Dearborn!"

"Really? What is it?"

"Seeds! So they are!"

"From you, Sheemie?"

"Oh, no."

Roland took the packet—just an envelope which had been folded over and sealed. There was nothing written on the front or back, and the tips of his fingers felt no seeds within.

"Who from, then?"

"Can't remember," said Sheemie, who then cast his eyes aside. His brains had been stirred just enough, Roland reflected, so that he would never be unhappy for long, and would never be able to lie at all. Then his eyes, hopeful and timid, came back to Roland's. "I remember what I was supposed to say to you, though."

"Aye? Then say it, Sheemie."

Speaking as one who recites a painfully memorized line, both proud and nervous, he said: "These are the seeds you scattered on the Drop."

Roland's eyes blazed so fiercely that Sheemie stumbled back a step. He gave his *sombrera* a quick tug, turned, and hurried back to the safety of his flowers. He liked Will Dearborn and Will's friends (especially Mr. Arthur Heath, who sometimes said things that made Sheemie laugh fit to split), but in that moment he saw something in Will-sai's eyes that frightened him badly. In that instant he understood that Will was as much a killer as the one in the cloak, or the one who had wanted Sheemie to lick his boots clean, or old white-haired Jonas with the trembly voice.

As bad as them, or even worse.

8

Roland slipped the "seed-packet" into his shirt and didn't open it until the three of them were back on the porch of the Bar K. In the distance, the thinny grumbled, making their horses twitch their ears nervously.

"Well?" Cuthbert asked at last, unable to restrain himself any longer.

Roland took the envelope from inside his shirt, and tore it open. As he did, he reflected that Susan had known exactly what to say. To a nicety.

The others bent in, Alain from his left and Cuthbert from his right, as he unfolded the single scrap of paper. Again he saw her simple, neatly made writing, the message not much longer than the previous one. Very different in content, however.

There is an orange grove a mile off the road on the town side of Citgo. Meet me there at moonrise. Come alone. S.

And below that, printed in emphatic little letters: BURN THIS.

"We'll keep a lookout," Alain said.

Roland nodded. "Aye. But from a distance."

Then he burned the note.

9

The orange grove was a neatly kept rectangle of about a dozen rows at the end of a partly overgrown cart-track. Roland arrived there after dark but still a good half hour before the rapidly thinning Peddler would haul himself over the horizon once more.

As the boy wandered along one of the rows, listening to the somehow skeletal sounds from the oilpatch to the north (squealing pistons, grinding gears, thudding driveshafts), he was struck by deep homesickness. It was the fragile fragrance of orange-blossoms—a bright runner laid over the darker stench of oil—that brought it on.

This toy grove was nothing like the great apple orchards of New Canaan . . . except somehow it was. There was the same feeling of dignity and civilization here, of much time devoted to something not strictly necessary. And in this case, he suspected, not very useful, either. Oranges grown this far north of the warm latitudes were probably almost as sour as lemons. Still, when the breeze stirred the trees, the smell made him think of Gilead with bitter longing, and for the first time he considered the possibility that he might never see home again—that he had become as much a wanderer as old Peddler Moon in the sky.

He heard her, but not until she was almost on top of him—if she'd been an enemy instead of a friend, he might still have had time to draw and fire, but it would have been close. He was filled with admiration, and as he saw her face in the starlight, he felt his heart gladden.

She halted when he turned and merely looked at him, her hands linked before her at her waist in a way that was sweetly and unconsciously childlike. He took a step toward her and they came up in what he took for alarm. He stopped, confused. But he had misread her gesture in the chancy light. She could have stopped then, but chose not to. She stepped toward him deliberately, a tall young woman in a split riding skirt and plain black boots. Her *sombrero* hung down on her back, against the bound rope of her hair.

"Will Dearborn, we are met both fair and ill," she said in a trembling voice, and then he was kissing her; they burned against one another as the Peddler rose in the famine of its last quarter.

10

Inside her lonely hut high on the Cöos, Rhea sat at her kitchen table, bent over the glass the Big Coffin Hunters had brought her a month and a half ago. Her face was bathed in its pink glow, and no one would have mistaken it for the face of a girl any longer. She had extraordinary vitality, and it had carried her for many years (only the longest-lived residents of Hambry had any idea of how old Rhea of the Cöos actually was, and they only the vaguest), but the glass was finally sapping it—sucking it out of her as a vampire sucks blood. Behind her, the hut's larger room was even dingier and more cluttered than usual. These days she had no time for even a pretense of cleaning; the glass ball took up all her time. When she wasn't looking into it, she was *thinking* of looking into it . . . and, oh! Such things she had seen!

Ermot twined around one of her scrawny legs, hissing with agitation, but she barely noticed him. Instead she bent even closer into the ball's poison pink glow, enchanted by what she saw there.

It was the girl who had come to her to be proved honest, and the young man she had seen the first time she'd looked into the ball. The one she had mistaken for a gunslinger, until she had realized his youth.

The foolish girl, who had come to Rhea singing and left in a more proper silence, had proved honest, and might well be honest yet (certainly she kissed and touched the boy with a virgin's mingled greed and timidity), but she wouldn't be honest much longer if they kept on the way they were going. And wouldn't Hart Thorin be in for a surprise when he took his supposedly pure young gilly to bed? There were ways to fool men about that (men practically *begged* to be fooled about that), a thimble of pig's blood would serve nicely, but *she* wouldn't know that. Oh, this was too good! And to think she could watch Miss Haughty brought low, right here, in this wonderful glass! Oh, it was too good! Too wonderful!

She leaned closer still, the deep sockets of her eyes

filling with pink fire. Ermot, sensing that she remained immune to his blandishments, crawled disconsolately away across the floor, in search of bugs. Musty pranced away from him, spitting feline curses, his six-legged shadow huge and misshapen on the firestruck wall.

II

Roland sensed the moment rushing at them. Somehow he managed to step away from her, and she stepped back from him, her eyes wide and her cheeks flushed—he could see that flush even in the light of the newly risen moon. His balls were throbbing. His groin felt full of liquid lead.

She half-turned away from him, and Roland saw that her *sombrero* had gone askew on her back. He reached out one trembling hand and straightened it. She clasped his fingers in a brief but strong grip, then bent to pick up her riding gloves, which she had stripped off in her need to touch him skin to skin. When she stood again, the wash of blood abruptly left her face, and she reeled. But for his hands on her shoulders, steadying her, she might have fallen. She turned toward him, eyes rueful.

"What are we to do? Oh, Will, what are we to do?"

"The best we can," he said. "As we both always have. As our fathers taught us."

"This is mad."

Roland, who had never felt anything so sane in his life—even the deep ache in his groin felt sane and right—said nothing.

"Do ye know how dangerous 'tis?" she asked, and went on before he could reply. "Aye, ye do. I can see ye do. If we were seen together at all, 'twould be serious. To be seen as we just were—"

She shivered. He reached for her and she stepped back. "Best ye don't, Will. If ye do, won't be nothing done between us but spooning. Unless that was your intention?"

"You know it wasn't."

She nodded. "Have ye set your friends to watch?"

"Aye," he said, and then his face opened in that unexpected smile she loved so well. "But not where they can watch *us*."

"Thank the gods for that," she said, and laughed rather distractedly. Then she stepped closer to him, so close that he was hard put not to take her in his arms again. She looked curiously up into his face. "Who are you, really, Will?"

"Almost who I say I am. That's the joke of this, Susan. My friends and I weren't sent here because we were drunk and helling, but we weren't sent here to uncover any fell plot or secret conspiracy, either. We were just boys to be put out of the way in a time of danger. All that's happened since—" He shook his head to show how helpless he felt, and Susan thought again of her father saying *ka* was like a wind—when it came it might take your chickens, your house, your barn. Even your life.

"And is Will Dearborn your real name?"

He shrugged. "One name's as good as another, I wot, if the heart that answers to it is true. Susan, you were at Mayor's House today, for my friend Richard saw you ride up—"

"Aye, fittings," she said. "For I am to be this year's Reaping Girl—it's Hart's choice, nothing I ever would have had on my own, mark I say it. A lot of foolishness, and hard on Olive as well, I warrant."

"You will make the most beautiful Reap-Girl that ever was," he said, and the clear sincerity in his voice made her tingle with pleasure; her cheeks grew warm again.

There were five changes of costume for the Reaping Girl between the noon feast and the bonfire at dusk, each more elaborate than the last (in Gilead there would have been nine; in that way, Susan didn't know how lucky she was), and she would have worn all five happily for Will, had he been the Reaping Lad. (This year's Lad was Jamie McCann, a pallid and whey-faced stand-in for Hart Thorin, who was approximately forty years too old and gray for the job.) Even more happily would she have worn the sixth—a silvery shift with wisp-thin straps and a hem that stopped high on her thighs. This was a costume no one but Maria, her maid, Conchetta, her seamstress, and Hart Thorin would ever see. It was the one she would be wearing when she went to the old man's couch as his gilly, after the feast was over.

"When you were up there, did you see the ones who call themselves the Big Coffin Hunters?"

"I saw Jonas and the one with the cloak, standing together in the courtyard and talking," she said.

"Not Depape? The redhead?"

She shook her head.

"Do you know the game Castles, Susan?"

"Aye. My father showed me when I was small."

"Then you know how the red pieces stand at one end of the board and the white at the other. How they come around the Hillocks and creep toward each other, setting screens for cover. What's going on here in Hambry is very like that. And, as in the game, it has now become a question of who will break cover first. Do you understand?"

She nodded at once. "In the game, the first one around his Hillock is vulnerable."

"In life, too. Always. But sometimes even staying in cover is difficult. My friends and I have counted nearly everything we dare count. To count the rest—"

"The horses on the Drop, for instance."

"Aye, just so. To count them would be to break cover. Or the oxen we know about—"

Her eyebrows shot up. "There are no oxen in Hambry. Ye must be mistaken about that."

"No mistake."

"Where?"

"The Rocking H."

Now her eyebrows drew back down, and knitted in a thoughtful frown. "That's Laslo Rimer's place."

"Aye—Kimba's brother. Nor are those the only treasures hidden away in Hambry these days. There are extra wagons, extra tack hidden in barns belonging to members of the Horsemen's Association, extra caches of feed—"

"Will, *no!*"

"Yes. All that and more. But to count them—to be *seen* counting them—is to break cover. To risk being Castled. Our recent days have been pretty nightmarish—we try to look profitably busy without moving over to the Drop side of Hambry, where most of the danger lies. It's harder and harder to do. Then we received a message—"

"A message? How? From whom?"

"Best you not know those things, I think. But it's led us to believe that some of the answers we're looking for may be at Citgo."

"Will, d'ye think that what's out here may help me to know more about what happened to my da?"

"I don't know. It's possible, I suppose, but not likely. All I know for sure is that I finally have a chance to count something that matters and not be seen doing it." His blood had cooled enough for him to hold out his hand to her; Susan's had cooled enough for her to take it in good confidence. She had put her glove back on again, however. Better safe than sorry.

"Come on," she said. "I know a path."

12

In the moon's pale half-light, Susan led him out of the orange grove and toward the thump and squeak of the oilpatch. Those sounds made Roland's back prickle; made him wish for one of the guns hidden under the bunkhouse floorboards back at the Bar K.

"Ye can trust me, Will, but that doesn't mean I'll be much help to ye," she said in a voice just a notch above a whisper. "I've been within hearing distance of Citgo my whole life, but I could count the number of times I've actually been in it on the fingers of both hands, so I could. The first two or three were on dares from my friends."

"And then?"

"With my da. He were always interested in the Old People, and my Aunt Cord always said he'd come to a bad end, meddling in their leavings." She swallowed hard. "And he did come to a bad end, although I doubt it were the Old People responsible. Poor Da."

They had reached a smoothwire fence. Beyond it, the gantries of the oil wells stood against the sky like sentinels the size of Lord Perth. How many had she said were still working? Nineteen, he thought. The sound of them was ghastly—the sound of monsters being choked to death. Of course it was the kind of place that kids dared each other to go into; a kind of open-air haunted house.

He held two of the wires apart so she could slip between them, and she did the same for him. As he passed through, he saw a line of white porcelain cylinders marching down the post closest to him. A fencewire went through each.

"You understand what these are? Were?" he asked Susan, tapping one of the cylinders.

"Aye. When there was electricity, some went through here." She paused, then added shyly: "It's how I feel when you touch me."

He kissed her cheek just below her ear. She shivered and pressed a hand briefly against his cheek before drawing away.

"I hope your friends will watch well."

"They will."

"Is there a signal?"

"The whistle of the nighthawk. Let's hope we don't hear it."

"Aye, be it so." She took his hand and drew him into the oilpatch.

13

The first time the gas-jet flared ahead of them, Will spat a curse under his breath (an obscenely energetic one she hadn't heard since her father died) and dropped the hand not holding hers to his belt.

"Be easy! It's only the candle! The gas-pipe!"

He relaxed slowly. "That they use, don't they?"

"Aye. To run a few machines—little more than toys, they are. To make ice, mostly."

"I had some the day we met the Sheriff."

When the flare licked out again—bright yellow with a bluish core—he didn't jump. He glanced at the three gas-storage tanks behind what Hambry-folk called "the candle" without much interest. Nearby was a stack of rusty canisters in which the gas could be bottled and carried.

"You've seen such before?" she asked.

He nodded.

"The Inner Baronies must be very strange and wonderful," Susan said.

"I'm beginning to think they're no stranger than those of the Outer Arc," he said, turning slowly. He pointed. "What's yon building down there? Left over from the Old People?"

"Aye."

To the east of Citgo, the ground dropped sharply down a thickly wooded slope with a lane cut through the middle of it—this lane was as clear in the moonlight as a part in hair. Not far from the bottom of the slope was a crumbling building surrounded by rubble. The tumble-and-strew was the detritus of many fallen smokestacks—that much could be extrapolated from the one which still stood. Whatever else the Old People had done, they had made lots of smoke.

"There were useful things in there when my da was a child," she said. "Paper and such—even a few ink-writers that would still work . . . for a little while, at least. If you shook them hard." She pointed to the left of the building, where there was a vast square of crumbled paving, and a few rusting hulks that had been the Old People's weird, horseless mode of travel. "Once there were things over there that looked like the gas-storage tanks, only much, much larger. Like huge silver cans, they were. They didn't rust like those that are left. I can't think what became of them, unless someone hauled them off for water storage. I never would. 'Twould be unlucky, even if they weren't contaminated."

She turned her face up to his, and he kissed her mouth in the moonlight.

"Oh, Will. What a pity this is for you."

"What a pity for both of us," he said, and then passed between them one of those long and aching looks of which only teenagers are capable. They looked away at last and walked on again, hand-in-hand.

She couldn't decide which frightened her more—

the few derricks that were still pumping or those dozens which had fallen silent. One thing she knew for sure was that no power on the face of the earth could have gotten her within the fence of this place without a friend close beside her. The pumps wheezed; every now and then a cylinder screamed like someone being stabbed; at periodic intervals "the candle" would fire off with a sound like dragon's breath, throwing their shadows out long in front of them. Susan kept her ears pitched for the nighthawk's piercing two-note whistle, and heard nothing.

They came to a wide lane—what had once undoubtedly been a maintenance road—that split the oilpatch in two. Running down the center was a steel pipe with rusting joints. It lay in a deep concrete trough, with the upper arc of its rusty circumference protruding above ground level.

"What's this?" he asked.

"The pipe that took the oil to yon building, I reckon. It means nothing, 'tis been dry for years."

He dropped to one knee, slid his hand carefully into the space between the concrete sleeve and the pipe's rusty side. She watched him nervously, biting her lip to keep herself from saying something which would surely come out sounding weak or womanish: What if there were biting spiders down there in the forgotten dark? Or what if his hand got stuck? What would they do then?

Of that latter there had been no chance, she saw when he pulled his hand free. It was slick and black with oil.

"Dry for years?" he asked with a little smile.

She could only shake her head, bewildered.

14

They followed the pipe toward a place where a rotten gate barred the road. The pipe (she could now see oil bleeding out of its old joints, even in the weak moonlight) ducked under the gate; they went over it. She thought his hands rather too intimate for polite company in their helping, and rejoiced at each touch. *If he doesn't stop, the top of my head will explode like "the candle,"* she thought, and laughed.

"Susan?"

" 'Tis nothing, Will, only nerves."

Another of those long glances passed between them as they stood on the far side of the gate, and then they went down the hill together. As they walked, she noticed an odd thing: many of the pines had been stripped of their lower branches. The hatchet marks and scabs of pine resin were clear in the moonlight, and looked new. She pointed this out to Will, who nodded but said nothing.

At the bottom of the hill, the pipe rose out of the ground and, supported on a series of rusty steel cradles, ran about seventy yards toward the abandoned building before stopping with the ragged suddenness of a battlefield amputation. Below this stopping point was what looked like a shallow lake of drying, tacky oil. That it had been there for awhile Susan could tell from the numerous corpses of birds she could see scattered across it— they had come down to investigate, become stuck, and stayed to die in what must have been an unpleasantly leisurely fashion.

She stared at this with wide, uncomprehending eyes until Will tapped her on the leg. He had hunkered down. She joined him knee-to-knee and followed the sweeping movement of his finger with growing disbelief and confusion. There were tracks here. Very big ones. Only one thing could have made them.

"Oxen," she said.

"Aye. They came from there." He pointed at the place where the pipe ended. "And they go—" He turned on the soles of his boots, still hunkered, and pointed back toward the slope where the woods started. Now that he pointed them out, she easily saw what she should have seen at once, horseman's daughter that she was. A perfunctory effort had been made to hide the tracks and the churned-up ground where something heavy had been dragged or rolled. Time had smoothed away more of the mess, but the marks were still clear. She even thought she knew what the oxen had been dragging, and she could see that Will knew, as well.

The tracks split off from the end of the pipe in two arcs. Susan and "Will Dearborn" followed the right-hand one. She wasn't surprised to see ruts mingled in with the tracks of the oxen. They were shallow—it had been a dry summer, by and large, and the ground was nearly as hard as concrete—but they were there. To still be able to see them at all meant that some goodly amount of weight had been moved. And aye, of course; why else would oxen be needed?

"Look," Will said as they neared the hem of forest at the foot of the slope. She finally saw what had caught his attention, but she had to get down on her hands and knees to do it—how sharp his eyes were! Almost supernaturally so. There were boot-tracks here. Not fresh, but they were a lot newer than the tracks of the oxen and the wheelruts.

"This was the one with the cape," he said, indicating a clear pair of tracks. "Reynolds."

"Will! Thee can't know it!"

He looked surprised, then laughed. "Sure I can. He

walks with one foot turned in a little—the left foot. And here it is." He stirred the air over the tracks with the tip of his finger, then laughed again at the way she was looking at him. " 'Tisn't sorcery, Susan daughter of Patrick; only trailcraft."

"How do ye know so much, so young?" she asked. "Who are ye, Will?"

He stood up and looked down into her eyes. He didn't have to look far; she was tall for a girl. "My name's not Will but Roland," he said. "And now I've put my life in your hands. That I don't mind, but mayhap I've put your own life at risk, as well. You must keep it a dead secret."

"Roland," she said wonderingly. Tasting it.

"Aye. Which do you like better?"

"Your real one," she said at once. " 'Tis a noble name, so it is."

He grinned, relieved, and this was the grin that made him look young again.

She raised herself on her toes and put her lips on his. The kiss, which was chaste and close-mouthed to begin with, bloomed like a flower: became open and slow and humid. She felt his tongue touch her lower lip and met it, shyly at first, with her own. His hands covered her back, then slipped around to her front. He touched her breasts, also shy to begin with, then slid his palms up their lower slopes to their tips. He uttered a small, moaning sigh directly into her mouth. And as he drew her closer and began to trail kisses down her neck, she felt the stone hardness of him below the buckle of his belt, a slim, warm length which exactly matched the melting she felt in the same place; those two places were meant for each other, as she was for him and he for her. It was *ka*, after all—*ka* like the wind, and she would go with it willingly, leaving all honor and promises behind.

She opened her mouth to tell him so, and then a

queer but utterly persuasive sensation enfolded her: they were being watched. It was ridiculous, but it was there; she even felt she knew who was watching. She stepped back from Roland, her booted heels rocking unsteadily on the half-eroded oxen tracks. "Get out, ye old bitch," she breathed. "If ye be spying on us in some way, I know not how, *get thee gone!*"

15

On the hill of the Cöos, Rhea drew back from the glass, spitting curses in a voice so low and harsh that she sounded like her own snake. She didn't know what Susan had said—no sound came through the glass, only sight— but she knew that the girl had sensed her. And when she did, all sight had been wiped out. The glass had flashed a brilliant pink, then had gone dark, and none of the passes she made over it would serve to brighten it again.

"Aye, fine, let it be so," she said at last, giving up. She remembered the wretched, prissy girl (not so prissy with the young man, though, was she?) standing hypnotized in her doorway, remembered what she had told the girl to do after she had lost her maidenhead, and began to grin, all her good humor restored. For if she lost her maidenhead to this wandering boy instead of to Hart Thorin, Lord High Mayor of Mejis, the comedy would be even greater, would it not?

Rhea sat in the shadows of her stinking hut and began to cackle.

16

Roland stared at her, wide-eyed, and as Susan explained about Rhea a little more fully (she left out the humiliating final examinations which lay at the heart of "proving honesty"), his desire cooled just enough for him to reassert control. It had nothing to do with jeopardizing the position he and his friends were trying to maintain in Hambry (or so he told himself) and everything to do with maintaining Susan's—her position was important, her honor even more so.

"I imagine it was your imagination," he said when she had finished.

"I think not." With a touch of coolness.

"Or conscience, even?"

At that she lowered her eyes and said nothing.

"Susan, I would not hurt you for the world."

"And ye love me?" Still without looking up.

"Aye, I do."

"Then it's best you kiss and touch me no more—not tonight. I can't stand it if ye do."

He nodded without speaking and held out his hand. She took it, and they walked on in the direction they had been going when they had been so sweetly distracted.

While they were still ten yards from the hem of the forest, both saw the glimmer of metal despite the dense foliage—*too dense,* she thought. *Too dense by far.*

It was the pine-boughs, of course; the ones which had been whacked from the trees on the slope. What they had been interlaced to camouflage were the big silver cans now missing from the paved area. The silver storage containers had been dragged over here—by the oxen, presumably—and then concealed. But why?

Roland inspected along the line of tangled pine

branches, then stopped and plucked several aside. This created an opening like a doorway, and he gestured her to go through. "Be sharp in your looks," he said. "I doubt if they've bothered to set traps or tripwires, but 'tis always best to be careful."

Behind the camouflaging boughs, the tankers had been as neatly lined up as toy soldiers at the end of the day, and Susan at once saw one reason why they had been hidden: they had been re-equipped with wheels, well-made ones of solid oak which came as high as her chest. Each had been rimmed with a thin iron strip. The wheels were new, so were the strips, and the hubs had been custom-made. Susan knew only one blacksmith in Barony capable of such fine work: Brian Hookey, to whom she had gone for Felicia's new shoes. Brian Hookey, who had smiled and clapped her on the shoulder like a *compadre* when she had come in with her da's shoebag hanging on her hip. Brian Hookey, who had been one of Pat Delgado's best friends.

She recalled looking around and thinking that times had been good for sai Hookey, and of course she had been right. Work in the blacksmithing line had been plentiful. Hookey had been making lots of wheels and rims, for one thing, and someone must have been paying him to do it. Eldred Jonas was one possibility; Kimba Rimer an even better one. Hart? She simply couldn't believe that. Hart had his mind—what little there was of it—fixed on other matters this summer.

There was a kind of rough path behind the tankers. Roland walked slowly along it, pacing like a preacher with his hands clasped at the small of his back, reading the incomprehensible words writ upon the tankers' rear decks: CITGO. SUNOCO. EXXON. CONOCO. He paused once and read aloud, haltingly: "Cleaner fuel for a better tomorrow." He snorted softly. "Rot! *This* is tomorrow."

"Roland—Will, I mean—what are they *for*?"

He didn't answer at first, but turned and walked back down the line of bright steel cans. Fourteen on this side of the mysteriously reactivated oil-supply pipe, and, she assumed, a like number on the other. As he walked, he rapped his fist on the side of each. The sound was dull and clunky. They were full of oil from the Citgo oilpatch.

"They were trigged quite some time ago, I imagine," he said. "I doubt if the Big Coffin Hunters did it all themselves, but they no doubt oversaw it . . . first the fitting of the new wheels to replace the old rotten rubber ones, then the filling. They used the oxen to line them up here, at the base of the hill, because it was convenient. As it's convenient to let the extra horses run free out on the Drop. Then, when we came, it seemed prudent to take the precaution of covering these up. Stupid babies we might be, but perhaps smart enough to wonder about twenty-eight loaded oil-carts with new wheels. So they came out here and covered them."

"Jonas, Reynolds, and Depape."

"Aye."

"But why?" She took him by the arm and asked her question again. "What are they *for*?"

"For Farson," Roland said with a calm he didn't feel. "For the Good Man. The Affiliation knows he's found a number of war-machines; they come either from the Old People or from some other where. Yet the Affiliation fears them not, because they don't work. They're silent. Some feel Farson has gone mad to put his trust in such broken things, but . . ."

"But mayhap they're not broken. Mayhap they only need this stuff. And mayhap Farson knows it."

Roland nodded.

She touched the side of one of the tankers. Her fingers came away oily. She rubbed the tips together, smelled them, then bent and picked up a swatch of grass to wipe her hands. "This doesn't work in our machines. It's been tried. It clogs them."

Roland nodded again. "My fa—my folk in the Inner Crescent know that as well. And count on it. But if Farson has gone to this trouble—*and* split aside a troop of men to come and get these tankers, as we have word he has done—he either knows a way to thin it to usefulness, or he thinks he does. If he's able to lure the forces of the Affiliation into a battle in some close location where rapid retreat is impossible, and if he can use machine-weapons like the ones that go on treads, he could win more than a battle. He could slaughter ten thousand horse-mounted fighting men and win the war."

"But surely yer fathers know this . . . ?"

Roland shook his head in frustration. How much their fathers knew was one question. What they made of what they knew was another. What forces drove them—necessity, fear, the fantastic pride which had also been handed down, father to son, along the line of Arthur Eld—was yet a third. He could only tell her his clearest surmise.

"I think they daren't wait much longer to strike Farson a mortal blow. If they do, the Affiliation will simply rot out from the inside. And if that happens, a good deal of Mid-World will go with it."

"But . . ." She paused, biting her lip, shaking her head. "Surely even Farson must know . . . understand . . ." She looked up at him with wide eyes. "The ways of the Old People are the ways of death. Everyone knows that, so they do."

Roland of Gilead found himself remembering a cook named Hax, dangling at the end of a rope while the rooks pecked up scattered breadcrumbs from beneath the dead man's feet. Hax had died for Farson. But before that, he had poisoned children for Farson.

"Death," he said, "is what John Farson's all about."

17

In the orchard again.

It seemed to the lovers (for so they now were, in all but the most physical sense) that hours had passed, but it had been no more than forty-five minutes. Summer's last moon, diminished but still bright, continued to shine above them.

She led him down one of the lanes to where she had tied her horse. Pylon nodded his head and whickered softly at Roland. He saw the horse had been rigged for silence—every buckle padded, and the stirrups themselves wrapped in felt.

Then he turned to Susan.

Who can remember the pangs and sweetness of those early years? We remember our first real love no more clearly than the illusions that caused us to rave during a high fever. On that night and beneath that fading moon, Roland Deschain and Susan Delgado were nearly torn apart by their desire for each other; they floundered for what was right and ached with feelings that were both desperate and deep.

All of which is to say that they stepped toward each other, stepped back, looked into each other's eyes with a kind of helpless fascination, stepped forward again, and stopped. She remembered what he had said with a kind of horror: that he would do anything for her but share her with another man. She would not—perhaps *could* not—break her promise to Mayor Thorin, and it seemed that Roland would not (or *could* not) break it for her. And here was the most horrible thing of all: strong as the wind of *ka* might be, it appeared that honor and the promises they had made would prove stronger.

"What will ye do now?" she asked through dry lips.

"I don't know. I must think, and I must speak with my friends. Will you have trouble with your aunt when you go home? Will she want to know where you've been and what you've been doing?"

"Is it me you're concerned about or yourself and yer plans, Willy?"

He didn't respond, only looked at her. After a moment, Susan dropped her eyes.

"I'm sorry, that was cruel. No, she'll not tax me. I often ride at night, although not often so far from the house."

"She won't know how far you've ridden?"

"Nay. And these days we tread carefully around each other. It's like having two powder magazines in the same house." She reached out her hands. She had tucked her gloves into her belt, and the fingers which grasped his fingers were cold. "This'll have no good end," she said in a whisper.

"Don't say that, Susan."

"Aye, I do. I must. But whatever comes, I love thee, Roland."

He took her in his arms and kissed her. When he released her lips, she put them to his ear and whispered, "If you love me, then love me. Make me break my promise."

For a long moment when her heart didn't beat, there was no response from him, and she allowed herself to hope. Then he shook his head—only the one time, but firmly. "Susan, I cannot."

"Is yer honor so much greater than yer professed love for me, then? Aye? Then let it be so." She pulled out of his arms, beginning to cry, ignoring his hand on her boot as she swung up into the saddle—his low call to wait, as well. She yanked free the slipknot with which Pylon had been tethered and turned him with one spurless foot. Roland was still calling to her, louder now, but she flung

Pylon into a gallop and away from him before her brief
flare of rage could go out. He would not take her used,
and her promise to Thorin had been made before she
knew Roland walked the face of the earth. That being so,
how dare he insist that the loss of honor and consequent
shame be hers alone? Later, lying in her sleepless bed,
she would realize he had insisted nothing. And she was
not even clear of the orange grove before raising her left
hand to the side of her face, feeling the wetness there,
and realizing that he had been crying, too.

18

Roland rode the lanes outside town until well past
moonset, trying to get his roaring emotions under some
kind of control. He would wonder for awhile what he
was going to do about their discovery at Citgo, and then
his thoughts would shift to Susan again. Was he a fool
for not taking her when she wanted to be taken? For
not sharing what she wanted to share? *If you love me, then
love me.* Those words had nearly torn him open. Yet in
the deep rooms of his heart—rooms where the clearest voice was that of his father—he felt he had not been
wrong. Nor was it just a matter of honor, whatever she
might think. But let her think that if she would; better
she should hate him a little, perhaps, than realize how
deep the danger was for both of them.

Around three o' the clock, as he was about to turn for
the Bar K, he heard the rapid drumming of hoofbeats
on the main road, approaching from the west. Without thinking about why it seemed so important to do
so, Roland swung back in that direction, then brought
Rusher to a stop behind a high line of run-to-riot hedges.
For nearly ten minutes the sound of the hoofbeats con-

tinued to swell—sound carried far in the deep quiet of early morning—and that was quite enough time for Roland to feel he knew who was riding toward Hambry hell-for-leather just two hours before dawn. Nor was he mistaken. The moon was down, but he had no trouble, even through the brambly interstices of the hedge, recognizing Roy Depape. By dawn the Big Coffin Hunters would be three again.

Roland turned Rusher back the way he had been heading, and rode to rejoin his own friends.

CHAPTER TEN

Bird and Bear
and Hare and Fish

I

The most important day of Susan Delgado's life—the day upon which her life turned like a stone upon a pivot—came about two weeks after her moonlit tour of the oilpatch with Roland. Since then she had seen him only half a dozen times, always at a distance, and they had raised their hands as passing acquaintances do when their errands bring them briefly into sight of one another. Each time this happened, she felt a pain as sharp as a knife twisting in her . . . and though it was no doubt cruel, she hoped he felt the same twist of the knife. If there was anything good about those two miserable weeks, it was only that her great fear—that gossip might begin about herself and the young man who called himself Will Dearborn—subsided, and she found herself actually sorry to feel it ebb. Gossip? There was nothing to gossip *about*.

Then, on a day between the passing of the Peddler's Moon and the rise of the Huntress, *ka* finally came and blew her away—house and barn and all. It began with someone at the door.

2

She had been finishing the washing—a light enough chore with only two women to do it for—when the knock came.

"If it's the ragman, send him away, ye mind!" Aunt Cord called from the other room, where she was turning bed-linen.

But it wasn't the ragman. It was Maria, her maid from Seafront, looking woeful. The second dress Susan was to wear on Reaping Day—the silk meant for luncheon at Mayor's House and the Conversational afterward—was ruined, Maria said, and she was in hack because of it. Would be sent back to Onnie's Ford if she wasn't lucky, and she the only support of her mother and father—oh, it was hard, much too hard, so it was. Could Susan come? Please?

Susan was happy to come—was always happy to get out of the house these days, and away from her aunt's shrewish, nagging voice. The closer Reaping came, the less she and Aunt Cord could abide each other, it seemed.

They took Pylon, who was happy enough to carry two girls riding double through the morning cool, and Maria's story was quickly told. Susan understood almost at once that Maria's position at Seafront wasn't really in much jeopardy; the little dark-haired maid had simply been using her innate (and rather charming) penchant for creating drama out of what was really not very dramatic at all.

The second Reaping dress (which Susan thought of as Blue Dress With Beads; the first, her breakfast dress, was White Dress With High Waist and Puffed Sleeves) had been kept apart from the others—it needed a bit of work yet—and something had gotten into the first-floor sewing room and gnawed it pretty much to rags. If this had been the costume she was to wear to the bonfire-lighting, or the one she was to wear to the ball-room dance after the bonfire had been lit, the matter would indeed have been serious. But Blue Dress With Beads was essentially just a fancified day receiving dress, and could easily be replaced in the two months between now and the Reap. Only two! Once—on the night the old witch had granted her her reprieve—it had seemed like eons before she would have to begin her bed-service to Mayor Thorin. And now it was only two months! She twisted in a kind of involuntary protest at the thought.

"Mum?" Maria asked. Susan wouldn't allow the girl to call her sai, and Maria, who seemed incapable of calling her mistress by her given name, had settled on this compromise. Susan found the term amusing, given the fact that she was only sixteen, and Maria herself probably just two or three years older. "Mum, are you all right?"

"Just a crick in my back, Maria, that's all."

"Aye, I get those. Fair bad, they are. I've had three aunts who've died of the wasting disease, and when I get those twinges, I'm always afeard that—"

"What kind of animal chewed up Blue Dress? Do ye know?"

Maria leaned forward so she could speak confidentially into her mistress's ear, as if they were in a crowded market-place alley instead of on the road to Seafront. "It's put about that a raccoon got in through a window that 'us opened during the heat of the day and was then forgot at day's end, but I had a good sniff of that room, and Kimba Rimer did, too, when he came down to inspect. Just before he sent me after you, that was."

"What did you smell?"

Maria leaned close again, and this time she actually whispered, although there was no one on the road to overhear: "Dog farts."

There was a moment of thunderstruck silence, and then Susan began to laugh. She laughed until her stomach hurt and tears went streaming down her cheeks.

"Are ye saying that W-W-Wolf . . . the Mayor's own *d-d-dog* . . . got into the downstairs seamstress's closet and chewed up my Conversational d-d—" But she couldn't finish. She was simply laughing too hard.

"Aye," Maria said stoutly. She seemed to find nothing unusual about Susan's laughter . . . which was one of the things Susan loved about her. "But he's not to be blamed, so I say, for a dog will follow his natural instincts, if the way is open for him to do so. The downstairs maids—" She broke off. "You'd not tell the Mayor or Kimba Rimer this, I suppose, Mum?"

"Maria, I'm shocked at you—ye play me cheap."

"No, Mum, I play ye dear, so I do, but it's always best to be safe. All I meant to say was that, on hot days, the downstairs maids sometimes go into that sewing closet for their fives. It lies directly in the shadow of the watchtower, ye know, and is the coolest room in the house—even cooler than the main receiving rooms."

"I'll remember that," Susan said. She thought of holding the Luncheon and Conversational in the seamstress's beck beyond the kitchen when the great day came, and began to giggle again. "Go on."

"No more to say, Mum," Maria told her, as if all else were too obvious for conversation. "The maids eat their cakes and leave the crumbs. I reckon Wolf smelled em and this time the door was left open. When the crumbs was gone, he tried the dress. For a second course, like."

This time they laughed together.

3

But she wasn't laughing when she came home.

Cordelia Delgado, who thought the happiest day of her life would be the one when she finally saw her troublesome niece out the door and the annoying business of her defloration finally over, bolted out of her chair and hurried to the kitchen window when she heard the gallop of approaching hoofs about two hours after Susan had left with that little scrap of a maid to have one of her dresses refitted. She never doubted that it was Susan returning, and she never doubted it was trouble. In ordinary circumstances, the silly twist would never gallop one of her beloved horses on a hot day.

She watched, nervously dry-washing her hands, as Susan pulled Pylon up in a very unDelgado–like scrunch, then dismounted in an unladylike leap. Her braid had come half undone, spraying that damned blonde hair that was her vanity (and her curse) in all directions. Her skin was pale, except for twin patches of color flaring high on her cheekbones. Cordelia didn't like the look of those at all. Pat had always flared in that same place when he was scared or angry.

She stood at the sink, now biting her lips as well as working her hands. Oh, 'twould be so good to see the back of that troublesome she. "Ye haven't made trouble, have ye?" she whispered as Susan pulled the saddle from Pylon's back and then led him toward the barn. "You better not have, Miss Oh So Young and Pretty. Not at this late date. You better not have."

4

When Susan came in twenty minutes later, there was no sign of her aunt's strain and rage; Cordelia had put them away as one might store a dangerous weapon—a gun, say—on a high closet shelf. She was back in her rocker, knitting, and the face she turned to Susan's entry had a surface serenity. She watched the girl go to the sink, pump cold water into the basin, and then splash it on her face. Instead of reaching for a towel to pat herself dry, Susan only looked out the window with an expression that frightened Cordelia badly. The girl no doubt fancied that look haunted and desperate; to Cordelia, it looked only childishly willful.

"All right, Susan," she said in a calm, modulated voice. The girl would never know what a strain it was to achieve that tone, let alone maintain it. Unless she was faced with a willful teenager of her own one day, that was. "What's fashed thee so?"

Susan turned to her—Cordelia Delgado, just sitting there in her rocker, calm as a stone. In that moment Susan felt she could fly at her aunt and claw her thin, self-righteous face to strings, screaming *This is your fault! Yours! All yours!* She felt soiled—no, that wasn't strong enough; she felt *filthy,* and nothing had really happened. In a way, that was the horror of it. Nothing had really happened *yet.*

"It shows?" was all she said.

"Of course it does," Cordelia replied. "Now tell me, girl. Has he been on thee?"

"Yes . . . no . . . no."

Aunt Cord sat in her chair, knitting in her lap, eyebrows raised, waiting for more.

At last Susan told her what had happened, speaking

in a tone that was mostly flat—a little tremble intruded toward the end, but that was all. Aunt Cord began to feel a cautious sort of relief. Perhaps more goose-girl nerves was all it came down to, after all!

The substitute gown, like all the substitutes, hadn't been finished off; there was too much else to do. Maria had therefore turned Susan over to blade-faced Conchetta Morgenstern, the chief seamstress, who had led Susan into the downstairs sewing room without saying anything—if saved words were gold, Susan had sometimes reflected, Conchetta would be as rich as the Mayor's sister was reputed to be.

Blue Dress With Beads was draped over a headless dressmaker's dummy crouched beneath one low eave, and although Susan could see ragged places on the hem and one small hole around to the back, it was by no means the tattered ruin she had been expecting.

"Can it not be saved?" she asked, rather timidly.

"No," Conchetta said curtly. "Get out of those trousers, girl. Shirt, too."

Susan did as she was bid, standing barefoot in the cool little room with her arms crossed over her bosom . . . not that Conchetta had ever shown the slightest interest in what she had, back or front, above or below.

Blue Dress With Beads was to be replaced by Pink Dress With Appliqué, it seemed. Susan stepped into it, raised the straps, and stood patiently while Conchetta bent and measured and muttered, sometimes using a bit of chalk to write numbers on a wall-stone, sometimes grabbing a swag of material and pulling it tighter against Susan's hip or waist, checking the look in the full-length mirror on the far wall. As always during this process, Susan slipped away mentally, allowing her mind to go where it wanted. Where it wanted to go most frequently these days was into a daydream of riding along the Drop with

Roland, the two of them side by side, finally stopping in a willow grove she knew that overlooked Hambry Creek.

"Stand there still as you can," Conchetta said curtly. "I be back."

Susan was hardly aware she was gone; was hardly aware she was in Mayor's House at all. The part of her that really mattered *wasn't* there. That part was in the willow grove with Roland. She could smell the faint half-sweet, half-acrid perfume of the trees and hear the quiet gossip of the stream as they lay down together forehead to forehead. He traced the shape of her face with the palm of his hand before taking her in his arms . . .

This daydream was so strong that at first Susan responded to the arms which curled around her waist from behind, arching her back as they first caressed her stomach and then rose to cup her breasts. Then she heard a kind of plowing, snorting breath in her ear, smelled tobacco, and understood what was happening. Not Roland touching her breasts, but Hart Thorin's long and skinny fingers. She looked in the mirror and saw him looming over her left shoulder like an incubus. His eyes were bulging, there were big drops of sweat on his forehead in spite of the room's coolness, and his tongue was actually hanging out, like a dog's on a hot day. Revulsion rose in her throat like the taste of rotten food. She tried to pull away and his hands tightened their hold, pulling her against him. His knuckles cracked obscenely, and now she could feel the hard lump at the center of him.

At times over the last few weeks, Susan had allowed herself to hope that, when the time came, Thorin would be incapable—that he would be able to make no iron at the forge. She had heard this often happened to men when they got older. The hard, throbbing column which lay against her bottom disabused her of that wistful notion in a hurry.

She had managed at least a degree of diplomacy by simply putting her hands over his and attempting to draw them off her breasts instead of pulling away from him again (Cordelia, impassive, not showing the great relief she felt at this).

"Mayor Thorin—Hart—you mustn't—this is hardly the place and not yet the time—Rhea said—"

"Balls to her and all witches!" His cultured politician's tones had been replaced by an accent as thick as that in the voice of any back-country farmhand from Onnie's Ford. "I must have something, a bonbon, aye, so I must. Balls to the witch, I say! Owlshit to 'er!" The smell of tobacco a thick reek around her head. She thought that she would vomit if she had to smell it much longer. "Just stand still, girl. Stand still, my temptation. Mind me well!"

Somehow she did. There was even some distant part of her mind, a part totally dedicated to self-preservation, that hoped he would mistake her shudders of revulsion for maidenly excitement. He had drawn her tight against him, hands working energetically on her breasts, his respiration a stinky steam-engine in her ear. She stood back to him, her eyes closed, tears squeezing out from beneath the lids and through the fringes of her lashes.

It didn't take him long. He rocked back and forth against her, moaning like a man with stomach cramps. At one point he licked the lobe of her ear, and Susan thought her skin would crawl right off her body in its revulsion. Finally, thankfully, she felt him begin to spasm against her.

"Oh, aye, get out, ye damned poison!" he said in a voice that was almost a squeal. He pushed so hard she had to brace her hands against the wall to keep from being driven face-first into it. Then he at last stepped back.

For a moment Susan only stood as she was, with

her palms against the rough cold stone of the sewing room wall. She could see Thorin in the mirror, and in his image she saw the ordinary doom that was rushing at her, the ordinary doom of which this was but a fore-taste: the end of girlhood, the end of romance, the end of dreams where she and Roland lay together in the willow grove with their foreheads touching. The man in the mirror looked oddly like a boy himself, one who's been up to something he wouldn't tell his mother about. Just a tall and gangly lad with strange gray hair and narrow twitching shoulders and a wet spot on the front of his trousers. Hart Thorin looked as if he didn't quite know where he was. In that moment the lust was flushed out of his face, but what replaced it was no better—that vacant confusion. It was as if he were a bucket with a hole in the bottom: no matter what you put in it, or how much, it always ran out before long.

He'll do it again, she thought, and felt an immense tiredness creep over her. *Now that he's done it once, he'll do it every chance he gets, likely. From now on coming up here is going to be like . . . well . . .*

Like Castles. Like playing at Castles.

Thorin looked at her a moment longer. Slowly, like a man in a dream, he pulled the tail of his billowy white shirt out of his pants and let it drop around him like a skirt, covering the wet spot. His chin gleamed; he had drooled in his excitement. He seemed to feel this and wiped the wetness away with the heel of one hand, look-ing at her with those empty eyes all the while. Then some expression at last came into them, and without another word he turned and left the room.

There was a little scuffling thud in the hall as he col-lided with someone out there. Susan heard him mutter "Sorry! Sorry!" under his breath (it was more apology than he'd given her, muttered or not), and then Conchetta stepped back into the room. The swatch of cloth she'd gone after was draped around her shoulders like a stole. She took in Susan's pale face and tearstained cheeks at once. *She'll say nothing,* Susan thought. *None of them will, just as none of them will lift a finger to help me off this stick I've run myself on. "Ye sharpened it yourself, gilly," they'd say if I called for help, and that'll be their excuse for leaving me to wriggle.*

But Conchetta had surprised her. "Life's hard, missy, so it is. Best get used to it."

5

Susan's voice—dry, by now pretty much stripped of emotion—at last ceased. Aunt Cord put her knitting aside, got up, and put the kettle on for tea.

"Ye dramatize, Susan." She spoke in a voice that strove to be both kind and wise, and succeeded at neither. "It's a trait ye get from your Manchester side—half of them fancied themselves poets, t'other half fancied themselves painters, and almost all of them spent their nights too drunk to tapdance. He grabbed yer titties and gave yer a dry-hump, that's all. Nothing to be so upset over. Certainly nothing to lose sleep over."

"How would you know?" Susan asked. It was disrespectful, but she was beyond caring. She thought she'd reached a point where she could bear anything from her aunt except that patronizing worldly-wise tone of voice. It stung like a fresh scrape.

Cordelia raised an eyebrow and spoke without rancor. "How ye do love to throw that up to me! Aunt Cord, the dry old stick. Aunt Cord the spinster. Aunt Cord the graying virgin. Aye? Well, Miss Oh So Young and Pretty, virgin I *might* be, but I had a lover or two back when I was young . . . before the world moved on, ye might say. Mayhap one was the great Fran Lengyll."

And mayhap not, Susan thought; Fran Lengyll was her aunt's senior by at least fifteen years, perhaps as many as twenty-five.

"I've felt old Tom's goat on my backside a time or two, Susan. Aye, and on my frontside as well."

"And were any of these lovers sixty, with bad breath and knuckles that cracked when they squeezed your titties, Aunt? Did any of them try to push you through the nearest wall when old Tom began to wag his beard and say baa-baa-baa?"

The rage she expected did not come. What did was worse—an expression close to the look of emptiness she had seen on Thorin's face in the mirror. "Deed's done, Susan." A smile, short-lived and awful, flickered like an eyelid on her aunt's narrow face. "Deed's done, aye."

In a kind of terror Susan cried: "My father would have hated this! *Hated* it! And hated you for allowing it to happen! For *encouraging* it to happen!"

"Mayhap," Aunt Cord said, and the awful smile winked at her again. "Mayhap so. And the only thing he'd hate more? The dishonor of a broken promise, the shame of a faithless child. He would want thee to go on with it, Susan. If thee would remember his face, thee *must* go on with it."

Susan looked at her, mouth drawn down in a trembling arc, eyes filling with tears again. *I've met someone I love!* That was what she would have told her if she could. *Don't you understand how that changes things? I've met someone I love!* But if Aunt Cord had been the sort of person to whom she could have said such a thing, Susan would likely never have been impaled on this stick to begin with. So she turned and stumbled from the house without saying anything, her streaming eyes blurring her vision and filling the late summer world with rueful color.

6

She rode with no conscious idea of where she was going, yet some part of her must have had a very specific destination in mind, because forty minutes after leaving her house, she found herself approaching the very grove of willows she had been daydreaming about when Thorin had crept up behind her like some bad elf out of a gammer's story.

It was blessedly cool in the willows. Susan tied Felicia (whom she had ridden out bareback) to a branch, then walked slowly across the little clearing which lay at the heart of the grove. Here the stream passed, and here she sat on the springy moss which carpeted the clearing. Of course she had come here; it was where she had brought all her secret griefs and joys since she had discovered the clearing at the age of eight or nine. It was here she had come, time and time again, in the nearly endless days after her father's death, when it had seemed to her that the very world—her version of it, at least—had ended with Pat Delgado. It was only this clearing that had heard the full and painful measure of her grief; to the stream she had spoken it, and the stream had carried it away.

Now a fresh spate of tears took her. She put her head on her knees and sobbed—loud, unladylike sounds like the caw of squabbling crows. In that moment she thought she would have given anything—*everything*—to have her father back for one minute, to ask him if she must go on with this.

She wept above the brook, and when she heard the sound of a snapping branch, she started and looked back over her shoulder in terror and chagrin. This was her secret place and she didn't want to be found here, especially not when she was bawling like a kiddie who has fallen and bumped her head. Another branch snapped. Someone was here, all right, invading her secret place at the worst possible time.

"Go away!" she screamed in a tear-clotted voice she barely recognized. "Go away, whoever ye are, be decent and leave me alone!"

But the figure—she could now see it—kept coming. When she saw who it was, she at first thought that Will Dearborn (*Roland,* she thought, *his real name is Roland*) must be a figment of her overstrained imagination. She wasn't entirely sure he was real until he knelt and put his arms around her. Then she hugged him with panicky tightness. "How did you know I was—"

"Saw you riding across the Drop. I was at a place where I go to think sometimes, and I saw you. I wouldn't have followed, except I saw that you were riding bareback. I thought something might be wrong."

"Everything's wrong."

Deliberately, with his eyes wide open and serious, he began kissing her cheeks. He had done it several times on both sides of her face before she realized he was kissing her tears away. Then he took her by the shoulders and held her back from him so he could look into her eyes.

"Say it again and I will, Susan. I don't know if that's a promise or a warning or both at the same time, but . . . say it again and I will."

There was no need to ask him what he meant. She seemed to feel the ground move beneath her, and later she would think that for the first and only time in her life she had actually felt *ka,* a wind that came not from the sky but from the earth. *It has come to me, after all,* she thought. *My* ka, *for good or ill.*

"Roland!"

"Yes, Susan."

She dropped her hand below his belt-buckle and grasped what was there, her eyes never leaving his.

"If you love me, then love me."

"Aye, lady. I will."

He unbuttoned his shirt, made in a part of Mid-World she would never see, and took her in his arms.

7

Ka:

They helped each other with their clothes; they lay naked in each other's arms on summer moss as soft as the finest goosedown. They lay with their foreheads touching, as in her daydream, and when he found his way into her, she felt pain melt into sweetness like some wild and exotic herb that may only be tasted once in each lifetime. She held that taste as long as she could, until at last the sweetness overcame it and she gave in to that, moaning deep in her throat and rubbing her forearms against the sides of his neck. They made love in the willow grove, questions of honor put aside, promises broken without so much as a look back, and at the end of it Susan discovered there was more than sweetness; there was a kind of delirious clinching of the nerves that began in the part of her that had opened before him like a flower; it began there and then filled her entire body. She cried out again and again, thinking there could not be so much pleasure in the mortal world; she would die of it. Roland added his voice to hers, and the sound of water rushing over stones wrapped around both. As she pulled him closer to her, locking her ankles together behind his knees and covering his face with fierce kisses, his going out rushed after hers as if trying to catch up. So were lovers joined in the Barony of Mejis, near the end of the last great age, and the green moss beneath the place where her thighs joined turned a pretty red as her virginity passed; so were they joined and so were they doomed.

Ka.

8

They lay together in each other's arms, sharing after-glow kisses beneath Felicia's mild gaze, and Roland felt himself drowsing. This was understandable—the strain on him that summer had been enormous, and he had been sleeping badly. Although he didn't know it then, he would sleep badly for the rest of his life.

"Roland?" Her voice, distant. Sweet, as well.

"Yes?"

"Will thee take care of me?"

"Yes."

"I can't go to him when the time comes. I can bear his touching, and his little thefts—if I have you, I can—but I can't go to him on Reap Night. I don't know if I've forgotten the face of my father or not, but I cannot go to Hart Thorin's bed. There are ways the loss of a girl's virginity can be concealed, I think, but I won't use them. I simply cannot go to his bed."

"All right," he said, "good." And then, as her eyes widened in startlement, he looked around. No one was there. He looked back at Susan, fully awake now. "What? What is it?"

"I might already be carrying your child," she said. "Has thee thought of that?"

He hadn't. Now he did. A child. Another link in the

chain stretching back into the dimness where Arthur Eld
had led his gunslingers into battle with the great sword
Excalibur raised above his head and the crown of All-
World on his brow. But never mind that; what would his
father think? Or Gabrielle, to know she had become a
grandmother?

A little smile had formed at the corners of his mouth,
but the thought of his mother drove it away. He thought
of the mark on her neck. When his mother came to his
mind these days, he *always* thought of the mark he'd
seen on her neck when he came unexpected into her
apartment. And the small, rueful smile on her face.

"If you carry my child, such is my good fortune," he said.

"And mine." It was her turn to smile, but it had a sad
look to it all the same, that smile. "We're too young, I
suppose. Little more than kiddies ourselves."

He rolled onto his back and looked up at the blue
sky. What she said might be true, but it didn't matter.
Truth was sometimes not the same as reality—this was
one of the certainties that lived in the hollow, cavey
place at the center of his divided nature. That he could
rise above both and willingly embrace the insanity of
romance was a gift from his mother. All else in his nature
was humorless . . . and, perhaps more important, without metaphor. That they were too young to be parents?
What of that? If he had planted a seed, it would grow.

"Whatever comes, we'll do as we must. And I'll always
love you, no matter what comes."

She smiled. He said it as a man would state any dry
fact: sky is up, earth is down, water flows south.

"Roland, how old *are* you?" She was sometimes troubled by the idea that, young as she herself was, Roland
was even younger. When he was concentrating on something, he could look so hard he frightened her. When
he smiled, he looked not like a lover but a kid brother.

"Older than I was when I came here," he said. "Older by far. And if I have to stay in sight of Jonas and his men another six months, I'll be hobbling and needing a boost in the arse to get aboard my horse."

She grinned at that, and he kissed her nose.

"And thee'll take care of me?"

"Aye," he said, and grinned back at her. Susan nodded, then also turned on her back. They lay that way, hip to hip, looking up at the sky. She took his hand and placed it on her breast. As he stroked the nipple with his thumb, it raised its head, grew hard, and began to tingle. This sensation slipped quickly down her body to the place that was still throbbing between her legs. She squeezed her thighs together and was both delighted and dismayed to find that doing so only made matters worse.

"Ye *must* take care of me," she said in a low voice. "I've pinned everything on you. All else is cast aside."

"I'll do my best," he said. "Never doubt it. But for now, Susan, you must go on as you have been. There's more time yet to pass; I know that because Depape is back and will have told his tale, but they still haven't moved in any way against us. Whatever he found out, Jonas still thinks it's in his interest to wait. That's apt to make him more dangerous when he *does* move, but for now it's still Castles."

"But after the Reaping Bonfire—Thorin—"

"You'll never go to his bed. That you can count on. I set my warrant on it."

A little shocked at her own boldness, she reached below his waist. "Here's a warrant ye can set on me, if ye would," she said.

He would. Could. And did.

When it was over (for Roland it had been even sweeter than the first time, if that was possible), he asked her: "That feeling you had out at Citgo, Susan—of being watched. Did you have it this time?"

She looked at him long and thoughtfully. "I don't know. My mind was in other places, ye ken." She touched him gently, then laughed as he jumped—the nerves in the half-hard, half-soft place where her palm stroked were still very lively, it seemed.

She took her hand away and looked up at the circle of sky above the grove. "So beautiful here," she murmured, and her eyes drifted closed.

Roland also felt himself drifting. It was ironic, he thought. This time she hadn't had that sensation of being watched . . . but the second time, he had. Yet he would have sworn there was no one near this grove.

No matter. The feeling, megrim or reality, was gone now. He took Susan's hand, and felt her fingers slip naturally through his, entwining.

He closed his eyes.

9

All of this Rhea saw in the glass, and wery interesting viewing it made, aye, wery interesting, indeed. But she'd seen shagging before—sometimes with three or four or even more doing it all at the same time (sometimes with partners who were not precisely alive)—and the hokey-pokey wasn't very interesting to her at her advanced age. What she was interested in was what would come *after* the hokey-pokey.

Is our business done? the girl had asked.

Mayhap there's one more little thing, Rhea had responded, and then she told the impudent trull what to do.

Aye, she'd given the girl very clear instructions as the two of them stood in the hut doorway, the Kissing Moon shining down on them as Susan Delgado slept the strange sleep and Rhea stroked her braid and whispered instructions in her ear. Now would come the fulfillment of that interlude . . . and that was what she wanted to see, not two babbies shagging each other like they were the first two on earth to discover how 'twas done.

Twice they did it with hardly a pause to natter in between (she would have given a good deal to hear that natter, too). Rhea wasn't surprised; at his young age, she supposed the brat had enough spunkum in his sack to give her a week's worth of doubles, and from the way the little slut acted, that might be to her taste. Some of them discovered it and never wanted aught else; this was one, Rhea thought.

But let's see how sexy you feel in a few minutes, you snippy bitch, she thought, and leaned deeper into the pulsing pink light thrown from the glass. She could sometimes feel that light aching in the very bones of her face . . . but it was a *good* ache. Aye, wery good indeed.

They were at last done . . . for the time being, at least. They clasped hands and drifted off to sleep.

"Now," Rhea murmured. "Now, my little one. Be a good girl and do as ye were told."

As if hearing her, Susan's eyes opened—but there was nothing in them. They woke and slept at the same time. Rhea saw her gently pull her hand free of the boy's. She sat up, bare breasts against bare thighs, and looked around. She got to her feet—

That was when Musty, the six-legged cat, jumped into Rhea's lap, *waowing* for either food or affection. The old woman shrieked with surprise, and the wizard's glass at once went dark—puffed out like a candleflame in a gust of wind.

Rhea shrieked again, this time with rage, and seized the cat before it could flee. She hurled it across the room, into the fireplace. That was as dead a hole as only a summer fireplace can be, but when Rhea cast a bony, misshapen hand at it, a yellow gust of flame rose from the single half-charred log lying in there. Musty screamed and fled from the hearth with his eyes wide and his split tail smoking like an indifferently butted cigar.

"Run, aye!" Rhea spat after him. "Begone, ye vile cusk!"

She turned back to the glass and spread her hands over it, thumb to thumb. But although she concentrated with all her might, willed until her heart was beating with a sick fury in her chest, she could do no more than bring back the ball's natural pink glow. No images appeared. This was bitterly disappointing, but there was nothing to be done. And in time she would be able to see the results with her own two natural eyes, if she cared to go to town and do so.

Everybody would be able to see.

Her good humor restored, Rhea returned the ball to its hiding place.

10

Only moments before he would have sunk too deep in sleep to have heard it, a warning bell went off in Roland's mind. Perhaps it was the faint realization that her hand was no longer entwined with his; perhaps it was raw intuition. He could have ignored that faint bell, and almost did, but in the end his training was too strong. He came up from the threshold of real sleep, fighting his way back to clarity as a diver kicks for the surface of a quarry. It was hard at first, but became easier; as he neared wakefulness, his alarm grew.

He opened his eyes and looked to his left. Susan was no longer there. He sat up, looked to his right, and saw nothing above the cut of the stream . . . yet he felt that she was in that direction, all the same.

"Susan?"

No response. He got up, looked at his pants, and Cort—a visitor he never would have expected in such a romantic bower as this—spoke up gruffly in his mind. *No time, maggot.*

He walked naked to the bank and looked down. Susan was there, all right, also naked, her back to him. She had unbraided her hair. It hung, loose gold, almost all the way to the lyre of her hips. The chill air rising from the surface of the stream shivered the tips of it like mist.

She was down on one knee at the edge of the running water. One arm was plunged into it almost to the elbow; she searched for something, it seemed.

"Susan!"

No answer. And now a cold thought came to him: *She's been infested by a demon. While I slept, heedless, beside her, she's been infested by a demon.* Yet he did not think he really believed that. If there had been a demon near this clearing, he would have felt it. Likely both of them would have felt it; the horses, too. But *something* was wrong with her.

She brought an object up from the streambed and held it before her eyes in her dripping hand. A stone. She examined it, then tossed it back—*plunk.* She reached in again, head bent, two sheaves of her hair now actually floating on the water, the stream prankishly tugging them in the direction it flowed.

"Susan!"

No response. She plucked another stone out of the stream. This one was a triangular white quartz, shattered into a shape that was almost like the head of a spear. Susan tilted her head to the left and took a sheaf of her hair in her hand, like a woman who means to comb out a nest of tangles. But there was no comb, only the rock with its sharp edge, and for a moment longer Roland remained on the bank, frozen with horror, sure that she meant to cut her own throat out of shame and guilt over what they'd done. In the weeks to come, he was haunted by a clear knowledge: if it *had* been her throat she'd intended, he wouldn't have been in time to stop her.

Then the paralysis broke and he hurled himself down the bank, unmindful of the sharp stones that gouged the soles of his feet. Before he reached her, she had already used the edge of the quartz to cut off part of the golden tress she held.

Roland seized her wrist and pulled it back. He could see her face clearly now. What could have been mistaken for serenity from the top of the bank now looked like what it really was: vacuity, emptiness.

When he took hold of her, the smoothness of her face was replaced by a dim and fretful smile; her mouth quivered as if she felt distant pain, and an almost form-less sound of negation came from her mouth: *"Nnnnn-nnnn—"*

Some of the hair she had cut off lay on her thigh like gold wire; most had fallen into the stream and been car-ried away. Susan pulled against Roland's hand, trying to get the sharp edge back to her hair, wanting to continue her mad barbering. The two of them strove together like arm-wrestlers in a barroom contest. And Susan was win-ning. He was physically the stronger, but not stronger than the enchantment which held her. Little by little the white triangle of quartz moved back toward her hanging hair. That frightening sound—*Nnnnnnnnnn*—kept drift-ing from her mouth.

"Susan! Stop it! Wake up!"

"Nnnnnnnn—"

Her bare arm quivering visibly in the air, the muscles bunched like hard little rocks. And the quartz moving closer and closer to her hair, her cheek, the socket of her eye.

Without thinking about it—it was the way he always acted most successfully—Roland moved his face close to the side of hers, giving up another four inches to the fist holding the stone in order to do it. He put his lips against the cup of her ear and then clucked his tongue against the roof of his mouth. Clucked sidemouth, in fact.

Susan jerked back from that sound, which must have gone through her head like a spear. Her eyelids fluttered rapidly, and the pressure she was exerting against Roland's grip eased a little. He took the chance and twisted her wrist.

"Ow! Owwww!"

The stone flew out of her opening hand and splashed into the water. Susan gazed at him, now fully awake, her eyes filled with tears and bewilderment. She was rubbing her wrist . . . which, Roland thought, was likely to swell.

"Ye hurt me, Roland! Why did ye hurt m . . ."

She trailed off, looking around. Now not just her face but the whole set of her body expressed bewilderment. She moved to cover herself with her hands, then realized they were still alone and dropped them to her sides. She glanced over her shoulder at the footprints—all of them bare—leading down the bank.

"How did I get down here?" she asked. "Did thee carry me, after I fell asleep? And why did thee hurt me? Oh, Roland, I love thee—why did ye hurt me?"

He picked up the strands of hair that still lay on her thigh and held them in front of her. "You had a stone with a sharp edge. You were trying to cut yourself with it, and you didn't want to stop. I hurt you because I was scared. I'm just glad I didn't break your wrist . . . at least, I don't think I did."

Roland took it and rotated it gently in either direction, listening for the grate of small bones.

He heard nothing, and the wrist turned freely. As Susan watched, stunned and confused, he raised it to his lips and kissed the inner part, above the delicate tracery of veins.

II

Roland had tied Rusher just far enough into the willows so the big gelding could not be seen by anyone who happened to come riding along the Drop.

"Be easy," Roland said, approaching. "Be easy a little longer, goodheart."

Rusher stamped and whickered, as if to say he could be easy until the end of the age, if that was what were required.

Roland flipped open his saddlebag and took out the steel utensil that served as either a pot or a frypan, depending on his needs. He started away, then turned back. His bedroll was tied behind Rusher's saddle—he had planned to spend the night camped out on the Drop, thinking. There had been a lot to think about, and now there was even more.

He pulled one of the rawhide ties, reached inside the blankets, and pulled out a small metal box. This he opened with a tiny key he drew from around his neck. Inside the box was a small square locket on a fine silver chain (inside the locket was a line-drawing of his mother), and a handful of extra shells—not quite a dozen. He took one, closed it in his fist, and went back to Susan. She looked at him with wide, frightened eyes.

"I don't remember anything after we made love the second time," she said. "Only looking up at the sky and thinking how good I felt and going to sleep. Oh, Roland, how bad does it look?"

"Not bad, I should think, but you'll know better than I. Here."

He dipped his cooker full of water and set it on the bank. Susan bent over it apprehensively, laying the hair on the left side of her head across her forearm, then moving the arm slowly outward, extending the tress in a band of bright gold. She saw the ragged cut at once. She examined it carefully, then let it drop with a sigh more relieved than rueful.

"I can hide it," she said. "When it's braided, no one will know. And after all, 'tis only hair—no more than woman's vanity. My aunt has told me so often enough, certainly. But Roland, *why*? Why did I do it?"

Roland had an idea. If hair was a woman's vanity, then hair-chopping would likely be a woman's bit of nastiness—a man would hardly think of it at all. The Mayor's wife, had it been her? He thought not. It seemed more likely that Rhea, up there on her height of land looking north toward the Bad Grass, Hanging Rock, and Eyebolt Canyon, had set this ugly trap. Mayor Thorin had been meant to wake up on the morning after the Reap with a hangover and a bald-headed gilly.

"Susan, can I try something?"

She gave him a smile. "Something ye didn't try already up yonder? Aye, what ye will."

"Nothing like that." He opened the hand he had held closed, showing the shell. "I want to try and find out who did this to you, and why." And other things, too. He just didn't know what they were yet.

She looked at the shell. Roland began to move it along the back of his hand, dancing it back and forth in a dexterous weaving. His knuckles rose and fell like the heddles of a loom. She watched this with a child's fascinated delight. "Where did ye learn that?"

"At home. It doesn't matter."

"Ye'd hypnotize me?"

"Aye . . . and I don't think it would be for the first time." He made the shell dance a bit faster—now east along his rippling knuckles, now west. "May I?"

"Aye," she said. "If you can."

12

He could, all right; the speed with which she went under confirmed that this had happened to Susan before, and recently. Yet he couldn't get what he wanted from her. She was perfectly cooperative *(some sleep eager,* Cort would have said), but beyond a certain point she would not go. It wasn't decorum or modesty, either—as she slept open-eyed before the stream, she told him in a far-off but calm voice about the old woman's examination, and the way Rhea had tried to "fiddle her up." (At this Roland's fists clenched so tightly his nails bit into his palms.) But there came a point where she could no longer remember.

She and Rhea had gone to the door of the hut, Susan said, and there they had stood with the Kissing Moon shining down on their faces. The old woman had been touching her hair, Susan remembered that much. The touch revolted her, especially after the witch's previous touches, but Susan had been unable to do anything about it. Arms too heavy to raise; tongue too heavy to speak. She could only stand there while the witch whispered in her ear.

"What?" Roland asked. "What did she whisper?"

"I don't know," Susan said. "The rest is pink."

"Pink? What do you mean?"

"Pink," she repeated. She sounded almost amused, as if she believed Roland was being deliberately dense. "She says, 'Aye, lovely, just so, it's a good girl y'are,' then everything's pink. Pink and bright."

"Bright."

"Aye, like the moon. And then . . ." She paused. "Then I think it *becomes* the moon. The Kissing Moon, mayhap. A bright pink Kissing Moon, as round and full as a grapefruit."

He tried other ways into her memory with no success—every path he tried ended in that bright pinkness, first obscuring her recollection and then coalescing into a full moon. It meant nothing to Roland; he'd heard of blue moons, but never pink ones. The only thing of which he was sure was that the old woman had given Susan a powerful command to forget.

He considered taking her deeper—she would go—but didn't dare. Most of his experience came from hypnotizing his friends—classroom exercises that were larky and occasionally spooky. Always there had been Cort or Vannay present to make things right if they went off-track. Now there were no teachers to step in; for better or worse, the students had been left in charge of the school. What if he took her deep and couldn't get her back up again? And he had been told there were demons in the below-mind as well. If you went down to where they were, they sometimes swam out of their caves to meet you . . .

All other considerations aside, it was getting late. It wouldn't be prudent to stay here much longer.

"Susan, do you hear me?"

"Aye, Roland, I hear you very well."

"Good. I'm going to say a rhyme. You'll wake up as I say it. When I'm done, you'll be wide awake and remember everything we've said. Do you understand?"

"Aye."

"Listen: Bird and bear and hare and fish, Give my love her fondest wish."

Her smile as she rose to consciousness was one of the

most beautiful things he had ever seen. She stretched, then put her arms around his neck and covered his face with kisses. "You, you, you, you," she said. "You're my fondest wish, Roland. You're my *only* wish. You and you, forever and ever."

They made love again there on the bank, beside the babbling stream, holding each other as tightly as they could, breathing into each other's mouths and living on each other's breath. *You, you, you, you.*

13

Twenty minutes later, he boosted her onto Felicia's back. Susan leaned down, took his face in her hands, and kissed him soundly.

"When will I see ye again?" she asked.

"Soon. But we must be careful."

"Aye. Careful as two lovers ever were, I think. Thank God thee's clever."

"We can use Sheemie, if we don't use him too often."

"Aye. And, Roland—do ye know the pavillion in Green Heart? Close to where they serve tea and cakes and things when the weather's fair?"

Roland did. Fifty yards or so up Hill Street from the jail and the Town Gathering Hall, Green Heart was one of the most pleasant places in town, with its quaint paths, umbrella-shaded tables, grassy dancing pavillion, and menagerie.

"There's a rock wall at the back," she said. "Between the pavillion and the menagerie. If you need me badly—"

"I'll always need you badly," he said.

She smiled at his gravity. "There's a stone on one of the lower courses—a reddish one. You'll see it. My friend Amy and I used to leave messages there for each other when we were little girls. I'll look there when I can. Ye do the same."

"Aye." Sheemie would work for awhile, if they were careful. The red rock might also work for awhile, if they were careful. But no matter how careful they were, they would slip eventually, because the Big Coffin Hunters now probably knew more about Roland and his friends than Roland ever would have wished. But he had to see her, no matter what the risks. If he didn't, he felt he might die. And he only had to look at her to know she felt the same.

"Watch special for Jonas and the other two," he said.

"I will. Another kiss, if ye favor?"

He kissed her gladly, and would just as gladly have pulled her off the mare's back for a fourth go-round . . . but it was time to stop being delirious and start being careful.

"Fare you well, Susan. I love y—" He paused, then smiled. "I love thee."

"And I thee, Roland. What heart I have is yours."

She had a great heart, he thought as she slipped through the willows, and already he felt its burden on his own. He waited until he felt sure she must be well away. Then he went to Rusher and rode off in the opposite direction, knowing that a new and dangerous phase of the game had begun.

14

Not too long after Susan and Roland had parted, Cordelia Delgado stepped out of the Hambry Mercantile with a box of groceries and a troubled mind. The troubled mind was caused by Susan, of course, always Susan, and Cordelia's fear that the girl would do something stupid before Reaping finally came around.

These thoughts were snatched out of her mind just as hands—strong ones—snatched the box of groceries from her arms. Cordelia cawed in surprise, shaded her eyes against the sun, and saw Eldred Jonas standing there between the Bear and Turtle totems, smiling at her. His hair, long and white (and beautiful, in her opinion), lay over his shoulders. Cordelia felt her heart beat a little faster. She had always been partial to men like Jonas, who could smile and banter their way to the edge of risquéness . . . but who carried their bodies like blades.

"I startled you. I cry your pardon, Cordelia."

"Nay," she said, sounding a little breathless to her own ears. "It's just the sun—so bright at this time of day—"

"I'd help you a bit on your way, if you give me leave. I'm only going up High as far as the corner, then I turn up the Hill, but may I help you that far?"

"With thanks," she said. They walked down the steps and up the board sidewalk, Cordelia looking around in little pecking glances to see who was observing them— she beside the handsome sai Jonas, who just happened to be carrying her goods. There was a satisfying number of onlookers. She saw Millicent Ortega, for one, looking out of Ann's Dresses with a satisfying O of surprise on her stupid cow's puss.

"I hope you don't mind me calling you Cordelia." Jonas shifted the box, which she'd needed two hands to carry, casually under one arm. "I feel, since the welcoming dinner at Mayor Thorin's house, that I know you."

"Cordelia's fine."

"And may I be Eldred to you?"

"I think 'Mr. Jonas' will do a bit longer," she said, then favored him with what she hoped was a coquettish smile. Her heart beat faster yet. (It did not occur to her that perhaps Susan was not the only silly goose in the Delgado family.)

"So be it," Jonas said, with a look of disappointment so comic that she laughed. "And your niece? Is she well?"

"Quite well, thank ye for asking. A bit of a trial, sometimes—"

"Was there ever a girl of sixteen who wasn't?"

"I suppose not."

"Yet you have additional burdens regarding her this fall. I doubt if *she* realizes that, though."

Cordelia said nothing—'twouldn't be discreet—but gave him a meaningful look that said much.

"Give her my best, please."

"I will." But she wouldn't. Susan had conceived a great (and irrational, in Cordelia's view) dislike for Mayor Thorin's regulators. Trying to talk her out of these feelings would likely do no good; young girls thought they knew everything. She glanced at the star peeking unobtrusively out from beneath the flap of Jonas's vest. "I understand ye've taken on an additional responsibility in our undeserving town, sai Jonas."

"Aye, I'm helping out Sheriff Avery," he agreed. His voice had a reedy little tremble which Cordelia found quite endearing, somehow. "One of his deputies—Claypool, his name is—"

"Frank Claypool, aye."

"—fell out of his boat and broke his leg. How do you fall out of a boat and break your leg, Cordelia?"

She laughed merrily (the idea that everyone in Hambry was watching them was surely wrong . . . but it felt that way, and the feeling was not unpleasant) and said she didn't know.

He stopped on the corner of High and Camino Vega, looking regretful. "Here's where I turn." He handed the box back to her. "Are you sure you can carry that? I suppose I could go on with you to your house—"

"No need, no need. Thank you. Thank you, *Eldred*."

The blush which crept up her neck and cheeks felt as hot as fire, but his smile was worth every degree of heat. He tipped her a little salute with two fingers and sauntered up the hill toward the Sheriff's office.

Cordelia walked on home. The box, which had seemed such a burden when she stepped out of the mercantile, now seemed to weigh next to nothing. This feeling lasted for half a mile or so, but by the time her house came into view, she was once again aware of the sweat trickling down her sides, and the ache in her arms. Thank the gods summer was almost over . . . and wasn't that Susan, just leading her mare in through the gate?

"Susan!" she called, now enough returned to earth for her former irritation with the girl to sound clear in her voice. "Come and help me, 'fore I drop this and break the eggs!"

Susan came, leaving Felicia to crop grass in the front yard. Ten minutes earlier, Cordelia would have noticed nothing of how the girl looked—her thoughts had been too wrapped up in Eldred Jonas to admit of much else. But the hot sun had taken some of the romance out of her head and returned her feet to earth. And as Susan took the box from her (handling it almost as easily as Jonas had done), Cordelia thought she didn't much care for the girl's appearance. Her temper had changed, for one thing—from the half-hysterical confusion in which she'd left to a pleasant and happy-eyed calmness. That was the Susan of previous years to the sleeve and seam . . . but not this year's moaning, moody breast-beater. There was nothing else Cordelia could put her finger on, except—

But there was, actually. One thing. She reached out and grasped the girl's braid, which looked uncharacteristically sloppy this afternoon. Of course Susan had been riding; that could explain the mess. But it didn't explain how dark her hair was, as if that bright mass of gold had begun to tarnish. And she jumped, almost guiltily, when she felt Cordelia's touch. Why, pray tell, was that?

"Yer hair's damp, Susan," she said. "Have ye been swimming somewhere?"

"Nay! I stopped and ducked my head at the pump outside Hookey's barn. He doesn't mind—'tis a deep well he has. It's so hot. Perhaps there'll be a shower later. I hope so. I gave Felicia to drink as well."

The girl's eyes were as direct and as candid as ever, but Cordelia thought there was something off in them, just the same. She couldn't say what. The idea that Susan might be hiding something large and serious did not immediately cross Cordelia's mind; she would have said her niece was incapable of keeping a secret any greater than a birthday present or a surprise party . . . and not even such secrets as those for more than a day or two. And yet something *was* off here. Cordelia dropped her fingers to the collar of the girl's riding shirt.

"Yet this is dry."

"I was careful," she said, looking at her aunt with a puzzled eye. "Dirt sticks worse to a wet shirt. You taught me that, Aunt."

"Ye flinched when I touched yer hair, Susan."

"Aye," Susan said, "so I did. The weird-woman touched it just that same way. I haven't liked it since. Now may I take these groceries in and get my horse out of the hot sun?"

"Don't be pert, Susan." Yet the edginess in her niece's voice actually eased her in some strange way. That feeling that Susan had changed, somehow—that feeling of *offness*—began to subside.

"Then don't be tiresome."

"Susan! Apologize to me!"

Susan took a deep breath, held it, then let it out. "Yes, Aunt. I do. But it's hot."

"Aye. Put those in the pantry. And thankee."

Susan went on toward the house with the box in her arms. When the girl had enough of a lead so they wouldn't have to walk together, Cordelia followed. It was all foolishness on her part, no doubt—suspicions brought on by her flirtation with Eldred—but the girl was at a dangerous age, and much depended on her good behavior over the next seven weeks. After that she would be Thorin's problem, but until then she was Cordelia's. Cordelia thought that, in the end, Susan would be true to her promise, but until Reaping Fair she would bear close watching. About such matters as a girl's virginity, it was best to be vigilant.

KANSAS, SOMEWHERE, SOMEWHEN

Eddie stirred. Around them the thinny still whined like an unpleasant mother-in-law; above them the stars gleamed as bright as new hopes . . . or bad intentions. He looked at Susannah, sitting with the stumps of her legs curled beneath her; he looked at Jake, who was eating a burrito; he looked at Oy, whose snout rested on Jake's ankle and who was looking up at the boy with an expression of calm adoration.

The fire was low, but still it burned. The same was true of Demon Moon, far in the west.

"Roland." His voice sounded old and rusty to his own ears.

The gunslinger, who had paused for a sip of water, looked at him with his eyebrows raised.

"How can you know every corner of this story?"

Roland seemed amused. "I don't think that's what you really want to know, Eddie."

He was right about that—old long, tall, and ugly made a habit of being right. It was, as far as Eddie was concerned, one of his most irritating characteristics. "All right. How long have you been talking? *That's* what I really want to know."

"Are you uncomfortable? Want to go to bed?"

He's making fun of me, Eddie thought . . . but even as the idea occurred to him, he knew it wasn't true. And

447

no, he *wasn't* uncomfortable. There was no stiffness in his joints, although he had been sitting cross-legged ever since Roland had begun by telling them about Rhea and the glass ball, and he didn't need to go to the toilet. Nor was he hungry. Jake was munching the single leftover burrito, but probably for the same reason folks climbed Mount Everest . . . because it was there. And why *should* he be hungry or sleepy or stiff? Why, when the fire still burned and the moon was not yet down?

He looked at Roland's amused eyes and saw the gunslinger was reading his thoughts.

"No, I don't want to go to bed. You know I don't. But, Roland . . . you've been talking a *long* time." He paused, looked down at his hands, then looked up again, smiling uneasily. "Days, I would have said."

"But time is different here. I've told you that; now you see for yourself. Not all nights are the same length just recently. Days, either . . . but we notice time more at night, don't we? Yes, I think we do."

"Is the thinny stretching time?" And now that he had mentioned it, Eddie could hear it in all its creepy glory—a sound like vibrating metal, or maybe the world's biggest mosquito.

"It might be helping, but mostly it's just how things are in my world."

Susannah stirred like a woman who rises partway from a dream that holds her like sweet quicksand. She gave Eddie a look that was both distant and impatient. "Let the man talk, Eddie."

"Yeah," Jake said. "Let the man talk."

And Oy, without raising his snout from Jake's ankle: "An. Awk."

"All right," Eddie said. "No problem."

Roland swept them with his eyes. "Are you sure? The

rest is . . ." He didn't seem able to finish, and Eddie realized that Roland was scared.

"Go on," Eddie told him quietly. "Let the rest be what it is. What it was." He looked around. Kansas, they were in Kansas. Somewhere, somewhen. Except he felt that Mejis and those people he had never seen—Cordelia and Jonas and Brian Hookey and Sheemie and Pettie the Trotter and Cuthbert Allgood—were very close now. That Roland's lost Susan was very close now. Because reality was thin here—as thin as the seat in an old pair of bluejeans—and the dark would hold for as long as Roland needed it to hold. Eddie doubted if Roland even noticed the dark, particularly. Why would he? Eddie thought it had been night inside of Roland's mind for a long, long time . . . and dawn was still nowhere near.

He reached out and touched one of those callused killer's hands. Gently he touched it, and with love.

"Go on, Roland. Tell your tale. All the way to the end."

"All the way to the end," Susannah said dreamily. "Cut the vein." Her eyes were full of moonlight.

"All the way to the end," Jake said.

"End," Oy whispered.

Roland held Eddie's hand for a moment, then let it go. He looked into the guttering fire without immediately speaking, and Eddie sensed him trying to find the way. Trying doors, one after another, until he found one that opened. What he saw behind it made him smile and look up at Eddie.

"True love is boring," he said.

"Say *what?*"

"True love is boring," Roland repeated. "As boring as any other strong and addicting drug. And, as with any other strong drug . . ."

PART THREE

COME, REAP

CHAPTER ONE

Beneath the Huntress Moon

I

True love, like any other strong and addicting drug, is boring—once the tale of encounter and discovery is told, kisses quickly grow stale and caresses tiresome . . . except, of course, to those who share the kisses, who give and take the caresses while every sound and color of the world seems to deepen and brighten around them. As with any other strong drug, true first love is really only interesting to those who have become its prisoners.

And, as is true of any other strong and addicting drug, true first love is dangerous.

2

Some called the Huntress the last moon of summer; some called it the first of fall. Whichever it was, it signalled a change in the life of the Barony. Men put out into the bay wearing sweaters beneath their oilskins as the winds began to turn more and more firmly into autumn's east-west alley, and to sharpen as they turned. In the great Barony orchards north of Hambry (and in smaller orchards owned by John Croydon, Henry Wertner, Jake White, and the morose but wealthy Coral

Thorin), the pickers began to appear in the rows, carrying their odd, off-kilter ladders; they were followed by horse-drawn carts full of empty barrels. Downwind of the cider-houses— especially downwind of the great Barony cider-mansion a mile north of Seafront—the breezy air was filled with the sweet tang of blems being pressed by the basketload. Away from the shore of the Clean Sea, the days remained warm as the Huntress waxed, skies were clear day and night, but summer's real heat had departed with the Peddler. The last cutting of hay began and was finished in the run of a week—that last one was always scant, and ranchers and freeholders alike would curse it, scratching their heads and asking themselves why they even bothered . . . but come rainy, blowsy old March, with the barn lofts and bins rapidly emptying, they always knew. In the Barony's gardens—the great ones of the ranchers, the smaller ones of the freeholders, and the tiny backyard plots of the townsfolk—men and women and children appeared in their old clothes and boots, their *sombreros* and *sombreras*. They came with the legs of their pants tied down firmly at the ankles, for in the time of the Huntress, snakes and scorpions in plentiful numbers wandered east from the desert. By the time old Demon Moon began to fatten, a line of rattlers would hang from the hitching posts of both the Travellers' Rest and the mercantile across the street. Other businesses would similarly decorate their hitching posts, but when the prize for the most skins was given on Reaping Day, it was always the inn or the market that won it. In the fields and gardens, baskets to pick into were cast along the rows by women with their hair tied up in kerchiefs and reap-charms hidden in their bosoms. The last of the tomatoes were picked, the last of the cucumbers, the last of the corn, the last of the parey and mingo. Waiting behind them, as the days sharpened and the autumn storms began to near, would come squash, sharproot, pumpkins, and potatoes. In Mejis the time of reaping had begun, while overhead, clearer and clearer on each starry night, the Huntress pulled her bow and looked east over those strange, watery leagues no man or woman of Mid-World had ever seen.

3

Those in the grip of a strong drug—heroin, devil grass, true love—often find themselves trying to maintain a precarious balance between secrecy and ecstasy as they walk the tightrope of their lives. Keeping one's balance on a tightrope is difficult under the soberest circumstances; doing so while in a state of delirium is all but impossible. *Completely* impossible, in the long run.

Roland and Susan were delirious, but at least had the thin advantage of knowing it. And the secret would not have to be kept forever, but only until Reaping Day Fair, at the very longest. Things might end even sooner than that, if the Big Coffin Hunters broke cover. The actual first move might be made by one of the other players, Roland thought, but no matter who moved first, Jonas and his men would be there, a part of it. The part apt to be most dangerous to the three boys.

Roland and Susan were careful—as careful as delirious people could be, at any rate. They never met in the same place twice in a row, they never met at the same time twice in a row, they never skulked on their way to their trysts. In Hambry, riders were common but skulkers were noticed. Susan never tried to cover her "riding out" by enlisting the help of a friend (although she had friends who would have done her this service); people who needed alibis were people keeping secrets. She had a sense that Aunt Cord was growing increasingly uneasy about her rides—particularly the ones she took in the early evenings—but so far she accepted Susan's oft-repeated reason for them: she needed time to be solitary, to meditate on her promise and to accept her responsibility. Ironically, these suggestions had originally come from the witch of the Cöos.

They met in the willow grove, in several of the abandoned boathouses which stood crumbling at the northern hook of the bay, in a herder's hut far out in the desolation of the Cöos, in an abandoned squatter's shack hidden in the Bad Grass. The settings were, by and large, as sordid as any of those in which addicts come together to practice their vice, but Susan and Roland didn't see the rotting walls of the shack or the holes in the roof of the hut or smell the mouldering nets in the corners of the old soaked boathouses. They were drugged, stone in love, and to them, every scar on the face of the world was a beauty-mark.

Twice, early on in those delirious weeks, they used the red rock in the wall at the back of the pavillion to arrange meetings, and then some deep voice spoke inside Roland's head, telling him there must be no more of it—the rock might have been just the thing for children playing at secrets, but he and his love were no longer children; if they were discovered, banishment would be the luckiest punishment they could hope for. The red rock was too conspicuous, and writing things down—even messages that were unsigned and deliberately vague—was horribly dangerous.

Using Sheemie felt safer to both of them. Beneath his smiling light-mindedness there was a surprising depth of . . . well, discretion. Roland had thought long and hard before settling on that word, and it was the right word: an ability to keep silent that was more dignified than mere cunning. Cunning was out of Sheemie's reach in any case, and always would be—a man who couldn't tell a lie without shifting his eyes away from yours was a man who would never be considered cunning.

They used Sheemie half a dozen times over the five weeks when their physical love burned at its hottest—three of those times were to make meetings, two were to change meeting-places, and one was to cancel a tryst when Susan spied riders from the Piano Ranch sweeping for strays near the shack in the Bad Grass.

That deep, warning voice never spoke to Roland about Sheemie as it had about the dangers of the red rock . . . but his conscience spoke to him, and when he finally mentioned this to Susan (the two of them wrapped in a saddle-blanket and lying naked in each other's arms), he found that her conscience had been troubling her, as well. It wasn't fair to put the boy in the way of their possible trouble. After coming to that conclusion, Roland and Susan arranged their meetings strictly between the two of them. If she could not meet him, Susan said, she would hang a red shirt over the sill of her window, as if to dry. If he could not meet her, he was to leave a white stone in the northeast corner of the yard, diagonally across the road from Hookey's Livery, where the town pump stood. As a last resort, they would use the red rock in the pavillion, risky or not, rather than bringing Sheemie into their affairs—their *affair*—again.

Cuthbert and Alain watched Roland's descent into addiction first with disbelief, envy, and uneasy amusement, then with a species of silent horror. They had been sent to what was supposed to have been safety and had discovered a place of conspiracy, instead; they had come to take census in a Barony where most of the aristocracy had apparently switched its allegiance to the Affiliation's bitterest enemy; they had made personal enemies of three hard men who had probably killed enough folks to populate a fair-sized graveyard. Yet they had felt equal to the situation, because they had come here under the leadership of their friend, who had attained near-mythic status in their minds by besting Cort—with a hawk as his weapon!—and becoming a gunslinger at the unheard of age of fourteen. That they had been given guns themselves for this mission had meant a great deal to them when they set out from Gilead, and nothing at all by the time they began to realize the scope of what was going on in Hambrytown and the Barony of which it was a part. When that realization came, Roland was the weapon they counted on. And now—

"He's like a revolver cast into water!" Cuthbert exclaimed one evening, not long after Roland had ridden away to meet Susan. Beyond the bunkhouse porch, Huntress rose in her first quarter. "Gods know if it'll ever fire again, even if it's fished out and dried off."

"Hush, wait," Alain said, and looked toward the porch rail. Hoping to jolly Cuthbert out of his bad temper (a task that was quite easy under ordinary circumstances), Alain said: "Where's the lookout? Gone to bed early for once, has he?"

This only irritated Cuthbert more. He hadn't seen the rook's skull in days—he couldn't exactly say how many—and he took its loss as an ill omen. "Gone, but not to bed," he replied, then looked balefully to the west, where Roland had disappeared aboard his big old galoot of a horse. "Lost, I reckon. Like a certain fellow's mind and heart and good sense."

"He'll be all right," Alain said awkwardly. "You know him as well as I do, Bert—known him our whole lives, we have. He'll be all right."

Quietly, without even a trace of his normal good humor, Cuthbert said: "I don't feel I know him now."

They had both tried to talk to Roland in their different ways; both received a similar response, which was no real response at all. The dreamy (and perhaps slightly troubled) look of abstraction in Roland's eyes during these one-sided discussions would have been familiar to anyone who has ever tried to talk sense to a drug addict. It was a look that said Roland's mind was occupied by the shape of Susan's face, the smell of Susan's skin, the feel of Susan's body. And *occupied* was a silly word for it, one that fell short. It wasn't an occupation but an obsession.

"I hate her a little for what she's done," Cuthbert said, and there was a note in his voice Alain had never heard before—a mixture of jealousy, frustration, and fear. "Perhaps more than a little."

"You mustn't!" Alain tried not to sound shocked, but couldn't help it. "She isn't responsible for—"

"Is she not? She went out to Citgo with him. She saw what he saw. God knows how much else he's told her after they've finished making the beast with two backs. And she's all the way around the world from stupid. Just the way she's managed her side of their affair shows that." Bert was thinking, Alain guessed, of her tidy little trick with the *corvette.* "She must know she's become part of the problem herself. She must *know* that!"

Now his bitterness was frighteningly clear. *He's jealous of her for stealing his best friend,* Alain thought, *but it doesn't stop there. He's jealous of his best friend, as well, because his best friend has won the most beautiful girl any of us have ever seen.*

Alain leaned over and grasped Cuthbert's shoulder. When Bert turned away from his morose examination of the dooryard to look at his friend, he was startled by the grimness on Alain's face. "It's *ka,*" Alain said.

Cuthbert almost sneered. "If I had a hot dinner for every time someone blamed theft or lust or some other stupidity on *ka*—"

Alain's grip tightened until it became painful. Cuthbert could have pulled away but didn't. He watched Alain closely. The joker was, temporarily, at least, gone. "Blame is exactly what we two can't afford," Alain said. "Don't you see that? And if it's *ka* that's swept them away, we needn't blame. We *can't* blame. We must rise above it. We need him. And we may need her, too."

Cuthbert looked into Alain's eyes for what seemed to be a very long time. Alain saw Bert's anger at war with his good sense. At last (and perhaps only for the time being), good sense won out.

"All right, fine. It's *ka*, everybody's favorite whipping-boy. That's what the great unseen world's for, after all, isn't it? So we don't have to take the blame for our acts of stupidity? Now let go of me, Al, before you break my shoulder."

Alain let go and sat back in his chair, relieved. "Now if we only knew what to do about the Drop. If we don't start counting there soon—"

"I've had an idea about that, actually," Cuthbert said. "It just needs a little working out. I'm sure Roland could help . . . if either of us can get his attention for a few minutes, that is."

They sat for awhile without speaking, looking out at the dooryard. Inside the bunkhouse, the pigeons—another bone of contention between Roland and Bert these days—cooed. Alain rolled himself a smoke. It was slow work, and the finished product looked rather comical, but it held together when he lit it.

"Your father would stripe you raw if he saw that in your hand," Cuthbert remarked, but he spoke with a certain admiration. By the time the following year's Huntress came around, all three of them would be confirmed smokers, tanned young men with most of the boyhood slapped out of their eyes.

Alain nodded. The strong Outer Crescent tobacco made him swimmy in the head and raw in the throat, but a cigarette had a way of calming his nerves, and right now his nerves could use some calming. He didn't know about Bert, but these days he smelled blood on the wind. Possibly some of it would be their own. He wasn't exactly frightened—not yet, at least—but he was very, very worried.

4

Although they had been honed like hawks toward the guns since early childhood, Cuthbert and Alain still carried an erroneous belief common to many boys their age: that their elders were also their betters, at least in such matters as planning and wit; they actually believed that grownups knew what they were doing. Roland knew better, even in his lovesickness, but his friends had forgotten that in the game of Castles, *both* sides wear the blindfold. They would have been surprised to find that at least two of the Big Coffin Hunters had grown extremely nervous about the three young men from In-World, and extremely tired of the waiting game both sides had been playing.

One early morning, as the Huntress neared the half, Reynolds and Depape came downstairs together from the second floor of the Travellers' Rest. The main public room was silent except for various snores and phlegmy wheezings. In Hambry's busiest bar, the party was over for another night.

Jonas, accompanied by a silent guest, sat playing Chancellors' Patience at Coral's table to the left of the batwing doors. Tonight he was wearing his duster, and his breath smoked faintly as he bent over his cards. It wasn't cold enough to frost—not quite yet—but the frost would come soon. The chill in the air left no doubt of that.

The breath of his guest also smoked. Kimba Rimer's skeletal frame was all but buried in a gray *serape* lit with faint bands of orange. The two of them had been on the edge of getting down to business when Roy and Clay (*Pinch and Jilly,* Rimer thought) showed up, their plowing and planting in the second-floor cribs also apparently over for another night.

"Eldred," Reynolds said, and then: "Sai Rimer."

Rimer nodded back, looking from Reynolds to Depape with thin distaste. "Long days and pleasant nights, gentlemen." Of course the world had moved on, he thought. To find such low culls as these two in positions of importance proved it. Jonas himself was only a little better.

"Might we have a word with you, Eldred?" Clay Reynolds asked. "We've been talking, Roy and I—"

"Unwise," Jonas remarked in his wavery voice. Rimer wouldn't be surprised to find, at the end of his life, that the Death Angel had such a voice. "Talking can lead to thinking, and thinking's dangerous for such as you boys. Like picking your nose with bullet-heads."

Depape donkeyed his damned hee-haw laughter, as if he didn't realize the joke was on him.

"Jonas, listen," Reynolds began, and then looked uncertainly at Rimer.

"You can talk in front of sai Rimer," Jonas said, laying out a fresh line of cards. "He is, after all, our chief employer. I play at Chancellors' Patience in his honor, so I do."

Reynolds looked surprised. "I thought . . . that is to say, I believed that Mayor Thorin was . . ."

"Hart Thorin wants to know none of the details of our arrangement with the Good Man," Rimer said. "A share of the profits is all he requires in that line, Mr. Reynolds. The Mayor's chief concern right now is that the Reaping

Day Fair go smoothly, and that his arrangements with the young lady be . . . smoothly consummated."

"Aye, that's a diplomatic turn o' speech for ye," Jonas said in a broad Mejis accent. "But since Roy looks a little perplexed, I'll translate. Mayor Thorin spends most of his time in the jakes these days, yanking his willy-pink and dreaming his fist is Susan Delgado's box. I'm betting that when the shell's finally opened and her pearl lies before him, he'll never pluck it—his heart'll explode from excitement, and he'll drop dead atop her, so he will. Yar!"

More donkey laughter from Depape. He elbowed Reynolds. "He's got it down, don't he, Clay? Sounds just like em!"

Reynolds grinned, but his eyes were still worried. Rimer managed a smile as thin as a scum of November ice, and pointed at the seven which had just popped out of the pack. "Red on black, my dear Jonas."

"I ain't your dear anything," Jonas said, putting the seven of diamonds on an eight of shadows, "and you'd do well to remember that." Then, to Reynolds and Depape: "Now what do you boys want? Rimer 'n me was just going to have us a little palaver."

"Perhaps we could *all* put our heads together," Reynolds said, putting a hand on the back of a chair. "Kind of see if our thinking matches up."

"I think not," Jonas said, sweeping his cards together. He looked irritated, and Clay Reynolds took his hand off the back of the chair in a hurry. "Say your say and be done with it. It's late."

"We was thinking it's time to go on out there to the Bar K," Depape said. "Have a look around. See if there's anything to back up what the old fella in Ritzy said."

"And see what else they've got out there," Reynolds put in. "It's gettin close now, Eldred, and we can't afford to take chances. They might have—"

"Aye? Guns? Electric lights? Fairy-women in bottles? Who knows? I'll think about it, Clay."

"But—"

"I said I'll think about it. Now go on upstairs, the both of you, back to your own fairy-women."

Reynolds and Depape looked at him, looked at each other, then backed away from the table. Rimer watched them with his thin smile.

At the foot of the stairs, Reynolds turned back. Jonas paused in the act of shuffling his cards and looked at him, tufted eyebrows raised.

"We underestimated em once and they made us look like monkeys. I don't want it to happen again. That's all."

"Your ass is still sore over that, isn't it? Well, so is mine. And I tell you again, they'll pay for what they did. I have the bill ready, and when the time comes, I'll present it to them, with all interest duly noted. In the meantime, they aren't going to spook me into making the first move. Time is on *our* side, not theirs. Do you understand that?"

"Yes."

"Will you try to remember it?"

"Yes," Reynolds repeated. He seemed satisfied.

"Roy? Do you trust me?"

"Aye, Eldred. To the end." Jonas had praised him for the work he had done in Ritzy, and Depape had rolled in it the way a male dog rolls in the scent of a bitch.

"Then go on up, the both of you, and let me palaver with the boss and be done with it. I'm too old for these late nights."

When they were gone, Jonas dealt out a fresh line of cards, then looked around the room. There were perhaps a dozen folks, including Sheb the piano-player and Barkie the bouncer, sleeping it off. No one was close enough to listen to the low-voiced conversation of the two men by the door, even if one of the snoring drunkards was for some reason only shamming sleep. Jonas put a red queen on a black knight, then looked up at Rimer. "Say your say."

"Those two said it for me, actually. Sai Depape will never be embarrassed by a surplus of brains, but Reynolds is fairly smart for a gunny, isn't he?"

"Clay's trig when the moon's right and he's had a shave," Jonas agreed. "Are you saying you came all the way from Seafront to tell me those three babbies need a closer looking at?"

Rimer shrugged.

"Perhaps they do, and I'm the man to do it, if so— right enough. But what's there to find?"

"That's to be seen," Rimer said, and tapped one of Jonas's cards. "There's a Chancellor."

"Aye. Near as ugly as the one I'm sitting with." Jonas put the Chancellor—it was Paul—above his run of cards. The next draw uncovered Luke, whom he put next to Paul. That left Peter and Matthew still lurking in the bush. Jonas looked at Rimer shrewdly. "You hide it better than my pals, but you're as nervous as they are, underneath. You want to know what's out at that bunkhouse? I'll tell you: extra boots, pictures of their mommies, socks that stink to high heaven, stiff sheets from boys who've been taught it's low-class to chase after the sheep . . . and guns hidden somewhere. Under the floorboards, like enough."

"You really think they have guns?"

"Aye, Roy got the straight of that, all right. They're from Gilead, they're likely from the line of Eld or from folk who like to think they're from it, and they're likely 'prentices to the trade who've been sent on with guns they haven't earned yet. I wonder a bit about the tall one with the I-don't-give-a-shit look in his eyes—he *might* already be a gunslinger, I suppose—but is it likely? I don't think so. Even if he is, I could take him in a fair go. I know it, and he does, too."

"Then why have they been sent here?"

"Not because those from the Inner Baronies suspect your treason, sai Rimer—be easy on that score."

Rimer's head poked out of his *serape* as he sat up straight, and his face stiffened. "How dare you call me a traitor? How *dare* you?"

Eldred Jonas favored Hambry's Minister of Inventory with an unpleasant smile. It made the white-haired man look like a wolverine. "I've called things by their right names my whole life, and I won't stop now. All that needs matter to you is that I've never double-crossed an employer."

"If I didn't believe in the cause of—"

"To hell with what you believe! It's late and I want to go to bed. The folk in New Canaan and Gilead haven't the foggiest idea of what does or doesn't go on out here on the Crescent; there aren't many of em who've ever been here, I'd wager. Them are too busy trying to keep everything from falling down around their ears to do much travelling these days. No, what they know is all from the picturebooks they was read out of when they 'us babbies themselves: happy cowboys galloping after stock, happy fishermen pulling whoppers into their boats, folks clogging at barn-raisings and drinking big pots o' *graf* in Green Heart pavillion. For the sake of the Man Jesus, Rimer, don't go dense on me—I deal with that day in and day out."

"They see Mejis as a place of quiet and safety."

"Aye, bucolic splendor, just so, no doubt about it. They know that their whole way o' life—all that nobility and chivalry and ancestor-worship—is on fire. The final battle may take place as much as two hundred wheels northwest of their borders, but when Farson uses his fire-carriages and robots to wipe out their army, trouble will come south fast. There are those from the Inner Baronies who've smelled this coming for twenty years or more. They didn't send these brats here to discover your secrets, Rimer; folks such as these don't send their babbies into danger on purpose. They sent em here to get em out of the way, that's all. That doesn't make em blind or stupid, but for the sake of the gods, let's be sane. They're *kiddies*."

"What else might you find, should you go out there?"

"Some way of sending messages, mayhap. A heliograph's the most likely. And out beyond Eyebolt, a shepherd or maybe a freeholder susceptible to a bribe— someone they've trained to catch the message and either flash it on or carry it afoot. But before long it'll be too late for messages to do any good, won't it?"

"Perhaps, but it's not too late yet. And you're right. Kiddies or not, they worry me."

"You've no cause, I tell you. Soon enough, I'll be wealthy and you'll be downright rich. Mayor yourself, if you want. Who'd stand to stop you? Thorin? He's a joke. Coral? She'd help you string him up, I wot. Or perhaps you'd like to be a Baron, if such offices be revived?" He saw a momentary gleam in Rimer's eyes and laughed. Matthew came out of the deck, and Jonas put him up with the other Chancellors. "Yar, I see that's what you've got your heart set on. Gems is nice, and for gold that goes twice, but there's nothing like having folk bow and scrape before ye, is there?"

Rimer said, "They should have been on the cowboy side by now."

Jonas's hands stopped above the layout of cards. It was a thought that had crossed his own mind more than once, especially over the last two weeks or so.

"How long do you think it takes to count our nets and boats and chart out the fish-hauls?" Rimer asked. "They should be over on the Drop, counting cows and horses, looking through barns, studying the foal-charts. They should have been there two weeks ago, in fact. Unless they already know what they'd find."

Jonas understood what Rimer was implying, but couldn't believe it. *Wouldn't* believe it. Not such a depth of slyness from boys who only had to shave once a week.

"No," he said. "That's your own guilty heart talking to you. They're just so determined to do it right that they're creeping along like old folks with bad eyes. They'll be over on the Drop soon enough, and counting their little hearts out."

"And if they're not?"

A good question. Get rid of them somehow, Jonas supposed. An ambush, perhaps. Three shots from cover, no more babbies. There'd be ill feeling afterward—the boys were well liked in town—but Rimer could handle that until Fair Day, and after the Reap it wouldn't matter. Still—

"I'll have a look around out at the Bar K," Jonas said at last. "By myself—I won't have Clay and Roy tramping along behind me."

"That sounds fine."

"Perhaps you'd like to come and lend a hand."

Kimba Rimer smiled his icy smile. "I think not."

Jonas nodded, and began to deal again. Going out to the Bar K would be a bit risky, but he didn't expect any real problem—especially if he went alone. They were only *boys*, after all, and gone for much of each day.

"When may I expect a report, sai Jonas?"

"When I'm ready to make it. Don't crowd me."

Rimer lifted his thin hands and held them, palms out, to Jonas. "Cry your pardon, sai," he said.

Jonas nodded, slightly mollified. He flipped up another card. It was Peter, Chancellor of Keys. He put the card in the top row and then stared at it, combing his fingers through his long white hair as he did. He looked from the card to Rimer, who looked back, eyebrows raised.

"You smile," Rimer said.

"Yar!" Jonas said, and began to deal again. "I'm happy! All the Chancellors are out. I think I'm going to win this game."

5

For Rhea, the time of the Huntress had been a time of frustration and unsatisfied craving. Her plans had gone awry, and thanks to her cat's hideously mistimed leap, she didn't know how or why. The young cull who'd taken Susan Delgado's cherry had likely stopped her from chopping her scurf . . . but how? And who was he really? She wondered that more and more, but her curiosity was secondary to her fury. Rhea of the Cöos wasn't used to being balked.

She looked across the room to where Musty crouched and watched her carefully. Ordinarily he would have relaxed in the fireplace (he seemed to like the cool drafts that swirled down the chimney), but since she had singed his fur, Musty preferred the woodpile. Given Rhea's mood, that was probably wise. "You're lucky I let ye live, ye warlock," the old woman grumbled.

She turned back to the ball and began to make passes above it, but the glass only continued to swirl with bright pink light—not a single image appeared. Rhea got up at last, went to the door, threw it open, and looked out on the night sky. Now the moon had waxed a little past the half, and the Huntress was coming clear on its bright face. Rhea directed the stream of foul language she didn't quite dare to direct at the glass (who knew what entity might lurk inside it, waiting to take offense at such talk?) up at the woman in the moon. Twice she slammed her bony old fist into the door-lintel as she cursed, dredging up every dirty word she could think of, even the potty-mouth words children throw at each other in the dust of the play yard. Never had she been so angry. She had given the girl a command, and the girl, for whatever reasons, had disobeyed. For standing against Rhea of the Cöos, the bitch deserved to die.

"But not right away," the old woman whispered. "First she should be rolled in the dirt, then pissed on until the dirt's mud and her fine blonde hair's full of it. Humiliated . . . hurt . . . spat on . . ."

She slammed her fist against the door's side again, and this time blood flew from the knuckles. It wasn't just the girl's failure to obey the hypnotic command. There was another matter, related but much more serious: Rhea herself was now too upset to use the glass, except for brief and unpredictable periods of time. The hand-passes she made over it and the incantations she muttered to it were, she knew, useless; the words and gestures were just the way she focused her will. That was what the glass responded to—will and concentrated thought. Now, thanks to the trollop of a girl and her boy lover, Rhea was too angry to summon the smooth concentration needed to part the pink fog which swirled inside the ball. She was, in fact, too angry to see.

"How can I make it like it was?" Rhea asked the half-glimpsed woman in the moon. "Tell me! *Tell me!*" But the Huntress told her nothing, and at last Rhea went back inside, sucking at her bleeding knuckles.

Musty saw her coming and squeezed into the cobwebby space between the woodpile and the chimney.

CHAPTER TWO

The Girl at the Window

I

Now the Huntress "filled her belly," as the old-timers said—even at noon she could be glimpsed in the sky, a pallid vampire woman caught in bright autumn sunlight. In front of businesses such as the Travellers' Rest and on the porches of such large ranch houses as Lengyll's Rocking B and Renfrew's Lazy Susan, stuffy-guys with heads full of straw above their old overalls began to appear. Each wore his *sombrero;* each held a basket of produce cradled in his arms; each looked out at the emptying world with stitched white-cross eyes.

Wagons filled with squashes clogged the roads; bright orange drifts of pumpkins and bright magenta drifts of sharproot lay against the sides of barns. In the fields, the potatocarts rolled and the pickers followed behind. In front of the Hambry Mercantile, reap-charms appeared like magic, hanging from the carved Guardians like wind-chimes.

All over Mejis, girls sewed their Reaping Night costumes (and sometimes wept over them, if the work went badly) as they dreamed of the boys they would dance with in the Green Heart pavillion. Their little brothers began to have trouble sleeping as they thought of the rides and the games and the prizes they might win at the

471

carnival. Even their elders sometimes lay awake in spite of their sore hands and aching backs, thinking about the pleasures of the Reap.

Summer had slipped away with a final flirt of her green-gown; harvest-time had arrived.

2

Rhea cared not a fig for Reaping dances or carnival games, but she could no more sleep than those who did. Most nights she lay on her stinking pallet until dawn, her skull thudding with rage. On a night not long after Jonas's conversation with Chancellor Rimer, she determined to drink herself into oblivion. Her mood was not improved when she found that her *graf* barrel was almost empty; she blistered the air with her curses.

She was drawing in breath for a fresh string of them when an idea struck her. A wonderful idea. A *brilliant* idea. She had wanted Susan Delgado to cut off her hair. That hadn't worked, and she didn't know why . . . but she did know *something* about the girl, didn't she? Something interesting, aye, so it was, wery interesting, indeed.

Rhea had no desire to go to Thorin with what she knew; she had a fond (and foolish, likely) hope that the Mayor had forgotten about his wonderful glass ball. But the girl's aunt, now . . . suppose Cordelia Delgado were to discover that not only was her niece's virginity lost, the girl was well on her way to becoming a practiced trollop? Rhea didn't think Cordelia would go to the Mayor, either—the woman was a prig but not a fool— yet it would set the cat among the pigeons just the same, wouldn't it?

"*Waow!*"

Thinking of cats, there was Musty, standing on the

stoop in the moonlight, looking at her with a mixture of hope and mistrust. Rhea, grinning hideously, opened her arms. "Come to me, my precious! Come, my sweet one!"

Musty, understanding all was forgiven, rushed into his mistress's arms and began to purr loudly as Rhea licked along his sides with her old and yellowing tongue. That night the Cöos slept soundly for the first time in a week, and when she took the glass ball into her arms the following morning, its mists cleared for her at once. She spent the day in thrall to it, spying on people she detested, drinking little and eating nothing. Around sunset, she came out of her trance enough to realize she had as yet done nothing about the saucy little jade. But that was all right; she saw how it *could* be done . . . and she could watch all the results in the glass! All the protests, all the shouting and recriminations! She would see Susan's tears. That would be the best, to see her tears.

"A little harvest of my own," she said to Ermot, who now came slithering up her leg toward the place where she liked him best. There weren't many men who could do you like Ermot could do you, no indeed. Sitting there with a lapful of snake, Rhea began to laugh.

3

"Remember your promise," Alain said nervously as they heard the approaching beat of Rusher's hoofs. "Keep your temper."

"I will," Cuthbert said, but he had his doubts. As Roland rode around the long wing of the bunkhouse and into the yard, his shadow trailing out in the sunset light, Cuthbert clenched his hands nervously. He willed them to open, and they did. Then, as he watched Roland dismount, they rolled themselves closed again, the nails digging into his palms.

Another go-round, Cuthbert thought. *Gods, but I'm sick of them. Sick to death.*

Last night's had been about the pigeons—again. Cuthbert wanted to use one to send a message back west about the oil tankers; Roland still did not. So they had argued. Except (here was another thing which infuriated him, that rubbed against his nerves like the sound of the thinny) Roland did not argue. These days Roland did not *deign* to argue. His eyes always kept that distant look, as if only his body was here. The rest of him—mind, soul, spirit, *ka*—was with Susan Delgado.

"No," he had said simply. "It's too late for such."

"You can't know that," Cuthbert had argued. "And even if it's too late for *help* to come from Gilead, it's not too late for *advice* to come from Gilead. Are you so blind you can't see that?"

"What advice can they send us?" Roland hadn't seemed to hear the rawness in Cuthbert's voice. His own voice was calm. Reasonable. And utterly disconnected, Cuthbert thought, from the urgency of the situation.

"If we knew that," he had replied, "we wouldn't have to ask, Roland, would we?"

"We can only wait and stop them when they make their move. It's comfort you're looking for, Cuthbert, not advice."

You mean wait while you fuck her in as many ways and in as many places as you can imagine, Cuthbert thought. *Inside, outside, rightside up and upside down.*

"You're not thinking clearly about this," Cuthbert had said coldly. He'd heard Alain's gasp. Neither of them had ever said such a thing to Roland in their lives, and once it was out, he'd waited uneasily for whatever explosion might follow.

None did. "Yes," Roland replied, "I am." And he had gone into the bunkhouse without another word.

Now, watching Roland uncinch Rusher's girths and pull the saddle from his back, Cuthbert thought: *You're not, you know. But you better think clearly about this. By all the gods, you'd better.*

"Hile," he said as Roland carried the saddle over to the porch and set it on the step. "Busy afternoon?" He felt Alain kick his ankle and ignored it.

"I've been with Susan," Roland said. No defense, no demur, no excuse. And for a moment Cuthbert had a vision of shocking clarity: he saw the two of them in a hut somewhere, the late afternoon sun shining through holes in the roof and dappling their bodies. She was on top, riding him. Cuthbert saw her knees on the old, spongy boards, and the tension in her long thighs. He saw how tanned her arms were, how white her belly. He saw how Roland's hands cupped the globes of her breasts, squeezing them as she rocked back and forth above him, and he saw how the sun lit her hair, turning it into a fine-spun net.

Why do you always have to be first? he cried at Roland in his mind. *Why does it always have to be you? Gods damn you, Roland! Gods damn you!*

"We were on the docks," Cuthbert said, his tone a thin imitation of his usual brightness. "Counting boots and marine tools and what are called clam-drags. What an amusing time of it we've had, eh, Al?"

"Did you need me to help you do that?" Roland asked. He went back to Rusher, and took off the saddle-blanket. "Is that why you sound angry?"

"If I sound angry, it's because most of the fishermen are laughing at us behind our backs. We keep coming back and coming back. Roland, they think we're fools."

Roland nodded. "All to the good," he said.

"Perhaps," Alain said quietly, "but Rimer doesn't think we're fools—it's in the way he looks at us when we pass. Nor does Jonas. And if they don't think we're fools, Roland, what *do* they think?"

Roland stood on the second step, the saddle-blanket hanging forgotten over his arm. For once they actually seemed to have his attention, Cuthbert thought. Glory be and will wonders never cease.

"They think we're avoiding the Drop because we already know what's there," Roland said. "And if they don't think it, they soon will."

"Cuthbert has a plan."

Roland's gaze—mild, interested, already starting to be not there again—shifted to Cuthbert. Cuthbert the joker. Cuthbert the 'prentice, who had in no way earned the gun he'd carried east to the Outer Crescent. Cuthbert the virgin and eternal second. *Gods, I don't want to hate him. I don't, but now it's so easy.*

"We two should go and see Sheriff Avery tomorrow," Cuthbert said. "We will present it as a courtesy visit. We have already established ourselves as three courteous, if slightly stupid, young fellows, have we not?"

"To a fault," Roland agreed, smiling.

"We'll say that we've finally finished with the seacoast side of Hambry, and we hope to be every bit as meticulous on the farm and cowboy side. But we certainly don't want to cause trouble or be in anyone's way. It is, after all, the busiest time of year—for ranchers as well as farmers—and even citified fools such as ourselves will be aware of that. So we'll give the good Sheriff a list—"

Roland's eyes lit up. He tossed the blanket over the porch rail, grabbed Cuthbert around the shoulders, and gave him a rough hug. Cuthbert could smell a lilac scent around Roland's collar and felt an insane but powerful urge to clamp his hands around Roland's throat and try to strangle him. Instead, he gave him a perfunctory clap on the back in return.

Roland drew away, grinning widely. "A list of the ranches we'll be visiting," he said. "Aye! And with forewarning, they can move any stock they'd like us not to see on to the next ranch, or the last one. The same for tack, feed, equipment . . . it's masterful, Cuthbert! You're a genius!"

"Far from that," Cuthbert said. "I've just spared a little time to think about a problem that concerns us all. That concerns the entire Affiliation, mayhap. We *need* to think. Wouldn't you say?"

Alain winced, but Roland didn't seem to notice. He was still grinning. Even at fourteen, such an expression on his face was troubling. The truth was that when Roland grinned, he looked slightly mad. "Do you know, they may even move in a fair number of muties for us to look at, just so we'll continue to believe the lies they've already told about the impurity of their stocklines." He paused, seeming to think, and then said: "Why don't you and Alain go and see the Sheriff, Bert? That would do very well, I think."

At this point Cuthbert nearly threw himself at Roland, wanting to scream *Yes, why not? Then you could spend tomorrow morning pronging her as well as tomorrow afternoon! You idiot! You thoughtless lovestruck idiot!*

It was Al who saved him—saved them all, perhaps.

"Don't be a fool," he said sharply, and Roland wheeled toward him, looking surprised. He wasn't used to sharpness from that quarter. "You're our leader, Roland—seen that way by Thorin, by Avery, by the townsfolk. Seen that way by us as well."

"No one appointed me—"

"No one needed to!" Cuthbert shouted. "You won your guns! These folk would hardly believe it—I hardly believe it myself just lately—but *you are a gunslinger.* You have to go! Plain as the nose on your face! It doesn't matter which of us accompanies you, but you have to go!" He could say more, much more, but if he did, where would it end? With their fellowship broken beyond repair, likely. So he clamped his mouth shut—no need for Alain to kick him this time—and once again waited for the explosion. Once again, none came.

"All right," Roland said in his new way—that mild it-doesn't-much-matter way that made Cuthbert feel like biting him to wake him up. "Tomorrow morning. You and I, Bert. Will eight suit you?"

"Down to the ground," Cuthbert said. Now that the discussion was over and the decision made, Bert's heart was beating wildly and the muscles in his upper thighs felt like rubber. It was the way he'd felt after their confrontation with the Big Coffin Hunters.

"We'll be at our prettiest," Roland said. "Nice boys from the Inners with good intentions but not many brains. Fine." And he went inside, no longer grinning (which was a relief) but smiling gently.

Cuthbert and Alain looked at each other and let out their breath in a mutual rush. Cuthbert cocked his head toward the yard, and went down the steps. Alain followed, and the two boys stood in the center of the dirt rectangle with the bunkhouse at their backs. To the east, the rising full moon was hidden behind a scrim of clouds.

"She's tranced him," Cuthbert said. "Whether she means to or not, she'll kill us all in the end. Wait and see if she don't."

"You shouldn't say such, even in jest."

"All right, she'll crown us with the jewels of Eld and we'll live forever."

"You have to stop being angry at him, Bert. You *have* to."

Cuthbert looked at him bleakly. "I can't."

4

The great storms of autumn were still a month or more distant, but the following morning dawned drizzly and gray. Roland and Cuthbert wrapped themselves in *serapes* and headed for town, leaving Alain to the few home place chores. Tucked in Roland's belt was the schedule of farms and ranches—beginning with the three small spreads owned by the Barony—the three of them had worked out the previous evening. The pace this schedule suggested was almost ludicrously slow—it would keep them on the Drop and in the orchards almost until Year's End Fair—but it conformed to the pace they had already set on the docks.

Now the two of them rode silently toward town, both lost in their own thoughts. Their way took them past the Delgado house. Roland looked up and saw Susan sitting in her window, a bright vision in the gray light of that fall morning. His heart leaped up and although he didn't know it then, it was how he would remember her most clearly forever after—lovely Susan, the girl at the window. So do we pass the ghosts that haunt us later in our lives; they sit undramatically by the roadside like poor beggars, and we see them only from the corners of our eyes, if we see them at all. The idea that they have been waiting there for us rarely if ever crosses our minds. Yet they do wait, and when we have passed, they gather up their bundles of memory and fall in behind, treading in our footsteps and catching up, little by little.

Roland raised a hand to her. It went toward his mouth at first, wanting to send her a kiss, but that would be madness.

He lifted the hand before it could touch his lips and

ticked a finger off his forehead instead, offering a saucy little salute.

Susan smiled and returned it in kind. None saw Cordelia, who had gone out in the drizzle to check on the last of her squash and sharproot. That lady stood where she was, a *sombrera* yanked down on her head almost to the eyeline, half-hidden by the stuffy-guy guarding the pumpkin patch. She watched Roland and Cuthbert pass (Cuthbert she barely saw; her interest was in the other one). From the boy on horseback she looked up to Susan, sitting there in her window, humming as blithely as a bird in a gilded cage.

A sharp splinter of suspicion whispered its way into Cordelia's heart. Susan's change of temperament—from alternating bouts of sorrow and fearful anger to a kind of dazed but mainly cheerful acceptance—had been so sudden. Mayhap it wasn't acceptance at all.

"Ye're mad," she whispered to herself, but her hand remained tight on the haft of the machete she held. She dropped to her knees in the muddy garden and abruptly began chopping sharproot vines, tossing the roots themselves toward the side of the house with quick, accurate throws. "There's nothing between em. I'd know. Children of such an age have no more discretion than . . . than the drunks in the Rest."

But the way they had smiled. The way they had smiled at *each other.*

"Perfectly normal," she whispered, chopping and throwing. She cut a sharproot nearly in half, ruining it, not noticing. The whispering was a habit she'd picked up only recently, as Reap Day neared and the stresses of coping with her brother's troublesome daughter mounted. "Folks smile at each other, that's all."

The same for the salute and Susan's returning wave. Below, the handsome cavalier, acknowledging the pretty

maid; above, the maid herself, pleased to be acknowledged by such as he. It was youth calling to youth, that
was all. And yet . . .

The look in his eyes . . . and the look in hers.

Nonsense, of course. But—

But you saw something else.

Yes, perhaps. For a moment it had seemed to her that
the young man was going to blow Susan a kiss . . . then
had remembered himself at the last moment and turned
it into a salute, instead.

*Even if ye did see such a thing, it means nothing. Young
cavaliers are saucy, especially when out from beneath the gaze of
their fathers. And these three already have a history, as ye well
know.*

All true enough, but none of it removed that chilly
splinter from her heart.

5

Jonas answered Roland's knock and let the two boys into
the Sheriff's office. He was wearing a Deputy's star on
his shirt, and looked at them with expressionless eyes.
"Boys," he said. "Come in out of the wet."

He stepped back to allow them entrance. His limp was
more pronounced than Roland had ever seen it; the wet
weather was playing it up, he supposed.

Roland and Cuthbert stepped in. There was a gas
heater in the corner—filled from "the candle" at Citgo,
no doubt—and the big room, which had been cool on
the day they had first come here, was stuporously hot. The
three cells held five woeful-looking drunks, two pairs of
men and a woman in the center cell by herself, sitting on
the bunk with her legs spread wide, displaying a broad
expanse of red drawers. Roland feared that if she got her

finger any farther up her nose, she might never retrieve it. Clay Reynolds was leaning against the notice-board, picking his teeth with a broomstraw. Sitting at the rolltop desk was Deputy Dave, stroking his chin and frowning through his monocle at the board which had been set up there. Roland wasn't at all surprised to see that he and Bert had interrupted a game of Castles.

"Well, look here, Eldred!" Reynolds said. "It's two of the In-World boys! Do your mommies know you're out, fellas?"

"They do," Cuthbert said brightly. "And you're looking very well, sai Reynolds. The wet weather's soothed your pox, has it?"

Without looking at Bert or losing his pleasant little smile, Roland shot an elbow into his friend's shoulder. "Pardon my friend, sai. His humor regularly transgresses the bounds of good taste; he doesn't seem able to help it. There's no need for us to scratch at one another— we've agreed to let bygones be bygones, haven't we?"

"Aye, certainly, all a misunderstanding," Jonas said. He limped back across to the desk and the game-board. As he sat down on his side of it, his smile turned to a sour little grimace. "I'm worse than an old dog," he said. "Someone ought to put me down, so they should. Earth's cold but painless, eh, boys?"

He looked back at the board and moved a man around to the side of his Hillock. He had begun to Castle, and was thus vulnerable . . . although not very, in this case, Roland thought; Deputy Dave didn't look like much in the way of competition.

"I see you're working for the Barony salt now," Roland said, nodding at the star on Jonas's shirt.

"Salt's what it amounts to," Jonas said, companionably enough. "A fellow went leg-broke. I'm helping out, that's all."

"And sai Reynolds? Sai Depape? Are they helping out as well?"

"Yar, I reckon," Jonas said. "How goes your work among the fisherfolk? Slow, I hear."

"Done at last. The work wasn't so slow as we were. But coming here in disgrace was enough for us—we have no intention of leaving that way. Slow and steady wins the race, they say."

"So they do," Jonas agreed. "Whoever 'they' are."

From somewhere deeper in the building there came the whoosh of a water-stool flushing. *All the comforts of home in the Hambry Sheriff's,* Roland thought. The flush was soon followed by heavy footsteps descending a staircase, and a few moments later, Herk Avery appeared. With one hand he was buckling his belt; with the other he mopped his broad and sweaty forehead. Roland admired the man's dexterity.

"Whew!" the Sheriff exclaimed. "Them beans I ate last night took the shortcut, I tell ye." He looked from Roland to Cuthbert and then back to Roland. "Why, boys! Too wet for net-counting, is it?"

"Sai Dearborn was just saying that their net-counting days are at an end," Jonas said. He combed back his long hair with the tips of his fingers. Beyond him, Clay Reynolds had resumed his slouch against the notice-board, looking at Roland and Cuthbert with open dislike.

"Aye? Well, that's fine, that's fine. What's next, youngsters? And is there any way we here can help ye? For that's what we like to do best, lend a hand where a hand's needed. So it is."

"Actually, you *could* help us," Roland said. He reached into his belt and pulled out the list. "We have to move on to the Drop, but we don't want to inconvenience anyone."

Grinning hugely, Deputy Dave slid his Squire all the

way around his own Hillock. Jonas Castled at once, ripping open Dave's entire left flank. The grin faded from Dave's face, leaving a puzzled emptiness. "How'd ye manage that?"

"Easy." Jonas smiled, then pushed back from the desk to include the others in his regard. "You want to remember, Dave, that I play to win. I can't help it; it's just my nature." He turned his full attention to Roland. His smile broadened. "Like the scorpion said to the maiden as she lay dying, 'You knowed I was poison when you picked me up.'"

6

When Susan came in from feeding the livestock, she went directly to the cold-pantry for the juice, which was her habit. She didn't see her aunt standing in the chimney corner and watching her, and when Cordelia spoke, Susan was startled badly. It wasn't just the unexpectedness of the voice; it was the coldness of it.

"Do ye know him?"

The juice-jug slipped in her fingers, and Susan put a steadying hand beneath it. Orange juice was too precious to waste, especially this late in the year. She turned and saw her aunt by the woodbox. Cordelia had hung her *sombrera* on a hook in the entryway, but she still wore her *serape* and muddy boots. Her *cuchillo* lay on top of the stacked wood, with green strands of sharproot vine still trailing from its edge. Her tone was cold, but her eyes were hot with suspicion.

A sudden clarity filled Susan's mind and all of her senses. *If you say "No," you're damned,* she thought. *If you even ask who, you may be damned. You must say—*

"I know them both," she replied in offhand fashion.

"I met them at the party. So did you. Ye frightened me, Aunt."

"Why did he salute ye so?"

"How can I know? Perhaps he just felt like it."

Her aunt bolted forward, slipped in her muddy boots, regained her balance, and seized Susan by the arms. Now her eyes were blazing. "Be'n't insolent with me, girl! Be'n't haughty with me, Miss Oh So Young and Pretty, or I'll—"

Susan pulled backward so hard that Cordelia staggered and might have fallen again, if the table had not been handy to grab. Behind her, muddy foot-tracks stood out on the clean kitchen floor like accusations. "Call me that again and I'll . . . I'll slap thee!" Susan cried. "So I will!"

Cordelia's lips drew back from her teeth in a dry, ferocious smile. "Ye'd slap your father's only living blood kin? Would ye be so bad?"

"Why not? Do ye not slap me, Aunt?"

Some of the heat went out of her aunt's eyes, and the smile left her mouth. "Susan! Hardly ever! Not half a dozen times since ye were a toddler who would grab anything her hands could reach, even a pot of boiling water on the—"

"It's with thy mouth thee mostly hits nowadays," Susan said. "I've put up with it—more fool me—but am done with it now. I'll have no more. If I'm old enough to be sent to a man's bed for money, I'm old enough for ye to keep a civil tongue when ye speak to me."

Cordelia opened her mouth to defend herself—the girl's anger had startled her, and so had her accusations—and then she realized how cleverly she was being led away from the subject of the boys. Of the *boy*.

"Ye only know him from the party, Susan? It's Dearborn I mean." *As I think ye well know.*

"I've seen him about town," Susan said. She met her

aunt's eyes steadily, although it cost her an effort; lies would follow half-truths as dark followed dusk. "I've seen all three of them about town. Are ye satisfied?"

No, Susan saw with mounting dismay, she was not.

"Do ye swear to me, Susan—on your father's name— that ye've not been meeting this boy Dearborn?"

All the rides in the late afternoon, Susan thought. *All the excuses. All the care that no one should see us. And it all comes down to a careless wave on a rainy morning. That easily all's put at risk. Did we think it could be otherwise? Were we that foolish?*

Yes . . . and no. The truth was they had been mad. And still were.

Susan kept remembering the look of her father's eyes on the few occasions when he had caught her in a fib. That look of half-curious disappointment. The sense that her fibs, innocuous as they might be, had hurt him like the scratch of a thorn.

"I will swear to nothing," she said. "Ye've no right to ask it of me."

"Swear!" Cordelia cried shrilly. She groped out for the table again and grasped it, as if for balance. "Swear it! Swear it! This is no game of jacks or tag or Johnny-jump-my-pony! Thee's not a child any longer! Swear to me! Swear that thee're still pure!"

"No," Susan said, and turned to leave. Her heart was beating madly, but still that awful clarity informed the world. Roland would have known it for what it was: she was seeing with gunslinger's eyes. There was a glass window in the kitchen, looking out toward the Drop, and in it she saw the ghostly reflection of Aunt Cord coming toward her, one arm raised, the hand at the end of it knotted into a fist. Without turning, Susan put up her own hand in a halting gesture. "Raise that not to me," she said. "Raise it not, ye bitch."

She saw the reflection's ghost-eyes widen in shock and dismay. She saw the ghost-fist relax, become a hand again, fall to the ghost-woman's side.

"Susan," Cordelia said in a small, hurt voice. "How can ye call me so? What's so coarsened your tongue and your regard for me?"

Susan went out without replying. She crossed the yard and entered the barn. Here the smells she had known since childhood—horses, lumber, hay—filled her head and drove the awful clarity away. She was tumbled back into childhood, lost in the shadows of her confusion again. Pylon turned to look at her and whickered. Susan put her head against his neck and cried.

7

"There!" Sheriff Avery said when sais Dearborn and Heath were gone. "It's as ye said—just slow is all they are; just creeping careful." He held the meticulously printed list up, studied it a moment, then cackled happily. "And look at this! What a beauty! Har! We can move anything we don't want em to see days in advance, so we can."

"They're fools," Reynolds said . . . but he pined for another chance at them, just the same. If Dearborn really thought bygones were bygones over that little business in the Travellers' Rest, he was way past foolishness and dwelling in the land of idiocy.

Deputy Dave said nothing. He was looking disconsolately through his monocle at the Castles board, where his white army had been laid waste in six quick moves. Jonas's forces had poured around Red Hillock like water, and Dave's hopes had been swept away in the flood.

"I'm tempted to wrap myself up dry and go over to Seafront with this," Avery said. He was still gloating over

the paper, with its neat list of farms and ranches and pro-
posed dates of inspection. Up to Year's End and beyond
it ran. Gods!

"Why don't ye do that?" Jonas said, and got to his feet.
Pain ran up his leg like bitter lightning.

"Another game, sai Jonas?" Dave asked, beginning to
reset the pieces.

"I'd rather play a weed-eating dog," Jonas said, and
took malicious pleasure at the flush that crept up Dave's
neck and stained his guileless fool's face. He limped
across to the door, opened it, and went out on the porch.
The drizzle had become a soft, steady rain. Hill Street
was deserted, the cobbles gleaming wetly.

Reynolds had followed him out. "Eldred—"

"Get away," Jonas said without turning.

Clay hesitated a moment, then went back inside and
closed the door.

What the hell's wrong with you? Jonas asked himself.

He should have been pleased at the two young pups
and their list—as pleased as Avery was, as pleased as
Rimer would be when he heard about this morning's
visit. After all, hadn't he told Rimer not three days ago
that the boys would soon be over on the Drop, counting their little hearts out? Yes. So why did he feel so
unsettled? So fucking jittery? Because there still hadn't
been any contact from Farson's man, Latigo? Because
Reynolds came back empty from Hanging Rock on one
day and Depape came back empty the next? Surely not.
Latigo would come, along with a goodly troop of men,
but it was still too soon for them, and Jonas knew it.
Reaping was still almost a month away.

*So is it just the bad weather working on your leg, stirring up
that old wound and making you ugly?*

No. The pain was bad, but it had been worse before.
The trouble was his head. Jonas leaned against a post

beneath the overhang, listened to the rain plinking on the tiles, and thought how, sometimes in a game of Castles, a clever player would peek around his Hillock for just a moment, then duck back. That was what this felt like—it was so right it smelled wrong. Crazy idea, but somehow not crazy at all.

"Are you trying to play Castles with me, sprat?" Jonas murmured. "If so, you'll soon wish you'd stayed home with your mommy. So you will."

8

Roland and Cuthbert headed back to the Bar K along the Drop—there would be no counting done today. At first, in spite of the rain and the gray skies, Cuthbert's good humor was almost entirely restored.

"Did you see them?" he asked with a laugh. "Did you see them, Roland . . . Will, I mean? They bought it, didn't they? Swallowed that honey whole, they did!"

"Yes."

"What do we do next? What's our next move?"

Roland looked at him blankly for a moment, as if startled out of a doze. "The next move is theirs. We count. And we wait."

Cuthbert's good cheer collapsed in a puff, and he once more found himself having to restrain a flood of recrimination, all whirling around two basic ideas: that Roland was shirking his duty so he could continue to wallow in the undeniable charms of a certain young lady, and—more important—that Roland had lost his wits when all of Mid-World needed them the most.

Except what duty was Roland shirking? And what made him so sure Roland was wrong? Logic? Intuition? Or just shitty old catbox jealousy? Cuthbert found himself thinking of the effortless way Jonas had ripped up Deputy Dave's army when Deputy Dave had moved too soon. But life was not like Castles . . . was it? He didn't know. But he thought he had at least one valid intuition: Roland was heading for disaster. And so they all were.

Wake up, Cuthbert thought. *Please, Roland, wake up before it's too late.*

CHAPTER THREE

Playing Castles

I

There followed a week of the sort of weather that makes folk apt to crawl back into bed after lunch, take long naps, and wake feeling stupid and disoriented. It was far from flood-weather, but it made the final phase of the apple-picking dangerous (there were several broken legs, and in Seven-Mile Orchard a young woman fell from the top of her ladder, breaking her back), and the potato-fields became difficult to work; almost as much time was spent freeing wagons stuck in the gluey rows as was spent actually picking. In Green Heart, what decorations had been done for the Reaping Fair grew sodden and had to be pulled down. The work volunteers waited with increasing nervousness for the weather to break so they could begin again.

It was bad weather for young men whose job it was to take inventory, although they were at least able to begin visiting barns and counting stock. It was good weather for a young man and young woman who had discovered the joys of physical love, you would have said, but Roland and Susan met only twice during the run of gray weather. The danger of what they were doing was now almost palpable.

The first time was in an abandoned boathouse on the Seacoast Road. The second was in the far end of the crumbling building below and to the east of Citgo—they made love with furious intensity on one of Roland's saddle-blankets, which was spread on the floor of what had once been the oil refinery's cafeteria. As Susan climaxed, she shrieked his name over and over. Startled pigeons filled the old, shadowy rooms and crumbling hallways with their soft thunder.

2

Just as it seemed that the drizzle would never end and the grinding sound of the thinny in the still air would drive everyone in Hambry insane, a strong wind—almost a gale—blew in off the ocean and puffed the clouds away. The town awoke one day to a sky as bright as blue steel and a sun that turned the bay to gold in the morning and white fire in the afternoon. That sense of lethargy was gone. In the potato-fields the carts rolled with new vigor. In Green Heart an army of women began once more to bedeck with flowers the podium where Jamie McCann and Susan Delgado would be acclaimed this year's Reaping Lad and Girl.

Out on the part of the Drop closest to Mayor's House, Roland, Cuthbert, and Alain rode with renewed purpose, counting the horses which ran with the Barony brand on their flanks. The bright skies and brisk winds filled them with energy and good cheer, and for a course of days—three, or perhaps four—they galloped together in a whooping, shouting, laughing line, their old good fellowship restored.

On one of these brisk and sunny days, Eldred Jonas stepped out of the Sheriff's office and walked up Hill

Street toward Green Heart. He was free of both Depape and Reynolds this morning—they had ridden out to Hanging Rock together, looking for Latigo's outriders, who must come soon, now—and Jonas's plan was simple: to have a glass of beer in the pavillion, and watch the preparations that were going on there: the digging of the roasting-pits, the laying of faggots for the bonfire, the arguments over how to set the mortars that would shoot off the fireworks, the ladies flowering the stage where this year's Lad and Girl would be offered for the town's adulation. Perhaps, Jonas thought, he might take a likely-looking flower-girl off for an hour or two of recreation. The maintenance of the saloon whores he left strictly to Roy and Clay, but a fresh young flower-girl of seventeen or so was a different matter.

The pain in his hip had faded with the damp weather; the painful, lurching stride with which he had moved for the last week or so had become a mere limp again. Perhaps just a beer or two in the open air would be enough, but the thought of a girl wouldn't quite leave his head. Young, clear-skinned, high-breasted. Fresh, sweet breath. Fresh, sweet lips—

"Mr. Jonas? Eldred?"

He turned, smiling, to the owner of the voice. No dewy-complexioned flower-girl with wide eyes and moist, parted lips stood there, but a skinny woman edging into late middle age—flat chest, flat bum, tight pale lips, hair scrooped so tight against her skull that it fair screamed. Only the wide eyes corresponded with his daydream. *I believe I've made a conquest,* Jonas thought sardonically.

"Why, Cordelia!" he said, reaching out and taking one of her hands in both of his. "How lovely you look this morning!"

Thin color came up in her cheeks and she laughed a little. For a moment she looked forty-five instead of sixty. *And she's not sixty,* Jonas thought. *The lines around her mouth and the shadows under her eyes . . . those are new.*

"You're very kind," she said, "but I know better. I haven't been sleeping, and when women my age don't sleep, they grow old rapidly."

"I'm sorry to hear you're sleeping badly," he said. "But now that the weather's changed, perhaps—"

"It's not the weather. Might I speak to you, Eldred? I've thought and thought, and you're the only one I dare turn to for advice."

His smile widened. He placed her hand through his arm, then covered it with his own. Now her blush was like fire. With all that blood in her head, she might talk for hours. And Jonas had an idea that every word would be interesting.

3

With women of a certain age and temperament, tea was more effective than wine when it came to loosening the tongue. Jonas gave up his plans for a lager (and, perhaps, a flower-girl) without so much as a second thought. He seated sai Delgado in a sunny corner of the Green Heart pavillion (it was not far from a red rock Roland and Susan knew well), and ordered a large pot of tea; cakes, too. They watched the Reaping Fair preparations go forward as they waited for the food and drink. The sunswept park was full of hammering and sawing and shouts and bursts of laughter.

"All Fair-Days are pleasant, but Reaping turns us all into children again, don't you find?" Cordelia asked.

"Yes, indeed," said Jonas, who hadn't felt like a child even when he had been one.

"What I still like best is the bonfire," she said, looking

toward the great pile of sticks and boards that was being constructed at the far end of the park, cater-corner from the stage. It looked like a large wooden tepee. "I love it when the townsfolk bring their stuffy-guys and throw them on. Barbaric, but it always gives me *such* a pleasant shiver."

"Aye," Jonas said, and wondered if it would give her a pleasant shiver to know that three of the stuffy-guys thrown onto the Reap Night bonfire this year were apt to smell like pork and scream like harpies as they burned. If his luck was in, the one that screamed the longest would be the one with the pale blue eyes.

The tea and cakes came, and Jonas didn't so much as glance at the girl's full bosom when she bent to serve. He had eyes only for the fascinating sai Delgado, with her nervous little shifting movements and odd, desperate look.

When the girl was gone, he poured out, put the teapot back on its trivet, then covered her hand with his. "Now, Cordelia," he said in his warmest tone. "I can see something troubles you. Out with it. Confide in your friend Eldred."

Her lips pressed so tightly together that they almost disappeared, but not even that effort could stop their trembling. Her eyes filled with tears; swam with them; overspilled. He took his napkin and, leaning across the table, wiped the tears away.

"Tell me," he said tenderly.

"I will. I must tell somebody or go mad. But you must make one promise, Eldred."

"Of course, molly." He saw her blush more furiously than ever at this harmless endearment, and squeezed her hand. "Anything."

"You mustn't tell Hart. That disgusting spider of a Chancellor, either, but especially not the Mayor. If I'm right in

what I suspect and he found out, he could send her west!"
She almost moaned this, as if comprehending it as a real
fact for the first time. "He could send us *both* west!"

Maintaining his sympathetic smile, he said: "Not a word
to Mayor Thorin, not a word to Kimba Rimer. Promise."

For a moment he thought that she wouldn't take the
plunge . . . or perhaps couldn't. Then, in a low, gaspy
voice that sounded like ripping cloth, she said a single
word. "Dearborn."

He felt his heart take a bump as the name that had
been so much in his mind now passed her lips, and
although he continued to smile, he could not forbear a
single hard squeeze of her fingers that made her wince.

"I'm sorry," he said. "It's just that you startled me a little. Dearborn . . . a well-spoken enough lad, but I wonder if he's entirely trustworthy."

"I fear he's been with my Susan." Now it was her turn
to squeeze, but Jonas didn't mind. He hardly felt it, in
fact. He continued to smile, hoping he did not look as
flabbergasted as he felt. "I fear he's been with her . . . as
a man is with a woman. Oh, how horrible this is!"

She wept with a silent bitterness, taking little pecking peeks around as she did to make sure they were not
being observed. Jonas had seen coyotes and wild dogs
look around from their stinking dinners in just that fashion. He let her get as much of it out of her system as
he could—he wanted her calm; incoherencies wouldn't
help him—and when he saw her tears slackening, he
held out a cup of tea. "Drink this."

"Yes. Thank you." The tea was still hot enough to
steam, but she drank it down greedily. *Her old throat must
be lined with slate,* Jonas thought. She set the cup down,
and while he poured out fresh, she used her frilly *pañuelo*
to scrub the tears almost viciously from her face.

"I don't like him," she said. "Don't like him, don't

trust him, none of those three with their fancy In-World bows and insolent eyes and strange ways of talking, but him in particular. Yet if anything's gone on betwixt the two of em (and I'm so afraid it has), it comes back to her, doesn't it? It's the woman, after all, who must refuse the bestial impulses."

He leaned over the table, looking at her with warm sympathy. "Tell me everything, Cordelia."

She did.

4

Rhea loved everything about the glass ball, but what she especially loved was the way it unfailingly showed her people at their vilest. Never in its pink reaches did she see one child comforting another after a fall at play, or a tired husband with his head in his wife's lap, or old people supping peacefully together at the end of the day; these things held no more interest for the glass, it seemed, than they did for her.

Instead she had seen acts of incest, mothers beating children, husbands beating wives. She had seen a gang of boys out west'rds of town (it would have amused Rhea to know these swaggering eight-year-olds called themselves the Big Coffin Hunters) go about enticing stray dogs with a bone and then cutting off their tails for a lark. She had seen robberies, and at least one murder: a wandering man who had stabbed his companion with a pitchfork after some sort of trivial argument. That had been on the first drizzly night. The body still lay mouldering in a ditch beside the Great Road West, covered with a layer of straw and weeds. It might be discovered before the autumn storms came to drown another year; it might not.

She also glimpsed Cordelia Delgado and that hard gun, Jonas, sitting in Green Heart at one of the outside tables and talking about . . . well, of course she didn't know, did she? But she could see the look in the spinster bitch's eyes. Infatuated with him, she was, all pink in the face. Gone all hot and sweet over a backshooter and failed gunslinger. It was comical, aye, and Rhea thought she would keep an eye on them, from time to time. Wery entertaining, it would likely be.

After showing her Cordelia and Jonas, the glass veiled itself once more. Rhea put it back in the box with the eye on the lock. Seeing Cordelia in the glass had reminded the old woman that she had unfinished business regarding Cordelia's sluttish niece. That Rhea still hadn't done that business was ironic but understandable—as soon as she had seen how to fix the young sai's wagon, Rhea's mind and emotions had settled again, the images in the ball had reappeared, and in her fascination with them Rhea had temporarily forgotten that Susan Delgado was alive. Now, however, she remembered her plan. Set the cat among the pigeons. And speaking of cats—

"Musty! Yoo-hoo, Musty, where are ye?"

The cat came oiling out of the woodpile, eyes glowing in the dirty dimness of the hut (when the weather turned fine again, Rhea had pulled her shutters to), forked tail waving. He jumped into her lap.

"I've an errand for ye," she said, bending over to lick the cat. The entrancing taste of Musty's fur filled her mouth and throat.

Musty purred and arched his back against her lips. For a six-legged mutie cat, life was good.

5

Jonas got rid of Cordelia as soon as he could—although not as soon as he would have liked, because he had to keep the scrawny bint sweetened up. She might come in handy another time. In the end he had kissed her on the corner of her mouth (which caused her to turn so violently red he feared she might have a brain-storm) and told her that he would check into the matter which so concerned her.

"But discreetly!" she said, alarmed.

Yes, he said, walking her home, he would be discreet; discretion was his middle name. He knew Cordelia wouldn't—*couldn't*—be eased until she knew for sure, but he guessed it would turn out to be nothing but vapor. Teenagers loved to dramatize, didn't they? And if the young lass saw that her aunt was afraid of something, she might well feed auntie's fears instead of allaying them.

Cordelia had stopped by the white picket fence that divided her garden-plot from the road, an expression of sublime relief coming over her face. Jonas thought she looked like a mule having its back scratched with a stiff brush.

"Why, I never thought of that . . . yet it's likely, isn't it?"

"Likely enough," Jonas had said, "but I'll still check into it most carefully. Better safe than sorry." He kissed the corner of her mouth again. "And not a word to the fellows at Seafront. Not a hint."

"Thank'ee, Eldred! Oh, thank'ee!" And she had hugged him before hurrying in, her tiny breasts pressing like stones against the front of his shirt. "Mayhap I'll sleep tonight, after all!"

She might, but Jonas wondered if he would.

He walked toward Hookey's stable, where he kept his horse, with his head down and his hands locked behind his back. A gaggle of boys came racing up the other side of the street; two of them were waving severed dog's tails with blood clotted at the ends.

"Coffin Hunters! We're Big Coffin Hunters just like you!" one called impudently across to him.

Jonas drew his gun and pointed it at them—it was done in a flash, and for a moment the terrified boys saw him as he really was: with his eyes blazing and his lips peeled back from his teeth, Jonas looked like a white-haired wolf in man's clothes.

"Get on, you little bastards!" he snarled. "Get on before I blow you loose of your shoes and give your fathers cause to celebrate!"

For a moment they were frozen, and then they fled in a howling pack. One had left his trophy behind; the dog's tail lay on the board sidewalk like a grisly fan. Jonas grimaced at the sight of it, holstered his gun, locked his hands behind him again, and walked on, looking like a parson meditating on the nature of the gods. And what in gods' name was he doing, pulling iron on a bunch of young hellions like that?

Being upset, he thought. *Being worried.*

He was worried, all right. The titless old biddy's suspicions had upset him greatly. Not on Thorin's account— as far as Jonas was concerned, Dearborn could fuck the girl in the town square at high noon of Reaping Fair Day—but because it suggested that Dearborn might have fooled him about other things.

Crept up behind you once, he did, and you swore it'd never happen again. But if he's been diddling that girl, it has *happened again. Hasn't it?*

Aye, as they said in these parts. If the boy had had the impertinence to begin an affair with the Mayor's gilly-

in-waiting, and the incredible slyness to get away with
it, what did that do to Jonas's picture of three In-World
brats who could barely find their own behinds with both
hands and a candle?

*We underestimated em once and they made us look like mon-
keys,* Clay had said. *I don't want it to happen again.*

Had it happened again? How much, really, did Dearborn and his friends know? How much had they found
out? And who had they told? If Dearborn had been able
to get away with pronging the Mayor's chosen . . . to
put something *that* large over on Eldred Jonas . . . on
everyone . . .

"Good day, sai Jonas," Brian Hookey said. He was
grinning widely, all but kowtowing before Jonas with his
sombrero crushed against his broad blacksmith's chest.
"Would ye care for fresh *graf,* sai? I've just gotten the
new pressing, and—"

"All I want is my horse," Jonas said curtly. "Bring it
quick and stop your quacking."

"Aye, so I will, happy to oblige, thankee-sai." He hurried off on the errand, taking one nervous, grinning look
back over his shoulder to make sure he wasn't going to
be shot out of hand.

Ten minutes later Jonas was headed west on the Great
Road. He felt a ridiculous but nevertheless strong desire
to simply kick his horse into a gallop and leave all this
foolishness behind him: Thorin the graying goat-boy,
Roland and Susan with their no-doubt mawkish teen-
age love, Roy and Clay with their fast hands and slow
wits, Rimer with his ambitions, Cordelia Delgado with
her ghastly visions of the two of them in some bosky dell,
him likely reciting poetry while she wove a garland of
flowers for his brow.

He had ridden away from things before, when intuition whispered; plenty of things. But there would be

no riding away this time. He had vowed vengeance on the brats, and while he had broken a bushel of promises made to others, he'd never broken one made to himself.

And there was John Farson to consider. Jonas had never spoken to the Good Man himself (and never wanted to; Farson was reputed to be whimsically, dangerously insane), but he had had dealings with George Latigo, who would probably be leading the troop of Farson's men that would arrive any day now. It was Latigo who had hired the Big Coffin Hunters in the first place, paying a huge cash advance (which Jonas hadn't yet shared with Reynolds and Depape) and promising an even larger piece of war-spoil if the Affiliation's major forces were wiped out in or around the Shavéd Mountains.

Latigo was a good-sized bug, all right, but nothing to the size of the bug trundling along behind him. And besides, no large reward was ever achieved without risk. If they delivered the horses, oxen, wagons of fresh vege-tables, the tack, the oil, the glass—most of all the wizard's glass—all would be well. If they failed, it was very likely that their heads would end up being whacked about by Farson and his aides in their nightly polo games. It could happen, and Jonas knew it. No doubt someday it *would* happen. But when his head finally parted company from his shoulders, the divorce wouldn't be caused by any such smarms as Dearborn and his friends, no matter *whose* bloodline they had descended from.

But if he's been having an affair with Thorin's autumn treat . . . if he's been able to keep such a secret as that, what others has he been keeping? Perhaps he is *playing Castles with you.*

If so, he wouldn't play for long. The first time young Mr. Dearborn poked his nose around his Hillock, Jonas would be there to shoot it off for him.

The question for the present was where to go first. Out to the Bar K, to take a long overdue look at the boys' living quarters? He could; they would be counting Bar-ony horses on the Drop, all three of them. But it wasn't over horses that he might lose his head, was it? No, the horses were just a small added attraction, as far as the Good Man was concerned.

Jonas rode for Citgo instead.

6

First he checked the tankers. They were just as had been and should be—lined up in a neat row with their new wheels ready to roll when the time came, and hid-den behind their new camouflage. Some of the screen-ing pine branches were turning yellow at the tips, but the recent spell of rain had kept most admirably fresh. There had been no tampering that Jonas could see.

Next he climbed the hill, walking beside the pipe-line and pausing more and more frequently to rest; by the time he reached the rotting gate between the slope and the oilpatch, his bad leg was paining him severely. He studied the gate, frowning over the smudges he saw on the top rung. They might mean nothing, but Jonas thought someone might have climbed over the gate rather than risk opening it and having it fall off its hinges.

He spent the next hour strolling around the der-ricks, paying especially close attention to those that still worked, looking for sign. He found plenty of tracks, but it was impossible (especially after a week of wet weather) to read them with any degree of accuracy. The In-World boys might have been out here; that ugly little band of brats from town might have been out here; Arthur Eld and the whole company of his knights might have been out here. The ambiguity put Jonas in a foul temper, as ambiguity (other than on a Castles board) always did.

He started back the way he'd come, meaning to descend the slope to his horse and ride back to town. His leg was aching like fury, and he wanted a stiff drink to quiet it down. The bunkhouse at the Bar K could wait another day.

He got halfway to the gate, saw the weedy spur track tying Citgo to the Great Road, and sighed. There would be nothing on that little strip of road to see, but now that he'd come all the way out here, he supposed he should finish the job.

Bugger finishing the job, I want a damned drink.

But Roland wasn't the only one who sometimes found his wishes overruled by training. Jonas sighed, rubbed at his leg, then walked back to the weedy twin ruts. Where, it seemed, there was something to find after all.

It lay in the grassy ditch less than a dozen paces from the place where the old road joined the Great Road. At first he saw only a smooth white shape in the weeds and thought it was a stone. Then he saw a black roundness that could only be an eyehole. Not a stone, then; a skull.

Grunting, Jonas knelt and fished it out while the few living derricks continued to squeal and thump behind him. A rook's skull. He had seen it before. Hell, he suspected most of the town had. It belonged to the showoff, Arthur Heath . . . who, like all showoffs, needed his little props.

"He called it the lookout," Jonas murmured. "Put it on the horn of his saddle sometimes, didn't he? And sometimes wore it around his neck like a pendant." Yes. The youngster had been wearing it so that night in the Travellers' Rest, when—

Jonas turned the bird's skull. Something rattled inside like a last lonely thought. Jonas tilted it, shook it over his open palm, and a fragment of gold chain dropped out. That was how the boy had been wearing it. At some point the chain had broken, the skull had fallen in the ditch, and sai Heath had never troubled to go looking for it. The thought that someone might find it had probably never crossed his mind. Boys were careless. It was a wonder any ever grew up to be men.

Jonas's face remained calm as he knelt there examining the bird's skull, but behind the unlined brow he was as furious as he had ever been in his life. They had been out here, all right—it was another thing he would have scoffed at just yesterday. He had to assume they had seen the tankers, camouflage or no camouflage, and if not for the chance of finding this skull, he never would have known for sure, one way or the other.

"When I finish with em, their eyesockets'll be as empty as yours, Sir Rook. I'll gouge em clean myself."

He started to throw the skull away, then changed his mind. It might come in handy. Carrying it in one hand, he started back to where he'd left his horse.

7

Coral Thorin walked down High Street toward the Travellers' Rest, her head thumping rustily and her heart sour in her breast. She had been up only an hour, but her hangover was so miserable it felt like a day already. She was drinking too much of late and she knew it—almost every night now—but she was very careful not to take more than one or two (and always light ones) where folks could see. So far, she thought no one suspected. And as long as no one suspected, she supposed she would keep on. How else to bear her idiotic brother? This idiotic town? And, of course, the knowledge that all of the ranchers in the Horsemen's Association and at least half of the large landowners were traitors? "Fuck the Affiliation," she whispered. "Better a bird in the hand."

But did she really have a bird in the hand? Did any of them? Would Farson keep his promises—promises made by a man named Latigo and passed on by their own inimitable Kimba Rimer? Coral had her doubts; despots had such a convenient way of forgetting their promises, and birds in the hand such an irritating way of pecking your fingers, shitting in your palm, and then flying away. Not that it mattered now; she had made her bed. Besides, folks would always want to drink and gamble and rut, regardless of who they bowed their knees to or in whose name their taxes were collected.

Still, when the voice of old demon conscience whispered, a few drinks helped to still its lips.

She paused outside Craven's Undertaking Parlor, looking upstreet at the laughing boys on their ladders, hanging paper lanterns from high poles and building eaves. These gay lamps would be lit on the night of the Reap Fair, filling Hambry's main street with a hundred shades of soft, conflicting light.

For a moment Coral remembered the child she had been, looking at the colored paper lanterns with wonder, listening to the shouts and the rattle of fireworks, listening to the dance-music coming from Green Heart as her father held her hand . . . and, on his other side, her big brother Hart's hand. In this memory, Hart was proudly wearing his first pair of long trousers.

Nostalgia swept her, sweet at first, then bitter. The child had grown into a sallow woman who owned a saloon and whorehouse (not to mention a great deal of land along the Drop), a woman whose only sexual partner of late was her brother's Chancellor, a woman whose chief goal upon arising these days was getting to the hair of the dog that bit her as soon as possible. How, exactly, had things turned out so? This woman whose eyes she used was the last woman the child she had been would have expected to become.

"Where did I go wrong?" she asked herself, and laughed. "Oh dear Man Jesus, where did this straying sinner-child go wrong? Can you say hallelujah." She sounded so much like the wandering preacher-woman that had come through town the year before—Pittston, her name had been, Sylvia Pittston—that she laughed again, this time almost naturally. She walked on toward the Rest with a better will.

Sheemie was outside, tending to the remains of his silk-flowers. He waved to her and called a greeting. She waved back and called something in return. A good enough lad, Sheemie, and although she could have found another easily enough, she supposed she was glad Depape hadn't killed him.

The bar was almost empty but brilliantly lit, all the gas-jets flaring. It was clean, as well. Sheemie would have emptied the spittoons, but Coral guessed it was the plump woman behind the bar who had done all the rest. The makeup couldn't hide the sallowness of that woman's cheeks, the hollowness of her eyes, or the way her neck had started to go all crepey (seeing that sort of liz-ardy skin on a woman's neck always made Coral shiver inside).

It was Pettie the Trotter tending bar beneath The Romp's stern glass gaze, and if allowed to do so, she would continue until Stanley appeared and banished her. Pettie had said nothing out loud to Coral—she knew better—but had made her wants clear enough just the same. Her whoring days were almost at an end. She desperately desired to go to work tending bar. There was precedent for it, Coral knew—a female bartender at Forest Trees in Pass o' the River, and there had been another at Glencove, up the coast in Tavares, until she had died of the pox. What Pettie refused to see was that Stanley Ruiz was younger by fifteen years and in far better health. He would be pouring drinks under The Romp long after Pettie was rotting (instead of Trotting) in a pauper's grave.

"Good even, sai Thorin," Pettie said. And before Coral could so much as open her mouth, the whore had put a shot glass on the bar and filled it full of whiskey. Coral looked at it with dismay. Did they all know, then?

"I don't want that," she snapped. "Why in Eld's name would I? Sun isn't even down! Pour it back into the bottle, for yer father's sake, and then get the hell out of here. Who d'ye think yer serving at five o' the clock, anyway? Ghosts?"

Pettie's face fell a foot; the heavy coat of her makeup actually seemed to crack apart. She took the funnel from under the bar, stuck it in the neck of the bottle, and poured the shot of whiskey back in. Some went onto the bar in spite of the funnel; her plump hands (now ringless; her rings had been traded for food at the mercantile across the street long since) were shaking. "I'm sorry, sai. So I am. I was only—"

"I don't care what ye was only," Coral said, then turned a bloodshot eye on Sheb, who had been sitting on his piano-bench and leafing through old sheet-music. Now he was staring toward the bar with his mouth hung open. "And what are *you* looking at, ye frog?"

"Nothing, sai Thorin. I—"

"Then go look at it somewhere else. Take this pig with'ee. Give her a bounce, why don't ye? It'll be good for her skin. It might even be good for yer own."

"I—"

"Get out! Are ye deaf? Both of ye!"

Pettie and Sheb went away toward the kitchen instead

of the cribs upstairs, but it was all the same to Coral. They could go to hell as far as she was concerned. Anywhere, as long as they were out of her aching face.

She went behind the bar and looked around. Two men playing cards over in the far corner. That hardcase Reynolds was watching them and sipping a beer. There was another man at the far end of the bar, but he was staring off into space, lost in his own world. No one was paying any especial attention to sai Coral Thorin, and what did it matter if they were? If Pettie knew, they all knew.

She ran her finger through the puddle of whiskey on the bar, sucked it, ran it through again, sucked it again. She grasped the bottle, but before she could pour, a spidery monstrosity with gray-green eyes leaped, hissing, onto the bar. Coral shrieked and stepped back, dropping the whiskey bottle between her feet . . . where, for a wonder, it didn't break. For a moment she thought her head would break, instead—that her swelling, throbbing brain would simply split her skull like a rotten eggshell. There was a crash as the card-players overturned their table getting up. Reynolds had drawn his gun.

"Nay," she said in a quavering voice she could hardly recognize. Her eyeballs were pulsing and her heart was racing. People *could* die of fright, she realized that now. "Nay, gentlemen, all's well."

The six-legged freak standing on the bar opened its mouth, bared its needle fangs, and hissed again.

Coral bent down (and as her head passed below the level of her waist, she was once more sure it was going to explode), picked up the bottle, saw that it was still a quarter full, and drank directly from the neck, no longer caring who saw her do it or what they thought.

As if hearing her thought, Musty hissed again. He was wearing a red collar this afternoon—on him it looked baleful rather than jaunty. Beneath it was tucked a white scrap of paper.

"Want me to shoot it?" a voice drawled. "I will if you like. One slug and won't be nothing left but claws." It was Jonas, standing just inside the batwings, and although he looked not a whole lot better than she felt, Coral had no doubt he could do it.

"Nay. The old bitch'll turn us all into locusts, or something like, if ye kill her familiar."

"What bitch?" Jonas asked, crossing the room.

"Rhea Dubativo. Rhea of the Cöos, she's called."

"Ah! Not the bitch but the witch."

"She's both."

Jonas stroked the cat's back. It allowed itself to be petted, even arching against his hand, but he only gave it the single caress. Its fur had an unpleasant damp feel.

"Would you consider sharing that?" he asked, nodding toward the bottle. "It's early, but my leg hurts like a devil sick of sin."

"Your leg, my head, early or late. On the house."

Jonas raised his white eyebrows.

"Count yer blessings and have at it, cully."

She reached toward Musty. He hissed again, but allowed her to draw the note out from under his collar. She opened it and read the five words that were printed there:

$$\text{I'm dry, send the boy}$$

"Might I see?" Jonas asked. With the first drink down and warming his belly, the world looked better.

"Why not?" She handed him the note. Jonas looked, then handed it back. He had almost forgotten Rhea, and that wouldn't have done at all. Ah, but it was hard to remember everything, wasn't it? Just lately Jonas felt less like a hired gun than a cook trying to make all nine courses of a state dinner come out at the same time. Luckily, the old hag had reminded him of her presence herself. Gods bless her thirst. And his own, since it had landed him here at the right time.

"Sheemie!" Coral bawled. She could also feel the whiskey working; she felt almost human again. She even wondered if Eldred Jonas might be interested in a dirty evening with the Mayor's sister . . . who knew what might speed the hours?

Sheemie came in through the batwings, hands grimy, pink *sombrera* bouncing on his back at the end of its *cuerda*. "Aye, Coral Thorin! Here I be!"

She looked past him, calculating the sky. Not tonight, not even for Rhea; she wouldn't send Sheemie up there after dark, and that was the end of it.

"Nothing," she said in a voice that was gentler than usual. "Go back to yer flowers, and see that ye cover them well. It bids frosty."

She turned over Rhea's note and scrawled a single word on it:

tomorrow

This she folded and handed to Jonas. "Stick it under that stink's collar for me, will ye? I don't want to touch him."

Jonas did as he was asked. The cat favored them with a final wild green look, then leaped from the bar and vanished beneath the batwings.

"Time is short," Coral said. She hadn't the slightest idea what she meant, but Jonas nodded in what appeared to be perfect understanding. "Would you care to go upstairs with a closet drunk? I'm not much in the looks department, but I can still spread em all the way to the edge of the bed, and I don't just lie there."

He considered, then nodded. His eyes were gleaming. This one was as thin as Cordelia Delgado . . . but what a difference, eh? What a difference! "All right."

"I've been known to say some nasty things—fair warning."

"Dear lady, I shall be all ears."

She smiled. Her headache was gone. "Aye. I'll just bet ye will."

"Give me a minute. Don't move a step." He walked across to where Reynolds sat.

"Drag up a chair, Eldred."

"I think not. There's a lady waiting."

Reynolds's gaze flicked briefly toward the bar. "You're joking."

"I never joke about women, Clay. Now mark me."

Reynolds sat forward, eyes intent. Jonas was grateful this wasn't Depape. Roy would do what you asked, and usually well enough, but only after you'd explained it to him half a dozen times.

"Go to Lengyll," he said. "Tell him we want to put about a dozen men—no less than ten—out at yon oilpatch. Good men who can get their heads down and keep them down and not snap the trap too soon on an ambush, if ambushing's required. Tell him Brian Hookey's to be in charge. He's got a level head, which is more than can be said for most of these poor things."

Reynolds's eyes were hot and happy. "You expect the brats?"

"They've been out there once, mayhap they'll be out again. If so, they're to be crossfired and knocked down dead. At once and with no warning. You understand?"

"Yar! And the tale after?"

"Why, that the oil and the tankers must have been

their business," Jonas said with a crooked smile. "To be taken to Farson, at their command and by confederates unknown. We'll be carried through the streets on the town's shoulders, come Reap. Hailed as the men who rooted out the traitors. Where's Roy?"

"Gone back to Hanging Rock. I saw him at noon. He says they're coming, Eldred; says when the wind swings into the east, he can hear approaching horse."

"Maybe he only hears what he wants to hear." But he suspected Depape was right. Jonas's mood, at rock bottom when he stepped into the Travellers' Rest, was now very much on the rebound.

"We'll start moving the tankers soon, whether the brats come or not. At night, and two by two, like the animals going on board Old Pa's Ark." He laughed at this. "But we'll leave some, eh? Like cheese in a trap."

"Suppose the mice don't come?"

Jonas shrugged. "If not one way, another. I intend to press them a little more tomorrow. I want them angry, and I want them confused. Now go on about your business. I have yon lady waiting."

"Better you than me, Eldred."

Jonas nodded. He guessed that half an hour from now, he would have forgotten all about his aching leg. "That's right," he said. "You she'd eat like fudge."

He walked back to the bar, where Coral stood with her arms folded. Now she unfolded them and took his hands. The right she put on her left breast. The nipple was hard and erect under his fingers. The forefinger of his left hand she put in her mouth, and bit down lightly.

"Shall we bring the bottle?" Jonas asked.

"Why not?" said Coral Thorin.

8

If she'd gone to sleep as drunk as had been her habit over the last few months, the creak of the bedsprings wouldn't have awakened her—a bomb-blast wouldn't have awakened her. But although they'd brought the bottle, it still stood on the night-table of the bedroom she maintained at the Rest (it was as big as any three of the whores' cribs put together), the level of the whiskey unchanged. She felt sore all over her body, but her head was clear; sex was good for that much, anyway.

Jonas was at the window, looking out at the first gray traces of daylight and pulling his pants up. His bare back was covered with crisscrossed scars. She thought to ask him who had administered such a savage flogging and how he'd survived it, then decided she'd do better to keep quiet.

"Where are ye off to?" she asked.

"I believe I'm going to start by finding some paint—any shade will do—and a street-mutt still in possession of its tail. After that, sai, I don't think you want to know."

"Very well." She lay down and pulled the covers up to her chin. She felt she could sleep for a week.

Jonas yanked on his boots and went to the door, buckling his gunbelt. He paused with his hand on the knob. She looked at him, grayish eyes already half-filled with sleep again.

"I've never had better," Jonas said.

Coral smiled. "No, cully," she said. "Nor I."

CHAPTER FOUR

Roland and Cuthbert

I

Roland, Cuthbert, and Alain came out onto the porch of the Bar K bunkhouse almost two hours after Jonas had left Coral's room at the Travellers' Rest. By then the sun was well up over the horizon. They weren't late risers by nature, but as Cuthbert put it, "We have a certain In-World image to maintain. Not laziness but *longiness.*"

Roland stretched, arms spread toward the sky in a wide Y, then bent and grasped the toes of his boots. This caused his back to crackle.

"I hate that noise," Alain said. He sounded morose and sleepy. In fact, he had been troubled by odd dreams and premonitions all night—things which, of the three of them, only he was prey to. Because of the touch, perhaps—with him it had always been strong.

"That's why he does it," Cuthbert said, then clapped Alain on the shoulder. "Cheer up, old boy. You're too handsome to be downhearted."

Roland straightened, and they walked across the dusty yard toward the stables. Halfway there, he came to a stop so sudden that Alain almost ran into his back. Roland was looking east. "Oh," he said in a funny, bemused voice. He even smiled a little.

"Oh?" Cuthbert echoed. "Oh what, great leader? Oh

515

joy, I shall see the perfumed lady anon, or oh rats, I must work with my smelly male companions all the livelong day?"

Alain looked down at his boots, new and uncomfortable when they had left Gilead, now sprung, trailworn, a little down at the heels, and as comfortable as workboots ever got. Looking at them was better than looking at his friends, for the time being. There was always an edge to Cuthbert's teasing these days; the old sense of fun had been replaced by something that was mean and unpleasant. Alain kept expecting Roland to flash up at one of Cuthbert's jibes, like steel that has been struck by sharp flint, and knock Bert sprawling. In a way, Alain almost wished for it. It might clear the air.

But not the air of this morning.

"Just oh," Roland said mildly, and walked on.

"Cry your pardon, for I know you'll not want to hear it, but I'd speak a further word about the pigeons," Cuthbert said as they saddled their mounts. "I still believe that a message—"

"I'll make you a promise," Roland said, smiling.

Cuthbert looked at him with some mistrust. "Aye?"

"If you still want to send by flight tomorrow morning, we'll do so. The one you choose shall be sent west to Gilead with a message of your devising banded to its leg. What do you say, Arthur Heath? Is it fair?"

Cuthbert looked at him for a moment with a suspicion that hurt Alain's heart. Then he also smiled. "Fair," he said. "Thank you."

And then Roland said something which struck Alain as odd and made that prescient part of him quiver with disquiet. "Don't thank me yet."

2

"I don't want to go up there, sai Thorin," Sheemie said. An unusual expression had creased his normally smooth face—a troubled and fearful frown. "She's a scary lady. Scary as a beary, she is. Got a wart on her nose, right here." He thumbed the tip of his own nose, which was small and smooth and well molded.

Coral, who might have bitten his head off for such hesitation only yesterday, was unusually patient today. "So true," she said. "But Sheemie, she asked for ye special, and she tips. Ye know she does, and well."

"Won't help if she turns me into a beetle," Sheemie said morosely. "Beetles can't spend coppers."

Nevertheless, he let himself be led to where Caprichoso, the inn's pack-mule, was tied. Barkie had loaded two small tuns over the mule's back. One, filled with sand, was just there for balance. The other held a fresh pressing of the *graf* Rhea had a taste for.

"Fair-Day's coming," Coral said brightly. "Why, it's not three weeks now."

"Aye." Sheemie looked happier at this. He loved Fair-Days passionately—the lights, the firecrackers, the dancing, the games, the laughter. When Fair-Day came, everyone was happy and no one spoke mean.

"A young man with coppers in his pocket is sure to have a good time at the Fair," Coral said.

"That's true, sai Thorin." Sheemie looked like someone who has just discovered one of life's great principles. "Aye, truey-true, so it is."

Coral put Caprichoso's rope halter into Sheemie's palm and closed the fingers over it. "Have a nice trip, lad. Be polite to the old crow, bow yer best bow . . . and make sure ye're back down the hill before dark."

"Long before, aye," Sheemie said, shivering at the very thought of still being up in the Cöos after nightfall. "Long before, sure as loaves 'n fishes."

"Good lad." Coral watched him off, his pink *sombrera* now clapped on his head, leading the grumpy old pack-mule by its rope. And, as he disappeared over the brow of the first mild hill, she said it again: "Good lad."

3

Jonas waited on the flank of a ridge, belly-down in the tall grass, until the brats were an hour gone from the Bar K. He then rode to the ridgetop and picked them out, three dots four miles away on the brown slope. Off to do their daily duty. No sign they suspected anything. They were smarter than he had at first given them credit for . . . but nowhere near as smart as they thought they were.

He rode to within a quarter mile of the Bar K—except for the bunkhouse and stable, a burned-out hulk in the bright sunlight of this early autumn day—and tethered his horse in a copse of cottonwoods that grew around the ranch house spring. Here the boys had left some washing to dry. Jonas stripped the pants and shirts off the low branches upon which they had been hung, made a pile of them, pissed on them, and then went back to his horse.

The animal stamped the ground emphatically when Jonas pulled the dog's tail from one of his saddlebags, as if saying he was glad to be rid of it. Jonas would be glad to be rid of it, too. It had begun giving off an unmistakable aroma. From the other saddlebag he took a small glass jar of red paint, and a brush. These he had obtained from Brian Hookey's eldest son, who was minding the livery stable today. Sai Hookey himself would be out to Citgo by now, no doubt.

Jonas walked to the bunkhouse with no effort at concealment . . . not that there was much in the way of concealment to be had out here. And no one to hide from, anyway, now that the boys were gone.

One of them had left an actual book—Mercer's *Homilies and Meditations*—on the seat of a rocking chair on the porch. Books were things of exquisite rarity in Mid-World, especially as one travelled out from the center. This was the first one, except for the few kept in Seafront, that Jonas had seen since coming to Mejis. He opened it. In a firm woman's hand he read: *To my dearest son, from his loving MOTHER.* Jonas tore this page out, opened his jar of paint, and dipped the tips of his last two fingers inside. He blotted out the word MOTHER with the pad of his third finger, then, using the nail of his pinky as a makeshift pen, printed CUNT above MOTHER. He poked this sheet on a rusty nailhead where it was sure to be seen, then tore the book up and stamped on the pieces. Which boy had it belonged to? He hoped it was Dearborn's, but it didn't really matter.

The first thing Jonas noticed when he went inside was the pigeons, cooing in their cages. He had thought they might be using a helio to send their messages, but pigeons! My! That was ever so much more trig!

"I'll get to you in a few minutes," he said. "Be patient, darlings; peck and shit while you still can."

He looked around with some curiosity, the soft coo of the pigeons soothing in his ears. Lads or lords? Roy had asked the old man in Ritzy. The old man had said maybe both. Neat lads, at the very least, from the way they kept their quarters, Jonas thought. Well trained. Three bunks, all made. Three piles of goods at the foot of each, stacked up just as neat. In each pile he found a picture of a mother—oh, such good fellows they were—and in one he found a picture of both parents.

He had hoped for names, possibly documents of some kind (even love letters from the girl, mayhap), but there was nothing like that. Lads or lords, they were careful enough. Jonas removed the pictures from their frames and shredded them. The goods he scattered to all points of the compass, destroying as much as he could in the limited time he had. When he found a linen handker-chief in the pocket of a pair of dress pants, he blew his nose on it and then spread it carefully on the toes of the boy's dress boots, so that the green splat would show to good advantage. What could be more aggravating—more *unsettling*—than to come home after a hard day spent tallying stock and find some stranger's snot on one of your personals?

The pigeons were upset now; they were incapable of scolding like jays or rooks, but they tried to flutter away from him when he opened their cages. It did no good, of course. He caught them one by one and twisted their heads off. That much accomplished, Jonas popped one bird beneath the strawtick pillow of each boy.

Beneath one of these pillows he found a small bonus: paper strips and a storage-pen, undoubtedly kept for the composition of messages. He broke the pen and flung it across the room. The strips he put in his own pocket. Paper always came in handy.

With the pigeons seen to, he could hear better. He began walking slowly back and forth on the board floor, head cocked, listening.

4

When Alain came riding up to him at a gallop, Roland ignored the boy's strained white face and burning, frightened eyes. "I make it thirty-one on my side," he said, "all with the Barony brand, crown and shield. You?"

"We have to go back," Alain said. "Something's wrong. It's the touch. I've never felt it so clear."

"Your count?" Roland asked again. There were times, such as now, when he found Alain's ability to use the touch more annoying than helpful.

"Forty. Or forty-one, I forget. And what does it matter? They've moved what they don't want us to count. Roland, didn't you hear me? We have to go back! Something's wrong! *Something's wrong at our place!*"

Roland glanced toward Bert, riding peaceably some five hundred yards away. Then he looked back at Alain, his eyebrows raised in a silent question.

"Bert? He's numb to the touch and always has been—you know it. I'm not. You know I'm not! Roland, please! Whoever it is will see the pigeons! Maybe find our *guns!*" The normally phlegmatic Alain was nearly crying in his excitement and dismay. "If you won't go back with me, give me leave to go back by myself! Give me leave, Roland, for your father's sake!"

"For *your* father's sake, I give you none," Roland said. "My count is thirty-one. Yours is forty. Yes, we'll say forty. Forty's a good number—good as any, I wot. Now we'll change sides and count again."

"What's wrong with you?" Alain almost whispered. He was looking at Roland as if Roland had gone mad.

"Nothing."

"You *knew!* You knew when we left this morning!"

"Oh, I might have seen something," Roland said. "A reflection, perhaps, but . . . do you trust me, Al? That's what matters, I think. Do you trust me, or do you think I lost my wits when I lost my heart? As he does?" He jerked his head in Cuthbert's direction. Roland was looking at

Alain with a faint smile on his lips, but his eyes were ruthless and distant—it was Roland's over-the-horizon look. Alain wondered if Susan Delgado had seen that expression yet, and if she had, what she made of it.

"I trust you." By now Alain was so confused that he didn't know for sure if that was a lie or the truth.

"Good. Then switch sides with me. My count is thirty-one, mind."

"Thirty-one," Alain agreed. He raised his hands, then dropped them back to his thighs with a slap so sharp his normally stolid mount laid his ears back and jigged a bit under him. "Thirty-one."

"I think we may go back early today, if that's any satisfaction to you," Roland said, and rode away. Alain watched him. He'd always wondered what went on in Roland's head, but never more than now.

5

Creak. Creak-creak.

Here was what he'd been listening for, and just as Jonas was about to give up the hunt. He had expected to find their hideyhole a little closer to their beds, but they were trig, all right.

He went to one knee and used the blade of his knife to pry up the board which had creaked. Under it were three bundles, each swaddled in dark strips of cotton cloth. These strips were damp to the touch and smelled fragrantly of gun-oil. Jonas took the bundles out and unwrapped each, curious to see what sort of calibers the youngsters had brought. The answer turned out to be serviceable but undistinguished. Two of the bundles contained single five-shot revolvers of a type then called (for no reason I know) "carvers." The third contained two guns, sixshooters of higher quality than the carvers. In fact, for one heart-stopping moment, Jonas thought he had found the big revolvers of a gunslinger—true-blue steel barrels, sandalwood grips, bores like mineshafts. Such guns he could not have left, no matter what the cost to his plans. Seeing the plain grips was thus something of a relief. Disappointment was never a thing you looked for, but it had a wonderful way of clearing the mind.

He rewrapped the guns and put them back, put the board back as well. A gang of ne'er-do-well clots from town might possibly come out here, and might possibly vandalize the unguarded bunkhouse, scattering what they didn't tear up, but find a hiding place such as this? No, my son. Not likely.

Do you really think they'll believe it was hooligans from town that did this?

They might; just because he had underestimated them to start with didn't mean he should turn about-face and begin overestimating them now. And he had the luxury of not needing to care. Either way, it would make them angry. Angry enough to rush full-tilt around their Hillock, perhaps. To throw caution to the wind . . . and reap the whirlwind.

Jonas poked the end of the severed dog's tail into one of the pigeon-cages, so it stuck up like a huge, mocking feather. He used the paint to write such charmingly boyish slogans as

SUCK my prick!

and

co home you ritch fuckers

on the walls. Then he left, standing on the porch for a moment to verify he still had the Bar K to himself. Of course he did. Yet for a blink or two, there at the end, he'd felt uneasy— almost as though he'd been scented. By some sort of In-World telepathy, mayhap.

There is such; you know it. The touch, it's called.

Aye, but that was the tool of gunslingers, artists, and lunatics. Not of boys, be they lords or just lads.

Jonas went back to his horse at a near-trot nevertheless, mounted, and rode toward town. Things were reaching the boil, and there would be a lot to do before Demon Moon rose full in the sky.

6

Rhea's hut, its stone walls and the cracked *guijarros* of its roof slimed with moss, huddled on the last hill of the Cöos. Beyond it was a magnificent view northwest—the Bad Grass, the desert, Hanging Rock, Eyebolt Canyon— but scenic vistas were the last thing on Sheemie's mind as he led Caprichoso cautiously into Rhea's yard not long after noon. He'd been hungry for the last hour or so, but now the pangs were gone. He hated this place worse than any other in Barony, even more than Citgo with its big towers always going creakedy-creak and clangety-clang.

"Sai?" he called, leading the mule into the yard. Capi balked as they neared the hut, planting his feet and lowering his neck, but when Sheemie tugged the halter, he came on again. Sheemie was almost sorry.

"Ma'am? Nice old lady that wouldn't hurt a fly? You therey-air? It's good old Sheemie with your *graf.*" He smiled and held out his free hand, palm up, to demonstrate his exquisite harmlessness, but from the hut there was still no response. Sheemie felt his guts first coil, then

cramp. For a moment he thought he was going to shit in
his pants just like a babby; then he passed wind and felt
a little better. In his bowels, at least.

He walked on, liking this less at every step. The yard
was rocky and the straggling weeds yellowish, as if the
hut's resident had blighted the very earth with her touch.
There was a garden, and Sheemie saw that the vegetables still in it—pumpkins and sharproot, mostly—were
muties. Then he noticed the garden's stuffy-guy. It was
also a mutie, a nasty thing with two straw heads instead
of one and what appeared to be a stuffed hand in a woman's satin glove poking out of the chest area.

Sai Thorin'll never talk me up here again, he thought. *Not
for all the pennies in the world.*

The hut's door stood open. To Sheemie it looked like
a gaping mouth. A sickish dank smell drifted out.

Sheemie stopped about fifteen paces from the house,
and when Capi nuzzled his bottom (as if to ask what was
keeping them), the boy uttered a brief screech. The
sound of it almost set him running, and it was only by
exercising all his willpower that he was able to stand his
ground. The day was bright, but up here on this hill,
the sun seemed meaningless. This wasn't his first trip up
here, and Rhea's hill had never been pleasant, but it was
somehow worse now. It made him feel the way the sound
of the thinny made him feel when he woke and heard
it in the middle of the night. As if something awful was
sliding toward him—something that was all insane eyes
and red, reaching claws.

"S-S-Sai? Is anyone here? Is—"

"Come closer." The voice drifted out of the open door.
"Come to where I can see you, idiot boy."

Trying not to moan or cry, Sheemie did as the voice
said. He had an idea that he was never going back down
the hill again. Caprichoso, perhaps, but not him. Poor

old Sheemie was going to end up in the cookpot—hot dinner tonight, soup tomorrow, cold snacks until Year's End. That's what he would be.

He made his reluctant way to Rhea's stoop on rubbery legs—if his knees had been closer together, they would have knocked like castanets. She didn't even *sound* the same.

"S-Sai? I'm afraid. So I a-a-am."

"So ye should be," the voice said. It drifted and drifted, slipping out into the sunlight like a sick puff of smoke. "Never mind, though—just do as I say. Come closer, Sheemie, son of Stanley."

Sheemie did so, although terror dragged at every step he took. The mule followed, head down. Capi had honked like a goose all the way up here—honked ceaselessly—but now he had fallen silent.

"So here ye be," the voice buried in those shadows whispered. "Here ye be, indeed."

She stepped into the sunlight falling through the open door, wincing for a moment as it dazzled her eyes. Clasped in her arms was the empty *graf* barrel. Coiled around her throat like a necklace was Ermot.

Sheemie had seen the snake before, and on previous occasions had never failed to wonder what sort of agonies he might suffer before he died if he happened to be bitten by such. Today he had no such thoughts. Compared to Rhea, Ermot looked normal. The old woman's face had sunken at the cheeks, giving the rest of her head the look of a skull. Brown spots swarmed out of her thin hair and over her bulging brow like an army of invading insects. Below her left eye was an open sore, and her grin showed only a few remaining teeth.

"Don't like the way I look, do'ee?" she asked. "Makes yer heart cold, don't it?"

"N-No," Sheemie said, and then, because that didn't

sound right: "I mean yes!" But gods, that sounded even worse. "You're beautiful, sai!" he blurted.

She chuffed nearly soundless laughter and thrust the empty tun into his arms almost hard enough to knock him on his ass. The touch of her fingers was brief, but long enough to make his flesh crawl.

"Well-a-day. They say handsome is as handsome does, don't they? And that suits me. Aye, right down to the ground. Bring me my *graf,* idiot child."

"Y-yes, sai! Right away, sai!" He took the empty tun back to the mule, set it down, then fumbled loose the cordage holding the little barrel of *graf.* He was very aware of her watching him, and it made him clumsy, but finally he got the barrel loose. It almost slid through his grasp, and there was a nightmarish moment when he thought it would fall to the stony ground and smash, but he caught his grip again at the last second. He took it to her, had just a second to realize she was no longer wearing the snake, then felt it crawling on his boots. Ermot looked up at him, hissing and baring a double set of fangs in an eerie grin.

"Don't move too fast, my boy. 'Twouldn't be wise— Ermot's grumpy today. Set the barrel just inside the door, here. It's too heavy for me. Missed a few meals of late, I have."

Sheemie bent from the waist *(bow yer best bow,* Sai Thorin had said, and here he was, doing just that), grimacing, not daring to ease the pressure on his back by moving his feet because the snake was still on them. When he straightened, Rhea was holding out an old and stained envelope. The flap had been sealed with a blob of red wax. Sheemie dreaded to think what might have been rendered down to make wax such as that.

"Take this and give it to Cordelia Delgado. Do ye know her?"

"A-Aye," Sheemie managed. "Susan-sai's auntie."

"That's right." Sheemie reached tentatively for the envelope, but she held it back a moment. "Can't read, can ye, idiot boy?"

"Nay. Words 'n letters go right out of my head."

"Good. Mind ye show this to no one who can, or some night ye'll find Ermot waiting under yer pillow. I see far, Sheemie, d'ye mark me? *I see far.*"

It was just an envelope, but it felt heavy and somehow dreadful in Sheemie's fingers, as if it were made out of human skin instead of paper. And what sort of letter could Rhea be sending Cordelia Delgado, anyway? Sheemie thought back to the day he'd seen sai Delgado's face all covered with cobwebbies, and shivered. The horrid creature lurking before him in the doorway of her hut could have been the very creature who'd spun those webs.

"Lose it and I'll know," Rhea whispered. "Show my business to another, and I'll know. Remember, son of Stanley, I see far."

"I'll be careful, sai." It might be better if he *did* lose the envelope, but he wouldn't. Sheemie was dim in the head, everyone said so, but not so dim that he didn't understand why he had been called up here: not to deliver a barrel of *graf,* but to receive this letter and pass it on.

"Would ye care to come in for a bit?" she whispered, and then pointed a finger at his crotch. "If I give ye a little bit of mushroom to eat—special to me, it is—I can look like anyone ye fancy."

"Oh, I can't," he said, clutching his trousers and smiling a huge broad smile that felt like a scream trying to get out of his skin. "That pesky thing fell off last week, that did."

For a moment Rhea only gawped at him, genuinely

surprised for one of the few times in her life, and then she once more broke out in chuffing bursts of laughter. She held her stomach in her waxy hands and rocked back and forth with glee. Ermot, startled, streaked into the house on his lengthy green belly. From somewhere in its depths, her cat hissed at it.

"Go on," Rhea said, still laughing. She leaned forward and dropped three or four pennies into his shirt pocket. "Get out of here, ye great galoophus! Don't ye linger, either, looking at flowers!"

"No, sai—"

Before he could say more, the door clapped to so hard that dust puffed out of the cracks between the boards.

7

Roland surprised Cuthbert by suggesting at two o' the clock that they go back to the Bar K. When Bert asked why, Roland only shrugged and would say nothing more. Bert looked at Alain and saw a queer, musing expression on the boy's face.

As they drew closer to the bunkhouse, a sense of foreboding filled Cuthbert. They topped a rise, and looked down at the Bar K. The bunkhouse door stood open.

"Roland!" Alain cried. He was pointing to the cottonwood grove where the ranch's spring was. Their clothes, neatly hung to dry when they left, were now scattered hell-to-breakfast.

Cuthbert dismounted and ran to them. Picked up a shirt, sniffed it, flung it away. "Pissed on!" he cried indignantly.

"Come on," Roland said. "Let's look at the damage."

8

There was a lot of damage to look at. *As you expected,* Cuthbert thought, gazing at Roland. Then he turned to Alain, who appeared gloomy but not really surprised. *As you* both *expected.*

Roland bent toward one of the dead pigeons, and plucked at something so fine Cuthbert at first couldn't see what it was.

Then he straightened up and held it out to his friends. A single hair. Very long, very white. He opened the pinch of his thumb and forefinger and let it waft to the floor. There it lay amid the shredded remains of Cuthbert Allgood's mother and father.

"If you knew that old corbie was here, why didn't we come back and end his breath?" Cuthbert heard himself ask.

"Because the time was wrong," Roland said mildly.

"*He* would have done it, had it been one of us in his place, destroying his things."

"We're not like him," Roland said mildly.

"I'm going to find him and blow his teeth out the back of his head."

"Not at all," Roland said mildly.

If Bert had to listen to one more mild word from Roland's mouth, he would run mad. All thoughts of fellowship and *ka-tet* left his mind, which sank back into his body and was at once obliterated by simple red fury. Jonas had been here. Jonas had pissed on their clothes, called Alain's mother a cunt, torn up their most treasured pictures, painted childish obscenities on their walls, killed their pigeons. Roland had known . . . done nothing . . . intended to *continue* doing nothing. Except fuck his gilly-girl. He would do plenty of that, aye, because now that was all he cared about.

But she won't like the look of your face the next time you climb into the saddle, Cuthbert thought. *I'll see to that.*

He drew back his fist. Alain caught his wrist. Roland turned away and began picking up scattered blankets, as if Cuthbert's furious face and cocked fist were simply of no account to him.

Cuthbert balled up his other fist, meaning to make Alain let go of him, one way or the other, but the sight of his friend's round and honest face, so guileless and dismayed, quieted his rage a little. His argument wasn't with Alain. Cuthbert was sure the other boy had known something bad was happening here, but he was also sure that Roland had insisted Alain do nothing until Jonas was gone.

"Come with me," Alain muttered, slinging an arm around Bert's shoulders. "Outside. For your father's sake, come. You have to cool off. This is no time to be fighting among ourselves."

"It's no time for our leader's brains to drain down into his prick, either," Cuthbert said, making no effort to lower his voice. But the second time Alain tugged him, Bert allowed himself to be led toward the door.

I'll stay my rage at him this one last time, he thought, *but I think—I* know—*that is all I can manage. I'll have Alain tell him so.*

The idea of using Alain as a go-between to his best friend—of knowing that things had come to such a pass—filled Cuthbert with an angry, despairing rage, and at the door to the porch he turned back to Roland. *"She has made you a coward,"* he said in the High Speech. Beside him, Alain drew in his breath sharply.

Roland stopped as if suddenly turned to stone, his back to them, his arms full of blankets. In that moment

Cuthbert was sure Roland would turn and rush toward him. They would fight, likely until one of them was dead or blind or unconscious. Likely that one would be him, but he no longer cared.

But Roland never turned. Instead, in the same speech, he said: *"He came to steal our guile and our caution. With you, he has succeeded."*

"No," Cuthbert said, lapsing back into the low speech. "I know that part of you really believes that, but it's not so. The truth is, you've lost your compass. You've called your carelessness love and made a virtue of irresponsibility. I—"

"For gods' sake, *come!*" Alain nearly snarled, and yanked him out the door.

9

With Roland out of sight, Cuthbert felt his rage veering toward Alain in spite of himself; it turned like a weathervane when the wind shifts. The two of them stood facing each other in the sunshiny dooryard, Alain looking unhappy and distracted, Cuthbert with his hands knotted into fists so tight they trembled at his sides.

"Why do you always excuse him? Why?"

"Out on the Drop, he asked if I trusted him. I said I did. And I do."

"Then you're a fool."

"And he's a gunslinger. If he says we must wait longer, we must."

"He's a gunslinger by accident! A freak! A mutie!"

Alain stared at him in silent shock.

"Come with me, Alain. It's time to end this mad game. We'll find Jonas and kill him. Our *ka-tet* is broken. We'll make a new one, you and I."

"It's not broken. If it does break, it'll be you responsible. And for that I'll never forgive you."

Now it was Cuthbert's turn to be silent.

"Go for a ride, why don't you? A long one. Give yourself time to cool off. So much depends on our fellowship—"

"Tell *him* that!"

"No, I'm telling *you*. Jonas wrote a foul word about my mother. Don't you think I'd go with you just to avenge that, if I didn't think that Roland was right? That it's what Jonas wants? For us to lose our wits and come charging blindly around our Hillock?"

"That's right, but it's wrong, too," Cuthbert said. Yet his hands were slowly unrolling, fists becoming fingers again. "You don't see and I don't have the words to explain. If I say that Susan has poisoned the well of our *ka-tet*, you would call me jealous. Yet I think she has, all unknowing and unmeaning. She's poisoned his mind, and the door to hell has opened. Roland feels the heat from that open door and thinks it's only his feeling for her . . . but we must do better, Al. We must *think* better. For him as well as for ourselves and our fathers."

"Are you calling her our enemy?"

"No! It would be easier if she was." He took a deep breath, let it out, took another, let it out, took a third and let it out. With each one he felt a little saner, a little more himself. "Never mind. There's no more to say on't for now. Your advice is good—I think I will take a ride. A long one."

Bert started toward his horse, then turned back.

"Tell him he's wrong. Tell him that even if he's right about waiting, he's right for the wrong reasons, and that makes him all the way wrong." He hesitated. "Tell him what I said about the door to hell. Say that's *my* piece of the touch. Will you tell him?"

"Yes. Stay away from Jonas, Bert."

Cuthbert mounted up. "I promise nothing."

"You're not a man." Alain sounded sorrowful; on the point of tears, in fact. "None of us are men."

"You better be wrong about that," Cuthbert said, "because men's work is coming."

He turned his mount and rode away at a gallop.

10

He went far up the Seacoast Road, to begin with trying not to think at all. He'd found that sometimes unexpected things wandered into your head if you left the door open for them. Useful things, often.

This afternoon that didn't happen. Confused, miserable, and without a fresh idea in his head (or even the hope of one), Bert at last turned back to Hambry. He rode the High Street from end to end, waving or speaking to people who hiled him. The three of them had met a lot of good people here. Some he counted as friends, and he rather felt the common folk of Hambrytown had adopted them—young fellows who were far from their own homes and families. And the more Bert knew and saw of these common folk, the less he suspected that they were a part of Rimer's and Jonas's nasty little game. Why else had the Good Man chosen Hambry in the first place, if not because it provided such excellent cover?

There were plenty of folk out today. The farmers' market was booming, the street-stalls were crowded, children were laughing at a Pinch and Jilly show (Jilly was currently chasing Pinch back and forth and bashing the poor old longsuffering fellow with her broom), and the Reaping Fair decorations were going forward at speed. Yet Cuthbert felt only a little joy and anticipation at the thought of the Fair. Because it wasn't his own, wasn't Gilead Reaping? Perhaps . . . but mostly just because his mind and heart were so heavy. If this was what growing up was like, he thought he could have skipped the experience.

   He rode on out of town, the ocean now at his back, the sun full in his face, his shadow growing ever longer behind him. He thought he'd soon veer off the Great Road and ride across the Drop to the Bar K. But before he could, here came his old friend, Sheemie, leading a mule. Sheemie's head was down, his shoulders slumped, his pink 'brera askew, his boots dusty. To Cuthbert he looked as though he had walked all the way from the tip of the earth.

   "Sheemie!" Cuthbert cried, already anticipating the boy's cheery grin and loony patter. "Long days and pleasant nights! How are y—"

   Sheemie lifted his head, and as the brim of his *sombrera* came up, Cuthbert fell silent. He saw the dreadful fear on the boy's face—the pale cheeks, the haunted eyes, the trembling mouth.

II

Sheemie could have been at the Delgado place two hours ago, if he'd wanted, but he had trudged along at a turtle's pace, the letter inside his shirt seeming to drag at his every step. It was awful, so awful. He couldn't even think about it, because his thinker was mostly broken, so it was.

   Cuthbert was off his horse in a flash, and hurrying to Sheemie. He put his hands on the boy's shoulders. "What's wrong? Tell your old pal. He won't laugh, not a bit."

   At the sound of "Arthur Heath's" kind voice and the sight of his concerned face, Sheemie began to weep. Rhea's strict command that he should tell no one flew out of his head. Still sobbing, he recounted everything that had happened since that morning. Twice Cuthbert had to ask him to slow down, and when Bert led the boy to a tree in whose shade the two of them sat together, Sheemie was finally able to do so. Cuthbert listened with growing unease. At the end of his tale, Sheemie produced an envelope from inside his shirt.

Cuthbert broke the seal and read what was inside, his eyes growing large.

12

Roy Depape was waiting for him at the Travellers' Rest when Jonas returned in good spirits from his trip to the Bar K. An outrider had finally shown up, Depape announced, and Jonas's spirits rose another notch. Only Roy didn't look as happy about it as Jonas would have expected. Not happy at all.

"Fellow's gone on to Seafront, where I guess he's expected," Depape said. "He wants you right away. I wouldn't linger here to eat, not even a popkin, if I were you. I wouldn't take a drink, either. You'll want a clear head to deal with this one."

"Free with your advice today, ain't you, Roy?" Jonas said. He spoke in a heavily sarcastic tone, but when Pettie brought him a tot of whiskey, he sent it back and asked for water instead. Roy had a bit of a look to him, Jonas decided. Too pale by half, was good old Roy. And when Sheb sat down at his piano-bench and struck a chord, Depape jerked in that direction, one hand dropping to the butt of his gun. Interesting. And a little disquieting.

"Spill it, son—what's got your back hair up?"

Roy shook his head sullenly. "Don't rightly know."

"What's this fellow's name?"

"I didn't ask, he didn't say. He showed me Farson's *sigul,* though. You know." Depape lowered his voice a little. "The eye."

Jonas knew, all right. He hated that wide-open staring eye, couldn't imagine what had possessed Farson to pick it in the first place. Why not a mailed fist? Crossed swords? Or a bird? A falcon, for instance—a falcon would have made a fine *sigul.* But that *eye*—

"All right," he said, finishing the glass of water. It went down better than whiskey would have done, anyway—dry as a bone, he'd been. "I'll find out the rest for myself, shall I?"

As he reached the batwing doors and pushed them open, Depape called his name. Jonas turned back.

"He looks like other people," Depape said.

"What do you mean?"

"I don't hardly know." Depape looked embarrassed and bewildered . . . but dogged, too. Sticking to his guns. "We only talked five minutes in all, but once I looked at him and thought it was the old bastard from Ritzy—the one I shot. Little bit later I th'ow him a glance and think, 'Hellfire, it's my old pa standin there.' Then that went by, too, and he looked like himself again."

"And how's that?"

"You'll see for yourself, I reckon. I don't know if you'll like it much, though."

Jonas stood with one batwing pushed open, thinking. "Roy, 'twasn't Farson himself, was it? The Good Man in some sort of disguise?"

Depape hesitated, frowning, and then shook his head. "No."

"Are you sure? We only saw him the once, remember, and not close-to." Latigo had pointed him out. Sixteen months ago that had been, give or take.

"I'm sure. You remember how big he was?"

Jonas nodded. Farson was no Lord Perth, but he was six feet or more, and broad across at both brace and basket.

"This man's Clay's height, or less. And he stays the same height no matter who he looks like." Depape hesitated a moment and said: "He laughs like a dead person. I could barely stand to hear him do it."

"What do you mean, like a dead person?"

Roy Depape shook his head. "Can't rightly say."

13

Twenty minutes later, Eldred Jonas was riding beneath COME IN PEACE and into the courtyard of Seafront, uneasy because he had expected Latigo . . . and unless Roy was very much mistaken, it wasn't Latigo he was getting.

Miguel shuffled forward, grinning his gummy old grin, and took the reins of Jonas's horse.

"Reconocimiento."

"Por nada, jefe."

Jonas went in, saw Olive Thorin sitting in the front parlor like a forlorn ghost, and nodded to her. She nodded back, and managed a wan smile.

"Sai Jonas, how well you look. If you see Hart—"

"Cry your pardon, lady, but it's the Chancellor I've come to see," Jonas said. He went on quickly upstairs toward the Chancellor's suite of rooms, then down a narrow stone hall lit (and not too well) with gas-jets.

When he reached the end of the corridor, he rapped on the door waiting there—a massive thing of oak and brass set in its own arch. Rimer didn't care for such as Susan Delgado, but he loved the trappings of power; that was what took the curve out of his noodle and made it straight. Jonas rapped.

"Come in, my friend," a voice—not Rimer's—called.

It was followed by a tittery laugh that made Jonas's flesh creep. *He laughs like a dead person,* Roy had said.

Jonas pushed open the door and stepped in. Rimer cared for incense no more than he cared for the hips and lips of women, but there was incense burning in here now—a woody smell that made Jonas think of court at Gilead, and functions of state in the Great Hall. The gas-jets were turned high. The draperies—purple velvet, the color of royalty, Rimer's absolute favorite—trembled minutely in the breath of sea breeze coming in through the open windows. Of Rimer there was no sign. Or of anyone else, come to that. There was a little balcony, but the doors giving on it were open, and no one was out there.

Jonas stepped a little farther into the room, glancing into a gilt-framed mirror on the far side to check behind him without turning his head. No one there, either. Ahead and to the left was a table with places set for two and a cold supper in place, but no one in either chair. Yet someone had spoken to him. Someone who'd been directly on the other side of the door, from the sound. Jonas drew his gun.

"Come, now," said the voice which had bid him enter. It came from directly behind Jonas's left shoulder. "No need for that, we're all friends here. All on the same side, you know."

Jonas whirled on his heels, suddenly feeling old and slow. Standing there was a man of medium height, powerfully built from the look of him, with bright blue eyes and the rosy cheeks of either good health or good wine. His parted, smiling lips revealed cunning little teeth which must have been filed to points—surely such points couldn't be natural. He wore a black robe, like the robe of a holy man, with the hood pushed back. Jonas's first thought, that the fellow was bald, had been wrong, he saw. The hair was simply cropped so stringently that it was nothing but fuzz.

"Put the beanshooter away," the man in black said. "We're friends here, I tell you—absolutely palsy-walsy. We'll break bread and speak of many things—oxen and oil-tankers and whether or not Frank Sinatra really *was* a better crooner than Der Bingle."

"Who? A better *what?*"

"No one you know; nothing that matters." The man in black tittered again. It was, Jonas thought, the sort of sound one might expect to hear drifting through the barred windows of a lunatic asylum.

He turned. Looked into the mirror again. This time he saw the man in black standing there and smiling at him, big as life. Gods, had he been there all along?

Yes, but you couldn't see him until he was ready to be seen. I don't know if he's a wizard, but he's a glamor-man, all right. Mayhap even Farson's sorcerer.

He turned back. The man in the priest's robe was still smiling. No pointed teeth now. But they *had* been pointed. Jonas would lay his watch and warrant on it.

"Where's Rimer?"

"I sent him away to work with young sai Delgado on her Reaping Day catechisms," the man in black said. He slung a chummy arm around Jonas's shoulders and began leading him toward the table. "Best we palaver alone, I think."

Jonas didn't want to offend Farson's man, but he couldn't bear the touch of that arm. He couldn't say why, but it was unbearable. Pestilential. He shrugged it off and went on to one of the chairs, trying not to shiver. No wonder Depape had come back from Hanging Rock looking pale. No damned wonder.

Instead of being offended, the man in black tittered again (*Yes,* Jonas thought, *he does laugh like the dead, very like, so he does).* For one moment Jonas thought it was Fardo, Cort's father, in this room with him—that it was the man who had sent him west all those years ago—and he reached for his gun again. Then it was just the man in black, smiling at him in an unpleasantly knowing way, those blue eyes dancing like the flame from the gas-jets.

"See something interesting, sai Jonas?"

"Aye," Jonas said, sitting down. "Eats." He took a piece of bread and popped it into his mouth. The bread stuck to his dry tongue, but he chewed determinedly all the same.

"Good boy." The other also sat, and poured wine, filling Jonas's glass first. "Now, my friend, tell me everything you've done since the three troublesome boys arrived, and everything you know, and everything you have planned. I would not have you leave out a single jot."

"First show me your *sigul.*"

"Of course. How prudent you are."

The man in black reached inside his robe and brought out a square of metal—silver, Jonas guessed. He tossed it onto the table, and it clattered across to Jonas's plate. Engraved on it was what he had expected—that hideous staring eye.

"Satisfied?"

Jonas nodded.

"Slide it back to me."

Jonas reached for it, but for once his normally steady hand resembled his reedy, unstable voice. He watched the fingers tremble for a moment, then lowered the hand quickly to the table.

"I . . . I don't want to."

No. He didn't want to. Suddenly he knew that if he touched it, the engraved silver eye would roll . . . and look directly at him.

The man in black tittered and made a come-along

gesture with the fingers of his right hand. The silver buckle (that was what it looked like to Jonas) slid back to him . . . and up the sleeve of his homespun robe.

"Abracadabra! Bool! The end! Now," the man in black went on, sipping his wine delicately, "if we have finished the tiresome formalities . . ."

"One more," Jonas said. "You know my name; I would know yours."

"Call me Walter," the man in black said, and the smile suddenly fell off his lips. "Good old Walter, that's me. Now let us see where we are, and where we're going. Let us, in short, palaver."

14

When Cuthbert came back into the bunkhouse, night had fallen. Roland and Alain were playing cards. They had cleaned the place up so that it looked almost as it had (thanks to turpentine found in a closet of the old foreman's office, even the slogans written on the walls were just pink ghosts of their former selves), and now were deeply involved in a game of *Casa Fuerte,* or Hot-patch, as it was known in their own part of the world. Either way, it was basically a two-man version of Watch Me, the card-game which had been played in barrooms and bunkhouses and around campfires since the world was young.

Roland looked up at once, trying to read Bert's emotional weather. Outwardly, Roland was as impassive as ever, had even played Alain to a draw across four difficult hands, but inwardly he was in a turmoil of pain and indecision. Alain had told him what Cuthbert had said while the two of them stood talking in the yard, and they were terrible things to hear from a friend, even when they came at second hand. Yet what haunted him more was what Bert had said just before leaving:

You've called your carelessness love and made a virtue of irresponsibility. Was there even a *chance* he had done such a thing? Over and over he told himself no—that the course he had ordered them to follow was hard but sensible, the only course that made sense. Cuthbert's shouting was just so much angry wind, brought on by nerves . . . and his fury at having their private place defiled so outrageously. Still . . .

Tell him he's right for the wrong reasons, and that makes him all the way wrong.

That couldn't be.

Could it?

Cuthbert was smiling and his color was high, as if he had galloped most of the way back. He looked young, handsome, and vital. He looked happy, in fact, almost like the Cuthbert of old—the one who'd been capable of babbling happy nonsense to a rook's skull until someone told him to please, *please* shut up.

But Roland didn't trust what he saw. There was something wrong with the smile, the color in Bert's cheeks could have been anger rather than good health, and the sparkle in his eyes looked like fever instead of humor. Roland showed nothing on his own face, but his heart sank. He'd hoped the storm would blow itself out, given a little time, but he didn't think it had. He shot a glance at Alain, and saw that Alain felt the same.

Cuthbert, it will be over in three weeks. If only I could tell you that.

The thought which returned was stunning in its simplicity: *Why can't you?*

He realized he didn't know. Why had he been holding back, keeping his own counsel? For what *purpose? Had* he been blind? Gods, *had* he?

"Hello, Bert," he said, "did you have a nice r—"

"Yes, very nice, a very nice ride, an *instructive* ride. Come outside. I want to show you something."

Roland liked the thin glaze of hilarity in Bert's eyes less and less, but he laid his cards in a neat facedown fan on the table and got up.

Alain pulled at his sleeve. "No!" His voice was low and panicky. "Do you not see how he looks?"

"I see," Roland said. And felt dismay in his heart.

For the first time, as he walked slowly toward the friend who no longer looked like a friend, it occurred to Roland that he had been making decisions in a state close akin to drunkenness. Or had he been making decisions at all? He was no longer sure.

"What is it you'd show me, Bert?"

"Something wonderful," Bert said, and laughed. There was hate in the sound. Perhaps murder. "You'll want a good close look at this. I know you will."

"Bert, what's wrong with you?" Alain asked.

"Wrong with me? Nothing wrong with *me*, Al—I'm as happy as a dart at sunrise, a bee in a flower, a fish in the ocean." And as he turned away to go back through the door, he laughed again.

"Don't go out there," Alain said. "He's lost his wits."

"If our fellowship is broken, any chance we might have of getting out of Mejis alive is gone," Roland said. "That being the case, I'd rather die at the hands of a friend than an enemy."

He went out. After a moment of hesitation, Alain followed. On his face was a look of purest misery.

15

Huntress had gone and Demon had not yet begun to show his face, but the sky was powdered with stars, and they threw enough light to see by. Cuthbert's horse, still saddled, was tied to the hitching rail. Beyond it, the square of dusty dooryard gleamed like a canopy of tarnished silver.

"What is it?" Roland asked. They weren't wearing guns, any of them. That was to be grateful for, at least. "What would you show me?"

"It's here." Cuthbert stopped at a point midway between the bunkhouse and the charred remains of the home place. He pointed with great assurance, but Roland could see nothing out of the ordinary. He walked over to Cuthbert and looked down.

"I don't see—"

Brilliant light—starshine times a thousand—exploded in his head as Cuthbert's fist drove against the point of his chin. It was the first time, except in play (and as very small boys), that Bert had ever struck him. Roland didn't lose consciousness, but he *did* lose control over his arms and legs. They were there, but seemingly in another country, flailing like the limbs of a rag doll. He went down on his back. Dust puffed up around him. The stars seemed strangely in motion, running in arcs and leaving milky trails behind them. There was a high ringing in his ears.

From a great distance he heard Alain scream: "Oh, you fool! You stupid *fool!*"

By making a tremendous effort, Roland was able to turn his head. He saw Alain start toward him and saw Cuthbert, no longer smiling, push him away. "This is between us, Al. You stay out of it."

"You sucker-punched him, you bastard!" Alain, slow to anger, was now building toward a rage Cuthbert might well regret. *I have to get up,* Roland thought. *I have to get between them before something even worse happens.* His arms and legs began to swim weakly in the dust.

"Yes—that's how he's played us," Cuthbert said. "I only returned the favor." He looked down. "That's what I wanted to show you, Roland. That particular piece of ground. That particular puff of dust in which you are now lying. Get a good taste of it. Mayhap it'll wake you up."

Now Roland's own anger began to rise. He felt the coldness that was seeping into his thoughts, fought it, and realized he was losing. Jonas ceased to matter; the tankers at Citgo ceased to matter; the supply conspiracy they had uncovered ceased to matter. Soon the Affiliation and the *ka-tet* he had been at such pains to preserve would cease to matter as well.

The surface numbness was leaving his feet and legs, and he pushed himself to a sitting position. He looked up calmly at Bert, his tented hands on the ground, his face set. Starshine swam in his eyes.

"I love you, Cuthbert, but I'll have no more insubordination and jealous tantrums. If I paid you back for all, I reckon you'd finish in pieces, so I'm only going to pay you for hitting me when I didn't know it was coming."

"And I've no doubt ye can, cully," Cuthbert said, falling effortlessly into the Hambry patois. "But first ye might want to have a peek at this." Almost contemptuously, he tossed a folded sheet of paper. It hit Roland's chest and bounced into his lap.

Roland picked it up, feeling the fine point of his developing rage lose its edge. "What is it?"

"Open and see. There's enough starlight to read by."

Slowly, with reluctant fingers, Roland unfolded the sheet of paper and read what was printed there.

pure no more! he's had every hole
of her has will Dearborn! How Do
Ye LIKE IT?

He read it twice. The second time was actually harder, because his hands had begun to tremble. He saw every place he and Susan had met—the boathouse, the hut, the shack—and now he saw them in a new light, knowing someone else had seen them, too. How clever he had believed they were being. How confident of their secrecy and their discretion. And yet someone had been watching all the time. Susan had been right. Someone had seen.

I've put everything at risk. Her life as well as our lives.

Tell him what I said about the doorway to hell.

And Susan's voice, too: Ka *like a wind . . . if you love me, then love me.*

So he had done, believing in his youthful arrogance that everything would turn out all right for no other reason—yes, at bottom he had believed this—than that *he* was *he,* and *ka* must serve his love.

"I've been a fool," he said. His voice trembled like his hands.

"Yes, indeed," Cuthbert said. "So you have." He dropped to his knees in the dust, facing Roland. "Now if you want to hit me, hit away. Hard as you want and as many as you can manage. I'll not hit back. I've done all I can to wake you up to your responsibilities. If you still sleep, so be it. Either way, I still love you." Bert put his hands on Roland's shoulders and briefly kissed his friend's cheek.

Roland began to cry. They were partly tears of gratitude, but mostly those of mingled shame and confusion; there was even a small, dark part of him that hated Cuthbert and always would. That part hated Cuthbert more on account of the kiss than because of the unexpected punch on the jaw; more for the forgiveness than the awakening.

He got to his feet, still holding the letter in one dusty hand, the other ineffectually brushing his cheeks and leaving damp smears there. When he staggered and Cuthbert put out a hand to steady him, Roland pushed him so hard that Cuthbert himself would have fallen, if Alain hadn't caught hold of his shoulders.

Then, slowly, Roland went back down again—this time in front of Cuthbert with his hands up and his head down.

"Roland, no!" Cuthbert cried.

"Yes," Roland said. "I have forgotten the face of my father, and cry your pardon."

"Yes, all right, for gods' sake, *yes!*" Cuthbert now sounded as if he were crying himself. "Just . . . please get up! It breaks my heart to see you so!"

And mine to be so, Roland thought. *To be humbled so. But I brought it on myself, didn't I? This dark yard, with my head throbbing and my heart full of shame and fear. This is mine, bought and paid for.*

They helped him up and Roland let himself be helped. "That's quite a left, Bert," he said in a voice that almost passed for normal.

"Only when it's going toward someone who doesn't know it's coming," Cuthbert replied.

"This letter—how did you come by it?"

Cuthbert told of meeting Sheemie, who had been dithering along in his own misery, as if waiting for *ka* to intervene . . . and, in the person of "Arthur Heath," *ka* had.

"From the witch," Roland mused. "Yes, but how did *she* know? For she never leaves the Cöos, or so Susan has told me."

"I can't say. Nor do I much care. What I'm most concerned about right now is making sure that Sheemie isn't hurt because of what he told me and gave me. After that, I'm concerned that what old witch Rhea has tried to tell once she doesn't try to tell again."

"I've made at least one terrible mistake," Roland said, "but I don't count loving Susan as another. That was beyond me to change. As it was beyond her. Do you believe that?"

"Yes," Alain said at once, and after a moment, almost reluctantly, Cuthbert said, "Aye, Roland."

"I've been arrogant and stupid. If this note had reached her aunt, she could have been sent into exile."

"And we to the devil, by way of hangropes," Cuthbert added dryly. "Although I know that's a minor matter to you by comparison."

"What about the witch?" Alain asked. "What do we do about her?"

Roland smiled a little, and turned toward the northwest. "Rhea," he said. "Whatever else she is, she's a first-class troublemaker, is she not? And troublemakers must be put on notice."

He started back toward the bunkhouse, trudging with his head down. Cuthbert looked at Alain, and saw that Al was also a little teary-eyed. Bert put out his hand. For a moment Alain only looked at it. Then he nodded—to himself rather than to Cuthbert, it seemed—and shook it.

"You did what you had to," Alain said. "I had my doubts at first, but not now."

Cuthbert let out his breath. "And I did it the way I had to. If I hadn't surprised him—"

"—he would have beaten you black and blue."

"So many more colors than that," Cuthbert said. "I would have looked like a rainbow."

"The Wizard's Rainbow, even," Alain said. "Extra colors for your penny."

That made Cuthbert laugh. The two of them walked back toward the bunkhouse, where Roland was unsaddling Bert's horse.

Cuthbert turned in that direction to help, but Alain held him back. "Leave him alone for a little while," he said. "It's best you do."

They went on ahead, and when Roland came in ten minutes later, he found Cuthbert playing his hand. And winning with it.

"Bert," he said.

Cuthbert looked up.

"We have a spot of business tomorrow, you and I. Up on the Cöos."

"Are we going to kill her?"

Roland thought, and thought hard. At last he looked up, biting his lip. "We should."

"Aye. We should. But are we going to?"

"Not unless we have to, I reckon." Later he would regret this decision—if it was a decision—bitterly, but there never came a time when he did not understand it. He had been a boy not much older than Jake Chambers during that Mejis fall, and the decision to kill does not come easily or naturally to most boys. "Not unless she makes us."

"Perhaps it would be best if she did," Cuthbert said. It was hard gunslinger talk, but he looked troubled as he said it.

"Yes. Perhaps it would. It's not likely, though, not in one as sly as her. Be ready to get up early."

"All right. Do you want your hand back?"

"When you're on the verge of knocking him out? Not at all."

Roland went past them to his bunk. There he sat,

looking at his folded hands in his lap. He might have been praying; he might only have been thinking hard. Cuthbert looked at him for a moment, then turned back to his cards.

16

The sun was just over the horizon when Roland and Cuthbert left the next morning. The Drop, still drenched with morning dew, seemed to burn with orange fire in the early light. Their breath and that of their horses puffed frosty in the air. It was a morning neither of them ever forgot. For the first time in their lives they went forth wearing holstered revolvers; for the first time in their lives they went into the world as gunslingers.

Cuthbert said not a word—he knew that if he started, he'd do nothing but babble great streams of his usual nonsense—and Roland was quiet by nature. There was only one exchange between them, and it was brief.

"I said I made at least one very bad mistake," Roland told him. "One that this note"—he touched his breast pocket— "brought home to me. Do you know what that mistake was?"

"Not loving her—not that," Cuthbert said. "You called that *ka,* and I call it the same." It was a relief to be able to say this, and a greater one to believe it. Cuthbert thought he could even accept Susan herself now, not as his best friend's lover, a girl he had wanted himself the first time he saw her, but as a part of their entwined fate.

"No," Roland said. "Not loving her, but thinking that love could somehow be apart from everything else. That I could live two lives—one with you and Al and our job here, one with her. I thought that love could lift me above *ka,* the way a bird's wings can take it above all the things that would kill it and eat it, otherwise. Do you understand?"

"It made you blind." Cuthbert spoke with a gentleness quite foreign to the young man who had suffered through the last two months.

"Yes," Roland said sadly. "It made me blind . . . but now I see. Come on, a little faster, if you please. I want to get this over."

17

They rode up the rutty cart-track along which Susan (a Susan who had known a good deal less about the ways of the world) had come singing "Careless Love" beneath the light of the Kissing Moon. Where the track opened into Rhea's yard, they stopped.

"Wonderful view," Roland murmured. "You can see the whole sweep of the desert from here."

"Not much to say about the view right here in front of us, though."

That was true. The garden was full of unpicked mutie vegetables, the stuffy-guy presiding over them either a bad joke or a bad omen. The yard supported just one tree, now moulting sickly-looking fall leaves like an old vulture shedding its feathers. Beyond the tree was the hut itself, made of rough stone and topped by a single sooty pot of a chimney with a hex-sign painted on it in sneering yellow. At the rear corner, beyond one overgrown window, was a woodpile.

Roland had seen plenty of huts like it—the three of them had passed any number on their way here from Gilead— but never one that felt as powerfully *wrong* as this. He saw nothing untoward, yet there was a feeling, too strong to be denied, of a presence. One that watched and waited.

Cuthbert felt it, too. "Do we have to go closer?" He swallowed. "Do we have to go in? Because . . . Roland, the door is open. Do you see?"

He saw. As if she expected them. As if she was inviting them in, wanting them to sit down with her to some unspeakable breakfast.

"Stay here." Roland gigged Rusher forward.

"No! I'm coming!"

"No, cover my back. If I need to go inside, I'll call you to join me . . . but if I need to go inside, the old woman who lives here will breathe no more. As you said, that might be for the best."

At every slow step Rusher took, the feeling of wrongness grew in Roland's heart and mind. There was a stench to the place, a smell like rotten meat and hot putrefied tomatoes. It came from the hut, he supposed, but it also seemed to come wafting out of the very ground. And at every step, the whine of the thinny seemed louder, as if the atmosphere of this place somehow magnified it.

Susan came up here alone, and in the dark, he thought. *Gods, I'm not sure I could have come up here in the dark with my friends for company.*

He stopped beneath the tree, looking through the open door twenty paces away. He saw what could have been a kitchen: the legs of a table, the back of a chair, a filthy hearthstone. No sign of the lady of the house. But she was there. Roland could feel her eyes crawling on him like loathsome bugs.

I can't see her because she's used her art to make herself dim . . . but she's there.

And just perhaps he *did* see her. The air had a strange shimmer just inside the door to the right, as if it had been heated. Roland had been told that you could see someone who was *dim* by turning your head and looking from the corner of your eye. He did that now.

"Roland?" Cuthbert called from behind him.

"Fine so far, Bert." Barely paying attention to the words he was saying, because . . . yes! That shimmer was clearer now, and it had almost the shape of a woman. It could be his imagination, of course, but . . .

But at that moment, as if understanding he'd seen her, the shimmer moved farther back into the shadows. Roland glimpsed the swinging hem of an old black dress, there and then gone.

No matter. He had not come to see her but only to give her her single warning . . . which was one more than any of their fathers would have given her, no doubt.

"Rhea!" His voice rolled in the harsh tones of old, stern and commanding. Two yellow leaves fell from the tree, as if shivered loose by that voice, and one fell in his black hair. From the hut came only a waiting, listening silence . . . and then the discordant, jeering yowl of a cat.

"Rhea, daughter of none! I've brought something back to you, woman! Something you must have lost!" From his shirt he took the folded letter and tossed it to the stony ground. "Today I've been your friend, Rhea— if this had gone where you had intended it to go, you would have paid with your life."

He paused. Another leaf drifted down from the tree. This one landed in Rusher's mane.

"Hear me well, Rhea, daughter of none, and understand me well. I have come here under the name of Will Dearborn, but Dearborn is not my name and it is the Affiliation I serve. More, 'tis all which lies behind the Affiliation—'tis the power of the White. You have crossed the way of our *ka,* and I warn you only this once: *do not cross it again.* Do you understand?"

Only that waiting silence.

"Do not touch a single hair on the head of the boy who carried your bad-natured mischief hence, or you'll die. Speak not another word of those things you know or think you know to anyone—not to Cordelia Delgado, nor to Jonas, nor to Rimer, nor to Thorin—or you'll die. Keep your peace and we will keep ours. Break it, and we'll still you. Do you understand?"

More silence. Dirty windows peering at him like eyes. A puff of breeze sent more leaves showering down around him, and caused the stuffy-guy to creak nastily on his pole. Roland thought briefly of the cook, Hax, twisting at the end of his rope.

"Do you understand?"

No reply. Not even a shimmer could he see through the open door now.

"Very well," Roland said. "Silence gives consent." He gigged his horse around. As he did, his head came up a little, and he saw something green shift above him among the yellow leaves. There was a low hissing sound.

"Roland look out! Snake!" Cuthbert screamed, but before the second word had left his mouth, Roland had drawn one of his guns.

He fell sideways in the saddle, holding with his left leg and heel as Rusher jigged and pranced. He fired three times, the thunder of the big gun smashing through the still air and then rolling back from the nearby hills. With each shot the snake flipped upward again, its blood dotting red across a background of blue sky and yellow leaves. The last bullet tore off its head, and when the snake fell for good, it hit the ground in two pieces. From within the hut came a wail of grief and rage so awful that Roland's spine turned to a cord of ice.

"You bastard!" screamed a woman's voice from the shadows. *"Oh, you murdering cull! My friend! My friend!"*

"If it was your friend, you oughtn't to have set it on me," Roland said. "Remember, Rhea, daughter of none."

The voice uttered one more shriek and fell silent.

Roland rode back to Cuthbert, holstering his gun. Bert's eyes were round and amazed. "Roland, what shooting! Gods, what shooting!"

"Let's get out of here."

"But we still don't know how she knew!"

"Do you think she'd tell?" There was a small but minute shake in Roland's voice. The way the snake had come out of the tree like that, right at him . . . he could still barely believe he wasn't dead. Thank gods for his hand, which had taken matters over.

"We could make her talk," Cuthbert said, but Roland could tell from his voice that Bert had no taste for such. Maybe later, maybe after years of trail-riding and gunslinging, but now he had no more stomach for torture than for killing outright.

"Even if we could, we couldn't make her tell the truth. Such as her lies as other folks breathe. If we've convinced her to keep quiet, we've done enough for today. Come on. I hate this place."

18

As they rode back toward town, Roland said: "We've got to meet."

"The four of us. That's what you mean, isn't it?"

"Yes. I want to tell everything I know and surmise. I want to tell you my plan, such as it is. What we've been waiting *for.*"

"That would be very good indeed."

"Susan can help us." Roland seemed to be speaking to himself. Cuthbert was amused to see that the lone, crownlike leaf was still caught in his dark hair. "Susan was *meant* to help us. Why didn't I see that?"

"Because love is blind," Cuthbert said. He snorted

laughter and clapped Roland on the shoulder. "Love is blind, old son."

19

When she was sure the boys were gone, Rhea crept out of her door and into the hateful sunshine. She hobbled across to the tree and fell on her knees by the tattered length of her snake, weeping loudly.

"Ermot, Ermot!" she cried. "See what's become of ye!"

There was his head, the mouth frozen open, the double fangs still dripping poison—clear drops that shone like prisms in the day's strengthening light. The glazing eyes glared. She picked Ermot up, kissed the scaly mouth, licked the last of the venom from the exposed needles, crooning and weeping all the while.

Next she picked up the long and tattered body with her other hand, moaning at the holes which had been torn into Ermot's satiny hide; the holes and the ripped red flesh beneath. Twice she put the head against the body and spoke incantations, but nothing happened. Of course not. Ermot had gone beyond the aid of her spells. Poor Ermot.

She held his head to one flattened old dug, and his body to the other. Then, with the last of his blood wetting the bodice of her dress, she looked in the direction the hateful boys had gone.

"I'll pay ye back," she whispered. "By all the gods that ever were, I'll pay ye back. When ye least expect it, there Rhea will be, and your screams will break your throats. Do you hear me? *Your screams will break your throats!*"

She knelt a moment longer, then got up and shuffled back toward her hut, holding Ermot to her bosom.

CHAPTER FIVE

Wizard's Rainbow

I

On an afternoon three days after Roland's and Cuthbert's visit to the Cöos, Roy Depape and Clay Reynolds walked along the upstairs hallway of the Travellers' Rest to the spacious bedroom Coral Thorin kept there. Clay knocked. Jonas called for them to come in, it was open.

The first thing Depape saw upon entering was sai Thorin herself, in a rocker by the window. She wore a foamy nightdress of white silk and a red *bufanda* on her head. She had a lapful of knitting. Depape looked at her in surprise. She offered him and Reynolds an enigmatic smile, said "Hello, gents," and returned to her needlework. Outside there was a rattle of firecrackers (young folks could never wait until the big day; if they had crackers in their hands, they had to set match to them), the nervous whinny of a horse, and the raucous laughter of boys.

Depape turned to Reynolds, who shrugged and then crossed his arms to hold the sides of his cloak. In this way he expressed doubt or disapproval or both.

"Problem?"

Jonas was standing in the doorway to the bathroom, wiping shaving soap from his face with the end of the towel laid over his shoulder. He was bare to the waist.

Depape had seen him that way plenty of times, but the old white crisscrossings of scars always made him feel a little sick to his stomach.

"Well . . . I knew we was using the lady's room, I just didn't know the lady came with it."

"She does." Jonas tossed the towel into the bathroom, crossed to the bed, and took his shirt from where it hung on one of the footposts. Beyond him, Coral glanced up, gave his naked back a single greedy look, then went back to her work once more. Jonas slipped into his shirt. "How are things at Citgo, Clay?"

"Quiet. But it'll get noisy if certain young *vagabundos* poke their nosy noses in."

"How many are out there, and how do they set?"

"Ten in the days. A dozen at night. Roy or I are out once every shift, but like I say, it's been quiet."

Jonas nodded, but he wasn't happy. He'd hoped to draw the boys out to Citgo before now, just as he'd hoped to draw them into a confrontation by vandalizing their place and killing their pigeons. Yet so far they still hid behind their damned Hillock. He felt like a man in a field with three young bulls. He's got a red rag, this would-be *torero*, and he's flapping it for all he's worth, and still the *toros* refuse to charge. Why?

"The moving operation? How goes that?"

"Like clockwork," Reynolds said. "Four tankers a night, in pairs, the last four nights. Renfrew's in charge, him of the Lazy Susan. Do you still want to leave half a dozen as bait?"

"Yar," Jonas said, and there was a knock at the door.

Depape jumped. "Is that—"

"No," Jonas said. "Our friend in the black robe has decamped. Perhaps he goes to offer comfort to the Good Man's troops before battle."

Depape barked laughter at that. By the window, the

woman in the nightgown looked down at her knitting and said nothing.

"It's open!" Jonas called.

The man who stepped in was wearing the *sombrero, serape,* and *sandalias* of a farmer or *vaquero,* but the face was pale and the lock of hair peeking out from beneath the *sombrero's* brim was blond. It was Latigo. A hard man and no mistake, but a great improvement over the laughing man in the black robe, just the same.

"Good to see you, gentlemen," he said, coming in and closing the door. His face—dour, frowning—was that of a man who hasn't seen anything good in years. Maybe since birth. "Jonas? Are you well? Do things march?"

"I am and they do," Jonas said. He offered his hand. Latigo gave it a quick, dry shake. He didn't do the same for Depape or Reynolds, but glanced at Coral instead.

"Long days and pleasant nights, lady."

"And may you have twice the number, sai Latigo," she said without looking up from her knitting.

Latigo sat on the end of the bed, produced a sack of tobacco from beneath his *serape,* and began rolling a cigarette.

"I won't stay long," he said. He spoke in the abrupt, clipped tones of northern In-World, where—or so Depape had heard—reindeer-fucking was still considered the chief sport. If you ran slower than your sister, that was. "It wouldn't be wise. I don't quite fit in, if one looks closely."

"No," Reynolds said, sounding amused. "You don't."

Latigo gave him a sharp glance, then returned his attention to Jonas. "Most of my party is camped thirty wheels from here, in the forest west of Eyebolt Canyon . . . what *is* that wretched noise inside the canyon, by the way? It frightens the horses."

"A thinny," Jonas said.

"It scares the men, too, if they get too close," Reynolds said. "Best to stay away, cap'n."

"How many are you?" Jonas asked.

"A hundred. And well armed."

"So, it's said, were Lord Perth's men."

"Don't be an ass."

"Have they seen any fighting?"

"Enough to know what it is," Latigo said, and Jonas knew he was lying. Farson had kept his veterans in their mountain boltholes. Here was a little expeditionary force where no doubt only the sergeants were able to do more with their cocks than run water through them.

"There are a dozen at Hanging Rock, guarding the tankers your men have brought so far," Latigo said.

"More than needed, likely."

"I didn't risk coming into this godforsaken shitsplat of a town in order to discuss my arrangements with you, Jonas."

"Cry your pardon, sai," Jonas replied, but perfunctorily. He sat on the floor next to Coral's rocker and began to roll a smoke of his own. She put her knitting aside and began to stroke his hair. Depape didn't know what there was about her that Eldred found so fascinating—when he himself looked he saw only an ugly bitch with a big nose and mosquito-bump titties.

"As to the three young men," Latigo said with the air of a fellow going directly to the heart of the matter. "The Good Man was extremely disturbed to learn there were visitors from In-World in Mejis. And now you tell me they aren't what they claim to be. So, just what *are* they?"

Jonas brushed Coral's hand away from his hair as though it were a troublesome insect. Undisturbed, she returned to her knitting. "They're not young men but mere boys, and if their coming here is *ka*—about which

I know Farson concerns himself deeply—then it may be our *ka* rather than the Affiliation's."

"Unfortunately, we'll have to forgo enlightening the Good Man with your theological conclusions," Latigo said. "We've brought radios, but they're either broken or can't work at this distance. No one knows which. I hate all such toys, anyway. The gods laugh at them. We're on our own, my friend. For good or ill."

"No need for Farson to worry unnecessarily," Jonas said.

"The Good Man wants these lads treated as a threat to his plans. I expect Walter told you the same thing."

"Aye. And I haven't forgotten a word. Sai Walter is an unforgettable sort of man."

"Yes," Latigo agreed. "He's the Good Man's under-liner. The chief reason he came to you was to underline these boys."

"And so he did. Roy, tell sai Latigo about your visit to the Sheriff day before yesterday."

Depape cleared his throat nervously. "The sheriff . . . Avery—"

"I know him, fat as a pig in Full Earth, he is," Latigo said. "Go on."

"One of Avery's deputies carried a message to the three boys as they counted horse on the Drop."

"What message?"

"Stay out of town on Reaping Day; stay off the Drop on Reaping Day; best to stay close to your quarters on Reaping Day, as Barony folk don't enjoy seeing outlanders, even those they like, when they keep their festivals."

"And how did they take it?"

"They agreed straight away to keep to themselves on Reaping," Depape said. "That's been their habit all along, to be just as agreeable as pie when something's asked of em. They know better, course they do—there's no more a custom here against outlanders on Reaping than there is anyplace else. In fact, it's quite usual to make strangers a part of the merry-making, as I'm sure the boys know. The idea—"

"—is to make them believe we plan to move on Fair-Day itself, yes, yes," Latigo finished impatiently. "What I want to know is *are* they convinced? Can you take them on the day *before* Reaping, as you've promised, or will they be waiting?"

Depape and Reynolds looked at Jonas. Jonas reached behind him and put his hand on Coral's narrow but not uninteresting thigh. Here it was, he thought. He would be held to what he said next, and without grace. If he was right, the Big Coffin Hunters would be thanked and paid . . . perhaps bonused, as well. If he was wrong, they would likely be hung so high and hard that their heads would pop off when they hit the end of the rope.

"We'll take them easy as birds on the ground," Jonas said. "Treason the charge. Three young men, all high-born, in the pay of John Farson. Shocking stuff. What could be more indicative of the evil days we live in?"

"One cry of treason and the mob appears?"

Jonas favored Latigo with a wintry smile. "As a concept, treason might be a bit of a reach for the common folk, even when the mob's drunk and the core's been bought and paid for by the Horsemen's Association. Murder, though . . . especially that of a much loved Mayor—"

Depape's startled eyes flew to the Mayor's sister.

"What a pity it will be," that lady said, and sighed. "I may be moved to lead the rabble myself."

Depape thought he finally understood Eldred's attraction: here was a woman every bit as cold-blooded as Jonas himself.

"One other matter," Latigo said. "A piece of the Good

Man's property was sent with you for safekeeping. A certain glass ball?"

Jonas nodded. "Yes, indeed. A pretty trifle."

"I understand you left it with the local *bruja*."

"Yes."

"You should take it back. Soon."

"Don't teach your grandpa to suck eggs," Jonas said, a bit testily. "I'm waiting until the brats are jugged."

Reynolds murmured curiously, "Have you seen it yourself, sai Latigo?"

"Not close up, but I've seen men who have." Latigo paused.

"One such ran mad and had to be shot. The only other time I saw anyone in such condition was thirty years ago, on the edge of the big desert. 'Twas a hut-dweller who'd been bitten by a rabid coyote."

"Bless the Turtle," Reynolds muttered, and tapped his throat three times. He was terrified of rabies.

"You won't bless anything if the Wizard's Rainbow gets hold of you," Latigo said grimly, and swung his attention back to Jonas. "You'll want to be even more careful taking it back than you were in giving it over. The old witch-woman's likely under its glam by now."

"I intend to send Rimer and Avery. Avery ain't much of a shake, but Rimer's a trig boy."

"I'm afraid that won't do," Latigo said.

"Won't it?" Jonas said. His hand tightened on Coral's leg and he smiled unpleasantly at Latigo. "Perhaps you could tell your 'umble servant *why* it won't do?"

It was Coral who answered. "Because," said she, "when the piece of the Wizard's Rainbow Rhea holds is taken back into custody, the Chancellor will be busy accompanying my brother to his final resting place."

"What's she talking about, Eldred?" Depape asked.

"That Rimer dies, too," Jonas said. He began to grin.

"Another foul crime to lay at the feet of John Farson's filthy spyboys."

Coral smiled in sweet agreement, put her hands over Jonas's, moved it higher on her thigh, and then picked up her knitting again.

2

The girl, although young, was married.

The boy, although fair, was unstable.

She met him one night in a remote place to tell him their affair, sweet as it had been, must end. He replied that it would never end, it was written in the stars. She told him that might be, but at some point the constellations had changed. Perhaps he began to weep. Perhaps she laughed—out of nervousness, very likely. Whatever the cause, such laughter was disastrously timed. He picked up a stone and dashed out her brains with it. Then, coming to his senses and realizing what he had done, he sat down with his back against a granite slab, drew her poor battered head into his lap, and cut his own throat as an owl looked on from a nearby tree. He died covering her face with kisses, and when they were found, their lips were sealed together with his life's blood and with hers.

An old story. Every town has its version. The site is usually the local lovers' lane, or a secluded stretch of riverbank, or the town graveyard. Once the details of what actually happened have been distorted enough to please the morbidly romantic, songs are made. These are usually sung by yearning virgins who play guitar or mando badly and cannot quite stay on key. Choruses tend to include such lachrymose refrains as *My-di-I-de-l-de-o, There they died together-o.*

The Hambry version of this quaint tale featured lovers

named Robert and Francesca, and had happened in the old days, before the world had moved on. The site of the supposed murder-suicide was the Hambry cemetery, the stone with which Francesca's brains had been dashed out was a slate marker, and the granite wall against which Robert had been leaning when he clipped his blowpipe had been the Thorin mausoleum. (It was doubtful there had been any Thorins in Hambry or Mejis five generations back, but folk-tales are, at best, generally no more than lies set in rhyme.)

True or untrue, the graveyard was considered haunted by the ghosts of the lovers, who could be seen (it was said) walking hand-in-hand among the markers, covered with blood and looking wistful. It was thus seldom visited at night, and was a logical spot for Roland, Cuthbert, Alain, and Susan to meet.

By the time the meeting took place, Roland had begun to feel increasingly worried . . . even desperate. Susan was the problem—or, more properly put, Susan's aunt. Even without Rhea's poisonous letter to help the process along, Cordelia's suspicions of Susan and Roland had hardened into a near certainty. On a day less than a week before the meeting in the cemetery, Cordelia had begun shrieking at Susan almost as soon as she stepped through the house door with her basket over her arm.

"Ye've been with him! Ye have, ye bad girl, it's written all over yer face!"

Susan, who had that day been nowhere near Roland, could at first only gape at her aunt. "Been with who?"

"Oh, be not coy with me, Miss Oh So Young and Pretty! Be not coy, I pray! Who does all but wiggle his tongue at ye when he passes our door? Dearborn, that's who! Dearborn! Dearborn! I'll say it a thousand times! Oh, shame on ye! Shame! Look at yer trousers! Green from the grass the two of ye have been rolling in, they are! I'm surprised they're not torn open at the crutch as well!" By then Aunt Cord had been nearly shrieking. The veins in her neck stood out like rope.

Susan, bemused, had looked down at the old khaki pants she was wearing.

"Aunt, it's paint—don't you see it is? Chetta and I've been making Fair-Day decorations up at Mayor's House. What's on my bottom got there when Hart Thorin—not Dearborn but *Thorin*—came upon me in the shed where the decorations and fireworks are stored. He decided it was as good a time and place as any to have another little wrestle. He got on top of me, shot his squirt into his pants again, and went off happy. Humming, he was." She wrinkled her nose, although the most she felt for Thorin these days was a kind of sad distaste. Her fear of him had passed.

Aunt Cord, meanwhile, had been looking at her with glittery eyes. For the first time, Susan found herself wondering consciously about Cordelia's sanity.

"A likely story," Cordelia whispered at last. There were little beads of perspiration above her eyebrows, and the nestles of blue veins at her temples ticked like clocks. She even had a smell, these days, no matter if she bathed or not—a rancid, acrid one. "Did ye work it out together as ye cuddled afterward, thee and him?"

Susan had stepped forward, grabbed her aunt's bony wrist, and clapped it to the stain on one of her knees. Cordelia cried out and tried to pull away, but Susan held fast. She then raised the hand to her aunt's face, holding it there until she knew Cordelia had smelled what was on her palm.

"Does thee smell it, Aunt? Paint! We used it on rice-paper for colored lanterns!"

The tension had slowly gone out of the wrist in Susan's hand. The eyes looking into hers regained a measure of clarity. "Aye," she had said at last. "Paint." A pause. "This time."

Since then, Susan had all too often turned her head to see a narrow-hipped figure gliding after her in the street, or one of her aunt's many friends marking her course with suspicious eyes. When she rode on the Drop, she now always had the sensation of being watched. Twice before the four of them came together in the graveyard, she had agreed to meet Roland and his friends. Both times she had been forced to break off, the second at the very last moment. On that occasion she had seen Brian Hookey's eldest son watching her in an odd, intent way. It had only been intuition . . . but *strong* intuition.

What made matters worse for her was that she was as frantic for a meeting as Roland himself, and not just for palaver. She needed to see his face, and to clasp one of his hands between both of hers. The rest, sweet as it was, could wait, but she needed to see him and touch him; needed to make sure he wasn't just a dream spun by a lonely, frightened girl to comfort herself.

In the end, Maria had helped her—gods bless the little maid, who perhaps understood more than Susan could ever guess. It was Maria who had gone to Cordelia with a note saying that Susan would be spending the night in the guest wing at Seafront. The note was from Olive Thorin, and in spite of all her suspicions, Cordelia could not quite believe it a forgery. As it was not. Olive had written it, listlessly and without questions, when Susan asked.

"What's wrong with my niece?" Cordelia had snapped.

"She tired, sai. And with the *dolor de garganta.*"

"Sore throat? So close before Fair-Day? Ridiculous! I don't believe it! Susan's never sick!"

"Dolor de garganta," Maria repeated, impassive as only a peasant woman can be in the face of disbelief, and

with that Cordelia had to be satisfied. Maria herself had no idea what Susan was up to, and that was just the way Susan liked it.

She'd gone over the balcony, moving nimbly down the fifteen feet of tangled vines growing up the north side of the building, and through the rear servants' door in the wall. There Roland had been waiting, and after two warm minutes with which we need not concern ourselves, they rode double on Rusher to the graveyard, where Cuthbert and Alain waited, full of expectation and nervous hope.

3

Susan looked first at the placid blond one with the round face, whose name was not Richard Stockworth but Alain Johns. Then at the other one—he from whom she had sensed such doubt of her and perhaps even anger at her. Cuthbert Allgood was his name.

They sat side by side on a fallen gravestone which had been overrun with ivy, their feet in a little brook of mist. Susan slid from Rusher's back and approached them slowly. They stood up. Alain made an In-World bow, leg out, knee locked, heel stiffly planted. "Lady," he said. "Long days—"

Now the other was beside him—thin and dark, with a face that would have been handsome had it not seemed so restless. His dark eyes were really quite beautiful.

"—and pleasant nights," Cuthbert finished, doubling Alain's bow. The two of them looked so like comic court-iers in a Fair-Day sketch that Susan laughed. She couldn't help herself. Then she curtseyed to them deeply, spreading her arms to mime the skirts she wasn't wearing. "And may you have twice the number, gentlemen."

Then they simply looked at each other, three young

people who were uncertain exactly how to proceed. Roland didn't help; he sat astride Rusher and only watched carefully.

Susan took a tentative step forward, not laughing now. There were still dimples at the corners of her lips, but her eyes were anxious.

"I hope you don't hate me," she said. "I'd understand it if you did—I've come into your plans . . . and between the three of you, as well—but I couldn't help it." Her hands were still out at her sides. Now she raised them to Alain and Cuthbert, palms up. "I love him."

"We don't hate you," Alain said. "Do we, Bert?"

For a terrible moment Cuthbert was silent, looking over Susan's shoulder, seeming to study the waxing Demon Moon. She felt her heart stop. Then his gaze returned to her and he gave a smile of such sweetness that a confused but brilliant thought (*If I'd met this one first*—, it began) shot through her mind like a comet.

"Roland's love is my love," Cuthbert said. He reached out, took her hands, and drew her forward so she stood between him and Alain like a sister with her two brothers. "For we have been friends since we wore cradle-clothes, and we'll continue as friends until one of us leaves the path and enters the clearing." Then he grinned like a kid. "Mayhap we'll all find the end of the path together, the way things are going."

"And soon," Alain added.

"Just so long," Susan Delgado finished, "as my Aunt Cordelia doesn't come along as our chaperone."

4

"We are *ka-tet*," Roland said. "We are one from many."

He looked at each in turn, and saw no disagreement

in their eyes. They had repaired to the mausoleum, and their breath smoked from their mouths and noses. Roland squatted on his hunkers, looking at the other three, who sat in a line on a stone meditation bench flanked by skeletal bouquets in stone pots. The floor was scattered with the petals of dead roses. Cuthbert and Alain, on either side of Susan, had their arms around her in quite unself-conscious fashion. Again Roland thought of one sister and two protective brothers.

"We're greater than we were," Alain said. "I feel that very strongly."

"I do, too," Cuthbert said. He looked around. "And a fine meeting-place, as well. Especially for such a *ka-tet* as ours."

Roland didn't smile; repartee had never been his strong suit. "Let's talk about what's going on in Hambry," he said, "and then we'll talk about the immediate future."

"We weren't sent here on a mission, you know," Alain said to Susan. "We were sent by our fathers to get us out of the way, that's all. Roland excited the enmity of a man who is likely a cohort of John Farson's—"

"'Excited the enmity of,'" Cuthbert said. "That's a good phrase. Round. I intend to remember it and use it at every opportunity."

"Control yourself," Roland said. "I've no desire to be here all night."

"Cry your pardon, O great one," Cuthbert said, but his eyes danced in a decidedly unrepentant way.

"We came with carrier pigeons for the sending and receiving of messages," Alain went on, "but I think the pigeons were laid on so our parents could be sure we were all right."

"Yes," Cuthbert said. "What Alain's trying to say is that we've been caught by surprise. Roland and I have had . . .

disagreements . . . about how to go on. He wanted to wait. I didn't. I now believe he was right."

"But for the wrong reasons," Roland said in a dry tone. "In any case, we've settled our differences."

Susan was looking back and forth between them with something like alarm. What her gaze settled upon was the bruise on Roland's lower left jaw, clearly visible even in the faint light which crept through the half-open *sepultura* door. "Settled them how?"

"It doesn't matter," Roland said. "Farson intends a battle, or perhaps a series of them, in the Shavéd Mountains, to the northwest of Gilead. To the forces of the Affiliation moving toward him, he will seem trapped. In a more ordinary course of things, that might even have been true. Farson intends to engage them, trap them, and destroy them with the weapons of the Old People. These he will drive with oil from Citgo. The oil in the tankers we saw, Susan."

"Where will it be refined so Farson can use it?"

"Someplace west of here along his route," Cuthbert said. "We think very likely the Vi Castis. Do you know it? It's mining country."

"I've heard of it, but I've never actually been out of Hambry in my life." She looked levelly at Roland. "I think that's to change soon."

"There's a good deal of machinery left over from the days of the Old People in those mountains," Alain said. "Most is up in the draws and canyons, they say. Robots and killer lights—razor-beams, such are called, because they'll cut you clean in half if you run into them. The gods know what else. Some of it's undoubtedly just legend, but where there's smoke, there's often fire. In any case, it seems the most likely spot for refining."

"And then they'd take it on to where Farson's waiting," Cuthbert said. "Not that that part matters to us; we've got all we can handle right here in Mejis."

"I've been waiting in order to get it all," Roland said. "Every bit of their damned plunder."

"In case you haven't noticed, our friend is just a wee nubbin ambitious," Cuthbert said, and winked.

Roland paid no attention. He was looking in the direction of Eyebolt Canyon. There was no noise from there this night; the wind had shifted onto its autumn course and away from town. "If we can fire the oil, the rest will go up with it . . . and the oil is the most important thing, anyway. I want to destroy it, then I want to get the hell out of here. The four of us."

"They mean to move on Reaping Day, don't they?" Susan asked.

"Oh yes, it seems so," Cuthbert said, then laughed. It was a rich, infectious sound—the laughter of a child— and as he did it, he rocked back and forth and held his stomach as a child would.

Susan looked puzzled. "What? What is it?"

"I can't tell," he said, chortling. "It's too rich for me. I'll laugh all the way through it, and Roland will be annoyed. You do it, Al. Tell Susan about our visit from Deputy Dave."

"He came out to see us at the Bar K," Alain said, smiling himself. "Talked to us like an uncle. Told us Hambryfolk don't care for outsiders at their Fairs, and we'd best keep right to our place on the day of the full moon."

"That's insane!" Susan spoke indignantly, as one is apt to when one hears one's hometown unjustly maligned. "We *welcome* strangers to our fairs, so we do, and always have! We're not a bunch of . . . of savages!"

"Soft, soft," Cuthbert said, giggling. "We know that, but Deputy Dave don't know we know, do he? He knows his wife makes the best white tea for miles around, and after that Dave's pretty much at sea. Sheriff Herk knows a *leetle* more, I sh'd judge, but not much."

"The pains they've taken to warn us off means two things," Roland said. "The first is that they intend to move on Reaping Fair-Day, just as you said, Susan. The second is that they think they can steal Farson's goods right out from under our noses."

"And then perhaps blame us for it afterward," Alain said.

She looked curiously from one to the other, then said: "What have you planned, then?"

"To destroy what they've left at Citgo as bait of our own and then to strike them where they gather," Roland said quietly. "That's Hanging Rock. At least half the tankers they mean to take west are there already. They'll have a force of men. As many as two hundred, perhaps, although I think it will turn out to be less. I intend that all these men should die."

"If they don't, we will," Alain said.

"How can the four of us kill two hundred soldiers?"

"We can't. But if we can start one or two of the clustered tankers burning, we think there'll be an explosion— mayhap a fearful one. The surviving soldiers will be terrified, and the surviving leaders infuriated. They'll see us, because we'll let ourselves be seen . . ."

Alain and Cuthbert were watching him breathlessly. The rest they had either been told or had guessed, but this part was the counsel Roland had, until now, kept to himself.

"What then?" she asked, frightened. *"What then?"*

"I think we can lead them into Eyebolt Canyon," Roland said. "I think we can lead them into the thinny."

5

Thunderstruck silence greeted this. Then, not without respect, Susan said: "You're mad."

"No," Cuthbert said thoughtfully. "He's not. You're thinking about that little cut in the canyon wall, aren't you, Roland? The one just before the jog in the canyon floor."

Roland nodded. "Four could scramble up that way without too much trouble. At the top, we'll pile a fair amount of rock. Enough to start a landslide down on any that should try following us."

"That's horrible," Susan said.

"It's survival," Alain replied. "If they're allowed to have the oil and put it to use, they'll slaughter every Affiliation man that gets in range of their weapons. The Good Man takes no prisoners."

"I didn't say wrong, only horrible."

They were silent for a moment, four children contemplating the murders of two hundred men. Except they wouldn't all be men; many (perhaps even most) would be boys roughly their own ages.

At last she said, "Those not caught in your rockslide will only ride back out of the canyon again."

"No, they won't." Alain had seen the lay of the land and now understood the matter almost completely. Roland was nodding, and there was a trace of a smile on his mouth.

"Why not?"

"The brush at the front of the canyon. We're going to set it on fire, aren't we, Roland? And if the prevailing winds are prevailing that day . . . the smoke . . ."

"It'll drive them the rest of the way in," Roland agreed. "Into the thinny."

"How will you set the brush-pile alight?" Susan asked. "I know it's dry, but surely you won't have time to use a sulfur match or your flint and steel."

"You can help us there," Roland said, "just as you can help us set the tankers alight. We can't count on touching off the oil with just our guns, you know; crude oil is a lot less volatile than people might think. And Sheemie's going to help you, I hope."

"Tell me what you want."

6

They talked another twenty minutes, refining the plan surprisingly little—all of them seemed to understand that if they planned too much and things changed suddenly, they might freeze. *Ka* had swept them into this; it was perhaps best that they count on *ka*—and their own courage—to sweep them back out again.

Cuthbert was reluctant to involve Sheemie, but finally went along—the boy's part would be minimal, if not exactly low-risk, and Roland agreed that they could take him with them when they left Mejis for good. A party of five was as fine as a party of four, he said.

"All right," Cuthbert said at last, then turned to Susan. "It ought to be you or me who talks to him."

"I will."

"Make sure he understands not to tell Coral Thorin so much as a word," Cuthbert said. "It isn't that the Mayor's her brother; I just don't trust that bitch."

"I can give ye a better reason than Hart not to trust her," Susan said. "My aunt says she's taken up with Eldred Jonas. Poor Aunt Cord! She's had the worst summer of her life. Nor will the fall be much better, I wot. Folk will call her the aunt of a traitor."

"Some will know better," Alain said. "Some always do."

"Mayhap, but my Aunt Cordelia's the sort of woman who never hears good gossip. No more does she speak it. She fancied Jonas herself, ye ken."

Cuthbert was thunderstruck. "Fancied Jonas! By all the fiddling gods! Can you imagine it! Why, if they hung folk for bad taste in love, your auntie would go early, wouldn't she?"

Susan giggled, hugged her knees, and nodded.

"It's time we left," Roland said. "If something chances that Susan needs to know right away, we'll use the red stone in the rock wall at Green Heart."

"Good," Cuthbert said. "Let's get out of here. The cold in this place eats into the bones."

Roland stirred, stretching life back into his legs. "The important thing is that they've decided to leave us free while they round up and run. That's our edge, and it's a good one. And now—"

Alain's quiet voice stopped him. "There's another matter. Very important."

Roland sank back down on his hunkers, looking at Alain curiously.

"The witch."

Susan started, but Roland only barked an impatient laugh. "She doesn't figure in our business, Al—I can't see how she could. I don't believe she's a part of Jonas's conspiracy—"

"Neither do I," Alain said.

"—and Cuthbert and I persuaded her to keep her mouth shut about Susan and me. If we hadn't, her aunt would have raised the roof by now."

"But don't you see?" Alain asked. "Who Rhea might have told isn't really the question. The question is *how she knew in the first place.*"

"It's pink," Susan said abruptly. Her hand was on her

hair, fingers touching the place where the cut ends had begun to grow out.

"What's pink?" Alain asked.

"The moon," she said, and then shook her head. "I don't know. I don't know what I'm talking about. Brainless as Pinch and Jilly, I am . . . Roland? What's wrong? What ails thee?"

For Roland was no longer hunkering; he had collapsed into a loose sitting position on the petal-strewn stone floor. He looked like a young man trying not to faint. Outside the mausoleum there was a bony rattle of fall leaves and the cry of a nightjar.

"Dear gods," he said in a low voice. "It can't be. *It can't be true.*" His eyes met Cuthbert's.

All the humor had washed out of the latter young man's face, leaving a ruthless and calculating bedrock his own mother might not have recognized . . . or might not have wanted to.

"Pink," Cuthbert said. "Isn't that interesting—the same word your father happened to mention just before we left, Roland, wasn't it? He warned us about the pink one. We thought it was a joke. *Almost.*"

"Oh!" Alain's eyes flew wide open. "Oh, *fuck!*" he blurted. He realized what he had said while sitting leg-to-leg with his best friend's lover and clapped his hands over his mouth. His cheeks flamed red.

Susan barely noticed. She was staring at Roland in growing fear and confusion. "What?" she asked. "What is it ye know? Tell me! *Tell me!*"

"I'd like to hypnotize you again, as I did that day in the willow grove," Roland said. "I want to do it right now, before we talk of this more and drag mud across what you remember."

Roland had reached into his pocket while she was speaking. Now he took out a shell, and it began to dance across the back of his hand once more. Her eyes went to it at once, like steel drawn to a magnet.

"May I?" he asked. "By your leave, dear."

"Aye, as ye will." Her eyes were widening and growing glassy. "I don't know why ye think this time should be any different, but . . ." She stopped talking, her eyes continuing to follow the dance of the shell across Roland's hand. When he stopped moving it and clasped it in his fist, her eyes closed. Her breath was soft and regular.

"Gods, she went like a stone," Cuthbert whispered, amazed.

"She's been hypnotized before. By Rhea, I think." Roland paused. Then: "Susan, do you hear me?"

"Aye, Roland, I hear ye very well."

"I want you to hear another voice, too."

"Whose?"

Roland beckoned to Alain. If anyone could break through the block in Susan's mind (or find a way around it), it would be him.

"Mine, Susan," Alain said, coming to Roland's side. "Do you know it?"

She smiled with her eyes closed. "Aye, you're Alain. Richard Stockworth that was."

"That's right." He looked at Roland with nervous, questioning eyes—*What shall I ask her?*—but for a moment Roland didn't reply. He was in two other places, both at the same time, and hearing two different voices.

Susan, by the stream in the willow grove: *She says, "Aye, lovely, just so, it's a good girl y'are," then everything's pink.*

His father, in the yard behind the Great Hall: *It's the grapefruit. By which I mean it's the pink one.*

The pink one.

7

Their horses were saddled and loaded; the three boys stood before them, outwardly stolid, inwardly feverish to be gone. The road, and the mysteries that lie along it, calls out to none as it calls to the young.

They were in the courtyard which lay east of the Great Hall, not far from where Roland had bested Cort, setting all these things in motion. It was early morning, the sun not yet risen, the mist lying over the green fields in gray ribbons. At a distance of about twenty paces, Cuthbert's and Alain's fathers stood sentry with their legs apart and their hands on the butts of their guns. It was unlikely that Marten (who had for the time being absented himself from the palace, and, so far as any knew, from Gilead itself) would mount any sort of attack on them—not here—but it wasn't entirely out of the question, either.

So it was that only Roland's father spoke to them as they mounted up to begin their ride east to Mejis and the Outer Arc.

"One last thing," he said as they adjusted their saddle girths. "I doubt you'll see anything that touches on our interests—not in Mejis—but I'd have you keep an eye out for a color of the rainbow. The Wizard's Rainbow, that is." He chuckled, then added: "It's the grapefruit. By which I mean it's the pink one."

"Wizard's Rainbow is just a fairy-tale," Cuthbert said, smiling in response to Steven's smile. Then—perhaps it was something in Steven Deschain's eyes—Cuthbert's smile faltered. "Isn't it?"

"Not all the old stories are true, but I think that of Maerlyn's Rainbow is," Steven replied. "It's said that once there were thirteen glass balls in it—one for each of the Twelve Guardians, and one representing the nexus-point of the Beams."

"One for the Tower," Roland said in a low voice, feeling gooseflesh. "One for the Dark Tower."

"Aye, Thirteen it was called when I was a boy. We'd tell stories about the black ball around the fire sometimes, and scare ourselves silly . . . unless our fathers caught us at it. My own da said it wasn't wise to talk about Thirteen, for it might hear its name called and roll your way. But Black Thirteen doesn't matter to you three . . . not now, at least. No, it's the pink one. Maerlyn's Grapefruit."

It was impossible to tell how serious he was . . . or if he was serious at all.

"If the other balls in the Wizard's Rainbow *did* exist, most are broken now. Such things never stay in one place or one pair of hands for long, you know, and even enchanted glass has a way of breaking. Yet at least three or four bends o' the Rainbow may still be rolling around this sad world of ours. The blue, almost certainly. A desert tribe of slow mutants—the Total Hogs, they called themselves—had that one less than fifty years ago, although it's slipped from sight again since. The green and the orange are reputed to be in Lud and Dis, respectively. And, just maybe, the pink one."

"What exactly do they do?" Roland asked. "What are they good for?"

"For seeing. Some colors of the Wizard's Rainbow are reputed to look into the future. Others look into the other worlds—those where the demons live, those where the Old People are supposed to have gone when they left our world. These may also show the location of the secret doors which pass between the worlds. Other colors, they say, can look far in our own world, and see things people would as soon keep secret. They never see the good; only the ill. How much of this is true and how much is myth no one knows for sure."

He looked at them, his smile fading.

"But this we do know: John Farson is said to have a talisman, something that glows in his tent late at night . . . sometimes before battles, sometimes before large movements of troop and horse, sometimes before momentous decisions are announced. And it glows pink."

"Maybe he has an electric light and puts a pink scarf over it when he prays," Cuthbert said. He looked around at his friends, a little defensively. "I'm not joking; there are people who do that."

"Perhaps," Roland's father said. "Perhaps that's all it is, or something like. But perhaps it's a good deal more. All I can say of my own knowledge is that he keeps beating us, he keeps slipping away from us, and he keeps turning up where he's least expected. If the magic is in him and not in some talisman he owns, gods help the Affiliation."

"We'll keep an eye out, if you like," Roland said, "but Farson's in the north or west. We're going east." As if his father did not know this.

"If it's a bend o' the Rainbow," Steven replied, "it could be anywhere—east or south's as likely as west. He can't keep it with him all the time, you see. No matter how much it would ease his mind and heart to do so. No one can."

"Why not?"

"Because they're alive, and hungry," Steven said. "One begins using em; one ends being used *by* em. If Farson has a piece of the Rainbow, he'll send it away and call it back only when he needs it. He understands the risk of losing it, but he also understands the risk of keeping it too long."

There was a question which the other two, constrained by politeness, couldn't ask. Roland could, and did. "You *are* serious about this, Dad? It's not just a leg-pull, is it?"

"I'm sending you away at an age when many boys still don't sleep well if their mothers don't kiss them good-night," Steven said. "I expect to see all three of you again, alive and well—Mejis is a lovely, quiet place, or was when I was a boy—but I can't be sure of it. As things are these days, no one can be sure of anything. I wouldn't send you away with a joke and a laugh. I'm surprised you think it."

"Cry your pardon," Roland said. An uneasy peace had descended between him and his father, and he would not rupture it. Still, he was wild to be off. Rusher jigged beneath him, as if seconding that.

"I don't expect you boys to see Maerlyn's glass . . . but I didn't expect to be seeing you off at fourteen with revolvers tucked in your bedrolls, either. *Ka's* at work here, and where *ka* works, anything is possible."

Slowly, slowly, Steven took off his hat, stepped back, and swept them a bow. "Go in peace, boys. And return in health."

"Long days and pleasant nights, sai," Alain said.

"Good fortune," Cuthbert said.

"I love you," Roland said.

Steven nodded. "Thankee-sai—I love you, too. My blessings, boys." He said this last in a loud voice, and the other two men—Robert Allgood and Christopher Johns, who had been known in the days of his savage youth as Burning Chris—added their own blessings.

So the three of them rode toward their end of the Great Road, while summer lay all about them, breath-less as a gasp. Roland looked up and saw something that made him forget all about the Wizard's Rainbow. It was his mother, leaning out of her apartment's bedroom win-dow: the oval of her face surrounded by the timeless gray

stone of the castle's west wing. There were tears coursing
down her cheeks, but she smiled and lifted one hand in
a wide wave. Of the three of them, only Roland saw her.

He didn't wave back.

8

"Roland!" An elbow struck him in the ribs, hard enough
to dispel these memories, brilliant as they were, and
return him to the present. It was Cuthbert. "Do something, if you mean to! Get us out of this deadhouse
before I shiver the skin right off my bones!"

Roland put his mouth close by Alain's ear. "Be ready
to help me."

Alain nodded.

Roland turned to Susan. "After the first time we were
together *an-tet,* you went to the stream in the grove."

"Aye."

"You cut some of your hair."

"Aye." That same dreaming voice. "So I did."

"Would you have cut it all?"

"Aye, every lick and lock."

"Do you know who told you to cut it?"

A long pause. Roland was about to turn to Alain when
she said, "Rhea." Another pause. "She wanted to fiddle
me up."

"Yes, but what happened later? What happened while
you stood in the doorway?"

"Oh, and something else happened before."

"What?"

"I fetched her wood," said she, and said no more.

Roland looked at Cuthbert, who shrugged. Alain
spread his hands. Roland thought of asking the latter
boy to step forward, and judged it still wasn't quite time.

"Never mind the wood for now," he said, "or all that came before. We'll talk of that later, mayhap, but not just yet. What happened as you were leaving? What did she say to you about your hair?"

"Whispered in my ear. And she had a Jesus-man."

"Whispered what?"

"I don't know. That part is pink."

Here it was. He nodded to Alain. Alain bit his lip and stepped forward. He looked frightened, but as he took Susan's hands in his own and spoke to her, his voice was calm and soothing.

"Susan? It's Alain Johns. Do you know me?"

"Aye—Richard Stockworth that was."

"What did Rhea whisper in your ear?"

A frown, faint as a shadow on an overcast day, creased her brow. "I can't see. It's pink."

"You don't need to see," Alain said. "Seeing's not what we want right now. Close your eyes so you can't do it at all."

"They *are* closed," she said, a trifle pettishly. *She's frightened,* Roland thought. He felt an urge to tell Alain to stop, to wake her up, and restrained it.

"The ones inside," Alain said. "The ones that look out from memory. Close those, Susan. Close them for your father's sake, and tell me not what you see but what you *hear.* Tell me what she *said.*"

Chillingly, unexpectedly, the eyes in her face opened as she closed those in her mind. She stared at Roland, and through him, with the eyes of an ancient statue. Roland bit back a scream.

"You were in the doorway, Susan?" Alain asked.

"Aye. So we both were."

"Be there again."

"Aye." A dreaming voice. Faint but clear. "Even with my eyes closed I can see the moon's light. 'Tis as big as a grapefruit."

It's the grapefruit, Roland thought. *By which I mean, it's the pink one.*

"And what do you hear? What does she say?"

"No, *I* say." The faintly petulant voice of a little girl. "First *I* say, Alain. I say 'And is our business done?' and she says 'Mayhap there's one more little thing,' and then . . . then . . ."

Alain squeezed gently down on her hands, using whatever it was he had in his own, his touch, sending it into her. She tried feebly to pull back, but he wouldn't let her. "Then what? What next?"

"She has a little silver medal."

"Yes?"

"She leans close and asks if I hear her. I can smell her breath. It reeks o' garlic. And other things, even worse." Susan's face wrinkled in distaste. "I say I hear her. Now I can see. I see the medal she has."

"Very well, Susan," Alain said. "What else do you see?"

"Rhea. She looks like a skull in the moonlight. A skull with hair."

"Gods," Cuthbert muttered, and crossed his arms over his chest.

"She says I should listen. I say I will listen. She says I should obey. I say I will obey. She says 'Aye, lovely, just so, it's a good girl y'are.' She's stroking my hair. All the time. My braid." Susan raised a dreaming, drowning hand, pale in the shadows of the crypt, to her blonde hair. "And then she says there's something I'm to do when my virginity's over. 'Wait,' she says, 'until he's asleep beside ye, then cut yer hair off yer head. Every strand. Right down to yer very skull.' "

The boys looked at her in mounting horror as her voice *became* Rhea's—the growling, whining cadences of the old woman of the Cöos. Even the face—except for the coldly dreaming eyes—had become a hag's face.

" 'Cut it all, girl, every whore's strand of it, aye, and go back to him as bald as ye came from yer mother! See how he likes ye then!' "

She fell silent. Alain turned his pallid face to Roland. His lips were trembling, but still he held her hands.

"Why is the moon pink?" Roland asked. "Why is the moon pink when you try to remember?"

"It's her glam." Susan seemed almost surprised, almost gay. Confiding. "She keeps it under her bed, so she does. She doesn't know I saw it."

"Are you sure?"

"Aye," Susan said, then added simply: "She would have killed me if she knew." She giggled, shocking them all. "Rhea has the moon in a box under her bed." She lilted this in the singsong voice of a small child.

"A pink moon," Roland said.

"Aye."

"Under her bed."

"Aye." This time she did pull her hands free of Alain's. She made a circle with them in the air, and as she looked up at it, a dreadful expression of greed passed over her face like a cramp. "I should like to have it, Roland. So I should. Lovely moon! I saw it when she sent me for the wood. Through her window. She looked . . . young." Then, once again: "I sh'd like to have such a thing."

"No—you wouldn't. But it's under her bed?"

"Aye, in a magic place she makes with passes."

"She has a piece of Maeriyn's Rainbow," Cuthbert said in a wondering voice. "The old bitch has what your da told us about—no wonder she knows all she does!"

"Is there more we need?" Alain asked. "Her hands have gotten very cold. I don't like having her this deep. She's done well, but . . ."

"I think we're done."

"Shall I tell her to forget?"

Roland shook his head at once—they were *ka-tet*, for good or ill. He took hold of her fingers, and yes, they *were* cold. "Susan?"

"Aye, dear."

"I'm going to say a rhyme. When I finish, you'll remember everything, as you did before. All right?"

She smiled and closed her eyes again. "Bird and bear and hare and fish . . ."

Smiling, Roland finished, "Give my love her fondest wish."

Her eyes opened. She smiled. "You," she said again, and kissed him. "Still you, Roland. Still you, my love."

Unable to help himself, Roland put his arms around her.

Cuthbert looked away. Alain looked down at his boots and cleared his throat.

9

As they rode back toward Seafront, Susan with her arms around Roland's waist, she asked: "Will you take the glass from her?"

"Best leave it where it is for now. It was left in her safe-keeping by Jonas, on behalf of Farson, I have no doubt. It's to be sent west with the rest of the plunder; I've no doubt of that, either. We'll deal with it when we deal with the tankers and Farson's men."

"Ye'd take it with us?"

"Take it or break it. I suppose I'd rather take it back to my father, but that has its own risks. We'll have to be careful. It's a powerful glam."

"Suppose she sees our plans? Suppose she warns Jonas or Kimba Rimer?"

"If she doesn't see us coming to take away her precious toy, I don't think she'll mind our plans one way or the other. I think we've put a scare into her, and if the ball has really gotten a hold on her, watching in it's what she'll mostly want to do with her time now."

"And hold onto it. She'll want to do that, too."

"Aye."

Rusher was walking along a path through the sea-cliff woods. Through the thinning branches they could glimpse the ivied gray wall surrounding Mayor's House and hear the rhythmic roar of waves breaking on the shingle below.

"You can get in safe, Susan?"

"No fear."

"And you know what you and Sheemie are to do?"

"Aye. I feel better than I have in ages. It's as if my mind is finally clear of some old shadow."

"If so, it's Alain you have to thank. I couldn't have done it on my own."

"There's magic in his hands."

"Yes." They had reached the servants' door. Susan dismounted with fluid ease. He stepped down himself and stood beside her with an arm around her waist. She was looking up at the moon.

"Look, it's fattened enough so you can see the beginning of the Demon's face. Does thee see it?"

A blade of nose, a bone of grin. No eye yet, but yes, he saw it.

"It used to terrify me when I was little." Susan was whispering now, mindful of the house behind the wall. "I'd pull the blind when the Demon was full. I was afraid that if he could see me, he'd reach down and take me up to where he was and eat me." Her lips were trembling. "Children are silly, aren't they?"

"Sometimes." He hadn't been afraid of Demon Moon himself as a small child, but he was afraid of this one.

The future seemed so dark, and the way through to the light so slim. "I love thee, Susan. With all my heart, I do."

"I know. And I love thee." She kissed his mouth with gentle open lips. Put his hand on her breast for a moment, then kissed the warm palm. He held her, and she looked past him at the ripening moon.

"A week until the Reap," she said. "*Fin de año* is what the vaqueros and *labradoros* call it. Do they call it so in your land?"

"Near enough," Roland said. "It's called closing the year. Women go about giving preserves and kisses."

She laughed softly against his shoulder. "Perhaps I'll not find things so different, after all."

"You must save all your best kisses for me."

"I will."

"Whatever comes, we'll be together," he said, but above them, Demon Moon grinned into the starry dark above the Clean Sea, as if he knew a different future.

CHAPTER SIX

Closing the Year

I

So now comes to Mejis *fin de año,* known in toward the center of Mid-World as closing the year. It comes as it has a thousand times before . . . or ten thousand, or a hundred thousand. No one can tell for sure; the world has moved on and time has grown strange. In Mejis their saying is "Time is a face on the water."

In the fields, the last of the potatoes are being picked by men and women who wear gloves and their heaviest *serapes,* for now the wind has turned firmly, blowing east to west, blowing hard, and always there's the smell of salt in the chilly air—a smell like tears. *Los campesinos* harvest the final rows cheerfully enough, talking of the things they'll do and the capers they'll cut at Reaping Fair, but they feel all of autumn's old sadness in the wind; the going of the year. It runs away from them like water in a stream, and although none speak of it, all know it very well.

In the orchards, the last and highest of the apples are picked by laughing young men (in these not-quite-gales, the final days of picking belong only to them) who bob up and down like crow's nest lookouts. Above them, in skies which hold a brilliant, cloudless blue, squadrons of geese fly south, calling their rusty *adieux.*

The small fishing boats are pulled from the water;

their hulls are scraped and painted by singing owners who mostly work stripped to the waist in spite of the chill in the air. They sing the old songs as they work—

> *I am a man of the bright blue sea,*
> *All I see, all I see,*
> *I am a man of the Barony,*
> *All I see is mine-o!*

> *I am a man of the bright blue bay,*
> *All I say, all I say,*
> *Until my nets are full I stay*
> *All I say is fine-o!*

—and sometimes a little cask of *graf* is tossed from dock to dock. On the bay itself only the large boats now remain, pacing about the big circles which mark their dropped nets as a working dog may pace around a flock of sheep. At noon the bay is a rippling sheet of autumn fire and the men on the boats sit cross-legged, eating their lunches, and know that all they see is theirs-o . . . at least until the gray gales of autumn come swarming over the horizon, coughing out their gusts of sleet and snow.

Closing, closing the year.

Along the streets of Hambry, the Reap-lights now burn at night, and the hands of the stuffy-guys are painted red. Reap-charms hang everywhere, and although women often kiss and are kissed in the streets and in both marketplaces—often by men they do not know— sexual intercourse has come to an almost complete halt. It will resume (with a bang, you might say) on Reap-Night. There will be the usual crop of Full Earth babies the following year as a result.

On the Drop, the horses gallop wildly, as if understanding (very likely they do) that their time of freedom is coming to an end. They swoop and then stand with their faces pointing west when the wind gusts, showing their asses to winter. On the ranches, porch-nets are taken down and shutters rehung. In the huge ranch kitchens and smaller farmhouse kitchens, no one is stealing Reap-kisses, and no one is even thinking about sex. This is the time of putting up and laying by, and the kitchens fume with steam and pulse with heat from before dawn until long after dark. There is the smell of apples and beets and beans and sharproot and curing strips of meat. Women work ceaselessly all day and then sleepwalk to bed, where they lie like corpses until the next dark morning calls them back to their kitchens.

Leaves are burned in town yards, and as the week goes on and Old Demon's face shows ever more clearly, red-handed stuffy-guys are thrown on the pyres more and more frequently. In the fields, cornshocks flare like torches, and often stuffies burn with them, their red hands and white-cross eyes rippling in the heat. Men stand around these fires, not speaking, their faces solemn. No one will say what terrible old ways and unspeakable old gods are being propitiated by the burning of the stuffy-guys, but they all know well enough. From time to time one of these men will whisper two words under his breath: *charyou tree.*

They are closing, closing, closing the year.

The streets rattle with firecrackers—and sometimes with a heftier "big-bang" that makes even placid carthorses rear in their traces—and echo with the laughter of children. On the porch of the mercantile and across the street at the Travellers' Rest, kisses—sometimes humidly open and with much sweet lashing of tongues—are exchanged, but Coral Thorin's whores ("cotton-gillies" is what the airy-fairy ones like Gert Moggins like to call themselves) are bored. They will have little custom this week.

This is not Year's End, when the winterlogs will

burn and Mejis will be barn-dances from one end to the other . . . and yet it is. This is the *real* year's end, *charyou tree,* and everyone, from Stanley Ruiz standing at the bar beneath The Romp to the farthest of Fran Lengyll's *vaqueros* out on the edge of the Bad Grass, knows it. There is a kind of echo in the bright air, a yearning for other places in the blood, a loneliness in the heart that sings like the wind.

But this year there's something else, as well: a sense of wrongness that no one can quite voice. Folks who never had a nightmare in their lives will awake screaming with them during the week of *fin de año;* men who consider themselves peaceful will find themselves not only in fistfights but instigating them; discontented boys who would only have dreamed of running away in other years will this year actually do it, and most will not come back after the first night spent sleeping raw.

There is a sense—inarticulate but very much there— that things have gone amiss this season. It is the closing of the year; it is also the closing of the peace. For it is here, in the sleepy Out-World Barony of Mejis, that Mid-World's last great conflict will shortly begin; it is from here that the blood will begin to flow. In two years, no more, the world as it has been will be swept away. It starts here. From its field of roses, the Dark Tower cries out in its beast's voice. Time is a face on the water.

2

Coral Thorin was coming down the High Street from the Bayview Hotel when she spied Sheemie, leading Caprichoso and heading in the opposite direction. The boy was singing "Careless Love" in a voice both high and sweet. His progress was slow; the barrels slung over

Capi's back were half again as large as the ones he had
carried up to the Cöos not long before.

Coral hailed her boy-of-all-work cheerily enough. She
had reason to be cheery; Eldred Jonas had no use for
fin de año abstinence. And for a man with a bad leg, he
could be very inventive.

"Sheemie!" she called "Where go ye? Seafront?"

"Aye," Sheemie said. "I've got the *graf* them asked for.
All parties come Reaping Fair, aye, tons of em. Dance a
lot, get hot a lot, drink *graf* to cool off a lot! How pretty
you look, sai Thorin, cheeks all pinky-pink, so they are."

"Oh, law! How kind of you to say, Sheemie!" She
favored him with a dazzling smile. "Go on, now, you
flatterer—don't linger."

"Noey-no, off I go."

Coral stood watching after him and smiling. *Dance a
lot, get hot a lot,* Sheemie had said. About the dancing
Coral didn't know, but she was sure this year's Reaping
would be hot, all right. Very hot indeed.

3

Miguel met Sheemie at Seafront's archway, gave him the
look of lofty contempt he reserved for the lower orders,
then pulled the cork from first one barrel and then the
other. With the first, he only sniffed from the bung; at
the second, he stuck his thumb in and then sucked it
thoughtfully. With his wrinkled cheeks hollowed inward
and his toothless old mouth working, he looked like an
ancient bearded baby.

"Tasty, ain't it?" Sheemie asked. "Tasty as a pasty, ain't
it, good old Miguel, been here a thousand years?"

Miguel, still sucking his thumb, favored Sheemie with
a sour look. *"Andale. Andale, simplon."*

Sheemie led his mule around the house to the kitchen. Here the breeze off the ocean was sharp and shiversome. He waved to the women in the kitchen, but not a one waved back; likely they didn't even see him. A pot boiled on every trink of the enormous stove, and the women— working in loose long-sleeved cotton garments like shifts and wearing their hair tied up in brightly colored clouts—moved about like phantoms glimpsed in fog.

Sheemie took first one barrel from Capi's back, then the other. Grunting, he carried them to the huge oak tank by the back door. He opened the tank's lid, bent over it, and then backed away from the eye-wateringly strong smell of elderly *graf.*

"Whew!" he said, hoisting the first barrel. "Ye could get drunk just on the smell o' that lot!"

He emptied in the fresh *graf,* careful not to spill. When he was finished, the tank was pretty well topped up. That was good, for on Reaping Night, apple-beer would flow out of the kitchen taps like water.

He slipped the empty barrels into their carriers, looked into the kitchen once more to be sure he wasn't being observed (he wasn't; Coral's simple-minded tavern-boy was the last thing on anyone's minds that morning), and then led Capi not back the way they'd come but along a path which led to Seafront's storage sheds.

There were three of them in a row, each with its own red-handed stuffy-guy sitting in front. The guys appeared to be watching Sheemie, and that gave him the shivers. Then he remembered his trip to crazy old bitch-lady Rhea's house. *She* had been scary. These were just old duds stuffed full of straw.

"Susan?" he called, low. "Are ye here?"

The door of the center shed was ajar. Now it trundled open a little. "Come in!" she called, also low. "Bring the mule! Hurry!"

He led Capi into a shed which smelled of straw and
beans and tack . . . and something else. Something
sharper. *Fireworks,* he thought. *Shooting-powder, too.*

Susan, who had spent the morning enduring final fittings, was dressed in a thin silk wrapper and large leather
boots. Her hair was done up in curling papers of bright
blue and red.

Sheemie tittered. "You look quite amusing, Susan,
daughter of Pat. Quite a chuckle for me, I think."

"Yes, I'm a picture for an artist to paint, all right,"
Susan said, looking distracted. "We have to hurry. I have
twenty minutes before I'm missed. I'll be missed before,
if that randy old goat is looking for me . . . let's be quick!"

They lifted the barrels from Capi's back. Susan took
a broken horse-bit from the pocket of her wrapper and
used the sharp end to pry off one of the tops. She tossed
the bit to Sheemie, who pried off the other. The apple-
tart smell of *graf* filled the shed.

"Here!" She tossed Sheemie a soft cloth. "Dry it out
as well as you can. Doesn't have to be perfect, they're
wrapped, but it's best to be safe."

They wiped the insides of the barrels, Susan stealing nervous glances at the door every few seconds. "All
right," she said. "Good. Now . . . there's two kinds. I'm
sure they won't be missed; there's enough stuff back
there to blow up half the world." She hurried back into
the dimness of the shed, holding the hem of her wrapper up with one hand, her boots clomping. When she
came back, her arms were full of wrapped packages.

"These are the bigger ones," she said.

He stored them in one of the casks. There were a
dozen packages in all, and Sheemie could feel round
things inside, each about the size of a child's fist. Big-
bangers. By the time he had finished packing and putting the top back on the barrel, she had returned with

an armload of smaller packages. These he stored in the other barrel. They were the little 'uns, from the feel, the ones that not only banged but flashed colored fire.

She helped him resling the barrels on Capi's back, still shooting those little glances at the shed door. When the barrels were secured to Caprichoso's sides, Susan sighed with relief and brushed her sweaty forehead with the backs of her hands. "Thank the gods that part's over," she said. "Now ye know where ye're to take them?"

"Aye, Susan daughter of Pat. To the Bar K. My friend Arthur Heath will put em safe."

"And if anyone asks what ye're doing out that way?"

"Taking sweet *graf* to the In-World boys, 'cause they've decided not to come to town for the Fair . . . why won't they, Susan? Don't they like Fairs?"

"Ye'll know soon enough. Don't mind it now, Sheemie. Go on—best be on your way."

Yet he lingered.

"What?" she asked, trying not to be impatient. "Sheemie, what is it?"

"I'd like to take *a fin de año* kiss from ye, so I would." Sheemie's face had gone an alarming shade of red.

Susan laughed in spite of herself, then stood on her toes and kissed the corner of his mouth. With that, Sheemie floated out to the Bar K with his load of fire.

4

Reynolds rode out to Citgo the following day, galloping with a scarf wrapped around his face so only his eyes peered out. He would be very glad to get out of this damned place that couldn't decide if it was ranchland or seacoast. The temperature wasn't all that low, but after coming in over the water, the wind cut like a razor. Nor was that all—there was a brooding quality to Hambry and all of Mejis as the days wound down toward the Reap; a haunted feeling he didn't care for a bit. Roy felt it, too. Reynolds could see it in his eyes.

No, he'd be glad to have those three baby knights so much ash in the wind and this place just a memory.

He dismounted in the crumbling refinery parking lot, tied his horse to the bumper of a rusty old hulk with the mystery-word CHEVROLET barely readable on its tailboard, then walked toward the oilpatch. The wind blew hard, chilling him even through the ranch-style sheepskin coat he wore, and twice he had to yank his hat down around his ears to keep it from blowing off. On the whole, he was glad he couldn't see himself; he probably looked like a fucking farmer.

The place seemed fine, though . . . which was to say, deserted. The wind made a lonely soughing sound as it combed through the firs on either side of the pipe. You'd never guess that there were a dozen pairs of eyes looking out at you as you strolled.

"Hai!" he called. "Come on out here, pard, and let's have some palaver."

For a moment there was no response; then Hiram Quint of the Piano Ranch and Barkie Callahan of the Travellers' Rest came ducking their way out through the trees. *Holy shit,* Reynolds thought, somewhere between awe and amusement. *There ain't that much beef in a butcher shop.*

There was a wretched old musketoon stuck into the waistband of Quint's pants; Reynolds hadn't seen one in years. He thought that if Quint was lucky, it would only misfire when he pulled the trigger. If he was unlucky, it would blow up in his face and blind him.

"All quiet?" he asked.

Quint replied in Mejis bibble-babble. Barkie listened,

then said: "All well, sai. He say he and his men grow impatient." Smiling cheerfully, his face giving no indication of what he was saying, Barkie added: "If brains was blackpowder, this ijit couldn't blow his nose."

"But he's a trustworthy idiot?"

Barkie shrugged. It might have been assent.

They went through the trees. Where Roland and Susan had seen almost thirty tankers, there were now only half a dozen, and of those six, only two actually had oil in them. Men sat on the ground or snoozed with their *sombreros* over their faces. Most had guns that looked about as trustworthy as the one in Quint's waistband. A few of the poorer *vaqs* had *bolas*. On the whole, Reynolds guessed they would be more effective.

"Tell Lord Perth here that if the boys come, it's got to be an ambush, and they'll only have one chance to do the job right," Reynolds said to Barkie.

Barkie spoke to Quint. Quint's lips parted in a grin, revealing a scarifying picket of black and yellow fangs. He spoke briefly, then put his hands out in front of them and closed them into huge, scarred fists, one above the other, as if wringing the neck of an invisible enemy. When Barkie began to translate, Clay Reynolds waved it away. He had caught only one word, but it was enough: *muerto*.

5

All that pre-Fair week, Rhea sat in front of the glass, peering into its depths. She had taken time to sew Ermot's head back onto his body with clumsy stitches of black thread, and she sat with the decaying snake around her neck as she watched and dreamed, not noticing the stench that began to arise from the reptile as time passed. Twice Musty came nigh, mewing for food, and each time Rhea batted the troublesome thing away without so much as a glance. She herself grew more and more gaunt, her eyes now looking like the sockets of the skulls stored in the net by the door to her bedroom. She dozed occasionally as she sat with the ball in her lap and the stinking snakeskin looped about her throat, her head down, the sharp point of her chin digging at her chest, runners of drool hanging from the loose puckers of her lips, but she never really slept. There was too much to see, far too much to see.

And it was hers for the seeing. These days she didn't even have to pass her hands above the glass to open its pink mists. All the Barony's meanness, all its petty (and not so petty) cruelties, all its cozening and lying lay before her. Most of what she saw was small and demeaning stuff—masturbating boys peeking through knotholes at their undressed sisters, wives going through husbands' pockets, looking for extra money or tobacco, Sheb the piano-player licking the seat of the chair where his favorite whore had sat for awhile, a maid at Seafront spitting into Kimba Rimer's pillowcase after the Chancellor had kicked her for being slow in getting out of his way.

These were all things which confirmed her opinion of the society she had left behind. Sometimes she laughed wildly; sometimes she spoke to the people she saw in the glass ball, as if they could hear her. By the third day of the week before Reaping, she had ceased her trips to the privy, even though she could carry the ball with her when she went, and the sour stench of urine began to rise from her.

By the fourth day, Musty had ceased coming near her.

Rhea dreamed in the ball and lost herself in her dreams, as others had done before her; deep in the petty pleasures of far-seeing, she was unaware that the pink ball was stealing the wrinkled remains of her *anima*. She likely would have considered it a fair trade if she had known. She saw all the things people did in the shadows, and they were the only things she cared for, and for them she almost certainly would have considered her life's force a fair trade.

6

"Here," the boy said, "let *me* light it, gods damn you." Jonas would have recognized the speaker; he was the lad who had waved a severed dog's tail across the street at Jonas and called, *We're Big Coffin Hunters just like you!*

The boy to whom this charming child had spoken tried to hold onto the piece of liver they had copped from the knacker's behind the Low Market. The first boy seized his ear and twisted. The second boy howled and held the chunk of liver out, dark blood running down his grimy knuckles as he did.

"That's better," the first boy said, taking it. "You want to remember who the *capataz* is, round here."

They were behind a bakery stall in the Low Market. Nearby, drawn by the smell of hot fresh bread, was a mangy mutt with one blind eye. He stared at them with hungry hope.

There was a slit in the chunk of raw meat. Poking out of it was a green big-bang fuse. Below the fuse, the liver bulged like the stomach of a pregnant woman. The first boy took a sulfur match, stuck it between his protruding front teeth, and lit it.

"He won't never!" said a third boy, in an agony of hope and anticipation.

"Thin as he is?" the first boy said. "Oh yes he will. Bet ye my deck of cards against yer hosstail."

The third boy thought it over and shook his head.

The first boy grinned. "It's a wise child ye are," he said, and lit the big-bang's fuse. "Hey, cully!" he called to the dog. "Want a bite o' sumpin good? Here ye go!"

He threw the chunk of raw liver. The scrawny dog never hesitated at the hissing fuse, but lunged forward with its one good eye fixed on the first decent food it had seen in days. As it snatched the liver out of the air, the big-bang the boys had slipped into it went off. There was a roar and a flash. The dog's head disintegrated from the jaws down. For a moment it continued to stand there, dripping, staring at them with its one good eye, and then it collapsed.

"Toadjer!" the first boy jeered. "Toadjer he'd take it! Happy Reap to us, eh?"

"What are you boys doing?" a woman's voice called sharply. "Get out of there, ye ravens!"

The boys fled, cackling, into the bright afternoon. They did sound like ravens.

7

Cuthbert and Alain sat their horses at the mouth of Eyebolt. Even with the wind blowing the sound of the thinny away from them, it got inside your head and buzzed there, rattling your teeth.

"I hate it," Cuthbert said through clenched teeth. "Gods, let's be quick."

"Aye," Alain said. They dismounted, bulky in their ranch-coats, and tied their horses to the brush which lay across the front of the canyon. Ordinarily, tethering wouldn't have been necessary, but both boys could see the horses hated the whining, grinding sound as much as they did. Cuthbert seemed to hear the thinny in his mind, speaking words of invitation in a groaning, horribly persuasive voice.

Come on, Bert. Leave all this foolishness behind: the drums, the pride, the fear of death, the loneliness you laugh at because laughing's all you can think to do. And the girl, leave her, too. You love her, don't you? And even if you don't, you want her. It's sad that she loves your friend instead of you, but if you come to me, all that will stop bothering you very soon. So come on. What are you waiting for?

"What am I waiting for?" he muttered.

"Huh?"

"I said, what are we waiting for? Let's get this done and get the holy hell out of here."

From their saddlebags they each took a small cotton bag. These contained gunpowder extracted from the smaller firecrackers Sheemie had brought them two days before. Alain dropped to his knees, pulled his knife, and began to crawl backward, digging a trench as far under the roll of brush as he could.

"Dig it deep," Cuthbert said. "We don't want the wind to blow it away."

Alain gave him a look which was remarkably hot. "Do you want to do it? Just so you can make sure it's done right?"

It's the thinny, Cuthbert thought. *It's working on him, too.*

"No, Al," he said humbly. "You're doing fine for someone who's both blind and soft in the head. Go on."

Alain looked at him fiercely a moment longer, then grinned and resumed the trench under the brush. "You'll die young, Bert."

"Aye, likely." Cuthbert dropped to his own knees and began to crawl after Alain, sprinkling gunpowder into the trench and trying to ignore the buzzy, cajoling voice of the thinny. No, the gunpowder probably wouldn't blow away, not unless there was a full gale. But if it rained, even the rolls of brush wouldn't be much protection. If it rained—

Don't think of that, he told himself. *That's* ka.

They finished loading gunpowder trenches under both sides of the brush barrier in only ten minutes, but it felt longer. To the horses as well, it seemed; they were stamping impatiently at the far end of their tethers, their ears laid back and their eyes rolling. Cuthbert and Alain untied them and mounted up. Cuthbert's horse actually bucked twice . . . except it felt more to Cuthbert as if the poor old thing were shuddering.

In the middle distance, bright sunshine twanged off bright steel. The tankers at Hanging Rock. They had been pulled in as tight to the sandstone outcrop as possible, but when the sun was high, most of the shadow disappeared, and concealment disappeared with it.

"I really can't believe it," Alain said as they started back. It would be a long ride, including a wide swing around Hanging Rock to make sure they weren't seen. "They must think we're blind."

"It's stupid they think we are," Cuthbert said, "but I suppose it comes to the same." Now that Eyebolt Canyon was falling behind them, he felt almost giddy with relief. Were they going in there a few days from now? Actually *going in,* riding to within mere yards of where that cursed puddle started? He couldn't believe it . . . and he made himself stop thinking about it before he could *start* believing it.

"More riders heading out to Hanging Rock," Alain said, pointing back toward the woods beyond the canyon. "Do you see them?"

They were small as ants from this distance, but Bert saw them very well. "Changing the guard. The important thing is that they don't see us—you don't think they can, do you?"

"Over here? Not likely."

Cuthbert didn't think so, either.

"They'll *all* be down come Reap, won't they?" Alain asked. "It won't do us much good to only catch a few."

"Yes—I'm pretty sure they all will."

"Jonas and his pals?"

"Them, too."

Ahead of them, the Bad Grass grew closer. The wind blew hard in their faces, making their eyes water, but Cuthbert didn't mind. The sound of the thinny was down to a faint drone behind him, and would soon be gone completely. Right now that was all he needed to make him happy.

"Do you think we'll get away with it, Bert?"

"Dunno," Cuthbert said. Then he thought of the gunpowder trenches lying beneath the dry rolls of brush, and grinned. "But I'll tell you one thing, Al: they'll know we were here."

8

In Mejis, as in every other Barony of Mid-World, the week before a Fair-Day was a political week. Important people came in from the farther corners of the Barony, and there were a good many Conversationals leading up to the main Conversational on Reaping Day. Susan was expected to be present at these—mostly as a decorative testimony to the Mayor's continuing puissance. Olive was also present, and, in a cruelly comic dumbshow that only the women truly appreciated, they sat on either side of the aging cockatoo, Susan pouring the coffee, Olive passing the cake, both of them gracefully accepting compliments on food and drink they'd had no hand in preparing.

Susan found it almost impossible to look at Olive's smiling, unhappy face. Her husband would never lie with Pat Delgado's daughter . . . but sai Thorin didn't know that, and Susan couldn't tell her. She had only to glimpse the Mayor's wife from the corner of her eye to remember what Roland had said that day on the Drop: *For a moment I thought she was my mother.* But that was the problem, wasn't it? Olive Thorin was nobody's mother. That was what had opened the door to this horrible situation in the first place.

There had been something much on Susan's mind to do, but with the round of activities at Mayor's House, it was but three days to Reaping before she got the chance. Finally, following this latest Conversational, she was able to slip out of Pink Dress with Appliqué (how she hated it! how she hated them all!) and jump back into jeans, a plain riding shirt, and a ranch-coat. There was no time to braid her hair, as she was expected back for Mayor's Tea, but Maria tied it back for her and off she had gone to the house she would shortly be leaving forever.

Her business was in the back room of the stable—the room her father had used as an office—but she went into the house first and heard what she'd hoped to hear: her aunt's ladylike, whistling snores. Lovely.

Susan got a slice of bread and honey and took it out to the barn-stable, protecting it as best she could from the clouds of dust that blew across the yard in the wind. Her aunt's stuffy-guy rattled on his post in the garden.

She ducked into the sweet-smelling shadows of the barn. Pylon and Felicia nickered hello, and she divided what she hadn't eaten between them. They seemed pleased enough to get it. She made especially of Felicia, whom she would soon be leaving behind.

She had avoided the little office since her father died, afraid of exactly the sort of pang that struck her when she lifted the latch and went in. The narrow windows were now covered with cobwebs, but they still let in autumn's bright light, more than enough for her to be able to see the pipe in the ashtray—the red one, his favorite, the one he called his thinking-pipe—and a bit of tack laid over the back of his desk chair. He had probably been mending it by gaslight, had put it by thinking to finish the next day . . . then the snake had done its dance under Foam's hoofs and there had never been a next day. Not for Pat Delgado.

"Oh, Da," she said in a small and broken voice. "How I do miss thee."

She crossed to the desk and ran her fingers along its surface, leaving trails of dust. She sat down in his chair, listened to it creak under her as it had always creaked under him, and that pushed her over the edge. For the next five minutes she sat there and wept, screwing her fists into her eyes as she had as a wee shim. Only now, of course, there was no Big Pat to come upon her and jolly her out of it, taking her on his lap and kissing her in that sensitive place under her chin (especially sensitive to the bristles on his upper lip, it had been) until her tears turned to giggles. Time was a face on the water, and this time it was the face of her father.

At last her tears tapered to sniffles. She opened the desk drawers, one after another, finding more pipes (many rendered useless by his constant stem-chewing), a hat, one of her own dolls (it had a broken arm Pat had apparently never gotten around to putting right), quill-pens, a little flask—empty but with a faint smell of whiskey still present around its neck. The only item of interest was in the bottom drawer: a pair of spurs. One still had its star rowel, but the other had been broken off. These were, she was almost positive, the spurs he had been wearing on the day he died.

If my da was here, she had begun that day on the Drop. *But he's not,* Roland had said. *He's dead.*

A pair of spurs, a broken-off rowel.

She bounced them in her hand, in her mind's eye seeing Ocean Foam rear, spilling her father (one spur catches in a stirrup; the rowel breaks free), then stumbling sideways and falling atop him. She saw this clearly, but she didn't see the snake Fran Lengyll had told them about. That she didn't see at all.

She put the spurs back where she had found them, got up, and looked at the shelf to the right of the desk, handy to Pat Delgado's smart hand. Here was a line of leather-bound ledgers, a priceless trove of books in a society that had forgotten how to make paper. Her father had been the man in charge of the Barony's horse for almost thirty years, and here were his stockline books to prove it.

Susan took down the last one and began to page through it. This time she almost welcomed the pang that struck her as she saw her father's familiar hand—the labored script, the steep and somehow more confident numbers.

Born of HENRIETTA, (2) foals both well Stillborn
of DELIA, a roan (MUTANT) Born of YOLANDA,
a THOROUGHBRED, a GOOD MALE COLT

And, following each, the date. So neat, he had been. So thorough. So . . .

She stopped suddenly, aware that she had found what she was looking for even without any clear knowledge of what she was doing in here. The last dozen pages of her da's final stockline book had been torn out.

Who had done it? Not her father; a largely self-taught man, he revered paper the way some people revered gods or gold.

And why had it been done?

That she thought she knew: horses, of courses. There were too many on the Drop. And the ranchers—Lengyll, Croydon, Renfrew—were lying about the threaded quality of the stockline. So was Henry Wertner, the man who had succeeded to her father's job.

If my da was here—

But he's not. He's dead.

She had told Roland she couldn't believe Fran Lengyll would lie about her father's death . . . but she could believe it now.

Gods help her, she could believe it now.

"What are ye doing in here?"

She gave a little scream, dropped the book, and whirled around. Cordelia stood there in one of her rusty black dresses. The top three buttons were undone, and Susan could see her aunt's collarbones sticking out above the plain white cotton of her shift. It was only on seeing those protruding bones that Susan realized how much weight Aunt Cord had lost over the last three months or so. She could see the red imprint of the pillow on her aunt's left cheek, like the mark of a slap. Her eyes glittered from dark, bruised-looking hollows of flesh.

"Aunt Cord! You startled me! You—"

"What are ye doing in here?" Aunt Cord repeated.

Susan bent and picked up the book. "I came to remember my father," she said, and put the book back on the shelf. Who had torn those pages out? Lengyll? Rimer? She doubted it. She thought it more likely that the woman standing before her right now had done it. Perhaps for as little as a single piece of red gold. *Nothing asked, nothing told, so all is well,* she would have thought, popping the coin into her moneybox, after first biting its edge to make sure it was true.

"Remember him? It's ask his forgiveness, ye should

do. For ye've forgotten his face, so ye have. Most griev-
ous have ye forgotten it, Sue."

Susan only looked at her.

"Have ye been with *him* today?" Cordelia asked in a brit-
tle, laughing voice. Her hand went to the red pillow-mark
on her cheek and began rubbing it. She had been getting
bad by degrees, Susan realized, but had become ever so
much worse since the gossip about Jonas and Coral Thorin
had started. "Have ye been with sai Dearborn? Is yer crack
still dewy from his spend? Here, let me see for myself!"

Her aunt glided forward—spectral in her black dress,
her bodice open, her slippered feet peeping—and
Susan pushed her back. In her fright and disgust, she
pushed hard. Cordelia struck the wall beside the cob-
webbed window.

"Ye should ask forgiveness yerself," Susan said. "To
speak to his daughter so in this place. *In this place.*" She
let her eyes turn to the shelf of ledgers, then return to
her aunt. The look of frightened calculation she saw
on Cordelia Delgado's face told her all she wanted or
needed to know. She hadn't been a party to her brother's murder, that Susan could not believe, but she had
known something of it. Yes, something.

"Ye faithless bitch," Cordelia whispered.

"No," Susan said, "I have been true."

And so, she realized, she had been. A great weight
seemed to slip off her shoulders at the thought. She
walked to the door of the office and turned back to her
aunt. "I've slept my last night here," she said. "I'll not listen to more such as this. Nor look at ye as ye are now. It
hurts my heart and steals the love I've kept for ye since
I was little, when ye did the best ye could to be my ma."

Cordelia clapped her hands over her face, as if looking at Susan hurt her.

"Get out, then!" she screamed. "*Go back to Seafront or*

wherever it is thee rolls with that boy! If I never see thy trollop's
face again, I'll count my life good!"

Susan led Pylon from the stable. When she got him
into the yard, she was sobbing almost too hard to mount
up. Yet mount she did, and she couldn't deny that there
was relief in her heart as well as sorrow. When she turned
onto the High Street and booted Pylon into a gallop, she
didn't look back.

9

In a dark hour of the following morning, Olive Thorin
crept from the room where she now slept to the one she
had shared for almost forty years with her husband. The
floor was cold under her bare feet and she was shivering by the time she reached the bed . . . but the chilly
floor wasn't the only reason she was shivering. She slid in
beside the gaunt, snoring man in the nightcap, and when
he turned away from her (his knees and back crackling
loudly as he did), she pressed against him and hugged
him tightly. There was no passion in this, but only a
need to share a bit of his warmth. His chest—narrow but
almost as well-known to her as her own plump one—
rose and fell under her hands, and she began to quiet
a little. He stirred, and she thought for a moment he
would wake and find her sharing his bed for the first
time in gods knew how long.

Yes, wake, she thought, *do.* She didn't dare wake him
of her own—all her courage had been exhausted just
getting here, creeping through the dark following one
of the worst dreams she had ever had in her life—but if
he woke, she would take it as a sign and tell him she had
dreamed of a vast bird, a cruel golden-eyed roc that flew
above the Barony on wings that dripped blood.

Wherever its shadow fell, there was blood, she would tell him, *and its shadow fell everywhere. The Barony ran with it, from Hambry all the way out to Eyebolt. And I smelled big fire in the wind. I ran to tell you and you were dead in your study, sitting by the hearth with your eyes gouged out and a skull in your lap.*

But instead of waking, in his sleep he took her hand, as he had used to do before he had begun to look at the young girls—even the serving-wenches—when they passed, and Olive decided she would only lie here and be still and let him hold her hand. Let it be like the old days for a bit, when everything had been right between them.

She slept a little herself. When she woke, dawn's first gray light was creeping in through the windows. He had dropped her hand—had, in fact, scooted away from her entirely, to his edge of the bed. It wouldn't do for him to wake and find her here, she decided, and the urgency of her nightmare was gone. She turned back the covers, swung her feet out, then looked at him once more. His nightcap had come askew. She put it right, her hands smoothing the cloth and the bony brow beneath. He stirred again. Olive waited until he had quieted, then got up. She slipped back to her own room like a phantom.

10

The midway booths opened in Green Heart two days before Reaping-Fair, and the first folks came to try their luck at the spinning wheel and the bottle-toss and the basket-ring. There was also a pony-train—a cart filled with laughing children, pulled along a figure-eight of narrow-gauge rails.

("Was the pony named Charlie?" Eddie Dean asked Roland.

("I think not," Roland said. "We have a rather unpleasant word that sounds like that in the High Speech."

("What word?" Jake asked.

("The one," said the gunslinger, "that means death.")

Roy Depape stood watching the pony plod its appointed rounds for a couple of turns, remembering with some nostalgia his own rides in such a cart as a child. Of course, most of his had been stolen.

When he had looked his fill, Depape sauntered on down to the Sheriff's office and went in. Herk Avery, Dave, and Frank Claypool were cleaning an odd and fantastical assortment of guns. Avery nodded at Depape and went back to what he was doing. There was something strange about the man, and after a moment or two Depape realized what it was: the Sheriff wasn't eating. It was the first time he'd ever come in here that the Sheriff didn't have a plate of grub close at hand.

"All ready for tomorrow?" Depape asked.

Avery gave him a half-irritated, half-smiling look. "What the hell kind of question is that?"

"One that Jonas sent me to ask," Depape said, and at that Avery's queer, nervy smile faltered a little.

"Aye, we're ready." Avery swept a meaty arm over the guns. "Don't ye see we are?"

Depape could have quoted the old saying about how the proof of the pudding was in the eating, but what was the point? Things would work out if the three boys were as fooled as Jonas thought they were; if they weren't fooled, they would likely carve Herk Avery's fat butt off the top of his legs and feed it to the handiest pack of wolverines. It didn't make much nevermind to Roy Depape one way or the other.

"Jonas also ast me to remind you it's early."

"Aye, aye, we'll be there early," Avery agreed. "These two and six more good men. Fran Lengyll's asked to go along, and he's got a machine-gun." Avery spoke this last with ringing pride, as if he himself had invented the machine-gun. Then he looked at Depape slyly. "What about you, coffin-hand? Want to go along? Won't take me more'n an eyeblink to deputize ye."

"I have another chore. Reynolds, too." Depape smiled. "There's plenty of work for all of us, Sheriff—after all, it's Reaping."

II

That afternoon, Susan and Roland met at the hut in the Bad Grass. She told him about the book with the torn-out pages, and Roland showed her what he'd left in the hut's north corner, secreted beneath a mouldering pile of skins.

She looked first at this, then at him with wide and frightened eyes. "What's wrong? What does thee *suspect* is wrong?"

He shook his head. *Nothing* was wrong . . . not that he could tell, anyway. And yet he had felt a strong need to do what he'd done, to leave what he'd left. It wasn't the touch, nothing like it, but only intuition.

"I think everything is all right . . . or as right as things can be when the odds may turn out fifty of them for each of us. Susan, our only chance is to take them by surprise. You're not going to risk that, are you? Not planning to go to Lengyll, waving your father's stockline book around?"

She shook her head. If Lengyll had done what she now suspected, he'd get his payback two days from now. There would be reaping, all right. Reaping aplenty. But this . . . this frightened her, and she said so.

"Listen." Roland took her face in his hands and looked into her eyes. "I'm only trying to be careful. If things go badly—and they could—you're the one most likely to get away clean. You and Sheemie. If that happens, Susan, you—*thee*—must come here and take my guns. Take them west to Gilead. Find my father. He'll know thee are who thee says by what thee shows. Tell him what happened here. That's all."

"If anything happens to thee, Roland, I won't be able to do anything. Except die."

His hands were still on her face. Now he used them to make her head shake slowly, from side to side. "You won't die," he said. There was a coldness in his voice and eyes that struck her not with fear but awe. She thought of his blood—of how old it must be, and how cold it must sometimes flow. "Not with this job undone. Promise me."

"I . . . I promise, Roland. I do."

"Tell me aloud what you promise."

"I'll come here. Get yer guns. Take them to yer da. Tell him what happened."

He nodded and let go of her face. The shapes of his hands were printed faintly on her cheeks.

"Ye frightened me," Susan said, and then shook her head. That wasn't right. "Ye *do* frighten me."

"I can't help what I am."

"And I wouldn't change it." She kissed his left cheek, his right cheek, his mouth. She put her hand inside his shirt and caressed his nipple. It grew instantly hard beneath the tip of her finger. "Bird and bear and hare and fish," she said, now making soft butterfly kisses all over his face. "Give your love her fondest wish."

After, they lay beneath a bearskin Roland had brought along and listened to the wind sough through the grass.

"I love that sound," she said. "It always makes me wish I could be part of the wind . . . go where it goes, see what it sees."

"This year, if *ka* allows, you will."

"Aye. And with thee." She turned to him, up on one elbow. Light fell through the ruined roof and dappled her face. "Roland, I love thee." She kissed him . . . and then began to cry.

He held her, concerned. "What is it? Sue, what troubles thee?"

"I don't know," she said, crying harder. "All I know is that there's a shadow on my heart." She looked at him with tears still flowing from her eyes. "Thee'd not leave me, would ye, dear? Thee'd not go without Sue, would ye?"

"No."

"For I've given all I have to ye, so I have. And my virginity's the very least of it, thee knows."

"I'd never leave you." But he felt cold in spite of the bearskin, and the wind outside—so comforting a moment ago—sounded like beast's breath. "Never, I swear."

"I'm frightened, though. Indeed I am."

"You needn't be," he said, speaking slowly and carefully . . . for suddenly all the wrong words wanted to come tumbling out of his mouth. *We'll leave this, Susan—not day after tomorrow, on Reaping, but now, this minute. Dress and we'll go crosswise to the wind; it's south we'll ride and never look back. We'll be—*

—haunted.

That's what they would be. Haunted by the faces of Alain and Cuthbert; haunted by the faces of all the men who might die in the Shavéd Mountains, massacred by weapons torn from the armory-crypts where they should have been left. Haunted most of all by the faces of their fathers, for all the rest of their lives. Not even the South Pole would be far enough to escape those faces.

"All you need do day after tomorrow is claim indisposition at lunch." They had gone over all this before, but now, in his sudden, pointless fright, it was all he could think of to say. "Go to your room, then leave as you did on the night we met in the graveyard. Hide up a little. Then, when it's three o' the clock, ride here, and look under the skins in yon corner. If my guns are gone—and they will be, I swear they will—then everything's all right. You'll ride to meet us. Come to the place above the canyon, the one we told you of. We'll—"

"Aye, I know all that, but something's wrong." She looked at him, touched the side of his face. "I fear for thee and me, Roland, and know not why."

"All will work out," he said. *"Ka—"*

"Speak not to me of *ka*!" she cried. "Oh please don't! *Ka* like a wind, my father said, it takes what it will and minds the plea of no man or woman. Greedy old *ka*, how I hate it!"

"Susan—"

"No, say no more." She lay back and pushed the bearskin down to her knees, exposing a body that far greater men than Hart Thorin might have given away kingdoms for. Beads of sunlight ran over her bare skin like rain. She held her arms out to him. Never had she looked more beautiful to Roland than she did then, with her hair spread about her and that haunted look on her face. He would think later: *She knew. Some part of her knew.*

"No more talking," she said. "Talking's done. If you love me, then love me."

And for the last time, Roland did. They rocked together, skin to skin and breath to breath, and outside the wind roared into the west like a tidal wave.

12

That evening, as the grinning Demon rose in the sky, Cordelia left her house and walked slowly across the lawn to her garden, detouring around the pile of leaves she had raked that afternoon. In her arms was a bundle of clothes. She dropped them in front of the pole to which her stuffy-guy was bound, then looked raptly up at the rising moon: the knowing wink of the eye, the ghoul's grin; silver as bone was that moon, a white button against violet silk.

It grinned at Cordelia; Cordelia grinned back. Finally, with the air of a woman awakening from a trance, she stepped forward and pulled the stuffy-guy off its pole. His head lolled limply against her shoulder, like the head of a man who has found himself too drunk to dance. His red hands dangled.

She stripped off the guy's clothes, uncovering a bulging, vaguely humanoid shape in a pair of her dead brother's long-handles. She took one of the things she had brought from the house and held it up to the moonlight. A red silk riding shirt, one of Mayor Thorin's presents to Miss Oh So Young and Pretty. One of those she wouldn't wear. Whore's clothes, she had called them. And what did that make Cordelia Delgado, who had taken care of her even after her bullheaded da had decided he must stand against the likes of Fran Lengyll and John Croydon? It made her a whorehouse madam, she supposed.

This thought led to an image of Eldred Jonas and Coral Thorin, naked and striving while a honky-tonk piano planked out "Red Dirt Boogie" below them, and Cordelia moaned like a dog.

She yanked the silk shirt over the stuffy's head. Next came one of Susan's split riding skirts. After the skirt, a pair of her slippers. And last, replacing the *sombrero,* one of Susan's spring bonnets.

Presto! The stuffy-guy was now a stuffy-gal.

"And caught red-handed ye are," she whispered. "I know. Oh yes, I know. I wasn't born yesterday."

She carried the stuffy from the garden to the pile of leaves on the lawn. She laid it close by the leaves, then scooped some up and pushed them into the bodice of the riding shirt, making rudimentary breasts. That done, she took a match from her pocket and struck it alight.

The wind, as if eager to cooperate, dropped. Cordelia touched the match to the dry leaves. Soon the whole pile was blazing. She picked the stuffy-gal up in her arms and stood with it in front of the fire. She didn't hear the rattling firecrackers from town, or the wheeze of the steam-organ in Green Heart, or the mariachi band playing in the Low Market; when a burning leaf rose and swirled past her hair, threatening to set it alight, she didn't seem to notice. Her eyes were wide and blank.

When the fire was at its height, she stepped to its edge and threw the stuffy on. Flame whumped up around it in bright orange gusts; sparks and burning leaves swirled skyward in a funnel.

"So let it be done!" Cordelia cried. The firelight on her face turned her tears to blood. *"Charyou tree!* Aye, just so!"

The thing in the riding clothes caught fire, its face charring, its red hands blazing, its white-cross eyes turning black. Its bonnet flared; the face began to burn.

Cordelia stood and watched, fists clenching and unclenching, heedless of the sparks that lit on her skin, heedless of the blazing leaves that swirled toward the house. Had the house caught fire, she would likely have ignored that as well.

She watched until the stuffy dressed in her niece's

clothes was nothing but ashes lying atop more ashes. Then, as slowly as a robot with rust in its works, she walked back to the house, lay down on the sofa, and slept like the dead.

13

It was three-thirty in the morning of the day before Reaping, and Stanley Ruiz thought he was finally done for the night. The last music had quit twenty minutes ago—Sheb had outlasted the mariachis by an hour or so, and now lay snoring with his face in the sawdust. Sai Thorin was upstairs, and there had been no sign of the Big Coffin Hunters; Stanley had an idea those were up to Seafront tonight. He also had an idea there was black work on offer, although he didn't know that for sure. He looked up at the glassy, two-headed gaze of The Romp. "Nor want to, old pal," he said. "All I want is about nine hours of sleep—tomorrow comes the real party, and they won't leave till dawn. So—"

A shrill scream rose from somewhere behind the building. Stanley jerked backward, thumping into the bar. Beside the piano, Sheb raised his head briefly, muttered "Wuzzat?" and dropped it back with a thump.

Stanley had absolutely no urge to investigate the source of the scream, but he supposed he would, just the same. It had sounded like that sad old bitch Pettie the Trotter. "I'd like to trot your saggy old ass right out of town," he muttered, then bent down to look under the bar. There were two stout ash-wood clubs here, The Calmer and The Killer. The Calmer was smooth burled wood, guaranteed to put out the lights for two hours any time you tapped some boisterous cull's head in the right place with it.

Stanley consulted his feelings and took the other club. It was shorter than The Calmer, wider at the top. And the business end of The Killer was studded with nails.

Stanley went down to the end of the bar, through the door, and across a dim supply-room stacked with barrels smelling of *graf* and whiskey. At the rear was a door giving on the back yard. Stanley approached it, took a deep breath, and unlocked it. He kept expecting Pettie to voice another head-bursting scream, but none came. There was only the sound of the wind.

Maybe you got lucky and she's kilt, Stanley thought. He opened the door, stepping back and raising the nail-studded club at the same time.

Pettie wasn't kilt. Dressed in a stained shift (a Pettie-skirt, one might say), the whore was standing on the path which led to the back privy, her hands clutched together above the swell of her bosom and below the drooping turkey-wattles of her neck. She was looking up at the sky.

"What is it?" Stanley asked, hurrying down to her. "Near scared ten years off my life, ye did."

"The moon, Stanley!" she whispered. "Oh, look at the moon, would ye!"

He looked up, and what he saw set his heart thumping, but he tried to speak reasonably and calmly. "Come now, Pettie, it's dust, that's all. Be reasonable, dear, ye know how the wind's blown these last few days, and no rain to knock down what it carries; it's dust, that's all."

Yet it didn't look like dust. "I know what I see," whispered Pettie. Above them, Demon Moon grinned and winked one eye through what appeared to be a shifting scrim of blood.

CHAPTER SEVEN

Taking the Ball

I

While a certain whore and certain bartender were still gaping up at the bloody moon, Kimba Rimer awoke sneezing.

Damn, a cold for Reaping, he thought. *As much as I have to be out over the next two days, I'll be lucky if it doesn't turn into—*

Something fluffed the end of his nose, and he sneezed again. Coming out of his narrow chest and dry slot of a mouth, it sounded like a small-caliber pistol-shot in the black room.

"Who's there?" he cried.

No answer. Rimer suddenly imagined a bird, something nasty and bad-tempered, that had gotten in here in daylight and was now flying around in the dark, fluttering against his face as he slept. His skin crawled—birds, bugs, bats, he hated them all—and he fumbled so energetically for the gas-lamp on the table by his bed that he almost knocked it off onto the floor.

As he drew it toward him, that flutter came again. This time puffing at his cheek. Rimer screamed and recoiled against the pillows, clutching the lamp to his chest. He turned the switch on the side, heard the hiss of gas, then pushed the spark. The lamp lit, and in the

625

thin circle of its radiance, he saw not a fluttering bird but Clay Reynolds sitting on the edge of the bed. In one hand Reynolds held the feather with which he had been tickling Mejis's Chancellor. His other was hidden in his cloak, which lay in his lap.

Reynolds had disliked Rimer from their first meeting in the woods far west of town—those same woods, beyond Eyebolt Canyon, where Farson's man Latigo now quartered the main contingent of his troops. It had been a windy night, and as he and the other Coffin Hunters entered the little glade where Rimer, accompanied by Lengyll and Croydon, were sitting by a small fire, Reynolds's cloak swirled around him. "*Sai Manto,*" Rimer had said, and the other two had laughed. It had been meant as a harmless joke, but it hadn't seemed harmless to Reynolds. In many of the lands where he had travelled, *manto* meant not "cloak" but "leaner" or "bender." It was, in fact, a slang term for homosexual. That Rimer (a provincial man under his veneer of cynical sophistication) didn't know this never crossed Reynolds's mind. He knew when people were making small of him, and if he could make such a person pay, he did so.

For Kimba Rimer, payday had come.

"Reynolds? What are you doing? How did you get in h—"

"You got to be thinking of the wrong cowboy," the man sitting on the bed replied. "No Reynolds here. Just *Señor Manto.*" He took out the hand which had been under his cloak. In it was a keenly honed *cuchillo.* Reynolds had purchased it in Low Market with this chore in mind. He raised it now and drove the twelve-inch blade into Rimer's chest. It went all the way through, pinning him like a bug. *A bedbug,* Reynolds thought.

The lamp fell out of Rimer's hands and rolled off the bed. It landed on the foot-runner, but did not break.

On the far wall was Kimba Rimer's distorted, struggling shadow. The shadow of the other man bent over it like a hungry vulture.

Reynolds lifted the hand which had held the knife. He turned it so the small blue tattooed coffin between thumb and forefinger was in front of Rimer's eyes. He wanted it to be the last thing Rimer saw on this side of the clearing.

"Let's hear you make fun of me now," Reynolds said. He smiled. "Come on. Let's just hear you."

2

Shortly before five o'clock, Mayor Thorin woke from a terrible dream. In it, a bird with pink eyes had been cruising slowly back and forth above the Barony. Wherever its shadow fell, the grass turned yellow, the leaves fell shocked from the trees, and the crops died. The shadow was turning his green and pleasant Barony into a waste land. *It may be my Barony, but it's my bird, too,* he thought just before awakening, huddled into a shuddery ball on one side of his bed. *My bird, I brought it here, I let it out of its cage.*

There would be no more sleep for him this night, and Thorin knew it. He poured himself a glass of water, drank it, then walked into his study, absently picking his nightgown from the cleft of his bony old ass as he went. The puff on the end of his nightcap bobbed between his shoulderblades; his knees cracked at every step.

As for the guilty feelings expressed by the dream . . . well, what was done was done. Jonas and his friends would have what they'd come for (and paid so handsomely for) in another day; a day after that, they'd be gone. Fly away, bird with the pink eyes and pestilent shadow; fly away to wherever you came from and take the Big Coffin Boys with you. He had an idea that by Year's End he'd be too busy dipping his wick to think much about such things. Or to dream such dreams.

Besides, dreams without visible sign were just dreams, not omens.

The visible sign might have been the boots beneath the study drapes—just the scuffed tips of them showing—but Thorin never looked in that direction. His eyes were fixed on the bottle beside his favorite chair. Drinking claret at five in the morning was no sort of habit to get into, but this once wouldn't hurt. He'd had a terrible dream, for gods' sake, and after all—

"Tomorrow's Reaping," he said, sitting in the wing-chair on the edge of the hearth. "I guess a man can jump a fence or two, come Reap."

He poured himself a drink, the last he'd ever take in this world, and coughed as the fire hit his belly and then climbed back up his throat, warming it. Better, aye, much. No giant birds now, no plaguey shadows. He stretched out his arms, laced his long and bony fingers together, and cracked them viciously.

"I *hate* it when you do that, you scrawny git," spoke a voice directly into Thorin's left ear.

Thorin jumped. His heart took its own tremendous leap in his chest. The empty glass flew from his hand, and there was no foot-runner to cushion its landing. It smashed on the hearth.

Before Thorin could scream, Roy Depape brushed off the mayoral nightcap, seized the gauzy remains of the mayoral mane, and yanked the mayoral head back. The knife Depape held in his other hand was much humbler than the one Reynolds had used, but it cut the old man's throat efficiently enough. Blood sprayed scarlet in the dim room. Depape let go of Thorin's hair, went back to the drapes he had been hiding behind, and picked something up off the floor. It was Cuthbert's lookout. Depape brought it back to the chair and put it in the dying Mayor's lap.

"Bird . . ." Thorin gargled through a mouthful of blood. "Bird!"

"Yar, old fella, and trig o' you to notice at a time like this, I will say." Depape pulled Thorin's head back again and took the old man's eyes out with two quick flips of his knife. One went into the dead fireplace; the other hit the wall and slid down behind the fire-tools. Thorin's right foot trembled briefly and was still.

One more job to do.

Depape looked around, saw Thorin's nightcap, and decided the ball on the end would serve. He picked it up, dipped it in the puddle of blood in the Mayor's lap, and drew the Good Man's *sigul*—

—on the wall.

"There," he murmured, standing back. "If that don't finish em, nothing on earth will."

True enough. The only question left unanswered was whether or not Roland's *ka-tet* could be taken alive.

3

Jonas had told Fran Lengyll exactly where to place his men, two inside the stable and six more out, three of these latter gents hidden behind rusty old implements, two hidden in the burnt-out remains of the home place, one—Dave Hollis—crouched on top of the stable itself, spying over the roofpeak. Lengyll was glad to see that the men in the posse took their job seriously. They were only boys, it was true, but boys who had on one occasion come off ahead of the Big Coffin Hunters.

Sheriff Avery gave a fair impression of being in charge of things until they got within a good shout of the Bar K. Then Lengyll, machine-gun slung over one shoulder (and as straight-backed in the saddle as he had been at twenty), took command. Avery, who looked nervous and sounded out of breath, seemed relieved rather than offended.

"I'll tell ye where to go as was told to me, for it's a good plan, and I've no quarrel with it," Lengyll had told his posse. In the dark, their faces were little more than dim blurs. "Only one thing I'll say to ye on my own hook. We don't need em alive, but it's best we have em so— it's the Barony we want to put paid to em, the common folk, and so put paid to this whole business, as well. Shut the door on it, if ye will. So I say this: if there's cause to shoot, shoot. But I'll flay the skin off the face of any man who shoots without cause. Do ye understand?"

No response. It seemed they did.

"All right," Lengyll had said. His face was stony. "I'll give ye a minute to make sure your gear's muffled, and then on we go. Not another word from here on out."

4

Roland, Cuthbert, and Alain came out of the bunkhouse at quarter past six that morning, and stood a-row on the porch. Alain was finishing his coffee. Cuthbert was yawning and stretching. Roland was buttoning his shirt and looking southwest, toward the Bad Grass. He was thinking not of ambushes but of Susan. Her tears. *Greedy old* ka, *how I hate it,* she had said.

His instincts did not awake; Alain's touch, which had sensed Jonas on the day Jonas had killed the pigeons, did not so much as quiver. As for Cuthbert—

"One more day of quiet!" that worthy exclaimed to the dawning sky. "One more day of grace! One more day of silence, broken only by the lover's sigh and the tattoo of horses' hoofs!"

"One more day of your bullshit," Alain said. "Come on."

They set off across the dooryard, sensing the eight pairs of eyes on them not at all. They walked into the stable past the two men flanking the door, one hidden behind an ancient harrow, the other tucked behind an untidy stack of hay, both with guns drawn.

Only Rusher sensed something was wrong. He stamped his feet, rolled his eyes, and, as Roland backed him out of his stall, tried to rear.

"Hey, boy," he said, and looked around. "Spiders, I reckon. He hates them."

Outside, Lengyll stood up and waved both hands forward.

Men moved silently toward the front of the stable. On the roof, Dave Hollis stood with his gun drawn. His monocle was tucked away in his vest pocket, so it should blink no badly timed reflection.

Cuthbert led his mount out of the stable. Alain followed. Roland came last, short-leading the nervous, prancy gelding.

"Look," Cuthbert said cheerily, still unaware of the men standing directly behind him and his friends. He was pointing north. "A cloud in the shape of a bear! Good luck for—"

"Don't move, cullies," Fran Lengyll called. "Don't so much as shuffle yer god-pounding feet."

Alain *did* begin to turn—in startlement more than anything else—and there was a ripple of small clicking sounds, like many dry twigs all snapping at once. The sound of cocking pistols and musketoons.

"No, Al!" Roland said. "Don't move! Don't!" In his throat despair rose like poison, and tears of rage stung at the corners of his eyes . . . yet he stood quiet. Cuthbert and Alain must stand quiet, too. If they moved, they'd be killed. "Don't move!" he called again. "Either of you!"

"Wise, cully." Lengyll's voice was closer now, and accompanied by several pairs of footfalls. "Put yer hands behind ye."

Two shadows flanked Roland, long in the first light. Judging by the bulk of the one on his left, he guessed it was being thrown by Sheriff Avery. He probably wouldn't be offering them any white tea this day. Lengyll would belong to the other shadow.

"Hurry up, Dearborn, or whatever yer name may be. Get em behind ye. Small of yer back. There's guns pointed at your pards, and if we end up taking in only two of yer instead of three, life'll go on."

Not taking any chances with us, Roland thought, and felt a moment of perverse pride. With it came a taste of something that was almost amusement. Bitter, though; that taste continued very bitter.

"Roland!" It was Cuthbert, and there was agony in his voice. "Roland, don't!"

But there was no choice. Roland put his hands behind his back. Rusher uttered a small, reproving whinny—as if to say all this was *highly* improper—and trotted away to stand beside the bunkhouse porch.

"You're going to feel metal on your wrists," Lengyll said. *"Esposas."*

Two cold circles slipped over Roland's hands. There was a click and suddenly the arcs of the handcuffs were tight against his wrists.

"All right," said another voice. "Now you, son."

"Be damned if I will!" Cuthbert's voice wavered on the edge of hysteria.

There was a thud and a muffled cry of pain. Roland turned around and saw Alain down on one knee, the heel of his left hand pressed against his forehead. Blood ran down his face.

"Ye want me to deal him another 'un?" Jake White asked. He had an old pistol in his hand, reversed so the butt was forward. "I can, you know; my arm is feeling wery limber for this early in the day."

"No!" Cuthbert was twitching with horror and something like grief. Ranged behind him were three armed men, looking on with nervous avidity.

"Then be a good boy an' get yer hands behind yer."

Cuthbert, still fighting tears, did as he was told. *Esposas* were put on him by Deputy Bridger. The other two men yanked Alain to his feet. He reeled a little, then stood firm as he was handcuffed. His eyes met Roland's, and Al tried to smile. In some ways it was the worst moment of that terrible ambush morning. Roland nodded back and made himself a promise: he would never be taken like this again, not if he lived to be a thousand years old.

Lengyll was wearing a trailscarf instead of a string tie this morning, but Roland thought he was inside the same box-tail coat he'd worn to the Mayor's welcoming party, all those weeks ago. Standing beside him, puffing with excitement, anxiety, and self-importance, was Sheriff Avery.

"Boys," the Sheriff said, "ye're arrested for transgressing the Barony. The specific charges are treason and murder."

"Who did we murder?" Alain asked mildly, and one of the posse uttered a laugh either shocked or cynical, Roland couldn't tell which.

"The Mayor and his Chancellor, as ye know quite well," Avery said. "Now—"

"How can you do this?" Roland asked curiously. It was Lengyll to whom he spoke. "Mejis is your home place; I've seen the line of your fathers in the town cemetery. How can you do this to your home place, sai Lengyll?"

"I've no intention of standing out here and making palaver with ye," Lengyll said. He glanced over Roland's shoulder. "Alvarez! Get his horse! Boys as trig as this bunch should have no problem riding with their hands behind their—"

"No, tell me," Roland interposed. "Don't hold back, sai Lengyll—these are your friends you've come with, and not a one who isn't inside your circle. How can you do it? Would you rape your own mother if you came upon her sleeping with her dress up?"

Lengyll's mouth twitched—not with shame or embarrassment but momentary prudish distaste, and then the old rancher looked at Avery. "They teach em to talk pretty in Gilead, don't they?"

Avery had a rifle. Now he stepped toward the handcuffed gunslinger with the butt raised. "I'll teach 'im how to talk proper to a man of the gentry, so I will! Knock the teef straight out of his head, if you say aye, Fran!"

Lengyll held him back, looking tired. "Don't be a fool. I don't want to bring him back laying over a saddle unless he's dead."

Avery lowered his gun. Lengyll turned to Roland.

"Ye're not going to live long enough to profit from advice, Dearborn," he said, "but I'll give'ee some, anyway: stick with the winners in this world. And know how the wind blows, so ye can tell when it changes direction."

"You've forgotten the face of your father, you scurrying little maggot," Cuthbert said clearly.

This got to Lengyll in a way Roland's remark about his mother had not—it showed in the sudden bloom of color in his weathered cheeks.

"Get em mounted!" he said. "I want em locked up tight within the hour!"

5

Roland was boosted into Rusher's saddle so hard he almost flew off on the other side—would have, if Dave Hollis had not been there to steady him and then to wedge Roland's boot into the stirrup. Dave offered the gunslinger a nervous, half-embarrassed smile.

"I'm sorry to see you here," Roland said gravely.

"It's sorry I am to be here," the deputy said. "If murder was your business, I wish you'd gotten to it sooner. And your friend shouldn't have been so arrogant as to leave his calling-card." He nodded toward Cuthbert.

Roland hadn't the slightest idea what Deputy Dave was referring to, but it didn't matter. It was just part of the frame, and none of these men believed much of it, Dave likely included. Although, Roland supposed, they would come to believe it in later years and tell it to their children and grandchildren as gospel. The glorious day they'd ridden with the posse and taken down the traitors.

The gunslinger used his knees to turn Rusher . . . and there, standing by the gate between the Bar K's dooryard and the lane leading to the Great Road, was Jonas himself. He sat astride a deep-chested bay, wearing a green felt drover's hat and an old gray duster. There was a rifle in the scabbard beside his right knee. The left side of the duster was pulled back to expose the butt of his revolver. Jonas's white hair, untied today, lay over his shoulders.

He doffed his hat and held it out to Roland in courtly greeting. "A good game," he said. "You played very well for someone who was taking his milk out of a tit not so long ago."

"Old man," Roland said, "you've lived too long."

Jonas smiled. "You'd remedy that if you could, wouldn't you? Yar, I reckon." He flicked his eyes at Lengyll. "Get their toys, Fran. Look specially sharp for knives. They've got guns, but not with em. Yet I know a bit more about those shooting irons than they might think. And funny boy's slingshot. Don't forget that, for gods' sake. He like to take Roy's head off with it not so long ago."

"Are you talking about the carrot-top?" Cuthbert asked. His horse was dancing under him; Bert swayed back and forth and from side to side like a circus rider to keep from tumbling off. "He never would have missed his head. His balls, maybe, but not his head."

"Probably true," Jonas agreed, watching as the spears and Roland's shortbow were taken into custody. The slingshot was on the back of Cuthbert's belt, tucked into a holster he had made for it himself. It was very well for Roy Depape that he hadn't tried Bert, Roland knew—Bert could take a bird on the wing at sixty yards. A pouch holding steel shot hung at the boy's left side. Bridger took it, as well.

While this was going on, Jonas fixed Roland with an amiable smile. "What's your real name, brat? Fess up—no harm in telling now; you're going to ride the handsome, and we both know it."

Roland said nothing. Lengyll looked at Jonas, eyebrows raised. Jonas shrugged, then jerked his head in the direction of town. Lengyll nodded and poked Roland with one hard, chapped finger. "Come on, boy. Let's ride."

Roland squeezed Rusher's sides; the horse trotted toward Jonas. And suddenly Roland knew something. As with all his best and truest intuitions, it came from nowhere and everywhere—absent at one second, all there and fully dressed at the next.

"Who sent you west, maggot?" he asked as he passed Jonas. "Couldn't have been Cort—you're too old. Was it his father?"

The look of slightly bored amusement left Jonas's face—*flew* from his face, as if slapped away. For one amazing moment the man with the white hair was a child again: shocked, shamed, and hurt.

"Yes, Cort's da—I see it in your eyes. And now you're here, on the Clean Sea . . . except you're really in the west. The soul of a man such as you can never leave the west."

Jonas's gun was out and cocked in his hand with such speed that only Roland's extraordinary eyes were capable of marking the movement. There was a murmur from the men behind them—partly shock, mostly awe.

"Jonas, don't be a fool!" Lengyll snarled. "You ain't killin em after we took the time and risk to hood em and tie their hooks, are ye?"

Jonas seemed to take no notice. His eyes were wide; the corners of his seamed mouth were trembling. "Watch your words, Will Dearborn," he said in a low, hoarse voice. "You want to watch em ever so close. I got two pounds of pressure on a three-pound trigger right this second."

"Fine, shoot me," Roland said. He lifted his head and looked down at Jonas. "Shoot, exile. Shoot, worm. Shoot, you failure. You'll still live in exile and die as you lived."

For a moment he was sure Jonas *would* shoot, and in that moment Roland felt death would be enough, an acceptable end after the shame of being caught so easily. In that moment Susan was absent from his mind. Nothing breathed in that moment, nothing called, nothing moved. The shadows of the men watching this confrontation, both on foot and on horseback, were printed depthless on the dirt.

Then Jonas dropped the hammer of his gun and slipped it back into its holster.

"Take em to town and jug em," he said to Lengyll. "And when I show up, I don't want to see one hair harmed on one head. If I could keep from killing this one, you can keep from hurting the rest. Now go on."

"Move," Lengyll said. His voice had lost some of its bluff authority. It was now the voice of a man who realizes (too late) that he has bought chips in a game where the stakes are likely much too high.

They rode. As they did, Roland turned one last time. The contempt Jonas saw in those cool young eyes stung him worse than the whips that had scarred his back in Garlan years ago.

6

When they were out of sight, Jonas went into the bunkhouse, pulled up the board which concealed their little armory, and found only two guns. The matched set of six-shooters with the dark handles—Dearborn's guns, surely—were gone.

You're in the west. The soul of a man such as you can never leave the west. You'll live in exile and die as you lived.

Jonas's hands went to work, disassembling the revolvers Cuthbert and Alain had brought west. Alain's had never even been worn, save on the practice-range. Outside, Jonas threw the pieces, scattering them every whichway. He threw as hard as he could, trying to rid himself of that cool blue gaze and the shock of hearing what he'd believed no man had known. Roy and Clay suspected, but even they hadn't known for sure.

Before the sun went down, everyone in Mejis would know that Eldred Jonas, the white-haired regulator with the tattooed coffin on his hand, was nothing but a failed gunslinger.

You'll live in exile and die as you lived.

"P'raps," he said, looking at the burned-out ranch house without really seeing it. "But I'll live longer than you, young Dearborn, and die long after your bones are rusting in the ground."

He mounted up and swung his horse around, sawing viciously at the reins. He rode for Citgo, where Roy and Clay would be waiting, and he rode hard, but Roland's eyes rode with him.

7

"Wake up! Wake up, sai! Wake up! Wake up!"

At first the words seemed to be coming from far away, drifting down by some magical means to the dark place where she lay. Even when the voice was joined by a rudely shaking hand and Susan knew she *must* wake up, it was a long, hard struggle.

It had been weeks since she'd gotten a decent night's sleep, and she had expected more of the same last night . . . *especially* last night. She had lain awake in her luxurious bedchamber at Seafront, tossing from side to side, possibilities—none good—crowding her mind. The nightgown she wore crept up to her hips and bunched at the small of her back. When she got up to use the commode, she took the hateful thing off, hurled it into a corner, and crawled back into bed naked.

Being out of the heavy silk nightgown had done the trick. She dropped off almost at once . . . and in this case, *dropped off* was exactly right: it was less like falling asleep than falling into some thoughtless, dreamless crack in the earth.

Now this intruding voice. This intruding arm, shaking her so hard that her head rolled from side to side on the pillow. Susan tried to slide away from it, pulling her knees up to her chest and mouthing fuzzy protests, but the arm followed. The shaking recommenced; the nagging, calling voice never stopped.

"Wake up, sai! Wake up! In the name of the Turtle and the Bear, wake up!"

Maria's voice. Susan hadn't recognized it at first because Maria was so upset. Susan had never heard her so, or expected to. Yet it *was* so; the maid sounded on the verge of hysteria.

Susan sat up. For a moment so much input—all of it wrong—crashed in on her that she was incapable of moving. The duvet beneath which she had slept tumbled into her lap, exposing her breasts, and she could do no more than pluck weakly at it with the tips of her fingers.

The first wrong thing was the light. It flooded through the windows more strongly than it ever had before . . . because, she realized, she had never been in this room so late before. Gods, it had to be ten o' the clock, perhaps later.

The second wrong thing was the sounds from below. Mayor's House was ordinarily a peaceful place in the morning; until noon one heard little but *casa vaqueros* leading the horses out for their morning exercise, the whicker-whicker-whick of Miguel sweeping the courtyard, and the constant boom and shush of the waves. This morning there were shouts, curses, galloping horses, the occasional burst of strange, jagged laughter. Somewhere outside her room—perhaps not in this wing, but close— Susan heard the running thud of booted feet.

The wrongest thing of all was Maria herself, cheeks ashy beneath her olive skin-tone, and her usually neat hair tangled and unbound. Susan would have guessed only an earthquake could make her look so, if that.

"Maria, what is it?"

"You have to go, sai. Seafront maybe not safe for you just now. Your own house maybe better. When I don't see you earlier, I think you gone there already. You chose a bad day to sleep late."

"Go?" Susan asked. Slowly, she pulled the duvet all the way up to her nose and stared at Maria over it with wide, puffy eyes. "What do you mean, go?"

"Out the back." Maria plucked the duvet from Susan's sleep-numbed hands again and this time stripped it all the way down to her ankles. "Like you did before. Now, missy, now! Dress and go! Those boys put away, aye, but what if they have friends? What if they come back, kill you, too?"

Susan had been getting up. Now all the strength ran out of her legs and she sat back down on the bed again. "Boys?" she whispered. "Boys kill who? *Boys kill who?*"

This was a good distance from grammatical, but Maria took her meaning.

"Dearborn and his pinboys," she said.

"Who are they supposed to have killed?"

"The Mayor and the Chancellor." She looked at Susan with a kind of distracted sympathy. "Now get up, I tell you. And get gone. This place gone *loco.*"

"They didn't do any such thing," Susan said, and only just restrained herself from adding, *It wasn't in the plan.*

"Sai Thorin and sai Rimer jus' as dead, whoever did it." There were more shouts below, and a sharp little explosion that didn't sound like a firecracker. Maria looked in that direction, then began to throw Susan her clothes. "The Mayor's eyes, they gouged right out of his head."

"They couldn't have! Maria, I know them—"

"Me, I don't know nothing about them and care less—

but I care about you. Get dressed and get out, I tell you. Quick as you can."

"What's happened to them?" A terrible thought came to Susan and she leaped to her feet, clothes falling all around her. She seized Maria by the shoulders. "They haven't been killed?" Susan shook her. "Say they haven't been killed!"

"I don't think so. There's been a t'ousan' shouts and ten t'ousan' rumors go the rounds, but I think jus' jailed. Only . . ."

There was no need for her to finish; her eyes slipped from Susan's, and that involuntary shift (along with the confused shouts from below) told all the rest. Not killed yet, but Hart Thorin had been greatly liked, and from an old family. Roland, Cuthbert, and Alain were strangers.

Not killed yet . . . but tomorrow was Reaping, and tomorrow night was Reaping Bonfire.

Susan began to dress as fast as she could.

8

Reynolds, who had been with Jonas longer than Depape, took one look at the figure cantering toward them through the skeletal oil derricks, and turned to his partner. "Don't ask him any questions—he's not in any mood for silly questions this morning."

"How do you know?"

"Never mind. Just keep your ever-fucking gob shut."

Jonas reined up before them. He sat slumped in his saddle, pale and thoughtful. His look prompted one question from Roy Depape in spite of Reynolds's caution. "Eldred, are you all right?"

"Is anyone?" Jonas responded, then fell silent again.

Behind them, Citgo's few remaining pumpers squalled tiredly.

At last Jonas roused himself and sat a little straighter in the saddle. "The cubs'll be stored supplies by now. I told Lengyll and Avery to fire a double set of pistol-shots if anything went wrong, and there hasn't been any shooting like that."

"We didn't hear none, either, Eldred," Depape said eagerly. "Nothing atall like that."

Jonas grimaced. "You wouldn't, would you? Not out in this noise. Fool!"

Depape bit his lip, saw something in the neighborhood of his left stirrup that needed adjusting, and bent to it.

"Were you boys seen at your business?" Jonas asked. "This morning, I mean, when you sent Rimer and Thorin off. Even a chance either of you was seen?"

Reynolds shook his head for both of them. " 'Twas clean as could be."

Jonas nodded as if the subject had been of only passing interest to him, then turned to regard the oilpatch and the rusty derricks. "Mayhap folks are right," he said in a voice almost too low to hear. "Mayhap the Old People *were* devils." He turned back to them. "Well, we're the devils now. Ain't we, Clay?"

"Whatever you think, Eldred," Reynolds said.

"I said what I think. *We're* the devils now, and by God, that's how we'll behave. What about Quint and that lot down there?" He cocked his head toward the forested slope where the ambush had been laid.

"Still there, pending your word," Reynolds said.

"No need of em now." He favored Reynolds with a dark look. "That Dearborn's a coozey brat. I wish I was going to be in Hambry tomorrow night just so I could lay a torch between his feet. I almost left him cold and dead at the Bar K. Would've if not for Lengyll. Coozey little brat is what he is."

Slumping as he spoke. Face growing blacker and blacker, like stormclouds drifting across the sun. Depape, his stirrup fixed, tossed Reynolds a nervous glance. Reynolds didn't answer it. What point? If Eldred went crazy now (and Reynolds had seen it happen before), there was no way they could get out of his killing-zone in time.

"Eldred, we got quite a spot more to do."

Reynolds spoke quietly, but it got through. Jonas straightened. He took off his hat, hung it on his saddle as if the horn were a coathook, and brushed absently through his hair with his fingers.

"Yar—quite a spot is right. Ride down there. Tell Quint to send for oxen to pull those last two full tankers out to Hanging Rock. He sh'd keep four men with him to hook em up and take em on to Latigo. The rest can go on ahead."

Reynolds now judged it safe to ask a question. "When do the rest of Latigo's men get there?"

"Men?" Jonas snorted. "Don't we wish, cully! The rest of Latigo's *boys'll* ride out to Hanging Rock by moonlight, pennons no doubt flying for all the coyotes and other assorted desert-dogs to see and be awed by. They'll be ready to do escort duty by ten tomorrow, I sh'd think . . . although if they're the sort of lads I'm expecting, fuck-ups are apt to be the rule of the day. The good news is that we don't much need em, anyway. Things look well in hand. Now go down there, get them about their business, and then ride back to me, just as fast's you can."

Jonas turned and looked toward the lumpy swell of hills to the northwest.

"We have business of our own," he said. "Soonest begun, boys, soonest done. I want to shake the dust of fucking Mejis off my hat and boots as soon as I can. I don't like the way it feels anymore. Not at all."

9

The woman, Theresa Maria Dolores O'Shyven, was forty years old, plump, pretty, mother of four, wife of Peter, a *vaquero* of laughing temperament. She was also a seller of rugs and draperies in the Upper Market; many of the prettier and more delicate appointments at Seafront had passed through Theresa O'Shyven's hands, and her family was quite well-to-do. Although her husband was a range-rider, the O'Shyven clan was what would have been called middle-class in another place and time. Her two oldest children were grown and gone, one right out o' Barony. The third eldest was sparking and hoping to marry his heart's delight at Year's End. Only the youngest suspected something was wrong with Ma, and this one had no idea how close Theresa was to complete obsessional madness.

Soon, Rhea thought, watching Theresa avidly in the ball. *She'll start doing it soon, but first she's got to get rid of the brat.*

There was no school at Reaptide, and the stalls opened only for a few hours in the afternoon, so Theresa sent her youngest daughter off with a pie. A Reaptide gift to a neighbor, Rhea surmised, although she couldn't hear the soundless instructions the woman gave her daughter as she pulled a knitted cap down over the girl's ears. And 'twouldn't be a neighbor too close, either; she'd want time, would Theresa Maria Dolores O'Shyven, time to be a-choring. It was a good-sized house, and there were a lot of corners in it that needed cleaning.

Rhea chuckled; the chuckle turned into a hollow

gust of coughing. In the corner, Musty looked at the old woman hauntedly. Although far from the emaciated skeleton that his mistress had become, Musty didn't look good at all.

The girl was shown out with the pie under her arm; she paused to give her mother a single troubled look, and then the door was shut in her face.

"Now!" Rhea croaked. "Them corners is waitin! Down on yer knees, woman, and get to business!"

First Theresa went to the window. When she was satisfied with what she saw—her daughter out the gate and down the High Street, likely—she turned back to her kitchen. She walked to the table and stood there, looking dreamy-eyed into space.

"No, none o' that, now!" Rhea cried impatiently. She no longer saw her own filthy hut, she no longer smelled either its rank aromas or her own. She had gone into the Wizard's Rainbow. She was with Theresa O'Shyven, whose cottage had the cleanest corners in all Mejis. Mayhap in all Mid-World.

"Hurry, woman!" Rhea half-screamed. "Get to yer housework!"

As if hearing, Theresa unbuttoned her housedress, stepped out of it, and laid it neatly over a chair. She pulled the hem of her clean, mended shift up over her knees, went to the corner, and got down on all fours.

"That's it, my *corazón!*" Rhea cried, nearly choking on a phlegmy mixture of coughing and laughter. "Do yer chores, now, and do em wery pert!"

Theresa O'Shyven poked her head forward to the full length of her neck, opened her mouth, stuck out her tongue, and began to lick the corner. She lapped it as Musty lapped his milk. Rhea watched this, slapping her knee and whooping, her face growing redder and redder as she rocked from side to side. Oh, Theresa was her favorite, aye! No doubt! For hours now she would crawl about on her hands and knees with her ass in the air, licking into the corners, praying to some obscure god—not even the Man-Jesus God—for forgiveness of who knew what as she did this, her penance. Sometimes she got splinters in her tongue and had to pause to spit blood into the kitchen basin. Up until now some sixth sense had always gotten her to her feet and back into her dress before any of her family returned, but Rhea knew that sooner or later the woman's obsession would take her too far, and she would be surprised. Perhaps today would be the day—the little girl would come back early, perhaps for a coin to spend in town, and discover her mother down on her knees and licking the corners. Oh, what a spin and raree! How Rhea wanted to see it! How she longed to—

Suddenly Theresa O'Shyven was gone. The interior of her neat little cottage was gone. *Everything* was gone, lost in curtains of shifting pink light. For the first time in weeks, the wizard's glass had gone blank.

Rhea picked the ball up in her scrawny, long-nailed fingers and shook it. "What's wrong with you, plaguey thing? *What's wrong?*"

The ball was heavy, and Rhea's strength was fading. After two or three hard shakes, it slipped in her grip. She cradled it against the deflated remains of her breasts, trembling.

"No, no, lovey," she crooned. "Come back when ye're ready, aye, Rhea lost her temper a bit but she's got it back now, she never meant to shake ye and she'd never *ever* drop ye, so ye just—"

She broke off and cocked her head, listening. Horses approaching. No, not approaching; *here*. Three riders, by the sound. They had crept up on her while she was distracted.

The boys? Those plaguey boys?

Rhea held the ball against her bosom, eyes wide, lips wet. Her hands were now so thin that the ball's pink glow shone through them, faintly illuminating the dark spokes that were her bones.

"Rhea! Rhea of the Cöos!"

No, not the boys.

"Come out here, and bring what you were given!"

Worse.

"Farson wants his property! We've come to take it!"

Not the boys but the Big Coffin Hunters.

"Never, ye dirty old white-haired prick," she whispered. "Ye'll never take it." Her eyes moved from side to side in small, shooting peeks. Scraggle-headed and tremble-mouthed, she looked like a diseased coyote driven into its final arroyo.

She looked down at the ball and a whining noise began to escape her. Now even the pink glow was gone. The sphere was as dark as a corpse's eyeball.

10

A shriek came from the hut.

Depape turned to Jonas with wide eyes, his skin prickling. The thing which had uttered that cry hardly sounded human.

"Rhea!" Jonas called again. "Bring it out here now, woman, and hand it over! I've no time to play games with you!"

The door of the hut swung open. Depape and Reynolds drew their guns as the old crone stepped out, blinking against the sunlight like something that's spent its whole life in a cave. She was holding John Farson's favorite toy high over her head. There were plenty of rocks in the dooryard she could throw it against, and even if her aim was bad and she missed them all, it might smash anyway.

This could be bad, and Jonas knew it—there were some people you just couldn't threaten. He had focused so much of his attention on the brats (who, ironically, had been taken as easy as milk) that it had never occurred to him to worry much about this part of it. And Kimba Rimer, the man who had suggested Rhea as the perfect custodian for Maerlyn's Rainbow, was dead. Couldn't lay it at Rimer's doorstep if things went wrong up here, could he?

Then, just to make things a little worse when he'd have thought they'd gone as far west as they could without dropping off the cold end of the earth, he heard the cocking sound of Depape drawing the hammer of his gun.

"Put that away, you idiot!" he snarled.

"But look at her!" Depape almost moaned. *"Look* at her, Eldred!"

He *was.* The thing inside the black dress appeared to be wearing the corpse of a putrefying snake around its throat for a necklace. She was so scrawny that she resembled nothing so much as a walking skeleton. Her peeling skull was only tufted with hair; the rest had fallen out. Sores clustered on her cheeks and brow, and there was a mark like a spider-bite on the left side of her mouth. Jonas thought that last might be a scurvy-bloom, but he didn't really care one way or another. What he cared about was the ball upraised in the dying woman's long and shivering claws.

II

The sunlight so dazzled Rhea's eyes that she didn't see the gun pointed at her, and when her vision cleared, Depape had put it away again. She looked at the men lined up across from her—the bespectacled redhead, the one in the cloak, and Old White-Hair Jonas—and uttered a dusty croak of laughter. Had she been afraid of them, these mighty Coffin Hunters? She supposed she had, but for gods' sake, why? They were men, that was all, just more men, and she had been beating such all her life. Oh, they thought they ruled the roost, all right—nobody in Mid-World accused anyone of forgetting the face of his *mother*—but they were poor things, at bottom, moved to tears by a sad song, utterly undone by the sight of a bare breast, and all the more capable of being manipulated simply because they were so sure they were strong and tough and wise.

The glass was dark, and as much as she hated that darkness, it had cleared her mind.

"Jonas!" she cried. "Eldred Jonas!"

"I'm here, old mother," he said. "Long days and pleasant nights."

"Never mind yer sops, time's too short for em." She came four steps farther and stopped with the ball still held over her head. Near her, a gray chunk of stone jutted from the weedy ground. She looked at it, then back at Jonas. The implication was unspoken but unmistakable.

"What do you want?" Jonas asked.

"The ball's gone dark," she said, answering from the side. "All the time I had it in my keeping, it was lively—aye, even when it showed nothing I could make out, it was passing lively, bright and pink—but it fell dark almost at the sound of yer voice. It doesn't want to go with ye."

"Nevertheless, I'm under orders to take it." Jonas's voice became soft and conciliating. It wasn't the tone he used when he was in bed with Coral, but it was close. "Think a minute, and you'll see my situation. Farson wants it, and who am I to stand against the wants of a man who'll be the most powerful in Mid-World when

Demon Moon rises next year? If I come back without it and say Rhea of the Cöos refused me it, I'll be killed."

"If ye come back and tell him I broke it in yer ugly old face, ye'll be killed, too," Rhea said. She was close enough for Jonas to see how far her sickness had eaten into her. Above the few remaining tufts of her hair, the wretched ball was trembling back and forth. She wouldn't be able to hold it much longer. A minute at most. Jonas felt a dew of sweat spring out on his forehead.

"Aye, mother. But d'you know, given a choice of deaths, I'd choose to take the cause of my problem with me. That's you, darling."

She croaked again—that dusty replica of laughter—and nodded appreciatively. " 'Twon't do Farson any good without me in any case," she said. "It's found its mistress, I wot—that's why it went dark at the sound of yer voice."

Jonas wondered how many others had believed the ball was just for them. He wanted to wipe the sweat from his brow before it ran in his eyes, but kept his hands in front of him, folded neatly on the horn of his saddle. He didn't dare look at either Reynolds or Depape, and could only hope they would leave the play to him. She was balanced on both a physical and mental knife-edge; the smallest movement would send her tumbling off in one direction or the other.

"Found the one it wants, has it?" He thought he saw a way out of this. If he was lucky. And it might be lucky for her, as well. "What should we do about that?"

"Take me with ye." Her face twisted into an expression of gruesome greed; she looked like a corpse that is trying to sneeze. *She doesn't realize she's dying,* Jonas thought. *Thank the gods for that.* "Take the ball, but take me, as well. I'll go with ye to Farson. I'll become his soothsayer, and nothing will stand before us, not with me to read the ball for him. Take me with ye!"

"All right," Jonas said. It was what he had hoped for. "Although what Farson decides is none o' mine. You know that?"

"Aye."

"Good. Now give me the ball. I'll give it back into your keeping, if you like, but I need to make sure it's whole."

She slowly lowered it. Jonas didn't think it was entirely safe even cradled in her arms, but he breathed a little easier when it was, all the same. She shuffled toward him, and he had to control an urge to gig his horse back from her.

He bent over in the saddle, holding his hands out for the glass. She looked up at him, her old eyes still shrewd behind their crusted lids. One of them actually drew down in a conspirator's wink. "I know yer mind, Jonas. Ye think, 'I'll take the ball, then draw my gun and kill her, what harm?' Isn't that true? Yet there *would* be harm, and all to you and yours. Kill me and the ball will never shine for Farson again. For someone, aye, someday, mayhap; but not for him . . . and will he let ye live if ye bring his toy back and he discovers it's broken?"

Jonas had already considered this. "We have a bargain, old mother. You go west with the glass . . . unless you die beside the trail some night. You'll pardon me for saying so, but you don't look well."

She cackled. "I'm better'n I look, oh yar! Years left 'fore this clock o' mine runs down!"

I think you may be wrong about that, old mother, Jonas thought. But he kept his peace and only held his hands out for the ball.

For a moment longer she held it. Their arrangement was made and agreed to on both sides, but in the end she could barely bring herself to ungrasp the ball. Greed shone in her eyes like moonlight through fog.

He held his hands out patiently, saying nothing, waiting for her mind to accept reality—if she let go, there was some chance. If she held on, very likely everyone in this stony, weedy yard would end up riding the handsome before long.

With a sigh of regret, she finally put the ball in his hands. At the instant it passed from her to him, an ember of pink light pulsed deep in the depths of the glass. A throb of pain drove into Jonas's head . . . and a shiver of lust coiled in his balls.

As from a great distance, he heard Depape and Reynolds cocking their pistols.

"Put those away," Jonas said.

"But—" Reynolds looked confused.

"They thought'ee was going to double-cross Rhea," the old woman said, cackling. "Good thing ye're in charge rather than them, Jonas . . . mayhap you know summat they don't."

He knew something, all right—how dangerous the smooth, glassy thing in his hands was. It could take him in a blink, if it wanted. And in a month, he would be like the witch: scrawny, raddled with sores, and too obsessed to know or care.

"Put them away!" he shouted.

Reynolds and Depape exchanged a glance, then reholstered their guns.

"There was a bag for this thing," Jonas said. "A drawstring bag laid inside the box. Get it."

"Aye," Rhea said, grinning unpleasantly at him. "But it won't keep the ball from takin ye if it wants to. Ye needn't think it will." She surveyed the other two, and her eye fixed on Reynolds. "There's a cart in my shed, and a pair of good gray goats to pull it." She spoke to Reynolds, but her eyes kept turning back to the ball, Jonas noticed . . . and now *his* damned eyes wanted to go there, too.

"You don't give me orders," Reynolds said.

"No, but *I* do," Jonas said. His eyes dropped to the ball, both wanting and fearing to see that pink spark of life deep inside. Nothing. Cold and dark. He dragged his gaze back up to Reynolds again. "Get the cart."

12

Reynolds heard the buzzing of flies even before he slipped through the shed's sagging door, and knew at once that Rhea's goats had finished their days of pulling. They lay bloated and dead in their pen, legs sticking up and the sockets of their eyes squirming with maggots. It was impossible to know when Rhea had last fed and watered them, but Reynolds guessed at least a week, from the smell.

Too busy watching what goes on in that glass ball to bother, he thought. *And what's she wearing that dead snake around her neck for?*

"I don't want to know," he muttered from behind his pulled-up neckerchief. The only thing he *did* want right now was to get the hell out of here.

He spied the cart, which was painted black and overlaid with cabalistic designs in gold. It looked like a medicine-show wagon to Reynolds; it also looked a bit like a hearse. He seized it by the handles and dragged it out of the shed as fast as he could. Depape could do the rest, by gods. Hitch his horse to the cart and haul the old woman's stinking freight to . . . where? Who knew? Eldred, maybe.

Rhea came tottering out of her hut with the drawstring bag they'd brought the ball in, but she stopped, head cocked, listening, when Reynolds asked his question.

Jonas thought it over, then said: "Seafront to begin, I

guess. Yar, that'll do for her, and this glass bauble as well, I reckon, until the party's over tomorrow."

"Aye, Seafront, I've never been there," Rhea said, moving forward again. When she reached Jonas's horse (which tried to shy away from her), she opened the bag. After a moment's further consideration, Jonas dropped the ball in. It bulged round at the bottom, making a shape like a teardrop.

Rhea wore a sly smile. "Mayhap we'll meet Thorin. If so, I might have something to show him in the Good Man's toy that'd interest him ever so much."

"If you meet him," Jonas said, getting down to help hitch Depape's horse to the black cart, "it'll be in a place where no magic is needed to see far."

She looked at him, frowning, and then the sly smile slowly resurfaced. "Why, I b'lieve our Mayor's met wiv a accident!"

"Could be," Jonas agreed.

She giggled, and soon the giggle turned into a full-throated cackle. She was still cackling as they drew out of the yard, cackling and sitting in the little black cart with its cabalistic decorations like the Queen of Black Places on her throne.

CHAPTER EIGHT

The Ashes

I

Panic is highly contagious, especially in situations when nothing is known and everything is in flux. It was the sight of Miguel, the old *mozo*, that started Susan down its greased slope. He was in the middle of Seafront's courtyard, clutching his broom of twigs against his chest and looking at the riders who passed to and fro with an expression of perplexed misery. His *sombrero* was twisted around on his back, and Susan observed with something like horror that Miguel—usually brushed and clean and neat as a pin—was wearing his *serape* inside out. There were tears on his cheeks, and as he turned this way and that, following the passing riders, trying to hile those he recognized, she thought of a child she had once seen toddle out in front of an oncoming stage. The child had been pulled back in time by his father; who would pull Miguel back?

She started for him, and a *vaquero* aboard a wild-eyed spotted roan galloped so close by her that one stirrup ticked off her hip and the horse's tail flicked her forearm. She voiced a strange-sounding little chuckle. She had been worried about Miguel and had almost been run down herself! Funny!

She looked both ways this time, started forward, then

657

drew back again as a loaded wagon came careering around the corner, tottering on two wheels at first. What it was loaded with she couldn't see—the goods in the wagon-bed were covered with a tarp—but she saw Miguel move toward it, still clutching his broom. Susan thought of the child in front of the stage again and shrieked an inarticulate cry of alarm. Miguel cringed back at the last moment and the cart flew by him, bounded and swayed across the courtyard, and disappeared out through the arch.

Miguel dropped his broom, clapped both hands to his cheeks, fell to his knees, and began to pray in a loud, lamenting voice. Susan watched him for a moment, her mouth working, and then sprinted for the stables, no longer taking care to keep against the side of the building. She had caught the disease that would grip almost all of Hambry by noon, and although she managed to do a fairly apt job of saddling Pylon (on any other day there would have been three stable-boys vying for the chance to help the pretty sai), any ability to think had left her by the time she heel-kicked the startled horse into a run outside the stable door.

When she rode past Miguel, still on his knees and praying to the bright sky with his hands upraised, she saw him no more than any other rider had before her.

2

She rode straight down the High Street, thumping her spur-less heels at Pylon's sides until the big horse was fairly flying. Thoughts, questions, possible plans of action . . . none of those had a place in her head as she rode. She was but vaguely aware of the people milling in the street, allowing Pylon to weave his own path through them. The only thing she was aware of was his name—

Roland, Roland, Roland!—ringing in her head like a
scream. Everything had gone upside down. The brave
little *ka-tet* they had made that night at the graveyard was
broken, three of its members jailed and with not long to
live (if they even *were* still alive), the last member lost and
confused, as crazy with terror as a bird in a barn.

If her panic had held, things might have turned out
in a much different fashion. But as she rode through the
center of town and out the other side, her way took her
toward the house she had shared with her father and
her aunt. That lady had been watching for the very rider
who now approached.

As Susan neared, the door flew open and Cordelia,
dressed in black from throat to toe, rushed down the
front walk to the street, shrieking with either horror or
laughter. Perhaps both. The sight of her cut through the
foreground haze of panic in Susan's mind . . . but not
because she recognized her aunt.

"*Rhea!*" she cried, and drew back on the reins so violently that the horse skidded, reared, and almost tilted
them over backward. That would likely have crushed the
life out of his mistress, but Pylon managed to keep at
least his back feet, pawing at the sky with his front ones
and whinnying loudly. Susan slung an arm around his
neck and hung on for dear life.

Cordelia Delgado, wearing her best black dress and a
lace mantilla over her hair, stood in front of the horse as
if in her own parlor, taking no notice of the hooves cutting the air less than two feet in front of her nose. In one
gloved hand she held a wooden box.

Susan belatedly realized that this wasn't Rhea, but
the mistake really wasn't that odd. Aunt Cord wasn't as
thin as Rhea (not yet, anyway), and more neatly dressed
(except for her dirty gloves—why her aunt was wearing
gloves in the first place Susan didn't know, let alone why

they looked so smudged), but the mad look in her eyes was horribly similar.

"Good day t'ye, Miss Oh So Young and Pretty!" Aunt Cord greeted her in a cracked, vivacious voice that made Susan's heart tremble. Aunt Cord curtseyed one-handed, holding the little box curled against her chest with the other. "Where go ye on this fine autumn day? Where go ye so speedy? To no lover's arms, that seems sure, for one's dead and the other ta'en!"

Cordelia laughed again, thin lips drawing back from big white teeth. Horse teeth, almost. Her eyes glared in the sunlight.

Her mind's broken, Susan thought. *Poor thing. Poor old thing.*

"Did thee put Dearborn up to it?" Aunt Cord asked. She crept to Pylon's side and looked up at Susan with luminous, liquid eyes. "Thee did, didn't thee? Aye! Perhaps thee even gave him the knife he used, after runnin yer lips o'er it for good luck. Ye're in it together—why not admit it? At least admit thee's lain with that boy, for I know it's true. I saw the way he looked at ye the day ye were sitting in the window, and the way ye looked back at him!"

Susan said, "If ye'll have truth, I'll give it to ye. We're lovers. And we'll be man and wife ere Year's End."

Cordelia raised one dirty glove to the blue sky and waved it as if saying hello to the gods. She screamed with mingled triumph and laughter as she waved. "And t'be *wed,* she thinks! Ooooo! Ye'd no doubt drink the blood of your victims on the marriage altar, too, would ye not? Oh, wicked! It makes me weep!" But instead of weeping she laughed again, a howl of mirth into the blind blue face of the sky.

"We planned no murders," Susan said, drawing—if only in her own mind—a line of difference between the

killings at Mayor's House and the trap they had hoped
to spring on Farson's soldiers. "And he *did* no murders.
No, this is the business of your friend Jonas, I wot. His
plan, his filthy work."

Cordelia plunged her hand into the box she held, and
Susan understood at once why the gloves she wore were
dirty: she had been grubbing in the stove.

"*I curse thee with the ashes!*" Cordelia cried, flinging a
black and gritty cloud of them at Susan's leg and the
hand which held Pylon's reins. "*I curse thee to darkness,
both of thee! Be ye happy together, ye faithless! Ye murderers! Ye
cozeners! Ye liars! Ye fornicators! Ye lost and renounced!*"

With each cry, Cordelia Delgado threw another handful of ashes. And with each cry, Susan's mind grew clearer,
colder. She held fast and allowed her aunt to pelt her; in
fact, when Pylon, feeling the gritty rain against his side,
attempted to pull away, Susan gigged him set. There were
spectators now, avidly watching this old ritual of renunci-
ation (Sheemie was among them, eyes wide and mouth
quivering), but Susan barely noticed. Her mind was her
own again, she had an idea of what to do, and for that
alone she supposed she owed her aunt some sort of thanks.

"I forgive ye, Aunt," she said.

The box of stove-ashes, now almost empty, tumbled
from Cordelia's hands as if Susan had slapped her.
"What?" she whispered. "What does thee say?"

"For what ye did to yer brother and my father," Susan
said. "For what ye were a part of."

She rubbed a hand on her leg and bent with the hand
held out before her. Before her aunt could pull away,
Susan had wiped ashes down one of her cheeks. The
smudge stood out there like a wide, dark scar. "But wear
that, all the same," she said. "Wash it off if ye like, but I
think ye'll wear it in yer heart yet awhile." She paused. "I
think ye already do. Goodbye."

"Where does thee think thee's going?" Aunt Cord was pawing at the soot-mark on her face with one gloved hand, and when she lunged forward in an attempt to grasp Pylon's reins, she stumbled over the box and almost fell. It was Susan, still bent over to her aunt's side, who grasped her shoulder and held her up. Cordelia pulled back as if from the touch of an adder. "Not to him! Ye'll not go to him now, ye mad goose!"

Susan turned her horse away. "None of yer business, Aunt. This is the end between us. But mark what I say: we'll be married by Year's End. Our firstborn is already conceived."

"Thee'll be married tomorrow night if thee goes nigh him! Joined in smoke, wedded in fire, bedded in the ashes! *Bedded in the ashes,* do ye hear me?"

The madwoman advanced on her, railing, but Susan had no more time to listen. The day was fleeting. There would be time to do the things that needed doing, but only if she moved at speed.

"Goodbye," she said again, and then galloped away. Her aunt's last words followed her: *In the ashes, do ye hear me?*

3

On her way out of town along the Great Road, Susan saw riders coming toward her, and got off the highway. This would not, she felt, be a good time to meet pilgrims. There was an old granary nearby; she rode Pylon behind it, stroked his neck, murmured for him to be quiet.

It took the riders longer to reach her position than she would have expected, and when they finally got there, she saw why. Rhea was with them, sitting in a black cart covered with magical symbols. The witch had been scary when Susan had seen her on the night of the Kissing

Moon, but still recognizably human; what the girl saw passing before her now, rocking from side to side in the black cart and clutching a bag in her lap, was an unsexed, sore-raddled creature that looked more like a troll than a human being. With her were the Big Coffin Hunters.

"To Seafront!" the thing in the cart screamed. "Hie you on, and at full speed! I'll sleep in Thorin's bed tonight or know the reason why! Sleep in it and piss in it, if I take a notion! Hie you on, I say!"

Depape—it was to his horse that the cart had been harnessed—turned around and looked at her with distaste and fear. "Still your mouth."

Her answer was a fresh burst of laughter. She rocked from side to side, holding a bag on her lap with one hand and pointing at Depape with the twisted, long-nailed index finger of the other. Looking at her made Susan feel weak with terror, and she felt the panic around her again, like some dark fluid that would happily drown her brain if given half a chance.

She worked against the feeling as best she could, holding onto her mind, refusing to let it turn into what it had been before and would be again if she let it—a brainless bird trapped in a barn, bashing into the walls and ignoring the open window through which it had entered.

Even when the cart was gone below the next hill and there was nothing left of them but dust hanging in the air, she could hear Rhea's wild cackling.

4

She reached the hut in the Bad Grass at one o' the clock. For a moment she just sat astride Pylon, looking at it. Had she and Roland been here hardly twenty-four hours ago? Making love and making plans? It was hard to believe, but when she dismounted and went in, the wicker basket in which she had brought them a cold meal confirmed it. It still sat upon the rickety table.

Looking at the hamper, she realized she hadn't eaten since the previous evening—a miserable supper with Hart Thorin that she'd only picked at, too aware of his eyes on her body. Well, they'd done their last crawl, hadn't they? And she'd never have to walk down another Seafront hallway wondering what door he was going to come bursting out of like Jack out of his box, all grabbing hands and stiff, randy prick.

Ashes, she thought. *Ashes and ashes. But not us, Roland. I swear, my darling, not us.*

She was frightened and tense, trying to put everything she now must do in order—a process to be followed just as there was a process to be followed when saddling a horse—but she was also sixteen and healthy. One look at the hamper and she was ravenous.

She opened it, saw there were ants on the two remaining cold beef sandwiches, brushed them off, and gobbled the sandwiches down. The bread had gotten rather stiff, but she hardly noticed. There was a half jar of sweet cider and part of a cake, as well.

When she had finished everything, she went to the north corner of the hut and moved the hides someone had begun to cure and then lost interest in. There was a hollow beneath. Within it, wrapped in soft leather, were Roland's guns.

If things go badly, thee must come here and take them west to Gilead. Find my father.

With faint but genuine curiosity, Susan wondered if Roland had really expected she would ride blithely off to Gilead with his unborn child in her belly while he and his friends were roasted, screaming and red-handed, on the Reap-Night bonfire.

She pulled one of the guns out of its holster. It took her a moment or two to see how to get the revolver open, but then the cylinder rolled out and she saw that each chamber was loaded. She snapped it back into place and checked the other one.

She concealed them in the blanket-roll behind her saddle, just as Roland had, then mounted up and headed east again. But not toward town. Not yet. She had one more stop to make first.

5

At around two o' the clock, word that Fran Lengyll would be speaking at the Town Gathering Hall began to sweep through the town of Mejis. No one could have said where this news (it was too firm and specific to be a rumor) began, and no one much cared; they simply passed it on.

By three o' the clock, the Gathering Hall was full, and two hundred or more stood outside, listening as Lengyll's brief address was relayed back to them in whispers. Coral Thorin, who had begun passing the news of Lengyll's impending appearance at the Travellers' Rest, was not there. She knew what Lengyll was going to say; had, in fact, supported Jonas's argument that it should be as simple and direct as possible. There was no need for rabble-rousing; the townsfolk would be a mob by sundown of Reaping Day, a mob always picked its own leaders, and it always picked the right ones.

Lengyll spoke with his hat held in one hand and a silver reap-charm hanging from the front of his vest. He was brief, he was rough, and he was convincing. Most folks in the crowd had known him all their lives, and didn't doubt a word he said.

Hart Thorin and Kimba Rimer had been murdered by Dearborn, Heath, and Stockworth, Lengyll told the crowd of men in denim and women in faded gingham. The crime had come home to them because of a certain item—a bird's skull—left in Mayor Thorin's lap.

Murmurs greeted this. Many of Lengyll's listeners had seen the skull, either mounted on the horn of Cuthbert's saddle or worn jauntily around his neck. They had laughed at his prankishness. Now they thought of how he had laughed back at them, and realized he must have been laughing at a different joke all along. Their faces darkened.

The weapon used to slit the Chancellor's throat, Lengyll continued, had belonged to Dearborn. The three young men had been taken that morning as they prepared to flee Mejis. Their motivations were not entirely clear, but they were likely after horses. If so, they would be for John Farson, who was known to pay well for good nags, and in cash. They were, in other words, traitors to their own lands and to the cause of the Affiliation.

Lengyll had planted Brian Hookey's son Rufus three rows back. Now, exactly on time, Rufus Hookey shouted out: "Has they confessed?"

"Aye," Lengyll said. "Confessed both murders, and spoke it most proud, so they did."

A louder murmur at this, almost a rumble. It ran backward like a wave to the outside, where it went from mouth to mouth: most proud, most proud, they had murdered in the dark of night and spoke it most proud.

Mouths were tucked down. Fists clenched.

"Dearborn said that Jonas and his friends had caught on to what they were doing, and took the word to Rimer. They killed Chancellor Rimer to shut him up while they finished their chores, and Thorin in case Rimer had passed word on."

This made little sense, Latigo had argued. Jonas had smiled and nodded. *No,* he had said, *not a mite of sense, but it doesn't matter.*

Lengyll was prepared to answer questions, but none were asked. There was only the murmur, the dark looks, the muted click and clink of reap-charms as people shifted on their feet.

The boys were in jail. Lengyll made no statement concerning what would happen to them next, and once again he was not asked. He said that some of the activities scheduled for the next day—the games, the rides, the turkey-run, the pumpkin-carving contest, the pig-scramble, the riddling competition, and the dance—had been cancelled out of respect for the tragedy. The things that really mattered would go on, of course, as they always had and must: the cattle and livestock judging, the horse-pull, the sheep-shearing, the stockline meetings, and the auctions: horse, pig, cow, sheep. And the bonfire at moonrise. The bonfire and the burning of the guys. *Charyou tree* was the end of Reaping Fair-Day, and had been since time out of mind. Nothing would stop it save the end of the world.

"The bonfire will burn and the stuffy-guys will burn on it," Eldred Jonas had told Lengyll. "That's all you're to say. It's all you *need* to say."

And he'd been right, Lengyll saw. It was on every face. Not just the determination to do right, but a kind of dirty eagerness. There were old ways, old rites of which the red-handed stuffy-guys were one surviving remnant. There were *los ceremoniosos: Charyou tree.* It had been generations since they had been practiced (except, every once and again, in secret places out in the hills), but sometimes when the world moved on, it came back to where it had been.

Keep it brief, Jonas had said, and it had been fine advice, fine advice indeed. He wasn't a man Lengyll would have wanted around in more peaceful times, but a useful one in times such as these.

"Gods give you peace," he said now, stepping back and folding his arms with his hands on his shoulders to show he had finished. "Gods give us all peace."

"Long days and peaceful nights," they returned in a low, automatic chorus. And then they simply turned and left, to go wherever folks went on the afternoon before Reaping. For a good many of them, Lengyll knew, it would be the Travellers' Rest or the Bayview Hotel. He raised a hand and mopped his brow. He hated to be out in front of people, and never so much as today, but he thought it had gone well. Very well, indeed.

6

The crowd streamed away without speaking. Most, as Lengyll had foreseen, headed for the saloons. Their way took them past the jail, but few looked at it . . . and those few who did did so in tiny, furtive glances. The porch was empty (save for a plump red-handed stuffy sprawled in Sheriff Avery's rocker), and the door stood ajar, as it usually did on warm and sunny afternoons. The boys were inside, no doubt about that, but there was no sign that they were being guarded with any particular zeal.

If the men passing on their way downhill to the Rest and the Bayview had banded together into one group, they could have taken Roland and his friends with no trouble whatsoever. Instead, they went by with their heads down, walking stolidly and with no conversation to where the drinks were waiting. Today was not the day. Nor tonight.

Tomorrow, however—

7

Not too far from the Bar K, Susan saw something on the Barony's long slope of grazing-land that made her rein up and simply sit in the saddle with her mouth open. Below her and much farther east of her position, at least three miles away, a band of a dozen cowboys had rounded up the biggest herd of Drop-runners she had ever seen: perhaps four hundred head in all. They ran lazily, going where the *vaqs* pointed them with no trouble.

Probably think they're going in for the winter, Susan thought.

But they weren't headed in toward the ranches running along the crest of the Drop; the herd, so large it flowed on the grass like a cloud-shadow, was headed west, toward Hanging Rock.

Susan had believed everything Roland said, but this made it true in a personal way, one she could relate directly to her dead father.

Horses, of courses.

"You bastards," she murmured. "You horse-thieving *bastards.*"

She turned Pylon and rode for the burned-out ranch. To her right, her shadow was growing long. Overhead, the Demon Moon glimmered ghostly in the daylight sky.

8

She had worried that Jonas might have left men at the Bar K—although why he would've she didn't really know, and the fear turned out to be groundless in any case. The ranch was as empty as it had been for the five or six years between the fire that had put paid to it and the arrival of the boys from In-World. She could see signs of that morning's confrontation, however, and when she went into the bunkhouse where the three of them had slept, she at once saw the gaping hole in the floorboards. Jonas had neglected to close it up again after taking Alain's and Cuthbert's guns.

She went down the aisle between the bunks, dropped to one knee, and looked into the hole. Nothing. Yet she doubted if what she had come for had been there in the first place—the hole wasn't big enough.

She paused, looking at the three cots. Which was Roland's? She supposed she could find out—her nose would tell her, she knew the smell of his hair and skin very well—but she thought she would do better to put such soft impulses behind her. What she needed now was to be hard and quick—to move without pausing or looking back.

Ashes, Aunt Cord whispered in her head, almost too faintly to hear. Susan shook her head impatiently, as if to clear that voice away, and walked out back.

There was nothing behind the bunkhouse, nothing behind the privy or to either side of it. She went around to the back of the old cook-shack next, and there she found what she'd come looking for, placed casually and with no attempt at concealment: the two small barrels she had last seen slung over Caprichoso's back.

The thought of the mule summoned the thought of Sheemie, looking down at her from his man's height and with his hopeful boy's face. *I'd like to take a* fin de año *kiss from ye, so I would.*

Sheemie, whose life had been saved by "Mr. Arthur Heath." Sheemie, who had risked the wrath of the witch by giving Cuthbert the note meant for her aunt. Sheemie, who had brought these barrels up here. They had been smeared with soot to partially camouflage them, and Susan got some on her hands and the sleeves of her shirt as she took off the tops—more ashes. But the firecrackers were still inside: the round, fist-sized big-bangers and the smaller lady-fingers.

She took plenty of both, stuffing her pockets until they bulged and carrying more in her arms. She stowed them in her saddlebags, then looked up at the sky. Three-thirty. She wanted to get back to Hambry no earlier than twilight, and that meant at least an hour to wait. There was a little time to be soft, after all.

Susan went back into the bunkhouse and found the bed which had been Roland's easily enough. She knelt beside it like a child saying bedtime prayers, put her face against his pillow, and inhaled deeply.

"Roland," she said, her voice muffled. "How I love thee. How I love thee, dear."

She lay on his bed and looked toward the window, watching the light drain away. Once she raised her hands in front of her eyes, examining the barrel-soot on her fingers. She thought of going to the pump in front of the cookhouse and washing, but decided not to. Let it stay. They were *ka-tet,* one from many—strong in purpose and strong in love.

Let the ashes stay, and do their worst.

9

My Susie has 'er faults, but she's always on time, Pat Delgado used to say. *Fearful punctual, that girl.*

It was true on the night before Reap. She skirted her own house and rode up to the Travellers' Rest not ten minutes after the sun had finally gone behind the hills, filling the High Street with thick mauve shadows.

The street was eerily deserted, considering it was the night before Reap; the band which had played in Green

Heart every night for the last week was silent; there were periodic rattles of firecrackers, but no yelling, laughing children; only a few of the many colored lamps had been lit.

Stuffy-guys seemed to peer from every shadow-thickened porch. Susan shivered at the sight of their blank white-cross eyes.

Doings at the Rest were similarly odd. The hitching-rails were crowded (even more horses had been tied at the rails of the mercantile across the street) and light shone from every window—so many windows and so many lights that the inn looked like a vast ship on a darkened sea—but there was none of the usual riot and jubilation, all set to the jagtime tunes pouring out of Sheb's piano.

She found she could imagine the customers inside all too well—a hundred men, maybe more—simply standing around and drinking. Not talking, not laughing, not chucking the dice down Satan's Alley and cheering or groaning at the result. No bottoms stroked or pinched; no Reap-kisses stolen; no arguments started out of loose mouths and finished with hard fists. Just men drinking, not three hundred yards from where her love and his friends were locked up. The men who were here wouldn't do anything tonight but drink, though. And if she was lucky . . . brave and lucky . . .

As she drew Pylon up in front of the saloon with a murmured word, a shape rose out of the shadows. She tensed, and then the first orangey light of the rising moon caught Sheemie's face. She relaxed again—even laughed a little, mostly at herself. He was a part of their *ka-tet;* she knew he was. Was it surprising that he should know, as well?

"Susan," he murmured, taking off his *sombrera* and holding it against his chest. "I been waiting for'ee."

"Why?" she asked.

" 'Cause I knew ye'd come." He looked back over his shoulder at the Rest, a black bulk spraying crazy light toward every point of the compass. "We're going to let Arthur and them free, ain't we?"

"I hope so," she said.

"We have to. The folks in there, they don't talk, but they don't *have* to talk. I knows, Susan, daughter of Pat. *I knows.*"

She supposed he did. "Is Coral inside?"

Sheemie shook his head. "Gone up to Mayor's House. She told Stanley she was going to help lay out the bodies for the funeral day after tomorrow, but I don't think she'll be here for the funeral. I think the Big Coffin Hunters is going and she'll go with 'em." He raised a hand and swiped at his leaking eyes.

"Your mule, Sheemie—"

"All saddled, and I got the long halter."

She looked at him, open-mouthed. "How did ye know—"

"Same way I knew ye'd be coming, Susan-sai. I just knew." He shrugged, then pointed vaguely. "Capi's around the back. I tied him to the cook's pump."

"That's good." She fumbled in the saddlebag where she had put the smaller firecrackers. "Here. Take some of these. Do'ee have a sulfur or two?"

"Aye." He asked no questions, simply stuffed the firecrackers into his front pocket. She, however, who had never been through the batwing doors of the Travellers' Rest in her whole life, had another question for him.

"What do they do with their coats and hats and *serapes* when they come in, Sheemie? They must take em off; drinking's warm work."

"Oh, aye. They puts em on a long table just inside the door. Some fights about whose is whose when they're ready to go home."

She nodded, thinking hard and fast. He stood before

her, still holding his *sombrera* against his chest, letting her do what he could not . . . at least not in the conventionally understood way. At last she raised her head again.

"Sheemie, if you help me, you're done in Hambry . . . done in Mejis . . . done in the Outer Arc. You go with us if we get away. You have to understand that. Do you?"

She saw he did; his face fairly shone with the idea. "Aye, Susan! Go with you and Will Dearborn and Richard Stockworth and my best friend, Mr. Arthur Heath! Go to In-World! We'll see buildings and statues and women in gowns like fairy princesses and—"

"If we're caught, we'll be killed."

He stopped smiling, but his eyes didn't waver. "Aye, killed we'll be if ta'en, most like."

"Will you still help me?"

"Capi's all saddled," he repeated. Susan reckoned that was answer enough. She took hold of the hand pressing the *sombrera* to Sheemie's chest (the hat's crown was pretty well crushed, and not for the first time). She bent, holding Sheemie's fingers with one hand and the horn of her saddle with the other, and kissed his cheek. He smiled up at her.

"We'll do our best, won't we?" she asked him.

"Aye, Susan daughter of Pat. We'll do our best for our friends. Our very best."

"Yes. Now listen, Sheemie. Very carefully."

She began to talk, and Sheemie listened.

10

Twenty minutes later, as the bloated orange moon struggled above the buildings of the town like a pregnant woman climbing a steep hill, a lone *vaquero* led a mule along Hill Street in the direction of the Sheriff's office.

This end of Hill Street was a pit of shadows. There was a little light around Green Heart, but even the park (which would have been thronged, noisy, and brilliantly lit in any other year) was mostly empty. Nearly all the booths were closed, and of those few that remained open, only the fortune-teller was doing any business. Tonight all fortunes were bad, but still they came—don't they always?

The *vaquero* was wearing a heavy serape; if this particular cowboy had the breasts of a woman, they were concealed. The *vaq* wore a large, sweat-stained *sombrero;* if this cowboy had the face of a woman, it was likewise concealed. Low, from beneath that hat's broad brim, came a voice singing "Careless Love."

The mule's small saddle was buried under the large bundle which had been roped to it—cloth or clothes of some kind, it might have been, although the deepening shadows made it impossible to say for sure. Most amusing of all was what hung around the mule's neck like some peculiar reap-charm: two *sombreros* and a drover's hat strung on a length of rope.

As the *vaq* neared the Sheriff's office, the singing ceased. The place might have been deserted if not for the single dim light shining through one window. In the porch rocker was a comical stuffy-guy wearing one of Herk Avery's embroidered vests and a tin star. There were no guards; absolutely no sign that the three most hated men in Mejis were sequestered within. And now, very faintly, the *vaquero* could hear the strum of a guitar.

It was blotted out by a thin rattle of firecrackers. The *vaq* looked over one shoulder and saw a dim figure. It waved. The *vaquero* nodded, waved back, then tied the mule to the hitching-post—the same one where Roland and his friends had tied their horses when they had come to introduce themselves to the Sheriff, on a summer day so long ago.

II

The door opened—no one had bothered to lock it—while Dave Hollis was trying, for about the two hundredth time, to play the bridge of "Captain Mills, You Bastard." Across from him, Sheriff Avery sat rocked back in his desk chair with his hands laced together on his paunch. The room flickered with mild orange lamplight.

"You keep it up, Deputy Dave, and there won't have to be any execution," Cuthbert Allgood said. He was standing at the door of one of the cells with his hands wrapped around the bars. "We'll kill ourselves. In self-defense."

"Shut up, maggot," Sheriff Avery said. He was half-dozing in the wake of a four-chop dinner, thinking of how he would tell his brother (and his brother's wife, who was killing pretty) in the next Barony about this heroic day. He would be modest, but he would still get it across to them that he'd played a central role; that if not for him, these three young *ladrones* might have—

"Just don't sing," Cuthbert said to Dave. "I'll confess to the murder of Arthur Eld himself if you just don't sing."

To Bert's left, Alain was sitting cross-legged on his bunk. Roland was lying on his with his hands behind his head, looking up at the ceiling. But at the moment the door's latch clicked, he swung to a sitting position. As if he'd only been waiting.

"That'll be Bridger," Deputy Dave said, gladly putting his guitar aside. He hated this duty and couldn't wait to be relieved. Heath's jokes were the worst. That he could continue to joke in the face of what was going to happen to them tomorrow.

"I think it's likely one of *them*," Sheriff Avery said, meaning the Big Coffin Hunters.

In fact, it was neither. It was a cowboy all but buried in

a *serape* that looked much too big for him (the ends actually dragged on the boards as he clumped in and shut the door behind him), and wearing a hat that came way down over his eyes. To Herk Avery, the fellow looked like somebody's idea of a cowboy stuffy.

"Say, stranger!" he said, beginning to smile . . . for this was surely someone's joke, and Herk Avery could take a joke as well as any man. Especially after four chops and a mountain of mashed. "Howdy! What business do ye—"

The hand which hadn't closed the door had been under the *serape*. When it came out, it was clumsily holding a gun all three of the prisoners recognized at once. Avery stared at it, his smile slowly fading. His hands unlaced themselves. His feet, which had been propped up on his desk, came down to the floor.

"Whoa, partner," he said slowly. "Let's talk about it."

"Get the keys off the wall and unlock the cells," the *vaq* said in a hoarse, artificially deep voice. Outside, unnoticed by all save Roland, more firecrackers rattled in a dry, popping string.

"I can't hardly do that," Avery said, easing open the bottom drawer of his desk with his foot. There were several guns, left over from that morning, inside. "Now, I don't know if that thing's loaded, but I don't hardly think a traildog like you—"

The newcomer pointed the gun at the desk and pulled the trigger. The report was deafening in the little room, but Roland thought—hoped—that with the door shut, it would sound like just another firecracker. Bigger than some, smaller than others.

Good girl, he thought. *Oh, good girl—but be careful. For gods' sake, Sue, be careful.*

All three of them standing in a line at the cell doors now, eyes wide and mouths tight.

The bullet struck the corner of the Sheriff's rolltop

and tore off a huge splinter. Avery screamed, tilted back in his chair again, and went sprawling. His foot remained hooked under the drawer-pull; the drawer shot out and overturned, spilling three ancient firearms across the board floor.

"Susan, look out!" Cuthbert shouted, and then: "No, Dave!"

At the end of his life, it was duty and not fear of the Big Coffin Hunters which propelled Dave Hollis, who had hoped to be Sheriff of Mejis himself when Avery retired (and, he sometimes told his wife, Judy, a better one than Fatso had ever dreamed of being). He forgot that he had serious questions about the way the boys had been taken as well as about what they might or might not have done. All he thought of then was that they were prisoners o' the Barony, and such would not be taken if he could help it.

He lunged for the cowboy in the too-big clothes, meaning to tear the gun out of his hands. And shoot him with it, if necessary.

12

Susan was staring at the yellow blaze of fresh wood on the corner of the Sheriff's desk, forgetting everything in her amazement—so much damage inflicted by the single twitch of a finger!—when Cuthbert's desperate shout awakened her to her position.

She shrank back against the wall, avoiding Dave's first swipe at the oversized *serape,* and, without thinking, pulled the trigger again. There was another loud explosion, and Dave Hollis—a young man only two years older than she herself—was flung backward with a smoking hole in his shirt between two points of the star he wore. His eyes were wide and unbelieving. His monocle lay by one outstretched hand on its length of black silk ribbon. One of his feet struck his guitar and knocked it to the floor with a thrum nearly as musical as the chords he had been trying to make.

"Dave," she whispered. "Oh Dave, I'm sorry, what did I do?"

Dave tried once to get up, then collapsed forward on his face. The hole going into the front of him was small, but the one she was looking at now, the one coming out the back, was huge and hideous, all black and red and charred edges of cloth . . . as if she had run him through with a blazing hot poker instead of shooting him with a gun, which was supposed to be merciful and civilized and was clearly neither one.

"Dave," she whispered. "Dave, I . . ."

"Susan look out!" Roland shouted.

It was Avery. He scuttled forward on his hands and knees, seized her around the calves, and yanked her feet out from under her. She came down on her bottom with a tooth-rattling crash and was face to face with him—his frog-eyed, large-pored face, his garlic-smelling hole of a mouth.

"Gods, ye're a *girl*," he whispered, and reached for her. She pulled the trigger of Roland's gun again, setting the front of her *serape* on fire and blowing a hole in the ceiling. Plaster dust drifted down. Avery's ham-sized hands settled around her throat, cutting off her wind. Somewhere far away, Roland shrieked her name.

She had one more chance.

Maybe.

One's enough, Sue, her father spoke inside of her head. *One's all ye need, my dear.*

She cocked Roland's pistol with the side of her thumb, socked the muzzle deep into the flab hanging from the underside of Sheriff Herk Avery's head, and pulled the trigger. The mess was considerable.

13

Avery's head dropped into her lap, as heavy and wet as a raw roast. Above it, she could feel growing heat. At the bottom edge of her vision was the yellow flicker of fire.

"On the desk!" Roland shouted, yanking the door of his cell so hard it rattled in its frame. "Susan, the water-pitcher! For your father's sake!"

She rolled Avery's head out of her lap, got to her feet, and staggered to the desk with the front of the *serape* burning. She could smell its charred stench and was grateful in some far corner of her mind that she'd had time, while waiting for dusk, to tie her hair behind her.

The pitcher was almost full, but not with water; she could smell the sweet-sour tang of *graf*. She doused her-self with it, and there was a brisk hissing as the liquid hit the flames. She stripped the *serape* off (the oversized *sombrero* came with it) and threw it on the floor. She looked at Dave again, a boy she had grown up with, one she might even have kissed behind the door of Hookey's, once upon an antique time.

"Susan!" It was Roland's voice, harsh and urgent. "The keys! Hurry!"

Susan grabbed the keyring from the nail on the wall. She went to Roland's cell first and thrust the ring blindly through the bars. The air was thick with smells of gun-smoke, burned wool, blood. Her stomach clenched helplessly at every breath.

Roland picked the right key, reached back through the bars with it, and plunged it into the lockbox. A moment later he was out, and hugging her roughly as her tears broke. A moment after that, Cuthbert and Alain were out, as well.

"You're an angel!" Alain said, hugging her himself.

"Not I," she said, and began to cry harder. She thrust the gun at Roland. It felt filthy in her hand; she never wanted to touch one again. "Him and me played together when we were berries. He was one of the good ones—never a braid-puller or a bully—and he grew up a good one. Now I've ended him, and who'll tell his wife?"

Roland took her back into his arms and held her there for a moment. "You did what you had to. If not him, then us. Does thee not know it?"

She nodded against his chest. "Avery, him I don't mind so much, but Dave . . ."

"Come on," Roland said. "Someone might recognize the gunshots for what they were. Was it Sheemie throwing firecrackers?"

She nodded. "I've got clothes for you. Hats and *serapes.*"

Susan hurried back to the door, opened it, peeked out in either direction, then slipped into the growing dark.

Cuthbert took the charred *serape* and put it over Deputy Dave's face. "Tough luck, partner," he said. "You got caught in between, didn't you? I reckon you wasn't so bad."

Susan came back in, burdened with the stolen gear which had been tied to Capi's saddle. Sheemie was already off on his next errand without having to be told. If the inn-boy was a halfwit, she'd known a lot of folks in her time who were running on quarters and eighths.

"Where'd you get this stuff?" Alain asked.

"The Travellers' Rest. And I didn't. Sheemie did." She held the hats out. "Come on, hurry."

Cuthbert took the headgear and passed it out. Roland and Alain had already slipped into the *serapes;* with the hats added and pulled well down over their faces, they could have been any Drop-*vaqs* in Barony.

"Where are we going?" Alain asked as they stepped out onto the porch. The street was still dark and deserted at this end; the gunshots had attracted no attention.

"Hookey's, to start with," Susan said. "That's where your horses are."

They went down the street together in a little group of four. Capi was gone; Sheemie had taken the mule along. Susan's heart was thudding rapidly and she could feel sweat standing out on her brow, but she still felt cold. Whether or no what she had done was murder, she had ended two lives this evening, and crossed a line that could never be recrossed in the other direction. She had done it for Roland, for her love, and simply knowing she could have done no different now offered some consolation.

Be happy together, ye faithless, ye cozeners, ye murderers. I curse thee with the ashes.

Susan seized Roland's hand, and when he squeezed, she squeezed back. And as she looked up at Demon Moon, its wicked face now draining from choleric red-orange to silver, she thought that when she had pulled the trigger on poor, earnest Dave Hollis, she had paid for her love with the dearest currency of all—had paid with her soul. If he left her now, her aunt's curse would be fulfilled, for only ashes would remain.

CHAPTER NINE

Reaping

I

As they stepped into the stable, which was lit by one dim gas lamp, a shadow moved out of one of the stalls. Roland, who had belted on both guns, now drew them. Sheemie looked at him with an uncertain smile, holding a stirrup in one hand. Then the smile broadened, his eyes flashed with happiness, and he ran toward them.

Roland holstered his guns and made ready to embrace the boy, but Sheemie ran past him and threw himself into Cuthbert's arms.

"Whoa, whoa," Cuthbert said, first staggering back comically and then lifting Sheemie off his feet. "You like to knock me over, boy!"

"She got ye out!" Sheemie cried. "Knew she would, so I did! Good old Susan!" Sheemie looked around at Susan, who stood beside Roland. She was still pale, but now seemed composed. Sheemie turned back to Cuthbert and planted a kiss directly in the center of Bert's forehead.

"Whoa!" Bert said again. "What's that for?"

" 'Cause I love you, good old Arthur Heath! You saved my life!"

"Well, maybe I did," Cuthbert said, laughing in an embarrassed way (his borrowed *sombrero,* too large to begin with, now sat comically askew on his head), "but if we don't get a move on, I won't have saved it for long."

"Horses are all saddled," Sheemie said. "Susan told me to do it and I did. I did it just right. I just have to put this stirrup on Mr. Richard Stockworth's horse, because the one on there's 'bout worn through."

"That's a job for later," Alain said, taking the stirrup. He put it aside, then turned to Roland. "Where do we go?"

Roland's first thought was that they should return to the Thorin mausoleum.

Sheemie reacted with instant horror. "The boneyard? And with Demon Moon at the full?" He shook his head so violently that his *sombrera* came off and his hair flew from side to side. "They're dead in there, sai Dearborn, but if ye tease em during the time of the Demon, they's apt to get up and walk!"

"It's no good, anyway," Susan said. "The women of the town'll be lining the way from Seafront with flowers, and filling the mausoleum, too. Olive will be in charge, if she's able, but my aunt and Coral are apt to be in the company. Those aren't ladies we want to meet."

"All right," Roland said. "Let's mount up and ride. Think about it, Susan. You too, Sheemie. We want a place where we can hide up until dawn, at least, and it should be a place we can get to in less than an hour. Off the Great Road, and in any direction from Hambry but northwest."

"Why not northwest?" Alain asked.

"Because that's where we're going now. We've got a job to do . . . and we're going to let them know we're doing it. Eldred Jonas most of all." He offered a thin blade of smile. "I want him to know the game is over. No more Castles. The *real* gunslingers are here. Let's see if he can deal with them."

2

An hour later, with the moon well above the trees, Roland's *ka-tet* arrived at the Citgo oilpatch. They rode out parallel to the Great Road for safety's sake, but, as it happened, the caution was wasted: they saw not one rider on the road, going in either direction. *It's as if Reaping's been cancelled this year,* Susan thought . . . then she thought of the red-handed stuffies, and shivered. They would have painted Roland's hands red tomorrow night, and still would, if they were caught. *Not just him, either. All of us. Sheemie, too.*

They left the horses (and Caprichoso, who had trotted ill-temperedly but nimbly behind them on a tether) tied to some long-dead pumping equipment in the southeastern corner of the patch, and then walked slowly toward the working derricks, which were clustered in the same area. They spoke in whispers when they spoke at all. Roland doubted if that was necessary, but whispers here seemed natural enough. To Roland, Citgo was far spookier than the graveyard, and while he doubted that the dead in that latter place awoke even when Old Demon was full, there were some *very* unquiet corpses here, squalling zombies that stood rusty-weird in the moonlight with their pistons going up and down like marching feet.

Roland led them into the active part of the patch, nevertheless, past a sign which read HOW'S YOUR HARD-HAT? and another reading WE PRODUCE OIL, WE REFINE SAFETY. They stopped at the foot of a derrick grinding so loudly that Roland had to shout in order to be heard.

"*Sheemie! Give me a couple of those big-bangers!*"

Sheemie had taken a pocketful from Susan's saddlebag and now handed a pair of them over. Roland took

Bert by the arm and pulled him forward. There was a square of rusty fencing around the derrick, and when the boys tried to climb it, the horizontals snapped like old bones. They looked at each other in the running shadows combined of machinery and moonlight, nervous and amused.

Susan twitched Roland's arm. *"Be careful!"* she shouted over the rhythmic *whumpa-whumpa-whumpa* of the derrick machinery. She didn't look frightened, he saw, only excited and alert.

He grinned, pulled her forward, and kissed the lobe of her ear. "Be ready to run," he whispered. "If we do this right, there's going to be a new candle here at Citgo. A hellacious big one."

He and Cuthbert ducked under the lowest strut of the rusty derrick tower and stood next to the equipment, wincing at the cacophony. Roland wondered that it hadn't torn itself apart years ago. Most of the works were housed in rusty metal blocks, but he could see a gigantic turning shaft of some kind, gleaming with oil that must be supplied by automated jets. Up this close, there was a gassy smell that reminded him of the jet that flared rhythmically on the other side of the oilpatch.

"Giant-farts!" Cuthbert shouted.

"What?"

"I said it smells like . . . aw, never mind! Let's do it if we can . . . can we?"

Roland didn't know. He walked toward the machinery crying out beneath metal cowls which were painted a faded, rusting green. Bert followed with some reluctance. The two of them slid into a short aisle, smelly and baking hot, that took them almost directly beneath the derrick. Ahead of them, the shaft at the end of the piston turned steadily, shedding oily teardrops down its smooth sides. Beside it was a curved pipe—almost surely an overflow pipe, Roland thought. An occasional drop of crude oil fell from its lip, and there was a black puddle on the ground beneath. He pointed at it, and Cuthbert nodded.

Shouting would do no good in here; the world was a roaring, squealing din. Roland curled one hand around his friend's neck and pulled Cuthbert's ear to his lips; he held a big-bang up in front of Bert's eyes with the other.

"Light it and run," he said. "I'll hold it, give you as much time as I can. That's for my benefit as much as for yours. I want a clear path back through that machinery, do you understand?"

Cuthbert nodded against Roland's lips, then turned the gunslinger's head so he could speak in the same fashion. "What if there's enough gas here to burn the air when I make a spark?"

Roland stepped back. Raised his palms in a "How-do-I-know?" gesture. Cuthbert laughed and drew out a box of sulfur matches which he had scooped off Avery's desk before leaving. He asked with his eyebrows if Roland was ready. Roland nodded.

The wind was blowing hard, but under the derrick the surrounding machinery cut it off and the flame from the sulfur rose straight. Roland held out the big-banger, and had a momentary, painful memory of his mother: how she had hated these things, how she had always been sure that he would lose an eye or a finger to one.

Cuthbert tapped his chest above his heart and kissed his palm in the universal gesture of good luck. Then he touched the flame to the fuse. It began to sputter. Bert turned, pretended to bang off a covered block of machinery—that was Bert, Roland thought; he would joke on the gallows—and then dashed back down the short corridor they'd used to get here.

Roland held the round firework as long as he dared,

then lobbed it into the overflow pipe. He winced as he turned away, half-expecting what Bert was afraid of: that the very air would explode. It didn't. He ran down the short aisle, came into the clear, and saw Cuthbert standing just outside the broken bit of fencing. Roland flapped both hands at him—*Go, you idiot, go!*—and then the world blew up behind him.

The sound was a deep, belching thud that seemed to shove his eardrums inward and suck the breath out of his throat. The ground rolled under his feet like a wave under a boat, and a large, warm hand planted itself in the center of his back and shoved him forward. He thought he ran with it for a step—maybe even two or three steps—and then he was lifted off his feet and hurled at the fence, where Cuthbert was no longer standing; Cuthbert was sprawled on his back, staring up at something behind Roland. The boy's eyes were wide and wondering; his mouth hung open. Roland could see all this very well, because Citgo was now as bright as in full daylight. They had lit their own Reaping bonfire, it seemed, a night early and much brighter than the one in town could ever hope to be.

He went skidding on his knees to where Cuthbert lay, and grabbed him under one arm. From behind them came a vast, ripping roar, and now chunks of metal began to fall around them. They got up and ran toward where Alain stood in front of Susan and Sheemie, trying to protect them.

Roland took a quick look back over his shoulder and saw that the remains of the derrick—about half of it still stood—were glowing blackish red, like a heated horseshoe, around a flaring yellow torch that ran perhaps a hundred and fifty feet into the sky. It was a start. He didn't know how many other derricks they could fire before folk began arriving from town, but he was determined to do as many as possible, no matter what the risks might be. Blowing up the tankers at Hanging Rock was only half the job. Farson's *source* had to be wiped out.

Further firecrackers dropped down further overflow pipes turned out not to be necessary. There was a network of inter-connected pipes under the oilpatch, most filled with natural gas that had leaked in through ancient, decaying seals. Roland and Cuthbert had no more than reached the others when there was a fresh explosion, and a fresh tower of flame erupted from a derrick to the right of the one they had set afire. A moment later, a third derrick—this one sixty full yards away from the first two—exploded with a dragon's roar. The ironwork tore free of its anchoring concrete pillars like a tooth pulled from a decayed gum. It rose on a cushion of blazing blue and yellow, attained a height of perhaps seventy feet, then heeled over and came crashing back down, spewing sparks in every direction.

Another. Another. And yet another.

The five young people stood in their corner, stunned, holding their hands up to shield their eyes from the glare. Now the oilpatch flared like a birthday cake, and the heat baking toward them was enormous.

"Gods be kind," Alain whispered.

If they lingered here much longer, Roland realized, they would be popped like corn. There were the horses to consider, too; they were well away from the main focus of the explosions, but there was no guarantee that the focus would stay where it was; already he saw two derricks that hadn't even been working engulfed in flames. The horses would be terrified.

Hell, *he* was terrified.

"Come on!" he shouted.

They ran for the horses through shifting yellow-orange brilliance.

3

At first Jonas thought it was going on in his own head—
that the explosions were part of their lovemaking.

Lovemaking, yar. Lovemaking, horseshit. He and
Coral made love no more than donkeys did sums. But it
was *something*. Oh yes indeed it was.

He'd been with passionate women before, ones who
took you into a kind of oven-place and then held you
there, staring with greedy intensity as they pumped their
hips, but until Coral he'd never been with a woman that
sparked such a powerfully harmonic chord in himself.
With sex, he had always been the kind of man who took
it when it came and forgot it when it didn't. But with
Coral he only wanted to take it, take it, and take it some
more. When they were together they made love like cats
or ferrets, twisting and hissing and clawing; they bit at
each other and cursed at each other, and so far none of
it was even close to enough. When he was with her, Jonas
sometimes felt as if he were being fried in sweet oil.

Tonight there had been a meeting with the Horsemen's
Association, which had pretty much become the Farson
Association in these latter days. Jonas had brought them
up to date, had answered their idiotic questions, and
had made sure they understood what they'd be doing
the next day. With that done, he had checked on Rhea,
who had been installed in Kimba Rimer's old suite. She
hadn't even noticed Jonas peering in at her. She sat in
Rimer's high-ceilinged, book-lined study—behind Rimer's ironwood desk, in Rimer's upholstered chair, looking as out of place as a whore's bloomers on a church
altar. On Rimer's desk was the Wizard's Rainbow. She was
passing her hands back and forth above it and muttering
rapidly under her breath, but the ball remained dark.

Jonas had locked her in and had gone to Coral. She had been waiting for him in the parlor where tomorrow's Conversational would have been held. There were plenty of bedrooms in that wing, but it was to her dead brother's that she had led him . . . and not by accident, either, Jonas was sure. There they made love in the canopied bed Hart Thorin would never share with his gilly.

It was fierce, as it had always been, and Jonas was approaching his orgasm when the first oil derrick blew. *Christ, she's something,* he thought. *There's never in the whole damned world been a woman like—*

Then two more explosions, in rapid succession, and Coral froze for a moment beneath him before beginning to thrust her hips again. "Citgo," she said in a hoarse, panting voice.

"Yar," he growled, and began to thrust with her. He had lost all interest in making love, but they had reached the point where it was impossible to stop, even under threat of death or dismemberment.

Two minutes later he was striding, naked, toward Thorin's little lick of a balcony, his half-erect penis wagging from side to side ahead of him like some halfwit's idea of a magic wand. Coral was a step behind him, as naked as he was.

"Why now?" she burst out as Jonas thrust open the balcony door. "I could have come three more times!"

Jonas ignored her. The countryside looking northwest was a moon-gilded darkness . . . except where the oilpatch was. There he saw a fierce yellow core of light. It was spreading and brightening even as he watched; one thudding explosion after another hammered across the intervening miles.

He felt a curious darkening in his mind—that feeling had been there ever since the brat, Dearborn, by some febrile leap of intuition, had recognized him for who and what he was. Making love to the energetic Coral melted that feeling a little, but now, looking at the burning tangle of fire which had five minutes ago been the Good Man's oil reserves, it came back with debilitating intensity, like a swamp-fever that sometimes quits the flesh but hides in the bones and never really leaves. *You're in the west,* Dearborn had said. *The soul of a man such as you can never leave the west.* Of course it was true, and he hadn't needed any such titmonkey as Will Dearborn to tell him . . . but now that it had been said, there was a part of his mind that couldn't stop thinking about it.

Fucking Will Dearborn. Where, exactly, was he now, him and his pair of good-mannered mates? In Avery's *calabozo?* Jonas didn't think so. Not anymore.

Fresh explosions ripped the night. Down below, men who had run and shouted in the wake of the early morning's assassinations were running and shouting again.

"It's the biggest Reaping firework that ever was," Coral said in a low voice.

Before Jonas could reply, there was a hard hammering on the bedroom door. It was thrown open a second later, and Clay Reynolds came clumping across the room, wearing a pair of blue jeans and nothing else. His hair was wild; his eyes were wilder.

"Bad news from town, Eldred," he said. "Dearborn and the other two In-World brats—"

Three more explosions, falling almost on top of each other. From the blazing Citgo oilpatch a great red-orange fireball rose lazily into the black of night, faded, disappeared. Reynolds walked out onto the balcony and stood between them at the railing, unmindful of their nakedness. He stared at the fireball with wide, wondering eyes until it was gone. As gone as the brats. Jonas felt that curious, debilitating gloom trying to steal over him again.

"How did they get away?" he asked. "Do you know? Does Avery?"

"Avery's dead. The deputy who was with him, too. 'Twas another deputy found em, Todd Bridger . . . Eldred, what's going on out there? What happened?"

"Oh, that's your boys," Coral said. "Didn't take em long to start their own Reaping party, did it?"

How much heart do they have? Jonas asked himself. It was a good question—maybe the only one that mattered. Were they now done making trouble . . . or just getting started?

He once more wanted to be out of here—out of Seafront, out of Hambry, out of Mejis. Suddenly, more than anything, he wanted to be miles and wheels and leagues away. He had bounded around his Hillock, it was too late to go back, and now he felt horribly exposed.

"Clay."

"Yes, Eldred?"

But the man's eyes—and his mind—were still on the conflagration at Citgo. Jonas took his shoulder and turned Reynolds toward him. Jonas felt his own mind starting to pick up speed, ticking past points and details, and welcomed the feeling. That queer, dark sense of fatalism faded and disappeared.

"How many men are here?" he asked.

Reynolds frowned, thought about it. "Thirty-five," he said. "Maybe."

"How many armed?"

"With guns?"

"No, with pea-blowers, you damned fool."

"Probably . . ." Reynolds pulled his lower lip, frowning more fiercely than ever. "Probably a dozen. That's guns likely to work, you ken."

"The big boys from the Horsemen's Association? Still all here?"

"I think so."

"Get Lengyll and Renfrew. At least you won't have to wake em up; they'll *all* be up, and most of em right down there." Jonas jerked a thumb at the courtyard. "Tell Renfrew to put together an advance party. Armed men. I'd like eight or ten, but I'll take five. Have that old woman's cart harnessed to the strongest, hardiest pony this place has got. Tell that old fuck Miguel that if the pony he chooses dies in the traces between here and Hanging Rock, he'll be using his wrinkled old balls for earplugs."

Coral Thorin barked brief, harsh laughter. Reynolds glanced at her, did a double-take at her breasts, then looked back at Jonas with an effort.

"Where's Roy?" Jonas asked.

Reynolds looked up. "Third floor. With some little serving maid."

"Kick him out," Jonas said. "It's his job to get the old bitch ready to ride."

"We're going?"

"Soon as we can. You and me first, with Renfrew's boys, and Lengyll behind, with the rest of the men. You just make sure Hash Renfrew's with us, Clay; that man's got sand in his craw."

"What about the horses out on the Drop?"

"Never mind the everfucking horses." There was another explosion at Citgo; another fireball floated into the sky. Jonas couldn't see the dark clouds of smoke which must be rushing up, or smell the oil; the wind, out of the east and into the west, would be carrying both away from town.

"But—"

"Just do as I say." Jonas now saw his priorities in clear, ascending order. The horses were on the bottom—Farson could find horses damned near anywhere. Above them were the tankers gathered at Hanging Rock. They were more important than ever now, because the source was gone. Lose the tankers, and the Big Coffin Hunters could forget going home.

Yet most important of all was Farson's little piece of the Wizard's Rainbow. It was the one truly irreplaceable item. If it was broken, let it be broken in the care of George Latigo, not that of Eldred Jonas.

"Get moving," he told Reynolds. "Depape rides after, with Lengyll's men. You with me. Go on. Make it happen."

"And me?" Coral asked.

He reached out and tugged her toward him. "I ain't forgot you, darlin," he said.

Coral nodded and reached between his legs, oblivious of the staring Clay Reynolds. "Aye," she said. "And I ain't forgot you."

4

They escaped Citgo with ringing ears and slightly singed around the edges but not really hurt, Sheemie riding double behind Cuthbert and Caprichoso clattering after, at the end of his long lead.

It was Susan who came up with the place they should go, and like most solutions, it seemed completely obvious . . . once someone had thought of it. And so, not long after Reaping Eve had become Reaping Morn, the five of them came to the hut in the Bad Grass where Susan and Roland had on several occasions met to make love.

Cuthbert and Alain unrolled blankets, then sat on them to examine the guns they had liberated from the Sheriff's office. They had also found Bert's slingshot.

"These're hard calibers," Alain said, holding one up with the cylinder sprung and peering one-eyed down the barrel. "If they don't throw too high or wide, Roland, I think we can do some business with them."

"I wish we had that rancher's machine-gun," Cuthbert said wistfully.

"You know what Cort would say about a gun like that?" Roland asked, and Cuthbert burst out laughing. So did Alain.

"Who's Cort?" Susan asked.

"The tough man Eldred Jonas only thinks he is," Alain said. "He was our teacher."

Roland suggested that they catch an hour or two of sleep—the next day was apt to be difficult. That it might also be their last was something he didn't feel he had to say.

"Alain, are you listening?"

Alain, who knew perfectly well that Roland wasn't speaking of his ears or his attention-span, nodded.

"Do you hear anything?"

"Not yet."

"Keep at it."

"I will . . . but I can't promise anything. The touch is flukey. You know that as well as I do."

"Just keep trying."

Sheemie had carefully spread two blankets in the corner next to his proclaimed best friend. "He's Roland . . . and *he's* Alain . . . who are you, good old Arthur Heath? Who are you really?"

"Cuthbert's my name." He stuck out his hand. "Cuthbert Allgood. How do y'do, and how do y'do, and how do y'do again?"

Sheemie shook the offered hand, then began giggling. It was a cheerful, unexpected sound, and made them all smile. Smiling hurt Roland a little, and he guessed that if he could see his own face, he'd observe a pretty good burn from being so close to the exploding derricks.

"Key-youth-bert," Sheemie said, giggling. "Oh my! Key-youth-bert, that's a funny name, no wonder you're such a funny fellow. Key-youth-bert, oh-aha-ha-ha, that's a pip, a real pip!"

Cuthbert smiled and nodded. "Can I kill him now, Roland, if we don't need him any longer?"

"Save him a bit, why don't you?" Roland said, then turned to Susan, his own smile fading. "Will thee walk out with me a bit, Sue? I'd talk to thee."

She looked up at him, trying to read his face. "All right." She held out her hand. Roland took it, they walked into the moonlight together, and beneath its light, Susan felt dread take hold of her heart.

5

They walked out in silence, through sweet-smelling grass that tasted good to cows and horses even as it was expanding in their bellies, first bloating and then killing them. It was high—at least a foot taller than Roland's head—and still green as summer. Children sometimes got lost in the Bad Grass and died there, but Susan had never feared to be here with Roland, even when there were no sky-markers to steer by; his sense of direction was uncannily perfect.

"Sue, thee disobeyed me in the matter of the guns," he said at last.

She looked at him, smiling, half-amused and half-angry. "Does thee wish to be back in thy cell, then? Thee and thy friends?"

"No, of course not. Such bravery!" He held her close and kissed her. When he drew back, they were both breathing hard. He took her by the arms and looked into her eyes. "But thee mustn't disobey me this time."

She looked at him steadily, saying nothing.

"Thee knows," he said. "Thee knows what I'd tell thee."

"Aye, perhaps."

"Say. Better you than me, maybe."

"I'm to stay at the hut while you and the others go. Sheemie and I are to stay."

He nodded. "Will you? Will *thee?*"

She thought of how unfamiliar and wretched Roland's gun had felt in her hand as she held it beneath the *serape*; of the wide, unbelieving look in Dave's eyes as the bullet she'd fired into his chest flung him backward; of how the first time she'd tried to shoot Sheriff Avery, the bullet had only succeeded in setting her own clothing afire, although he had been right there in front of her. They didn't have a gun for her (unless she took one of Roland's), she couldn't use one very well in any case . . . and, more important, she didn't *want* to use one. Under those circumstances, and with Sheemie to think about, too, it was best she just stay out of the way.

Roland was waiting patiently. She nodded. "Sheemie and I'll wait for thee. It's my promise."

He smiled, relieved.

"Now pay me back with honesty, Roland."

"If I can."

She looked up at the moon, shuddered at the ill-omened face she saw, and looked back at Roland. "What chance thee'll come back to me?"

He thought about this very carefully, still holding to her arms. "Far better than Jonas thinks," he said at last. "We'll wait at the edge of the Bad Grass and should be able to mark his coming well enough."

"Aye, the herd o' horses I saw—"

"He may come without the horses," Roland said, not knowing how well he had matched Jonas's thinking, "but his folk will make noise even if they come without the herd. If there's enough of them, we'll see them, as well—they'll cut a line through the grass like a part in hair."

Susan nodded. She had seen this many times from the Drop—the mysterious parting of the Bad Grass as groups of men rode through it.

"If they're looking for thee, Roland? If Jonas sends scouts ahead?"

"I doubt he'll bother." Roland shrugged. "If they do, why, we'll kill them. Silent, if we can. Killing's what we were trained to do; we'll do it."

She turned her hands over, and now she was gripping his arms instead of the other way around. She looked impatient and afraid. "Thee hasn't answered my question. What chance I'll see thee back?"

He thought it over. "Even toss," he said at last.

She closed her eyes as if struck, drew in a breath, let it out, opened her eyes again. "Bad," she said, "yet maybe not as bad as I thought. And if thee doesn't come back? Sheemie and I go west, as thee said before?"

"Aye, to Gilead. There'll be a place of safety and respect for you there, dear, no matter what . . . but it's especially important that you go if you *don't* hear the tankers explode. Thee knows that, doesn't thee?"

"To warn yer people—thy *ka-tet.*"

Roland nodded.

"I'll warn them, no fear. And keep Sheemie safe, too. He's as much the reason we've got this far as anything I've done."

Roland was counting on Sheemie for more than she knew. If he and Bert and Alain *were* killed, it was Sheemie who would stabilize her, give her reason to go on.

"When does thee leave?" Susan asked. "Do we have time to make love?"

"We have time, but perhaps it's best we don't," he said. "It's going to be hard enough to leave thee again without. Unless you really want to . . ." His eyes half-pleaded with her to say yes.

"Let's just go back and lie down a bit," she said, and took his hand. For a moment it trembled on her lips to tell him that she was kindled with his child, but at the last moment she kept silent. There was enough for him to think about without that added, mayhap . . . and she didn't want to pass such happy news beneath such an ugly moon. It would surely be bad luck.

They walked back through high grass that was already springing together along their path. Outside the hut, he turned her toward him, put his hands on her cheeks, and softly kissed her again.

"I will love thee forever, Susan," he said. "Come whatever storms."

She smiled. The upward movement of her cheeks spilled a pair of tears from her eyes. "Come whatever storms," she agreed. She kissed him again, and they went inside.

6

The moon had begun to descend when a party of eight rode out beneath the arch with COME IN PEACE writ upon it in the Great Letters. Jonas and Reynolds were in the lead. Behind them came Rhea's black wagon, drawn by a trotting pony that looked strong enough to go all night and half the next day. Jonas had wanted to give her a driver, but Rhea refused—"Never was an animal I didn't get on with better than any man ever could," she'd told him, and that seemed to be true. The reins lay limp in her lap; the pony worked smart without them. The other five men consisted of Hash Renfrew, Quint, and three of Renfrew's best *vaqueros*.

Coral had wanted to come as well, but Jonas had different ideas. "If we're killed, you can go on more or less as before," he'd said. "There'll be nothing to tie you to us."

"Without ye, I'm not sure there'd be any reason *to* go on," she said.

"Ar, quit that schoolgirl shit, it don't become you. You'd find plenty of reasons to keep staggerin down the path, if you had to put your mind to it. If all goes well—as I expect it will—and you still want to be with me, ride out of here as soon as you get word of our success. There's a town west of here in the Vi Castis Mountains. Ritzy. Go there on the fastest horse you can swing a leg over. You'll be there ahead of us by days, no matter how smart we're able to push along. Find a respectable inn that'll take a woman on her own . . . if there is such a thing in Ritzy. Wait. When we get there with the tankers, you just fall into the column at my right hand. Have you got it?"

She had it. One woman in a thousand was Coral Thorin—sharp as Lord Satan, and able to fuck like Satan's favorite harlot. Now if things only turned out to be as simple as he'd made them sound.

Jonas fell back until his horse was pacing alongside the black cart. The ball was out of its bag and lay in Rhea's lap. "Anything?" he asked. He both hoped and dreaded to see that deep pink pulse inside it again.

"Nay. It'll speak when it needs to, though—count on it."

"Then what good are *you,* old woman?"

"Ye'll know when the time comes," Rhea said, looking at him with arrogance (and some fear as well, he was happy to see).

Jonas spurred his horse back to the head of the little column. He had decided to take the ball from Rhea at the slightest sign of trouble. In truth, it had already inserted its strange, addicting sweetness into his head; he thought about that single pink pulse of light he'd seen far too much.

Balls, he told himself. *Battlesweat's all I've got. Once this business is over, I'll be my old self again.*

Nice if true, but . . .

. . . but he had, in truth, begun to wonder.

Renfrew was now riding with Clay. Jonas nudged his horse in between them. His dicky leg was aching like a bastard; another bad sign.

"Lengyll?" he asked Renfrew.

"Putting together a good bunch," Renfrew said, "don't you fear Fran Lengyll. Thirty men."

"Thirty! God Harry's body, I told you I wanted forty! Forty at least!"

Renfrew measured him with a pale-eyed glance, then winced at a particularly vicious gust of the freshening wind. He pulled his neckerchief up over his mouth and nose. The *vaqs* riding behind had already done so. "How afraid of these three boys are you, Jonas?"

"Afraid for both of us, I guess, since you're too stupid to know who they are or what they're capable of." He raised his own neckerchief, then forced his voice into a more reasonable timbre. It was best he do so; he needed these bumpkins yet awhile longer. Once the ball was turned over to Latigo, that might change. "Though mayhap we'll never see them."

"It's likely they're already thirty miles from here and riding west as fast as their horses'll take em," Renfrew agreed. "I'd give a crown to know how they got loose."

What does it matter, you idiot? Jonas thought, but said nothing.

"As for Lengyll's men, they'll be the hardest boys he can lay hands on—if it comes to a fight, those thirty will fight like sixty."

Jonas's eyes briefly met Clay's. *I'll believe it when I see it,* Clay's brief glance said, and Jonas knew again why he had always liked this one better than Roy Depape.

"How many armed?"

"With guns? Maybe half. They'll be no more than an hour behind us."

"Good." At least their back door was covered. It would have to do. And he couldn't wait to be rid of that thrice-cursed ball.

Oh? whispered a sly, half-mad voice from a place much deeper than his heart. *Oh, can't you?*

Jonas ignored the voice until it stilled. Half an hour later, they turned off the road and onto the Drop. Several miles ahead, moving in the wind like a silver sea, was the Bad Grass.

7

Around the time that Jonas and his party were riding down the Drop, Roland, Cuthbert, and Alain were swinging up into their saddles. Susan and Sheemie stood by the doorway to the hut, holding hands and watching them solemnly.

"Thee'll hear the explosions when the tankers go, and smell the smoke," Roland said. "Even with the wind the wrong way, I think thee'll smell it. Then, no more than an hour later, more smoke. There." He pointed. "That'll be the brush piled in front of the canyon's mouth."

"And if we don't see those things?"

"Into the west. But thee will, Sue. I swear thee will."

She stepped forward, put her hands on his thigh, and looked up at him in the latening moonlight. He bent; put his hand lightly against the back of her head; put his mouth on her mouth.

"Go thy course in safety," Susan said as she drew back from him.

"Aye," Sheemie added suddenly. "Stand and be true,

all three." He came forward himself and shyly touched Cuthbert's boot.

Cuthbert reached down, took Sheemie's hand, and shook it. "Take care of her, old boy."

Sheemie nodded seriously. "I will."

"Come on," Roland said. He felt that if he looked at her solemn, upturned face again, he would cry. "Let's go."

They rode slowly away from the hut. Before the grass closed behind them, hiding it from view, he looked back a final time.

"Sue, I love thee."

She smiled. It was a beautiful smile. "Bird and bear and hare and fish," she said.

The next time Roland saw her, she was caught inside the Wizard's glass.

8

What Roland and his friends saw west of the Bad Grass had a harsh, lonely beauty. The wind was lifting great sheets of sand across the stony desert floor; the moonlight turned these into footracing phantoms. At moments Hanging Rock was visible some two wheels distant, and the mouth of Eyebolt Canyon two wheels farther on. Sometimes both were gone, hidden by the dust. Behind them, the tall grass made a soughing, singing sound.

"How do you boys feel?" Roland asked. "All's well?"

They nodded.

"There's going to be a lot of shooting, I think."

"We'll remember the faces of our fathers," Cuthbert said.

"Yes," Roland agreed, almost absently. "We'll remember them very well." He stretched in the saddle. "The wind's in our favor, not theirs—that's one good thing.

We'll hear them coming. We must judge the size of the group. All right?"

They both nodded.

"If Jonas has still got his confidence, he'll come soon, in a small party—whatever gunnies he can put together on short notice—and he'll have the ball. In that case, we'll ambush them, kill them all, and take the Wizard's Rainbow."

Alain and Cuthbert sat quiet, listening intently. The wind gusted, and Roland clapped a hand to his hat to keep it from flying off. "If he fears more trouble from us, I think he's apt to come later on, and with a bigger party of riders. If that happens, we'll let them pass . . . then, if the wind is our friend and keeps up, we'll fall in behind them."

Cuthbert began to grin. "Oh Roland," he said. "Your father would be proud. Only fourteen, but cozy as the devil!"

"Fifteen come next moonrise," Roland said seriously. "If we do it this way, we may have to kill their drogue riders. Watch my signals, all right?"

"We're going to cross to Hanging Rock as part of their party?" Alain asked. He had always been a step or two behind Cuthbert, but Roland didn't mind; sometimes reliability was better than quickness. "Is that it?"

"If the cards fall that way, yes."

"If they've got the pink ball with em, you'd better hope it doesn't give us away," Alain said.

Cuthbert looked surprised. Roland bit his lip, thinking that sometimes Alain was plenty quick. Certainly he had come up with this unpleasant little idea ahead of Bert . . . ahead of Roland, too.

"We've got a lot to hope for this morning, but we'll play our cards as they come off the top of the pack."

They dismounted and sat by their horses there on the

edge of the grass, saying little. Roland watched the silver clouds of dust racing each other across the desert floor and thought of Susan. He imagined them married, living in a freehold somewhere south of Gilead. By then Farson would have been defeated, the world's strange decline reversed (the childish part of him simply assumed that making an end to John Farson would somehow see to that), and his gunslinging days would be over. Less than a year it had been since he had won the right to carry the six-shooters he wore on his hips—and to carry his father's great revolvers when Steven Deschain decided to pass them on—and already he was tired of them. Susan's kisses had softened his heart and quickened him, some-how; had made another life possible. A better one, perhaps. One with a house, and kiddies, and—

"They're coming," Alain said, snapping Roland out of his reverie.

The gunslinger stood up, Rusher's reins in one fist. Cuthbert stood tensely nearby. "Large party or small? Does thee . . . do you know?"

Alain stood facing southeast, hands held out with the palms up. Beyond his shoulder, Roland saw Old Star just about to slip below the horizon. Only an hour until dawn, then.

"I can't tell yet," Alain said.

"Can you at least tell if the ball—"

"No. Shut up, Roland, let me listen!"

Roland and Cuthbert stood and watched Alain anx-iously, at the same time straining their ears to hear the hooves of horses, the creak of wheels, or the mur-mur of men on the passing wind. Time spun out. The wind, rather than dropping as Old Star disappeared and dawn approached, blew more fiercely than ever. Roland looked at Cuthbert, who had taken out his slingshot and was playing nervously with the pull. Bert raised one shoulder in a shrug.

"It's a small party," Alain said suddenly. "Can either of you touch them?"

They shook their heads.

"No more than ten, maybe only six."

"Gods!" Roland murmured, and pumped a fist at the sky. He couldn't help it. "And the ball?"

"I can't touch it," Alain said. He sounded almost as though he were sleeping himself. "But it's with them, don't you think?"

Roland did. A small party of six or eight, probably travelling with the ball. It was perfect.

"Be ready, boys," he said. "We're going to take them."

9

Jonas's party made good time down the Drop and into the Bad Grass. The guide-stars were brilliant in the autumn sky, and Renfrew knew them all. He had a click-line to measure between the two he called The Twins, and he stopped the group briefly every twenty minutes or so to use it. Jonas hadn't the slightest doubt the old cowboy would bring them out of the tall grass pointed straight at Hanging Rock.

Then, about an hour after they'd entered the Bad Grass, Quint rode up beside him. "That old lady, she want to see you, sai. She say it's important."

"Do she, now?" Jonas asked.

"Aye." Quint lowered his voice. "That ball she got on her lap all glowy."

"Is that so? I tell you what, Quint—keep my old trail-buddies company while I see what's what." He dropped back until he was pacing beside the black cart. Rhea raised her face to him, and for a moment, washed as it was in the pink light, he thought it the face of a young girl.

"So," she said. "Here y'are, big boy. I thought ye'd show up pretty smart." She cackled, and as her face broke into its sour lines of laughter, Jonas again saw her as she really was—all but sucked dry by the thing in her lap. Then he looked down at it himself . . . and was lost. He could feel that pink glow radiating into all the deepest passages and hollows of his mind, lighting them up in a way they'd never been lit up before. Even Coral, at her dirty busiest, couldn't light him up that way.

"Ye like it, don't ye?" she half-laughed, half-crooned. "Aye, so ye do, so would anyone, such a pretty glam it is! But what do ye *see*, sai Jonas?"

Leaning over, holding to the saddle-horn with one hand, his long hair hanging down in a sheaf, Jonas looked deeply into the ball. At first he saw only that luscious, labial pink, and then it began to draw apart. Now he saw a hut surrounded by tall grass. The sort of hut only a hermit could love. The door—it was painted a peeling but still bright red—stood open. And sitting there on the stone stoop with her hands in her lap, her blankets on the ground at her feet, and her unbound hair around her shoulders was . . .

"I'll be damned!" Jonas whispered. He had now leaned so far out of the saddle that he looked like a trick rider in a circus show, and his eyes seemed to have disappeared; there were only sockets of pink light where they had been.

Rhea cackled delightedly. "Aye, it's Thorin's gilly that never was! Dearborn's lovergirl!" Her cackling stopped abruptly. "Lovergirl of the young proddy who killed my Ermot. And he'll pay for it, aye, so he will. Look closer, sai Jonas! Look closer!"

He did. Everything was clear now, and he thought he should have seen it earlier. Everything this girl's aunt had feared had been true. Rhea had known, although why she hadn't told anyone the girl had been screwing one of the In-World boys, Jonas didn't know. And Susan had done more than just screw Will Dearborn; she'd helped him escape, him and his trail-mates, and she might well have killed two lawmen for him, into the bargain.

The figure in the ball swam closer. Watching that made him feel a little dizzy, but it was a pleasant dizziness. Beyond the girl was the hut, faintly lit by a lamp which had been turned down to the barest core of flame. At first Jonas thought someone was sleeping in one corner, but on second glance he decided it was only a heap of hides that looked vaguely human.

"Do'ee spy the boys?" Rhea asked, seemingly from a great distance. "Do'ee spy em, m'lord sai?"

"No," he said, his own voice seeming to come from that same distant place. His eyes were pinned to the ball. He could feel its light baking deeper and deeper into his brain. It was a good feeling, like a hot fire on a cold night. "She's alone. Looks as if she's waiting."

"Aye." Rhea gestured above the ball—a curt dusting-off movement of the hands—and the pink light was gone. Jonas gave a low, protesting cry, but no matter; the ball was dark again. He wanted to stretch his hands out and tell her to make the light return—to beg her, if necessary—and held himself back by pure force of will. He was rewarded by a slow return of his wits. It helped to remind himself that Rhea's gestures were as meaningless as the puppets in a Pinch and Jilly show. The ball did what *it* wanted, not what *she* wanted.

Meanwhile, the ugly old woman was looking at him with eyes that were perversely shrewd and clear. "Waiting for what, do'ee suppose?" she asked.

There was only one thing she *could* be waiting for, Jonas thought with rising alarm. The boys. The three beardless sons of bitches from In-World. And if they weren't with her, they might well be up ahead, doing their own waiting.

Waiting for him. Possibly even waiting for—

"Listen to me," he said. "I'll only speak once, and you best answer true. Do they know about that thing? *Do those three boys know about the Rainbow?*"

Her eyes shifted away from his. It was answer enough in one way, but not in another. She had had things her way all too long up there on her hill; she had to know who was boss down here. He leaned over again and grabbed her shoulder. It was horrible—like grabbing a bare bone that somehow still lived—but he made himself hold on all the same. And squeeze. She moaned and wriggled, but he held on.

"Tell me, you old bitch! Run your fucking gob!"

"They might know of it," she whined. "The girl might've seen something the night she came to be— arrr, let go, ye're killing me!"

"If I wanted to kill you, you'd be dead." He took another longing glance at the ball, then sat up straight in the saddle, cupped his hands around his mouth, and called: "Clay! Hold up!" As Reynolds and Renfrew reined back, Jonas raised a hand to halt the *vaqs* behind him.

The wind whispered through the grass, bending it, rippling it, whipping up eddies of sweet smell. Jonas stared ahead into the dark, even though he knew it was fruitless to look for them. They could be anywhere, and Jonas didn't like the odds in an ambush. Not one bit.

He rode to where Clay and Renfrew were waiting. Renfrew looked impatient. "What's the problem? Dawn'll be breaking soon. We ought to get a move-on."

"Do you know the huts in the Bad Grass?"

"Aye, most. Why—"

"Do you know one with a red door?"

Renfrew nodded and pointed northish. "Old Soony's place. He had some sort of religious conversion—a dream or a vision or something. That's when he painted the door of his hut red. He's gone to the Mannifolk these last five years." He no longer asked why, at least; he had seen something on Jonas's face that had shut up his questions.

Jonas raised his hand, looked at the blue coffin tattooed there for a second, then turned and called for Quint. "You're in charge," Jonas told him.

Quint's shaggy eyebrows shot up. *"Me?"*

"Yar. But you're not going on—there's been a change of plan."

"What—"

"Listen and don't open your mouth again unless there's something you don't understand. Get that damned black cart turned around. Put your men around it and hie on back the way we came. Join up with Lengyll and his men. Tell them Jonas says wait where you find em until he and Reynolds and Renfrew come. Clear?"

Quint nodded. He looked bewildered but said nothing.

"Good. Get about it. And tell the witch to put her toy back in its bag." Jonas passed a hand over his brow. Fingers which had rarely shaken before had now picked up a minute tremble. "It's distracting."

Quint started away, then looked back when Jonas called his name.

"I think those In-World boys are out here, Quint. Probably ahead of where we are now, but if they're back the way you're going, they'll probably set on you."

Quint looked nervously around at the grass, which rose higher than his head. Then his lips tightened and he returned his attention to Jonas.

"If they attack, they'll try to take the ball," Jonas continued. "And sai, mark me well: any man who doesn't die protecting it will wish he had." He lifted his chin at the *vaqs*, who sat astride their horses in a line behind the black cart. "Tell them that."

"Aye, boss," Quint said.

"When you reach Lengyll's party, you'll be safe."

"How long should we wait for yer if ye don't come?"

"Til hell freezes over. Now go." As Quint left, Jonas turned to Reynolds and Renfrew. "We're going to make a little side-trip, boys," he said.

10

"Roland." Alain's voice was low and urgent. "They've turned around."

"Are you sure?"

"Yes. There's another group coming along behind them. A much larger one. That's where they're headed."

"Safety in numbers, that's all," Cuthbert said.

"Do they have the ball?" Roland asked. "Can you touch it yet?"

"Yes, they have it. It makes them easy to touch even though they're going the other way now. Once you find it, it glows like a lamp in a mineshaft."

"Does Rhea still have the keeping of it?"

"I think so. It's awful to touch her."

"Jonas is afraid of us," Roland said. "He wants more men around him when he comes. That's what it is, what it must be." Unaware that he was both right and badly out in his reckoning. Unaware that for one of the few times since they had left Gilead, he had lapsed into a teenager's disastrous certainty.

"What do we do?" Alain asked.

"Sit here. Listen. Wait. They'll bring the ball this way
again if they're going to Hanging Rock. They'll have to."

"Susan?" Cuthbert asked. "Susan and Sheemie? What
about them? How do we know they're all right?"

"I suppose that we don't." Roland sat down, cross-
legged, with Rusher's trailing reins in his lap. "But Jonas
and his men will be back soon enough. And when they
come, we'll do what we must."

II

Susan hadn't wanted to sleep inside—the hut felt
wrong to her without Roland. She had left Sheemie
huddled under the old hides in the corner and taken
her own blankets outside. She sat in the hut's doorway
for a little while, looking up at the stars and praying for
Roland in her own fashion. When she began to feel a
little better, she lay down on one blanket and pulled
the other over her. It seemed an eternity since Maria
had shaken her out of her heavy sleep, and the open-
mouthed, glottal snores drifting out of the hut didn't
bother her much. She slept with her head pillowed on
one arm, and didn't wake when, twenty minutes later,
Sheemie came to the doorway, blinked at her sleepily,
and then walked off into the grass to urinate. The only
one to notice him was Caprichoso, who stuck out his
long muzzle and took a nip at Sheemie's butt as the boy
passed him. Sheemie, still mostly asleep, reached back
and pushed the muzzle away. He knew Capi's tricks well
enough, so he did.

Susan dreamed of the willow grove—bird and bear
and hare and fish—and what woke her wasn't Sheemie's
return from his necessary but a cold circle of steel pressing into her neck. There was a loud click that she rec-

ognized at once from the Sheriff's office: a pistol being cocked. The willow grove faded from the eye of her mind.

"Shine, little sunbeam," said a voice. For a moment her bewildered, half-waking mind tried to believe it was yesterday, and Maria wanted her to get up and out of Seafront before whoever had killed Mayor Thorin and Chancellor Rimer could come back and kill her, as well.

No good. It wasn't the strong light of midmorning that her eyes opened upon, but the ash-pallid glow of five o'clock. Not a woman's voice but a man's. And not a hand shaking her shoulder but the barrel of a gun against her neck.

She looked up and saw a lined, narrow face framed by white hair. Lips no more than a scar. Eyes the same faded blue as Roland's. Eldred Jonas. The man standing behind him had bought her own da drinks once upon a happier time: Hash Renfrew. A third man, one of Jonas's *ka-tet,* ducked into the hut. Freezing terror filled her midsection—some for her, some for Sheemie. She wasn't sure the boy would even understand what was happening to them. *These are two of the three men who tried to kill him,* she thought. *He'll understand that much.*

"Here you are, Sunbeam, here you come," Jonas said companionably, watching her blink away the sleepfog. "Good! You shouldn't be napping all the way out here on your own, not a pretty sai such as yourself. But don't worry, I'll see you get back to where you belong."

His eyes flicked up as the redhead with the cloak stepped out of the hut. Alone. "What's she got in there, Clay? Anything?"

Reynolds shook his head. "All still on the hoss, I reckon."

Sheemie, Susan thought. *Where are you, Sheemie?*

Jonas reached out and caressed one of her breasts briefly. "Nice," he said. "Tender and sweet. No wonder Dearborn likes you."

"Get yer filthy blue-marked hand off me, you bastard."

Smiling, Jonas did as she bid. He turned his head and regarded the mule. "I know this one; it belongs to my good friend Coral. Along with everything else, you've turned livestock thief! Shameful, shameful, this younger generation. Don't you agree, sai Renfrew?"

But her father's old associate said nothing. His face was carefully blank, and Susan thought he might be just the tiniest tad ashamed of his presence here.

Jonas turned back to her, his thin lips curved in the semblance of a benevolent smile. "Well, after murder I suppose stealing a mule comes easy, don't it?"

She said nothing, only watched as Jonas stroked Capi's muzzle.

"What all were they hauling, those boys, that it took a mule to put it on?"

"Shrouds," she said through numb lips. "For you and all yer friends. A fearful heavy load it made, too—near broke the poor animal's back."

"There's a saying in the land I come from," Jonas said, still smiling. "Clever girls go to hell. Ever heard it?" He went on stroking Capi's nose. The mule liked it; his neck was thrust out to its full length, his stupid little eyes half-closed with pleasure. "Has it crossed your mind that fellows who unload their pack animal, split up what it was carrying, and take the goods away usually ain't coming back?"

Susan said nothing.

"You've been left high and dry, Sunbeam. Fast fucked is usually fast forgot, sad to say. Do you know where they went?"

"Yes," she said. Her voice was low, barely a whisper.

Jonas looked pleased. "If you was to tell, things might go easier for you. Would you agree, Renfrew?"

"Aye," Renfrew said. "They're traitors, Susan—for the

Good Man. If you know where they are or what they're up to, tell us."

Keeping her eyes fixed on Jonas, Susan said: "Come closer." Her numbed lips didn't want to move and it came out sounding like *Cung gloser,* but Jonas understood and leaned forward, stretching his neck in a way that made him look absurdly like Caprichoso. When he did, Susan spat in his face.

Jonas recoiled, lips twisting in surprise and revulsion. *"Arrr! BITCH!"* he cried, and launched a full-swung, open-handed blow that drove her to the ground. She landed at full length on her side with black stars exploding across her field of vision. She could already feel her right cheek swelling like a balloon and thought, *If he'd hit an inch or two lower, he might've broken my neck. Mayhap that would've been best.* She raised her hand to her nose and wiped blood from the right nostril.

Jonas turned to Renfrew, who had taken a single step forward and then stopped himself. "Put her on her horse and tie her hands in front of her. Tight." He looked down at Susan, then kicked her in the shoulder hard enough to send her rolling toward the hut. "Spit on me, would you? Spit on Eldred Jonas, would you, you bitch?"

Reynolds was holding out his neckerchief. Jonas took it, wiped the spittle from his face with it, then dropped into a hunker beside her. He took a handful of her hair and carefully wiped the neckerchief with it. Then he hauled her to her feet. Tears of pain now peeped from the corners of her eyes, but she kept silent.

"I may never see your friend again, sweet Sue with the tender little titties, but I've got you, ain't I? Yar. And if Dearborn gives us trouble, I'll give you double. And make sure Dearborn knows. You may count on it."

His smile faded, and he gave her a sudden, bitter shove that almost sent her sprawling again.

"Now get mounted, and do it before I decide to change your face a little with my knife."

12

Sheemie watched from the grass, terrified and silently crying, as Susan spit in the bad Coffin Hunter's face and was knocked to the ground, hit so hard the blow might have killed her. He almost rushed out then, but something—it could have been his friend Arthur's voice in his head—told him that would only get *him* killed.

He watched as Susan mounted. One of the other men—not a Coffin Hunter but a big rancher Sheemie had seen in the Rest from time to time—tried to help, but Susan pushed him away with the sole of her boot. The man stood back with a red face.

Don't make em mad, Susan, Sheemie thought. *Oh gods, don't do that, they'll hit ye some more! Oh, yer poor face! And ye got a nosebleed, so you do!*

"Last chance," Jonas told her. "Where are they, and what do they mean to do?"

"Go to hell," she said.

He smiled—a thin, hurty smile. "Likely I'll find you there when I arrive," he said. Then, to the other Coffin Hunter: "You checked the place careful?"

"Whatever they had, they took it," the redhead answered. "Only thing they left was Dearborn's punch-bunny."

That made Jonas laugh meany-mean as he climbed on board his own horse. "Come on," he said, "let's ride."

They went back into the Bad Grass. It closed around them, and it was as if they had never been there . . . except that Susan was gone, and so was Capi. The big rancher riding beside Susan had been leading the mule.

When he was sure they weren't going to return, Sheemie walked slowly back into the clearing, doing up the button on top of his pants as he came. He looked from the way Roland and his friends had gone to the one in which Susan had been taken. Which?

A moment's thought made him realize there was no choice. The grass out here was tough and springy. The path Roland and Alain and good old Arthur Heath (so Sheemie still thought of him, and always would) had taken was gone. The one made by Susan and her captors, on the other hand, was still clear. And perhaps, if he followed her, he could do something for her. Help her.

Walking at first, then jogging as his fear that they might double back and catch him dissipated, Sheemie went in the direction Susan had been taken. He would follow her most of that day.

13

Cuthbert—not the most sanguine of personalities in any situation—grew more and more impatient as the day brightened toward true dawn. *It's Reaping,* he thought. *Finally Reaping, and here we sit with our knives sharpened and not a thing in the world to cut.*

Twice he asked Alain what he "heard." The first time Alain only grunted. The second time he asked what Bert *expected* him to hear, with someone yapping away in his ear like that.

Cuthbert, who did not consider two enquiries fifteen minutes apart as "yapping away," wandered off and sat morosely in front of his horse. After a bit, Roland came over and sat down beside him.

"Waiting," Cuthbert said. "That's what most of our time in Mejis has been about, and it's the thing I do worst."

"You won't have to do it much longer," Roland said.

14

Jonas's company reached the place where Fran Lengyll's party had made a temporary camp about an hour after the sun had topped the horizon. Quint, Rhea, and Renfrew's *vaqs* were already there and drinking coffee, Jonas was glad to see.

Lengyll started forward, saw Susan riding with her hands tied, and actually drew back a step, as if he wanted to find a corner to hide in. There were no corners out here, however, so he stood fast. He did not look happy about it, however.

Susan nudged her horse forward with her knees, and when Reynolds tried to grab her shoulder, she dipped it to the side, temporarily eluding him.

"Why, Francis Lengyll! Imagine meeting you here!"

"Susan, I'm sorry to see ye so," Lengyll said. His flush crept closer and closer to his brow, like a tide approaching a seawall. "It's bad company ye've fallen in with, girl . . . and in the end, bad company always leaves ye to face the music alone."

Susan actually laughed. "Bad company!" she said. "Aye, ye'd know about that, wouldn't ye, Fran?"

He turned, awkward and stiff in his embarrassment. She raised one booted foot and, before anyone could stop her, kicked him squarely between the shoulder-blades. He went down on his stomach, his whole face widening in shocked surprise.

"No ye don't, ye bold cunt!" Renfrew shouted, and fetched her a wallop to the side of the head—it was on the left, and at least evened things up a bit, she would think later when her mind cleared and she was capable of thinking. She swayed in the saddle, but kept her seat. And she never looked at Renfrew, only at Lengyll, who had now managed to get to his hands and knees. He wore a deeply dazed expression.

"You killed my father!" she screamed at him. *"You killed my father, you cowardly, sneaking excuse for a man!"* She looked at the party of ranchers and *vaqs*, all of them staring at her now. *"There he is, Fran Lengyll, head of the Horsemen's Association, as low a sneak as ever walked! Low as coyote shit! Low as—"*

"That's enough," Jonas said, watching with some interest as Lengyll scuttled back to his men—and yes, Susan was bitterly delighted to see, it was a full-fledged scuttle—with his shoulders hunched. Rhea was cackling, rocking from side to side and making a sound like fingernails on a piece of slate. The sound shocked Susan, but she wasn't a bit surprised by Rhea's presence in this company.

"It could never be enough," she said, looking from Jonas to Lengyll with an expression of contempt so deep it seemed bottomless. "For him it could never be enough."

"Well, perhaps, but you did quite well in the time you had, lady-sai. Few could have done better. And listen to the witch cackle! Like salt in his wounds, I wot . . . but we'll shut her up soon enough." Then, turning his head: "Clay!"

Reynolds rode up.

"Think you can get Sunbeam back to Seafront all right?"

"I think so." Reynolds tried not to show the relief he felt at being sent back east instead of west. He had begun to have a bad feeling about Hanging Rock, Latigo, the tankers . . . about the whole show, really. God knew why. "Now?"

"Give it another minute," Jonas said. "Mayhap there's going to be a spot of killing right here. Who knows? But it's the unanswered questions that makes it worthwhile getting up in the morning, even when a man's leg aches like a tooth with a hole in it. Wouldn't you say so?"

"I don't know, Eldred."

"Sai Renfrew, watch our pretty Sunbeam a minute. I have a piece of property to take back."

His voice carried well—he had meant that it should—and Rhea's cackles cut off suddenly, as if severed out of her throat with a hooking-knife. Smiling, Jonas walked his horse toward the black cart with its jostling show of gold symbols. Reynolds rode on his left, and Jonas sensed rather than saw Depape fall in on his right. Roy was a good enough boy, really; his head was a little soft, but his heart was in the right place, and you didn't have to tell him *everything.*

For every step forward Jonas's horse took, Rhea shrank back a little in the cart. Her eyes shifted from side to side in their deep sockets, looking for a way out that wasn't there.

"Keep away from me, ye charry man!" she cried, raising a hand toward him. With the other she clutched the sack with the ball in it ever more tightly. "Keep away, or I'll bring the lightning and strike ye dead where ye sit yer horse! Yer harrier friends, too!"

Jonas thought Roy hesitated briefly at that, but Clay never did, nor did Jonas himself. He guessed there was a great lot she could do . . . or that there had been, at one time. But that was before the hungry glass had entered her life.

"Give it up to me," he said. He reached the side of her wagon and held his hand out for the bag. "It's not yours and never was. One day you'll doubtless have the Good Man's thanks for keeping it so well as you have, but now you must give it up."

She screamed—a sound of such piercing intensity that several of the *vaqueros* dropped their tin coffee-cups and clapped their hands over their ears. At the same time she knotted her hand through the drawstring and raised the bag over her head. The curved shape of the ball swung back and forth at the bottom of it like a pendulum.

"I'll not!" she howled. *"I'll smash it on the ground before I give it up to the likes o' you!"*

Jonas doubted if the ball would break, not hurled by her weak arms onto the trampled, springy mat of the Bad Grass, but he didn't think he would have occasion to find out, one way or the other.

"Clay," he said. "Draw your gun."

He didn't need to look at Clay to see that he'd done it; he saw the frantic way her eyes shifted to the left, where Clay sat his horse.

"I'm going to have a count," Jonas said. "Just a short one; if I get to three and she hasn't passed that bag over, blow her ugly head off."

"Aye."

"One," Jonas said, watching the ball pendulum back and forth at the bottom of the upheld bag. It was glowing; he could see dull pink even through the cloth. "Two. Enjoy hell, Rhea, goodbye. Thr—"

"Here!" she screamed, thrusting it out toward him and shielding her face with the crooked hook of her free hand. *"Here, take it! And may it damn you the way it's damned me!"*

"Thankee-sai."

He grabbed the bag just below the draw top and yanked. Rhea screamed again as the string skinned her knuckles and tore off one of her nails. Jonas hardly heard. His mind was a white explosion of exultation. For the first time in his long professional life he forgot his job, his surroundings, and the six thousand things that could get him killed on any day. He had it; he had it; by all the graves of all the gods, he had the fucking thing!

Mine! he thought, and that was all. He somehow

restrained the urge to open the bag and stick his head
inside it, like a horse sticking its head into a bag of oats,
and looped the drawstring over the pommel of his saddle twice instead. He took in a breath as deep as his lungs
would allow, then expelled it. Better. A little.

"Roy."

"Aye, Jonas."

It would be good to get out of this place, Jonas thought,
and not for the first time. To get away from these hicks.
He was sick of *aye* and *ye* and *so it is*, sick to his bones.

"Roy, we'll give the bitch a ten-count this time. If she
isn't out of my sight by then, you have my permission to
blow her ass off. Now, let's see if you can do the counting. I'll be listening close, so mind you don't skip any!"

"One," Depape said eagerly. "Two. Three. Four."

Spitting curses, Rhea snatched up the reins of the cart
and spanked the pony's back with them. The pony laid
its ears back and jerked the cart forward so vigorously
that Rhea went tumbling backward off the cantboard,
her feet up, her white and bony shins showing above
her ankle-high black shoes and mismatched wool stock-
ings. The *vaqueros* laughed. Jonas laughed himself. It was
pretty funny, all right, seeing her on her back with her
pins in the air.

"Fuh-fuh-five," Depape said, laughing so hard he was
hiccupping. "Sih-sih-*six*!"

Rhea climbed back up, flopped onto the cantboard
again with all the grace of a dying fish, and peered
around at them, wall-eyed and sneering.

"I curse ye all!" she screamed. It cut through them, still-
ing their laughter even as the cart bounced toward the
edge of the trampled clearing. *"Every last one of ye! Ye . . .
and ye . . . and ye!"* Her crooked finger pointed last at
Jonas. *"Thief! Miserable thief!"*

As though it was yours, Jonas marveled (although

"Mine!" was the first word to occur to him, once he had taken possession of it). *As though such a wonder could ever belong to a back-country reader of rooster-guts such as you.*

The cart bounced its way into the Bad Grass, the pony pulling hard with its ears laid back; the old woman's screams served to drive it better than any whip could have done. The black slipped into the green. They saw the cart flicker like a conjurer's trick, and then it was gone. For a long time yet, however, they heard her shrieking her curses, calling death down upon them beneath the Demon Moon.

15

"Go on," Jonas told Clay Reynolds. "Take our Sunbeam back. And if you want to stop on the way and make some use of her, why, be my guest." He glanced at Susan as he said this, to see what effect it might be having, but he was disappointed—she looked dazed, as if the last blow Renfrew had dealt her had scrambled her brains, at least temporarily. "Just make sure she gets to Coral at the end of all the fun."

"I will. Any message for sai Thorin?"

"Tell her to keep the wench someplace safe until she hears from me. And . . . why don't you stay with her, Clay? Coral, I mean—come tomorrow, I don't think we'll have to worry about this 'un anymore, but Coral . . . ride with her to Ritzy when she goes. Be her escort, like."

Reynolds nodded. Better and better. Seafront it would be, and that was fine. He might like a little taste of the girl once he got her there, but not on the way. Not under the ghostly-full daytime Demon Moon.

"Go on, then. Get started."

Reynolds led her across the clearing, aiming for a

point well away from the bent swath of grass where Rhea
had made her exit. Susan rode silently, downcast eyes
fixed on her bound wrists.

Jonas turned to face his men. "The three young fellows from In-World have broken their way out of jail,
with that haughty young bitch's help," he said, pointing
at Susan's departing back.

There was a low, growling murmur from the men.
That "Will Dearborn" and his friends were free they had
known; that sai Delgado had helped them escape they
had not . . . and it was perhaps just as well for her that
Reynolds was at that moment leading her into the Bad
Grass and out of sight.

"Never mind!" Jonas shouted, pulling their attention
back to him. He reached out a stealthy hand and caressed
the curve at the bottom of the drawstring bag. Just touching the ball made him feel as if he could do anything,
and with one hand tied behind his back, at that.

"Never mind her, and never mind them!" His eyes
moved from Lengyll to Wertner to Croydon to Brian
Hookey to Roy Depape. "We're close to forty men, going
to join another hundred and fifty. They're three, and not
one a day over sixteen. Are you afraid of three little boys?"

"*No!*" they cried.

"If we run on em, my cullies, what will we do?"

"*KILL THEM!*" The shout so loud that it sent rooks
rising up into the morning sun, cawing their displeasure
as they commenced the hunt for more peaceful surroundings.

Jonas was satisfied. His hand was still on the sweet
curve of the ball, and he could feel it pouring strength
into him. *Pink strength,* he thought, and grinned.

"Come on, boys. I want those tankers in the woods
west of Eyebolt before the home folks light their Reap-
Night Bonfire."

16

Sheemie, crouched down in the grass and peering into the clearing, was nearly run over by Rhea's black wagon; the screaming, gibbering witch passed so close to him that he could smell her sour skin and dirty hair. If she had looked down, she couldn't have missed seeing him and undoubtedly would have turned him into a bird or a bumbler or maybe even a mosquito.

The boy saw Jonas pass custody of Susan to the one in the cloak, and began working his way around the edge of the clearing. He heard Jonas haranguing the men (many of whom Sheemie knew; it shamed him to know how many Mejis cowboys were doing that bad Coffin Hunter's bidding), but paid no attention to what he was saying. Sheemie froze in place as they mounted up, momentarily scared they would come in his direction, but they rode the other way, west. The clearing emptied almost as if by magic . . . except it wasn't *entirely* empty. Caprichoso had been left behind, his lead trailing on the beaten grass. Capi looked after the departing riders, brayed once—as if to tell them they could all go to hell—then turned and made eye-contact with Sheemie, who was peering out into the clearing. The mule flicked his ears at the boy, then tried to graze. He lipped the Bad Grass a single time, raised his head, and brayed at Sheemie, as if to say this was all the inn-boy's fault.

Sheemie stared thoughtfully at Caprichoso, thinking of how much easier it was to ride than to walk. Gods, yes . . . but that second bray decided him against it. The mule might give one of his disgusted cries at the wrong time and alert the man who had Susan.

"You'll find your way home, I reckon," Sheemie said. "So long, pal. So long, good old Capi. See you farther down the path."

He found the path made by Susan and Reynolds, and began to trot after them once more.

17

"They're coming again," Alain said a moment before Roland sensed it himself—a brief flicker in his head like pink lightning. "All of them."

Roland hunkered in front of Cuthbert. Cuthbert looked back at him without even a suggestion of his usual foolish good humor.

"Much of it's on you," Roland said, then tapped the slingshot. "And on that."

"I know."

"How much have you got in the armory?"

"Almost four dozen steel balls." Bert held up a cotton bag which had, in more settled times, held his father's tobacco. "Plus assorted fireworks in my saddlebag."

"How many big-bangers?"

"Enough, Roland." Unsmiling. With the laughter gone from them, he had the hollow eyes of just one more killer. "Enough."

Roland ran a hand down the front of the *serape* he wore, letting his palm reacquaint itself with the rough weave. He looked at Cuthbert's, then at Alain's, telling himself again that it could work, yes, as long as they held their nerve and didn't let themselves think of it in terms of three against forty or fifty, it could work.

"The ones out at Hanging Rock will hear the shooting once it starts, won't they?" Al asked.

Roland nodded. "With the wind blowing from us to them, there's no doubt of that."

"We'll have to move fast, then."

"We'll go as best we can." Roland thought of standing between the tangled green hedges behind the Great Hall, David the hawk on his arm and a sweat of terror trickling down his back. *I think you die today,* he had told the hawk, and he had told it true. Yet he himself had lived, and passed his test, and walked out of the testing corridor facing east. Today it was Cuthbert and Alain's turn to be tested—not in Gilead, in the traditional place of proving behind the Great Hall, but here in Mejis, on the edge of the Bad Grass, in the desert, and in the canyon. Eyebolt Canyon.

"Prove or die," Alain said, as if reading the run of the gunslinger's thoughts. "That's what it comes down to."

"Yes. That's what it always comes down to, in the end. How long before they get here, do you think?"

"An hour at least, I'd say. Likely two."

"They'll be running a 'watch-and-go.' "

Alain nodded. "I think so, yes."

"That's not good," Cuthbert said.

"Jonas is afraid of being ambushed in the grass," Roland said. "Maybe of us setting fire to it around him. They'll loosen up when they get into the clear."

"You hope," Cuthbert said.

Roland nodded gravely. "Yes. I hope."

18

At first Reynolds was content to lead the girl along the broken backtrail at a fast walk, but about thirty minutes after leaving Jonas, Lengyll, and the rest, he broke into a trot. Pylon matched Reynolds's horse easily, and just as easily when, ten minutes later, he upped their speed to a light but steady run.

Susan held to the horn of her saddle with her bound hands and rode easily at Reynolds's right, her hair streaming out behind her. She thought her face must be quite colorful; the skin of her cheeks felt raised at least two inches higher than usual, welted and tender. Even the passing wind stung a little.

At the place where the Bad Grass gave way to the Drop, Reynolds stopped to give the horses a blow. He dismounted himself, turned his back to her, and took a piss. As he did, Susan looked up along the rise of land and saw the great herd, now untended and unravelling at the edges. They had done that much, perhaps. It wasn't much, but it was something.

"Do you need to do the necessary?" Reynolds asked. "I'll help you down if you do, but don't say no now and whine about it later."

"Ye're afraid. Big brave regulator that ye are, ye're scared, ain't ye? Aye, coffin tattoo and all."

Reynolds tried a contemptuous grin. It didn't fit his face very well this morning. "You ort to leave the fortune-telling to those that are good at it, missy. Now do you need a necessary stop or not?"

"No. And ye *are* afraid. Of what?"

Reynolds, who only knew that his bad feeling hadn't left him when he left Jonas, as he'd hoped it would, bared his tobacco-stained teeth at her. "If you can't talk sensible, just shut up."

"Why don't ye let me go? Perhaps my friends will do the same for you, when they catch us up."

This time Reynolds grunted laughter which was almost genuine. He swung himself into his saddle, hawked, spat. Overhead, Demon Moon was a pale and bloated ball in the sky. "You can dream, miss'sai," he said, "dreaming's free. But you ain't never going to see those three again. They're for the worms, they are. Now let's ride."

They rode.

19

Cordelia hadn't gone to bed at all on Reaping Eve. She sat the night through in her parlor chair, and although there was sewing on her lap, she had put not a single stitch in nor picked one out. Now, as morning's light brightened toward ten o' the clock, she sat in the same chair, looking out at nothing. What was there to look at, anyway? Everything had come down with a smash—all her hopes of the fortune Thorin would settle on Susan and Susan's child, perhaps while he still lived, certainly in his dead-letter; all her hopes of ascending to her proper place in the community; all her plans for the future. Swept away by two wilful young people who couldn't keep their pants up.

She sat in her old chair with her knitting on her lap and the ashes Susan had smeared on her cheek standing out like a brand, and thought: *They'll find me dead in this chair, someday—old, poor, and forgotten. That ungrateful child! After all I did for her!*

What roused her was a weak scratching at the window. She had no idea how long it had been going on before it finally intruded on her consciousness, but when it did, she laid her needlework aside and got up to see. A bird, perhaps. Or children playing Reaping jokes, unaware that the world had come to an end. Whatever it was, she would shoo it away.

Cordelia saw nothing at first. Then, as she was about to turn away, she spied a pony and cart at the edge of the yard. The cart was a little disquieting—black, with gold symbols overpainted—and the pony in the shafts stood with its head lowered, not grazing, looking as if it had been run half to death.

She was still frowning out at this when a twisted, filthy hand rose in the air directly in front of her and began to scratch at the glass again. Cordelia gasped and clapped both hands to her bosom as her heart took a startled leap in her chest. She backed up a step, and gave a little shriek as her calf brushed the fender of the stove.

The long, dirty nails scratched twice more, then fell away.

Cordelia stood where she was for a moment, irresolute, then went to the door, stopping at the woodbox to pick up a chunk of ash which fitted her hand. Just in case. Then she jerked the door open, went to the corner of the house, drew in a deep, steadying breath, and went around to the garden side, raising the ash-chunk as she did.

"Get out, whoever ye are! Scat before I—"

Her voice was stilled by what she saw: an incredibly old woman crawling through the frost-killed flowerbed next to the house—crawling toward her. The crone's stringy white hair (what remained of it) hung in her face. Sores festered on her cheeks and brow; her lips had split and drizzled blood down her pointed, warty chin. The corneas of her eyes had gone a filthy gray-yellow, and she panted like a cracked bellows as she moved.

"Good woman, help me," this specter gasped. "Help me if ye will, for I'm about done up."

The hand holding the chunk of ash sagged. Cordelia could hardly believe what she was seeing. "Rhea?" she whispered. "Is it Rhea?"

"Aye," Rhea whispered, crawling relentlessly through the dead silkflowers, dragging her hands through the cold earth. "Help me."

Cordelia retreated a step, her makeshift bludgeon now hanging at her knee. "No, I . . . I can't have such as thee in my house . . . I'm sorry to see ye so, but . . . but I have a reputation, ye ken . . . folk watch me close, so they do . . ."

She glanced at the High Street as she said this, as if expecting to see a line of townspeople outside her gate, watching eagerly, avid to fleet their wretched gossip on its lying way, but there was no one there. Hambry was quiet, its walks and byways empty, the customary joyous noise of Reaping Fair-Day stilled. She looked back at the thing which had fetched up in her dead flowers.

"Yer niece . . . did this . . ." the thing in the dirt whispered. "All . . . her fault . . ."

Cordelia dropped the chunk of wood. It clipped the side of her ankle, but she hardly noticed. Her hands curled into fists before her.

"Help me," Rhea whispered. "I know . . . where she is . . . we . . . we have work, us two . . . women's . . . work . . ."

Cordelia hesitated a moment, then went to the woman, knelt, got an arm around her, and somehow got her to her feet. The smell coming off her was reeky and nauseating—the smell of decomposing flesh.

Bony fingers caressed Cordelia's cheek and the side of her neck as she helped the hag into the house. Cordelia's flesh crawled, but she didn't pull away until Rhea collapsed into a chair, gasping from one end and farting from the other.

"Listen to me," the old woman hissed.

"I am." Cordelia drew a chair over and sat beside her. At death's door she might be, but once her eye fell on you, it was strangely hard to look away. Now Rhea's fingers dipped inside the bodice of her dirty dress, brought out a silver charm of some kind, and began to move it back and forth rapidly, as if telling beads. Cordelia, who hadn't felt sleepy all night, began to feel that way now.

"The others are beyond us," Rhea said, "and the ball

has slipped my grasp. But *she*—! Back to Mayor's House she's been ta'en, and mayhap we could see to her—we could do that much, aye."

"You can't see to anything," Cordelia said distantly. "You're dying."

Rhea wheezed laughter and a trickle of yellowish drool. "Dying? Nay! Just done up and in need of a refreshment. Now listen to me, Cordelia daughter of Hiram and sister of Pat!"

She hooked a bony (and surprisingly strong) arm around Cordelia's neck and drew her close. At the same time she raised her other hand, twirling the silver medallion in front of Cordelia's wide eyes. The crone whispered, and after a bit Cordelia began to nod her understanding.

"Do it, then," the old woman said, letting go. She slumped back in her chair, exhausted. "Now, for I can't last much longer as I am. And I'll need a bit o' time after, mind ye. To revive, like."

Cordelia moved across the room to the kitchen area. There, on the counter beside the hand-pump, was a wooden block in which were sheathed the two sharp knives of the house. She took one and came back. Her eyes were distant and far, as Susan's had been when she and Rhea stood in the open doorway of Rhea's hut in the light of the Kissing Moon.

"Would ye pay her back?" Rhea asked. "For that's why I've come to ye."

"Miss Oh So Young and Pretty," Cordelia murmured in a barely audible voice. The hand not holding the knife floated up to her face and touched her ash-smeared cheek. "Yes. I'd be repaid of her, so I would."

"To the death?"

"Aye. Hers or mine."

" 'Twill be hers," Rhea said, "never fear it. Now refresh me, Cordelia. Give me what I need!"

Cordelia unbuttoned her dress down the front, pushing it open to reveal an ungenerous bosom and a middle which had begun to curve out in the last year or so, making a tidy little potbelly. Yet she still had the vestige of a waist, and it was here she used the knife, cutting through her shift and the top layers of flesh beneath. The white cotton began to bloom red at once along the slit.

"Aye," Rhea whispered. "Like roses. I dream of them often enough, roses in bloom, and what stands black among em at the end of the world. Come closer!" She put her hand on the small of Cordelia's back, urging her forward. She raised her eyes to Cordelia's face, then grinned and licked her lips. "Good. Good enough."

Cordelia looked blankly over the top of the old woman's head as Rhea of the Cöos buried her face against the red cut in the shift and began to drink.

20

Roland was at first pleased as the muted jingle of harness and buckle drew closer to the place where the three of them were hunkered down in the high grass, but as the sounds drew closer still—close enough to hear murmuring voices as well as soft-thudding hooves—he began to be afraid. For the riders to pass close was one thing, but if they were, through foul luck, to come right upon them, the three boys would likely die like a nest of moles uncovered by the blade of a passing plow.

Ka surely hadn't brought them all this way to end in such fashion, had it? In all these miles of Bad Grass, how could that party of oncoming riders possibly strike the one point where Roland and his friends had pulled up? But still they closed in, the sound of tack and buckle and men's voices growing ever sharper.

Alain looked at Roland with dismayed eyes and pointed to the left. Roland shook his head and patted his hands toward the ground, indicating they would stay put. They *had* to stay put; it was too late to move without being heard.

Roland drew his guns.

Cuthbert and Alain did the same.

In the end, the plow missed the moles by sixty feet. The boys could actually see the horses and riders flashing through the thick grass; Roland easily made out that the party was led by Jonas, Depape, and Lengyll, riding three abreast. They were followed by at least three dozen others, glimpsed as roan flashes and the bright red and green of *serapes* through the grass. They were strung out pretty well, and Roland thought he and his friends could reasonably hope they'd string out even more once they reached open desert.

The boys waited for the party to pass, holding their horses' heads in case one of them took it in mind to whicker a greeting to the nags so close by. When they were gone, Roland turned his pale and unsmiling face to his friends.

"Mount up," he said. "Reaping's come."

21

They walked their horses to the edge of the Bad Grass, meeting the path of Jonas's party where the grass gave way first to a zone of stunted bushes and then to the desert itself.

The wind howled high and lonesome, carrying big drifts of gritty dust under a cloudless dark blue sky. Demon Moon stared down from it like the filmed eye of a corpse. Two hundred yards ahead, the drogue riders backing Jonas's party were spread out in a line of three, their *sombreros* jammed down tight on their heads, their shoulders hunched, their *serapes* blowing.

Roland moved so that Cuthbert rode in the middle of their trio. Bert had his slingshot in his hand. Now he handed Alain half a dozen steel balls, and Roland another half-dozen. Then he raised his eyebrows questioningly. Roland nodded and they began to ride.

Dust blew past them in rattling sheets, sometimes turning the drogue riders into ghosts, sometimes obscuring them completely, but the boys closed in steadily. Roland rode tense, waiting for one of the drogues to turn in his saddle and see them, but none did—none of them wanted to put his face into that cutting, grit-filled wind. Nor was there sound to warn them; there was sandy hardpack under the horses' hooves now, and it didn't give away much.

When they were just twenty yards behind the drogues, Cuthbert nodded—they were close enough for him to work. Alain handed him a ball. Bert, sitting ramrod straight in the saddle, dropped it into the cup of his slingshot, pulled, waited for the wind to drop, then released. The rider ahead on the left jerked as if stung, raised one hand a little, then toppled out of his saddle. Incredibly, neither of his two *compañeros* seemed to notice. Roland saw what he thought was the beginning of a reaction from the one on the right when Bert drew again, and the rider in the middle collapsed forward onto his horse's neck. The horse, startled, reared up. The rider flopped bonelessly backward, his *sombrero* tumbling off, and fell. The wind dropped enough for Roland to hear his knee snap as his foot caught in one of his stirrups.

The third rider now began to turn. Roland caught a glimpse of a bearded face—a dangling cigarette, unlit because of the wind, one astonished eye—and then

Cuthbert's sling *thupped* again. The astonished eye was replaced by a red socket. The rider slid from his saddle, groping for the horn and missing it.

Three gone, Roland thought.

He kicked Rusher into a gallop. The others did the same, and the boys rode forward into the dust a stirrup's width apart. The horses of the ambushed drogue riders veered off to the south in a group, and that was good. Riderless horses ordinarily didn't raise eyebrows in Mejis, but when they were saddled—

More riders up ahead: a single, then two side by side, then another single.

Roland drew his knife, and rode up beside the fellow who was now drogue and didn't know it.

"What news?" he asked conversationally, and when the man turned, Roland buried his knife in his chest. The *vaq's* brown eyes widened above the bandanna he'd pulled up outlaw-style over his mouth and nose, and then he tumbled from his saddle.

Cuthbert and Alain spurred past him, and Bert, not slowing, took the two riding ahead with his slingshot. The fellow beyond them heard something in spite of the wind, and swivelled in his saddle. Alain had drawn his own knife and now held it by the tip of the blade. He threw hard, in the exaggerated full-arm motion they had been taught, and although the range was long for such work—twenty feet at least, and in windy air—his aim was true. The hilt came to rest protruding from the center of the man's bandanna. The *vaq* groped for it, making choked gargling sounds around the knife in his throat, and then he too dropped from the saddle.

Seven now.

Like the story of the shoemaker and the flies, Roland thought. His heart was beating slow and hard in his chest as he caught up with Alain and Cuthbert. The wind gusted a lonely whine. Dust flew, swirled, then dropped with the wind. Ahead of them were three more riders, and ahead of them the main party.

Roland pointed at the next three, then mimed the slingshot. Pointed beyond them and mimed firing a revolver. Cuthbert and Alain nodded. They rode forward, once again stirrup-to-stirrup, closing in.

22

Bert got two of the three ahead of them clean, but the third jerked at the wrong moment, and the steel ball meant for the back of his head only clipped his earlobe on the way by. Roland had drawn his gun by then, however, and put a bullet in the man's temple as he turned. That made ten, a full quarter of Jonas's company before the riders even realized trouble had begun. Roland had no idea if it would be enough of an advantage, but he knew that the first part of the job was done. No more stealth; now it was a matter of raw killing.

"Hile! Hile!" he screamed in a ringing, carrying voice. *"To me, gunslingers! To me! Ride them down! No prisoners!"*

They spurred toward the main party, riding into battle for the first time, closing like wolves on sheep, shooting before the men ahead of them had any slight idea of who had gotten in behind them or what was happening. The three boys had been trained as gunslingers, and what they lacked in experience they made up for with the keen eyes and reflexes of the young. Under their guns, the desert east of Hanging Rock became a killing-floor.

Screaming, not a single thought among them above the wrists of their deadly hands, they sliced into the unprepared Mejis party like a three-sided blade, shooting as they went. Not every shot killed, but not a one went entirely

wild, either. Men flew out of their saddles and were
dragged by boots caught in stirrups as their horses bolted;
other men, some dead, some only wounded, were trampled beneath the feet of their panicky, rearing mounts.

Roland rode with both guns drawn and firing, Rusher's reins gripped in his teeth so they wouldn't fall over-
side and trip the horse up. Two men dropped beneath
his fire on his left, two more on the right. Ahead of them,
Brian Hookey turned in his saddle, his beard-stubbly face
long with amazement. Around his neck, a reap-charm in
the shape of a bell swung and tinkled as he grabbed for
the shotgun which hung in a scabbard over one burly
blacksmith's shoulder. Before he could do more than
get a hand on the gunstock, Roland blew the silver bell
off his chest and exploded the heart which lay beneath
it. Hookey pitched out of his saddle with a grunt.

Cuthbert caught up with Roland on the right side and
shot two more men off their horses. He gave Roland a
fierce and blazing grin. *"Al was right!"* he shouted. *"These
are hard calibers!"*

Roland's talented fingers did their work, rolling the
cylinders of the guns he held and reloading at a full
gallop—doing it with a ghastly, supernatural speed—
and then beginning to fire again. Now they had come
almost all the way through the group, riding hard, laying men low on both sides and straight ahead as well.
Alain dropped back a little and turned his horse, covering Roland and Cuthbert from behind.

Roland saw Jonas, Depape, and Lengyll reining
around to face their attackers. Lengyll was clawing at
his machine-gun, but the strap had gotten tangled in
the wide collar of the duster he wore, and every time
he grabbed for the stock, it bobbed out of his reach.
Beneath his heavy gray-blond mustache, Lengyll's mouth
was twisted with fury.

Now, riding between Roland and Cuthbert and these three, holding a huge blued-steel five-shot in one hand, came Hash Renfrew.

"Gods damn you!" Renfrew cried. "Oh, you rotten sister-fuckers!" He dropped his reins and laid the five-shot in the crook of one elbow to steady it. The wind gusted viciously, wrapping him in an envelope of swirling brown grit.

Roland had no thought of retreating, or perhaps jigging to one side or the other. He had, in fact, no thoughts at all. The fever had descended over his mind and he burned with it like a torch inside a glass sleeve. Screaming through the reins caught in his teeth, he galloped toward Hash Renfrew and the three men behind him.

23

Jonas had no clear idea of what was happening until he heard Will Dearborn screaming

(Hile! To me! No prisoners!)

a battle-cry he knew of old. Then it fell into place and the rattle of gunfire made sense. He reined around, aware of Roy doing the same beside him . . . but most aware of the ball in its bag, a thing both powerful and fragile, swinging back and forth against the neck of his horse.

"It's those *kids!*" Roy exclaimed. His total surprise made him look more stupid than ever.

"*Dearborn, you bastard!*" Hash Renfrew spat, and the gun in his hand thundered a single time.

Jonas saw Dearborn's sombrero rise from his head, its brim chewed away. Then the kid was firing, and he was good—better than anyone Jonas had ever seen in his life. Renfrew was hammered back out of his saddle with both legs kicking, still holding onto his monster gun, firing it twice at the dusty-blue sky before hitting the ground on his back and rolling, dead, on his side.

Lengyll's hand dropped away from the elusive wire stock of his speed-shooter and he only stared, unable to believe the apparition bearing down on him out of the dust. "Get back!" he cried. "In the name of the Horsemen's Association, I tell you—" Then a large black hole appeared in the center of his forehead, just above the place where his eyebrows tangled together. His hands flew up to his shoulders, palms out, as if he were declaring surrender. That was how he died.

"Son of a bitch, oh you little sister-fucking son of a bitch!" Depape howled. He tried to draw and his revolver got caught in his *serape*. He was still trying to pull it free when a bullet from Roland's gun opened his mouth in a red scream almost all the way down to his adam's apple.

This can't be happening, Jonas thought stupidly. *It can't, there are too many of us.*

But it *was* happening. The In-World boys had struck unerringly at the fracture-line; were performing what amounted to a textbook example of how gunslingers were supposed to attack when the odds were bad. And Jonas's coalition of ranchers, cowboys, and town tough-boys had shattered. Those not dead were fleeing to every point of the compass, spurring their horses as if a hundred devils paroled from hell were in pursuit. They were far from a hundred, but they *fought* like a hundred. Bodies were scattered in the dust everywhere, and as Jonas watched, he saw the one serving as their back door—Stockworth— ride down another man, bump him out of his saddle, and put a bullet in his head as he fell. *Gods of the earth,* he thought, *that was Croydon, him that owns the Piano Ranch!*

Except he didn't own it anymore.

And now Dearborn was bearing down on Jonas with his gun drawn.

Jonas snatched the drawstring looped around the horn of his saddle and unwound it with two fast, hard snaps of the wrist. He held the bag up in the windy air, his teeth bared and his long white hair streaming.

"*Come any closer and I'll smash it! I mean it, you damned puppy! Stay where you are!*"

Roland never hesitated in his headlong gallop, never paused to think; his hands did his thinking for him now, and when he remembered all this later, it was distant and silent and queerly warped, like something seen in a flawed mirror . . . or a wizard's glass.

Jonas thought: *Gods, it's him! It's Arthur Eld himself come to take me!*

And as the barrel of Roland's gun opened in his eye like the entrance to a tunnel or a mineshaft, Jonas remembered what the brat had said to him in the dusty dooryard of that burned-out ranch: *The soul of a man such as you can never leave the west.*

I knew, Jonas thought. *Even then I knew my* ka *had pretty well run out. But surely he won't risk the ball . . . he* can't *risk the ball, he's the* dinh *of this* ka-tet *and he can't risk it . . .*

"*To me!*" Jonas screamed. "*To me, boys! They're only three, for gods' sake! To me, you cowards!*"

But he was alone—Lengyll killed with his idiotic machine-gun lying by his side, Roy a corpse glaring up at the bitter sky, Quint fled, Hookey dead, the ranchers who had ridden with them gone. Only Clay still lived, and he was miles from here.

"*I'll smash it!*" he shrieked at the cold-eyed boy bearing down on him like death's sleekest engine. "*Before all the gods, I'll—*"

Roland thumbed back the hammer of his revolver and fired. The bullet struck the center of the tattooed hand holding the drawstring cord and vaporized the palm, leaving only fingers that twitched their random way out of a spongy red mass. For just a moment Roland saw the blue coffin, and then it was covered by downspilling blood.

The bag dropped. And, as Rusher collided with Jonas's horse and slewed it to the side, Roland caught the bag deftly in the crook of one arm. Jonas, screaming in dismay as the prize left him, grabbed at Roland, caught his shoulder, and almost succeeded in turning the gunslinger out of his saddle. Jonas's blood rained across Roland's face in hot drops.

"Give it back, you brat!" Jonas clawed under his *serape* and brought out another gun. *"Give it back, it's mine!"*

"Not anymore," Roland said. And, as Rusher danced around, quick and delicate for such a large animal, Roland fired two point-blank rounds into Jonas's face. Jonas's horse bolted out from under him and the man with the white hair landed spreadeagled on his back with a thump. His arms and legs spasmed, jerked, trembled, then stilled.

Roland looped the bag's drawstring over his shoulder and rode back toward Alain and Cuthbert, ready to give aid . . . but there was no need. They sat their horses side by side in the blowing dust, at the end of a scattered road of dead bodies, their eyes wide and dazed—eyes of boys who have passed through fire for the first time and can hardly believe they have not been burned. Only Alain had been wounded; a bullet had opened his left cheek, a wound that healed clean but left a scar he bore until his dying day. He could not remember who had shot him, he said later on, or at what point of the battle. He had been lost to himself during the shooting, and had only vague memories of what had happened after the charge began. Cuthbert said much the same.

"Roland," Cuthbert said now. He passed a shaky hand down his face. "Hile, gunslinger."

"Hile."

Cuthbert's eyes were red and irritated from the sand,

as if he had been crying. He took back the unspent silver slingshot balls when Roland handed them to him without seeming to know what they were. "Roland, we're alive."

"Yes."

Alain was looking around dazedly. "Where did the others go?"

"I'd say at least twenty-five of them are back there," Roland said, gesturing at the road of dead bodies. "The rest—" He waved his hand, still with a revolver in it, in a wide half-circle. "They've gone. Had their fill of Mid-World's wars, I wot."

Roland slipped the drawstring bag off his shoulder, held it before him on the bridge of his saddle for a moment, and then opened it. For a moment the bag's mouth was black, and then it filled with the irregular pulse of a lovely pink light.

It crept up the gunslinger's smooth cheeks like fingers and swam in his eyes.

"Roland," Cuthbert said, suddenly nervous, "I don't think you should play with that. Especially not now. They'll have heard the shooting out at Hanging Rock. If we're going to finish what we started, we don't have time for—"

Roland ignored him. He slipped both hands into the bag and lifted the wizard's glass out. He held it up to his eyes, unaware that he had smeared it with drop-lets of Jonas's blood. The ball did not mind; this was not the first time it had been blood-touched. It flashed and swirled formlessly for a moment, and then its pink vapors opened like curtains. Roland saw what was there, and lost himself within it.

CHAPTER TEN

Beneath the Demon Moon (II)

I

Coral's grip on Susan's arm was firm but not painful. There was nothing particularly cruel about the way she was moving Susan along the downstairs corridor, but there was a relentlessness about it that was disheartening. Susan didn't try to protest; it would have been useless. Behind the two women were a pair of *vaqueros* (armed with knives and *bolas* rather than guns; the available guns had all gone west with Jonas). Behind the *vaqs,* skulking along like a sullen ghost which lacks the necessary psychic energy to fully materialize itself, came the late Chancellor's older brother, Laslo. Reynolds, his taste for a spot of journey's-end rape blunted by his growing sense of disquiet, had either remained above or gone off to town.

"I'm going to put ye in the cold pantry until I know better what to do with'ee, dear," Coral said. "Ye'll be quite safe there . . . and warm. How fortunate ye wore a *serape.* Then . . . when Jonas gets back . . ."

"Ye'll never see sai Jonas again," Susan said. "He won't ever—"

Fresh pain exploded in her sensitive face. For a moment it seemed the entire world had blown up. Susan reeled back against the dressed stone wall of the lower corridor, her vision first blurred, then slowly clearing. She could feel blood flowing down her cheek from a wound opened by the stone in Coral's ring when Coral had backhanded her. And her nose. *That* cussed thing was bleeding again, too.

Coral was looking at her in a chilly this-is-all-business-to me fashion, but Susan believed she saw something different in the woman's eyes. Fear, mayhap.

"Don't talk to me about Eldred, missy. He's sent to catch the boys who killed my brother. The boys *you* set loose."

"Get off it." Susan wiped her nose, grimaced at the blood pooled in her palm, and wiped it on the leg of her pants. "I know who killed Hart as well as ye do yerself, so don't pull mine and I won't yank yer own." She watched Coral's hand rise, ready to slap, and managed a dry laugh. "Go on. Cut my face open on the other side, if ye like. Will that change how ye sleep tonight with no man to warm the other side of the bed?"

Coral's hand came down fast and hard, but instead of slapping, it seized Susan's arm again. Hard enough to hurt, this time, but Susan barely felt it. She had been hurt by experts this day, and would suffer more hurt gladly, if that would hasten the moment when she and Roland could be together again.

Coral hauled her the rest of the way down the corridor, through the kitchen (that great room, which would have been all steam and bustle on any other Reaping Day, now stood uncannily deserted), and to the ironbound door on the far side. This she opened. A smell of potatoes and gourds and sharp-root drifted out.

"Get in there. Go smart, before I decide to kick yer winsome ass square."

Susan looked her in the eye, smiling.

"I'd damn ye for a murderer's bed-bitch, sai Thorin,

but ye've already damned yerself. Ye know it, too—'tis written in yer face, to be sure. So I'll just drop ye a curt-sey"—still smiling, she suited action to the words—"and wish ye a very good day."

"*Get in and shut up yer saucy mouth!*" Coral cried, and pushed Susan into the cold pantry. She slammed the door, ran the bolt, and turned her blazing eyes upon the *vaqs*, who stood prudently away from her.

"Keep her well, *muchachos*. Mind ye do."

She brushed between them, not listening to their assurances, and went up to her late brother's suite to wait for Jonas, or word of Jonas. The whey-faced bitch sit-ting down there amongst the carrots and potatoes knew nothing, but her words

(*ye'll never see sai Jonas again*)

were in Coral's head now; they echoed and would not leave.

2

Twelve o' the clock sounded from the squat bell-tower atop the Town Gathering Hall. And if the unaccustomed silence which hung over the rest of Hambry seemed strange as that Reap morning passed into afternoon, the silence in the Travellers' Rest was downright eerie. Better than two hundred souls were packed together beneath the dead gaze of The Romp, all of them drink-ing hard, yet there was hardly a sound among them save for the shuffle of feet and the impatient rap of glasses on the bar, indicating that another drink was wanted.

Sheb had tried a hesitant tune on the piano—"Big Bot-tle Boogie," everyone liked that one—and a cowboy with a mutie-mark on one cheek had put the tip of a knife in his ear and told him to shut up that noise if he wanted to keep what passed for his brains on the starboard side of his eardrum. Sheb, who would be happy to go on drawing breath for another thousand years if the gods so allowed, quit his piano-bench at once, and went to the bar to help Stanley and Pettie the Trotter serve up the booze.

The mood of the drinkers was confused and sullen. Reaping Fair had been stolen from them, and they didn't know what to do about it. There would still be a bonfire, and plenty of stuffy-guys to burn on it, but there were no Reap-kisses today and would be no dancing tonight; no riddles, no races, no pig-wrestle, no jokes . . . no good cheer, dammit! No hearty farewell to the end of the year! Instead of joviality there had been murder in the dark, and the escape of the guilty, and now only the hope of retribution instead of the certainty of it. These folk, sullen-drunk and as potentially dangerous as storm-clouds filled with lightning, wanted someone to focus on, someone to tell them what to do.

And, of course, someone to toss on the fire, as in the days of Eld.

It was at this point, not long after the last toll of noon had faded into the cold air, that the batwing doors opened and two women came in. A good many knew the crone in the lead, and several of them crossed their eyes with their thumbs as a ward against her evil look. A murmur ran through the room. It was the Cöos, the old witch-woman, and although her face was pocked with sores and her eyes sunk so deep in their sockets they could barely be seen, she gave off a peculiar sense of vitality. Her lips were red, as if she had been eating win-terberries.

The woman behind her walked slowly and stiffly, with one hand pressed against her midsection. Her face was as white as the witch-woman's mouth was red.

Rhea advanced to the middle of the floor, passing the

gawking trailhands at the Watch Me tables without so much as a glance. When she reached the center of the bar and stood directly beneath The Romp's glare, she turned to look at the silent drovers and townsfolk.

"Most of ye know me!" she cried in a rusty voice which stopped just short of stridency. "Those of ye who don't have never wanted a love-potion or needed the ram put back in yer rod or gotten tired of a nagging mother-in-law's tongue. I'm Rhea, the wise-woman of the Cöos, and this lady beside me is aunt to the girl who freed three murderers last night . . . this same girl who murdered yer town's Sheriff and a good young man—married, he was, and with a kid on the way. He stood before her with 'is defenseless hands raised, pleadin for his life on behalf of his wife and his babby to come, and still she shot 'im! Cruel, she is! Cruel and heartless!"

A mutter ran through the crowd. Rhea raised her twisted old claws and it stilled at once. She turned in a slow circle to see them all, hands still raised, looking like the world's oldest, ugliest prizefighter.

"Strangers came and ye welcomed em in!" she cried in her rusty crow's voice. "Welcomed em and gave em bread to eat, and it's ruin they've fed ye in return! The deaths of those ye loved and depended on, spoilage to the time of the harvest, and gods know what curses upon the time to follow *fin de año!*"

More murmurs, now louder. She had touched their deepest fear: that this year's evil would spread, might even snarl the newly threaded stock which had so slowly and hopefully begun to emerge along the Outer Arc.

"But they've gone and likely won't be back!" Rhea continued. "Mayhap just as well—why should their strange blood taint our ground? But there's this other . . . one raised among us . . . a young woman gone traitor to her town and rogue among her own kind."

Her voice dropped to a hoarse whisper on this last phrase; her listeners strained forward to hear, faces grim, eyes big. And now Rhea pulled the pallid, skinny woman in the rusty black dress forward. She stood Cordelia in front of her like a doll or a ventriloquist's dummy, and whispered in her ear . . . but the whisper travelled, somehow; they all heard it.

"Come, dear. Tell em what ye told me."

In a dead, carrying voice, Cordelia said: "She said she wouldn't be the Mayor's gilly. He wasn't good enough for such as her, she said. And then she seduced Will Dearborn. The price of her body was a fine position in Gilead as his consort . . . and the murder of Hart Thorin. Dearborn paid her price. Lusty as he was for her, he paid gladly. His friends helped; they may have had the use of 'er as well, for all I know. Chancellor Rimer must have gotten in their way. Or p'rhaps they just saw him, and felt like doing him, too."

"Bastards!" Pettie cried. "Sneaking young culls!"

"Now tell em what's needed to clarify the new season before it's sp'iled, dearie," Rhea said in a crooning voice.

Cordelia Delgado raised her head and looked around at the men. She took a breath, pulling the sour, intermingled smells of *graf* and beer and smoke and whiskey deep into her spinster's lungs.

"Take her. Ye must take her. I say it in love and sorrow, so I do."

Silent. Their eyes.

"Paint her hands."

The glass gaze of the thing on the wall, looking its stuffed judgment over the waiting room.

"Charyou tree," Cordelia whispered.

They did not cry their agreement but sighed it, like autumn wind through stripped trees.

3

Sheemie ran after the bad Coffin Hunter and Susan-sai until he could literally run no more—his lungs were afire and the stitch which had formed in his side turned into a cramp. He pitched forward onto the grass of the Drop, his left hand clutching his right armpit, grimacing with pain.

He lay there for some time with his face deep in the fragrant grass, knowing they were getting farther and farther ahead but also knowing it would do him no good to get up and start running again until the stitch was good and gone. If he tried to hurry the process, the stitch would simply come back and lay him low again. So he lay where he was, lifting his head to look at the tracks left by Susan-sai and the bad Coffin Hunter, and he was just about ready to try his feet when Caprichoso bit him. Not a nip, mind you, but a good healthy chomp. Capi had had a difficult twenty-four hours, and he hadn't much liked to see the author of all his misery lying on the grass, apparently taking a nap.

"Yeee-OWWWW-by-damn!" Sheemie cried, and rocketed to his feet. There was nothing so magical as a good bite on the ass, a man of more philosophic bent might have reflected; it made all other concerns, no matter how heavy or sorrowful, disappear like smoke.

He whirled about. "Why did you do that, you mean old sneak of a Capi?" Sheemie was rubbing his bottom vigorously, and large tears of pain stood out in his eyes. "That hurts like . . . like a big old *sonovabitch!*"

Caprichoso extended his neck to its maximum length, bared his teeth in the satanic grin which only mules and dromedaries can command, and brayed. To Sheemie that bray sounded very like laughter.

The mule's lead still trailed back between his sharp lit-

tle hoofs. Sheemie reached for it, and when Capi dipped
his head to inflict another bite, the boy gave him a good
hard whack across the side of his narrow head. Capi
snorted and blinked.

"You had that coming, mean old Capi," Sheemie said.
"I'll have to shit from a squat for a week, so I will. Won't
be able to sit on the damned jakes." He doubled the lead
over his fist and climbed aboard the mule. Capi made
no attempt to buck him off, but Sheemie winced as his
wounded part settled atop the ridge of the mule's spine.
This was good luck just the same, though, he thought
as he kicked the animal into motion. His ass hurt, but
at least he wouldn't have to walk . . . or try to run with a
stitch in his side.

"Go on, stupid!" he said. "Hurry up! Fast as you can,
you old sonovabitch!"

In the course of the next hour, Sheemie called Capi
"you old sonovabitch" as often as possible—he had discovered, as many others had before him, that only the
first cussword is really hard; after that, there's nothing
quite like them for relieving one's feelings.

4

Susan's trail cut diagonally across the Drop toward the
coast and the grand old adobe that rose there. When
Sheemie reached Seafront, he dismounted outside the
arch and only stood, wondering what to do next. That
they had come here, he had no doubt—Susan's horse,
Pylon, and the bad Coffin Hunter's horse were tethered
side by side in the shade, occasionally dropping their
heads and blowing in the pink stone trough that ran
along the courtyard's ocean side.

What to do now? The riders who came and went

beneath the arch (mostly white-headed *vaqs* who'd been considered too old to form a part of Lengyll's party) paid no attention to the inn-boy and his mule, but Miguel might be a different story. The old *mozo* had never liked him, acted as if he thought Sheemie would turn thief, given half a chance, and if he saw Coral's slop-and-carry-boy skulking in the courtyard, Miguel would very likely drive him away.

No, he won't, he thought grimly. *Not today, today I can't let him boss me. I won't go even if he hollers.*

But if the old man *did* holler and raised an alarm, what then? The bad Coffin Hunter might come and kill him. Sheemie had reached a point where he was willing to die for his friends, but not unless it served a purpose.

So he stood in the cold sunlight, shifting from foot to foot, irresolute, wishing he was smarter than he was, that he could think of a plan. An hour passed this way, then two. It was slow time, each passing moment an exercise in frustration. He sensed any opportunity to help Susan-sai slipping away, but didn't know what to do about it. Once he heard what sounded like thunder from the west . . . although a bright fall day like this didn't seem right for thunder.

He had about decided to chance the courtyard any-way—it was temporarily deserted, and he might be able to make it across to the main house—when the man he had feared came staggering out of the stables.

Miguel Torres was festooned with reap-charms and was very drunk. He approached the center of the court-yard in rolling side-to-side loops, the tugstring of his *sombrero* twisted against his scrawny throat, his long white hair flying. The front of his *chibosa* was wet, as if he had tried to take a leak without remembering that you had to unlimber your dingus first. He had a small ceramic jug in one hand. His eyes were fierce and bewildered.

"Who done this?" Miguel cried. He looked up at the afternoon sky and the Demon Moon which floated there. Little as Sheemie liked the old man, his heart cringed. It was bad luck to look directly at old Demon, so it was. "Who done this thing? I ask that you tell me, *señor*! *Por favor!*" A pause, then a scream so powerful that Miguel reeled on his feet and almost fell. He raised his fists, as if he would box an answer out of the winking face in the moon, then dropped them wearily. Corn liquor slopped from the neck of the jug and wet him further. *"Maricon,"* he muttered. He staggered to the wall (almost tripping over the rear legs of the bad Coffin Hunter's horse as he went), then sat down with his back against the adobe wall. He drank deeply from the jug, then pulled his *sombrero* up and settled it over his eyes. His arm twitched the jug, then settled it back, as if in the end it had proved too heavy. Sheemie waited until the old man's thumb came unhooked from the jughandle and the hand flopped onto the cobbles. He started forward, then decided to wait even a little longer. Miguel was old and Miguel was mean, but Sheemie guessed Miguel might also be tricky. Lots of folks were, especially the mean ones.

He waited until he heard Miguel's dusty snores, then led Capi into the courtyard, wincing at every clop of the mule's hooves. Miguel never stirred, however. Sheemie tied Capi to the end of the hitching rail (wincing again as Caprichoso brayed a tuneless greeting to the horses tied there), then walked quickly across to the main door, through which he had never in his life expected to pass. He put his hand on the great iron latch, looked back once more at the old man sleeping against the wall, then opened the door and tiptoed in.

He stood for a moment in the oblong of sun the open door admitted, his shoulders hunched all the way up to his ears, expecting a hand to settle on the scruff of his neck (which bad-natured folk always seemed able to find, no matter how high you hunched your shoulders) at any moment; an angry voice would follow, asking what he thought he was doing here.

The foyer stood empty and silent. On the far wall was a tapestry depicting *vaqueros* herding horses along the Drop; against it leaned a guitar with a broken string. Sheemie's feet sent back echoes no matter how lightly he walked. He shivered. This was a house of murder now, a bad place. There were likely ghosts.

Still, Susan was here. Somewhere.

He passed through the double doors on the far side of the foyer and entered the reception hall. Beneath its high ceiling, his footfalls echoed more loudly than ever. Long-dead mayors looked down at him from the walls; most had spooky eyes that seemed to follow him as he walked, marking him as an intruder. He knew their eyes were only paint, but still . . .

One in particular troubled him: a fat man with clouds of red hair, a bulldog mouth, and a mean glare in his eye, as if he wanted to ask what some halfwit inn-boy was doing in the Great Hall at Mayor's House.

"Quit looking at me that way, you big old sonuvabitch," Sheemie whispered, and felt a little better. For the moment, at least.

Next came the dining hall, also empty, with the long trestle tables pushed back against the wall. There was the remains of a meal on one—a single plate of cold chicken and sliced bread, half a mug of ale. Looking at those few bits of food on a table that had served dozens at various fairs and festivals—that should have served dozens this very day—brought the enormity of what had happened home to Sheemie. And the sadness of it, too. Things had changed in Hambry, and would likely never be the same again.

These long thoughts did not keep him from gobbling the leftover chicken and bread, or from chasing it with what remained in the alepot. It had been a long, food-less day.

He belched, clapped both hands over his mouth, eyes making quick and guilty side-to-side darts above his dirty fingers, and then walked on.

The door at the far end of the room was latched but unlocked. Sheemie opened it and poked his head out into the corridor which ran the length of Mayor's House. The way was lit with gas chandeliers, and was as broad as an avenue. It was empty—at least for the moment—but he could hear whispering voices from other rooms, and perhaps other floors, as well. He supposed they belonged to the maids and any other servants that might be about this afternoon, but they sounded very ghostly to him, just the same. Perhaps one belonged to Mayor Thorin, wandering the corridor right in front of him (if Sheemie could but see him . . . which he was glad he couldn't). Mayor Thorin wandering and wondering what had hap-pened to him, what this cold jellylike stuff soaking into his nightshirt might be, who—

A hand gripped Sheemie's arm just above the elbow. He almost shrieked.

"Don't!" a woman whispered. "For your father's sake!"

Sheemie somehow managed to keep the scream in. He turned. And there, wearing jeans and a plain checked ranch-shirt, her hair tied back, her pale face set, her dark eyes blazing, stood the Mayor's widow.

"S-S-Sai Thorin . . . I . . . I . . . I . . ."

There was nothing else he could think of to say. *Now she'll call for the guards o' the watch, if there be any left,* he thought. In a way, it would be a relief.

"Have ye come for the girl? The Delgado girl?"

Grief had been good to Olive, in a terrible way—had

made her face seem less plump, and oddly young. Her dark eyes never left his, and forbade any attempt at a lie. Sheemie nodded.

"Good. I can use your help, boy. She's down below, in the pantry, and she's guarded."

Sheemie gaped, not believing what he was hearing.

"Do you think I believe she had anything to do with Hart's murder?" Olive asked, as if Sheemie had objected to her idea. "I may be fat and not so speedy on my pins anymore, but I'm not a complete idiot. Come on, now. Seafront's not a good place for sai Delgado just now—too many people from town know where she is."

5

"Roland."

He will hear this voice in uneasy dreams for the rest of his life, never quite remembering what he has dreamed, only knowing that the dreams leave him feeling ill somehow—walking restlessly, straightening pictures in loveless rooms, listening to the call to muzzein *in alien town squares.*

"Roland of Gilead."

This voice, which he almost recognizes; a voice so like his own that a psychiatrist from Eddie's or Susannah's or Jake's when-and-where would say it is his voice, the voice of his subconscious, but Roland knows better; Roland knows that often the voices that sound the most like our own when they speak in our heads are those of the most terrible outsiders, the most dangerous intruders.

"Roland, son of Steven."

The ball has taken him first to Hambry and to Mayor's House, and he would see more of what is happening there, but then it takes him away—calls him away in that strangely familiar voice, and he has to go. There is no choice because, unlike

Rhea or Jonas, he is not watching the ball and the creatures who speak soundlessly within it; he is inside *the ball, a part of its endless pink storm.*

"Roland, come. Roland, see."

And so the storm whirls him first up and then away. He flies across the Drop, rising and rising through stacks of air first warm and then cold, and he is not alone in the pink storm which bears him west along the Path of the Beam. Sheb flies past him, his hat cocked back on his head; he is singing "Hey Jude" at the top of his lungs as his nicotine-stained fingers plink keys that are not there—transported by his tune, Sheb doesn't seem to realize that the storm has ripped his piano away.

"Roland, come,"

the voice says—the voice of the storm, the voice of the glass— and Roland comes. The Romp flies by him, glassy eyes blazing with pink light. A scrawny man in farmer's overalls goes flying past, his long red hair streaming out behind him. "Life for you, and for your crop," he says—something like that, anyway—and then he's gone. Next, spinning like a weird windmill, comes an iron chair (to Roland it looks like a torture device) equipped with wheels, and the boy gunslinger thinks The Lady of Shadows *without knowing why he thinks it, or what it means.*

Now the pink storm is carrying him over blasted mountains, now over a fertile green delta where a broad river runs its oxbow squiggles like a vein, reflecting a placid blue sky that turns to the pink of wild roses as the storm passes above. Ahead, Roland sees an uprushing column of darkness and his heart quails, but this is where the pink storm is taking him, and this is where he must go.

I want to get out, *he thinks, but he's not stupid, he realizes the truth: he may* never *get out. The wizard's glass has swallowed him. He may remain in its stormy, muddled eye forever.*

I'll shoot my way out, if I have to, *he thinks, but no—he has no guns. He is naked in the storm, rushing bareass toward that virulent blue-black infection that has buried all the landscape beneath it.*

And yet he hears singing.

Faint but beautiful—a sweet harmonic sound that makes him shiver and think of Susan: bird and bear and hare and fish.

Suddenly Sheemie's mule (Caprichoso, *Roland thinks, a* beautiful name) *goes past, galloping on thin air with his eyes as bright as firedims in the storm's* lumbre fuego. *Following him, wearing a* sombrera *and riding a broom festooned with fluttering reap-charms, comes Rhea of the Cöos. "I'll get you, my pretty!" she screams at the fleeing mule, and then, cackling, she is gone, zooming and brooming.*

Roland plunges into the black, and suddenly his breath is gone. The world around him is noxious darkness; the air seems to creep on his skin like a layer of bugs. He is buffeted, boxed to and fro by invisible fists, then driven downward in a dive so violent he fears he will be smashed against the ground: so fell Lord Perth.

Dead fields and deserted villages roll up out of the gloom; he sees blasted trees that will give no shade—oh, but all is shade here, all is death here, this is the edge of End-World, where some dark day he will come, and all is death here.

"Gunslinger, this is Thunderclap."

"Thunderclap," he says.

"Here are the unbreathing; the white faces."

"The unbreathing. The white faces."

Yes. He knows that, somehow. This is the place of slaughtered soldiers, the cloven helm, the rusty halberd; from here come the pale warriors. This is Thunderclap, where clocks run backward and the graveyards vomit out their dead.

Ahead is a tree like a crooked, clutching hand; on its topmost branch a billy-bumbler has been impaled. It should be dead, but as the pink storm carries Roland past, it raises its head and looks at him with inexpressible pain and weariness. "Oy!" it cries, and then it, too, is gone and not to be remembered for many years.

"Look ahead, Roland—see your destiny."

*Now, suddenly, he knows that voice—it is the voice of the
Turtle.*

*He looks and sees a brilliant blue-gold glow piercing the dirty
darkness of Thunderclap. Before he can do more than register it,
he breaks out of the darkness and into the light like something
coming out of an egg, a creature at last being born.*

"Light! Let there be light!"

*the voice of the Turtle cries, and Roland has to put his hands to
his eyes and peek through his fingers to keep from being blinded.
Below him is a field of blood—or so he thinks then, a boy of
fourteen who has that day done his first real killing.* This is the
blood that has flowed out of Thunderclap and threatens
to drown our side of the world, *he thinks, and it will not be
for untold years that he will finally rediscover his time inside the
ball and put this memory together with Eddie's dream and tell
his* compadres, *as they sit in the turnpike breakdown lane at
the end of the night, that he was wrong, that he had been fooled
by the brilliance, coming as it did, so hard on the heels of Thunderclap's shadows. "It wasn't blood but roses," he tells Eddie,
Susannah, and Jake.*

"Gunslinger, look—look there."

*Yes, there it is, a dusty gray-black pillar rearing on the hori-
zon: the Dark Tower, the place where all Beams, all lines of force,
converge. In its spiraling windows he sees fitful electric blue fire
and hears the cries of all those pent within; he senses both the
strength of the place and the wrongness of it; he can feel how it is
spooling error across everything, softening the divisions between
the worlds, how its potential for mischief is growing stronger
even as disease weakens its truth and coherence, like a body
afflicted with cancer; this jutting arm of dark gray stone is the
world's great mystery and last awful riddle.*

*It is the Tower, the Dark Tower rearing to the sky, and as
Roland rushes toward it in the pink storm, he thinks:* I will
enter you, me and my friends, if *ka* wills it so; we will
enter you and we will conquer the wrongness within you.

It may be years yet, but I swear by bird and bear and hare
and fish, by all I love that—

*But now the sky fills with flaggy clouds which flow out of
Thunderclap, and the world begins to go dark; the blue light
from the Tower's rising windows shines like mad eyes, and
Roland hears thousands of screaming, wailing voices.*

"You will kill everything and everyone you love," *says the
voice of the Turtle, and now it is a cruel voice, cruel and hard.*

"and still the Tower will be pent shut against you."

*The gunslinger draws in all his breath and draws together
all his force; when he cries his answer to the Turtle, he does
so for all the generations of his blood:* "NO! IT WILL NOT
STAND! WHEN I COME HERE IN MY BODY, IT WILL
NOT STAND! I SWEAR ON MY FATHER'S NAME, IT
WILL NOT STAND!"

"Then die,"

*the voice says, and Roland is hurled at the gray-black stone
flank of the Tower, to be smashed there like a bug against a rock.
But before that can happen—*

6

Cuthbert and Alain stood watching Roland with increasing concern. He had the piece of Maerlyn's Rainbow
raised to his face, cupped in his hands as a man might
cup a ceremonial goblet before making a toast. The drawstring bag lay crumpled on the dusty toes of his boots; his
cheeks and forehead were washed in a pink glow that
neither boy liked. It seemed alive, somehow, and hungry.

They thought, as if with one mind: *I can't see his eyes.
Where are his eyes?*

"Roland?" Cuthbert repeated. "If we're going to get
out to Hanging Rock before they're ready for us, you
have to put that thing away."

Roland made no move to lower the ball. He muttered something under his breath; later, when Cuthbert and Alain had a chance to compare notes, they both agreed it had been *thunderclap.*

"Roland?" Alain asked, stepping forward. As gingerly as a surgeon slipping a scalpel into the body of a patient, he slipped his right hand between the curve of the ball and Roland's bent, studious face. There was no response. Alain pulled back and turned to Cuthbert.

"Can you touch him?" Bert asked.

Alain shook his head. "Not at all. It's like he's gone somewhere far away."

"We have to wake him up." Cuthbert's voice was dust-dry and shaky at the edges.

"Vannay told us that if you wake a person from a deep hypnotic trance too suddenly, he can go mad," Alain said. "Remember? I don't know if I dare—"

Roland stirred. The pink sockets where his eyes had been seemed to grow. His mouth flattened into the line of bitter determination they both knew well.

"No! It will not stand!" he cried in a voice that made gooseflesh ripple the skin of the other two boys; that was not Roland's voice at all, at least not as he was now; that was the voice of a man.

"No," Alain said much later, when Roland slept and he and Cuthbert sat up before the campfire. "That was the voice of a king."

Now, however, the two of them only looked at their absent, roaring friend, paralyzed with fright.

"When I come here in my body, it will not stand! I swear on my father's name, IT WILL NOT STAND!"

Then, as Roland's unnaturally pink face contorted, like the face of a man who confronts some unimaginable horror, Cuthbert and Alain lunged forward. It was no longer a question of perhaps destroying him in an effort to save him; if they didn't do something, the glass would kill him as they watched.

In the dooryard of the Bar K, it had been Cuthbert who clipped Roland; this time Alain did the honors, administering a hard right to the center of the gunslinger's forehead. Roland tumbled backward, the ball spilling out of his loosening hands and the terrible pink light leaving his face. Cuthbert caught the boy and Alain caught the ball. Its heavy pink glow was weirdly insistent, beating at his eyes and pulling at his mind, but Alain stuffed it resolutely into the drawstring bag again without looking at it . . . and as he pulled the cord, yanking the bag's mouth shut, he saw the pink light wink out, as if it knew it had lost. For the time being, at least.

He turned back, and winced at the sight of the bruise puffing up from the middle of Roland's brow. "Is he—"

"Out cold," Cuthbert said.

"He better come to soon."

Cuthbert looked at him grimly, with not a trace of his usual amiability. "Yes," he said, "you're certainly right about that."

7

Sheemie waited at the foot of the stairs which led down to the kitchen area, shifting uneasily from foot to foot and waiting for sai Thorin to come back, or to call him. He didn't know how long she'd been in the kitchen, but it felt like forever. He wanted her to come back, and more than that—more than anything—he wanted her to bring Susan-sai with her. Sheemie had a terrible feeling about this place and this day; a feeling that darkened like the sky, which was now all obscured with smoke in the west. What was happening out there, or if it had anything to do with the thundery sounds he'd heard earlier, Sheemie didn't know, but he wanted to be out of here before the smoke-hazed sun went down and the *real* Demon Moon, not its pallid day-ghost, rose in the sky.

One of the swinging doors between the corridor and the kitchen pushed open and Olive came hurrying out. She was alone.

"She's in the pantry, all right," Olive said. She raked her fingers through her graying hair. "I got that much out of those two *pupuras,* but no more. I knew it was going to be that way as soon as they started talking that stupid crunk of theirs."

There was no proper word for the dialect of the Mejis *vaqueros,* but "crunk" served well enough among the Barony's higher-born citizens. Olive knew both of the *vaqs* guarding the pantry, in the vague way of a person who has once ridden a lot and passed gossip and weather with other Drop-riders, and she knew damned well these old boys could do better than crunk. They had spoken it so they could pretend to misunderstand her, and save both them and her the embarrassment of an outright refusal. She had gone along with the deception for much the same reason, although she could have responded with crunk of her own perfectly well—and called them some names their mothers never used—had she wanted.

"I told them there were men upstairs," she said, "and I thought maybe they meant to steal the silver. I said I wanted the *maloficios* turned out. And still they played dumb. *No habla, sai.* Shit. *Shit!*"

Sheemie thought of calling them a couple of big old sonuvabitches, and decided to keep silent. She was pacing back and forth in front of him and throwing an occasional burning look at the closed kitchen doors. At last she stopped in front of Sheemie again.

"Turn out your pockets," she said. "Let's see what you have for hopes and garlands."

Sheemie did as she asked, producing a little pocket-knife (a gift from Stanley Ruiz) and a half-eaten cookie from one. From the other he brought out three lady-finger firecrackers, a big-banger, and a few sulfur matches.

Olive's eyes gleamed when she saw these. "Listen to me, Sheemie," she said.

8

Cuthbert patted Roland's face with no result. Alain pushed him aside, knelt, and took the gunslinger's hands. He had never used the touch this way, but had been told it was possible—that one could reach another's mind, in at least some cases.

Roland! Roland, wake up! Please! We need you!

At first there was nothing. Then Roland stirred, muttered, and pulled his hands out of Alain's. In the moment before his eyes opened, both of the other two boys were struck by the same fear of what they might see: no eyes at all, only raving pink light.

But they were Roland's eyes, all right—those cool blue shooter's eyes.

He struggled to gain his feet, and failed the first time. He held out his hands. Cuthbert took one, Alain the other. As they pulled him up, Bert saw a strange and frightening thing: there were threads of white in Roland's hair. There had been none that morning; he would have sworn to it. The morning had been a long time ago, however.

"How long was I out?" Roland touched the bruise in the center of his forehead with the tips of his fingers and winced.

"Not long," Alain said. "Five minutes, maybe. Roland, I'm sorry I hit you, but I had to. It was . . . I thought it was killing you."

"Mayhap 'twas. Is it safe?"

Alain pointed wordlessly to the drawstring bag.

"Good. It's best one of you carry it for now. I might be . . ." He searched for the right word, and when he found it, a small, wintry smile touched the corners of his mouth—"tempted," he finished. "Let's ride for Hanging Rock. We've got work yet to finish."

"Roland . . ." Cuthbert began.

Roland turned, one hand on the horn of his horse's saddle.

Cuthbert licked his lips, and for a moment Alain didn't think he would be able to ask. *If you don't I will,* Alain thought . . . but Bert managed, bringing the words out in a rush.

"What did you see?"

"Much," Roland said. "I saw much, but most of it is already fading out of my mind, the way dreams do when you wake up. What I do remember I'll tell you as we ride. You must know, because it changes everything. We're going back to Gilead, but not for long."

"Where after that?" Alain asked, mounting.

"West. In search of the Dark Tower. If we survive today, that is. Come on. Let's take those tankers."

9

The two *vaqs* were rolling smokes when there was a loud bang from upstairs. They both jumped and looked at each other, the tobacco from their works-in-progress sifting down to the floor in small brown flurries. A woman shrieked. The doors burst open. It was the Mayor's widow again, this time accompanied by a maid. The *vaqs* knew her well—Maria Tomas, the daughter of an old *compadre* from the Piano Ranch.

"The thieving bastards have set the place on fire!" Maria cried, speaking to them in crunk. "Come and help!"

"Maria, sai, we have orders to guard—"

"A *putina* locked in the pantry?" Maria shouted, her eyes blazing. "Come, ye stupid old donkey, before the whole place catches! Then ye can explain to Señor Lengyll why ye stood here using yer thumbs for fart-corks while Seafront burned down around yer ears!"

"Go on!" Olive snapped. "Are you cowards?"

There were several smaller bangs as, above them in the great parlor, Sheemie set off the lady-fingers. He used the same match to light the drapes.

The two *viejos* exchanged a glance. *"Andelay,"* said the older of the two, then looked back at Maria. He no longer bothered with the crunk. "Watch this door," he said.

"Like a hawk," she agreed.

The two old men bustled out, one gripping the cords of his *bolas,* the other pulling a long knife from the scabbard on his belt.

As soon as the women heard their footsteps on the stairs at the end of the hall, Olive nodded to Maria and they crossed the room. Maria threw the bolts; Olive pulled the door open. Susan came out at once, looking from one to the other, then smiling tentatively. Maria gasped at the sight of her mistress's swelled face and the blood crusted around her nose.

Susan took Maria's hand before the maid could touch her face and squeezed her fingers gently. "Do ye think Thorin would want me now?" she asked, and then seemed to realize who her other rescuer was. "Olive . . . sai Thorin . . . I'm sorry. I didn't mean to be cruel. But ye must believe that Roland, him ye know as Will Dearborn, would never—"

"I know it well," Olive said, "and there's no time for this now. Come on."

She and Maria led Susan out of the kitchen, away from the stairs ascending to the main house and toward the storage rooms at the far north end of the lower level. In the drygoods storage room, Olive told the two of them to wait. She was gone for perhaps five minutes, but to Susan and Maria it seemed an eternity.

When she came back, Olive was wearing a wildly colored *serape* much too big for her—it might have been her husband's, but Susan thought it looked too big for the late Mayor, as well. Olive had tucked a piece of it into the side of her jeans to keep from stumbling over it. Slung over her arm like blankets, she had two more, both smaller and lighter. "Put these on," she said. "It's going to be cold."

Leaving the drygoods store, they went down a narrow servants' passageway toward the back courtyard. There, if they were fortunate (and if Miguel was still unconscious), Sheemie would be waiting for them with mounts. Olive hoped with all her heart that they would be fortunate. She wanted Susan safely away from Hambry before the sun went down.

And before the moon rose.

10

"Susan's been taken prisoner," Roland told the others as they rode west toward Hanging Rock. "That's the first thing I saw in the glass."

He spoke with such an air of absence that Cuthbert almost reined up. This wasn't the ardent lover of the last few months. It was as if Roland had found a dream to ride through the pink air within the ball, and part of him rode it still. *Or is it riding him?* Cuthbert wondered.

"What?" Alain asked. "Susan taken? How? By whom? Is she all right?"

"Taken by Jonas. He hurt her some, but not too badly. She'll heal . . . and she'll live. I'd turn around in a second if I thought her life was in any real danger."

Ahead of them, appearing and disappearing in the dust like a mirage, was Hanging Rock. Cuthbert could see the sunlight pricking hazy sunstars on the tankers, and he could see men. A lot of them. A lot of horses, as well. He patted the neck of his own mount, then glanced across to make sure Alain had Lengyll's machine-gun. He did. Cuthbert reached around to the small of his back, making sure of the slingshot. It was there. Also his deerskin ammunition bag, which now contained a number of the big-bangers Sheemie had stolen as well as steel shot.

He's using every ounce of his will to keep from going back, anyway, Cuthbert thought. He found the realization comforting—sometimes Roland scared him. There was something in him that went beyond steel. Something like madness. If it was there, you were glad to have it on your side . . . but often enough you wished it wasn't there at all. On *anybody's* side.

"Where is she?" Alain asked.

"Reynolds took her back to Seafront. She's locked in the pantry . . . or *was* locked there. I can't say which, exactly, because . . ." Roland paused, thinking. "The ball sees far, but sometimes it sees more. Sometimes it sees a future that's already happening."

"How can the future already be happening?" Alain asked.

"I don't know, and I don't think it was always that way.

I think it's more to do with the world than Maerlyn's Rainbow. Time is strange now. We *know* that, don't we? How things sometimes seem to . . . slip. It's almost as if there's a thinny everywhere, breaking things down. But Susan's safe. I know that, and that's enough for me. Sheemie is going to help her . . . or *is* helping her. Somehow Jonas missed Sheemie, and he followed Susan all the way back."

"Good for Sheemie!" Alain said, and pumped his fist into the air. "Hurrah!" Then: "What about us? Did you see us in this future?"

"No. This part was all quick—I hardly snatched more than a glance before the ball took me away. *Flew* me away, it seemed. But . . . I saw smoke on the horizon. I remember that. It could have been the smoke of burning tankers, or the brush piled in front of Eyebolt, or both. I think we're going to succeed."

Cuthbert was looking at his old friend in a queerly distraught way. The young man so deeply in love that Bert had needed to knock him into the dust of the courtyard in order to wake him up to his responsibilities . . . where was that young man, exactly? What had changed him, given him those disturbing strands of white hair?

"If we survive what's ahead," Cuthbert said, watching the gunslinger closely, "she'll meet us on the road. Won't she, Roland?"

He saw the pain on Roland's face, and now understood: the lover was here, but the ball had taken away his joy and left only grief. That, and some new purpose— yes, Cuthbert felt it very well—which had yet to be stated.

"I don't know," Roland said. "I almost hope not, because we can never be as we were."

"What?" This time Cuthbert *did* rein up.

Roland looked at him calmly enough, but now there were tears in his eyes.

"We are fools of *ka*," the gunslinger said. "*Ka* like a wind, Susan calls it." He looked first at Cuthbert on his left, then at Alain on his right. "The Tower is our *ka;* mine especially. But it isn't hers, nor she mine. No more is John Farson our *ka*. We're not going toward his men to defeat him, but only because they're in our way." He raised his hands, then dropped them again, as if to say, *What more do you need me to tell you?*

"There *is* no Tower, Roland," Cuthbert said patiently. "I don't know what you saw in that glass ball, but there *is* no Tower. Well, as a symbol, I suppose—like Arthur's Cup, or the Cross of the man-Jesus—but not as a real thing, a real building—"

"Yes," Roland said. "It's real."

They looked at him uncertainly, and saw no doubt on his face.

"It's real, and our fathers know. Beyond the dark land—I can't remember its name now, it's one of the things I've lost—is End-World, and in End-World stands the Dark Tower. Its existence is the great secret our fathers keep; it's what has held them together as *ka-tet* across all the years of the world's decline. When we return to Gilead—*if* we return, and I now think we will—I'll tell them what I've seen, and they'll confirm what I say."

"You saw all that in the glass?" Alain asked in an awe-hushed voice.

"I saw much."

"But not Susan Delgado," Cuthbert said.

"No. When we finish with yonder men and she finishes with Mejis, her part in our *ka-tet* ends. Inside the ball, I was given a choice: Susan, and my life as her husband and father of the child she now carries . . . or the Tower." Roland wiped his face with a shaking hand. "I would choose Susan in an instant, if not for one thing: the Tower is crumbling, and if it falls, everything we know will be swept away. There will be chaos beyond our imagining. We must go . . . *and we will go.*" Above his young and unlined cheeks, below his young and unlined brow, were the ancient killer's eyes that Eddie Dean would first glimpse in the mirror of an airliner's bathroom. But now they swam with childish tears.

There was nothing childish in his voice, however.

"I choose the Tower. I must. Let her live a good life and long with someone else—she will, in time. As for me, I choose the Tower."

II

Susan mounted on Pylon, which Sheemie had hastened to bring around to the rear courtyard after lighting the draperies of the great parlor on fire. Olive Thorin rode one of the Barony geldings with Sheemie double-mounted behind her and holding onto Capi's lead. Maria opened the back gate, wished them good luck, and the three trotted out. The sun was westering now, but the wind had pulled away most of the smoke that had risen earlier. Whatever had happened in the desert, it was over now . . . or happening on some other layer of the same present time.

Roland, be thee well, Susan thought. *I'll see thee soon, dear . . . as soon as I can.*

"Why are we going north?" she asked after half an hour's silent riding.

"Because Seacoast Road's best."

"But—"

"Hush! They'll find you gone and search the house first . . . if t'asn't burned flat, that is. Not finding you there, they'll send west, along the Great Road." She cast an eye on Susan that was not much like the dithery, slightly confabulated Olive Thorin that folks in Hambry knew . . . or thought they knew. "If I know that's the direction you'd choose, so will others we'd do well to avoid."

Susan was silent. She was too confused to speak, but Olive seemed to know what she was about, and Susan was grateful for that.

"By the time they get around to sniffing west, it'll be dark. Tonight we'll stay in one of the sea-cliff caves five miles or so from here. I grew up a fisherman's daughter, and I know all those caves, none better." The thought of the caves she'd played in as a girl seemed to cheer her. "Tomorrow we'll cut west, as you like. I'm afraid you're going to have a plump old widow as a chaperone for a bit. Better get used to the idea."

"Thee's too good," Susan said. "Ye should send Sheemie and I on alone, sai."

"And go back to what? Why, I can't even get two old trail-hands on kitchen-duty to follow my orders. Fran Lengyll's boss of the shooting-match now, and I've no urge to wait and see how he does at it. Nor if he decides he'd be better off with me adjudged mad and put up safe in a *haci* with bars on the windows. Or shall I stay to see how Hash Renfrew does as Mayor, with his boots up on my tables?" Olive actually laughed.

"Sai, I'm sorry."

"We shall all be sorry later on," Olive said, sounding remarkably cheery about it. "For now, the most important thing is to reach those caves unobserved. It must seem that we vanished into thin air. Hold up."

Olive checked her horse, stood in the stirrups, looked around to make sure of her position, nodded, then twisted in the saddle so she could speak to Sheemie.

"Young man, it's time for ye to mount yer trusty mule and go back to Seafront. If there are riders coming after us, ye must turn em aside with a few well-chosen words. Will'ee do that?"

Sheemie looked stricken. "I don't have any well-chosen words, sai Thorin, so I don't. I hardly have any words at all."

"Nonsense," Olive said, and kissed Sheemie's forehead. "Go back at a goodish trot. If'ee spy no one coming after us by the time the sun touches the hills, then turn north again and follow. We shall wait for ye by the signpost. Do ye know where I mean?"

Sheemie thought he did, although it marked the outmost northern boundary of his little patch of geography. "The red 'un? With the *sombrero* on it, and the arrow pointing back for town?"

"The very one. Ye won't get that far until after dark, but there'll be plenty of moonlight tonight. If ye don't come right away, we'll wait. But ye must go back, and shift any men that might be chasing us off our track. Do ye understand?"

Sheemie did. He slid off Olive's horse, clucked Caprichoso forward, and climbed on board, wincing as the place the mule had bitten came down. "So it'll be, Olive-sai."

"Good, Sheemie. Good. Off'ee go, then."

"Sheemie?" Susan said. "Come to me a moment, please."

He did, holding his hat in front of him and looking up at her worshipfully. Susan bent and kissed him not on the forehead but firmly on the mouth. Sheemie came close to fainting.

"Thankee-sai," Susan said. "For everything."

Sheemie nodded. When he spoke, he could manage nothing above a whisper. " 'Twas only *ka*," he said. "I know that . . . but I love you, Susan-sai. Go well. I'll see you soon."

"I look forward to it."

But there was no soon, and no later for them, either. Sheemie took one look back as he rode his mule south, and waved. Susan lifted her own hand in return. It was the last Sheemie ever saw of her, and in many ways, that was a blessing.

12

Latigo had set pickets a mile out from Hanging Rock, but the blond boy Roland, Cuthbert, and Alain encountered as they closed in on the tankers looked confused and unsure of himself, no danger to anyone. He had scurvy-blossoms around his mouth and nose, suggesting that the men Farson had sent on this duty had ridden hard and fast, with little in the way of fresh supplies.

When Cuthbert gave the Good Man's *sigul*—hands clasped to the chest, left above right, then both held out to the person being greeted—the blond picket did the same, and with a grateful smile.

"What spin and raree back there?" he asked, speaking with a strong In-World accent—to Roland, the boy sounded like a Nordite.

"Three boys who killed a couple of big bugs and then hied for the hills," Cuthbert replied. He was an eerily good mimic, and gave the boy back his own accent faultlessly. "There were a fight. It be over now, but they did fight fearful."

"What—"

"No time," Roland said brusquely. "We have dispatches." He crossed his hands on his chest, then held them out. "Hile! Farson!"

"Good Man!" the blond returned smartly. He gave

back the salute with a smile that said he would have asked Cuthbert where he was from and who he was related to, if there had been more time. Then they were past him and inside Latigo's perimeter. As easy as that.

"Remember that it's hit-and-run," Roland said. "Slow down for nothing. What we don't get must be left—there'll be no second pass."

"Gods, don't even suggest such a thing," Cuthbert said, but he was smiling. He pulled his sling out of its rudimentary holster and tested its elastic draw with a thumb. Then he licked the thumb and hoisted it to the wind. Not much problem there, if they came in as they were; the wind was strong, but at their backs.

Alain unslung Lengyll's machine-gun, looked at it doubtfully, then yanked back the slide-cock. "I don't know about this, Roland. It's loaded, and I think I see how to use it, but—"

"Then use it," Roland said. The three of them were picking up speed now, the hooves of their horses drumming against the hardpan. The wind gusted, belling the fronts of their *serapes*. "This is the sort of work it was meant for. If it jams, drop it and use your revolver. Are you ready?"

"Yes, Roland."

"Bert?"

"Aye," Cuthbert said in a wildly exaggerated Hambry accent, "so I am, so I am."

Ahead of them, dust puffed as groups of riders passed before and behind the tankers, readying the column for departure. Men on foot looked around at the oncomers curiously but with a fatal lack of alarm.

Roland drew both revolvers. *"Gilead!"* he cried. *"Hile! Gilead!"*

He spurred Rusher to a gallop. The other two boys did the same. Cuthbert was in the middle again, sitting

on his reins, slingshot in hand, lucifer matches radiating
out of his tightly pressed lips.

The gunslingers rode down on Hanging Rock like
furies.

13

Twenty minutes after sending Sheemie back south, Susan
and Olive came around a sharp bend and found themselves face to face with three mounted men in the road.
In the late-slanting sun, she saw that the one in the middle had a blue coffin tattooed on his hand. It was Reynolds. Susan's heart sank.

The one on Reynolds's left—he wore a stained white
drover's hat and had a lazily cocked eye—she didn't
know, but the one on the right, who looked like a stony-
hearted preacher, was Laslo Rimer. It was Rimer that
Reynolds glanced at, after smiling at Susan.

"Why, Las and I couldn't even get us a drink to send his
late brother, the Chancellor of Whatever You Want and
the Minister of Thank You Very Much, on with a word,"
Reynolds said. "We hadn't hardly hit town before we got
persuaded out here. I wasn't going to go, but . . . damn!
That old lady's something. Could talk a corpse into giving a blowjob, if you'll pardon the crudity. I think your
aunt may have lost a wheel or two off her cart, though,
sai Delgado. She—"

"Your friends are dead," Susan told him.

Reynolds paused, shrugged. "Wellnow. Maybe *si* and
maybe *no*. Me, I think I've decided to travel on without
em even if they ain't. But I might hang around here one
more night. This Reaping business . . . I've heard so
much about the way folks do it in the Outers. 'Specially
the bonfire part."

The man with the cocked eye laughed phlegmily.

"Let us pass," Olive said. "This girl has done nothing, and neither have I."

"She helped Dearborn escape," Rimer said, "him who murdered your own husband and my brother. I wouldn't call that nothing."

"The gods may restore Kimba Rimer in the clearing," Olive said, "but the truth is he looted half of this town's treasury, and what he didn't give over to John Farson, he kept for himself."

Rimer recoiled as if slapped.

"Ye didn't know I knew? Laslo, I'd be angry at how little any of ye thought of me . . . except why would I want to be thought of by the likes of you, anyway? I knew enough to make me sick, leave it at that. I know that the man you're sitting beside—"

"Shut up," Rimer muttered.

"—was likely the one who cut yer brother's black heart open; sai Reynolds was seen that early morning in that wing, so I've been told—"

"Shut up, you cunt!"

"—and so I believe."

"Better do as he says, sai, and hold your tongue," Reynolds said. Some of the lazy good humor had left his face. Susan thought: *He doesn't like people knowing what he did. Not even when he's the one on top and what they know can't hurt him. And he's less without Jonas. A lot less. He knows it, too.*

"Let us pass," Olive said.

"No, sai, I can't do that."

"I'll help ye, then, shall I?"

Her hand had crept beneath the outrageously large *serape* during the palaver, and now she brought out a huge and ancient *pistola*, its handles of yellowed ivory, its filigreed barrel of old tarnished silver. On top was a brass powder-and-spark.

Olive had no business even drawing the thing—it caught on her *serape,* and she had to fight it free. She had no business cocking it, either, a process that took both thumbs and two tries. But the three men were utterly flummoxed by the sight of the elderly blunderbuss in her hands, Reynolds as much as the other two; he sat his horse with his jaw hanging slack. Jonas would have wept.

"Get her!" a cracked old voice shrieked from behind the men blocking the road. *"What's wrong with ye, ye stupid culls? GET HER!"*

Reynolds started at that and went for his gun. He was fast, but he had given Olive too much of a headstart and was beaten, beaten cold. Even as he cleared leather with the barrel of his revolver, the Mayor's widow held the old gun out in both hands, and, squinching her eyes shut like a little girl who is forced to eat something nasty, pulled the trigger.

The spark flashed, but the damp powder only made a weary *floop* sound and disappeared in a puff of blue smoke. The ball—big enough to have taken Clay Reynolds's head off from the nose on up, had it fired—stayed in the barrel.

In the next instant his own gun roared in his fist. Olive's horse reared, whinnying. Olive went off the gelding head over boots, with a black hole in the orange stripe of her *serape*—the stripe which lay above her heart.

Susan heard herself screaming. The sound seemed to come from very far away. She might have gone on for some time, but then she heard the clop of approaching pony-hooves from behind the men in the road . . . and knew. Even before the man with the lazy eye moved aside to show her, she knew, and her screams stopped.

The galloped-out pony that had brought the witch back to Hambry had been replaced by a fresh one, but it was the same black cart, the same golden cabalistic symbols, the same driver. Rhea sat with the reins in her claws, her head ticking from side to side like the head of a rusty old robot, grinning at Susan without humor. Grinning as a corpse grins.

"Hello, my little sweeting," she said, calling her as she had all those months ago, on the night Susan had come to her hut to be proved honest. On the night Susan had come running most of the way, out of simple high spirits. Beneath the light of the Kissing Moon she had come, her blood high from the exercise, her skin flushed; she had been singing "Careless Love."

"Yer pallies and screw-buddies have taken my ball, ye ken," Rhea said, clucking the pony to a stop a few paces ahead of the riders. Even Reynolds looked down on her with uneasiness. "Took my lovely glam, that's what those bad boys did. Those bad, bad boys. But it showed me much while yet I had it, aye. It sees far, and in more ways than one. Much of it I've forgot . . . but not which way ye'd come, my sweeting. Not which way that precious old dead bitch laying yonder on the road would bring ye. And now ye must go to town." Her grin widened, became something unspeakable. "It's time for the fair, ye ken."

"Let me go," Susan said. "Let me go, if ye'd not answer to Roland of Gilead."

Rhea ignored her and spoke to Reynolds. "Bind her hands before her and stand her in the back of the cart. There's people that'll want to see her. A good look is what they'll want, and a good look is just what they'll have. If her aunt's done a proper job, there'll be a lot of them in town. Get her up, now, and be smart about it."

14

Alain had time for one clear thought: *We could have gone around them—if what Roland said is true, then only the wizard's glass matters, and we have that. We could have gone around them.*

Except, of course, that was impossible. A hundred generations of gunslinger blood argued against it. Tower or no Tower, the thieves must not be allowed to have their prize. Not if they could be stopped.

Alain leaned forward and spoke directly into his horse's ear. "Jig or rear when I start shooting, and I'll knock your fucking brains out."

Roland led them in, outracing the other two on his stronger horse. The clot of men nearest by—five or six mounted, a dozen or more on foot and examining a pair of the oxen which had dragged the tankers out here—gazed at him stupidly until he began to fire, and then they scattered like quail. He got every one of the riders; their horses fled in a widening fan, trailing their reins (and, in one case, a dead soldier). Somewhere someone was shouting, "Harriers! Harriers! Mount up, you fools!"

"Alain!" Roland screamed as they bore down. In front of the tankers, a double handful of riders and armed men were coming together—*milling* together—in a clumsy defensive line. *"Now! Now!"*

Alain raised the machine-gun, seated its rusty wire stock in the hollow of his shoulder, and remembered what little he knew about rapid-fire weapons: aim low, swing fast and smooth.

He touched the trigger and the speed-shooter bellowed into the dusty air, recoiling against his shoulder in a series of rapid thuds, shooting bright fire from the end of its perforated barrel. Alain raked it from left to right, running the sight above the scattering, shouting defenders and across the high steel hides of the tankers.

The third tanker actually blew up on its own. The sound it made was like no explosion Alain had ever heard: a guttural, muscular ripping sound accompanied by a brilliant flash of orange-red fire. The steel shell rose in two halves. One of these spun thirty yards through the air and landed on the desert floor in a furiously burning hulk; the other rose straight up into a column of greasy black smoke. A burning wooden wheel spun across the sky like a plate and came back down trailing sparks and burning splinters.

Men fled, screaming—some on foot, others laid flat along the necks of their nags, their eyes wide and panicky.

When Alain reached the end of the line of tankers, he reversed the track of the muzzle. The machine-gun was hot in his hands now, but he kept his finger pressed to the trigger. In this world, you had to use what you could while it still worked. Beneath him, his horse ran on as if it had understood every word Alain had whispered in its ear.

Another! I want another!

But before he could blow another tanker, the gun ceased its chatter—perhaps jammed, probably empty. Alain threw it aside and drew his revolver. From beside him there came the *thuppp* of Cuthbert's slingshot, audible even over the cries of the men, the hoofbeats of the horses, the *whoosh* of the burning tanker. Alain saw a sputtering big-bang arc into the sky and come down exactly where Cuthbert had aimed: in the oil puddling around the wooden wheels of a tanker marked SUNOCO. For a moment Alain could clearly see the line of nine or a dozen holes in the tanker's bright side—holes he had put there with sai Lengyll's speed-shooter—and then there was a crack and a flash as the big-bang exploded. A moment later, the holes running along the bright flank of the tanker began to shimmer. The oil beneath them was on fire.

"Get out!" a man in a faded campaign hat yelled. *"She's gointer blow! They're all going to b—"*

Alain shot him, exploding the side of his face and knocking him out of one old, sprung boot. A moment later the second tanker blew up. One burning steel panel shot out sidewards, landed in the growing puddle of crude oil beneath a third tanker, and then that one exploded, as well. Black smoke rose in the air like the fumes of a funeral pyre; it darkened the day and drew an oily veil across the sun.

15

All six of Farson's chief lieutenants had been carefully described to Roland—to all fourteen gunslingers in training—and he recognized the man running for the *remuda* at once: George Latigo. Roland could have shot him as he ran, but that, ironically, would have made possible a getaway that was cleaner than he wanted.

Instead, he shot the man who ran to meet him.

Latigo wheeled on the heels of his boots and stared at Roland with blazing, hate-filled eyes. Then he ran again, hiling another man, shouting for the riders who were huddled together beyond the burning zone.

Two more tankers exploded, whamming at Roland's ear-drums with dull iron fists, seeming to suck the air back from his lungs like a riptide. The plan had been for Alain to perforate the tankers and for Cuthbert to then shoot in a steady, arcing stream of big-bangers, lighting the spilling oil. The one big-banger he actually shot seemed to confirm that the plan had been feasible, but it was the last slingshot-work Cuthbert did that day. The ease with which the gunslingers had gotten inside the enemy's perimeter and the confusion which greeted their original charge could have been chalked up to inexperience and exhaustion, but the placing of the tankers had been Latigo's mistake, and his alone. He had drawn them tight without even thinking about it, and now they blew tight, one after another. Once the conflagration began, there was no chance of stopping it. Even before Roland raised his left arm and circled it in the air, signalling for Alain and Cuthbert to break off, the work was done. Latigo's encampment was an oily inferno, and John Farson's plans for a motorized assault were so much black smoke being tattered apart by the *fin de año* wind.

"*Ride!*" Roland screamed. "*Ride, ride, ride!*"

They spurred west, toward Eyebolt Canyon. As they went, Roland felt a single bullet drone past his left ear. It was, so far as he knew, the only shot fired at any of them during the assault on the tankers.

16

Latigo was in an ecstasy of fury, a perfect brain-bursting rage, and that was probably merciful—it kept him from thinking of what the Good Man would do when he learned of this fiasco. For the time being, all Latigo cared about was catching the men who had ambushed him . . . if an ambush in desert country was even possible.

Men? No.

The *boys* who had done this.

Latigo knew who they were, all right; he didn't know how they had gotten out here, but he knew who they were, and their run would stop right here, east of the woods and rising hills.

"Hendricks!" he bawled. Hendricks had at least managed to hold his men—half a dozen of them, all mounted—near the *remuda. "Hendricks, to me!"*

As Hendricks rode toward him, Latigo spun the other way and saw a huddle of men standing and watching the burning tankers. Their gaping mouths and stupid young sheep faces made him feel like screaming and dancing up and down, but he refused to give in to that. He held a narrow beam of concentration, one aimed directly at the raiders, who must not under any circumstances be allowed to escape.

"You!" he shouted at the men. One of them turned; the others did not. Latigo strode to them, drawing his pistol as he went. He slapped it into the hand of the man who had turned toward the sound of his voice, and pointed at random to one of those who had not. "Shoot that fool."

Dazed, his face that of a man who believes he is dreaming, the soldier raised the pistol and shot the man to whom Latigo had pointed. That unlucky fellow went down in a heap of knees and elbows and twitching hands. The others turned.

"Good," Latigo said, taking his gun back.

"Sir!" Hendricks cried. *"I see them, sir! I have the enemy in clear view!"*

Two more tankers exploded. A few whickering shards of steel flew in their direction. Some of the men ducked; Latigo did not so much as twitch. Nor did Hendricks. A good man. Thank God for at least one such in this nightmare.

"Shall I hie after them, sir?"

"I'll take your men and hie after them myself, Hendricks. Mount these hoss-guts before us." He swept an arm at the standing men, whose doltish attention had been diverted from the burning tankers to their dead comrade. "Pull in as many others as you can. Do you have a bugler?"

"Yes, sir, Raines, sir!" Hendricks looked around, beckoned, and a pimply, scared-looking boy rode forward. A dented bugle on a frayed strap hung askew on the front of his shirt.

"Raines," Latigo said, "you're with Hendricks."

"Yes, sir."

"Get as many men as you can, Hendricks, but don't linger over the job. They're headed for that canyon, and I believe someone told me it's a box. If so, we're going to turn it into a shooting gallery."

Hendricks's lips spread in a twisted grin. "Yes, sir."

Behind them, the tankers continued to explode.

17

Roland glanced back and was astonished by the size of the black, smoky column rising into the air. Ahead he could clearly see the brush blocking most of the canyon's mouth. And although the wind was blowing the wrong way, he could now hear the maddening mosquito-whine of the thinny.

He patted the air with his outstretched hands, signalling for Cuthbert and Alain to slow down. While they were both still looking at him, he took off his bandanna, whipped it into a rope, and tied it so it would cover his ears. They copied him. It was better than nothing.

The gunslingers continued west, their shadows now running out behind them as long as gantries on the desert floor. Looking back, Roland could see two groups of riders streaming in pursuit. Latigo was at the head of the first, Roland thought, and he was deliberately holding his riders back a little, so that the two groups could merge and attack together.

Good, he thought.

The three of them rode toward Eyebolt in a tight line, continuing to hold their own horses in, allowing their pursuers to close the distance. Every now and then another thud smote the air and shivered through the ground as one of the remaining tankers blew up. Roland was amazed at how easy it had been—even after the battle with Jonas and Lengyll, which should have put the men out here on their mettle, it had been easy. It made him think of a Reaptide long ago, he and Cuthbert surely no more than seven years old, running along a line of stuffy-guys with sticks, knocking them over one after the other, bang-bang-bangety-bang.

The sound of the thinny was warbling its way into his brain in spite of the bandanna over his ears, making his eyes water. Behind him, he could hear the whoops and shouts of the pursuing men. It delighted him. Latigo's men had counted the odds—two dozen against three, with many more of their own force riding hard to join the battle—and their peckers were up once more.

Roland faced front and pointed Rusher at the slit in the brush marking the entrance to Eyebolt Canyon.

18

Hendricks fell in beside Latigo, breathing hard, cheeks glaring with color. "Sir! Beg to report!"

"Then do it."

"I have twenty men, and there are p'raps three times that number riding hard to join us."

Latigo ignored all of this. His eyes were bright blue

flecks of ice. Under his mustache was a small, greedy smile. "Rodney," he said, speaking Hendricks's first name almost with the caress of a lover.

"Sir?"

"I think they're going in, Rodney. Yes . . . look. I'm sure of it. Two more minutes and it'll be too late for them to turn back." He raised his gun, laid the muzzle across his forearm, and threw a shot at the three riders ahead, mostly in exuberance.

"Yes, sir, very good, sir." Hendricks turned and waved viciously for his men to close up, close up.

19

"Dismount!" Roland shouted when they reached the line of tangled brush. It had a smell that was at once dry and oily, like a fire waiting to happen. He didn't know if their failure to ride their horses into the canyon would put Latigo's wind up or not, and he didn't care. These were good mounts, fine Gilead stock, and over these last months, Rusher had become his friend. He would not take him or any of the horses into the canyon, where they would be caught between the fire and the thinny.

The boys were off the horses in a flash, Alain pulling the drawstring bag free of his saddle-horn and slinging it over one shoulder. Cuthbert's and Alain's horses ran at once, whinnying, parallel to the brush, but Rusher lingered for a moment, looking at Roland. "Go on." Roland slapped him on the flank. "Run."

Rusher ran, tail streaming out behind him. Cuthbert and Alain slipped through the break in the brush. Roland followed, glancing down to make sure that the powder-trail was still there. It was, and still dry—there had been not a drop of rain since the day they'd laid it.

"Cuthbert," he said. "Matches."

Cuthbert gave him some. He was grinning so hard it was a wonder they hadn't fallen out of his mouth. "We warmed up their day, didn't we, Roland? Aye!"

"We did, indeed," Roland said, grinning himself. "Go on, now. Back to that chimney-cut."

"Let me do it," Cuthbert said. "Please, Roland, you go with Alain and let me stay. I'm a firebug at heart, always have been."

"No," Roland said. "This part of it's mine. Don't argue with me. Go on. And tell Alain to mind the wizard's glass, no matter what."

Cuthbert looked at him for a moment longer, then nodded. "Don't wait too long."

"I won't."

"May your luck rise, Roland."

"May yours rise twice."

Cuthbert hurried away, boots rattling on the loose stone which carpeted the floor of the canyon. He reached Alain, who lifted a hand to Roland. Roland nodded back, then ducked as a bullet snapped close enough to his temple to flick his hatbrim.

He crouched to the left of the opening in the brush and peered around, the wind now striking full in his face. Latigo's men were closing rapidly. More rapidly than he had expected. If the wind blew out the lucifers—

Never mind the ifs. Hold on, Roland . . . hold on . . . wait for them . . .

He held on, hunkering with an unlit match in each hand, now peering out through a tangle of interlaced branches. The smell of mesquite was strong in his nostrils. Not far behind it was the reek of burning oil. The drone of the thinny filled his head, making him feel dizzy, a stranger to himself. He thought of how it had been inside the pink storm, flying through the air . . .

how he had been snatched away from his vision of Susan. *Thank God for Sheemie,* he thought distantly. *He'll make sure she finishes the day someplace safe.* But the craven whine of the thinny seemed somehow to mock him, to ask him if there had been more to see.

Now Latigo and his men were crossing the last three hundred yards to the canyon's mouth at a full-out gallop, the ones behind closing up fast. It would be hard for the ones riding point to stop suddenly without the risk of being ridden down.

It was time. Roland stuck one of the lucifers between his front teeth and raked it forward. It lit, spilling one hot and sour spark onto the wet bed of his tongue. Before the lucifer's head could burn away, Roland touched it to the powder in the trench. It lit at once, running left beneath the north end of the brush in a bright yellow thread.

He lunged across the opening—which might be wide enough for two horses running flank to flank—with the second lucifer already poised behind his teeth. He struck it as soon as he was somewhat blocked from the wind, dropped it into the powder, heard the splutter-hiss, then turned and ran.

20

Mother and father, was Roland's first shocked thought— memory so deep and unexpected it was like a slap. *At Lake Saroni.*

When had they gone there, to beautiful Lake Saroni in the northern part of Gilead Barony? That Roland couldn't remember. He knew only that he had been very small, and that there had been a beautiful stretch of sandy beach for him to play on, perfect for an aspiring

young castle-builder such as he. That was what he had
been doing on one day of their

*(vacation? was it a vacation? did my parents once upon a
time actually take a vacation?)*

trip, and he had looked up, something—maybe only
the cries of the birds circling over the lake—had made
him look up, and there were his mother and father, Steven and Gabrielle Deschain, at the water's edge, standing with their backs to him and their arms around each
other's waists, looking out at blue water beneath a blue
summer sky. How his heart had filled with love for them!
How infinite was love, twining in and out of hope and
memory like a braid with three strong strands, so much
the Bright Tower of every human's life and soul.

It wasn't love he felt now, however, but terror. The figures standing before him as he ran back to where the
canyon ended (where the *rational* part of the canyon
ended) weren't Steven of Gilead and Gabrielle of Arten
but his mollies, Cuthbert and Alain. They didn't have
their arms around each other's waists, either, but their
hands were clasped, like the hands of fairy-tale children
lost in a threatening fairy-tale wood. Birds circled, but
they were vultures, not gulls, and the shimmering, mist-
topped stuff before the two boys wasn't water.

It was the thinny, and as Roland watched, Cuthbert
and Alain began to walk toward it.

"Stop!" he screamed. *"For your fathers' sakes, stop!"*

They did not stop. They walked hand-in-hand toward
the white-edged hem of the smoky green shimmer. The
thinny whined its pleasure, murmured endearments,
promised rewards. It baked the nerves numb and picked
at the brain.

There was no time to reach them, so Roland did the
only thing he could think of: raised one of his guns and
fired it over their heads. The report was a hammer-blow

in the canyon's enclosure, and for a moment the rico-
chet whine was louder than that of the thinny. The two
boys stopped only inches from its sick shimmer. Roland
kept expecting it to reach out and grab them, as it had
grabbed the low-flying bird when they had been here on
the night of the Peddler's Moon.

He triggered two more shots into the air, the reports
hitting the walls and rolling back. *"Gunslingers!"* he cried.
"To me! To me!"

It was Alain who turned toward him first, his dazed
eyes seeming to float in his dust-streaked face. Cuthbert
continued forward another step, the tips of his boots disappearing in the greenish-silver froth at the edge of the
thinny (the whingeing grumble of the thing rose half a
note, as if in anticipation), and then Alain yanked him
back by the tugstring of his *sombrero*. Cuthbert tripped
over a good-sized chunk of fallen rock and landed hard.
When he looked up, his eyes had cleared.

"Gods!" he murmured, and as he scrambled to his
feet, Roland saw that the toes of his boots were gone,
clipped off neatly, as if with a pair of gardening shears.
His great toes stuck out.

"Roland," he gasped as he and Alain stumbled toward
him. "Roland, we were almost gone. It *talks!*"

"Yes. I've heard it. Come on. There's no time."

He led them to the notch in the canyon wall, praying
that they could get up quick enough to avoid being riddled with bullets . . . as they certainly would be, if Latigo
arrived before they could get up at least part of the way.

A smell, acrid and bitter, began to fill the air—an
odor like boiling juniper berries. And the first tendrils
of whitish-gray smoke drifted past them.

"Cuthbert, you first. Alain, you next. I'll come last.
Climb fast, boys. Climb for your lives."

21

Latigo's men poured through the slot in the wall of brush like water pouring into a funnel, gradually widening the gap as they came. The bottom layer of the dead vegetation was already on fire, but in their excitement none of them saw these first low flames, or marked them if they did. The pungent smoke also went unnoticed; their noses had been deadened by the colossal stench of the burning oil. Latigo himself, in the lead with Hendricks close behind, had only one thought; two words that pounded at his brain in a kind of vicious triumph: *Box canyon! Box canyon! Box canyon!*

Yet something began to intrude on this mantra as he galloped deeper into Eyebolt, his horse's hooves clattering nimbly through the scree of rocks and

(bones)

whitish piles of cow-skulls and ribcages. This was a kind of low buzzing, a maddening, slobbering whine, insectile and insistent. It made his eyes water. Yet, strong as the sound was (if it *was* a sound; it almost seemed to be coming from *inside* him), he pushed it aside, holding onto his mantra

(box canyon box canyon got em in a box canyon)

instead. He would have to face Walter when this was over, perhaps Farson himself, and he had no idea what his punishment would be for losing the tankers . . . but all that was for later. Now he wanted only to kill these interfering bastards.

Up ahead, the canyon took a jog to the north. They would be beyond that point, and probably not far beyond, either. Backed up against the canyon's final wall, trying to squeeze themselves behind what fallen rocks there might be. Latigo would mass what guns he had and drive them out into the open with ricochets. They would probably come with their hands up, hoping for mercy. They would hope in vain. After what they'd done, the trouble they'd caused—

As Latigo rode around the jog in the canyon's wall, already levelling his pistol, his horse screamed—like a woman, it screamed—and reared beneath him. Latigo caught the saddle-horn and managed to stay up, but the horse's rear hooves slid sideways in the scree and the animal went down. Latigo let go of the horn and threw himself clear, already aware that the sound which had been creeping into his ears was suddenly ten times stronger, buzzing loud enough to make his eyeballs pulse in their sockets, loud enough to make his balls tingle unpleasantly, loud enough to blot out the mantra which had been beating so insistently in his head.

The insistence of the thinny was far, far greater than any George Latigo could have managed.

Horses flashed around him as he landed in a kind of sprawling squat, horses that were shoved forward willy-nilly by the oncoming press from behind, by riders that squeezed through the gap in pairs (then trios as the hole in the brush, now burning all along its length, widened) and then spread out again once they were past the bottleneck, none of them clearly realizing that the entire *canyon* was a bottleneck.

Latigo got a confused glimpse of black tails and gray forelegs and dappled fetlocks; he saw chaps, and jeans, and boots jammed into stirrups. He tried to get up and a horseshoe clanged against the back of his skull. His hat saved him from unconsciousness, but he went heavily to his knees with his head down, like a man who means to pray, his vision full of stars and the back of his neck instantly soaked with blood from the gash the passing hoof had opened in his scalp.

Now he heard more screaming horses. Screaming men, as well. He got up again, coughing out the dust raised by the passing horses (such acrid dust, too; it clawed his throat like smoke), and saw Hendricks trying to spur his horse south and east against the oncoming tide of riders. He couldn't do it. The rear third of the canyon was some sort of swamp, filled with greenish steaming water, and there must be quicksand beneath it, because Hendricks's horse seemed stuck. It screamed again, and tried to rear. Its hindquarters slewed sideways. Hendricks crashed his boots into the animal's sides again and again, attempting to get it in motion, but the horse didn't—or couldn't—move. That hungry buzzing sound filled Latigo's ears, and seemed to fill the world.

"Back! Turn back!"

He tried to scream the words, but they came out in what was little more than a croak. Still the riders pounded past him, raising dust that was too thick to be *only* dust. Latigo pulled in breath so he could scream louder—they *had* to go back, something was dreadfully wrong in Eyebolt Canyon—and hacked it out without saying anything.

Screaming horses.

Reeking smoke.

And everywhere, filling the world like lunacy, that whining, whingeing, cringing buzz.

Hendricks's horse went down, eyes rolling, bit-parted teeth snapping at the smoky air and splattering curds of foam from its lips. Hendricks fell into the steaming stagnant water, and it wasn't water at all. It came alive, somehow, as he struck it; grew green hands and a green, shifty mouth; pawed his cheek and melted away the flesh, pawed his nose and tore it off, pawed at his eyes and stripped them from their sockets. It pulled Hendricks under, but before it did, Latigo saw his denuded jawbone, a bloody piston to drive his screaming teeth.

Other men saw, and tried to wheel away from the green trap. Those who managed to do so in time were broadsided by the next wave of men—some of whom were, incredibly, still yipping or bellowing full-throated battle cries. More horses and riders were driven into the green shimmer, which accepted them eagerly. Latigo, standing stunned and bleeding like a man in the middle of a stampede (which was exactly what he was), saw the soldier to whom he had given his gun. This fellow, who had obeyed Latigo's order and shot one of his *compadres* in order to awaken the rest of them, threw himself from his saddle, howling, and crawled back from the edge of the green stuff even as his horse plunged in. He tried to get to his feet, saw two riders bearing down on him, and clapped his hands across his face. A moment later he was ridden down.

The shrieks of the wounded and dying echoed in the smoky canyon, but Latigo hardly heard them. What he heard mostly was that buzzing, a sound that was almost a voice. Inviting him to jump in. To end it here. Why not? It was over, wasn't it? All over.

He struggled away instead, and was now able to make some headway; the stream of riders packing its way into the canyon was easing. Some of the riders fifty or sixty yards back from the jog had even been able to turn their horses. But these were ghostly and confused in the thickening smoke.

The cunning bastards have set the brush on fire behind us. Gods of heaven, gods of earth, I think we're trapped in here.

He could give no commands—every time he drew in breath to try, he coughed it wordlessly back out again— but he was able to grab a passing rider who looked all of seventeen and yank him out of his saddle. The boy went down headfirst and smashed his brow open on a jutting chunk of rock. Latigo was mounted in his place before the kid's feet had stopped twitching.

He jerked the horse's head around and spurred for the front of the canyon, but the smoke thickened to a choking white cloud before he got more than twenty yards. The wind was driving it this way. Latigo could make out—barely—the shifting orange glare of the burning brush at the desert end.

He wheeled his new horse back the way it had come. More horses loomed out of the fog. Latigo crashed into one of them and was thrown for the second time in five minutes. He landed on his knees, scrambled to his feet, and staggered back downwind, coughing and retching, eyes red and streaming.

It was a little better beyond the canyon's northward jog, but wouldn't be for much longer. The edge of the thinny was a tangle of milling horses, many with broken legs, and crawling, shrieking men. Latigo saw several hats floating on the greenish surface of the whining organism that filled the back of the canyon; he saw boots; he saw wristlets; he saw neckerchiefs; he saw the bugle-boy's dented instrument, still trailing its frayed strap.

Come in, the green shimmer invited, and Latigo found its buzz strangely attractive . . . intimate, almost. *Come in and visit, squat and hunker, be at rest, be at peace, be at one.*

Latigo raised his gun, meaning to shoot it. He didn't believe it could be killed, but he would remember the face of his father and go down shooting, all the same.

Except he didn't. The gun dropped from his relaxing fingers and he walked forward—others around him were now doing the same—into the thinny. The buzzing rose and rose, filling his ears until there was nothing else.

Nothing else at all.

22

They saw it all from the notch, where Roland and his friends had stopped in a strung-out line about twenty feet below the top. They saw the screaming confusion, the panicky milling, the men who were trampled, the men and horses that were driven into the thinny . . . and the men who, at the end, walked willingly into it.

Cuthbert was closest to the top of the canyon's wall, then Alain, then Roland, standing on a six-inch shelf of rock and holding an outcrop just above him. From their vantage-point they could see what the men struggling in their smoky hell below them could not: that the thinny was growing, reaching out, crawling eagerly toward them like an incoming tide.

Roland, his battle-lust slaked, did not want to watch what was happening below, but he couldn't turn away. The whine of the thinny—cowardly and triumphant at the same time, happy and sad at the same time, lost and found at the same time—held him like sweet, sticky ropes. He hung where he was, hypnotized, as did his friends above him, even when the smoke began to rise, and its pungent tang made him cough dryly.

Men shrieked their lives away in the thickening smoke below. They struggled in it like phantoms. They faded as the fug thickened, climbing the canyon walls like water. Horses whinnied desperately from beneath that acrid white death. The wind swirled its surface in prankish whirlpools. The thinny buzzed, and above where it lay, the surface of the smoke was stained a mystic shade of palest green.

Then, at long last, John Farson's men screamed no more.

We killed them, Roland thought with a kind of sick and fascinated horror. Then: *No, not we. I. I killed them.*

How long he might have stayed there Roland didn't know—perhaps until the rising smoke engulfed him as well, but then Cuthbert, who had begun to climb again, called down three words from above him; called down in a tone of surprise and dismay.

"Roland! *The moon!*"

Roland looked up, startled, and saw that the sky had darkened to a velvety purple. His friend was outlined against it and looking east, his face stained fever-orange with the light of the rising moon.

Yes, orange, the thinny buzzed inside his head. *Laughed* inside his head. *Orange as 'twas when it rose on the night you came out here to see me and count me. Orange like a fire. Orange like a bonfire.*

How can it be almost dark? he cried inside himself, but he knew—yes, he knew very well. Time had slipped back together, that was all, like layers of ground embracing once more after the argument of an earthquake.

Twilight had come.

Moonrise had come.

Terror struck Roland like a closed fist aimed at the heart, making him jerk backward on the small ledge he'd found. He groped for the horn-shaped outcrop above him, but that act of rebalancing was far away; most of him was inside the pink storm again, before he had been snatched away and shown half the cosmos. Perhaps the wizard's glass had only shown him what stood worlds far away in order to keep from showing him what might soon befall so close to home.

I'd turn around if I thought her life was in any real danger, he had said. *In a second.*

And if the ball knew that? If it couldn't lie, might it

not misdirect? Might it not take him away and show him a dark land, a darker tower? And it had shown him something else, something that recurred to him only now: a scrawny man in farmer's overalls who had said . . . what? Not quite what he'd thought, not what he had been used to hearing all his life; not *Life for you and life for your crop,* but . . .

"Death," he whispered to the stones surrounding him. "Death for you, life for my crop. *Charyou tree.* That's what he said, *Charyou tree.* Come, Reap."

Orange, gunslinger, a cracked old voice laughed inside his head. The voice of the Cöos. *The color of bonfires.* Charyou tree, fin de año, *these are the old ways of which only the stuffy-guys with their red hands remain . . . until tonight. Tonight the old ways are refreshed, as the old ways must be, from time to time.* Charyou tree, *you damned babby,* charyou tree: *tonight you pay for my sweet Ermot. Tonight you pay for all. Come, Reap.*

"Climb!" he screamed, reaching up and slapping Alain's behind. "Climb, climb! For your father's sake, *climb!*"

"Roland, what—?" Alain's voice was dazed, but he did begin to climb, going from handhold to handhold and rattling small pebbles down into Roland's upturned face. Squinting against their fall, Roland reached and swatted Al's bottom again, driving him like a horse.

"*Climb,* gods damn you!" he cried. "It mayn't be too late, even now!"

But he knew better. Demon Moon had risen, he had seen its orange light shining on Cuthbert's face like delirium, and he knew better. In his head the lunatic buzz of the thinny, that rotting sore eating through the flesh of reality, joined with the lunatic laughter of the witch, and he knew better.

Death for you, life for the crop. Charyou tree.

Oh, Susan—

23

Nothing was clear to Susan until she saw the man with the long red hair and the straw hat which did not quite obscure his lamb-slaughterer's eyes; the man with the cornshucks in his hands. He was the first, just a farmer (she had glimpsed him in the Lower Market, she thought; had even nodded to him, as countryfolk do, and he back to her), standing by himself not far from the place where Silk Ranch Road and the Great Road intersected, standing in the light of the rising moon. Until they came upon him, nothing was clear; after he hurled his bundle of cornshucks at her as she passed, standing in the slowly rolling cart with her hands bound in front of her and her head lowered and a rope around her neck, everything was clear.

"Charyou tree," he called, almost sweetly uttering words of the Old People she hadn't heard since her childhood, words that meant "Come, Reap" . . . and something else, as well. Something hidden, something secret, something to do with that root word, *char,* that word which meant only death. As the dried shucks fluttered around her boots, she understood the secret very well; understood also that there would be no baby for her, no wedding for her in the fairy-distant land of Gilead, no hall in which she and Roland would be joined and then saluted beneath the electric lights, no husband, no more nights of sweet love; all that was over. The world had moved on and all that was over, done before fairly begun.

She knew that she had been put in the back of the cart, *stood* in the back of the cart, and that the surviving Coffin Hunter had looped a noose around her neck. "Don't try to sit," he had said, sounding almost apologetic. "I have no desire to choke you, girly. If the wagon bumps and you fall, I'll try to keep the knot loose, but if you try to sit, I'll have to give you a pinching. *Her* orders." He nodded to Rhea, who sat erect on the seat of the cart, the reins in her warped hands. "*She's* in charge now."

And so she had been; so, as they neared town, she still was. Whatever the possession of her glam had done to her body, whatever the loss of it had done to her mind, it had not broken her power; that seemed to have increased, if anything, as if she'd found some other source from which she could feed, at least for awhile. Men who could have broken her over one knee like a stick of kindling followed her commands as unquestioningly as children.

There were more and more men as that Reaping afternoon wound its shallow course to night: half a dozen ahead of the cart, riding with Rimer and the man with the cocked eye, a full dozen riding behind it with Reynolds, the rope leading to her neck wound around his tattooed hand, at their head. She didn't know who these men were, or how they had been summoned.

Rhea had taken this rapidly increasing party north a little farther, then turned southwest on the old Silk Ranch Road, which wound back toward town. On the eastern edge of Hambry, it rejoined the Great Road. Even in her dazed state, Susan had realized the harridan was moving slowly, measuring the descent of the sun as they went, not clucking at the pony to hurry but actually reining it in, at least until afternoon's gold had gone. When they passed the farmer, thin-faced and alone, a good man, no doubt, with a freehold farm he worked hard from first gleam to last glow and a family he loved (but oh, there were those lamb-slaughterer eyes below the brim of his battered hat), she understood this leisurely course of travel, too. Rhea had been waiting for the moon.

With no gods to pray to, Susan prayed to her father.

Da? If thee's there, help me to be strong as I can be, and help

me hold to him, to the memory of him. Help me to hold to myself
as well. Not for rescue, not for salvation, but just so as not to
give them the satisfaction of seeing my pain and my fear. And
him, help him as well . . .

"Help keep him safe," she whispered. "Keep my love
safe; take my love safe to where he goes, give him joy in
who he sees, and make him a cause of joy in those who
see him."

"Praying, dearie?" the old woman asked without turning on the seat. Her croaking voice oozed false com-
passion. "Aye, ye'd do well t'make things right with the
Powers while ye still can—before the spit's burned right
out of yer throat!" She threw back her head and cackled,
the straggling remains of her broomstraw hair flying out
orange in the light of the bloated moon.

24

Their horses, led by Rusher, had come to the sound of
Roland's dismayed shout. They stood not far away, their
manes rippling in the wind, shaking their heads and
whinnying their displeasure whenever the wind dropped
enough for them to get a whiff of the thick white smoke
rising from the canyon.

Roland paid no attention to the horses or the smoke.
His eyes were fixed on the drawstring sack slung over
Alain's shoulder. The ball inside had come alive again;
in the growing dark, the bag seemed to pulse like some
weird pink firefly. He held out his hands for it.

"Give it to me!"

"Roland, I don't know if—"

"Give it to me, damn your face!"

Alain looked at Cuthbert, who nodded . . . then lifted
his hands skyward in a weary, distracted gesture.

Roland tore the bag away before Alain could do more than begin to shrug it off his shoulder. The gunslinger dipped into it and pulled the glass out. It was glowing fiercely, a pink Demon Moon instead of an orange one.

Behind and below them, the nagging whine of the thinny rose and fell, rose and fell.

"Don't look directly into that thing," Cuthbert muttered to Alain. "Don't, for your father's sake."

Roland bent his face over the pulsing ball, its light running over his cheeks and brow like liquid, drowning his eyes in its dazzle.

In Maerlyn's Rainbow he saw her—Susan, horse-drover's daughter, lovely girl at the window. He saw her standing in the back of a black cart decorated with gold symbols, the old witch's cart. Reynolds rode behind her, holding the end of a rope that was noosed around her neck. The cart was rolling toward Green Heart, making its way with processional slowness. Hill Street was lined with people of whom the farmer with the lamb-slaughterer's eyes had been only the first—all those folk of Hambry and Mejis who had been deprived of their fair but were now given this ancient dark attraction in its stead: *charyou tree,* come, Reap, death for you, life for our crops.

A soundless whispering ran through them like a gathering wave, and they began to pelt her—first with corn-husks, then with rotting tomatoes, then with potatoes and apples. One of these latter struck her cheek. She reeled, almost fell, then stood straight again, now raising her swollen but still lovely face so the moon painted it. She looked straight ahead.

"Charyou tree," they whispered. Roland couldn't hear them, but he could see the words on their lips. Stanley Ruiz was there, and Pettie, and Gert Moggins, and Frank Claypool, the deputy with the broken leg; Jamie McCann,

who was to have been this year's Reap Lad. Roland saw a hundred people he had known (and mostly liked) during his time in Mejis. Now these people pelted his love with cornshucks and vegetables as she stood, hands bound before her, in the back of Rhea's cart.

The slowly rolling cart reached Green Heart, with its colored paper lanterns and silent carousel where no laughing children rode . . . no, not this year. The crowd, still speaking those two words—*chanting* them now, it appeared—parted. Roland saw the heaped pyramid of wood that was the unlit bonfire. Sitting around it, their backs propped on the central column, their lumpy legs outstretched, was a ring of red-handed stuffy-guys. There was a single hole in the ring; a single waiting vacancy.

And now a woman emerged from the crowd. She wore a rusty black dress and held a pail in one hand. A smear of ash stood out on one of her cheeks like a brand. She—

Roland began to shriek. It was a single word, over and over again: *No, no, no, no, no, no!* The ball's pink light flashed brighter with each repetition, as if his horror refreshed and strengthened it. And now, with each of those pulses, Cuthbert and Alain could see the shape of the gunslinger's skull beneath his skin.

"We have to take it away from him," Alain said. "We have to, it's sucking him dry. It's killing him!"

Cuthbert nodded and stepped forward. He grabbed the ball, but couldn't take it from Roland's hands. The gunslinger's fingers seemed welded to it.

"Hit him!" he told Alain. "Hit him again, you have to!"

But Alain might as well have been hitting a post. Roland didn't even rock back on his heels. He continued to cry out that single negative—"*No! No! No! No*"—and the ball flashed faster and faster, eating its way into him through the wound it had opened, sucking up his grief like blood.

25

"Charyou tree!" Cordelia Delgado cried, darting forward from where she had been waiting. The crowd cheered her, and beyond her left shoulder Demon Moon winked, as if in complicity. *"Charyou tree,* ye faithless bitch! *Charyou tree!"*

She flung the pail of paint at her niece, splattering her pants and dressing her tied hands in a pair of wet scarlet gloves. She grinned up at Susan as the cart rolled past. The smear of ash stood out on her cheek; in the center of her pale forehead, a single vein pulsed like a worm.

"Bitch!" Cordelia screamed. Her fists were clenched; she danced a kind of hilarious jig, feet jumping, bony knees pumping beneath her skirt. *"Life for the crops! Death for the hitch!* Charyou tree! *Come, Reap!"*

The cart rolled past her; Cordelia faded from Susan's sight, just one more cruel phantasm in a dream that would soon end. *Bird and bear and hare and fish,* she thought. *Be safe, Roland; go with my love. That's my fondest wish.*

"Take her!" Rhea screamed. "Take this murdering bitch and cook her red-handed! *Charyou tree!"*

"Charyou tree!" the crowd responded. A forest of willing hands grew in the moonlit air; somewhere firecrackers rattled and children laughed excitedly.

Susan was lifted from the cart and handed toward the waiting woodpile above the heads of the crowd, passed by uplifted hands like a heroine returned triumphantly home from the wars. Her hands dripped red tears upon their straining, eager faces. The moon overlooked it all, dwarfing the glow of the paper lanterns.

"Bird and bear and hare and fish," she murmured as she was first lowered and then slammed against the pyramid of dry wood, put in the place which had been left for her—the whole crowd chanting in unison now, *"Charyou TREE! Charyou TREE! Charyou TREE!"*

"Bird and bear and hare and fish."

Trying to remember how he had danced with her that night. Trying to remember how he had loved with her in the willow grove. Trying to remember that first meeting on the dark road: *Thankee-sai, we're well met,* he had said, and yes, in spite of everything, in spite of this miserable ending with the folk who had been her neighbors turned into prancing goblins by moonlight, in spite of pain and betrayal and what was coming, he had spoken the truth: they had been well met, they had been very well met, indeed.

"Charyou TREE! Charyou TREE! Charyou TREE!"

Women came and piled dry cornshucks around her feet. Several of them slapped her (it didn't matter; her bruised and puffy face seemed to have gone numb), and one—it was Misha Alvarez, whose daughter Susan had taught to ride—spat into her eyes and then leaped prankishly away, shaking her hands at the sky and laughing. For a moment she saw Coral Thorin, festooned with reap-charms, her arms filled with dead leaves which she threw at Susan; they fluttered down around her in a crackling, aromatic shower.

And now came her aunt again, and Rhea beside her. Each held a torch. They stood before her, and Susan could smell sizzling pitch.

Rhea raised her torch to the moon. *"CHARYOU TREE!"* she screamed in her rusty old voice, and the crowd responded, *"CHARYOU TREE!"*

Cordelia raised her own torch. *"COME, REAP!"*

"COME, REAP!" they cried back to her.

"Now, ye bitch," Rhea crooned. "Now comes warmer kisses than any yer love ever gave ye."

"Die, ye faithless," Cordelia whispered. "Life for the crops, death for you."

It was she who first flung her torch into the cornshucks which were piled as high as Susan's knees; Rhea flung hers a bare second later. The cornshucks blazed up at once, dazzling Susan with yellow light.

She drew in a final breath of cool air, warmed it with her heart, and loosed it in a defiant shout: *"ROLAND, I LOVE THEE!"*

The crowd fell back, murmuring, as if uneasy at what they had done, now that it was too late to take it back; here was not a stuffy-guy but a cheerful girl they all knew, one of their own, for some mad reason backed up against the Reap-Night bonfire with her hands painted red. They might have saved her, given another moment— some might have, anyway—but it was too late. The dry wood caught; her pants caught; her shirt caught; her long blonde hair blazed on her head like a crown.

"ROLAND, I LOVE THEE!"

At the end of her life she was aware of heat but not pain. She had time to consider his eyes, eyes of that blue which is the color of the sky at first light of morning. She had time to think of him on the Drop, riding Rusher flat-out with his black hair flying back from his temples and his neckerchief rippling; to see him laughing with an ease and freedom he would never find again in the long life which stretched out for him beyond hers, and it was his laughter she took with her as she went out, fleeing the light and heat into the silky, consoling dark, calling to him over and over as she went, calling bird and bear and hare and fish.

26

There was no word, not even *no,* in his screams at the end: he howled like a gutted animal, his hands welded to the ball, which beat like a runaway heart. He watched in it as she burned.

Cuthbert tried again to take the cursed thing away, and couldn't. He did the only other thing he could think of—drew his revolver, pointed it at the ball, and thumbed back the hammer. He would likely wound Roland, and the flying glass might even blind him, but there was no other choice. If they didn't do something, the glam would kill him.

But there was no need. As if seeing Cuthbert's gun and understanding what it meant, the ball went instantly dark and dead in Roland's hands. Roland's stiff body, every line and muscle trembling with horror and outrage, went limp. He dropped like a stone, his fingers at last letting go of the ball. His stomach cushioned it as he struck the ground; it rolled off him and trickled to a stop by one of his limp, outstretched hands. Nothing burned in its darkness now except for one baleful orange spark—the tiny reflection of the rising Demon Moon.

Alain looked at the glass with a species of disgusted, frightened awe; looked at it as one might look at a vicious animal that now sleeps . . . but will wake again, and bite when it does.

He stepped forward, meaning to crush it to powder beneath his boot.

"Don't you dare," Cuthbert said in a hoarse voice. He was kneeling beside Roland's limp form but looking at Alain. The rising moon was in his eyes, two small, bright stones of light. "Don't you dare, after all the misery and death we've gone through to get it. Don't you even *think* of it."

Alain looked at him uncertainly for a moment, thinking he should destroy the cursed thing, anyway—misery suffered did not justify misery to come, and as long as the thing on the ground remained whole, misery was all it would bring anyone. It was a *misery-machine,* that was what it was, and it had killed Susan Delgado. He hadn't seen what Roland had seen in the glass, but he had seen his friend's face, and that had been enough. It had killed Susan, and it would kill more, if left whole.

But then he thought of *ka* and drew back. Later he would bitterly regret doing so.

"Put it in the bag again," Cuthbert said, "and then help me with Roland. We have to get out of here."

The drawstring bag lay crumpled on the ground nearby, fluttering in the wind. Alain picked up the ball, hating the feel of its smooth, curved surface, expecting it to come alive under his touch. It didn't, though. He put it in the bag, and looped it over his shoulder again. Then he knelt beside Roland.

He didn't know how long they tried unsuccessfully to bring him around—until the moon had risen high enough in the sky to turn silver again, and the smoke roiling out of the canyon had begun to dissipate, that was all he knew. Until Cuthbert told him it was enough; they would have to sling him over Rusher's saddle and ride with him that way. If they could get into the heavily forested lands west o' Barony before dawn, Cuthbert said, they would likely be safe . . . but they had to get at least that far. They had smashed Farson's men apart with stunning ease, but the remains would likely knit together again the following day. Best they be gone before that happened.

And that was how they left Eyebolt Canyon, and the

seacoast side of Mejis; riding west beneath the Demon
Moon, with Roland laid across his saddle like a corpse.

27

The next day they spent in Il Bosque, the forest west of
Mejis, waiting for Roland to wake up. When afternoon
came and he remained unconscious, Cuthbert said: "See
if you can touch him."

Alain took Roland's hands in his own, marshalled all
his concentration, bent over his friend's pale, slumber-
ing face, and remained that way for almost half an hour.
Finally he shook his head, let go of Roland's hands, and
stood up.

"Nothing?" Cuthbert asked.

Alain sighed and shook his head.

They made a travois of pine branches so he wouldn't
have to spend another night riding oversaddle (if nothing
else, it seemed to make Rusher nervous to be carrying his
master in such a way), and went on, not travelling on the
Great Road—that would have been far too dangerous—
but parallel to it. When Roland remained unconscious the
following day (Mejis falling behind them now, and both
boys feeling a deep tug of homesickness, inexplicable but
as real as tides), they sat on either side of him, looking at
each other over the slow rise and fall of his chest.

"Can an unconscious person starve, or die of thirst?"
Cuthbert asked. "They can't, can they?"

"Yes," Alain said. "I think they can."

It had been a long, nerve-wracking night of travel. Neither boy had slept well the previous day, but on this one
they slept like the dead, with blankets over their heads
to block the sun. They awoke minutes apart as the sun
was going down and Demon Moon, now two nights past

the full, was rising through a troubled rack of clouds that presaged the first of the great autumn storms.

Roland was sitting up. He had taken the glass from the drawstring bag. He sat with it cradled in his arms, a darkened bit of magic as dead as the glass eyes of The Romp. Roland's own eyes, also dead, looked indifferently off into the moonlit corridors of the forest. He would eat but not sleep. He would drink from the streams they passed but not speak. And he would not be parted from the piece of Maerlyn's Rainbow which they had brought out of Mejis at such great price. It did not glow for him, however.

Not, Cuthbert thought once, *while Al and I are awake to see it, anyway.*

Alain couldn't get Roland's hands off the ball, and so he laid his own on Roland's cheeks, touching him that way. Except there was nothing to touch, nothing there. The thing which rode west with them toward Gilead was not Roland, or even a ghost of Roland. Like the moon at the close of its cycle, Roland had gone.

PART FOUR

ALL GOD'S CHILLUN GOT SHOES

CHAPTER ONE

Kansas in the Morning

I

For the first time in

(hours? days?)

the gunslinger fell silent. He sat for a moment looking toward the building to the east of them (with the sun behind it, the glass palace was a black shape surrounded by a gold nimbus) with his forearms propped on his knees. Then he took the waterskin which lay on the pavement beside him, held it over his face, opened his mouth, and upended it.

He drank what happened to go in his mouth—the others could see his adam's apple working as he lay back in the breakdown lane, still pouring—but drinking didn't seem to be his primary purpose. Water streamed down his deeply lined forehead and bounced off his closed eyelids. It pooled in the triangular hollow at the base of his throat and ran back from his temples, wetting his hair and turning it darker.

At last he put the waterskin aside and only lay there, eyes closed, arms stretched out high above his head, like a man surrendering in his sleep. Steam rose in delicate tendrils from his wet face.

"Ahhh," he said.

"Feel better?" Eddie asked.

The gunslinger's lids rose, disclosing those faded yet somehow alarming blue eyes. "Yes. I do. I don't understand how that can be, as much as I dreaded this telling . . . but I do."

"An ologist-of-the-psyche could probably explain it to you," Susannah said, "but I doubt you'd listen." She put her hands in the small of her back, stretched and winced . . . but the wince was only reflex. The pain and stiffness she'd expected weren't there, and although there was one small creak near the base of her spine, she didn't get the satisfying series of snaps, crackles, and pops she had expected.

"Tell you one thing," Eddie said, "this gives a whole new meaning to 'Get it off your chest.' How long have we been here, Roland?"

"Just one night."

" 'The spirits have done it all in a single night,' " Jake said in a dreamy voice. His legs were crossed at the ankles; Oy sat in the diamond shape made by the boy's bent knees, looking at him with his bright gold-black eyes.

Roland sat up, wiping at his wet cheeks with his neckerchief and looking at Jake sharply. "What is it you say?"

"Not me. A guy named Charles Dickens wrote that. In a story called *A Christmas Carol.* All in a single night, huh?"

"Does any part of your body say it was longer?"

Jake shook his head. No, he felt pretty much the way he did any morning—better than on some. He had to take a leak, but his back teeth weren't exactly floating, or anything like that.

"Eddie? Susannah?"

"I feel good," Susannah said. "Surely not as if I stayed up all night, let alone many of em."

Eddie said, "It reminds me of the time I spent as a junkie, in a way—"

"Doesn't everything?" Roland asked dryly.

"Oh, that's funny," Eddie said. "A real howl. Next train that goes crazy on us, *you* can ask it the silly questions. What I meant was that you'd spend so many nights high that you got used to feeling like ten pounds of shit in a nine-pound bag when you got up in the morning—bad head, stuffy nose, thumping heart, glass in the old spine. Take it from your pal Eddie, you can tell just from the way you feel in the morning how good dope is for you. Anyway, you'd get so used to that—*I* did, anyway—that when you actually took a night off, you'd wake up the next morning and sit there on the edge of the bed, thinking, 'What the fuck's wrong with me? Am I sick? I feel weird. Did I have a stroke in the night?' "

Jake laughed, then clapped a hand over his mouth so violently that it was as if he wanted not just to hold the sound in but call it back. "Sorry," he said. "That made me think of my dad."

"One of my people, huh?" Eddie said. "Anyway, I expect to be sore, I expect to be tired, I expect to creak when I walk . . . but I actually think all I need to put me right is a quick pee in the bushes."

"And a bite to eat?" Roland asked.

Eddie had been wearing a small smile. Now it faded. "No," he said. "After that story, I'm not all that hungry. In fact, I'm not hungry at ail."

2

Eddie carried Susannah down the embankment and popped her behind a stand of laurel bushes to do her necessary. Jake was sixty or seventy yards east, in a grove of birches. Roland had said he would use the remedial strip to do his morning necessary, then raised his eyebrows when his New York friends laughed.

Susannah wasn't laughing when she came out of the bushes. Her face was streaked with tears. Eddie didn't ask her; he knew. He had been fighting the feeling himself. He took her gently in his arms and she put her face against the side of his neck. They stayed that way for a little while.

"Charyou tree," she said at last, pronouncing it as Roland had: chair-you tree, with a little upturned vowel at the end.

"Yeah," Eddie said, thinking that a Charlie by any other name was still a Charlie. As, he supposed, a rose was a rose was a rose. "Come, Reap."

She raised her head and began to wipe her swimming eyes. "To have gone through all that," she said, keeping her voice low . . . and looking once at the turnpike embankment to make sure Roland wasn't there, looking down at them. "And *at fourteen.*"

"Yeah. It makes my adventures searching for the elusive dime bag in Tompkins Square look pretty tame. In a way, though, I'm almost relieved."

"Relieved? Why?"

"Because I thought he was going to tell us that he killed her himself. For his damned Tower."

Susannah looked squarely into his eyes. "But he thinks that's what he did. Don't you understand that?"

3

When they were back together again and there was food actually in sight, all of them decided they could eat a bit, after all. Roland shared out the last of the burritos (*Maybe later today we can stop in at the nearest Boing Boing Burgers and see what they've got for leftovers,* Eddie thought), and they dug in. All of them, that was, except Roland.

He picked up his burrito, looked at it, then looked away. Eddie saw an expression of sadness on the gunslinger's face that made him look both old and lost. It hurt Eddie's heart, but he couldn't think what to do about it.

Jake, almost ten years younger, could. He got up, went to Roland, knelt beside him, put his arms around the gunslinger's neck, and hugged him. "I'm sorry you lost your friend," he said.

Roland's face worked, and for a moment Eddie was sure he was going to lose it. A long time between hugs, maybe. Mighty long. Eddie had to look away for a moment. *Kansas in the morning,* he told himself. *A sight you never expected to see. Dig on that for awhile, and let the man be.*

When he looked back, Roland had it together again. Jake was sitting beside him, and Oy had his long snout on one of the gunslinger's boots. Roland had begun to eat his burrito. Slowly, and without much relish . . . but he was eating.

A cold hand—Susannah's—crept into Eddie's. He took it and folded his fingers over it.

"One night," she marvelled.

"On our body-clocks, at least," Eddie said. "In our heads . . ."

"Who knows?" Roland agreed. "But storytelling always changes time. At least it does in my world." He smiled. It was unexpected, as always, and as always, it transformed his face into something nearly beautiful. Looking at that, Eddie mused, you could see how a girl might have fallen in love with Roland, once upon a time. Back when he had been long and going on tall but maybe not so ugly; back when the Tower hadn't yet got its best hold on him.

"I think it's that way in all worlds, sugar," Susannah said. "Could I ask you a couple of questions, before we get rolling?"

"If you like."

"What happened to you? How long were you . . . gone?"

"I was certainly gone, you're right about that. I was travelling. *Wandering.* Not in Maerlyn's Rainbow, exactly . . . I don't think I ever would have returned from there, if I'd gone into it while I was still . . . sick . . . but everyone has a wizard's glass, of course. Here." He tapped his forehead gravely, just above the space between his eyebrows. "That's where I went. That's where I travelled while my friends travelled east with me. I got better there, little by little. I held onto the ball, and I travelled inside my head, and I got better. But the glass never glowed for me until the very end . . . when the battlements of the castle and the towers of the city were actually in sight. If it had awakened earlier . . ."

He shrugged.

"If it had awakened before I'd started to get some of my strength of mind back, I don't think I'd be here now. Because any world—even a pink one with a glass sky— would have been preferable to one where there was no Susan. I suppose the force that gives the glass its life knew that . . . and waited."

"But when it *did* glow for you again, it told you the rest," Jake said. "It must have. It told you the parts that you weren't there to see."

"Yes. I know as much of the story as I do because of what I saw in the ball."

"You told us once that John Farson wanted your head on a pole," Eddie said. "Because you stole something from him. Something he held dear. It was the glass ball, wasn't it?"

"Yes. He was more than furious when he found out. He was insane with rage. In your parlance, Eddie, he 'went nuclear.'"

"How many more times *did* it glow for you?" Susannah asked.

"And what happened to it?" Jake added.

"I saw in it three times after we left Mejis Barony," Roland said. "The first was on the night before we came home to Gilead. That was when I travelled in it the longest, and it showed me what I've told you. A few things I've only guessed at, but most I was shown. It showed me these things not to teach or enlighten, but to hurt and wound. The remaining pieces of the Wizard's Rainbow are all evil things. Hurt enlivens them, somehow. It waited until my mind was strong enough to understand and *withstand* . . . and then it showed me all the things I missed in my stupid adolescent complacency. My lovesick daze. My prideful, murderous conceit."

"Roland, don't," Susannah said. "Don't let it hurt you still."

"But it does. It always will. Never mind. It doesn't matter now; that tale is told.

"The second time I saw into the glass—*went* into the glass—was three days after I came home. My mother wasn't there, although she was due that evening. She had gone into Debaria—a kind of retreat for women—to wait and pray for my return. Nor was Marten there. He was in Cressia, with Farson."

"The ball," Eddie said. "Your father had it by then?"

"No-o," Roland said. He looked down at his hands, and Eddie observed a faint flush rising into his cheeks. "I didn't give it to him at first. I found it . . . hard to give up."

"I bet," Susannah said. "You and everyone else who ever looked into the goddam thing."

"On the third afternoon, before we were to be banqueted to celebrate our safe return—"

"I bet you were really in a mood to party, too," Eddie said.

Roland smiled without humor, still studying his hands. "At around four o' the clock, Cuthbert and Alain came to my rooms. We were a trio for an artist to paint, I wot—windburned, hollow-eyed, hands covered with healing cuts and scrapes from our climb up the side of the canyon, scrawny as scarecrows. Even Alain, who tended toward stoutness, all but disappeared when he turned sideways. They confronted me, I suppose you'd say. They'd kept the secret of the ball to that point— out of respect for me and for the loss I'd suffered, they told me, and I believed them—but they would keep it no longer than that night's meal. If I wouldn't give it up voluntarily, it would be a question for our fathers to decide. They were horribly embarrassed, especially Cuthbert, but they were determined.

"I told them I'd give it over to my own father before the banquet—before my mother arrived by coach from Debaria, even. They should come early and see that I kept my promise. Cuthbert started to hem and haw and say that wouldn't be necessary, but of course it *was* necessary—"

"Yeah," Eddie said. He had the look of a man who understood this part of the story perfectly. "You can go into the crapper on your own, but it's a lot easier to actually flush all the bad shit down the toilet if you have somebody with you."

"Alain, at least, knew it would be better for me—easier—if I didn't have to hand the ball over alone. He hushed Cuthbert up and said they'd be there. And they were. And I gave it over, little as I wanted to. My father went as pale as paper when he looked into the bag and saw what was there, then excused himself and took it away. When he came back, he picked up his glass of wine and went on talking to us of our adventures in Mejis as if nothing had happened."

"But between the time your friends talked to you about it and the time you gave it up, you looked into it," Jake said. *"Went* into it. Travelled in it. What did it show you that time?"

"First the Tower again," Roland said, "and the beginning of the way there. I saw the fall of Gilead, and the triumph of the Good Man. We'd put those things back a mere twenty months or so by destroying the tankers and the oilpatch. I could do nothing about that, but it showed me something I *could* do. There was a certain knife. The blade had been treated with an especially potent poison, something from a distant Mid-World Kingdom called Garlan. Stuff so strong even the tiniest cut would cause almost instant death. A wandering singer—in truth, John Farson's eldest nephew—had brought this knife to court. The man he gave it to was the castle's chief of domestic staff. This man was to pass the knife on to the actual assassin. My father was not meant to see the sun come up on the morning after the banquet." He smiled at them grimly. "Because of what I saw in the Wizard's Glass, the knife never reached the hand that would have used it, and there was a new chief of domestics by the end of that week. These are pretty tales I tell you, are they not? Aye, very pretty, indeed."

"Did you see the person the knife was meant for?" Susannah asked. "The actual killer?"

"Yes."

"Anything else? Did you see anything else?" Jake asked. The plan to murder Roland's father didn't seem to hold much interest for him.

"Yes." Roland looked puzzled. "Shoes. Just for a minute. Shoes tumbling through the air. At first I thought they were autumn leaves. And when I saw what they really were, they were gone and I was lying on my bed with the ball hugged in my arms . . . pretty much the way

I carried it back from Mejis. My father . . . as I've said, his surprise when he looked inside the bag was very great, indeed."

You told him who had the knife with the special poison on it, Susannah thought, *Jeeves the Butler, or whoever, but you didn't tell him who was supposed to actually use it, did you, sugar? Why not? Because you wanted to take care of* dat *little spot o' work yo ownself?* But before she could ask, Eddie was asking a question of his own.

"Shoes? Flying through the air? Does that mean anything to you now?"

Roland shook his head.

"Tell us about the rest of what you saw in it," Susannah said.

He gave her a look of such terrible pain that what Susannah had only suspected immediately solidified to fact in her mind. She looked away from him and groped for Eddie's hand.

"I cry your pardon, Susannah, but I cannot. Not now. For now, I've told all I can."

"All right," Eddie said. "All right, Roland, that's cool."

"Ool," Oy agreed.

"Did you ever see the witch again?" Jake asked.

For a long time it seemed Roland would not answer this, either, but in the end he did.

"Yes. She wasn't done with me. Like my dreams of Susan, she followed me. All the way from Mejis, she followed me."

"What do you mean?" Jake asked in a low, awed voice. "Cripes, Roland, what do you mean?"

"Not now." He got up. "It's time we were on our way again." He nodded to the building which floated ahead of them; the sun was just now clearing its battlements. "Yon glitter-dome's a good distance away, but I think we can reach it this afternoon, if we move brisk. 'Twould be

best. It's not a place I'd reach after nightfall, if that can
be avoided."

"Do you know what it is yet?" Susannah asked.

"Trouble," he repeated. "And in our road."

4

For awhile that morning, the thinny warbled so loudly
that not even the bullets in their ears would entirely
stop up the sound; at its worst, Susannah felt as if the
bridge of her nose would simply disintegrate, and when
she looked at Jake, she saw he was weeping copiously—
not crying the way people do when they're sad, but the
way they do when their sinuses are in total revolt. She
couldn't get the saw-player the kid had mentioned out
of her mind. *Sounds Hawaiian,* she thought over and
over again as Eddie pushed her grimly along in the new
wheelchair, weaving in and out of the stalled vehicles.
*Sounds Hawaiian, doesn't it? Sounds fucking Hawaiian,
doesn't it, Miss Oh So Black and Pretty?*

On both sides of the turnpike the thinny lapped all
the way up to the embankment, casting its twitching,
misshapen reflections of trees and grain elevators, seeming to watch the pilgrims pass as hungry animals in a
zoo might watch plump children. Susannah would find
herself thinking of the thinny in Eyebolt Canyon, reaching out hungrily through the smoke for Latigo's milling
men, pulling them in (and some going in on their own,
walking like zombies in a horror movie), and then, she
would find herself thinking of the guy in Central Park
again, the wacko with the saw. *Sounds Hawaiian, doesn't
it? Counting one thinny, and it sounds Hawaiian, doesn't it?*

Just when she thought she could stand it not a moment
longer, the thinny began to draw back from I-70 again,

and its humming warble at last began to fade. Susannah was eventually able to pull the bullets out of her ears. She tucked them into the side-pocket of her chair with a hand that shook slightly.

"That was a bad one," Eddie said. His voice sounded clogged and weepy. She looked around at him and saw his cheeks were wet, his eyes red. "Take it easy, Suzie-pie," he said. "It's my sinuses, that's all. That sound kills em."

"Me, too," Susannah said.

"My sinuses are okay, but my head aches," Jake said. "Roland, do you have any more aspirin?"

Roland stopped, rummaged, and found the bottle.

"Did you ever see Clay Reynolds again?" Jake asked, after swallowing the pills with water from the skin he carried.

"No, but I know what happened to him. He got a bunch together, some of them deserters from Farson's army, went to robbing banks . . . in toward our part of the world, this was, but by then bank-thieves and stage-robbers didn't have much to fear from gunslingers."

"The gunslingers were busy with Farson," Eddie said.

"Yes. But Reynolds and his men were trapped by a smart sheriff who turned the main street of a town called Oakley into a killing-zone. Six of the ten in the gang were killed outright. The rest were hung. Reynolds was one of those. This was less than a year later, during the time of Wide Earth." He paused, then said: "One of those shot dead in the killing-zone was Coral Thorin. She had become Reynolds's woman; rode and killed with the rest of them."

They went on in silence for a bit. In the distance, the thinny warbled its endless song. Jake suddenly ran ahead to a parked camper. A note had been left under the wiper blade on the driver's side. By standing on his toes, he was just able to reach it. He scanned it, frowning.

"What does it say?" Eddie asked.

Jake handed it over. Eddie looked, then passed it to Susannah, who read it in turn and gave it to Roland. He looked, then shook his head. "I can make out only a few words—*old woman, dark man*. What does the rest say? Read it to me."

Jake took it back. " 'The old woman from the dreams is in Nebraska. Her name is Abagail.' " He paused. "Then, down here, it says, 'The dark man is in the west. Maybe Vegas.' "

Jake looked up at the gunslinger, the note fluttering in his hand, his face puzzled and uneasy. But Roland was looking toward the palace which shimmered across the highway—the palace that was not in the west but in the east, the palace that was light, not dark.

"In the west," Roland said. "Dark man, Dark Tower, and always in the west."

"Nebraska's west of here, too," Susannah said hesitantly. "I don't know if that matters, this Abagail person, but . . ."

"I think she's part of another story," Roland said.

"But a story close to this one," Eddie put in. "Next door, maybe. Close enough to swap sugar for salt . . . or start arguments."

"I'm sure you're right," Roland said, "and we may have business with the 'old woman' and the 'dark man' yet . . . but today our business is east. Come on."

They began walking again.

5

"What about Sheemie?" Jake asked after awhile.

Roland laughed, partly in surprise at the question, partly in pleased remembrance. "He followed us. It couldn't have been easy for him, and it must have been damned scary in places—there were wheels and wheels of wild country between Mejis and Gilead, and plenty of wild folks, too. Worse than just folks, mayhap. But *ka* was with him, and he showed up in time for Year's End Fair. He and that damned mule."

"Capi," Jake said.

"Appy," Oy repeated, padding along at Jake's heel.

"When we went in search of the Tower, I and my friends, Sheemie was with us. As a sort of squire, I suppose you'd say. He . . ." But Roland trailed off, biting at his lip, and of that he would say no more.

"Cordelia?" Susannah asked. "The crazy aunt?"

"Dead before the bonfire had burned down to embers. It might have been a heart-storm, or a brain-storm—what Eddie calls a stroke."

"Perhaps it was shame," Susannah said. "Or horror at what she'd done."

"It may have been," Roland said. "Waking to the truth when it's too late is a terrible thing. I know that very well."

"Something up there," Jake said, pointing at a long stretch of road from which the cars had been cleared. "Do you see?"

Roland did—with his eyes he seemed to see everything—but it was another fifteen minutes or so before Susannah began to pick up the small black specks ahead in the road. She was quite sure she knew what they were, although what she thought was less vision than intuition. Ten minutes after that, she was sure.

They were shoes. Six pairs of shoes placed neatly in a line across the eastbound lanes of Interstate 70.

CHAPTER TWO

Shoes in the Road

I

They reached the shoes at mid-morning. Beyond them, clearer now, stood the glass palace. It glimmered a delicate green shade, like the reflection of a lily pad in still water. There were shining gates in front of it; red pennons snapped from its towers in a light breeze.

The shoes were also red.

Susannah's impression that there were six pairs was understandable but wrong—there were actually four pairs and one quartet. This latter—four dark red booties made of supple leather—was undoubtedly meant for the four-footed member of their *ka-tet*. Roland picked one of them up and felt inside it. He didn't know how many bumblers had worn shoes in the history of the world, but he was willing to guess that none had ever been gifted with a set of silk-lined leather booties.

"Bally, Gucci, eat your heart out," Eddie said. "This is great stuff."

Susannah's were easiest to pick out, and not just because of the feminine, sparkly swoops on the sides. They weren't really shoes at all—they had been made to fit over the stumps of her legs, which ended just above the knees.

"Now look at this," she marvelled, holding one up

so the sun could flash on the rhinestones with which the shoes were decorated . . . if they *were* rhinestones. She had a crazy notion that maybe they were diamond chips. "Cappies. After four years of gettin along in what my friend Cynthia calls 'circumstances of reduced leg-room,' I finally got myself a pair of cappies. Think of that."

"Cappies," Eddie mused. "Is that what they call em?"

"That's what they call em, sugar."

Jake's were bright red Oxfords—except for the color, they would have looked perfectly at home in the well-bred classrooms of The Piper School. He flexed one, then turned it over. The sole was bright and unmarked. There was no manufacturer's stamp, nor had he really expected one. His father had maybe a dozen pairs of fine handmade shoes. Jake knew them when he saw them.

Eddie's were low boots with Cuban heels *(Maybe in this world you call them* Mejis *heels,* he thought) and pointed toes . . . what, back in his other life, had been known as "street-boppers." Kids from the midsixties—an era Odetta/Detta/Susannah had just missed—might have called them "Beatle-boots."

Roland's, of course, were cowboy boots. Fancy ones—you'd go dancing rather than droving in such as these. Looped stitching, side decorations, narrow, haughty arches. He examined them without picking them up, then looked at his fellow travellers and frowned. They were looking at each other. You would have said three people couldn't do that, only a pair . . . but you only would have said it if you'd never been part of a *ka-tet.*

Roland still shared *khef* with them; he felt the powerful current of their mingled thought, but could not understand it. *Because it's of their world. They come from different whens of that world, but they see something here that's common to all three of them.*

"What is it?" he asked. "What do they mean, these shoes?"

"I don't think any of us know *that*, exactly," Susannah said.

"No," Jake said. "It's another riddle." He looked at the weird, blood-red Oxford shoe in his hands with distaste. "Another goddamned riddle."

"Tell what you know." He looked toward the glass palace again. It was perhaps fifteen New York miles away, now, shining in the clear day, delicate as a mirage, but as real as . . . well, as real as shoes. "Please, tell me what you know about these shoes."

"I got shoes, *you* got shoes, all God's chillun got shoes," Odetta said. "That's the prevailin opinion, anyway."

"Well," Eddie said, *"we* got em, anyway. And you're thinking what I'm thinking, aren't you?"

"I guess I am."

"You, Jake?"

Instead of answering with words, Jake picked up the other Oxford (Roland had no doubt that all the shoes, including Oy's, would fit perfectly) and clapped them briskly together three times. It meant nothing to Roland, but both Eddie and Susannah reacted violently, looking around, looking especially at the sky, as if expecting a storm born out of this bright autumn sunshine. They ended up looking at the glass palace again . . . and then at each other, in that knowing, round-eyed way that made Roland feel like shaking them both until their teeth rattled. Yet he waited. Sometimes that was all a man could do.

"After you killed Jonas, you looked into the ball," Eddie said, turning to him.

"Yes."

"*Travelled* in the ball."

"Yes, but I don't want to talk about that again now; it has nothing to do with these—"

"I think it does," Eddie said. "You flew inside a pink storm. Inside a pink *gale,* you could say. Gale is a word you might use for a storm, isn't it? Especially if you were making up a riddle."

"Sure," Jake said. He sounded dreamy, almost like a boy who talks in his sleep. "When does Dorothy fly over the Wizard's Rainbow? When she's a Gale."

"We ain't in Kansas anymore, sugar," Susannah said, and then voiced a strange, humorless bark which Roland supposed was a species of laughter. "May look a little like it, but Kansas was never . . . you know, this *thin.* "

"I don't understand you," Roland said. But he felt cold, and his heart was beating too fast. There were thinnies everywhere now, hadn't he told them that? Worlds melting into one another as the forces of the Tower weakened? As the day when the rose would be plowed under drew nearer?

"You saw things as you flew," Eddie said. "Before you got to the dark land, the one you called Thunderclap, you saw things. The piano-player, Sheb. Who turned up again later in your life, didn't he?"

"Yes, in Tull."

"And the dweller with the red hair?"

"Him, too. He had a bird named Zoltan. But when we met, he and I, we said the normal. 'Life for you, life for your crop,' that sort of thing. I thought I heard the same when he flew by me in the pink storm, but he really said something else." He glanced at Susannah. "I saw your wheelchair, too. The old one."

"And you saw the witch."

"Yes. I—"

In a creaky chortle that reminded Roland unnervingly of Rhea, Jake Chambers cried: "I'll get you, my pretty! And your little dog, too!"

Roland stared at him, trying not to gape.

"Only in the movie, the witch wasn't riding a broom," Jake said. "She was on her bike, the one with the basket on the back."

"Yeah, no reap-charms, either," Eddie said. "Would have been a nice touch, though. I tell you, Jake, when I was a kid, I used to have nightmares about the way she laughed."

"It was the monkeys that gave me the creeps," Susannah said. "The flying monkeys. I'd get thinkin about em, and then have to crawl into bed with my mom and dad. They'd still be arguin 'bout whose bright idea it was to take me to that show in the foist place when I fell asleep between em."

"I wasn't worried about clapping the heels together," Jake said. "Not a bit." It was Susannah and Eddie he was speaking to; for the time being, it was as if Roland wasn't even there. "I wasn't wearing them, after all."

"True," Susannah said, sounding severe, "but you know what my daddy always used to say?"

"No, but I have a feeling we're going to find out," Eddie said.

She gave Eddie a brief, severe look, then turned her attention back to Jake. " 'Never whistle for the wind unless you want it to blow,' " she said. "And it's good advice, no matter what Young Mister Foolish here may think."

"Spanked again," Eddie said, grinning.

"Panked!" Oy said, eyeing Eddie severely.

"Explain this to me," Roland said in his softest voice. "I would hear. I would share your *khef*. And I would share it *now*."

2

They told him a story almost every American child of the twentieth century knew, about a Kansas farmgirl named Dorothy Gale who had been carried away by a cyclone and deposited, along with her dog, in the Land of Oz. There was no I-70 in Oz, but there was a yellow brick road which served much the same purpose, and there were witches, both good and bad. There was a *ka-tet* comprised of Dorothy, Toto, and three friends she met along the way: the Cowardly Lion, the Tin Woodman, and the Scarecrow. They each had

(bird and bear and hare and fish)

a fondest wish, and it was with Dorothy's that Roland's new friends (and Roland himself, for that matter) identified the most strongly: she wanted to find her way home again.

"The Munchkins told her that she had to follow the yellow brick road to Oz," Jake said, "and so she went. She met the others along the way, sort of like you met us, Roland—"

"Although you don't look much like Judy Garland," Eddie put in.

"—and eventually they got there. To Oz, the Emerald Palace, and the guy who lived in the Emerald Palace." He looked toward the glass palace ahead of them, greener and greener in the strengthening light, and then back to Roland.

"Yes, I understand. And was this fellow, Oz, a powerful *dinh?* A Baron? Perhaps a King?"

Again, the three of them exchanged a glance from which Roland was excluded. "That's complicated," Jake said. "He was sort of a humbug—"

"A bumhug? What's that?"

"Humbug," Jake said, laughing. "A faker. All talk, no action. But maybe the important thing is that the Wizard actually came from—"

"Wizard?" Roland asked sharply. He grasped Jake's shoulder with his diminished right hand. "Why do you call him so?"

"Because that was his title, sug," Susannah said. "The Wizard of Oz." She lifted Roland's hand gently but firmly from Jake's shoulder. "Let him tell it, now. He don't need you to squeeze it out of him."

"Did I hurt you? Jake, I cry your pardon."

"Nah, I'm fine," Jake said. "Don't worry about it. Anyway, Dorothy and her friends had a lot of adventures before finding out the Wizard was a, you know, a bumhug." Jake giggled at this with his hands clapped to his forehead and pushing back his hair, like a child of five. "He couldn't give the Lion courage, the Scarecrow a brain, or the Tin Woodman a heart. Worst of all, he couldn't send Dorothy back to Kansas. The Wizard had a balloon, but he went without her. I don't think he meant to, but he did."

"It seems to me, from your telling of the tale," Roland said, speaking very slowly, "that Dorothy's friends had the things they wanted all along."

"That's the moral of the story," Eddie said. "Maybe what makes it a great story. But Dorothy was stuck in Oz, you see. Then Glinda showed up. Glinda the Good. And, as a present for smooshing one of the bad witches under her house and melting another one, Glinda told Dorothy how to use the ruby slippers. The ones Glinda gave her."

Eddie raised the red Cuban-heeled street-boppers which had been left for him on the dotted white line of I-70.

"Glinda told Dorothy to click the heels of the ruby slippers together three times. That would take her back to Kansas, she said. And it did."

"And that's the end of the tale?"

"Well," Jake said, "it was so popular that the guy who wrote it went ahead and wrote about a thousand more Oz stories—"

"Yeah," Eddie said. "Everything but *Glinda's Guide to Firm Thighs.*"

"—and there was this crazy remake called *The Wiz,* starring black people—"

"Really?" Susannah asked. She looked bemused. "What a *peculiar* concept."

"—but the only one that really matters is the first one, I think," Jake finished.

Roland hunkered and put his hands into the boots which had been left for him. He lifted them, looked at them, put them down again. "Are we supposed to put them on, do you think? Here and now?"

His three friends from New York looked at each other doubtfully. At last Susannah spoke for them—fed him the *khef* which he could feel but not quite share on his own.

"Best not to right now, maybe. Too many badass spirits here."

"*Takuro* spirits," Eddie murmured, mostly to himself. Then: "Look, let's just take em along. If we're supposed to put em on, I think we'll know when the time comes. In the meantime, I think we ought to beware of bumhugs bearing gifts."

It cracked Jake up, as Eddie had known it would; sometimes a word or an image got into your funnybone like a virus and just lived there awhile. Tomorrow the word "bumhug" might mean nothing to the kid; for the rest of today, however, he was going to laugh every time he heard it. Eddie intended to use it a lot, especially when ole Jake wasn't expecting it.

They picked up the red shoes which had been left

for them in the eastbound lanes (Jake took Oy's) and moved on again toward the shimmering glass castle.

Oz, Roland thought. He searched his memory, but he didn't think it was a name he had ever heard before, or a word of the High Speech that had come in disguise, as *char* had come disguised as Charlie. Yet it had a sound that belonged in this business; a sound more of his world than of Jake's, Susannah's, and Eddie's, from whence the tale had come.

3

Jake kept expecting the Green Palace to begin looking normal as they drew closer to it, the way the attractions in Disney World began to look normal as you drew close to them—not *ordinary,* necessarily, but *normal,* things which were as much a part of the world as the corner bus stop or mailbox or park bench, stuff you could touch, stuff you could write FUCK PIPER on, if you took a notion.

But that didn't happen, wasn't *going* to happen, and as they neared the Green Palace, Jake realized something else: it was the most beautiful, radiant thing he had ever seen in his life. Not trusting it—and he did not—didn't change the fact. It was like a drawing in a fairy-tale book, one so good it had become real, somehow. And, like the thinny, it hummed . . . except that this sound was far fainter, and not unpleasant.

Pale green walls rose to battlements that jutted and towers that soared, seeming almost to touch the clouds floating over the Kansas plains. These towers were topped with needles of a darker, emerald green; it was from these that the red pennants flickered. Upon each pennant the symbol of the open eye had been

traced in yellow.

It's the mark of the Crimson King, Jake thought. *It's really his* sigul, *not John Farson's.* He didn't know how he knew this (how could he, when Alabama's Crimson Tide was the only Crimson *anything* he knew?), but he did.

"So beautiful," Susannah murmured, and when Jake glanced at her, he thought she was almost crying. "But not nice, somehow. Not right. Maybe not downright *bad,* the way the thinny is, but . . ."

"But not nice," Eddie said. "Yeah. That works. Not a red light, maybe, but a bright yellow one just the same." He rubbed the side of his face (a gesture he had picked up from Roland without even realizing it) and looked puzzled. "It feels almost not serious—a practical joke."

"I doubt it's a joke," Roland said. "Do you think it's a copy of the place where Dorothy and her *ka-tet* met the false wizard?"

Again, the three erstwhile New Yorkers seemed to exchange a single glance of consultation. When it was over, Eddie spoke for all of them. "Yeah. Yeah, probably. It's not the same as the one in the movie, but if this thing came out of our minds, it wouldn't be. Because we see the one from L. Frank Baum's book, too. Both from the illustrations in the book . . ."

"And the ones from our imaginations," Jake said.

"But that's it," Susannah said. "I'd say we're definitely off to see the Wizard."

"You bet," Eddie said. "Because-because-because-because-*because*—"

"*Because of the wonderful things he does!*" Jake and Susannah finished in unison, then laughed, delighted with each other, while Roland frowned at them, feeling puzzled and looking left out.

"But I have to tell you guys," Eddie said, "that it's only gonna take about one more wonderful thing to send me around to the dark side of the Psycho Moon. Most likely for good."

4

As they drew closer, they could see Interstate 70 stretching away into the pale green depths of the castle's slightly rounded outer wall; it floated there like an optical illusion. Closer yet, and they could hear the pennants snapping in the breeze and see their own ripply reflections, like drowned folk who somehow walk at the bottoms of watery tropical graves.

There was an inner redoubt of dark blue glass—it was a color Jake associated with the bottles fountain-pen ink came in—and a rust-hued wall-walk between the redoubt and the outer wall. That color made Susannah think of the bottles Hires root-beer had come in when she was a little girl.

The way in was blocked by a barred gate that was both huge and ethereal: it looked like wrought iron which had been turned to glass. Each cunningly made stake was a different color, and these colors seemed to come from the *inside,* as if the bars were filled with some bright gas or liquid.

The travellers stopped before it. There was no sign of the turnpike beyond it; instead of roadway, there was a courtyard of silver glass—a huge flat mirror, in fact. Clouds floated serenely through its depths; so did the image of the occasional swooping bird. Sun reflected off this glass courtyard and ran across the green castle walls in ripples.

On the far side, the wall of the palace's inner ward rose in a glimmery green cliff, broken by narrow loophole windows of jet-black glass. There was also an arched entry in this wall that made Jake think of St. Patrick's Cathedral.

To the left of the main doorway was a sentry-box made of cream-colored glass shot through with hazy orange threads. Its door, painted with red stripes, stood open. The phone-booth-sized room inside was empty, although there was something on the floor which looked to Jake like a newspaper.

Above the entry, flanking its darkness, were two crouching, leering gargoyles of darkest violet glass. Their pointed tongues poked out like bruises.

The pennants atop the towers flapped like schoolyard flags.

Crows cawed over empty cornfields now a week past the Reap.

Distant, the thinny whined and warbled.

"Look at the bars of this gate," Susannah said. She sounded breathless and awestruck. "Look very closely."

Jake bent toward the yellow bar until his nose nearly touched it and a faint yellow stripe ran down the middle of his face. At first he saw nothing, and then he gasped. What he had taken for motes of some kind were creatures—living creatures—imprisoned inside the bar, swimming in tiny schools. They looked like fish in an aquarium, but they also *(their heads,* Jake told himself, *I think it's mostly their heads)* looked oddly, disquietingly human. As if, Jake thought, he were looking into a vertical golden sea, all the ocean in a glass rod—and living myths no bigger than grains of dust swimming within it. A tiny woman with a fish's tail and long blonde hair streaming out behind her swam to her side of the glass, seemed to peer out at the giant boy (her eyes were round, startled, and beautiful), and then flipped away again.

Jake felt suddenly dizzy and weak. He closed his eyes until the feeling of vertigo went away, then opened them again and looked around at the others. "Cripes! Are they all the same?"

"All different, I think," said Eddie, who had already peered into two or three. He bent close to the purple rod, and his cheeks lit up as if in the glow of an old-fashioned fluoroscope. "These guys here look like birds—little tiny birds."

Jake looked and saw that Eddie was right: inside the gate's purple upright were flocks of birds no bigger than summer minges. They swooped giddily about in their eternal twilight, weaving over and under one another, their wings leaving tiny silver trails of bubbles.

"Are they really there?" Jake asked breathlessly. "Are they, Roland, or are we only imagining them?"

"I don't know. But I know what this gate has been made to look like."

"So do I," Eddie said. He surveyed the shining posts, each with its own column of imprisoned light and life. Each of the gate's wings consisted of six colored bars. The one in the center—broad and flat instead of round, and made to split in two when the gate was opened—was the thirteenth. This one was dead black, and in this one nothing moved.

Oh, maybe not that you can see, *but there are things moving around in there, all right,* Jake thought. *There's life in there,* terrible *life. And maybe there are roses, too. Drowned ones.*

"It's a Wizard's Gate," Eddie said. "Each bar has been made to look like one of the balls in Maerlyn's Rainbow. Look, here's the pink one."

Jake leaned toward it, hands propped on his thighs. He knew what would be inside even before he saw them: horses, of courses. Tiny herds of them, galloping through that strange pink stuff that was neither light nor liquid. Horses running in search of a Drop they would never find, mayhap.

Eddie stretched his hands out to grasp the sides of the central post, the black one.

"Don't!" Susannah called sharply.

Eddie ignored her, but Jake saw his chest stop for a moment and his lips tighten as he wrapped his hands around the black bar and waited for something—some force perhaps sent Special Delivery all the way from the Dark Tower itself—to change him, or even to strike him dead. When nothing happened, he breathed deep again, and risked a smile. "No electricity, but . . ." He pulled; the gate held fast. "No give, either. I see where it splits down the middle, but I get nothing. Want to take a shot, Roland?"

Roland reached for the gate, but Jake put a hand on his arm and stopped him before the gunslinger could do more than give it a preliminary shake. "Don't bother. That's not the way."

"Then what is?"

Instead of answering, Jake sat down in front of the gate, near the place where this strange version of I-70 ended, and began putting on the shoes which had been left for him. Eddie watched a moment, then sat down beside him. "I guess we ought to try it," he said to Jake, "even though it'll probably turn out to be just another bumhug."

Jake laughed, shook his head, and began to tighten the laces of the blood-red Oxfords. He and Eddie both knew it was no bumhug. Not this time.

5

"Okay," Jake said when they had all put on their red shoes (he thought they looked extraordinarily stupid, especially Eddie's pair). "I'll count to three, and we'll click our heels together. Like this." He clicked the Oxfords together once, sharply . . . and the gate shivered like a loosely fastened shutter blown by a strong wind. Susannah cried out. There followed a low, sweet chiming sound from the Green Palace, as if the walls themselves had vibrated.

"I guess this'll do the trick, all right," Eddie said. "I warn you, though, I'm not singing 'Somewhere Over the Rainbow.' That's not in my contract."

"The rainbow is here," the gunslinger said softly, stretching his diminished hand out to the gate.

It wiped the smile off Eddie's face. "Yeah, I know. I'm a little scared, Roland."

"So am I," the gunslinger said, and indeed, Jake thought he looked pale and ill.

"Go on, sugar," Susannah said. "Count before we all lose our nerve."

"One . . . two . . . *three*"

They clicked their heels together solemnly and in unison: *tock, tock, tock.* The gate shivered more violently this time, the colors in the uprights brightening perceptibly. The chime that followed was higher, sweeter—the sound of fine crystal tapped with the haft of a knife. It echoed in dreamy harmonics that made Jake shiver, half with pleasure and half with pain.

But the gate didn't open.

"What—" Eddie began.

"I know," Jake said. "We forgot Oy."

"Oh Christ," Eddie said. "I left the world I knew to watch a kid try to put booties on a fucked-up weasel. Shoot me, Roland, before I breed."

Roland ignored him, watching Jake closely as the boy sat down on the turnpike and called, "Oy! To me!"

The bumbler came willingly enough, and although he

had surely been a wild creature before they had met him on the Path of the Beam, he allowed Jake to slip the red leather booties onto his paws without making trouble: in fact, once he got the idea, he stepped into the last two. When all four of the little red shoes were in place (they looked, in fact, the most like Dorothy's ruby slippers), Oy sniffed at one of them, then looked attentively back at Jake.

Jake clicked his heels together three times, looking at the bumbler as he did so, ignoring the rattle of the gate and the soft chime from the walls of the Green Palace.

"You, Oy!"

"Oy!"

He rolled over on his back like a dog playing dead, then simply looked at his own feet with a kind of disgusted bewilderment. Looking at him, Jake had a sharp memory: trying to pat his stomach and rub his head at the same time, and his father making fun of him when he couldn't do it right away.

"Roland, help me. He knows what he's supposed to do, but he doesn't know how to do it." Jake glanced up at Eddie. "And don't make any smart remarks, okay?"

"No," Eddie said. "No smart remarks, Jake. Do you think just Oy has to do it this time, or is it still a group effort?"

"Just him, I think."

"But it wouldn't hurt us to kind of click along with Mitch," Susannah said.

"Mitch who?" Eddie asked, looking blank.

"Never mind. Go on, Jake, Roland. Give us a count again."

Eddie grasped Oy's forepaws. Roland gently grasped the bumbler's rear paws. Oy looked nervous at this—as if he perhaps expected to be swung briskly into the air and given the old heave-ho—but he didn't struggle.

"One, two, *three.*"

Jake and Roland gently patted Oy's forepaws and rear paws together in unison. At the same time they clicked the heels of their own footwear. Eddie and Susannah did the same.

This time the harmonic was a deep, sweet bong, like a glass church bell. The black glass bar running down the center of the gate did not split open but shattered, spraying crumbs of obsidian glass in all directions. Some rattled against Oy's hide. He sprang up in a hurry, yanking out of Jake's and Roland's grip and trotting a little distance away. He sat on the broken white line between the travel lane and the passing lane of the highway, his ears laid back, looking at the gate and panting.

"Come on," Roland said. He went to the left wing of the gate and pushed it slowly open. He stood at the edge of the mirror courtyard, a tall, lanky man in cow-poke jeans, an ancient shirt of no particular color, and improbable red cowboy boots. "Let's go in and see what the Wizard of Oz has to say for himself."

"If he's still here," Eddie said.

"Oh, I think he's here," Roland murmured. "Yes, I think he's here."

He ambled toward the main door with the empty sentry-box beside it. The others followed, welded to their own downward reflections by the red shoes like sets of Siamese twins.

Oy came last, skipping nimbly along in his ruby slippers, pausing once to sniff down at his own reflected snout.

"Oy!" he cried to the bumbler floating below him, and then hurried after Jake.

CHAPTER THREE

The Wizard

I

Roland stopped at the sentry-box, glanced in, then picked up the thing which was lying on the floor. The others caught up with him and clustered around. It had looked like a newspaper, and that was just what it was . . . although an exceedingly odd one. No Topeka *Capital-Journal* this, and no news of a population-levelling plague.

𝕿𝖍𝖊 𝕺𝖟 𝕯𝖆𝖎𝖑𝖞 𝕭𝖚𝖟𝖟

Vol. MDLXVIII No. 96 "Daily Buzz, Daily Buzz, Handsome Iz as Handsome Duuzz" Weather: Here today, gone tomorrow Lucky Numbers: None Prognosis: Bad

Blah blah blah blah blah blah blah blah blah blah blah blah blah blah blah blah blah blah blah blah blah blah blah blah blah blah blah blah blah blah blah blah blah blah blah blah blah blah blah blah blah yak yak yak yak yak yak yak yak yak yak yak yak yak yak yak yak yak yak blah blah blah good is bad bad is good all the stuff's the same good is bad bad is good all the stuff's the same go slow past the drawers all the stuff's the same blah blah blah blah blah blah

blah blah Blaine is a pain all the stuff's the same yak yak yak yak yak yak yak yak yak yak charyou tree all the stuff's the same blah yak blah blah yak yak blah blah blah yak yak yak baked turkey cooked goose all the stuff's the same blah blah yak yak ride a train die in pain all the stuff's the same blah blah blah blah blah blah blah blah blah blah blah blah blah blah blame blame blame blame blame blame blah blah blah blah blah blah blah yak yak blah blah blah blah blah blah blah blah blah blah blah. (Related story p. 6)

Below this was a picture of Roland, Eddie, Susannah, and Jake crossing the mirrored courtyard, as if this had happened the day before instead of only minutes ago. Beneath it was a caption reading: **Tragedy in Oz: Travellers Arrive Seeking Fame and Fortune; Find Death Instead.**

"I like that," Eddie said, adjusting Roland's revolver in the holster he wore low on his hip. "Comfort and encouragement after days of confusion. Like a hot drink on a cold fucking night."

"Don't be afraid of this," Roland said. "This *is* a joke."

"I'm not afraid," Eddie said, "but it's a little more than a joke. I lived with Henry Dean for a lot of years, and I know when there's a plot to psych me out afoot. I know it very well." He looked curiously at Roland. "I hope you don't mind me saying this, but *you're* the one who looks scared, Roland."

"I'm terrified," Roland said simply.

2

The arched entryway made Susannah think of a song which had been popular ten years or so before she had been yanked out of her world and into Roland's. *Saw an eyeball peepin through a smoky cloud behind the Green Door,* the lyric went. *When I said "Joe sent me," someone laughed out loud behind the Green Door.* There were actually two doors here instead of one, and no peephole through which an eyeball could look in either. Nor did Susannah try that old speakeasy deal about how Joe had sent her. She did, however, bend forward to read the sign hanging from one of the circular glass door-pulls. BELL OUT OF ORDER, PLEASE KNOCK, it said.

"Don't bother," she said to Roland, who had actually doubled up his fist to do as the sign said. "It's from the story, that's all."

Eddie pulled her chair back slightly, stepped in front of it, and took hold of the circular pulls. The doors opened easily, the hinges rolling in silence. He took a step forward into what looked like a shadowy green grotto, cupped his hands to his mouth, and called: *"Hey!"*

The sound of his voice rolled away and came back changed . . . small, echoing, lost. Dying, it seemed.

"Christ," Eddie said. "Do we have to do this?"

"If we want to get back to the Beam, I think so." Roland looked paler than ever, but he led them in. Jake helped Eddie lift Susannah's chair over the sill (a milky block of jade-colored glass) and inside. Oy's little shoes flashed dim red on the green glass floor. They had gone only ten paces when the doors slammed shut behind them with a no-question-about-it boom that rolled past them and went echoing away into the depths of the Green Palace.

3

There was no reception room; only a vaulted, cavernous hallway that seemed to go on forever. The walls were lit with a faint green glow. *This is just like the hallway in the movie,* Jake thought, *the one where the Cowardly Lion got so scared when he stepped on his own tail.*

And, adding a little extra touch of verisimilitude Jake could have done without, Eddie spoke up in a trembly (and better than passable) Bert Lahr imitation: "Wait a minute, fellas, I wuz just thinkin—I really don't wanna see the Wizard this much. I better wait for you outside!"

"Stop it," Jake said sharply.

"Oppit!" Oy agreed. He walked directly at Jake's heel, swinging his head watchfully from side to side as he went. Jake could hear no sound except for their own passage . . . yet he sensed something: a sound that *wasn't*. It was, he thought, like looking at a wind-chime that wants only the slightest puff of breeze to set it tinkling.

"Sorry," Eddie said. "Really." He pointed. "Look down there."

About forty yards ahead of them, the green corridor *did* end, in a narrow green doorway of amazing height— perhaps thirty feet from the floor to its pointed tip. And from behind it, Jake could now hear a steady thrumming sound. As they drew closer and the sound grew louder, his dread grew. He had to make a conscious effort to take the last dozen steps to the door. He knew this sound; he knew it from the run he'd made with Gasher under Lud, and from the run he and his friends had made on Blaine the Mono. It was the steady beat-beat-beat of slo-trans engines.

"It's like a nightmare," he said in a small, close-to-tears voice. "We're right back where we started."

"No, Jake," the gunslinger said, touching his hair. "Never think it. What you feel is an illusion. Stand and be true."

The sign on this door wasn't from the movie, and only Susannah knew it was from Dante. ABANDON HOPE, ALL YE WHO ENTER HERE, it said.

Roland reached out with his two-fingered right hand and pulled the thirty-foot door open.

4

What lay beyond it was, to the eyes of Jake, Susannah, and Eddie, a weird combination of *The Wizard of Oz* and Blaine the Mono. A thick rug (pale blue, like the one in the Barony Coach) lay on the floor. The chamber was like the nave of a cathedral, soaring to impenetrable heights of greenish-black. The pillars which supported the glowing walls were great glass ribs of alternating green and pink light; the pink was the exact shade of Blaine's hull. Jake saw these supporting pillars had been carven with a billion different images, none of them comforting; they jostled the eye and unsettled the heart. There seemed to be a preponderance of screaming faces.

Ahead of them, dwarfing the visitors, turning them into creatures that seemed no bigger than ants, was the chamber's only furnishing: an enormous green glass throne. Jake tried to estimate its size and was unable— he had no reference-points to help him. He thought that the throne's back might be fifty feet high, but it could as easily have been seventy-five or a hundred. It was marked with the open eye symbol, this time traced in red instead of yellow. The rhythmic thrusting of the light made the eye seem alive; to be beating like a heart.

Above the throne, rising like the pipes of a mighty medieval organ, were thirteen great cylinders, each pulsing a different color. Each, that was, save for the pipe which ran directly down in back of the throne's center. That one was black as midnight and as still as death.

"Hey!" Susannah shouted from her chair. "Anyone here?"

At the sound of her voice, the pipes flashed so brilliantly that Jake had to shield his eyes. For a moment the entire throneroom glared like an exploding rainbow. Then the pipes went out, went dark, went dead, just as the wizard's glass in Roland's story had done when the glass (or the force inhabiting the glass) decided to shut up for awhile. Now there was only the column of blackness, and the steady green pulse of the empty throne.

Next, a somehow tired humming sound, as of a very old servomechanism being called into use one final time, began to whine its way into their ears. Panels, each at least six feet long and two feet wide, slid open in the arms of the throne. From the black slots thus revealed, a rosecolored smoke began to drift out and up. As it rose, it darkened to a bright red. And in it, a terribly familiar zigzag line appeared. Jake knew what it was even before the words

(Lud Candleton Rilea The Falls of the Hounds Dasherville Topeka)

appeared, glowing smoke-bright.

It was Blaine's route-map.

Roland could say all he wanted about how things had changed, how Jake's feeling of being trapped in a nightmare

(this is the worst nightmare of my life, and that is the truth)

was just an illusion created by his confused mind and frightened heart, but Jake knew better. This place might look a little bit like the throneroom of Oz the Great and Terrible, but it was really Blaine the Mono. They were back aboard Blaine, and soon the riddling would begin all over again.

Jake felt like screaming.

5

Eddie recognized the voice that boomed out of the smoky route-map hanging above the green throne, but he believed it was Blaine the Mono no more than he believed it was the Wizard of Oz. *Some* wizard, perhaps, but this wasn't the Emerald City, and Blaine was just as dead as dogshit. Eddie had sent him home with a fuckin rupture.

"HELLO THERE AGAIN, LITTLE TRAILHANDS!"

The smoky route-map pulsed, but Eddie no longer associated it with the voice, although he guessed they were supposed to. No, the voice was coming from the pipes.

He glanced down, saw Jake's paper-white face, and knelt beside him. "It's crap, kid," he said.

"N-No . . . it's Blaine . . . not dead . . ."

"He's dead, all right. This is nothing but an amplified version of the after-school announcements . . . who's got detention and who's supposed to report to Room Six for Speech Therapy. You dig?"

"What?" Jake looked up at him, lips wet and trembling, eyes dazed. "What do you—"

"Those pipes are *speakers.* Even a pipsqueak can sound big through a twelve-speaker Dolby sound-system; don't you remember the movie? It has to sound big because it's a bumhug, Jake—just a bumhug."

"WHAT ARE YOU TELLING HIM, EDDIE OF NEW YORK? ONE OF YOUR STUPID, NASTY-MINDED LITTLE JOKES? ONE OF YOUR UNFAIR RIDDLES?"

"Yeah," Eddie said. "The one that goes, 'How many dipolar computers does it take to screw in a lightbulb?' Who are you, buddy? I know goddam well you're not Blaine the Mono, so who are you?"

"I . . . AM . . . OZ!" the voice thundered. The glass columns flashed; so did the pipes behind the throne. "OZ THE GREAT! OZ THE POWERFUL! WHO ARE YOU?"

Susannah rolled forward until her wheelchair was at the base of the dull green steps leading up to a throne that would have dwarfed even Lord Perth.

"I'm Susannah Dean, the small and crippled," she said, "and I was raised to be polite, but not to suffer bull-shit. We're here because we're *s'pozed* to be here—why else did we get left the shoes?"

"WHAT DO YOU WANT OF ME, SUSANNAH? WHAT WOULD YOU HAVE, LITTLE COWGIRL?"

"*You* know," she said. "We want what everyone wants, so far as I know—to go back home again, 'cause there's no place like home. We—"

"You can't go home," Jake said. He spoke in a rapid, frightened murmur. "You can't go home again, Thomas Wolfe said that, and that is the truth."

"It's a *lie,* sug," Susannah said. "A flat-out lie. You *can* go home again. All you have to do is find the right rain-bow and walk under it. We've found it; the rest is just, you know, footwork."

"WOULD YOU GO BACK TO NEW YORK, SUSAN-NAH DEAN? EDDIE DEAN? JAKE CHAMBERS? IS THAT WHAT YOU ASK OF OZ, THE MIGHTY AND POWERFUL?"

"New York isn't home for us anymore," Susannah said. She looked very small yet very fearless as she sat in her new wheelchair at the foot of the enormous, pulsing throne. "No more than Gilead is home for Roland. Take us back to the Path of the Beam. That's where we want to go, because that's our way home. Only way home we got."

"GO AWAY!" cried the voice from the pipes. "GO AWAY AND COME BACK TOMORROW! WE'LL DISCUSS THE BEAM THEN! FIDDLE-DE-DEE, SAID SCARLETT, WE'LL TALK ABOUT THE BEAM TOMORROW, FOR TOMORROW IS ANOTHER DAY!"

"No," Eddie said. "We'll talk about it now."

"DO NOT AROUSE THE WRATH OF THE GREAT AND POWERFUL OZ!" the voice cried, and the pipes flashed furiously with each word. Susannah was sure this was supposed to be scary, but she found it almost amusing, instead. It was like watching a salesman demonstrate a child's toy. *Hey, kids! When you talk, the pipes flash bright colors! Try it and see!*

"Sugar, you best listen, now," Susannah said. "What *you* don't want to do is arouse the wrath of folks with guns. Especially when you be livin in a glass house."

"I SAID COME BACK TOMORROW!"

Red smoke once more began to boil out of the slots in the arms of the throne. It was thicker now. The shape which had been Blaine's route-map melted apart and joined it. The smoke formed a face, this time. It was narrow and hard and watchful, framed by long hair.

It's the man Roland shot in the desert, Susannah thought wonderingly. *It's that man Jonas. I know it is.*

Now Oz spoke in a slightly trembling voice: "DO YOU PRESUME TO THREATEN THE GREAT OZ?" The lips of the huge, smoky face hovering over the throne's seat parted in a snarl of mingled menace and contempt. "YOU UNGRATEFUL CREATURES! OH, YOU UNGRATEFUL CREATURES!"

Eddie, who knew smoke and mirrors when he saw them, had glanced in another direction. His eyes widened and he gripped Susannah's arm above the elbow. "Look," he whispered. "Christ, Suze, look at Oy!"

The billy-bumbler had no interest in smoke-ghosts,

whether they were monorail route-maps, dead Coffin Hunters, or just Hollywood special effects of the pre–World War II variety. He had seen (or smelled) something that was more interesting.

Susannah grabbed Jake, turned him, and pointed at the bumbler. She saw the boy's eyes widen with understanding a moment before Oy reached the small alcove in the left wall. It was screened from the main chamber by a green curtain which matched the glass walls. Oy stretched his long neck forward, caught the curtain's fabric in his teeth, and yanked it back.

6

Behind the curtain red and green lights flashed; cylinders spun inside glass boxes; needles moved back and forth inside long rows of lighted dials. Yet Jake barely noticed these things. It was the man who took all his attention, the one sitting at the console, his back to them. His filthy hair, streaked with dirt and blood, hung to his shoulders in matted clumps. He was wearing some sort of headset, and was speaking into a tiny mike which hung in front of his mouth. His back was to them, and at first he had no idea that Oy had smelled him out and uncovered his hiding place.

"GO!" thundered the voice from the pipes . . . except now Jake saw where it was *really* coming from. "COME BACK TOMORROW IF YOU LIKE, BUT GO NOW! I WARN YOU!"

"It *is* Jonas, Roland must not have killed him after all," Eddie whispered, but Jake knew better. He had recognized the voice. Even distorted by the amplification of the colored pipes, he had recognized the voice. How could he have ever believed it to be the voice of Blaine?

"I WARN YOU, IF YOU REFUSE—"

Oy barked, a sharp and somehow forbidding sound. The man in the equipment alcove began to turn.

Tell me, cully, Jake remembered this voice saying before its owner had discovered the dubious attractions of amplification. *Tell me all you know about dipolar computers and transitive circuits. Tell me and I'll give you a drink.*

It wasn't Jonas, and it wasn't the Wizard of anything. It was David Quick's grandson. It was the Tick-Tock Man.

7

Jake stared at him, horrified. The coiled, dangerous creature who had lived beneath Lud with his mates—Gasher and Hoots and Brandon and Tilly—was gone. This might have been that monster's ruined father . . . or grandfather. His left eye—the one Oy had punctured with his claws—bulged white and misshapen, partly in its socket and partly on his unshaven cheek. The right side of his head looked half-scalped, the skull showing through in a long, triangular strip. Jake had a distant, panicdarkened memory of a flap of skin falling over the side of Tick-Tock's face, but he had been on the edge of hysteria by that point . . . and was again now.

Oy had also recognized the man who had tried to kill him and was barking hysterically, head down, teeth bared, back bowed. Tick-Tock stared at him with wide, stunned eyes.

"Pay no attention to that man behind the curtain," said a voice from behind them, and then tittered. "My friend Andrew is having another in a long series of bad days. Poor boy. I suppose I was wrong to bring him out of Lud, but he just looked so *lost* . . ." The owner of the voice tittered again.

Jake swung around and saw that there was now a man sitting in the middle of the great throne, with his legs casually crossed in front of him. He was wearing jeans, a dark jacket that belted at the waist, and old, rundown cowboy boots. On his jacket was a button that showed a pig's head with a bullet-hole between the eyes. In his lap this newcomer held a drawstring bag. He rose, standing in the seat of the throne like a child in daddy's chair, and the smile dropped away from his face like loose skin. Now his eyes blazed, and his lips parted over vast, hungry teeth.

"Get them, Andrew! Get them! Kill them! Every sister-fucking one of them!"

"My life for you!" the man in the alcove screamed, and for the first time Jake saw the machine-gun propped in the corner. Tick-Tock sprang for it and snatched it up. *"My life for you!"*

He turned, and Oy was on him once again, leaping forward and upward, sinking his teeth deep into Tick-Tock's left thigh, just below the crotch.

Eddie and Susannah drew in unison, each raising one of Roland's big guns. They fired in concert, not even the smallest overlap in the sound of their shots. One of them tore off the top of Tick-Tock's miserable head, buried itself in the equipment, and created a loud but mercifully brief snarl of feedback. The other took him in the throat.

He staggered forward one step, then two. Oy dropped to the floor and backed away from him, snarling. A third step took Tick-Tock out into the throneroom proper. He raised his arms toward Jake, and the boy could read Ticky's hatred in his remaining green eye; the boy thought he could hear the man's last, hateful thought: *Oh, you fucking little squint—*

Then Tick-Tock collapsed forward, as he had collapsed in the Cradle of the Grays . . . only this time he would rise no more.

"Thus fell Lord Perth, and the earth did shake with that thunder," said the man on the throne.

Except he's not a man, Jake thought. *Not a man at all. We've found the Wizard at last, I think. And I'm pretty sure I know what's in the bag he has.*

"Marten," Roland said. He held out his left hand, the one which was still whole. "Marten Broadcloak. After all these years. After all these *centuries.*"

"Want this, Roland?"

Eddie put the gun he had used to kill the Tick-Tock Man in Roland's hand. A tendril of blue smoke was still rising from the barrel. Roland looked at the old revolver as if he had never seen it before, then slowly lifted it and pointed it at the grinning, rosy-cheeked figure sitting cross-legged on the Green Palace's throne.

"Finally," Roland breathed, thumbing back the trigger. "Finally in my sights."

8

"That six-shooter will do you no good, as I think you know," the man on the throne said. "Not against *me.* Only misfires against *me,* Roland, old fellow. How's the family, by the way? I seem to have lost touch with them over the years. I was always such a *lousy* correspondent. Someone ought to take a hosswhip to me, aye, so they should!"

He threw back his head and laughed. Roland pulled the trigger of the gun in his hand. When the hammer fell there was only a dull click.

"Toadjer," the man on the throne said. "I think you must have gotten some of those wet slugs in there by accident, don't you? The ones with the flat powder? Good for blocking the sound of the thinny, but not so good for shooting old wizards, are they? Too bad. And your hand, Roland, look at your *hand!* Short a couple of fingers, by the look. My, this *has* been hard on you, hasn't it? Things could get easier, though. You and your friends could have a fine, fruitful life—and, as Jake would say, that is the truth. No more lobstrosities, no more mad trains, no more disquieting—not to mention dangerous—trips to other worlds. All you have to do is give over this stupid and hopeless quest for the Tower."

"No," Eddie said.

"No," Susannah said.

"No," Jake said.

"No!" Oy said, and added a bark.

The dark man on the green throne continued to smile, unperturbed. "Roland?" he asked. "What about you?" Slowly, he raised the drawstring bag. It looked dusty and old. It hung from the wizard's fist like a teardrop, and now the thing in its pouch began to pulse with pink light. "Cry off, and they need never see what's inside this—they need never see the last scene of that sad long-ago play. Cry off. Turn from the Tower and go your way."

"No," Roland said. He began to smile, and as his smile broadened, that of the man sitting on the throne began to falter. "You can enchant my guns, those of this world, I reckon," he said.

"Roland, I don't know what you're thinking of, laddie, but I warn you not to—"

"Not to cross Oz the Great? Oz the Powerful? But I think I will, Marten . . . or Maerlyn . . . or whoever you call yourself now . . ."

"Flagg, actually," the man on the throne said. "And we've met before." He smiled. Instead of broadening his face, as smiles usually did, it contracted Flagg's features into a narrow and spiteful grimace. "In the wreck of Gilead. You and your surviving pals—that laughing donkey Cuthbert Allgood made one of your party, I remember, and DeCurry, the fellow with the birthmark, made another—were on your way west, to seek the Tower. Or, in the parlance of Jake's world, you were off to see the Wizard. I know you saw me, but I doubt you knew until now that I saw you, as well."

"And will again, I reckon," Roland said. "Unless, that is, I kill you now and put an end to your interference."

Still holding his own gun out in his left hand, he went for the one tucked in the waistband of his jeans—Jake's Ruger, a gun from another world and perhaps immune to this creature's enchantments—with his right. And he was fast as he had always been fast, his speed blinding.

The man on the throne shrieked and cringed back. The bag fell from his lap, and the glass ball—once held by Rhea, once held by Jonas, once held by Roland himself—slipped out of its mouth. Smoke, green this time instead of red, billowed from the slots in the arms of the throne. It rose in obscuring fumes. Yet Roland still might have shot the figure disappearing into the smoke if he had made a clean draw. He didn't, however; the Ruger slid in the grip of his reduced hand, then twisted. The front sight caught on his belt-buckle. It took only an extra quarter-second for him to free the snag, but that was the quarter-second he had needed. He pumped three shots into the billowing smoke, then ran forward, oblivious of the shouts of the others.

He waved the smoke aside with his hands. His shots had shattered the back of the throne into thick green slabs of glass, but the man-shaped creature which had called itself Flagg was gone. Roland found himself already beginning to wonder if he—or it—had been there in the first place.

The ball was still there, however, unharmed and glowing the same enticing pink he remembered from so long ago—from Mejis, when he had been young and in love. This survivor of Maerlyn's Rainbow had rolled almost to the edge of the throne's seat; two more inches and it would have plunged over and shattered on the floor. Yet it had not; still it remained, this bewitched thing Susan Delgado had first glimpsed through the window of Rhea's hut, under the light of the Kissing Moon.

Roland picked it up—how well it fit his hand, how natural it felt against his palm, even after all these years—and looked into its cloudy, troubled depths. "You always did have a charmed life," he whispered to it. He thought of Rhea as he had seen her in this ball—her ancient, laughing eyes. He thought of the flames from the Reap-Night bonfire rising around Susan, making her beauty shimmer in the heat. Making it shiver like a mirage.

Wretched glam! he thought. *If I dashed you to the floor, surely we would drown in the sea of tears that would pour out of your split belly . . . the tears of all those you've put to ruin.*

And why not do it? Left whole, the nasty thing might be able to help them back to the Path of the Beam, but Roland didn't believe they actually *needed* it. He thought that Tick-Tock and the creature which had called itself Flagg had been their last challenge in that regard. The Green Palace was their door back to Mid-World . . . and it was theirs, now. They had conquered it by force of arms.

But you can't go yet, gunslinger. Not until you've finished your story, told the last scene.

Whose voice was that? Vannay's? No. Cort's? No. Nor was it the voice of his father, who had once turned him naked out of a whore's bed. That was the hardest voice, the one he often heard in his troubled dreams, the one he wanted so to please and so seldom could. No, not that voice, not this time.

This time what he heard was the voice of *ka*—*ka* like a wind. He had told so much of that awful fourteenth year . . . but he hadn't finished the tale. As with Detta Walker and the Blue Lady's forspecial plate, there was one more thing. A hidden thing. The question wasn't, he saw, whether or not the five of them could find their way out of the Green Palace and recover the Path of the Beam; the question was whether or not they could go on as *ka-tet*. If they were to do that, there could be nothing hidden; he would have to tell them of the final time he had looked into the wizard's glass in that long-ago year. Three nights past the welcoming banquet, it had been. He would have to tell them—

No, Roland, the voice whispered. *Not just tell. Not this time. You know better.*

Yes. He knew better.

"Come," he said, turning to them.

They drew slowly around him, their eyes wide and filling with the ball's flashing pink light. Already they were half-hypnotized by it, even Oy.

"We are *ka-tet*," Roland said, holding the ball toward them. "We are one from many. I lost my one true love at the beginning of my quest for the Dark Tower. Now look into this wretched thing, if you would, and see what I lost not long after. See it once and for all; see it very well."

They looked. The ball, cupped in Roland's upraised hands, began to pulse faster. It gathered them in and swept them away. Caught and whirled in the grip of that pink storm, they flew over the Wizard's Rainbow to the Gilead that had been.

CHAPTER FOUR

The Glass

Jake of New York stands in an upper corridor of the Great Hall of Gilead—more castle, here in the green land, than Mayor's House. He looks around and sees Susannah and Eddie standing by a tapestry, their eyes big, their hands tightly entwined. And Susannah is standing; she has her legs back, at least for now, and what she called "cappies" have been replaced by a pair of ruby slippers exactly like those Dorothy wore when she stepped out upon her version of the Great Road to find the Wizard of Oz, that bumhug.

She has her legs because this is a dream, *Jake thinks, but knows it is no dream. He looks down and sees Oy looking up at him with his anxious, intelligent, gold-ringed eyes. He is still wearing the red booties. Jake bends and strokes Oy's head. The feel of the bumbler's fur under his hand is clear and real. No, this isn't a dream.*

Yet Roland is not here, he realizes; they are four instead of five. He realizes something else as well: the air of this corridor is faintly pink, and small pink halos revolve around the funny, old-fashioned lightbulbs that illuminate the corridor. Something is going to happen; some story is going to play out in front of their eyes. And now, as if the very thought had summoned them, the boy hears the click of approaching footfalls.

It's a story I know, *Jake thinks.* One I've been told before.

As Roland comes around the corner, he realizes what story it is: the one where Marten Broadcloak stops Roland as Roland

865

passes by on his way to the rooftop, where it will perhaps be cooler. "You, boy," Marten will say. "Come in! Don't stand in the hall! Your mother wants to speak to you." But of course that isn't the truth, was never the truth, will never be the truth, no matter how much time slips and bends. What Marten wants is for the boy to see his mother, and to understand that Gabrielle Deschain has become the mistress of his father's wizard. Marten wants to goad the boy into an early test of manhood while his father is away and can't put a stop to it; he wants to get the puppy out of his way before it can grow teeth long enough to bite.

Now they will see all this; the sad comedy will go its sad and preordained course in front of their eyes. I'm too young, *Jake thinks, but of course he is not too young; Roland will be only three years older when he comes to Mejis with his friends and meets Susan upon the Great Road. Only three years older when he loves her; only three years older when he loses her.*

I don't care, I don't want to see it—

And won't he realizes as Roland draws closer; all that has already happened. For this is not August, the time of Full Earth, but late fall or early winter. He can tell by the serape *Roland wears, a souvenir of his trip to the Outer Arc, and by the vapor that smokes from his mouth and nose each time he exhales: no central heating in Gilead, and it's cold up here.*

There are other changes as well: Roland is now wearing the guns which are his birthright, the big ones with the sandal-wood grips. His father passed them on at the banquet, *Jake thinks. He doesn't know how he knows this, but he does. And Roland's face, although still that of a boy, is not the open, untried face of the one who idled up this same corridor five months before; the boy who was ensnared by Marten has been through much since then, and his battle with Cort has been the very least of it.*

Jake sees something else, too: the boy gunslinger is wearing the red cowboy boots. He doesn't know it, though. Because this isn't really happening.

Yet somehow it is. They are inside the wizard's glass, they are inside the pink storm (those pink halos revolving around the light fixtures remind Jake of The Falls of the Hounds, and the moonbows revolving in the mist), and this is happening all over again.

"Roland!" Eddie calls from where he and Susannah stand by the tapestry. Susannah gasps and squeezes his shoulder, wanting him to be silent, but Eddie ignores her. "No, Roland! Don't! Bad idea!"

"No! Olan!" Oy yaps.

Roland ignores both of them, and he passes by Jake a hand's breadth away without seeing him. For Roland, they are not here; red boots or no red boots, this ka-tet *is far in his future.*

He stops at a door near the end of the corridor, hesitates, then raises his fist and knocks. Eddie starts down the corridor toward him, still holding Susannah's hand . . . now he looks almost as if he is dragging her.

"Come on, Jake," says Eddie.

"No, I don't want to."

"It's not about what you want, and you know it. We're supposed to see. If we can't stop him, we can at least do what we came here to do. Now come on!"

Heart heavy with dread, his stomach clenched in a knot, Jake comes along. As they approach Roland—the guns look enormous on his slim hips, and his unlined but already tired face somehow makes Jake feel like weeping—the gunslinger knocks again.

"She ain't there, sugar!" Susannah shouts at him. "She ain't there or she ain't answering the door, and which one it is don't matter to you! Leave it! Leave her! *She ain't worth it! Just bein your mother don't make her worth it! Go away!"*

But he doesn't hear her, either, and he doesn't go away. As Jake, Eddie, Susannah, and Oy gather unseen behind him, Roland tries the door to his mother's room and finds it unlocked. He opens it, revealing a shadowy chamber decorated with silk hangings. On the floor is a rug that looks like the Persians beloved of Jake's mother . . . only this rug, Jake knows, comes from the Province of Kashamin.

On the far side of the parlor, by a window which has been shuttered against the winter winds, Jake sees a low-backed chair and knows it is the one she was in on the day of Roland's manhood test; it is where she was sitting when her son observed the love-bite on her neck.

The chair is empty now, but as the gunslinger takes another step into the room and turns to look toward the apartment's bedroom, Jake observes a pair of shoes—black, not red—beneath the drapes flanking the shuttered window.

"Roland!" he shouts. "Roland, behind the drapes! Someone behind the drapes! Look out!"

But Roland doesn't hear.

"Mother?" he calls, and even his voice is the same, Jake would know it anywhere . . . but it is such a magically freshened version of it! Young and uncracked by all the years of dust and wind and cigarette smoke. "Mother, it's Roland! I want to talk to you!"

Still no answer. He walks down the short hall which leads to the bedroom. Part of Jake wants to stay here in the parlor, to go to that drape and yank it aside, but he knows this isn't the way it's supposed to go. Even if he tried, he doubts it would do any good; his hand would likely pass right through, like the hand of a ghost.

"Come on," Eddie says. "Stay with him."

They go in a cluster that might have been comic under other circumstances. Not under these; here it is a case of three people desperate for the comfort of friends.

Roland stands looking at the bed against the room's left wall. He looks at it as if hypnotized. Perhaps he is trying to imagine Marten in it with his mother; perhaps he is remembering Susan, with whom he never slept in a proper bed, let alone a canopied luxury such as this. Jake can see the gunslinger's dim profile in a three-paneled mirror across the room, in an alcove. This triple glass stands in front of a small table the boy recognizes from his mother's side of his parents' bedroom; it is a vanity.

The gunslinger shakes himself and comes back from whatever thoughts have seized his mind. On his feet are those terrible boots; in this dim light, they look like the boots of a man who has walked through a creek of blood.

"Mother!"

He takes a step toward the bed and actually bends a little, as if he thinks she might be hiding under it. If she's been hiding, however, it wasn't there; the shoes which Jake saw beneath the drape were women's shoes, and the shape which now stands at the end of the short corridor, just outside the bedroom door, is wearing a dress. Jake can see its hem.

And he sees more than that. Jake understands Roland's troubled relationship with his mother and father better than Eddie or Susannah ever could, because Jake's own parents are peculiarly like them: Elmer Chambers is a gunslinger for the Network, and Megan Chambers has a long history of sleeping with sick friends. This is nothing Jake has been told, but he knows, somehow; he has shared khef *with his mother and father, and he knows what he knows.*

He knows something about Roland, as well: that he saw his mother in the wizard's glass. It was Gabrielle Deschain, fresh back from her retreat in Debaria, Gabrielle who would confess to her husband the errors of her ways and her thinking after the banquet, who would cry his pardon and beg to be taken back to his bed . . . and, when Steven drowsed after their lovemaking, she would bury the knife in his breast . . . or perhaps only lightly scratch his arm with it, not even waking him. With that knife, it would come to the same either way.

Roland had seen it all in the glass before finally turning the wretched thing over to his father, and Roland had put a stop to it. To save Steven Deschain's life, Eddie and Susannah would have said, had they seen so far into the business, but Jake has the unhappy wisdom of unhappy children and sees further. To save his mother's life as well. To give her one last chance to recover her sanity, one last chance to stand at her husband's side and be true. One last chance to repent of Marten Broadcloak.

Surely she will, surely she must! Roland saw her face that day, how unhappy she was, and surely she must! Surely she cannot have chosen *the magician! If he can only make her* see . . .

So, unaware that he has once more lapsed into the unwisdom of the very young—Roland cannot grasp that unhappiness and shame are often no match for desire—he has come here to speak to his mother, to beg her to come back to her husband before it's too late. He has saved her from herself once, he will tell her, but he cannot do it again.

And if she still won't go, *Jake thinks,* or tries to brave it out, pretend she doesn't know what he's talking about, he'll give her a choice: leave Gilead with his help—now, tonight—or be clapped in chains tomorrow morning, a traitor so outrageous she will almost certainly be hung as Hax the cook was hung.

"Mother?" he calls, still unaware of the shape standing in the shadows behind him. He takes one further step into the room, and now the shape moves. The shape raises its hands. There is something in its hands. Not a gun, Jake can tell that much, but it has a deadly look to it, a snaky *look, somehow—*

"Roland, watch out!" Susannah shrieks, and her voice is like a magical switch. There is something on the dressing table—the glass, of course; Gabrielle has stolen it, it's what she'll bring to her lover as a consolation prize for the murder her son prevented—and now it lights as if in response to Susannah's voice. It sprays brilliant pink light up the triple mirror and casts its glow back into the room. In that light, in that triple glass, Roland finally sees the figure behind him.

"Christ!" *Eddie Dean shrieks, horrified.* "Oh Christ, Roland! That's not your mother! That's—"

It's not even a woman, not really, not anymore; it is a kind of living corpse in a road-filthy black dress. There are only a few straggling tufts of hair left on her head and there's a gaping hole where her nose used to be, but her eyes still blaze, and the snake she holds wriggling between her hands is very *lively. Even in his own horror, Jake has time to wonder if she got it from under the same rock where she found the one Roland killed.*

It is Rhea who has been waiting for the gunslinger in his mother's apartment; it is the Cöos, come not just to retrieve her glam but to finish with the boy who has caused her so much trouble.

"Now, ye trollop's get!" she cries shrilly, cackling. "Now ye'll pay!"

But Roland has seen her, in the glass he has seen her, Rhea betrayed by the very ball she came to take back, and now he is whirling, his hands dropping to his new guns with all their deadly speed. He is fourteen, his reflexes are the sharpest and quickest they'll ever be, and he goes off like exploding gunpowder.

"No, Roland, don't!" *Susannah screams.* "It's a trick, it's a glam!"

Jake has just time to look from the mirror to the woman actually standing in the doorway; has just time to realize he, too, has been tricked.

Perhaps Roland also understands the truth at the last split-second—that the woman in the doorway really is *his mother after all, that the thing in her hands isn't a snake but a belt, something she has made for him, a peace offering, mayhap, that the glass has lied to him in the only way it* can *. . . by reflection.*

In any case, it's too late. The guns are out and thundering, their bright yellow flashes lighting the room. He pulls the trigger of each gun twice before he can stop, and the four slugs drive Gabrielle Deschain back into the corridor with the hopeful can-we-make-peace smile still on her face.

She dies that way, smiling.

Roland stands where he is, the smoking guns in his hands, his face cramped in a grimace of surprise and horror, just begin-

ning to get the truth of what he must carry with him the rest of his life: he has used the guns of his father to kill his mother.

Now cackling laughter fills the room. Roland does not turn; he is frozen by the woman in the blue dress and black shoes who lies bleeding in the corridor of her apartment; the woman he came to save and has killed, instead. She lies with the hand-woven belt draped across her bleeding stomach.

Jake turns for him, and is not surprised to see a green-faced woman in a pointed black hat swimming inside the ball. It is the Wicked Witch of the East; it is also, he knows, Rhea of the Cöos. She stares at the boy with the guns in his hands and bares her teeth at him in the most terrible grin Jake has ever seen in his life.

"I've burned the stupid girl ye loved—aye, burned her alive, I did—and now I've made ye a matricide. Do ye repent of killing my snake yet, gunslinger? My poor, sweet Ermot? Do ye regret playing yer hard games with one more trig than ye'll ever be in yer miserable life?"

He gives no sign that he hears, only stares at his lady mother. Soon he will go to her, kneel by her, but not yet; not yet.

The face in the ball now turns toward the three pilgrims, and as it does it changes, becomes old and bald and raddled— becomes, in fact, the face Roland saw in the lying mirror. The gunslinger has been unable to see his future friends, but Rhea sees them; aye, she sees them very well.

"Cry it off!" she croaks—it is the caw of a raven sitting on a leafless branch beneath a winter-dimmed sky. "Cry it off! Renounce the Tower!"

"Never, you bitch," Eddie says.

"Ye see what he is! What a monster he is! And this is only the beginning of it, ye ken! Ask him what happened to Cuthbert! To Alain—Alain's touch, clever as 'twas, saved him not in the end, so it didn't! Ask him what happened to Jamie De Curry! He never had a friend he didn't kill, never had a lover who's not dust in the wind!"

"Go your way," Susannah says, "and leave us to ours."

Rhea's green, cracked lips twist in a horrible sneer. "He's killed his own mother! What will he do to you, ye stupid brown-skinned bitch?"

"He didn't kill her," Jake said. "You killed her. Now go!"

Jake takes a step toward the ball, meaning to pick it up and dash it to the floor . . . and he can do that, he realizes, for the ball is real. It's the one thing in this vision that is. But before he can put his hands to it, it flashes a soundless explosion of pink light. Jake throws his hands up in front of his face to keep from being blinded, and then he is

(melting I'm melting what a world oh what a world)

falling, he is being whirled down through the pink storm, out of Oz and back to Kansas, out of Oz and back to Kansas, out of Oz and back to—

CHAPTER FIVE

The Path of the Beam

I

"—home," Eddie muttered. His voice sounded thick and punch-drunk to his own ears. "Back home, because there's no place like home, no indeed."

He tried to open his eyes and at first couldn't. It was as if they were glued shut. He put the heel of his hand to his forehead and pushed up, tightening the skin on his face. It worked; his eyes popped open. He saw neither the throne-room of the Green Palace nor (and this was what he had really expected) the richly appointed but somehow claustrophobic bedroom in which he had just been.

He was outside, lying in a small clearing of winter-white grass. Nearby was a little grove of trees, some still with their last brown leaves clinging to the branches. And one branch with an odd white leaf, an albino leaf. There was a pretty trickle of running water farther into the grove. Standing abandoned in the high grass was Susannah's new and improved wheelchair. There was mud on the tires, Eddie saw, and a few late leaves, crispy and brown, caught in the spokes. A few swatches of grass, too. Overhead was a skyful of still white clouds, every bit as interesting as a laundry-basket full of sheets.

The sky was clear when we went inside the Palace, he thought, and realized time had slipped again. How much or how little, he wasn't sure he wanted to know—Roland's world was like a transmission with its gear-teeth all but stripped away; you never knew when time was going to pop into neutral or race you away in overdrive.

Was this Roland's world, though? And if it was, how had they gotten back to it?

"How should I know?" Eddie croaked, and got slowly to his feet, wincing as he did so. He didn't think he was hungover, but his legs were sore and he felt as if he had just taken the world's heaviest Sunday afternoon nap.

Roland and Susannah lay on the ground under the trees. The gunslinger was stirring, but Susannah lay on her back, arms spread extravagantly wide, snoring in an unladylike way that made Eddie grin. Jake was nearby, with Oy sleeping on his side by one of the kid's knees. As Eddie looked at them, Jake opened his eyes and sat up. His gaze was wide but blank; he was awake, but had been so heavily asleep he didn't know it yet.

"Gruz," Jake said, and yawned.

"Yep," Eddie said, "that works for me." He turned in a slow circle, and had gotten three quarters of the way back to where he'd started when he saw the Green Palace on the horizon. From here it looked very small, and its brilliance had been robbed by the sunless day. Eddie guessed it might be thirty miles away. Leading toward them from that direction were the tracks of Susannah's wheelchair.

He could hear the thinny, but faintly. He thought he could see it, as well—a quicksilver shimmer like bogwater, stretching across the flat, open land . . . and finally drying up about five miles away. Five miles west of here? Given the location of the Green Palace and the fact that they had been travelling east on I-70, that was the natural assumption, but who really knew, especially with no visible sun to use for orientation?

"Where's the turnpike?" Jake asked. His voice sounded thick and gummy. Oy joined him, stretching first one rear leg, then the other. Eddie saw he had lost one of his booties at some point.

"Maybe it was cancelled due to lack of interest."

"I don't think we're in Kansas anymore," Jake said. Eddie looked at him sharply, but didn't believe the kid was consciously riffing on *The Wizard of Oz.* "Not the one where the Kansas City Royals play, not the one where the Monarchs play, either."

"What gives you that idea?"

Jake hoisted a thumb toward the sky, and when Eddie looked up, he saw that he had been wrong: it wasn't *all* still white overcast, boring as a basket of sheets. Directly above their heads, a band of clouds was moiling toward the horizon as steadily as a conveyor belt.

They were back on the Path of the Beam.

2

"Eddie? Where you at, sugar?"

Eddie looked down from the lane of clouds in the sky and saw Susannah sitting up, rubbing the back of her neck. She looked unsure of where she was. Perhaps even of *who* she was. The red cappies she was wearing looked oddly dull in this light, but they were still the brightest things in Eddie's view . . . until he looked down at his own feet and saw the street-boppers with their Cuban heels. Yet these also looked dull, and Eddie no longer thought it was just the day's cloudy light that made them seem so. He looked at Jake's shoes, Oy's remaining three slippers, Roland's cowboy boots (the gunslinger was sitting up now, arms crossed around his knees, looking blankly off into the distance). All the same ruby red, but a *lifeless* red, somehow. As if some magic essential to them had been used up.

Suddenly, Eddie wanted them off his feet.

He sat down beside Susannah, gave her a kiss, and said: "Good morning, Sleeping Beauty. Or afternoon, if it's that." Then, quickly, almost hating to touch them (it was like touching dead skin, somehow), Eddie yanked off the street-boppers. As he did, he saw that they were scuffed at the toes and muddy at the heels, no longer new-looking. He'd wondered how they'd gotten here; now, feeling the ache in the muscles of his legs and remembering the wheelchair tracks, he knew. They had walked, by God. Walked in their sleep.

"That," Susannah said, "is the best idea you've had since . . . well, in a long time." She stripped off the cappies. Close by, Eddie saw Jake taking off Oy's booties. "Were we there?" Susannah asked him. "Eddie, were we really there when he . . ."

"When I killed my mother," Roland said. "Yes, you were there. As I was. Gods help me, I was there. I did it." He covered his face with his hands and began to voice a series of harsh sobs.

Susannah crawled across to him in that agile way that was almost a version of walking. She put an arm around him and used her other hand to take his hands away from his face. At first Roland didn't want to let her do that, but she was persistent, and at last his hands—those killer's hands—came down, revealing haunted eyes which swam with tears.

Susannah urged his face down against her shoulder. "Be easy, Roland," she said. "Be easy and let it go. This part is over now. You past it."

"A man doesn't get past such a thing," Roland said. "No, I don't think so. Not ever."

"You didn't kill her," Eddie said.

"That's too easy." The gunslinger's face was still against Susannah's shoulder, but his words were clear enough. "Some responsibilities can't be shirked. Some *sins* can't be shirked. Yes, Rhea was there—in a way, at least—but I can't shift it all to the Cöos, much as I might like to."

"It wasn't her, either," Eddie said. "That's not what I mean."

Roland raised his head. "What in hell's name are you talking about?"

"*Ka,*" Eddie said. "*Ka* like a wind."

3

In their packs there was food none of them had put there—cookies with Keebler elves on the packages, Saran Wrapped sandwiches that looked like the kind you could get (if you were desperate, that was) from turnpike vending machines, and a brand of cola neither Eddie, Susannah, nor Jake knew. It tasted like Coke and came in a red and white can, but the brand was Nozz-A-La.

They ate a meal with their backs to the grove and their faces to the distant glam-gleam of the Green Palace, and called it lunch. *If we start to lose the light in an hour or so, we can make it supper by voice vote,* Eddie thought, but he didn't believe they'd need to. His interior clock was running again now, and that mysterious but usually accurate device suggested that it was early afternoon.

At one point he stood up and raised his soda, smiling into an invisible camera. "When I'm travelling through the Land of Oz in my new Takuro Spirit, I drink Nozz-A-La!" he proclaimed. "It fills me up but never fills me out! It makes me happy to be a man! It makes me know

God! It gives me the outlook of an angel and the balls of a tiger! When I drink Nozz-A-La, I say 'Gosh! Ain't I glad to be alive!' I say—"

"Sit down, you bumhug," Jake said, laughing.

"Ug," Oy agreed. His snout was on Jake's ankle, and he was watching the boy's sandwich with great interest.

Eddie started to sit, and then that strange albino leaf caught his eye again. *That's no leaf,* he thought, and walked over to it. No, not a leaf but a scrap of paper. He turned it over and saw columns of "blah blah" and "yak yak" and "all the stuff's the same." Usually newspapers weren't blank on one side, but Eddie wasn't surprised to find this one was—the Oz *Daily Buzz* had only been a prop, after all.

Nor was the blank side blank. Printed on it in neat, careful letters, was this message:

Next time I won't leave. Renounce the Tower. This is your last warning. And have a _great_ day! —R.F.

Below that, a little drawing:

Eddie brought the note back to where the others were eating. Each of them looked at it. Roland held it last, ran his thumb over it thoughtfully, feeling the texture of the paper, then gave it back to Eddie.

"R.F.," Eddie said. "The man who was running Tick-Tock. This is from him, isn't it?"

"Yes. He must have brought the Tick-Tock Man out of Lud."

"Sure," Jake said darkly. "That guy Flagg looked like someone who'd know a first-class bumhug when he found one. But how did they get here before us? What could be faster than Blaine the Mono, for cripe's sake?"

"A door," Eddie said. "Maybe they came through one of those special doors."

"Bingo," Susannah said. She held her hand out, palm up, and Eddie slapped it.

"In any case, what he suggests is not bad advice," Roland said. "I urge you to consider it most seriously. And if you want to go back to your world, I will allow you to go."

"Roland, I can't believe you," Eddie said. "This, after you dragged me and Suze over here, kicking and screaming? You know what my brother would say about you? That you're as contrary as a hog on ice-skates."

"I did what I did before I learned to know you as friends," Roland said. "Before I learned to love you as I loved Alain and Cuthbert. And before I was forced to . . . to revisit certain scenes. Doing that has . . ." He paused, looking down at his feet (he had put his old boots back on again) and thinking hard. At last he looked up again. "There was a part of me that hadn't moved or spoken in a good many years. I thought it was dead. It isn't. I have learned to love again, and I'm aware that this is probably my last chance to love. I'm slow—Vannay and Cort knew that; so did my father—but I'm not stupid."

"Then don't act that way," Eddie said. "Or treat us as if we were."

"What you call 'the bottom line,' Eddie, is this: I get my friends killed. And I'm not sure I can even risk doing that again. Jake especially . . . I . . . never mind. I don't have the words. For the first time since I turned around in a dark room and killed my mother, I may have found something more important than the Tower. Leave it at that."

"All right, I guess I can respect that."

"So can I," Susannah said, "but Eddie's right about *ka*." She took the note and ran a finger over it thoughtfully. "Roland, you can't talk about that—*ka*, I mean—then turn around and take it back again, just because you get a little low on willpower and dedication."

"Willpower and dedication are good words," Roland remarked. "There's a bad one, though, that means the same thing. That one is *obsession*."

She shrugged it away with an impatient twitch of her shoulders. "Sugarpie, either this whole business is *ka*, or none of it is. And scary as *ka* might be—the idea of fate with eagle eyes and a bloodhound's nose—I find the idea of no *ka* even scarier." She tossed the R.F. note aside on the matted grass.

"Whatever you call it, you're just as dead if it runs you over," Roland said. "Rimer . . . Thorin . . . Jonas . . . my mother . . . Cuthbert . . . Susan. Just ask them. Any of them. If you only could."

"You're missing the biggest part of this," Eddie said. "You *can't* send us back. Don't you realize that, you big galoot? Even if there was a door, we wouldn't go through it. Am I wrong about that?"

He looked at Jake and Susannah. They shook their heads. Even Oy shook his head. No, he wasn't wrong.

"We've *changed*," Eddie said. "We . . ." Now he was the one who didn't know how to go on. How to express his need to see the Tower . . . and his other need, just as strong, to go on carrying the gun with the sandalwood insets. *The big iron* was how he'd come to think of it. Like in that old Marty Robbins song about the man with the big iron on his hip. "It's *ka*," he said. It was all he could think of that was big enough to cover it.

"Kaka," Roland replied, after a moment's consideration. The three of them stared at him, mouths open.

Roland of Gilead had made a joke.

4

"There's one thing I don't understand about what we saw," Susannah said hesitantly. "Why did your mother hide behind that drape when you came in, Roland? Did she mean to . . ." She bit her lip, then brought it out. "Did she mean to kill you?"

"If she'd meant to kill me, she wouldn't have chosen a belt as her weapon. The very fact that she had made me a present—and that's what it was, it had my initials woven into it—suggests that she meant to ask my forgiveness. That she had had a change of heart."

Is that what you know, or only what you want to believe? Eddie thought. It was a question he would never ask. Roland had been tested enough, had won their way back to the Path of the Beam by reliving that terrible final visit to his mother's apartment, and that was enough.

"I think she hid because she was ashamed," the gunslinger said. "Or because she needed a moment to think of what to say to me. Of how to explain."

"And the ball?" Susannah asked him gently. "Was it on the vanity table, where we saw it? And did she steal it from your father?"

"Yes to both," Roland said. "Although . . . *did* she steal it?" He seemed to ask this question of himself. "My father knew a great many things, but he sometimes kept what he knew to himself."

"Like him knowing that your mother and Marten were seeing each other," Susannah said.

"Yes."

"But, Roland . . . you surely don't believe that your father would knowingly have allowed *you* to . . . to . . ."

Roland looked at her with large, haunted eyes. His tears had gone, but when he tried to smile at her question, he was unable. "Have knowingly allowed his son to kill his wife?" he asked. "No, I can't say that. Much as I'd like to, I can't. That he should have *caused* such a thing to have happened, to have deliberately set it in motion, like a man playing Castles . . . that I cannot believe. But would he allow *ka* to run its course? Aye, most certainly."

"What happened to the ball?" Jake asked.

"I don't know. I fainted. When I awoke, my mother and I were still alone, one dead and one alive. No one had come to the sound of the shots—the walls of that place were thick stone, and that wing mostly empty as well. Her blood had dried. The belt she'd made me was covered with it, but I took it, and I put it on. I wore that bloodstained gift for many years, and how I lost it is a tale for another day—I'll tell it to you before we have done, for it bears on my quest for the Tower.

"But although no one had come to investigate the gunshots, someone had come for another reason. While I lay fainted away by my mother's corpse, that someone came in and took the wizard's glass away."

"Rhea?" Eddie asked.

"I doubt she was so close in her body . . . but she had a way of making friends, that one. Aye, a way of making friends. I saw her again, you know." Roland explained no further, but a stony gleam arose in his eyes. Eddie had seen it before, and knew it meant killing.

Jake had retrieved the note from R.F. and now gestured at the little drawing beneath the message. "Do you know what this means?"

"I have an idea it's the *sigul* of a place I saw when I first travelled in the wizard's glass. The land called Thunderclap." He looked around at them, one by one. "I think it's there that we'll meet this man—this *thing*—named Flagg again."

Roland looked back the way they had come, sleep-walking in their fine red shoes. "The Kansas we came through was *his* Kansas, and the plague that emptied out that land was *his* plague. At least, that's what I believe."

"But it might not stay there," Susannah said.

"It could travel," Eddie said.

"To *our* world," Jake said.

Still looking back toward the Green Palace, Roland said: "To your world, or any other."

"Who's the Crimson King?" Susannah asked abruptly.

"Susannah, I know not."

They were quiet, then, watching Roland look toward the palace where he had faced a false wizard and a true memory and somehow opened the door back to his own world by so doing.

Our world, Eddie thought, slipping an arm around Susannah. *Our world now. If we go back to America, and perhaps we'll have to before this is over, we'll arrive as strangers in a strange land, no matter what when it is. This is our world now. The world of the Beams, and the Guardians, and the Dark Tower.*

"We got some daylight left," he said to Roland, and put a hesitant hand on the gunslinger's shoulder. When Roland immediately covered it with his own hand, Eddie smiled. "You want to use it, or what?"

"Yes," Roland said. "Let's use it." He bent and shouldered his pack.

"What about the shoes?" Susannah asked, looking doubtfully at the little red pile they had made.

"Leave them here," Eddie said. "They've served their purpose. Into your wheelchair, girl." He put his arms around her and helped her in.

"All God's children have shoes," Roland mused. "Isn't that what you said, Susannah?"

"Well," she said, settling herself, "the correct dialect adds a soupçon of flavor, but you've got the essence, honey, yes."

"Then we'll undoubtedly find more shoes as God wills it," Roland said.

Jake was looking into his knapsack, taking inventory of the foodstuffs that had been added by some unknown hand. He held up a chicken leg in a Baggie, looked at it, then looked at Eddie. "Who do you suppose packed this stuff?"

Eddie raised his eyebrows, as if to ask Jake how he could possibly be so stupid. "The Keebler Elves," he said. "Who else? Come on, let's go."

5

They clustered near the grove, five wanderers on the face of an empty land. Ahead of them, running across the plain, was a line in the grass which exactly matched the lane of rushing clouds in the sky. This line was nothing so obvious as a path . . . but to the awakened eye, the way that everything bent in the same direction was as clear as a painted stripe.

The Path of the Beam. Somewhere ahead, where this Beam intersected all the others, stood the Dark Tower. Eddie thought that, if the wind were right, he would almost be able to smell its sullen stone.

And roses—the dusky scent of roses.

He took Susannah's hand as she sat in her chair; Susannah took Roland's; Roland took Jake's. Oy stood two paces before them, head up, scenting the autumn air that combed his fur with unseen fingers, his gold-ringed eyes wide.

"We are *ka-tet*," Eddie said. It crossed his mind to wonder at how much he'd changed; how he had become a stranger, even to himself. "We are one from many."

"*Ka-tet*," Susannah said. "We are one from many."

"One from many," Jake said. "Come on, let's go."

Bird and bear and hare and fish, Eddie thought.

With Oy in the lead, they once more set out for the Dark Tower, walking along the Path of the Beam.

AFTERWORD

The scene in which Roland bests his old teacher, Cort, and goes off to roister in the less savory section of Gilead was written in the spring of 1970. The one in which Roland's father shows up the following morning was written in the summer of 1996. Although only sixteen hours pass between the two occurrences in the world of the story, twenty-six *years* had passed in the life of the story's teller. Yet the moment finally came, and I found myself confronting myself across a whore's bed—the unemployed schoolboy with the long black hair and beard on one side, the successful popular novelist ("America's shlockmeister," as I am affectionately known by my legions of admiring critics) on the other.

I mention this only because it sums up the essential weirdness of the Dark Tower experience for me. I have written enough novels and short stories to fill a solar system of the imagination, but Roland's story is my Jupiter—a planet that dwarfs all the others (at least from my own perspective), a place of strange atmosphere, crazy landscape, and savage gravitational pull. Dwarfs the others, did I say? I think there's more to it than that, actually. I am coming to understand that Roland's world (or worlds) actually *contains* all the others of my making; there is a place in Mid-World for Randall Flagg, Ralph Roberts, the wandering boys from *The Eyes of the Dragon,* even Father Callahan, the damned priest from *'Salem's Lot,* who rode out of New England on a Greyhound Bus and wound up dwelling on the border of a terrible Mid-World land called Thunderclap. This seems to be where they all finish up, and why not? Mid-World was here first, before all of them, dreaming under the blue gaze of Roland's bombardier eyes.

This book has been too long in coming—a good many readers who enjoy Roland's adventures have all but howled in frustration—and for that I apologize. The reason is best summed up by Susannah's thought as she prepares to tell Blaine the first riddle of their contest: *It is hard to begin.* There's nothing in these pages that I agree with more.

I knew that *Wizard and Glass* meant doubling back to Roland's young days, and to his first love affair, and I was scared to death of that story. Suspense is relatively easy, at least for me; love is hard. Consequently I dallied, I temporized, I procrastinated, and the book remained unwritten.

I began at last, working in motel rooms on my Macintosh PowerBook, while driving cross-country from Colorado to Maine after finishing my work on the miniseries version of *The Shining.* It occurred to me as I drove north through the deserted miles of western Nebraska (where I also happened to be, driving back from Colorado, when I got the idea for a story called "Children of the Corn"), that if I didn't start soon, I would never write the book at all.

But I no longer know the truth of romantic love, I told myself. *I know about marriage, and mature love, but forty-eight has a way of forgetting the heat and passion of seventeen.*

I will help you with that part, came the reply. I didn't know who that voice belonged to on that day outside Thetford, Nebraska, but I do now, because I have looked into his eyes across a whore's bed in a land that exists very clearly in my imagination. Roland's love for Susan Delgado (and hers for him) is what was told to me by the boy who began this story. If it's right, thank him. If it's wrong, blame whatever got lost in the translation.

Also thank my friend Chuck Verrill, who edited the book and hung with me every step of the way. His encouragement and help were invaluable, as was the encouragement of Elaine Koster, who has published all of these cowboy romances in paperback.

Most thanks of all go to my wife, who supports me in this madness as best she can and helped me on this book in a way she doesn't even know. Once, in a dark time, she gave me a funny little rubber figure that made me smile. It's Rocket J. Squirrel, wearing his blue aviator's hat and with his arms bravely outstretched. I put that figure on my manuscript as it grew (and grew . . . and *grew*), hoping some of the love that came with it would kind of fertilize the work. It must have worked, at least to a degree; the book is here, after all. I don't know if it's good or bad—I lost all sense of perspective around page four hundred—but it's here. That alone seems like a miracle. And I have started to believe I might actually live to complete this cycle of stories. (Knock on wood.)

There are three more to be told, I think, two set chiefly in Mid-World and one almost entirely in our world— that's the one dealing with the vacant lot on the corner of Second and Forty-sixth, and the rose that grows there. That rose, I must tell you, is in terrible danger.

In the end, Roland's *ka-tet* will come to the nightscape which is Thunderclap . . . and to what lies beyond it. All may not live to reach the Tower, but I believe that those who do reach it will stand and be true.

—Stephen King
Lovell, Maine, October 27, 1996

ACKNOWLEDGMENTS

The lyrics from "The Green Door," words by Marvin Moore, music by Bob Davie, copyright © Alley Music Corp. and Trio Music Co., Inc., 1956. Copyright renewed. All rights reserved. Used by permission.

The lyrics from "Whole Lot-ta Shakin' Goin' On" by Dave Williams and Sonny David, copyright © 1957.

ABOUT THE AUTHOR

Stephen King is the author of more than fifty books, all of them worldwide bestsellers. His recent work includes the short story collection *The Bazaar of Bad Dreams, End of Watch, Finders Keepers, Mr. Mercedes* (an Edgar Award winner for Best Novel), *Revival, Doctor Sleep,* and *Under the Dome.* His novel *11/22/63* was named a top ten book of 2011 by *The New York Times Book Review* and won the Los Angeles Times Book Prize for best Mystery/Thriller. He is the recipient of the 2014 National Medal of Arts and the 2003 National Book Foundation Medal for Distinguished Contribution to American Letters. He lives in Bangor, Maine, with his wife, novelist Tabitha King.